Until the Colors Fade

Also by Tim Jeal

LIVINGSTONE

SOMEWHERE BEYOND REPROACH

FOR LOVE OR MONEY

Until the Colors Fade

A NOVEL BY

Tim Jeal

DELACORTE PRESS/NEW YORK

Designed by Ann Spinelli

Library of Congress Cataloging in Publication Data

Jeal, Tim.
Until the colors fade.

I. Title.
PZ4.J428Un3   [PR6060.E2]   823'.9'14   76-17621
ISBN: 0-440-09299-X

PART ONE

The Election

One

A stranger visiting Rigton Bridge in the early 1850s would have been surprised to learn, as he sniffed the smoke in the air, that so large a manufacturing town had been little more than a straggling village thirty years before. Only the main street, with its two inns, church and market-place, remained as evidence of the days when the butcher's stock-in-trade was a half-sheep and the solitary hardware shop kept such rural oddities as sheep nets and gunpowder. Now these countrified shops had gone; there was no grocer selling bread, and the tailor, who had proudly displayed bonnets and stays alongside swallowtail coats, had lost his feminine custom to three smart London milliners' shops with wide plate-glass windows. Even the market cross had vanished—demolished to make way for the new "classical" Town Hall. But more remarkable than these changes, stranger even than the construction of an entirely new suburb of neat villas west of the town, was the disappearance of the water meadows. Here, the once deserted banks of the river were lined with coal wharfs and timber yards, and on the blackened water floated strings of barges filled with raw cotton in sacks and square bales of woven calico. Close at hand, vast barrack-like mills imposed their many-windowed cliffs of blackened brick upon the surrounding houses.

Behind the mills, the streets were cobbled and faultlessly regular, row upon parallel row of small back-to-back houses all gently sloping down toward the factories as though deliberately lined up to draw attention to the source of the town's wealth. Only on the far side of the river had the victorious march of bricks and mortar been temporarily checked by stubborn pockets of undeveloped countryside, where dunghills and cow-sheds stood their ground against the advancing tile yards and brickfields, and in half-finished streets an unyielding mixture of cinders and frozen mud hampered the efforts of the builders.

The most arresting symbol of the new era—more noticeable even than the twenty or so tall factory chimneys—was the soaring railway viaduct with its wide arches etched hard and black against the sky. The elegantly gabled railway station, built in a style bizarrely combining medieval and Tudor elements, was not to be found in the center of the town but two miles to the northeast, a position dictated partly by the height of the hills surrounding the low-lying town, and partly by the refusal of a local landowner to sell the railway company the only other feasible site.

From this station, in the late afternoon of 7 November 1852, a batch of strikers convicted of riot and arson were to be conveyed by train to Wakefield. Rigton Bridge also had its prison, but, because of the explosive situation in the town, the authorities had thought it advisable to accommodate the prisoners elsewhere.

The present trouble followed a pattern that had been familiar throughout the previous decade, when large fluctuations in the demand for finished cotton had led periodically to lower wages and dismissals. Now in Rigton Bridge a reduction in wages had been answered by a concerted strike at three mills, an action the masters had countered with dismissals and then with the replacement of those discharged by Irishmen from Belfast and Liverpool. There had been riots at one mill; the gates had been broken down, the fires put out and the boilers destroyed. The yeomanry had been called out and arrests made. Those convicted were the men about to be transferred by rail to Wakefield.

In normal circumstances such incidents, while deplored, were frequent enough not to excite undue alarm. But industrial unrest with a Parliamentary election pending was another matter; and when, furthermore, as was the case, one of the candidates was also the owner of the very mill where the worst violence had taken place, the situation was considered potentially disastrous. Because of the strike, now backed by the Spinners' Union, every cotton operative in the town could be expected to be on the streets on polling day, and since every one of them was barred from voting by the property qualification, the chances of them watching peacefully while the small shopkeepers and other small householders elected the wealthiest manufacturer in the town to Parliament were thought exceptionally remote, even given the dampening influence that regular cavalry might provide.

* * *

The light was fading and a porter had already lit the gas lamps outside the ticket hall, when half a dozen yeomanry troopers under a sergeant rode into the station yard, dismounted and formed up in line, grumbling about the cold. After the sergeant had checked with the stationmaster that the train was not due for another half hour, they went into the waiting room to sit by the small coal fire. Not many minutes later a pale young man with dark curling hair, and wearing a brown caped overcoat, pulled up his horse a hundred yards from the station, jumped down from the saddle and led the animal into a turnip field where he tethered him. Then he walked on across country until he reached the railway track, which he did not cross, but, keeping in the shadow of the embankment, he followed it until he reached the end of the station platform. Here he paused to see that he was not observed and then clambered up onto the platform and concealed himself behind some milk churns, from which position he could see much of the station yard and platform.

There could not be many occasions, Tom Strickland reflected, on which an artist must need feel obliged to conceal himself in order to witness a scene he might later wish to paint from memory, but today was undoubtedly one of them. Should news of his presence on the platform reach the ears of his current patron, there would be some embarrassing questions asked, especially because Joseph Braithwaite, whose portrait Strickland was working on, was the millowner whose property had suffered at the hands of the prisoners expected at the station. Caution was especially called for since George, Joseph Braithwaite's only son, was the officer in command of the convicts' yeomanry escort. Although Tom did not like George, who viewed artists as no better than superior tradesmen, he felt some sympathy with him for being obliged to perform the invidious task of guarding the men who had damaged one of his father's mills; but, with his commanding officer out of town, George, as the only captain in Rigton Bridge, had had no choice. Tom's interest in George's predicament was nonetheless limited, and he did not feel any concern for how the part-timers of the yeomanry

—mostly the sons of tenant farmers and local shopkeepers—would deal with a situation out of the usual run of field days, church parades and other social functions, which, occasional disturbances apart, formed their only experience of soldiering.

Tom's reason for crouching behind the milk churns on a cold November evening would have been viewed as madness by the Braithwaites: he wanted to see and memorize the faces of men who had risked so much and would now have to pay so heavily for their despairing attack on the cotton masters' domination of the town. In Paris, two years before, Tom had been overwhelmed by the power of Daumier's and Meissonier's paintings of the 1848 revolution, and, on his return to London, he had deserted the realms of idealized historical painting for unsentimental pictures of everyday life. Not only had this work been brutally criticized as squalid and devoid of all beauty and moral content, but he had failed to sell more than two large canvases in the following year. Heavily in debt he had been obliged to seek portrait commissions, and at the time had thought himself lucky to be employed by a manufacturer as wealthy as Joseph Braithwaite. But with the right theme, he still hoped to achieve the force of the best work he had seen at the Salon in 1850. These men, on their way to a decade of imprisonment for an hour's surrender to blind rage, might provide just such a theme. While slightly uncomfortable at the idea of using their misery, Tom was encouraged by the thought that, by preparing to paint them, he was defying Joseph Braithwaite, whose fury would be considerable should he ever discover that his protégé considered convicted criminals a fitter subject for art than his own noble face.

Fifteen minutes before the train was expected, Tom noticed the soldiers leave the waiting room and take up positions outside the ticket hall. Shortly afterward he heard the clatter of approaching hooves and saw a dozen mounted troopers sweep into the station yard just ahead of two horse-drawn omnibuses with shuttered windows. On each side of these vehicles rode six outriders and behind them came the main body of the troop, with George Braithwaite, resplendent in a deep blue Light Dragoon uniform, in front of them and immediately behind the second omnibus. At George's word of command, the leading riders dismounted and Tom saw them disappear into the station and then emerge on the platform. Two came toward him but stopped fifteen yards short of his hiding place. Two others made for the other end of the platform and the rest jumped down onto the track and fanned out on the opposite side to cut off any prisoner who might try to make a break. In the yard the gates had been closed and men were being placed at intervals around the fence, the remaining forty or so dismounting and forming up on each side of the omnibuses.

Hearing a faint whistle, Tom gazed away toward the distant gray smudge of Rigton Bridge and the arches of the viaduct, on which he saw silhouetted a squat black engine with a tall smokestack and behind it the yellow and green carriages strung out like toys, small against the darkening sky.

When the train clanked and sighed to a halt in the station, no move was made to remove the prisoners from the omnibuses until the passengers getting out had left the platform. Just over a dozen people stepped down from the open-sided, second-class carriages; only one left the single first-class coach. Tom watched this tall elegant man indicating to the porter with his gold-topped cane which boxes and portmanteaus to get down from the roof. Catching sight of the soldiers, this stranger showed no marked interest, but buttoned his fashionable dark green pilot coat, pulled on his kid gloves and adjusted his top hat before sauntering out into the yard where he engaged the only fly in sight. The other passengers settled themselves in the station omnibus, which like the fly was prevented from leaving the yard by the closed gates.

Once the shuttered omnibuses were unlocked, Tom was astounded by the speed and brutality with which the soldiers used the butts of their carbines to push and buffet their twenty-odd handcuffed prisoners to the train. So sudden was their emergence and so rapid their progress to the two extra mail coaches set aside for their reception that Tom caught sight of little more than a few haggard, unshaven faces and some worn fustian coats. Because he had expected cursing and defiant jeers, the uncomplaining silence of these men, driven like cattle across the platform, shocked Tom deeply. The only facial expressions he saw were not of anger or outraged dignity, but conveyed more the hunted fear and suspicion of trapped animals waiting for blows. Only one or two looked sullen. For the most part their eyes were fixed and expressionless, making them seem remote and strangely anonymous. Shaken by what he had seen and ashamed that he had expected more, Strickland crept down from behind the churns and retraced his steps beside the track.

It was much darker now and it took him longer than he had expected

to find the field leading into the one where he had left his hired hack, but
in spite of the delay he still calculated that the yeomanry would not have
left the station yet and that there would therefore be no danger of
blundering into George on the road back into Rigton Bridge. He had
been riding little more than two minutes when he heard a crash followed
by terrified screams coming from the road ahead. Overcoming a powerful urge to leave the road at once and ride as hard as he could across
country in the opposite direction, he pressed on at a cautious trot, his
heart pounding. Rounding a sharp bend he saw barely two hundred
yards in front of him a scene of indescribable confusion. The road at
this point cut into the side of a steep hill and was retained by a tall
embankment of granite blocks. Beneath this embankment the two shuttered omnibuses, which had been on their way back to the town, were
halted by a barrier across the road. A number of troopers, apparently no
more than a quarter of the troop, were desperately struggling to clear
away the pile of rocks and branches blocking their path, while above
them, on top of the embankment, indistinct shapes of men with
burning torches were visible, some of them levering up granite blocks
with iron bars and sending them hurtling down onto the roofs of the
stationary vehicles. The omnibus full of railway passengers had stopped
just short of the most exposed part of the road, but its occupants, taking
no chances, were tumbling out and slithering down the slope to the right
of the road. Seconds later rioters were leaping down onto the road from
the embankment and soon the hopelessly outnumbered troopers were
struggling with a formidable mob, their slashing sabers no match for
such numbers. One of the troopers' horses shied and became entangled
with the thrashing hooves of a fallen omnibus hack, eventually crashing
down on its flank. Another horse was hit by a rock as Tom watched.
Too stunned to think at first, Tom turned his horse blindly and dug in
his heels with all his strength. Halfway to the station he met the fly
which the well-dressed gentleman had hired, and yelled to the driver to
stop; then, without waiting to see whether he did, galloped on to warn
the rest of the troop. A minute or so later he saw them riding toward
him in the distance. Tom reined in his horse and turned, ready to ride up
beside George when he came level.

Braithwaite did not at first recognize Tom in the near darkness, but,
when he did, his pale blue watery eyes bulged with anger.

"What the devil are you doing here, Strickland?"

Tom did not answer the question but hurriedly told him what he had seen. George nodded, as though to assure Tom that he had expected as much.

"Hadn't you better order your men to stop?" Tom asked hesitantly, as they approached the final bend that would reveal the chaos ahead. Strickland looked about him uneasily and was shocked not to see any sign of the fly, for they had passed the point at which he had shouted to the driver.

"I know what I'm about," drawled George dismissively, taking a hand from his reins and tugging at his drooping, sandy mustache, a gesture which Tom supposed was intended to convey nonchalance, but which in fact gave the impression of nervousness. The affected stiffness of George's posture and his absurdly elaborate uniform with its enormous epaulets filled Tom with uncontrollable fury.

"Stay on this road and you'll be killed," he blurted out.

George turned to him scornfully and was about to shout back when he drew in his breath sharply. They had reached the bend where the embankment began and George had gained his first view of the scene of bloodshed and confusion, now luridly illuminated by the fiercely burning omnibuses. By the time George turned to his trumpeter, the troopers behind had already halted without waiting for the order. George too had pulled up his horse and was gazing ahead with stupefaction, evidently having thought that Strickland had been exaggerating. In spite of the cold, beads of sweat had broken out around the band of his plumed shako. He had supposed that he would be able to leave the road to get around any obstacle placed there, but the sheer embankment to the left ruled out any attempt to get up behind the rioters, and, the road itself being impassable, his only other option was the precipitous slope to the right. Even in daylight horses would probably stumble and fall on the loose stones and rocks; at night it would be suicidal to try. It was no more than ten seconds since they had halted, but it seemed immeasurably longer. George apparently had no idea what to do, and Tom could think of nothing. It was then that he noticed the fly pulled up to the side of the road under the shadow of the embankment some fifty yards away. A moment later the impeccably dressed man in the silk top hat and green pilot coat got out, and, seemingly oblivious to any danger, walked calmly up to them.

"Better dismount, I daresay," said the stranger, as though perfectly aware of George's dilemma. "Should be able to get a shot at the embankment from down there," he went on, pointing down the slope to his right with his cane to a place where the rocky ground flattened out into a small plateau.

Braithwaite listened speechless and the blood rushed to his cheeks; nor, Tom imagined, would the soundness of this dandified civilian's advice improve George's temper.

"I know my duty, sir," snapped George and then barked out the order to dismount and draw carbines. While the troopers fumbled with their ramrods and cartridges, the stranger said with quiet emphasis,

"Some shots in the air to start with might discourage them, I suppose?"

"I'm no butcher," George replied stiffly.

"I hope not, Mr. Braithwaite," replied the other with a hint of a smile. "Wouldn't care to be a witness in the coroner's court."

Tom noticed George's face freeze as he recognized his adviser.

"Crawford," he gasped.

The gentleman raised his hat a fraction before turning on his heel and walking back to the fly with the same unhurried step.

As the troopers started to slide down the wet rocks to the flatter ground below, Tom was wondering what he should do when the driver of the fly came up to him, touched his hat and murmured,

"Gen'lman wants a word with you."

Strickland dismounted and the driver took his horse's bridle. The interior of the fly was dimly lit by reflected light from the carriage lamp outside. A sudden feeling of unease made him pause before mounting the step. He heard an impatient voice,

"Come on, man; those fools are nervous enough to shoot at anything that moves." Tom sat down on the worn leather seat. His host smiled reassuringly, displaying a glimpse of white and very regular teeth. "Yeomanry regiments are all the same."

The silence that followed, although embarrassing Tom, evidently did not have that effect on his neighbor, for when Tom made as if to speak, he was silenced with a wave of the hand. Irritated at first by this gesture, Tom soon realized that the other was listening for the soldiers' shots. He had heard George call this stranger Crawford, and this intrigued him, since George hoped to marry a Miss Catherine Crawford. From George

—who was lonely as well as rich, and, when drunk, condescended to treat his father's humble artist with a measure of familiarity—Tom knew something of the Crawfords. The head of the family was Rear Admiral Sir James Crawford, a widower, at present at sea. Catherine lived in her father's house, four miles from Rigton Bridge, with her brother, Charles, a naval officer, currently ashore on half-pay. From the frequency with which George spoke of Charles's excellent professional prospects and his future as heir to his father's baronetcy, Tom had assumed that if they were not already friends, George had such a relationship in mind. Strangely George had never mentioned another brother. But possibly this newly arrived Crawford was a cousin or more remote relative. As he was pondering the stranger's identity, Tom heard two stuttering volleys ring out. Then an eerie silence was followed by a distant roar of rage and fear, broken by the screams of a man who must have been hit. At this sound, Crawford leaped from his seat and flung open the door, his face contorted with anger. Tom got out too, in time to see torches being flung away on the embankment, and figures running pell-mell along the parapet and jumping down into the road on the far side of the blazing vehicles.

"That's that then," said Crawford with a shrug of the shoulders, apparently in control of his indignation, but then bursting out, "Should have used regular troops. Any half-wit ought to have guessed what was coming when he saw no crowd at the station."

Tom was uncertain whether Crawford's anger stemmed from a fastidious dislike of military bungling or from sympathy with the rioters, who had been so easily routed by an incompetent force.

"Do you know about the prisoners?" he asked quietly.

"Don't need to. Rioters, strikers, looters—makes no difference. No magistrate transfers prisoners unless he expects trouble in a town."

Three more shots came from the lower ground to the right. Crawford compressed his lips and led Tom back to the fly.

"God knows when they'll get the road cleared," he sighed.

Crawford had a peculiar effect on Tom; he was impressed by his decisiveness and air of authority, but chilled by his manner, which he found aloof and cold. He could not fathom him at all; there was something enigmatic about him, an almost frightening quality. In the fitful light cast by the flames outside, Tom had noticed Crawford's eyes: a deep blue-gray color, under dark lashes—eyes at times remote and dull, as if he were weary and bored, at others, glinting with a sharpness that was disconcerting. The two men sitting side by side were very different in appearance, Strickland's features being softer, less angular, his lips fuller and his expressions and mannerisms gentler, more fleeting and less precise. Crawford's skin was bronzed, Tom's of an ivory pallor by contrast with his dark eyes and the black loose curls that framed his face. Crawford's hair was cut severely short, not waved nor brushed forward in the new fashion. He looked, Tom thought, about thirty, roughly five years older than himself.

Tom found the damp confined interior of the carriage oppressive with its smell of straw and musty leather. The silence worried him, and he was wondering whether he had been asked into the fly solely because it offered a degree of cover from stray shots, when Crawford turned to him abruptly and extended a gloved hand.

"My name's Crawford. Magnus Crawford."

"Thomas Strickland."

"My people come from Trawden way. Yours?"

How typical of his class, thought Tom, that he should have named the nearest village, when the house, Leaholme Hall, was one of the three largest in the neighborhood.

"My parents are dead. I come from London."

"You're a friend of Braithwaite?"

"His father's sitting for me. I'm an artist."

Magnus pulled out a flat silver flask and tossed it to Tom.

"Some brandy, Mr. Strickland?"

Tom refused, not knowing whether the offer had been made purely as a matter of form because Crawford wanted some himself, or whether he was really expected to accept. During the moment or two that he held the flask, he made out a few words of an inscription "*. . . Presented to Major Crawford . . . brother officers . . . garrison at Kandy . . . esteem and gratitude . . .*" There was also a date, which he could not read.

Crawford frowned, evidently noticing the direction of Tom's eyes and the slight hesitation before he returned the flask.

"Ever been to Ceylon, Mr. Strickland? Visitors usually enjoy the scenery. Excellent for pictures, I daresay."

Tom shook his head and felt his cheeks burning, at what he thought was a reproof. After all the man had offered him the thing.

"Shouldn't I have read it? I'd be pleased if people were grateful to me for anything."

"Wouldn't that depend on what they were grateful for?" asked Magnus with a trace of mockery. "I led two companies against a mob of ill-fed, badly armed natives. A riot really; the government called it a rebellion. The ones who didn't run away were tried and most of them shot. I carried out some of those sentences." He had said this with a harshness that did not conceal the pain the memory caused him. "I was not being mock-modest, Mr. Strickland."

"Why on earth have you kept it, feeling as you do?"

"In case I grow forgetful. You see I'm not going back. I've sold my commission."

Tom had a sudden recollection of something in the papers about a recent House of Commons Select Committee. The governor of Ceylon had been recalled because of the evidence of two army officers. Improper land confiscations and illegal courts-martial—something of that sort had been leveled at him.

"You gave evidence against the Colonial Government?"

"I did. After the damage had been done."

Crawford deftly poured himself some brandy into the top, which was in the shape of a thimble-like cup, and swallowed hard. Then, having screwed on the top again, he gave Tom an appraising look, which seemed to say more clearly than words: *I've told you something, now it's your turn.* So, when Magnus asked him to tell him precisely what was happening in the town, Tom was not in the least surprised, and the eager intentness with which Crawford listened was very understandable given the situation outside.

Tom had briefly recounted what he knew about the origins of the violence and was telling him about the complication of Joseph Braith-waite's candidature in the forthcoming election, when Magnus asked sharply,

"Who's behind old Braithwaite's adoption?"

"I'm not sure," replied Tom guardedly. He disliked being devious and was therefore bad at concealment. Crawford grinned at his embarrassment.

"What about Lord Goodchild?" He paused. "Well, Braithwaite couldn't stand without his support, could he?"

Tom nodded reluctant agreement. The following day he hoped to secure Lord Goodchild's commission to paint his wife's portrait. He owed this chance to Joseph Braithwaite's recommendation. Braithwaite was the wealthiest manufacturer in the district, Goodchild the largest landowner. With two such lucrative commissions in close succession, Tom hoped to be able to devote the best part of a year to work of his own choosing. He did not intend to jeopardize these prospects by committing indiscretions. A year free of financial anxieties mattered a great deal to him. Six months ago he had been reduced to sign painting and tinting architects' plans. Before that he had been living on a diet of bread and milk.

"It's a strange thing," mused Crawford. "Goodchild used to like the Braithwaites about as much as the cholera. He's short of money, I daresay." He shot Tom a questioning glance.

"You know these people far better than I." Tom realized as he finished speaking that he had said this more pointedly than he had intended, but he was nonetheless astonished when Crawford leaned toward him with burning eyes and said with a gentleness utterly at variance with the obsessive determination of his expression:

"Listen, Strickland, I know you need Braithwaite's money. I know what it's like to be frightened . . . like last year when I did nothing until matters ended . . . I told you how." He paused and looked at Tom with a softer expression. "You must see that there'll be a bloodbath on polling day unless the strike ends or Braithwaite withdraws his candidature."

"What have I to do with such things?" cried Tom, stung by Crawford's moralistic tone, feeling anger, but, in spite of himself, an inner blush of shame.

"If Braithwaite bought Goodchild, tell me," implored Magnus.

"How could I possibly know?"

"You're staying in his house, aren't you?"

Tom tossed back his head in exasperation.

"To him I'm no more important than a governess or music teacher. Would he tell me anything?"

"Does George ever talk to you?"

"I'm no use to you, I tell you. I accept the world as it is. Baronets' sons may get governors recalled and play politics. I have other things to do." Although Tom was sure that Crawford must be aware that he was trembling with suppressed fury, he showed no sign of being put out, but said calmly,

"Understand this. A man like Braithwaite, whose power depends on an absence of will in others, ends up as their servant not their master. I'd no right to ask anything of you until better acquainted, but what if we're not to meet again?"

"When you've worked for Mr. Braithwaite perhaps you will then tell me about servants and masters with more authority." Tom regretted the bitterness of his tone but could not help it. Normally pacific and courteous, he was appalled by the power of the emotions which Crawford's challenge had aroused in him. Doubtless the man had personal reasons for wishing to confound Braithwaite. Then let him pursue the matter on his own without enlisting the help of the first likely looking accomplice, with no thought for what it might cost him. The look of disappointment on Crawford's face was so obviously genuine that Tom could not help being disturbed by it.

"If you want to find out anything about George," he said, "ask your sister." Tom had meant the suggestion to contain a slight irony, but when he saw the amazement with which it was received, he wished he had remained silent. Miss Crawford had promised George an answer to his proposal in three months, quite long enough surely for her to have written to her brother, even as far away as Ceylon. But apparently neither she nor Charles Crawford had said anything to him. He would have been several weeks in London giving evidence to the Select Committee. Confused and mortified to have been indiscreet after all, Tom added quietly, "George Braithwaite hopes to marry your sister."

"Has Miss Crawford accepted?" Magnus asked shakily.

"She gives her answer next month."

Crawford let out his breath in a long sigh of relief.

"Well, Mr. Strickland," he said, "you've told me something anyway."

A moment later there was a loud tapping at the window, and Tom saw a soldier's face under a plumed shako.

"Cap'n Braithwaite wants summat wi' you, sir!" the man shouted through the glass, seeing Crawford in the far corner. Tom caught Crawford's eye, and was surprised to find himself smiling. Seconds afterward, Magnus had left the fly and was following the trooper down the road. As Tom stepped out, he saw George Braithwaite come up to Crawford, and heard him say,

"Mr. Crawford, I fear I must ask you to give up your carriage."

Half a dozen frightened troopers were stumbling toward the fly carrying three of their comrades. As they laid the wounded men down, Crawford bent over one, whose arm had been hanging limply and was now twisted to one side at an unnatural angle. Tom saw that the sleeve had been ripped open at the elbow, where the arm was a mess of lacerated flesh; blood was still welling steadily, and Tom thought he saw fragments of shattered bone. He had taken this in in a moment and looked away at once, feeling sick and faint. Not so Crawford, who grasped one of the troopers by the shoulder and shouted,

"Your shirt, man, take off your shirt."

The man hesitated; it was a cold night; but when Magnus tore open his tunic, the soldier hastened to oblige him. Magnus snatched the garment from him and ripped off a thin strip. With another man's saber he cut away the upper part of the wounded trooper's sleeve and tied this crude tourniquet firmly around the arm above the wound. While Crawford had been at work, the other two, who seemed less seriously hurt, had been placed on the floor of the fly under several fur-lined pelisses. The gravely wounded man was laid on the seat. Magnus took out his flask and helped the men on the floor to drink; when he had finished he turned furiously on Braithwaite.

"These men owe their injuries to you, sir."

Tom saw George flinch as though he had been struck.

"Those fellows on the hill had nothing to do with it?" George retorted, recovering some of his composure. Crawford's eyes narrowed. Tom noticed dark bloodstains on his previously spotless gloves.

"You sent a small detachment ahead in darkness on this road. Why?"

Braithwaite fiddled with the chin strap of his shako; his face looked drawn and ghastly.

"Damn it, Mr. Crawford, we were surprised."

"You had no hostile demonstrations going to the station?"

"On my honor, none."

Crawford's sardonic smile showed what he thought of George's denial.

"And where's the man you hit? Or can I congratulate you on killing any others?" Crawford pulled off his ruined gloves and tossed them away.

"We fired high. We found no wounded."

"I suppose they'd leave men behind to spend years behind bars if they recovered? Better to risk mortifying wounds in some filthy cellar than that."

"Good God, Crawford, they *chose* to attack us." Braithwaite sounded more bewildered than angry. Tom expected Magnus to tell him that incompetence was an invitation, his plans amateur and negligent and his inexperience a crime, but, to his surprise, Crawford merely wiped his hands on the shirt and sighed. Tom's premonition of what Magnus would say to his sister, about the man who had proposed to her, made him wince. Having told George that the trooper's arm needed immediate amputation, Crawford asked for a horse and suggested that his luggage be sent to Leaholme Hall the following day. He sounded tired and downcast. Although three horses had had to be shot, two men would be going with the wounded in the fly, so there was no difficulty about finding Crawford a horse and the troop sergeant soon led one up to him.

As soon as Magnus had mounted he started the horse at a brisk trot. Braithwaite ran beside him.

"I must entreat you to stop. We must escort you."

With a gesture in the direction of the burned-out omnibuses, Crawford shook his head, and, giving his horse a light flick with his cane, cantered into the darkness.

After the chaos of the past hour, the profound silence of the road ahead seemed strange to Magnus, and he had trouble getting used to the darkness now that the blazing vehicles were out of sight. At the first crossroads he turned his horse to the right and struck out across country. Earlier there had been clouds, but now the stars shone brightly from a clear frosty sky. In the distance he could make out well-remembered landmarks: the spire of Trawden church sharp against the skyline, the massive barn at Blayshaw Farm and behind it the dark line of woods skirting the rugged moorland beyond. The windows of isolated cottages glowed palely with the light of smoking mutton dips and rush tapers within. From across the fields he heard a shepherd's dog barking. The horse's hooves thudded on the grassy track. But, though Magnus had not been in this once familiar country for almost seven years, he felt no emotion: all that had been spent on the station road. On his hands he was aware of the slight tackiness of dry blood. The bizarre coincidence of the riot with his return, and the shock of hearing that George Braithwaite had proposed to Catherine, had left Magnus distraught and dazed.

His sister was the only member of his family for whom he felt real love, and it hurt him deeply to suspect that she might be considering marrying solely for convenience, even if thereby escaping a restricted life of dependence on her family. He hated this suspicion, but, because she had not refused George outright, could not rid himself of it. He had been away too long to be sure that the girl he had known had not changed. Another thought haunted him: his powerful premonition of devastating violence on polling day. The two preoccupations seemed at first quite separate, and yet he could not help their merging in his mind. He was struck by the strange fact that the father of the man whom his sister might marry also held the key to the wider problems in the town.

Magnus reined in his horse, and, while the animal pawed fretfully at the ground, he sat motionless, deep in thought. Action in one sphere might influence events in the other. Hadn't he known enough corruption in Ceylon to be able to sniff out the same infection in Rigton Bridge? His hatred of the Braithwaites was a long-standing one. A moment later he was trembling with excitement. If he could prove Joseph guilty of electoral corruption—and few elections were free of bribery—he could defeat not only George's marriage plans, but also his father's political ambitions. Nor could he be accused of personal spite; if Braithwaite was forced to stand down and abandon his candidature, there would be no bloodshed on polling day, and Catherine would be saved a wretched and loveless marriage, since she would never marry into a family dishonored by fraudulence. The perfect solution: private and public disaster averted by the same means.

The simplicity of the idea astounded and yet dismayed Magnus. There would be much he would never be able to find out. He felt suddenly despondent. Joseph Braithwaite would know how to cover his tracks. Then Magnus smiled. The artist. Of course. And the man had clearly known far more than he had been prepared to say. He had been evasive, certainly; but there had been an openness about him too, something very appealing. Magnus could not quite put his finger on it, but he had an intuitive hunch that, if faced with a clear-cut moral decision, Strickland would side with the angels. He was amused by his memory of the young man's righteous remarks about baronets' sons not understanding the vulnerable position of those without means. If he only knew my real situation, thought Magnus, my God, if he only knew. But he will soon enough, if I need him; he will then.

Soon Magnus came to a decision not to return to Leaholme Hall that evening but to spend the night in Rigton Bridge. It would be better not to see Catherine until he had first made some inquiries in town. After so many years a day would be forgiven, and he had only specified the week during which he could be expected. Several hours before, Magnus had felt close to despair; he had been returning home, not just to see his brother and sister, but because he could think of nowhere else to go; now matters seemed quite different. Old Braithwaite would be a formidable adversary, but there was always great consolation in having nothing to lose. The cold air stung Magnus's hands and face as he rode, but he did not care. A rabbit crossed the track in front of him; in the distance he could see the lights of Rigton Bridge.

* * *

As he rode beside George, Tom Strickland made no attempts at conversation. Braithwaite's morose silence suited him. If it persisted he might never have to explain why he had been at the station; if George were to ask, he had decided to fob him off with flattery about having been interested in his yeomanry duties, but reluctant to mention this in case George had felt imposed upon. In fact Tom was confident that George's only wish would be to forget the events of the past few hours as swiftly as he knew how, and in any case Tom was still too disconcerted by his conversation with Crawford to give much thought to George.

While remaining as certain as ever he had been that it was harder to paint, with even average competence, than to perform the most exacting military duty, Tom could not help feeling that, by being unforthcoming with Magnus, he had missed an opportunity—worse still, that, where an important principle had been involved, he had let himself down. He was not proud to be working for Joseph Braithwaite, whom he knew to be ruthless and unscrupulous, and this increased his discomfort. Only when Tom thought of the work he would be doing in a few months' time, while living on Braithwaite's money, did his conscience disturb him less. He had a duty—as onerous as any military one and more compelling because self-imposed—to convey his feelings in paint. There was nothing intellectual about it; he felt it as an emotional and intuitive necessity.

In the past year, without an adequate income, he had been constantly diverted and debilitated by the struggle to survive. Endless interruptions caused by the need to earn a few pounds had made him almost despair of ever having a long enough period to mount a concentrated attack on particular problems which he had so far failed to solve: not just technicalities involving light and mass, but a way to make others see things through his eyes. He remembered the individuality of the men on the platform and yet their anonymity. To convey the tragedy of that paradox . . . that was something to dream about. His recent failures had left him afraid that he had been trying to attain standards beyond his abilities, and this had terrified him. When his work had been rejected not just by the Academy and the British Institution, but by the lesser private galleries too, he had found it hard to produce anything. His sustaining hope had been then, and was still, that with the fair chance, which a modest level of security would bring, he would be able to confront his terror of failure and prove that his faith in himself was grounded upon solid rock.

If George Braithwaite should say disparaging things about Crawford, Tom knew that he would not contradict him; if need be, he would add criticisms of his own. Joseph Braithwaite's patronage meant more to him than money—far more. If he succeeded in securing Lord Goodchild's commission too, he would have his long-awaited chance within sight. Nobody could divert me then, he told himself, not Crawford nor an army of such men.

Soon they were crossing the iron bridge over the river, the horses' hooves ringing out on the macadam. Tom clenched his teeth. A man in the fly had started to scream, the agony of the sound mocked by its echo returning from the black, clifflike walls of the mills on the far shore.

❦ *Two* ❧

The elaborate wrought-iron gates with their tall flanking piers and heraldic griffins lay behind him, and, ahead, the drive described a gentle
curve across a mile of level parkland. Driving the Braithwaites' new
dogcart with its high red wheels and wasplike body, Tom Strickland
smiled to himself as he gained his first sight of the honey-colored stone
of the east front of Hanley Park.

In the center, a fine portico—four slender Corinthian columns supporting a pediment—was crowned by a statue of Juno or Diana, and, on
each side, symmetrical wings, in the same neo-Palladian style, were
topped with an elegant balustrade, its limits at each end marked by
massive stone urns. The peaceful park and the formal grace of this
classical building, glowing in the pale morning sunshine, contrasted so
strangely with the industrial town five miles away that Tom, in spite of
being nervous and very well aware of the purpose of his visit, could not
escape a powerful sense of unreality—as though he were driving toward
no real house, but through the frame of an eighteenth century painting
into another world: an impression enhanced by the ornamental lake to
his right and the green dome of a temple, glimpsed through the bare
branches of a screen of beech trees.

If Tom had once been tempted to suppose that the elegant spacious-
ness of such surroundings must produce a corresponding self-develop-
ment in their possessors, George Braithwaite had done his best to
disabuse him of the idea. Lord Goodchild, George had assured Tom,
would neither humiliate him with educated talk and scintillating wit, nor
even shock him with refined scandal—his lordship's pleasures, as be-
fitted one of the leading sportsmen of the age, being entirely physical. A
year ago, on a snow-covered road, he had beaten Lord Shrewsbury's

four-in-hand team, driving twenty miles in less than an hour. In his youth, it was said that he had been able to give any pugilist in the country a good fight, and had often amused himself by taking friends to pothouses in London's dockland and starting brawls. Marriage had mellowed him somewhat, but George had relished telling Tom that Goodchild still enjoyed heavy gambling, liaisons with married women and riding in steeplechases.

On the subject of Lady Goodchild, George had been less forthcoming. He had admitted that her reputation as a beauty was not exaggerated, but had then confessed his failure to discover any redeeming qualities to offset her natural coldness and arrogance—unless a mordantly scathing sense of humor could be said to be a redeeming quality. George had made it clear to Tom that, although his father's recommendation to Lord Goodchild would be enough to persuade his lordship to commission a portrait, the final decision would still lie with her ladyship. If she happened to find Tom commonplace or tiresome, there would be no commission, and a lady who had been known to throw bootjacks at her lady's maid and to grind a miniature of her mother-in-law under her heel in front of numerous spectators was not somebody who could be relied upon to be charitable.

Because his future hopes so much depended upon this commission, Tom was naturally depressed by this description, and his despondency was the greater for having allowed himself to imagine aristocratic generosity to rival Lady Holland's championing of the young Watts; but he had by no means abandoned hope of success. His best frock coat might be shabby and his flowing necktie conceal a shirt with similar shortcomings, but he had had ample proof in the past of being attractive to women. While the thought of any close relationship with Lady Goodchild did not enter his mind, he was comforted to know that his mistress, one of the leading singers in London's music halls, cared a great deal more for him than he did for her, and this in spite of propositions from numerous affluent and eminent men.

While many young men strained to appear mature men of the world —often in consequence merely seeming bored and vapid—Tom did not try to emulate anybody. Being shy by nature, any attempts to seem nonchalant and loftily self-confident would in any case have been hopeless. In fact his unaffected enthusiasm and unfeigned reticence usually achieved better results. Since he rarely liked people who pretended to great refinement, he tried to avoid similar excesses of gentility; but his desire to please did sometimes lead him to be too zealously polite, and a lot of his hesitance stemmed from the basic conflict between this eagerness to please and an equally strong inclination to be honest. This ambiguity, although he did not know it, gave his modest and deferential manner a disconcertingly ironic edge, especially when he occasionally slipped an entirely candid remark into an otherwise blandly tactful conversation. Nor could he from time to time help laughing when he had been listening with great seriousness to a lengthy monologue which he secretly viewed as anything but serious. After such behavior he was usually far more embarrassed and confused than the affronted person.

But laughter was very far from his mind as he approached the broad steps under the portico, having left his vehicle in the stables. He had never met anybody of Lord Goodchild's rank and was not unaware of the fact that he had been asked to call in the morning, a time usually reserved for tradesmen. Friends and acquaintances generally called in the afternoon. As he stood under the tall Corinthian columns it was some consolation to him to imagine that many of the aristocrats, whose scrapbooks Turner and Landseer had deigned to draw in, would have thought it the artist's privilege rather than their own to use those books.

As Tom reached the top step and saw a liveried footman with powdered hair and white stockings open the glass-paneled door, he vowed not to allow his pride to make him defensive, and prayed that neither the grandeur of the house nor his desperate eagerness to get the commission would overawe him into behaving with a servility which would later make him ashamed.

*   *   *

Lord Goodchild stormed out of his steward's office and stalked across the wide domed rotunda, his top boots echoing on the marble floor. In his right hand was a wad of letters and papers, and on his face a fixed angry frown. Dressed in hunting pink with a massive ivory-handled whip in his left hand, Henry Audley Fitzwarine Grandison, 5th Baron Goodchild, Justice of the Peace, Lieutenant Colonel of Her Majesty's 17th Lancers and Master of Foxhounds of the Pembury Hunt, cut an impressive figure. Although almost forty, hardly a squire in the county looking at his sweeping whiskers, slender waist and upright carriage did not envy him. But on this November morning his lordship felt far from self-satisfied. He had already missed the hunt breakfast and would now probably be late for the meet too, a sin that, as master, he had a punctilious horror of committing. But this sporting discourtesy to the members of the hunt was not at present uppermost in his mind.

Half an hour earlier a letter from the Reverend Francis St. Clare, the chief magistrate in Rigton Bridge, had arrived by special courier with a description of a riot which had taken place on the station road the evening before. With his letter, St. Clare had enclosed a more deadly communication, originally sent by the home secretary to Lord Delamere, the general commanding the Northern District.

> Whitehall 8th November 1852
>
> My Lord,
>
> In consequence of acts of outrage and violence which have suspended the employment of labour in the town of Rigton Bridge, I am commanded by Her Majesty to impress upon your lordship the necessity of taking effectual and immediate measures for the repression of tumult during the forthcoming Parliamentary election, and for the protection of property. Your lordship is advised to hold in readiness such regiments of regular troops as you may deem necessary. . . .

There were two cavalry regiments stationed in Manchester: Goodchild's own 17th Lancers and a regiment of Light Dragoons, and these therefore would be the regiments to be "held in readiness." Goodchild had no sympathy with strikers, but the thought of ordering cavalry to disperse an unarmed mob on polling day was utterly repugnant to him, and this was what he now fully expected to have to do. Various personal considerations would make such a duty particularly invidious. While it was public knowledge that his lordship had supported Joseph Braithwaite's adoption as Tory candidate, it was less widely appreciated that the grateful manufacturer had subsequently lent the obliging peer twenty thousand pounds on the security of that nobleman's Belgravia town house. Three years before, Goodchild had lost thirty thousand in the 1849 railway stock fiasco, and, with his Irish estates already heavily mortgaged and his racing stud and stables alone costing him four thousand a year, so large a loss had brought him to the verge of bankruptcy. Some land sales had bought time, but only Joseph Braithwaite's interest-free loan had saved him. Joseph's price had been his lordship's political support. Without the votes of Goodchild's tenant farmers, Braithwaite had known that he could not be sure of winning the poll; with Lord Goodchild's public support, those votes would be safe.

Goodchild was not an imaginative man, but it was very clear to him that if he had to deploy his regiment to keep the peace on polling day, the mob would be unlikely to enjoy being constrained by men under the command of a lieutenant colonel who was also the unpopular candidate's proposer. With this thought in mind, Goodchild had resigned himself to missing the hunt breakfast in order to write two letters. The first, addressed to Joseph Braithwaite, had been a plea to do whatever was necessary to end the cotton operatives' strike, even acceding to some of their demands if need be, the alternative being further acts of violence, which might jeopardize his election. Goodchild believed Braithwaite to be incapable of compromise, but for all that had felt bound to try to persuade him. The second letter was to St. Clare, and in it Lord Goodchild suggested that the magistrate lay charges against as few of the station road rioters as he could conscientiously contrive. Many men committed for trial would merely increase the tensions in the town, as would the premature dispatch of troops from Manchester. Lord Delamere, Goodchild advised St. Clare, should be warned to send no troops for two weeks and better still none until the eve of polling day itself.

Having written those letters, Goodchild had visited his secretary in the steward's office to ask whether he had heard any news of the riot from any other sources. He had not, but before Goodchild could leave the room, the man had requested his master's signature to a check for almost five hundred pounds made out in favor of a London dressmaker. Lord Goodchild, within his limited capacity for such things, had been attempting to reduce his own expenditure during the past year, and this bill, announcing so clearly that his wife had not done likewise, following so hard on the heels of the morning's other unwelcome news, had sent his lordship hurrying across the rotunda, cursing under his breath.

He was about to open the door of the morning room, where he expected to find Lady Goodchild, when a footman came up behind him and begged to inform his lordship that a Mr. Strickland was asking to see him. Goodchild, who had forgotten that the painter existed, and had in any case intended his wife to interview the man, snapped out, "He must wait," and threw open the morning room door.

As he entered, he saw Helen Goodchild's reflection in the pier glass between the tall windows. She was sitting reading near the fire, her face protected from the direct heat of the flames by an oval fire-screen. In his agitated frame of mind the peace and stillness of the room irritated Goodchild.

"My dear, not gone yet?" murmured his wife, laying aside her book and smiling at him with a mixture of concern and covert amusement. "Surely the meet is not canceled?"

To any outsider, seeing Helen's brown questioning eyes and pale, upturned face—redeemed from classic perfection by a sprinkling of faint freckles across the bridge of her nose—these questions would have seemed entirely innocent, but to Lord Goodchild they contained unpleasant traces of mockery.

"And why, pray, might the meet be canceled?" he asked curtly.

Lady Goodchild shot him a surprised and reproachful glance.

"A bad frost perhaps? The ground too hard for the scent to lie well?" She gave a little shrug. "You're the one who knows everything about such things." She raised a hand to her temple where a lock of auburn hair had escaped from the narrow bandeau of lace serving as a cap. The studied grace and calmness of this movement made Goodchild grit his teeth. No worries for her about last night's violence or the approaching election. He threw down his whip and moved closer to her.

"I am asked to settle an account of yours to the tune of five hundred pounds. Is it in order, madam? I daresay you have looked it through?"

"Do *you* look through tradesmen's bills?" she asked, as though surprised that he should be suggesting such an unfamiliar procedure.

"I have recently made such matters my business," he muttered, stung by the irony of her tone, and reddening as he saw her nod understandingly and then raise the tips of her fingers to her lips as if to conceal a smile. But he detected no amusement a moment later when she said,

"Am I reproved for dressing as your wife ought to dress? I have done so out of respect for your position, not from vanity."

"Position be damned. If you wore rags you'd still be my wife. Clothes don't come into it."

She stiffened and he saw a hard glint in her eyes.

"You spend as much on pelisses for your troopers."

"It's expected, Helen."

"And what may I expect?" she asked after a sharp intake of breath.

"If I may see the bill," he replied calmly, "I will tell you."

Helen rose and moved toward the bellpull by the marble mantelpiece.

"Don't ring. I would prefer you bring it yourself."

"Cooper does not read my letters," she replied with offended dignity. When she started toward the mantelpiece again, he moved in front of her. She flashed him a contemptuous look and turned on her heel. "Since you are clearly determined to be unreasonable, I will go for it."

On her return, Goodchild took the thick white envelope and pulled out its contents, reading in silence for a while, then bursting out,

"Fifteen guineas for a Honiton fichu. What in the name of all that's reasonable is a fichu? A handkerchief, isn't it? Must you pay that for a miserable scrap of lace?"

"Large enough to cover the neck and shoulders, but no matter."

"A French cambric peignoir trimmed with Valenciennes: twenty guineas." The thick creamy paper shook in his hand. "Twenty guineas for the gown you wear when you have your hair dressed. It's preposterous, incredible."

She tossed back her head with apparent indifference to his remarks.

"I wear it to breakfast. Should I be careless of my appearance at the only meal we take alone together?"

He laughed derisively and stabbed at the paper with a finger.

"I see you're not careless of your appearance when we've company either. Dinner dresses at sixty guineas. A *manteau de cour*, whatever that may be: forty guineas. Nice round figures these." He unfolded another sheet. "Great God, it's endless . . . Lined with ivory satin, trimmed with handworked embroidery of wild flowers on Brussels net." He flung down the pages and sank down onto a chaise longue opposite the fire, resting his head in his hands.

He heard her come toward him and then felt a gentle hand on his shoulder. Her anger he could bear, but the sound of her pained voice enraged him.

"Harry," she whispered, "how do you expect me to sympathize? Tell me honestly how much you spend on the hunt each year, how much on the stables? What economies have you made there?"

"How can I turn away men who've worked for the family since I was a boy? To defray the stud's expenses, I've as near as damn it sold out to the Braithwaites. Must I do more?"

"Yet you bought a new mail phaeton easily enough."

He jumped to his feet, trembling with rage.

"I am not quite a beggar yet." His awareness of the fact that, by questioning her he had left himself open to similar criticism, did not diminish his sense of humiliation. She had turned away, as though implying that his behavior was too gross to be witnessed.

"You have every comfort in Manchester, people say," she said quietly.

"I live no better than most of my officers when I am with the regiment."

"I have heard otherwise."

"Then you heard lies," he shouted, storming toward the door, but stopping short, realizing that to leave now, just when Helen had hinted at knowledge of the Manchester villa he kept for entertaining his current mistress, would be playing into her hands. In front of him, on the top of a lacquered Chinese cabinet, was an ivory chess set on a mother-of-pearl board. He picked up a knight and examined it with as much calmness as he could contrive, knowing that he had made himself absurd. Then replacing the piece, he looked at his wife and sighed. If only she could make herself more obliging and less critical, but it was always the same with women who thought too much. The intelligence and sharpness of tongue that had once attracted him, now had the opposite effect. Still beautiful at thirty-two—not even he could deny that—but to him it seemed a chill beauty in comparison with the opulent and more blatant charms of his Manchester doctor's wife. When told of his troubles, Dolly Carstairs would not blame him for bringing them on himself, as Helen had so often done, but would give him the comfort and sympathy he craved.

Goodchild did not want to return to the subject of the dressmaker's bill, but, since he was determined not to leave meekly, as if cowed by his wife's hints, and could think of no other grounds on which to attack her, he could see nothing for it. He had noticed that the morning dress she was wearing—a dark blue jacket bodice, edged with bands of lace converging at her slim waist—was not one he had seen before, and this gave him an idea.

"Before you brand me a profligate," he said, "answer me this: what do you do with your fichus and fripperies?"

"Wear them."

"How many times?"

"As often as I please."

"Afterward. That's what I meant. What then?"

She smiled easily.

"I give them to Cooper or Dowson. Should I burn them?"

Goodchild glanced upward at the delicate plaster medallions on the ceiling.

"Your generosity is overwhelming. I'm sure your waiting maid is the toast of the servants' hall in a sixty-guinea evening dress."

"She wears such things only when she is free to visit friends in Flixton or Rigton Bridge."

"There must be girls all over the county who would pay us for the privilege of Cooper's place."

Helen pursed her lips and made an impatient movement with her hands.

"And does Rogers not wear your castoffs, Harry?"

"No valet of mine gets an item of clothing from me until it is well worn."

Helen bent down and handed her husband his whip.

"I am keeping you from your sport." She paused and looked at him intently. "You know well enough what you must do to make me obliging."

"What pray?"

"Withdraw your threat to sell Audley House."

"How can I?" he snorted. "You know we cannot afford a London establishment."

"I care nothing for the establishment. Reduce the stables to a single carriage and pair, discharge as many servants as you please, close half the rooms, but keep the house." She fixed her eyes on his and moved closer. "I will not be left here while you are with the regiment or anywhere that pleases you."

"Not be left here?" he cried. "Is this a hovel?"

"You know my meaning." She treated him to a simpering society smile. "Who will call this afternoon, think you? Lady Markham to admire my ferns and pelargoniums? And will she talk about the plot of the latest three-volume novel from Mudie's? Mrs. Halpin, I daresay, will bring her new piece of needlework, and, God help me, her dumpy daughter—the one who sings French songs. Remember? Afterward will I take my drive in the barouche, reclining like some jaded dowager? Or drive myself in the park phaeton? Such luxury of choice." She clasped her hands together and whispered, "For mercy's sake, Harry. These people are nothing to me. You have your life, let me keep mine in Belgravia. Do not sell the house."

He studied the figured veneers on the bureau cabinet against the far wall and shook his head, still unable to face her.

"I have no choice; none," he said brusquely, before turning and making for the nearest door, wishing fervently that he could have had the good sense to have controlled his immediate anger on seeing the bill. By now he might have been at the meet and this scene would not have occurred. He hurried through the dining room, into the billiard room and from there into the hall.

A groom was waiting on the gravel carriage sweep with the horse he would ride to the meet. His favorite hunter had been sent on ahead two hours earlier to be fresh for the hunt. He was a few yards from the glass door when he heard a man's voice,

"Lord Goodchild?"

He spun around, irritated to be detained, and saw a young man in a brown frock coat with long curling hair getting up from an uncomfortable "Grecian" stool in the apse facing the door.

"Who are you, sir?"

"My name is Strickland, my lord. I'm here to see you. Mr. Braithwaite most kindly . . ."

"Why are you waiting here?"

"I have your secretary's letter saying . . ."

"No, no, I meant you should have been shown to an anteroom. Well, no matter."

Lord Goodchild shook his head at the discourtesy of his servants and opened the door. The young man stepped forward and began firmly,

"The letter says most definitely that . . ."

"Very likely, but I can't help that." Goodchild slapped his whip against his thigh and then smiled, as though he had hit on a solution that would be ideal for both of them. "Today week. Yes. Come today week at the same time. I'll see you then. Good day."

Without waiting for any further objection he went out and hurried down the steps, seeing the groom run forward to hold his stirrup. Moments later he was in the saddle and the groom clambering up onto his own mount. Tom Strickland watched the two men cantering down the drive and bit his lips. His face was white with anger and disappointment. Tom blinked furiously, mortified to feel his eyes filling. After waiting hopefully for almost an hour, so sudden and contemptuous a dismissal had shocked and stung him almost with the pain of a physical lash across the face.

Hearing a low cough to his left, he looked up from the black and white marble floor and saw the splendid footman who had first let him in and asked him to wait. The man's white cravat and silver-corded tailcoat offended him less than his air of supercilious civility. The thought that this silent functionary had probably witnessed his humiliation sent the blood racing to Tom's cheeks. The footman was looking at him with an expectant expression—his formal subserviency, Tom suspected, disguising definite satisfaction at what had taken place, confirming that not only those in livery did Lord Goodchild's bidding.

Tom advanced on him with a positive tread and said loudly,

"Tell Lady Goodchild that Mr. Strickland wishes to speak with her about her portrait." The man favored him with a low bow. "And say that he waited for his lordship to no purpose, and had his lordship's letter promising an interview."

Helen Goodchild, who had been in no pleasant temper after her husband's departure, had not hesitated to refuse to see Joseph Braithwaite's artist—a decision which her conviction that Joseph was to blame for many of her husband's troubles made still less surprising. Her manner had been so peremptory that she was genuinely astonished to see the same footman return ten minutes later with the perplexing information that Mr. Strickland had no other pressing appointments and would gladly wait until her ladyship might find a convenient moment to see him.

Short of having this persistent person ejected, a course which Helen did not consider, she knew that she would have to receive him. After all his request to see her was not unreasonable; he had come by appointment. Her mind made up, Helen decided to summon him to the Red Drawing Room, a far more formidable setting than the morning room in which she had exchanged words with her husband. She was not concerned to impress this stranger, but was determined that he should relay to Joseph Braithwaite an account of the interview which would discomfort the manufacturer. To receive Joseph's protégé in style, and then to refuse his services with exquisite courtesy, would give her the double satisfaction of offending Braithwaite and distressing her husband, whose dearest wish seemed to be to avoid differences with his benefactor. Having been born into a far humbler family than her husband's, Helen felt the indignity of their indebtedness to the nouveau riche Braithwaites far more keenly than Harry himself appeared to do.

The Red Drawing Room—"red" because its walls were lined with faded crimson Spitalfields silk—was not only the largest reception room in the house, but also, with its gilded Empire furniture, boulle cabinets, Aubusson carpet and glittering Waterford chandeliers, the most imposing. Four windows, almost reaching the rococo ceiling, were separated from each other by identical marble-topped console tables, supporting tall mirrors in frames decorated with gilded acanthus leaves. But the room's principal glory was not the furniture, nor even the Sèvres, but the pictures, for these included a *Magdalene* by Titian, Rembrandt's *Head of a Jew*, a group of classical figures by Poussin, and Canaletto's *Market Place at Padua*.

When Mr. Strickland was announced, and entered, holding his hat nervously in his hands, Helen glanced briefly at him and motioned to him to be seated on a small upright chair next to an elegant card table near the center of the room. His appearance gave her a shock which she was careful to conceal. She had somehow expected any artist employed by the Braithwaites to be of stolid and workmanlike mien, but here was a young man, whose pale, sensitive face and dark eyes would certainly fulfill any impressionable young lady's ideal of what a romantic poet ought to look like. Without raising her eyes from the carpet, Helen asked pleasantly,

"Tell me, Mr. Strickland, how Mr. Braithwaite came to give you the privilege of immortalizing him?"

"He saw some work of mine."

"Where?"

"The Theatre Royal in Manchester."

"Pictures in a theater, Mr. Strickland?"

Helen noticed that he seemed embarrassed and decided to devote more conversational attention to Joseph Braithwaite.

"I painted the frieze over the proscenium arch, my lady. The choice of subject was provided: Shakespeare enthroned between two elephantine figures of Tragedy and Comedy."

He had spoken in such a matter-of-fact way that Helen could not decide whether he was being ironic; perhaps he disliked painting murals.

"Need they have been . . . elephantine?" she asked quietly.

"The theater manager has a fondness for draperies."

"A taste evidently shared by Mr. Braithwaite." Helen could not help smiling. "Perhaps you are painting him in a toga?"

Because of his previous seriousness, Helen was surprised when Strickland laughed.

"He has enough draperies in his library. I painted three panels for him there: Truth, Temperance and Humility all in billowing folds."

"Is Mr. Braithwaite's portrait to be part of this sequence of virtues? Representing Thrift perhaps?" She had said this with no trace of amusement and was impressed when the artist replied in the same manner.

"These are female figures, my lady. Mr. Braithwaite would feel out of place. His will be a plain portrait."

She could guess from the movements of his hands as he held his hat on his knee that Strickland was nervous, but his answers had surprised her as much as his appearance had done. Nervous and yet assured—a strange combination. It occurred to her that unless she could lead him into making the gauche and boorish remarks she had expected, she would find it hard to send him away empty-handed.

"I suppose," she said, "painting a manufacturer must pose certain problems. Admirals can study their charts, statesmen flourish scrolls, but what can the millowner exhibit? A hank of cotton? Or should he be resting his hands on an operative's head in the manner of prints of Wilberforce blessing a kneeling slave?"

"Mr. Braithwaite wishes to be painted in his park with his house behind him, just as many gentlemen of recent prosperity liked to have it done a century ago."

Although his tone had been pleasant, Helen felt reproved by it. She had attempted to ridicule Braithwaite and now she was placed in the wrong. There were plenty of pictures of Harry's ancestors displaying their wealth, usually through their clothes. Ostentation had only recently become vulgar. Before the manufacturers had been able to spend as much as the aristocracy, it had been quite respectable. The very room they sat in proved that point. Lady Goodchild decided on another approach.

"I have heard it said that daguerreotypes will soon make portrait painting a dead art. What is your opinion, Mr. Strickland?"

"If the rich decide to hand such things on their staircases and in their passages, your ladyship's prophecy will come true."

She raised her eyebrows with feigned surprise.

"Is custom all that keeps the art alive?"

"If it is dying, what else could save it?"

His calmness disconcerted her. She had supposed that he would fly to the defense of portraiture, but he had merely returned her questions to her.

"Is it dying?" she insisted.

"Compare daguerreotypes and painted portraits and your ladyship can judge as well as I."

She rose and looked at him imperiously.

"I asked for *your* opinion, Mr. Strickland; I need not inquire of you for my own."

She walked to the nearest window and gazed across the lawn to where a gardener was sweeping leaves. She felt dissatisfied and annoyed; she had intended to be courteous and now she had been rude. She had attacked his livelihood and he had cleverly avoided arguing with her; behavior she had rewarded with bullying. She thought he would not answer, but a moment later heard him say,

"The camera records each detail just the same, each one with perfect accuracy. The value of an artist's work is its imperfections. He stresses some things and ignores others."

She turned and smiled.

"You mean if my nose is large, you will enhance my eyes if they are nicely shaped?"

She detected confusion and surprise in his face, as though he could not understand why she seemed determined to misinterpret him. She told herself that it was ridiculous to bother about what he felt or thought, but could not help herself. Perhaps the commission would be important to him. It was not his fault that she disliked Braithwaite; before his arrival she had not thought of him as anything other than a means of annoying the millowner. Now the recollection troubled her. She had not been Lady Goodchild long enough to have forgotten a poor childhood. Her mother, a naval officer's widow, had only received a small pension and Helen well remembered the condescension of children in the larger houses in the neighborhood, and mothers who used their position to give them immunity from plain speaking. She also recalled with embarrassment how her own mother had considered the worst offenders to be those women who had married above them. Revenge for past affronts, when not so happily situated, had been her explanation, that and a feeling that it was necessary to prove themselves equal to their exalted role. Helen realized with embarrassment that Strickland had been speaking. She caught something about the eye selecting and not taking in everything like a lens.

"The daguerreotype freezes the sitter in a momentary attitude. The painter hopes to find an expression that conveys several moods. When I see a face, I see many faces . . . just as I have while watching your ladyship. I have to try to convey as much of this as I can on a single canvas. I select details not to flatter but to be truthful. The eye is no camera."

As he finished, she lowered her eyes, unable to think of any argument to use against what he had said, and not wishing to contradict him anymore. His manner was so unassuming and his voice so gentle that she wondered why she had not abandoned her earlier hostility at the outset. The argument with Harry, she supposed, still feeling anger when she thought of it. She moved closer to Strickland and said briskly,

"You have brought work for me to see?"

"Yes, in the hall. I didn't like to bring it up in case . . ." He fell silent, evidently uncertain how to frame what he had been going to say.

"In case I sent you about your business after a few words? I can see that an artist would prefer his person to be rejected, rather than his work." She was pleased by his smile of gratitude. Her guess had obviously been a good one. He got up, but did not move toward the door.

She had not rung for a servant to collect his portfolio and wondered whether he felt insulted. Her motive had been the simple fear that a footman would take far longer to find it. He was still holding his hat.

"You may put it down, you know," she murmured.

He did so absently.

"I was wondering," he said hesitantly, "whether it might be better for me to sketch your ladyship this morning? You could tell more from that."

"It will not take long?" He shook his head. "Very well. If you have not hidden your things, I will ring for them."

His relief and happiness were so obvious that she felt a tremor of alarm. She had no intention of employing him unless she liked his work.

"I have not made up my mind, you understand," she said abruptly.

"Oh, no, I didn't think that. I was afraid you weren't going to see what I can do. Now I'm to have a proper chance, I feel quite satisfied. It was just having a chance, you see, your ladyship."

His eagerness to avoid seeming presumptuous amused her, but she kept this to herself, and after a footman had been dispatched for the artist's things, resumed her position at the window with her back to the room. In two hours she would be entertaining a dozen or so members of the hunt and their wives. Already she imagined the clash of their boots and their laughter echoing in the tall, marble-paved hall, as they tossed aside their whips and jocularly threw their hats onto the heads of the row of classical busts at the foot of the stairs. And at their center would be Harry's bright smile and good-natured voice. Whether talking to women, playing cards, shooting with a keeper or sipping Madeira with a friend, he was always cheerful and self-assured, always when there was company, and yet, alone with her, his buoyancy deserted him. If he could only confess his fears, she thought, perhaps then . . . She closed her eyes, imagining herself politely inquiring about the chase. Who had been first at the kill, who had fallen at Dinsley Water, who had not fallen at Dinsley Water, who had taken the brush? How had Colonel Yates's new mare run, had those in carriages been able to see much? Then they would eat and later she would dispense tea and then they would play cards, and some dine, and all the time her face would ache with smiling and her mind be numbed by the triviality of everything she was saying. She heard Strickland come up.

"Now where should I sit, Mr. Strickland? Wherever the light is best, tell me. Anything can be moved."

* * *

Although the sun was quite warm, there were still long white streamers of mist lying along the banks of the distant river. Poised at the top of a gently sloping plowed field, the ragged line of scarlet-, green- and mulberry-coated riders held their horses in check, while grooms tightened girths, attended to stirrup leathers and examined saddles and reins. Flasks were handed around and several gentlemen lit cigars. Below them, several hundred yards across the field, was Swaleham Gorse, a nine-acre covert of gorse, blackberry bushes and stunted blackthorns, overshadowed by a few tall and spiky Scotch firs. Except for the occasional snort of a horse, or a spur clinking against a stirrup iron, all was quiet.

Even an indifferent judge of a horse would have admired the solitary hunter several paces in front of the other mounts. His accurate and easy step, dark brown muzzle, gleaming coat and silky mane, marked him out as a horse worthy of his rider: the master of the hunt. From his back, Lord Goodchild watched one of his whips canter over to the right of the covert and rein in behind a thick blackthorn screen. From inside the thicket came the faint crack of twigs and branches as the other two whips wound their way through the tangled undergrowth. Although there were eighteen couple of hounds in there with them, and a fox had been scented, they had not managed to force him from his stronghold. For minutes at a time no hound was visible; then one or two would come into view, noses down and sterns up, as they crossed a thinner part of the evergreen.

As Goodchild gazed out across his land toward the twisting river and the distant hills, his anticipation of the coming chase was marred by other thoughts. If Helen really did refuse to accept the loss of Audley House, what then? Would she prove mad enough to try to force a separation? Even if she could establish his adultery with Dolly Carstairs, she would not have grounds for a divorce; the law might be an ass, but at least it protected husbands from spiteful and jealous wives. Not that Helen was jealous, but she would still use any weapon she could to retain Audley House, possibly blackmail. While Goodchild could face a scandal, he knew that Joseph Braithwaite could not, with the election growing closer. His nonconformist voters would not take it kindly if his proposer were to be exposed as a philanderer. The upshot of the matter might be the withdrawal of Joseph's loan and that would place more than Audley House in jeopardy. As it was, Dolly's husband was extracting five hundred a year in exchange for his complicity. Then there was the horror of polling day itself. Goodchild shuddered as he thought of the web of difficulties that hemmed him in. Seconds later he heard a single note of the huntsman's horn from the covert, followed by several sharp shrill blasts as the fox broke and ran.

He watched fascinated as the animal hesitated for a moment in the clear light of the open field; a second and he might have darted back to safety, but then he saw the first of the hounds streaking out of the thicket, cutting off his retreat. For the first time in his life, Goodchild felt that he knew what it was like to be a fox. His whip was raised and his heels poised, as he saw, at the far end of the line of riders, a bolting horse careering toward the hounds.

"Hold hard, Goddammit, hold hard!" he roared.

Another moment and the fox would be headed, and either get back into the covert or run straight into the mouths of the hounds. He was shouting again when he recognized the rider: Humphrey, his own son. The boy's teeth were clenched together with rage and terror as he pulled at the reins twisted around his whitened knuckles; he was trying with all his might to turn the animal, but in vain; no cuts of the whip or use of his spurs made the horse obey the reins. A loud groan rose from all the riders as the fox bolted into the midst of the pack where he was torn apart. Goodchild cantered across to the huntsman and shouted,

"Send back the hounds, there will be no run today."

Humphrey's face was wet with tears and anger as his father rode past him with averted eyes. Never had Goodchild so much wanted to see a fox have a fair run. He had never asked the boy to excel with his tutor, never sworn at him if he knew no Cicero and less Virgil, never asked that he should do anything except ride decently to hounds. A year ago, shortly after Humphrey's twelfth birthday, Goodchild had pressed Helen hard to consent to her only child going away to Eton or Rugby, but she had refused. No blacking other boys' boots or cleaning their candlesticks for her boy, her Humphrey. No wonder the fool was good for nothing. For a few moments Goodchild's fury made him forget everything else, but then he saw George Braithwaite riding toward him; he turned his horse at once, seeing several of his tenant farmers doff their hats as he passed. To have to endure George's cheerfulness on such a morning would be beyond endurance. He could imagine what Helen would say when he got in. "I see that the world is quite over when a morning's sport is lost; perhaps you would like to flog your son like one of your troopers." He was thinking of Dolly Carstairs when George's voice sounded in his ear.

"I say, my lord, you're in a deuced hurry to be off. Why not draw the covert again? Devilish shame if we don't get a run, wouldn't you say?"

Goodchild's eye passed from the black silk facings of George's scarlet coat to his waistcoat, which was not only embroidered with foxes' masks, but also sported fox-teeth buttons. Longing to scream at him, Goodchild forced a smile.

"All gone to earth I'd say, George. Too bad."

"Wouldn't care to be in Master Humphrey's boots," chuckled George, evidently intent on humoring Goodchild.

"You might find them a trifle small," muttered the peer.

George laughed, delighted to have been answered with a joke.

"So they would be, so they would. He'll need even smaller ones when you've cut him down to size. No more top boots, eh? Half boots for Master Humphrey now."

"Surprised you're not with Miss Crawford, George," replied Goodchild, certain this was the best way to be rid of him.

"I say, where?"

"With the carriages."

Goodchild pointed with his whip and watched with satisfaction as George raised his hat and turned his horse. In fact he had not seen Catherine Crawford. He even felt a little guilt as George went off hopefully. The man was not the fool he sometimes seemed to be. Nervousness did strange things to people. Must watch my own nerves, he thought, as he rode on. Helen would be sure to keep hers.

*   *   *

After dressing, on the morning of the meet, Charles Crawford had been disturbed to learn that a tin-lined chest and portmanteau belonging to his brother had been delivered an hour earlier. He had anticipated Magnus's arrival sometime during the week and so had not been altogether taken by surprise; but the fact that Magnus, after so long an absence, had chosen to send on his luggage, while himself remaining in Rigton Bridge, had struck Charles, who knew nothing of the riot, as thoughtless and eccentric behavior. His relations with his younger brother had been indifferent since adolescence, but Charles still felt insulted and annoyed.

For this reason he had decided against abandoning his previous intention of riding to Hanley Park during the morning. Charles's timing of this visit, to coincide with the hunt, was deliberate, since he wished to see Helen Goodchild alone, and knew his chances would be best when both her husband and her son were riding to hounds.

Having left his horse at the stables, Charles did not make straight for the portico, but instead walked round to a small opening in the beech hedge screening the formal gardens to the west of the house and slipped through. His object was not to enter the house undetected but to gain more time in which to think about what he would say to Lady Goodchild. The ideal place for doing so unobserved was the area within the box hedges, which encircled the central lily pond.

Thirteen years before, when Helen had married Lord Goodchild, Charles Crawford had not been conspicuous among those offering their congratulations, and few people had been surprised. Charles's obsessive desire to marry Helen had been no secret in the neighborhood. As Sir James Crawford's goddaughter, Helen had regularly come to stay with the family during childhood, and Charles's love had dated from that time. Perhaps it had been the knowledge that he was his father's favorite that had led Charles to believe that no ambition of his could remain ungratified, if pursued with the ruthless and egotistical single-mindedness for which he so much prided himself. In any case Goodchild's success with Helen and his own failure had been a blow from which he had never fully recovered. He would have been a better loser if he had been able to believe that Helen had chosen his rival because a rich peer was a better catch than a baronet's heir, or because Goodchild had been superior to him in worthiness of character, dedication to duty or in other solidly conventional ways; but his sense of humiliation had been the greater for his conviction that Goodchild had succeeded precisely because he had been less earnest and dedicated, gifted only with a superficial charm and reckless gaiety.

Twice during the decade following his rejection, Charles had come close to marrying others, but a lack of enthusiasm at a critical time had lost him his first choice, and the second had not been prepared to come out to Zanzibar when he had been serving as first lieutenant in a frigate on the East African Station. After that, in emulation of his father—by then an admiral—Charles had replaced love with duty and had lavished the major part of his affections on the navy; but even then, always at the back of his mind had been the thought, never much more than a wishful dream, that one day Helen and Goodchild might separate.

The past three months had been the only prolonged period, since the start of his naval career, in which Charles had been without a ship; and, during this time, what had hitherto seemed a remote and foolish hope had come to look more substantial. A far less observant man than Charles, who missed little, would have noted the scarcely veiled hostility between Lord and Lady Goodchild on the few occasions on which they appeared together away from Hanley Park. Having made various clandestine inquiries, Charles had decided that Helen might very well wish to separate. If she did, Charles was confident that he could suggest a way in which she would be able to get a reasonable settlement, without the scandal and indignity of a divorce by private Act of Parliament—for which, in any case, there were probably insufficient grounds. It was to acquaint Helen with his plan that Charles had come to Hanley Park. His continuing doubts, about how best to broach so delicate a matter, accounted for his last-minute delay in the garden.

Of course, even if Helen agreed to follow his advice, Charles knew that he might still not win her for himself, but he was equally well aware that, if he did nothing, he would also achieve nothing. Gratitude and dependence were supposed to be reliable keys to the heart and he had resolved to see if he could make them fit.

At intervals along the boxhedge, statues had been placed: a marble faun with a missing arm, a moss-eaten Cupid leaning drunkenly toward a similarly eroded Psyche, as if yearning for a never-to-be-consummated kiss. Having little time for symbolism or allegory, Charles saw no ironic comment on his own mission. In the middle of the pond, a statue of a bearded Triton released a fitful trickle of water from the lip of a large

stone vase clutched under a green and slimy arm. Charles stepped forward and looked down at his reflection in the murky water. A face
reddened by his years at sea, and coarser-featured than his brother's.
The same piercing blue-gray eyes of all the Crawford family, and hair as
thick as Magnus's but fairer; fairer too were his pale, almost white,
eyebrows and eyelashes. Tall and broad-shouldered, Charles looked as
formidable as he liked to be thought. His one feeling of physical inadequacy was caused by two missing fingers on his left hand—these had
been crushed in an accident at sea; and, although he had kept his flattened signet ring as a memento, he was still morbidly sensitive about the
disfigurement.

His thoughts finally in order, Charles turned and walked purposefully
away from the pond and emerged from the shelter of the hedge on the
open lawn in front of the west wing. He was wondering whether the
garden door would be locked when he caught sight of Helen through a
window. She was standing behind a young man sitting on a chair, and
was looking at some sort of paper he was holding up for her. A moment
later the man got up and Helen laughed over something he had said.
Charles's view was not improved by reflections of the sky in the panes of
glass, but, moving closer, he was surprised to see that Lady Goodchild's
companion was an artist who had been pointed out to him at Braithwaite's house a week before. While Charles did not for a moment suppose that her ladyship could be attracted to a man of Strickland's class
and profession, he felt irritated to find him at Hanley Park, especially on
this particular morning; and, momentarily forgetting that she owed her
rank to her neglectful husband, he was indignant that Helen should
lower herself, by allowing an artist to see that she found him amusing.
But then Helen had never been conventional, as the identities of many
of those permitted to dine at her table in London had already amply
proved. It was in spite of such things that Charles cared deeply for her.

Finding the garden door locked, he had to retrace his steps to the
beech hedge and go in at the main hall.

Helen came toward Charles as soon as he had been announced.

"An unexpected pleasure, Charles. I believe you have not met Mr.
Strickland. Captain Crawford, permit me to introduce Mr. Strickland."

Charles nodded briskly to Tom and put down his hat and cane on a small table by the door, making it evident, Tom thought, that he was too insignificant to be accorded the privilege of shaking hands. In fact he had seen Crawford at a large reception given by Joseph Braithwaite but had not been told his name. Now he found it incredible to discover that this man, with his awkward movements and set face, was the brother of the poised and graceful traveler he had met so recently on the station road. Tom saw Crawford murmur something to Lady Goodchild, who nodded and then turned to him apologetically:

"Mr. Strickland, I fear you must excuse me for a moment."

Tom thought she looked irritated as she led Charles from the room, but though he would have liked to have continued sketching her, he was too happy to feel any serious disappointment. After seeing two rough sketches, Lady Goodchild had agreed to sit for her portrait.

Helen ushered Charles along a covered colonnade until they reached the tall glass doors of the conservatory. She motioned to him to be seated on an ornate white iron seat but remained standing herself. He looked at her against the lush and improbable background of broad leaves and serrated fronds. Everything about her appearance pleased him: her complexion, her hair, the way her clothes always emphasized the perfection of her figure. She was waiting for him to speak. Seeing that the doors were still open, he got up and closed them.

"Helen, forgive me for intruding into what is clearly none of my business, but, as an old friend, perhaps you will bear with me. I know you will think me absurd for asking this, but the question has some bearing on another matter of great importance." He paused awkwardly, covering his embarrassment by resuming his seat. "Has your husband employed any new male servants in recent months?"

She frowned and shook her head, as though trying to clear it.

"Am I to understand, Charles, that you have come to talk about our servants?"

"Believe me, Helen, the subject is serious enough," he replied, wounded by her incredulity.

She gave him a resigned smile, which reminded him of a patient governess with an obtuse pupil, and sat down next to him.

"Since the matter is obviously of such interest to you—Harry does not interview servants. Our steward employs male staff; the housekeeper takes on the maids, except those who wait on me—naturally I interview them." She smiled. "I had almost forgotten to say that cook chooses her kitchen maids."

"But there have been new servants engaged recently?" he asked, persevering in spite of her ironic tone.

"They come and go," she replied with obvious impatience. "Ought I to be counting spoons and forks?"

"Have any new servants been seen skulking around doors?"

Helen threw up her hands in amazement.

"Heavens above, Charles, servants have always listened at doors and always will. Imagine how dull they would be without that amusement." She paused and stared at him with a directness that made him lower his eyes. "Spare me your insinuations, Charles, and speak plainly. You think Harry is having me spied upon. Is that not so?"

The sudden change from superior amusement to indignation and deadly earnestness shook Charles.

"I have no positive proof," he murmured, noticing that she was blushing.

"But you must think he has good reason for suspicion. Otherwise why should you wish to warn me?"

Charles could feel his heart thumping and an unpleasant tightness in his throat. He had hoped to manage matters more smoothly.

"Suspect you of anything, Helen? Nothing could be further from my mind. You ask me to be plain with you and I will try, although I confess to speak of such matters pains me beyond words." He paused and looked down at the tessellated floor of the conservatory. When he continued it was rapidly, as though he were eager to be done with what he had to say. "Lord Goodchild is at present embarrassed by the possibility of an action being brought against him by a Manchester physician."

Charles saw her smooth her dress nervously and then gaze at him as if uncertain that she had heard him aright; then, recovering herself, she asked in a level voice,

"May I ask the nature of this action?"

"Crim con," he replied, with burning cheeks.

She stared at him with sudden anger.

"Come, Charles, our grandmothers used that term. May we not say adultery? This man's wife is Harry's mistress, I suppose?" He nodded.

"And Harry is likely to be cited in divorce proceedings brought against her by her husband? Have I understood you?"

"You take this calmly, Helen," he replied with open admiration.

"Was it not bound to happen sooner or later?"

"Perhaps." He paused and groaned inwardly at how very differently he had envisaged her reacting. He had imagined tears and his comforting arm on her shoulder. "Matters are not quite as straightforward as I may have led you to believe," he went on. "Lord Goodchild will do all he can to stop the proceedings; he has many reasons for wishing to do so."

"Mr. Braithwaite would not approve, I daresay," said Helen with a bitter smile.

"Harry also has ambitions to be appointed general for the district when Delamere goes. A scandal would do little for his chances. Obviously he will bribe the doctor to prevent the action."

A silence followed, only broken by the chirping of small birds sheltering in the conservatory from the cold outside. Charles was alarmed by the strange expression on Helen's face.

"Why have you told me this?" she whispered. "To make me wretched? What possible gain can there be in my knowing?"

"Bear with me, Helen," he murmured, knowing that the critical moment had arrived. Now he could no longer delay telling her his plan. His eyes gleamed with excitement as he leaned toward her. "Should you try to force a separation now, Harry could not resist your demand, if you threaten to make his behavior public."

He watched her face intently not knowing what to expect. When she spoke, the soft sadness of her voice contrasted strangely with the harshness of what she had to say.

"You must think me desperate indeed to dare suggest such a dishonorable course to me."

"I only do so," he cried, "because I cannot bear to see you humiliated." He gazed at her with tender entreaty. "Let me talk to this doctor, Helen. I will say that, unless he goes on with his divorce and tells Harry that he is going to, I intend to inform his superiors that he is taking bribes. To avoid the loss of his medical license, he will oblige me."

Helen shook her head and frowned.

"How can it help me if he does cite Harry? A wife cannot seek a divorce on the grounds of adultery alone."

Charles's hopes rose again with what he took to be acquiescence on her part. He turned to her, his normally impassive face glowing with animation.

"Tell Harry that only you can prevent the case being brought. Explain your hold over the man. If you do that, I'd stake my life Harry will consent to a separation in a month or two and make you a generous settlement. He has too much to lose to dare gamble on whether you are in earnest. Everything's on your side—Harry's reliance on old Braith-waite, the election . . . everything." He jumped up unable to hide his feverish excitement. "Your chance may not come again. A few months' time and Harry will snap his fingers at any threat of scandal. You must act now or not at all." Her thoughtful silence maddened him. "What do you say, Helen?"

She hung her head for a moment and then said quietly,

"I will not pretend to maidenly outrage at your proposition. I can't tell you what I think now. I hardly know myself. I must have a few days to consider."

"You will send word then?"

"Yes."

Charles walked toward the doors, exulting in his success. Standing with his hands clasped behind his back—a pose that concealed his mutilated fingers—he said,

"Now perhaps you will appreciate my mention of the servants. Harry knows his present danger well enough. It would suit him to be able to produce trumped-up evidence against you if you prove awkward."

"I have nothing to conceal."

"Much can be made of little," he replied with a grim smile. "I would suggest that after this meeting you receive no gentlemen if you are alone. I would also advise you not to sit for your portrait, if that is your intention."

"Nobody would believe that I would . . ." She left the sentence unfinished, seeing his skeptical expression. "Harry would not stoop to using perjured statements," she ended, regaining her composure.

"If I am to help you, Helen, I think you should abide by my advice," he said gently.

"Very well," she sighed, "I will do as you ask, although I know you are no friend to Harry."

"If I were, you would hardly trust me."

Taking her silence for assent, Charles bowed to her and pushed open the doors. On reaching the Red Drawing Room, he did not bother to say anything to Strickland, but picked up his hat and cane and left the room. On his way to the stables, his elation was so great that he would have thrown his hat into the air or slashed the bushes with his cane, if he had not feared being observed.

When Helen returned to the room, Tom could see that whatever Crawford might have said had made a deep impression on her. Her former gaiety and sharpness of observation had given way to a self-absorbed and indifferent mood. He almost felt that she had forgotten his presence until she sat down in a chair close to him and said absently,

"I fear that I shall after all be too much engaged during the next few weeks to sit for you."

Tom looked at her aghast. She had made this devastating announcement with the distant unconcern that might have been appropriate for a remark about a change in the weather or the unexpected addition of another guest for dinner. The cruelty of the *volte-face* astonished and enraged him.

"If your ladyship would rather another artist . . ." he replied with icy control, deliberately leaving his sentence unfinished.

"I told you your work pleased me," she replied sharply. "I have not changed my mind. The timing is all that is in question."

"Your ladyship knew that I would be leaving for London in two weeks and told me distinctly that you could spare the necessary . . ."

"Perhaps even you have overlooked things on occasion, Mr. Strickland," she cut in, evidently annoyed that he should have pressed her.

"Indeed," he conceded with a show of contrition. "I hope your ladyship will not think me unreasonable if I ask you during which month at least I should expect . . ."

"I'm afraid I cannot tell you anything at present."

Although Tom thought he could detect a hint of apology in her voice, her refusal to give him even the vaguest commitment convinced him that he had been rejected. If she had any intention of employing him, she would surely prefer to guess now and change the dates later rather than say nothing. No reason could explain her behavior satisfactorily, except an inability to tell him to his face that she had changed her mind. The initial shock had passed, and his hands shook with anger as he took his sketchbook and ripped away the top three pages.

"In case any further events prevent you sitting at all, please allow me to leave these with you as some reward for what will then prove to have been a wasted hour." He got up and placed the sketches on his chair. Now he was eager to leave as quickly as possible. The room with its boulle tables and scantly appreciated works of art made him want to shout his disgust.

"I will keep them carefully, Mr. Strickland."

Tom picked up his hat and moved toward the doorway, where he turned.

"It may be unbecoming of me to make such an observation, your ladyship, but it might be less painful for any artist you may consider commissioning in the future if you withhold your appreciation until you are able to make some firm undertaking." His memory of Goodchild's treatment of him added to this rebuff made his lower lip tremble.

She rose and came several steps toward him, and said very softly,

"Mr. Strickland, not everything is always just as it seems."

"I have had proof of that today," he returned, refusing to be won over by the slight hint of pathos and appeal in her voice. How delightfully capricious to make a riddle out of a straightforward rejection; how amusing to try to make a man feel that his fall from favor is in some obscure and mysterious way impossible to explain; how enigmatic. Perhaps she thinks I will blame myself in the end, he thought bitterly, shutting the door behind him.

Alone, Helen raised clenched fists to her face and pressed them against her eyes. She did not suppose that in Strickland's position she would have behaved very differently. She cursed Charles and her husband silently and then with a sinking heart remembered what had been said in the conservatory. There were few things that she desired less than being beholden to Charles Crawford. But then, if Charles could be so resourceful, might she not be the same? The steward's books must surely have some record of payments to a Manchester physician. They would look quite innocent there. Men paid dearly for their health, particularly those like Harry who set such store on physical prowess. She could discover this doctor's name; yes, and see him too . . . herself. She breathed deeply, feeling suddenly sick as she remembered Charles saying that he could not bear to see her humiliated. Perhaps he would not have to bear it after all.

Not long afterward she heard the sound of raised voices coming from the hall; the members of the hunt were returning. She rested her forehead against the cold marble mantelpiece for several seconds and then went out to meet them, a smile already on her lips.

∾ *Three* ∾

Three miles from Hanley Park was Leaholme Hall, a smaller house but two centuries older, although the Crawfords had owned it for a mere seventy years. When the first baronet had bought the hall, the trees in the park had been wastefully and wantonly cut down, leaving the place naked and unsheltered on its low eminence, and, since then, his successors had done little to remedy this, beyond planting a few scraggy poplars and light-leaved birches, which now formed an interrupted screen to the southwest. The only old tree near the house was an ancient cedar, whose dark foliage conveniently obscured the modern brickwork of the new wing. Two stories high for the most part, with small, leaded panes set in mullioned windows, the house was too low and rambling to be imposing, and too large to be idiosyncratically homely, like so many smaller Elizabethan halls and manor houses.

As his gaze passed from the dark outer hedge of the topiary garden to the small clock tower above the stables, Magnus slowed his horse to a trot. His heart was full of misgiving, and, apart from his eagerness to see his sister, he took little pleasure in his homecoming. In any case Leaholme Hall was his home only in the most limited sense, since it, like his father's title and most of his possessions, would finally pass to Charles as Sir James Crawford's heir. But, as Magnus rode under the shadow of the squat central tower, resentment of the inferior prospects of a younger son had little to do with his despondent mood; the roots of that lay in the host of memories summoned up by the creeper-covered walls of his childhood home.

Even as children, Magnus and Charles had been markedly different: Magnus devoted to his mother and sister, Charles, four years his senior, concerned only with an assiduous emulation of their father. When

Charles had gone to sea as a boy of thirteen, Magnus had remained at home, rarely seeing his brother for more than a month or two every three years. The navy had also separated Magnus from his father, who, like Charles, had disapproved of his remaining at home; but Magnus's mother had encouraged him to do so and had employed a succession of tutors rather than have him sent away to school.

Magnus had been sixteen when his father took command of the blockading squadron, engaged in suppressing the West African Slave Trade. His mother, in spite of her younger son's pleas, had gone out to join her husband. Six months later Magnus had opened his father's letter telling him that she had died of fever. The dangers of the African coastal towns had been well known, and Magnus had never forgiven his father for allowing her to go. At Oxford, the following year, Magnus had embarked on what an outsider might have thought a frenzied course of self-destruction, but which was in truth aimed at his father. Sir James had considered him a coddled and oversensitive youth, and now Magnus set about showing him something different.

More innocent, because of his sheltered upbringing, than most of his contemporaries, Magnus had at first been forced to assume a cynical air of sophistication to avoid being hurt and ridiculed; but before long the pose seemed to have become the reality. Working not at all, drinking to excess and gambling with a recklessness unusual even among the richest aristocratic set, Magnus had gone down with no degree and debts of over two thousand pounds. His father had settled them on condition that his son take a post in the colonial service. The best Indian regiments being considered too expensive, he had been bought a commission in the Ceylon Rifles. He had served with distinction and had satisfied his conscience by testifying against the governor of the colony at the Commons Select Committee Inquiry into the recent disturbances there. Now, seven years after he had sailed from Southampton, he was returning home with little more than the sum raised by the sale of his commission—returning to live at his father's expense while Sir James's term as admiral on the North American Station lasted. His future seemed uncertain and ominously empty.

On learning from the butler that Captain Crawford was not at home, and that Miss Catherine had been riding earlier in the afternoon, but might by now be back at the stables, Magnus immediately made his way there. She was not in the yard, so he walked on toward the thick haw-thorn hedge enclosing the two paddocks. He opened the gate of the smaller one but did not at first see his sister. In the center of the field, a groom was ringing a colt. A bolster had been strapped to the animal's back to get him used to carrying weight, and he was lunging and dancing around at the end of a long halter, vainly striving to dislodge the un-familiar object. As Magnus glanced to his right, he saw Catherine watch-ing the proceedings from the gate leading into the adjacent paddock. He shouted to her and then started running across the rough grass.

They embraced on meeting, and Magnus, finding himself close to tears, could not imagine how he had felt such gloom approaching the house. In a neat black riding habit and soft dove-gray hat with a feath-ered plume, Catherine stood before him, and suddenly his time away seemed a brief interval of weeks not years. She smiled at him, cheeks flushed with excitement, and took both his hands in hers. The same vivid blue eyes, the same silvery blonde hair dressed in ringlets, the same Catherine, after seven years. The same, he repeated to himself, as if seeking conviction. Yet, even at this moment of meeting, he could not forget that George Braithwaite had proposed to her. Twenty-five, thought Magnus, and she was eighteen when I left.

As they walked in the direction of the house, Catherine turned to him and squeezed his arm.

"You must stay ever so long, Magnus."

"I'm not going back," he murmured.

"The hero of Kandy not going back?" she laughed, evidently suspect-ing a joke until she saw the seriousness of his face. "But why?" she asked in astonishment.

"I sent you the extracts from my evidence printed in *The Times*."

"I read them."

"Then you know why I can't return. The very men who praise me to my face for doing what I did, snarl at me behind my back."

"Poor Magnus."

"I'm not going to force any more natives to work on roads while their rice harvest rots. The coffee planters need the roads; they can get them built without me."

The sun was sinking, an indistinct red sphere, and the wind seemed colder. Dead leaves rustled across the gravel path, swirling in wide circles.

"So what will you do?" she asked with a nervous frown.

Her concern touched him, but Magnus had no wish to mull over his future so soon after his arrival. He shrugged his shoulders.

"Become a briefless barrister or make my fortune in the Australian goldfields," he answered with a laugh, and then stared at her with a parody of sternness. "Since I have come so far to see you, I trust you have given thought to my entertainment."

Catherine opened her eyes very wide and simpered coyly:

"Oh, yes, indeed, but I fear you will find us very dull with our muslin work and piano pieces from Donizetti and Bellini."

"On the contrary," he objected with great earnestness, "muslin and Donizetti are both absolute passions with me. In Ceylon I felt the absence of them sorely."

He gazed at her intensely until they both started to laugh. Then, arm in arm, they resumed their walk toward the house. Once they had laughed a great deal together. Magnus stopped as they reached the carriage sweep. From where they stood the sun's reflections in the diamond-shaped windowpanes made them glow like dull points of fire in the dark facade.

Most of the rooms in the house were narrow and low-ceilinged, but not so the Great Hall, which was still used for dining. With its high, oak, hammer-beam roof, carved screen and minstrels' gallery, it dated from that remote period when the family had sat at a high table on a dais, while their servants ate below them in the main body of the hall. Now there was only a single mahogany table, in the center of the room, immediately beneath a massive brass chandelier holding two dozen candles. Yet, not even with added light from the candelabra on the table and from oil lamps on the sideboard was more than a fraction of the cavernous room well lit. In the somber grandeur of this ancestral hall, Magnus dined with his brother and sister.

As the meal drew to a close the atmosphere was tense and uneasy. Charles had argued that his decision to leave Ceylon was a virtual confession of failure, just as Magnus had supposed he would. Principles, in his view, ought not to come into what was a matter of common sense. Whatever the shortcomings of officials and planters, Magnus would be a fool to throw away years of experience without having any alternative profession to take up. While Charles held forth, Catherine said nothing, and Magnus merely gazed at Beechey's portrait of the first baronet above the wide Tudor fireplace, recalling how much he had infuriated his father by comparing their ancestor's eighteenth-century admiral's full-dress uniform with the cocked hat and broad facings of a modern beadle's outfit.

He had vowed that, whatever his brother might say, he would not lose his temper. So when Charles had finished with Ceylon to his satisfaction, Magnus did not argue, but instead steered the conversation back to the troubles in Rigton Bridge, which had received an airing earlier, when he had told them about the riot. Wishing to find out Catherine's opinion of the Braithwaites indirectly, he thought this could be achieved by speaking of the strike. As though quite unversed in such things, he asked Charles humbly whether he thought the strikers would give in before the election. The naval officer snorted derisively.

"Not a chance. They're stubborn as mules."

"Couldn't the masters make concessions?"

Charles filled his glass from a decanter and pushed the coaster toward Magnus.

"Of course not. They can't afford to lose face."

Magnus glanced at Catherine but learned nothing from her impassive expression. They had finished eating and she might choose at any moment to withdraw, so that the cloth could be removed and port set out for the brothers to drink alone.

"Won't the union also worry about loss of face?" asked Magnus mildly.

"They're just out to intimidate sensible men who want to work." The slight flush on Charles's cheeks might have been from the claret, but Magnus thought it indicated strong feelings about the troubles. He placed his elbows on the table and leaned forward.

"But surely, Charles, not even sensible men can work when Irishmen fill their places?"

"I told you, the union stopped local men selling their labor." Charles sipped his claret thoughtfully and smiled. "With respect, Magnus, I don't think a colonial soldier is ideally equipped to make judgments about an English strike."

"Judgments? I didn't know that I'd even expressed an opinion," he replied, struggling to suppress his mounting irritation. He had never forgotten the way Charles had used his superior years to deride his views in childhood. "But I'll tell you my opinion, in case you misunderstand me. Unless Braithwaite discharges the Irishmen, last night's violence will be a trivial hors d'oeuvre to the feast we can expect on polling day." He turned to Catherine and asked quietly, "Does your opinion differ?" He could tell from the way she refused to meet his eye that she knew that he was asking a question that was partly a challenge and partly an appeal for her loyalty. She looked down at the table and hesitated a moment before saying rapidly,

"My opinion can neither differ or agree. I know nothing of trade." She rose and smiled briefly before withdrawing.

When she had gone and the butler had removed the cloth and set glasses in front of them, Magnus still felt stunned by her reply. Her genteel and prim assertion, that trade was too far beneath her to be considered, had been out of character. She had listened to their conversation patiently enough until he had mentioned Joseph Braithwaite specifically. Only then had she decided to leave. There could now be little doubt that she was seriously considering George's proposal. Not wanting to have to talk, Magnus asked his brother when he thought he would next have a ship; and soon, as he had expected, Charles was embarked on a lengthy monologue about the inadequacies and vacillations of the Board of Admiralty. The subject would undoubtedly last them until they joined Catherine again and possibly longer. While Charles talked, it occurred to Magnus that his brother would almost certainly favor a marriage to George Braithwaite, since if Catherine were to remain a spinster, the ultimate responsibility for her support would fall on him. With her mother dead and her father almost always away from home, Catherine was not well placed to have many London seasons. None of this would have escaped Charles, if, as seemed probable, he had assessed the possible alternatives to George.

Two hours later, when Charles eventually rang for the chamber candlesticks to be brought to light them to bed, no word had been spoken by anybody about George Braithwaite. But Magnus remained certain that Strickland had told him the truth the previous evening. He had been prepared to let matters rest awhile, because, in spite of some doubts, he believed that he knew a way to end Braithwaite's chances.

Earlier that day in Rigton Bridge, he had visited the offices of the

Rigton Independent, the town's only radical newspaper, with the intention of finding out more about the troubles. Instead he had discovered something of equal interest—something that involved George in a racing fraud.

The fact that racehorse owners often found it more profitable to enter an animal to lose a race rather than to win it was well known to him. To encourage heavy betting, the owner would make every public effort to persuade punters that the horse was a certain winner. Such bets would then be taken up by the owner's friends, who would of course be very careful not to appear as such. In the race the jockey's instructions would be to hold the horse back. According to one of Braithwaite's grooms, who had tipped off the *Independent*, George had followed this unsporting procedure in the Yorkshire Stakes, and had won more money, by laying against his own horse, than he would have done if he had taken the prize. The paper had printed the groom's story in the sure belief that Braithwaite would not sue. Few owners liked to gain still greater notoriety by suing their detractors for libel, but George had done just this; and, since the jockey could not be found, and none of those who had taken up bets could be linked directly with Braithwaite, the case had gone against the paper. The lack of evidence had disturbed Magnus; in such cases something unpleasant always came out; but if the groom had been *told* to tip off the paper, everything fell into place. The editor could not pay the fine and would therefore have to liquidate at a very convenient time for George's father, whose electoral prospects would be the better for the disappearance of the town's only radical newspaper. If George and Joseph Braithwaite had really planned such a thing, Magnus did not consider it unlikely that they had also provoked the strike deliberately to frighten electors into voting for the manufacturer, as the reactionary candidate more likely to be firm with lawbreakers and to restore order in the town.

Although Magnus instinctively mistrusted George, he knew little about him. When Magnus had sailed for Ceylon, George had been a youth of seventeen. But for Joseph Braithwaite, Magnus entertained no such vague feelings. When Magnus had been an undergraduate, Joseph had suspected, incorrectly as it happened, that the young man had designs on his daughter Annette. Since the girl had been plain, and her father at that time considerably less affluent, she had often been ignored at balls and other social functions. Out of kindness, Magnus had made it his business to talk to her and to ask her to dance. The idea that marriage to her would solve many of his problems had crossed his mind, but he had taken no deliberate steps to achieve this end. When, therefore, Joseph had warned him off with remarks about avaricious fortune-seekers and penniless younger sons, ready to stoop to any mean act and deception to gain their objectives, he had been furiously angry, and even after eight years had not forgiven the slight. Together with his present suspicions, the memory of that interview accounted for Magnus's inflexible determination to stop Catherine marrying George.

Once in his bedroom, Magnus lit more candles with a spill from the fire, and then, intent on clarifying his thoughts, sat down at the small davenport writing desk by the window and began to note down the information about which he already felt certain. Ten minutes later, he heard a soft knock at the door and looked up to see Catherine enter. She moved across the room without speaking, and, as the light from the fire patterned her dark velvet dress, he was surprised to notice that she had fastened a silver chatelaine around her waist, as though to remind him that this shining silver belt would be her badge of office if she were to remain unmarried, its hanging keys, to the safes, jewel boxes and linen chests, symbols of her future life as Charles's housekeeper. Waiting for her to speak, he had idly started to melt sealing wax over a candle. Taking a seal from a compartment in the desk, he brought it down with a thump on a blob of wax which had fallen on some paper.

"You're angry with me," she said quietly, resting her hands on the back of a prie-dieu close to the tall canopied bed. Her high-necked dress, with its small collar of lace and white cuffs, reminded him powerfully of dresses she had worn years ago; its color too, blue, had always been a favorite of hers.

"No, I'm not angry," he replied with a sigh. "When we choose to voice our opinions honestly is our own affair."

"One may have an opinion and not be free to voice it," she replied, encouraged by his gentle tone. "Mr. Braithwaite recently told Charles that the duty on chicory was to be doubled and advised him to buy all he could at the old price so he could sell at the new. He will have nothing said against Joseph."

"I thought you knew nothing of trade," said Magnus in a flat voice, getting up as he did so, as if overcome with impatience, and pacing across the room. He turned in front of a large tapestry. "You gave no opinion because you intend to marry George Braithwaite."

He watched her draw herself up very straight.

"And if I do?" she asked in a defiant whisper.

"You will become the wife of somebody whose father is as unscrupulous as he is ruthless."

"But the son is not the father, Magnus."

"The resemblance is closer than you may suppose."

She raised her hands to her face and laughed.

"Really, you're too absurd, Magnus. You've scarcely been in the neighborhood a day and you begin making solemn pronouncements about this person and that as though, forgive me, you're God Himself."

"Several people, besides God, know that George sued the *Independent* and bribed the most important witness to hide himself."

"All *I* know is that he was libeled and had the courage to sue." The silence, which followed this vehement exchange, was heavy with embarrassment. Realizing that Magnus was not going to speak, she came toward him with a placating smile. "Because there was so much dishonesty in Ceylon, you must not suppose that all the world is as bad. We should be happy, Magnus. Tonight of all nights we should not be arguing. How can we speak like this on the day of your return?"

"Because if we do not," he said, hiding his agitation, "we may as well say nothing in the weeks to come."

She did not reply but moved to the dressing table and sat down. Pulling the candle bracket closer to the mirror, Catherine stared at her reflection and secured her falling ringlets behind her ears, in the severer manner of older women.

"You have no right to reprove me for doing what the world so regularly applauds. Am I so angelic and rare a creature to escape the general rule of marrying for an establishment? At twenty-five should I still be swooning with the kind of love poets describe?" She shot him an ironic, questioning glance. "Love in a cottage may exist, but when the tiniest villa on the Thames cannot be had under two hundred a year, cottage love has become a luxury."

To give himself time to think, he put more coals on the fire.

"If Father becomes port admiral at Plymouth or Portsmouth, you will have your pick of naval officers. You will be his hostess."

She smiled at him and shook her head slowly.

"Father take a dull dockyard when he may yet hoist his flag off Spithead or Valetta? When I am fifty he may accept Portsmouth and then I may still take my pick, I suppose?"

The pallor of her face, her silvery hair, and slender hands moving restlessly in the candlelight gave an impression of such ghostly fragility that Magnus found it hard to take in her words, coming, it seemed, from an alien world, in which she had no place: a world of crude exchange and ill-considered pledges, savagely redeemed.

"Can you not try one more season?" he asked.

"Why one? Three or four might be better, but who will pay? And will Aunt Warren be ready to drag me from ball to soirée so I may run through my accomplishments yet again? You know her age and disposition." She tilted back the mirror, so she could no longer see herself. "George is too much influenced by his father, but I can wean him from it. He is rich, good-natured and loves me." She looked up at his sad face and reached out for his hand. "If I stay here I shall go mad; not all at once; only a little at a time. Not next year, nor the year after, but every day a little more, for ten, fifteen, twenty years in this house. Ministries may fall, armies perish, the Nile's source be found, while I remain the same. Is that your wish?" With sudden violence she ripped the chatelaine from her waist and flung it at his feet. "Would it please you to see that chain about my waist and hear me prattle about my housekeeping duties? Then you might ask yourself why I never married George. But I will be too busy to remember, too concerned whether a parlor-maid is dishonest or the butler watering Charles's best claret." She breathed deeply, trying to calm herself, but her eyes were still brilliant and her lips trembling. "No," she cried. "I refuse that empty life. Because you think me pure and innocent must I sacrifice myself to save your illusions? Time didn't stand still because you were away. You might like to, but we can't return to what we were when Mother was alive. Would you have ruined yourself at Oxford, if she'd shielded you less? Even cosseted children must grow up. So don't make her mistake with me. I don't want your protection."

She had spoken so rapidly that he had found himself snatching at isolated words, aware of her eyes all the time and compelled to silence by them, though he longed to stop her. To his surprise she now seemed absorbed in thought, as though trying to remember something, but then she roused herself and laughed unexpectedly.

"I never meant to say anything of the sort. I wanted to be calm and quiet, I . . . I can't remember what I planned to say." She frowned and raised a hand to her forehead, before suddenly brightening. "Of course I can't remember . . . It doesn't matter, you see, because I said what I really thought. There." She smiled and kissed him lightly on the cheek. "Now we can be friends. I told you what you asked for."

Magnus was so startled by this change of mood that he merely nodded. Only when she had gone, did he see that nothing had changed. He picked up the chatelaine and examined its tiny silver pencil and ivory note pad. She had used it cleverly to prove her point but the choice had not been a real one. George was not the last man alive. She would have other chances. Yet to try to convince her of that would be hopeless. He sat down absently at the davenport and looked at the mess of sealing wax. She had thought of the matter only from her own point of view, but her justification did not make a jot of difference to what the Braithwaites were, to Joseph's power-seeking and George's acquiescence, to the violence that would inevitably grow worse. While she had been speaking, Catherine had overwhelmed him, but now he saw his way clearly. If he could not persuade Catherine, then he would try with George. He would see what that young man was made of soon enough, and afterward . . . maybe Joseph Braithwaite himself. He recognized the same blend of fear and excitement he had known riding through the silent countryside after the riot. In any struggle with the Braithwaites, far more would be at stake than Catherine's future. Charles thought him a coward for leaving Ceylon. Perhaps, before the election was over, he would have to revise that estimate.

When Magnus had snuffed out the candles, it was not only the wind rattling the panes in their leaden frames, or the strangeness of being home, which kept him awake so long.

∾ *Four* ∾

In the small market town of Slaithworth, two miles north of the junction of the Rigton Bridge turnpike with the Oldham to Manchester road, the grocer's daughter and the butcher's boy stopped gossiping and stared up the street, past the saddler's and the smithy, toward the pond and the church. A resplendently turned-out traveling chariot thundered into view, forcing the carrier's wagon against the churchyard wall, and, without slackening speed, scattering some pigs being driven to the market square. On each of the two near-side horses rode an immaculately dressed postilion in white "leathers," tight scarlet jackets and tall, narrow-brimmed beaver hats. Each man held a whip of plaited leather with half a dozen polished silver bands between ferrule and thong. By the time the draper and his white-aproned assistant had come out to watch, the black and yellow chariot with its crested panels had passed the Star Inn and was speeding toward Gibbet Hill, leaving a swirling cloud of dust in its wake.

Two hours later the same carriage, proceeding at a more sedate pace, entered the small gravel sweep in front of a modern mansion in a genteel Manchester suburb. Helen Goodchild looked out of the chariot's window at the new red brick house with its stone window casings, many chimney pots and tall flight of steps leading up to a heavily studded door with a small brass plate in the center. For a visit to her own doctor Helen would have chosen an unostentatious brougham, but for a meeting with Dr. Carstairs she had wished to emphasize her position; for this purpose the emblazoned chariot with its four bay horses and two postilions could not be bettered.

Since Charles's visit Helen had debated for several days about whether to accept his help, but in the end had decided not to expose herself to complicated future obligations. If Charles could frighten a provincial doctor, she could do the same. It was for her to force her husband to a settlement and not for any outsider, whoever he might be. After enduring the humiliation of sending away Strickland, her fears and apprehension had given way to angry resentment, and this was still her dominant mood. Without informing her husband, she had ordered the reluctant steward to open his books to her, and had threatened him with dismissal unless he answered certain questions about any unrecorded payments her husband might have made to a Manchester physician. The sums paid to a Dr. James Carstairs had fully confirmed Charles's claims.

Helen's lady's maid got down from the rumble seat and rang the bell. The door was opened by a gray-haired housekeeper, who was joined a moment later by a bald manservant wearing striped trousers and a black tailcoat. After a brief conversation the lady's maid came back down the steps and opened the carriage door.

"Dr. Carstairs is with a patient, your ladyship."

"Tell his people to inform him that if he is with the queen's uncle I will still be admitted."

After further discussion, the maid returned and told one of the postilions to let down the carriage steps.

Carstairs had spent an absorbing morning in his attic laboratory, examining under a microscope organisms in the evacuations of three cholera victims, and comparing them with organic matter in samples of drinking water taken from neighboring standpipes. During the past six months, only his passionate desire to discover how the disease was transmitted had given him the strength to endure the disruption of his domestic life caused by his wife's infatuation with Lord Goodchild. A clever man, Carstairs owed his large and fashionable practice to his successful use of modern treatments. He had been the first doctor in the town to employ ether during surgery and to use chloroform to assist mothers in difficult childbirth. More recently he had gained a reputation for curing muscular pain with charges from galvanic batteries. He was still bent over his microscope when his housekeeper came in with the painfully unwelcome news that Lady Goodchild's coach-and-four was at present standing in front of the house. His first reaction was to delay seeing her by claiming he was with a patient, but that could only be a temporary expedient.

He crossed the room to a small zinc basin and washed his hands. Of course he could affect complete ignorance of his wife's adultery and feign shock and blazing anger; but then instant action would be expected, and that was a course to which he was entirely opposed. The woman herself might be ignorant of the situation: a prospect in its way even more horrifying. But on reflection he doubted whether she had come as a bona fide patient. But what could she possibly hope to gain by confronting him? This time it was his valet who came up to tell him that her ladyship would not wait. Carstairs ran a hand through his thinning hair and put on his silver-rimmed pince-nez. Then with a sigh he rolled down his shirt sleeves and put on a gray frock coat over his black waistcoat. Whatever her intentions, her ladyship could be relied upon, with the rest of her caste, to look down on him as a "sawbones" or jumped-up apothecary.

When he received her in his consulting room, Carstairs felt still more confused. That Goodchild should have preferred Dolly to the woman who now stood in front of the shelves of glass jars and bottles beside the door seemed fantastic to him. Dolly was so much plumper, with features coarse and blunt by comparison, and without any of Lady Goodchild's evident dignity. But perhaps it was this very lack of hauteur and reserve which the peer found attractive. There was no mistaking Dolly's bubbling laughter and her zest for all life's pleasures, however questionable some of them might be considered for a woman. Lady Goodchild, with her ivory smooth skin and black mantle edged with astrakhan, looked elegantly graceful in a way which Mrs. Carstairs could never hope to emulate, whoever her dressmaker might be.

"Your ladyship, I am sorry to have been prevented from seeing you sooner," said Carstairs, rising from his chair behind an imposing mahogany desk and indicating with a nod an upright leather chair beside the red curtain which hid his examination couch.

"You have no need to apologize, Doctor. I came without warning." She sat stiffly on the edge of the chair and glanced hesitantly down at her gloved hands. "I have come to speak of matters painful to both of us." She looked up and fixed his eye with unblushing directness. "You know of my husband's adultery with your wife?"

"I do, madam," he returned quietly, disturbed by the forthrightness of her question. Without dropping her gaze, she said sternly,

"And do you not intend to remind your wife of her duty to you?"

"I have done so, ma'am," he replied with a flicker of resentment in his eyes. Helen understood his feelings but did not soften her manner.

"May I ask with what result?"

"None, I fear, your ladyship. Mrs. Carstairs is of an independent frame of mind. I am afraid that talk of duty amuses rather than chastens her." Carstairs was surprised to see that instead of angering his visitor, his remark had made her smile.

"Wives may be spirited, Doctor, but never independent. By law even her property belongs to you." Her smile died on her lips. "Perhaps that fact might amuse her less than notions of duty."

Unlike most of his patients, Carstairs was never distressed by a woman's assumption of intellectual equality. He removed his pince-nez and rubbed the bridge of his nose.

"By law, Lady Goodchild, I might imprison her in this house, but I doubt whether it would be conducive to my happiness or peace of mind."

While Helen admired the ease with which he had turned her attack to his own advantage, she had no intention of showing him anything other than a formal superiority. Charles, she recalled, had supposed that Carstairs had genuinely wished to begin divorce proceedings and had only been dissuaded by her husband's bribery. Now it seemed that the doctor had merely given this impression to extort money. She said harshly,

"*You* may be ready to tolerate ignominy and humiliation, Dr. Carstairs; I am not."

"I envy your security, but my own freedom is circumscribed. If I bring an action against your husband, I endanger my livelihood. The rich entrust their souls to a parson and their bodies to a physician, and from both they expect unimpeachable domestic lives. Like a sensible tradesman, l must practice what my customers desire, and never disappoint them for quixotic personal considerations." He opened a black instrument case and held up a small scalpel. He caught her concealed alarm and smiled. "If my morality is not as bright and spotless as this knife, I might as well turn it on myself." He made a feint with it towards his throat, making her raise both hands to her mouth. Then he replaced it carefully in its proper compartment. "I might take physical measures to prevent my wife seeing your husband, but then I would run the risk of her eloping. Lord Goodchild, I daresay, has adequate means to place her in a villa and to supply her other needs. This would be as detrimental to my professional interests as any crim con proceedings. I prefer what you call humiliation to ruin."

Helen was angry with herself for showing her fear when he had taken out the scalpel, and was also mortified not to have disposed of the argument to which he had just treated her before he could use it.

"You are being less than honest with me, sir. My husband is buying your silence."

The scorn in her voice stung him into replying with a raised voice,

"I must contradict that. Your husband's sensuality could end my career. He owes me compensation."

She shot him a glance of disdainful incredulity and said with an impatient toss of the head,

"Lord Goodchild would never pay a man a farthing as charity . . . compensation—call it what you will—unless he believed himself forced to it to prevent public scandal."

"I am sure he would suffer far less than I in such an event."

"You are evidently unfamiliar with men of my husband's standing. He would never consider a provincial doctor's inconveniences anything but trifling when set beside his own. A king who falls from a mountain feels little sympathy for a peasant who stumbles from a molehill."

"Is that your ladyship's view?" asked Carstairs with a wry smile at the arrogance of her comparison.

"You give me small credit for thought, Doctor. I understand very well that a landowner needs no public approval to keep his land, but a physician must have it to retain his patients."

Carstairs nodded with grateful approval.

"I am glad your ladyship understands my reluctance to act."

"Certainly I understand it, but I think you are entirely mistaken in supposing that Lord Goodchild will never realize it too. His payments will cease but not his attentions to your wife. You would do better to tell him you intend to bring an action."

"And if he still sees Mrs. Carstairs and refuses to believe I am in earnest?"

"Why, bring your action, of course," she replied as if amazed by his obtuseness. She gave him a smile of sympathetic encouragement. "Your fears are groundless. Will anyone think less of you for refusing to be humiliated by my husband's philandering? People will admire your pluck rather than deride you—you deserve their derision now. Manufacturers, I believe, have little love for landowners. You will gain more patients than you lose, and the scandal-lovers and tuft-hunters will beg to be treated by the man whose wife was once the object of a peer's amorous attentions."

"My lady is doubtless a philanthropist," he remarked dryly, "but perhaps her gains from such proceedings would be more certain."

"I am sure you are an excellent physician, Doctor, but I would hardly have come for the pleasure of your acquaintance." She stared past him at the naked trees in the garden, which looked, she thought, appropriately like the diagram of the body's veins and blood vessels on the wall behind him. Without altering the direction of her gaze, she went on in a soft and distant voice, "If you do nothing, it will be my painful conclusion that my husband's payments are responsible for your inactivity." She switched her attention to the carvings on the legs of his desk. "I will of course see that the payments are stopped, and also if need be inform your professional superiors that you are receiving money for unprofessional services." She faced him and said, with a gentleness completely at variance with her words, "You have your license from the Royal College of Physicians, if your door-plate is correct. Such licenses can be revoked."

Carstairs looked down at some papers on his desk and sighed.

"Your ladyship may take it that I shall begin proceedings against your husband as soon as the matter of witnesses has been suitably arranged."

"I am most relieved, Doctor. I bear you no ill will, but I cannot allow an intolerable and shameful situation to continue." The passion with which she had said this left Carstairs in no doubt about her sincerity and determination. She inclined her head a little and frowned. "If you use the next few days to warn Lord Goodchild, I will not take it kindly; and should there be a sudden cooling of his ardor, I will think the coincidence too singular to be credible."

He bowed his head more in resignation than in deference and murmured,

"I shall endeavor to please you, ma'am."

"Thank you, Doctor."

Carstairs accompanied her to the hall and watched a liveried postilion leap forward to open the carriage door and check the firmness of the steps. As Helen got in her maid lifted her skirt to see that it did not catch on anything. An industrious physician, even in a great city like Manchester, might labor night and day for years and never own such a vehicle, which she so casually accepted as her right. Surrounded by her obsequious and retiring servants, no wonder she felt that she could dictate to all those living in other circumstances. Only when seated once more at his microscope did he feel composed again. The tiny moving shapes under the glass could teach equality and humility even to the proudest woman alive.

Leaving the city, Helen drew down the blinds of her carriage and tore off her bonnet. She wanted to talk to a friend, but could think of nobody in whom to confide. Charles would censure her for going in person and would see her action as a deliberate rejection. All her other friends in the north, and these were not numerous, were shared with her husband. Whatever her son's love for her, no thirteen-year-old boy could understand her fears or contradictory emotions nor give her advice and support. She thought of the large and empty house and felt weak with loneliness. An empty house? Better by far that it should be empty. For all her servants, was she a whit less isolated? Always the deferential masquerade must be observed unless familiarity should breed, as all the world knows, contempt. Only the proper frigid reserve and distance could command respectful and attentive service. She wondered suddenly whether, if by chance she passed a servant out of her uniform in Rigton Bridge, she would recognize her. Probably not; and yet she might be the same housemaid who had dusted her dressing table for a year. What did they think or talk about? What was their opinion of her? Two feet behind her, muffled up to the ears, was Lucy, her lady's maid, perched on the open rumble seat shivering with cold. Did she feel resentment? Lucy bathed her, dressed her, warmed her body linen before the fire and combed her hair. They talked of fashions and Lucy's family. But what, what did Lucy *think?* Helen buried her head in her hands and wept. She heard a refined voice, like her own, saying: *As though it matters what they think. Let them think what they like provided they know their place and are prompt and respectful.* Her husband doesn't care about her, so now for the first time in her life she wonders whether her servants like her or say unkind things behind her back, not, mark you, because she cares a jot for them. Helen thought with horror of the conversation she would soon have to have with her husband. Possibly the steward had already told his master about her questions.

Only later did she suddenly feel resilient and confident again. Had she really thought only of loneliness and desolation, when for the first time in years she had done something to change her position? She shook her head in amazement, and then lowered the window and shouted to the second postilion to stop. Then she turned around and called out,

"Cooper, you must be cold. You may sit with me."

Lucy clambered down from the rumble and got in diffidently. Helen could think of nothing else to say, so looked at the passing country outside.

~ *Five* ~

Friday night was always a significant one for George Braithwaite since it marked his weekly visit to Bentley's gambling hell. Because of his limited means, Tom Strickland had never thought it likely that he would be invited to accompany George in the pursuit of this particular pleasure; but, when the unexpected had happened, he had accepted. Although he had no intention of risking his own money on the tables, ever since Crawford's plea for information, during the riot, Tom had made a point of talking with George whenever the opportunity arose, in the hope that he might let slip unguarded remarks about his father's election methods. Already Tom suspected that Joseph Braithwaite was employing intimidation: mainly threatening not to renew shopkeepers' leases unless they voted for him; and from several things George had said when drunk, Tom also guessed that those voters, immune from threats, would be bought. Yet, even if these suspicions became more definite, Tom was not sure that he would have the courage to tell Crawford what he knew. If Joseph ever found out about such treachery, his desire for vengeance would surely not be sated by a mere withdrawal of patronage. "Accidents," which had befallen several of the leaders of the strike, were clear warnings. For the present, Tom told himself, he was finding things out purely for his own edification.

Having left George's brougham in the stable yard at the Green Dragon, Tom followed his patron's son into the High Street, and walked beside him past the darkened shop windows, heavily shuttered after closing, since the start of the recent disturbances. Across the echoing street a watchman with a lantern was methodically examining the chains and locks, checking that all was secure. In the exclusively working-class districts of Rigton Bridge, down by the mills and south of the river, the gin shops would still be crowded and noisy, but here, in the old town, the final stroke of eleven from St. John's Church lingered and died over silent, empty streets.

Near the old Corn Exchange and the Assembly Rooms, they cut through a cobbled alley and down the ill-lit Cockpit Steps into Lower Street, where the gas brackets were less frequent and the uneven sets sloped down toward the center of the street, forming a shallow drain. The smell of stagnant liquid and garbage mingled with the haze of coal smoke in the damp night air. Tom started as a rat scuttled across the narrow opening to a hidden court.

They passed a pawnbroker's and a tailor's before George stopped to listen outside an apparently closed cigar shop. Above, the first-floor windows were shuttered but Tom could just hear the muted sound of voices from within. An alley ran to the side of the shop, and facing onto it, in an otherwise grimy blank wall, was an unexceptional-looking door. George pushed it open and they entered a narrow passage lit by a naked gas jet high up on the wall beneath the sooty panes of a cracked fanlight. Ahead of them was another door with a small metal grille. Lifting his cane, George rapped on the grating and was soon rewarded by the appearance of an ugly, flat-nosed face pressed against the bars. A moment later the bolts were shot back and they were ushered up a flight of stairs to a landing where another former pugilist was sitting hunched over a desk; unlike the doorkeeper this man was smartly dressed in a black tailcoat with a rose in his buttonhole and next to it a spotted cravat held in place by a large gold pin. After signing his name in the book and handing over a sovereign, George led Tom through a green, baize-covered door into a long, low-ceilinged room, which evidently occupied the entire space above both the cigar shop and the tailor's next to it.

The furnishings were certainly nothing like the splendid, many-mirrored, red-carpeted, plush and gilt of the St. James's gambling hells, but, for a town like Rigton Bridge, George considered Bentley's a very satisfactory substitute. Immediately in front of him was the oval hazard table, and at the far end of the room, scarcely visible through the clouds of tobacco smoke, were tables for roulette and rouge et noir. On a long sideboard were dishes of cold game, beef and ham, with a fine supporting cast of salads, preserves, creams and jellies. All this food was provided free for the players, as were cigars but not wine. George glanced at Strickland and was pleased to see that he seemed impressed.

The hazard table, lit by a green-shaded gasolier, was the center of attention for the thirty or forty gentlemen present—most of them, officers in the 22nd Hussars, recently arrived from London to do garrison duty in neighboring Oldham. Bentley, himself, was as usual the principal croupier at the hazard table, and, as George heard his rasping and slightly breathless voice, he felt a pleasant flutter of anticipation in his stomach.

"The caster is backing in at seven, gentlemen. I'll take on the nick."

Then the rattle of dice, the bang of the box on the table, the quick announcement of the point and the raking in of counters from the losing columns. In this room, during the week of Rigton Races, George had once won almost two thousand pounds and had lost as much on other occasions. As always, Bentley was watching the betting habits of his clients: noting lower stakes, or too feverish a reaction to a lost point; if such symptoms coincided with less punctually paid checks, not many days would pass before the gambler in question would be refused admission by the doorkeeper. George admired Bentley for knowing his business so well.

Gambling constituted George's only escape from his father's influence and domination, being in direct opposition to Joseph's thriftiness and puritanical condemnation of all forms of aristocratic profligacy. Because the past few weeks had been particularly harrowing, George's favorite pastime had become still more important to him. Not only had his father forced him to sue the *Independent* against his own judgment, but he had also given him the dangerous and delicate task of negotiating with the secret confederacy into which the recently qualified voters had banded themselves for the purpose of selling their votes collectively and thus obtaining a higher price for them.

George watched the play in silence, savoring the moment. How much would he bet? Which game would he play? Would he terrify the other players by taking astonishing risks? His heart had started to beat faster, but the sensation was still agreeable and one to be relished. In a moment he would decide. After the next throw. His heart beat slightly faster as he reached into his pocket and pulled out a thick wad of notes. A thousand pounds. His breath came faster and a sudden surge of intense and yet fearful excitement sent a shiver down his spine. As he moved toward the cashier's table to get his counters, he was free of all other thoughts and cares, above all free of his father.

He was checking his counters when he felt a hand on his arm, and, thinking it was Strickland, without looking around, thrust out five guineas in ivory disks—after all the man ought to have something to play with—then George froze. Magnus Crawford was looking at him with an amused smile.

"I'd quite given you up, Mr. Braithwaite. I came yesterday too; but now you're here, perhaps we can talk."

He indicated a small side table, on which stood two glasses and a bottle in an ice bucket. George felt angry to be interrupted at such a moment, and, at the same time, acutely uneasy. The last person he would have wished to see in his favorite haunt was Magnus Crawford. In a matter of seconds all his pleasure and anticipation had been destroyed. Instead he found himself thinking of Crawford's humiliatingly decisive behavior during the riot, and worse than that of Catherine. Only on his evenings at Bentley's could George ever manage to forget the misery which her refusal to give him an immediate decision caused him. What the hell could Crawford want in any case? George did not care to admit it to himself, but he felt afraid.

"I don't come here to talk," he replied gruffly. "Hardly the place for it."

"It suits me well enough. Not many places I'd find you alone."

George was rattling his counters impatiently in the palms of his hands, when a sudden recollection made him gasp at his former lack of confidence. Charles Crawford had told him that his brother had returned home almost penniless.

"Some throws with you, Mr. Crawford? Play first and talk later." He had said this firmly to make it clear that this was his condition for a conversation. Noting Crawford's hesitation, and knowing that he was proud, George added in an undertone, "Low stakes, if you like." Seeing Crawford grow pale, George knew that he had found his mark. He wouldn't be so condescending after he'd lost heavily.

Magnus saw at a glance that Braithwaite was holding something approaching eight or nine hundred pounds in counters. The seconds dragged on and Magnus experienced the same terrifying indecision he had known years ago at Oxford before starting to play; the identical choking tension was there—tension in the end acute enough to make delay unendurable and a decision almost involuntary: a card snatched on impulse, mechanically, as if by a stranger. Afterward relief would be as great as fear. Magnus felt a sickening giddiness and a tingling sensation in the back of his thighs. His decision had been made before he knew it.

"Well?" George inquired with a hint of derision.

Refuse, Magnus told himself. Make a cutting remark about a man's means having little to do with his courage and still less with his common sense. But instead he returned Braithwaite's gaze and walked over to the cashier's table. When he sat down at the hazard table he had signed a check for four hundred pounds and now ranged that quantity of counters in front of him in three neat piles. He had felt an unreal detachment as he had made out the check, but now panic fluttered in his chest, spreading an alarming weakness to his limbs. He was sure that if he tried to hold out his hand, it would shake uncontrollably. Just this fear when he had stepped out from the front rank of his men and walked forward alone toward the ragged rebel line strung across the dusty white road. Only a fool, he told himself, would have tried to talk a crowd into dispersing before shooting first . . . a gamble. The agony had passed the moment the first bullets sang past his ears. And now with about half his assets on the table in front of him, Magnus prayed for the tension to snap and play to begin.

"You'd like to be caster, I suppose?" asked George, with the same trace of superiority.

"You may have the dice, Mr. Braithwaite," Magnus replied, amazed as he said this at his folly. George could now choose how much to put down and Magnus would have to match it with an equal sum. Pride, the insanity of pride, and yet Magnus did not repent. If George ever had to gamble with half his fortune, would he ever remain as outwardly calm?

Silence fell as George placed counters to the value of two hundred pounds in the central circle. Magnus pushed forward the same number. Bentley impassively flicked a few stray chips over the line with his rake.

"Six's the main," called out George as he threw the dice. Double sixes, double threes or a two and a four would give George all the money in the middle. Magnus did not look as the dice thudded onto the green cloth but he let out a long breath as he heard Bentley rasp out,

"Seven's the nick, gentlemen."

Since George had not managed to throw the exact main he had called, Magnus took that main for his chance, and his opponent adopted seven, the number of his second throw, as his new main. The odds were calculated so that a player could win or "nick" all the money with other combinations, eleven was a nick to a main of seven, just as double six was a nick to the mains of six or eight. Others were now placing side bets on the columns. The dice were replaced and Braithwaite threw again. A five and a six.

"The caster nicks it at eleven," announced Bentley, pushing all the counters across to Braithwaite. Almost all the side bets, Magnus realized, had been laid against him; as he looked at the exultant faces of the winners, he saw Strickland walk up to the table; he had not noticed him before, but supposed he had come with George. The caster had three throws for a complete "box hand," so Braithwaite had a final throw to clean out his opponent. He laid down a further two hundred and shouted,

"Seven's the main."

This time he won outright with a six and an ace. This shattering loss was so sudden that Magnus hardly took it in until Bentley had raked away the counters to George's side of the table. Only when this had happened did Magnus see that Strickland had placed a twenty-pound bet against his patron's son; this would be a heavy loss for a man of his vocation. George handed the dice box to Magnus.

"Your throw, Mr. Crawford," he said, trying in vain to conceal the satisfaction he felt. Magnus wrote out a promissory note and handed it to Bentley who stared searchingly at him before allowing him three hundred more in counters. If these were lost, there would be no others. He watched George's stubby white fingers idly drumming the table by his large pile of chips.

"Some new dice, please," Magnus said to the second croupier, more in the hope of changing his luck than because he thought the old ones were cogged. "A cigar," he added, once the replacement dice were in the box. Only when the cigar was between his lips and he had taken several unhurried puffs did he pick up the box and lean forward to place two

hundred in the circle. Such sums were lost and won often enough in Pall
Mall or Hanover Square, but in Rigton Bridge the absolute silence of the
crowded room was a tribute to the unprecedented scale of the betting.
Had any of the bystanders understood that Magnus was now committing
very nearly every penny he possessed, their amazement would have been
still greater. Braithwaite, who now had just short of fifteen hundred
pounds in black, green and red counters, could afford to look nonchalant as he matched Magnus's sum. As Magnus raised the box, the only
noises audible were the hissing jets of the gasolier overhead and the
rattling dice.

"Nine's the main," he cried as the dice rolled, toppled and finally fell
into place. His mouth was horribly dry and the box almost slipped from
his hand, so moist had it become with sweat. Magnus had thrown a five,
so that now became his main, while George took nine as his. As he
shook the box Magnus did not think of winning, but wondered how he
would be able to reach the door without his face betraying the crushing
magnitude of his loss. Before he released the dice he saw that once again
Strickland had backed him and was comforted that one or two others
were doing the same. Perhaps after all he did not look like a man whom
luck had utterly deserted. Even while the dice were falling Magnus saw
the needed patterns passing before his eyes, double fives, two and three,
or four and one, and then the dots at last resolved themselves. A sudden
roar of talk and exclamation broke as the spectators and side betters
saw that he had thrown three and two.

"The caster has nicked it at five, gentlemen."

For the first time Magnus saw the incredible sight of counters passing
to his side of the table. But his confidence was checked when with his
last throw he achieved deuce aces thus losing his own and Braithwaite's
two hundred pounds to the house. He was now down four hundred and
had three hundred left. He had turned catastrophe into a less serious
disaster, but disaster nonetheless. George was fiddling with the gold
chains across his damson-colored, flowered-silk waistcoat.

"What about it, Mr. Crawford?"

Magnus had known from the moment he asked that he would hand
him back the box; he would either win back his loss or lose everything.
This time Braithwaite staked three hundred and for the second time that
evening there were no counters left in front of him as Magnus matched

the bet. It cost him no effort to imagine how George would enjoy telling Charles about his triumph and how his brother in turn would take grim delight in informing their father, but worst of all was the certainty that a loss during this box hand would destroy every plan he had made. This was where his idiot scorn had got him; his disdain for the man had not even permitted him to allow George the spurious satisfaction of goading him a little with his superior wealth. So he had taken up his challenge on that hopelessly unequal ground. If he lost again, George would offer to accept a written note and then another if he lost again. The thought almost made Magnus's stomach turn over. Two hours ago his thoughts had ranged across the town, calculating quite different risks, trying to predict every possibility involving the strikers, the candidates and the military, but now all he saw, and it seemed would ever care about, centered on the pool of light cast on that green oval table with its delicately demarcated circle.

He caught the flash of George's white cuff and the movement of his frilled shirt as he cast the dice. The main called had been eight, but three had been thrown. Eight was now Magnus's main. Strickland was betting again and this fact comforted Magnus a little. The next throw produced no result, and since his box hand was over, George gave the box back to Magnus.

"The caster is still backing it at eight, gentlemen," came Bentley's dry thin voice as he sat with his rake poised and ready. A six and a two lay on the table when Magnus opened his eyes. Six hundred pounds was moved from the center of the table. He still had two throws left, and whereas before his success he would gladly have agreed to stop the moment he wiped out the worst of his loss, now he saw matters in a different light. He wanted to force George to write out a check for more counters. For a moment he even saw himself playing through the night and beggaring the man. When with his next throw he won six hundred pounds and a further three hundred with the last, he felt sure that anything was possible. He had noticed that Strickland had not placed a bet on the final throw and now wanted to see if he could catch his eye to reprove him for his lack of faith, but he had left the table and had his back turned. A sudden superstitious fear made Magnus get up. Strickland had backed him from his lowest ebb to the point where he was now eight hundred up on the evening and now he was stopping playing. If any gambler needed an omen, this was surely it.

"Allow me to give you more satisfaction," said George with a set face.

"I am sure you have given me enough," Magnus replied, feeling a sudden wave of exhaustion after the tension and excitement of the haz-ard table. For the first time in an hour he was aware of the room again. The table of food, the wall candelabras and the smoke-stained ceiling now became as real as the solitary circle of green cloth.

"Will you settle now, gentlemen?" asked Bentley, coming up to them. Magnus handed him five sovereigns for their box hands, before going over to the cashier. He paid over seven hundred in counters in return for his promissory note and check, the balance of eight hundred was given to him in coin and notes. George would have been astounded had he known that his opponent, who was now pocketing his winnings with such unconcern, had just doubled his total assets. Braithwaite wrote out a check for the two hundred he had lost above the counters he had started with.

"And now our conversation," said Magnus, guiding George to his side table. "I shall be to the point." A waiter took the champagne bottle from its ice bucket and filled their glasses. On the table, between them, was a cigar cutter and a small glass jar filled with toothpicks. Magnus leaned forward and said quietly,

"You wish to marry my sister."

George tugged at his sandy-colored mustache and met Magnus's eyes.

"That is a matter which concerns Miss Crawford, her father and myself."

Magnus nodded affably and lifted his glass to his lips.

"Formally, I daresay that's so, Mr. Braithwaite, but a brother may interest himself in a sister's doings, I suppose." He put down his glass abruptly. "Frankly, Braithwaite, if she accepts you, it'll be for your fortune. Do you want her on those terms?"

George's face was scarlet and his hand clasped so tightly around his glass that Magnus thought it would break. A second later, Braithwaite flung the glass to the ground, and roared,

"I'll not drink with a man who dares dishonor his sister's good name."

"I appreciate your feelings, but my motives are not dishonorable. I've invented nothing; she told me herself. I know it's a scandalous breach of confidence, but it's worse for a man to be deceived, and a woman to sell herself."

"What harm have I ever done you?" whispered George in a quavering, breaking voice. His face was still contorted with rage, but there were tears in his eyes. Magnus looked down at the table.

"None," he murmured gently, "but does that justify a loveless marriage?"

George let out a choking groan, as much of grief as anger. Then he brought down his fist on the table, sending the jar of toothpicks, and Magnus's glass, crashing to the floor. People gazed at them furtively, evidently supposing that they were arguing about their recent game.

"You're lying about her. Do you think I don't understand you, Crawford? You hate my father and you hate his class because your own is dying; you're sick with a pauper's envy, but you still think I'm not good enough for your sister. Well, to hell with you and your patrician airs."

George was breathing hard and still very angry, but Magnus judged that his outburst had helped him, and waited a moment until he was still further recovered, then he said with slow firm emphasis,

"I swear she's no more love for you than I have. Withdraw your proposal."

"Never," cried George violently. He lowered his eyes and then looked at Magnus with a calmer, but intensely absorbed expression. "I think I care for her enough," he said softly, "even to forgive what you've just said."

The man's genuine emotion shook Magnus badly. He had been about to threaten to lay new evidence before a magistrate concerning the conduct of the case against the *Independent* unless George complied with his wishes. But now he knew he would not be able to bring himself to say that. He had no definite proof against George, and much of his earlier hostility had drained away. Yet he was still disquieted. Not many minutes ago, George would happily have beggared him.

"If I've misjudged you, I have a proposition to make by which you may prove my mistake." George stared at him, as if puzzled by this apparent change of heart. Magnus smiled. "Persuade your father to discharge his Irishmen and I'll not hinder you with Miss Crawford. You have my word."

"What does the strike mean to you?"

Magnus laughed at George's confusion.

"You mean what do I stand to gain by ending it?" George nodded. "An egotist's private pleasure in influencing events . . . a moralist's satisfaction in averting bloodshed. You remember how it was the other night?" He paused. "Stand up to your father, and I'll know you're a better man than I took you for."

George stood up wearily and sighed.

"You know him very little, Crawford, that's plain enough."

"I've faith in you. I'll meet you at the Bull in three days. Monday at noon. Think of Miss Crawford, man."

Magnus walked briskly to the green baize door, leaving George standing motionless by the table.

When Crawford and George had been talking together, Tom Strickland had collected his winnings. Earlier he had signed a note for forty pounds and had staked it all in side bets on Magnus's throws; after an initial loss of twenty pounds, he had finished by winning just over a hundred. As the money was handed to him, he was still trembling with excitement. Never before had he risked so much with so little reason; a total loss could have cost him six months' painting. When he had seen Crawford lose again and again, and still match George's bets, Tom had scarcely dared watch as the dice fell; longing to tear himself away, the man's polished calmness had held him spellbound, until, unable to remain inactive while feeling such involvement, he had started to play.

Immediately afterward he had longed to talk to Crawford and share with him the ecstatic pleasure of winning, but, by then, he had been sitting with George. Tom was surprised that, though he neither knew nor understood the man, he nonetheless felt intuitively that, like him, Crawford had no place in the rigid stratification which birth, wealth and privilege sought to impose on all would-be absconders. For this reason, after Magnus had gone, he was not only disappointed to have been unable to speak to him, but also dismayed by the look of brooding malignity on George's normally impassive face. Tom had often heard it said that George could be as vindictive as his father. Without stopping to assess the risks of George guessing where he had gone, Tom quietly left the room and hurried down the stairs, intent on warning Crawford and disclosing his suspicions about Joseph's intimidation.

Halfway along Lower Street, Magnus heard rapidly approaching footsteps behind him; he turned at once, wondering whether George had suddenly taken it into his head to horsewhip him into a more convenient frame of mind, but instead he saw Strickland hurrying toward him, casting an occasional glance over his shoulder.

"Forgive me for following you, Mr. Crawford." He sounded breathless and uneasy.

"Provided you leave my money in my pocket, I shall be honored by your attentions."

Strickland did not smile at this, but drew Magnus aside out of the flickering gaslight into the dark shadow of an overhanging shop front.

"The Braithwaites aren't people to quarrel with."

The suddenness of this melodramatic announcement, coupled with Strickland's lowered voice and earnest expression, made Magnus want to laugh.

"Your desire to save your employer any inconvenience does your loyalty credit, Mr. Strickland."

"My concern is for your welfare, not his."

"Forgive my levity. An evening at Bentley's rarely leads to gravity of any sort." After the champagne, Magnus wished that he had found time to eat something. Apart from the wine, his encounter with George had left him light-headed and limp. The church clock was striking two. Strickland was looking at him anxiously.

"Old Braithwaite has a gang of paid thugs, former navvies and bargees mostly. He's already used them on individual strikers. One was found drowned in the canal."

For a moment Magnus felt the same dizziness and fear he had experienced on first seeing George's fistfuls of counters; Strickland might be telling the truth, might even wish to warn him, although the idea that the Braithwaites would dare treat him in the way they might men who had set fire to their property seemed farfetched. He felt suddenly suspicious. Perhaps George was using Strickland.

"You know this positively?" he asked sharply.

"I've heard the same story more than once."

"People tend to speak ill of masters during strikes."

Crawford's harsh and dismissive tone surprised and wounded Tom. Barely a week ago, the man had asked for such information, implored him for it.

"I'm sure that electors are being intimidated," he went on, until Crawford snapped back,

"Why should that concern me?"

"I thought from what you said . . ."

"Fiascoes like that don't encourage rational thinking, Mr. Strickland. Best forget what I said."

A moment later, Tom was amazed to find himself grasped by the coat and thrust back against the shop door, with Crawford's cane across his throat.

"Braithwaite sent you after me, didn't he?"

"But why?" asked Tom in amazement, laying his hands on the ends of the cane, but not attempting to free himself.

"To worm your way into my confidence and tell him what I say. You weren't very eager to tell me anything last time we met. A strange change since then, wouldn't you say?"

"Would I have told you what I have?" cried Tom.

"What's the use of rumors which can't be proved?"

"Nor can my goodwill," objected Tom, pressing down the cane so that it was against his chest. Magnus stepped back abruptly but did not look less suspicious. "I said nothing before," continued Tom, "because I wanted more work from Braithwaite. I've changed my mind."

"A man of principle," murmured Magnus, with what Tom thought was a sneer. He felt angry and humiliated.

"I took *you* for that," he replied warmly, derision and disappointment in his voice.

From a nearby court came the yowling of fighting cats; Magnus said nothing but stared down at the damp paving stones. He was confused and worried; he believed he had been mistaken about the man, but something still disturbed him. He felt angry with him, and yet he was so mild and gentle. Strickland had stung his pride.

"If people are being bribed and threatened, what am I supposed to be able to do? I have no mysterious power to prevent such abuses. I have no money beyond twice that which I was foolish enough to risk tonight, no friends here . . . nothing, do you understand?"

Strickland surprised him by smiling at this.

"You won a great deal tonight. A fortune to me."

"I see, and a few hundreds give me power, do they?" He laughed bitterly. "To do what?"

Tom said, almost without thinking, for George had talked about the paper earlier that day,

"A few hundreds could buy the *Independent*."

"Buy a newspaper? Me? You're raving."

"George sued for . . ."

"Yes, yes," cut in Magnus impatiently, "and the editor can't pay the fine. I've heard all that."

"But *you* could," whispered Tom, his eyes suddenly glowing with excitement.

"You mean pay the fine?" Tom nodded. "And make George Braithwaite howl like a stuck pig. There are cheaper ways of annoying him, surely?"

"But don't you see?" laughed Tom. "It's absurd, ridiculous, almost the first thing that entered my head when you asked what you could do with your money. . . . I thought it ridiculous too, just as you did; but if the rumors are true, you could print them. Would that be nothing?"

The breathless rapidity and feverish enthusiasm with which Strickland had spoken convinced Magnus that the idea had indeed just occurred to him; and, seeing the young man's earnest and expectant face, willing him to agree, Magnus could not help being infected by the same mood; but he showed none of this as he said with studied weariness,

"Do you want me to be sued as well, and ruined?"

Strickland looked momentarily downcast, but then he brightened.

"Old Braithwaite wouldn't risk appearing in court to deny allegations of corruption just before the election. Well, would he?"

"Why should he bother? *The Rigton Independent* is not *The Times*, I believe."

"Of course not, but only one man in six has the vote here; the paper could provide for most of them surely?"

Having never so much as given a thought to these matters until a moment previously, Tom was amazed to have managed impromptu answers to Crawford's objections, and his success added fuel to his conviction that the idea was workable. When, therefore, Crawford looked at him with quizzical amusement, Tom was puzzled and irritated.

"You're a strange man, Mr. Strickland, a mouse one day, a lion the next. I wonder what the future will bring?" He rattled the coins in his pockets and let out a low chuckle. "Of course your suggestion is laughable."

"I think the Braithwaites might find it less amusing," replied Tom angrily.

"Ah, but I have a sense of humor and they don't." Magnus laughed again and straightened his hat. Unable to understand his sudden high spirits, Tom lowered his eyes and feigned indifference. "No, please, forgive me," murmured Magnus, his eyes still sparkling with good humor. "I'm grateful for your warning, but you ought to go. I wouldn't like to delay George tonight if I were you. Losers at hazard are rarely sweet-tempered. . . . I ought to thank you for betting on my throws. When we meet again I'll be more serious. Tonight I can't think at all." He caught Tom's look of incomprehension and smiled. "We will meet again, you can be sure of that. I find your company most congenial." He shook his head and laughed again. "A wicked idea . . . quite wicked. To buy the paper he sued, with the money I've taken out of his pockets. Really you look so nice too, Mr. Strickland." He thrust out his hand. "Well, good night."

Moments later, Crawford's footsteps were dying away as he headed for Cockpit Steps. With hunched shoulders and his hands thrust deep in his coat, Tom retraced his steps to Bentley's; finding George gone, Tom set out for the inn where they had left the brougham.

In the yard of the Green Dragon, Braithwaite kicked over buckets and cursed the ostlers for their stupidity. When shutters were thrown open in the gallery above, and guests in nightshirts came out onto the balcony to complain about the noise, he roared back abuse. He prodded the head groom with his cane and shouted,

"Where the hell else would he be if he ain't at the Bull?"

"Would this be the gen'lman?" called out the boots as Tom walked in under the arch.

"Looked for you up and down the place, Strickland. Where the devil have you been?"

"Walking here."

"Thought I'd left you, I suppose?"

"It crossed my mind."

George flung open the door of the brougham and Tom climbed in.

"Nobody walks anywhere in this town at night, unless they're mad or drunk or both. You should have followed me. Damned artists are all fools."

The carriage jerked forward and in a moment the noise of the horses' hooves rang out under the archway. George was breathing heavily and every now and then he cursed out loud. He took several gulps from a flask and then beat on the roof to exhort the coachman to drive faster. The brougham swayed and lurched as the iron-edged wheels ground into ruts and pot-holes and sliced through heavy mud on the road.

Tom sat silently in his corner holding onto the hand strap beside the window. He was used to being insulted by George and took it philosophically. To Braithwaite it was quite incomprehensible that anybody should choose to earn his living in a field where talent and luck decreed whether he succeeded or failed. Money and influence were far more reliable bases on which to proceed. If George were to praise a picture as "clever," he meant no more than appreciation of a detail or a choice of subject, rather as though a critic were to applaud a book for its binding. To be patronized by both George and Crawford on the same night was insufferable. His anger temporarily made him forget his winnings, but when he remembered, Tom smiled to himself. After Joseph's portrait was finished, he really would be free to go, and then the Goodchilds, Braithwaites and Crawfords could play whatever game they chose without him.

He glanced at George with secret satisfaction and then caught his breath. The man's face was wet with tears.

⌒ *Six* ⌒

Lord Goodchild, dressed in his favorite baggy green shooting jacket and stained moleskins, led the way through a narrow cattle gap into a boggy, gorse-brown pasture. Trudging behind him, strung out in line, came his son, Humphrey, his head gamekeeper and an underkeeper, both weighed down with guns, powder horns and shot pouches; his lordship's valet brought up the rear, carrying a hamper containing chicken sandwiches, seltzer water, East India sherry and a large flask of brandy.

Just as two weeks before thoughts of his wife had spoiled Goodchild's anticipation of the hunt, today Helen's shadow loomed darker still over his sporting enjoyment. He had recently returned from Manchester, where he had been stunned to be refused admission by Dr. Carstairs, who had told him bluntly, with no reason given, that in future he would not be welcome. The following day at Hanley Park, Goodchild had not only heard from his head coachman that her ladyship had been to Manchester, but had also been informed by his steward that Lady Goodchild had asked for details about certain payments. After these revelations, Carstairs' behavior had no longer seemed inexplicable. Murderously angry though he had been, Goodchild had nevertheless controlled himself, and since that day had done his utmost to avoid being alone with Helen, using his regimental duties as an excuse for prolonged absence. If she was bent on forcing him to a separation or on compelling him to renounce his mistress, Goodchild knew that he would better be able to resist her if he could avoid a decisive confrontation before the election. Today he had only risked returning home for some shooting with Humphrey, because he was alarmed that, unless he spent some time with his son, he might lose the boy's affection entirely after the inevitable rift with his mother.

The ground they were walking across was heavy and clinging, and

Goodchild's new boots felt stiff and not fully broken in, although they had been worn a week by his manservant. Out in front, his lordship's two favorite pointers sniffed their way across the wet grass. Suddenly they froze and crouched like statues, their right feet raised, and muzzles pointing toward a rushy patch in the middle of the pasture.

The underkeeper handed his master a loaded gun and retired. Goodchild cocked it. As he moved forward a hare bounded off toward the hedge. A sharp scream followed the second shot and the animal crumpled and twisted in midstride.

"Seek dead," he murmured to the nearest pointer with a wave of the hand and the dog raced away and retrieved. Goodchild handed the gun back to the underkeeper and took another, which he held out to his son. The boy received it without a word.

Five minutes later as they were crossing a field of stubble, a covey of partridges rose with a loud whir. Humphrey missed with both barrels and the head keeper handed him a second gun, but, before he could discharge it, his father had fired into the rapidly dispersing flight of birds. One checked, dipped and then plummeted downward in a corkscrew dive, suddenly heavy after being so light. Humphrey heard the soft thud as it landed. Again at a word, a dog streaked away to collect.

"Won't get easier shots than that," muttered Goodchild, unable, for all his good intentions, to hide his displeasure.

"I'm sorry, sir."

"No need for that. You'll get more chances I wager."

In spite of his father's conciliatory tone, the boy said nothing but stared down at his feet with compressed lips and coloring cheeks. Goodchild thought he detected as much defiance as contrition in the expression, and wondered whether Humphrey had missed on purpose to annoy him. On the two brief occasions on which he had spoken to him, after he had headed the fox at the hunt, he had found his son unusually sullen and withdrawn even for him. A short silence ended when Palmer, the head keeper, started telling Goodchild about the barbarous new method poachers were using to take his pheasants: scattering raisins transfixed with a sharp pin or fishhook, which choked the birds as they swallowed. Palmer detailed the measures he was taking to kill poachers' dogs, including the nocturnal placing of poisoned rabbits' livers near gates where poachers set snares and nets to catch hares.

"You might poison a fox," objected Goodchild.

"Kill a poacher's dog, your lordship, and he won't train another under a year."

"A dead fox here and there is worth a hundred pheasants saved, I suppose," conceded Goodchild.

They walked on in silence over a wide turnip field, the heavy soil adhering to their boots making walking a laborious business. Overhead the slate gray sky seemed to promise snow. They stopped at a stile beside the Flixton road and the valet got out the sandwiches and brandy.

"Come here, my boy." Humphrey sat down beside his father on the stile, while the servants withdrew into a separate group. "If you don't care for it, you need not come shooting."

"I must persevere, sir."

"Perhaps I am too hard on you," said Goodchild gently. The boy looked at him suspiciously, as though sensing a trap if he spoke his mind.

"I'm sure a gentleman should be a good sportsman," he replied tactfully.

The valet handed them both sandwiches and a glass of brandy each. Humphrey did not like the taste but took the proffered glass without objecting.

"I think so," went on Goodchild, "but others might not agree. Your mother for one, I fancy."

Humphrey bit into his sandwich and did not reply. He wished he had some water to get rid of the unpleasant burning sensation left in his mouth by the brandy. Goodchild looked at his son's disgruntled face and cursed himself for having allowed him to become so dependent on his mother, but for this he knew he only had himself to blame. His long absences had hardly served to win his son's confidence. Now it might well be too late. If Helen lost him Joseph Braithwaite's financial support, they would be ruined. He tried to imagine a life with Hanley Park sold up and the land over which he had shot and hunted since boyhood closed to him forever. He waved to his valet to refill his glass but the brandy did not help him.

"Perhaps we've had enough sport for this morning," he said turning to Humphrey.

"As you wish, sir."

"What do *you* wish?" he snapped back, unable to bear his son's chilling formal obedience.

"I should like to return."

"Then why did you not say so?"

"I did not want to spoil your sport."

"You do so by refusing to speak your mind."

Humphrey, who had been gazing into his brandy, looked up with a flash of his mother's directness and said vehemently,

"Then I can no longer shoot with you."

"Why pray?"

"I dislike doing what I am not good at. You asked me to speak my mind."

"I did, and I applaud your decision. There's no pleasure dragging a reluctant boy after one."

"Nor being dragged, sir."

Goodchild felt confused and saddened. He had magnanimously offered the boy exemption from shooting but at first this had been refused. Then when he had repeated his offer, Humphrey had accepted, not with gratitude but with curt insolence.

"It would have been better if you had been truthful from the beginning and saved yourself the hypocrisy of deceiving me into believing that you enjoyed our sport."

"Had I done so, we would never have seen each other."

"And now that thought no longer distresses you?"

"Not when my presence only angers you."

"Should I be pleased by bad shooting?"

"Indeed not."

"You have mistaken criticism of your marksmanship for personal disapproval."

"Following game, little except shooting signifies."

A long silence, broken only by the wind in the leafless hedgerow. Goodchild's brief flicker of anger had spent itself and now only an empty helplessness remained. His voice was more appealing than peremptory as he said,

"If we neither ride nor shoot together, what can we do?"

"Nothing, I'm sure."

"We could walk."

The same look of suspicion, as though the remark had been ironic.

"I would have little of interest to say." Humphrey was surprised by his father's unexpected burst of laughter.

"The struggle, I assure you, would not be one-sided." Goodchild tipped back his brandy and smiled. "Good God, nothing to talk of. What do you know of the foresters or the ditchers? Have you seen a warrener at work? We'll find subjects enough."

"I shall enjoy it."

Goodchild looked at his son's diffident smile and had no idea whether he was being sincere. Another four years and the boy would be grown up, and by then any chance of getting to know him would have been irretrievably lost. He tossed his glass to the valet and jumped down from the stile. Soon they were on their way back to the house. Passing through a field of recently sowed winter wheat, Humphrey saw a boy, little younger than himself, perched on top of a gate; he had been hired to scare rooks from the seed. The underkeeper waved and the boy rotated his wooden rattle: a small sound in the empty landscape. When they reached the road, Goodchild took Humphrey's arm.

"I could never talk to my father. Do you think it runs in the family?"

"I hope not, sir."

"So do I, my boy." He sighed. "D'you know what I have to do in a week's time?"

"No, Father."

"Stand up in the market square and propose Mr. Braithwaite as Tory candidate."

"What will you say?"

"The usual Nomination Day nonsense; there'll be too much shouting and groaning for anybody to hear much."

"Will people throw things?" asked Humphrey with a trace of anxiety.

"I expect so," laughed Goodchild.

"I'd be frightened."

"I'm not looking forward to it myself."

They walked on in silence; they were sheltered from the first gusts of sleet by a fence of rotting wattles. At his age, thought Goodchild, I was betting on how many rats the best village terrier could kill in a minute, and laying money on whether any of the grooms could ride a hack round the edge of the paddock without using reins. A dirty, black-nailed boy, smelling of the stables, with half a cigar in his pocket and some filthy chewed toffee wrapped in a handkerchief, a boy whose main aversions had been dress coats, piano playing and his tutor. Yet Humphrey might almost belong to a different species with his love of books and dislike of rural pastimes. Goodchild heard his son say,

"Couldn't somebody else propose Mr. Braithwaite? Mother can't abide him."

Goodchild looked glumly at the rutted surface of the road.

"I'll explain a lot to you one day, Humphrey. I can't now, but I will; I will though, I promise you that."

As they tramped on, fresh flurries of sleet made their cheeks and ears smart. Coming into the park, the gray portico of the house was just visible through the bare black branches of some trees. Goodchild glanced at Humphrey and frowned. Would he ever be able to admit that his folly had endangered the boy's inheritance? Perhaps not, but he knew that he would have to be more truthful in future, if his past omissions were to be forgiven. At any rate a start had been made, a small one, but a start.

*   *   *

Goodchild had lunched with his wife, secure in the knowledge that Humphrey's presence would prevent her raising any objectionable topic of conversation. Afterward he retired at once to his smoking room, confident that he would not be disturbed in his private sanctum. Her ladyship had her dressing rooms and boudoir, where her husband never intruded, and she accorded him the same privilege in his smoking room and study.

Goodchild closed the door and sat down on the raised fender seat in front of the fire. In an hour he planned to return to Manchester to try to talk some sense into Carstairs, but in the meantime, before his journey, he intended to rest in his favorite room with its shelf of bound copies of *Bell's Life*, its gun cases and trophies. On the walls were sporting prints, so numerous that their frames touched, and by the hearth a fine tiger skin. A wide selection of crops and hunting whips sprouted from an elephant's foot near the door, and on the mantelpiece were ranged his lordship's collection of enamel and amber Turkish pipes. Goodchild lit a cigar and poured some brandy. Soothed by the warmth of the fire and the pleasant aroma of cigar smoke, he sank down in his leather chair. Later he began to doze; his eyes were still closed when the door opened and Helen entered.

"What the devil . . ." he muttered, sitting up and rubbing his eyes.

"Since you choose to avoid me at all times when we might otherwise talk privately, I have been obliged to seek you out."

"To what purpose?" he asked, forewarned of trouble to come by the silky gentleness of her voice. She smiled at his question.

"To speak privately, of course. I believe it is not unusual for husbands and wives to wish to talk to one another occasionally out of their servants' hearing."

"Say what you wish."

"Will you still sell Audley House?" she asked with sudden sharpness.

"A London establishment is impossible. You know that."

"I know that you have told me so." She moved closer to him and went on in the same unemotional voice, "I fear you will have a lean time of it with Dr. Carstairs."

"Your meaning, madam?" he snapped, jumping to his feet.

"He will bring an action against you unless I dissuade him."

"Unless *you* dissuade him?" he repeated incredulously.

"Poor man, he seemed most anxious in case details of your payments to him should reach the ears of his professional superiors."

Her self-possession and feigned sadness at being the cause of his indignation brought Goodchild to the verge of screaming, but he controlled himself and said in a level voice,

"Spite and jealousy do not become you, Helen."

She inclined her head as though thinking hard what reason he might have for this statement.

"Jealousy? I think not, Harry." She turned to him with a look he could not fathom: part sadness, part derision. "Can you remember when I last waited up long into the night listening for the wheels of your phaeton?" She paused as though trying vainly to recollect the precise date. "I think it was a month or two before you discovered that you could sleep so much better in your dressing room. That would make it three years and a bit over. I was jealous then, I don't deny it." She flashed him a mocking smile. "I could have killed Lady Stratton and I wouldn't have been unhappy to have done the same to Lady Constance

Mowbray, but when she became so upset about Mrs. Darcy, I felt quite sorry for her. I daresay I'm spiteful, Harry, but my modest stock of jealousy is sadly depleted."

"I fear I am a poor audience for your polished ironies, Helen; they do not however affect the facts of the matter in question." He had spoken with a languid air, but there was no more nonchalance as he continued. "If scandal diminishes the benefit which Braithwaite expects to derive from my support in the election, he will seek repayment; and then you may bid farewell to Hanley Park as well as Audley House. Think of our son, madam, before you contrive our ruin."

She flung back her head defiantly and said with icy scorn,

"When did *you* think of him, Harry? Is it my fault that you must grovel to Braithwaite? The debts are your doing, not mine."

"They exist, regardless of their origin," he replied impatiently. "I cannot keep Audley House, nor maintain you anywhere but here."

"Then you must suffer the consequences," she replied in a low, trembling voice. In spite of the fury and hatred in her eyes, he met them resolutely.

"Since they will fall as heavily on you, I will bear them as best I can."

Goodchild had expected another outburst of anger to greet his dry response, but instead she gazed at him remotely with a confused and perplexed expression. Then she raised her eyes and stared at him with astonishment, as if seeing him for the first time.

"You really would prefer that . . . the loss of everything . . . prefer that to giving way an inch to me. Whatever it cost you, you'll always be too proud to bargain with me."

"I was not aware," he replied curtly, "that your terms allowed me that latitude." He leaned with an elbow against the mantelpiece and looked down into the fire for a moment before facing her abruptly. "Your circumstances will be much reduced, but, if you wish it, I will have my solicitor set out the basis for a separation."

"When?"

"January."

"No," she cried vehemently. "You will do it before the election."

"I will do it," he shouted, "when I please or not at all."

She laughed harshly and pressed her hands together, seeking to suppress her despairing anger.

"And what persuasion may I use with you when that time comes? None I think."

"Do you doubt my word of honor?"

"Honor, of course, how foolish of me to doubt you. Gentlemen call their gambling debts 'debts of honor.' It surprises me how often their notes are not honored by their banks." She paused breathlessly, feeling tears pricking. "What honor is there in your dealings with your doctor's wife? In your toadying to Braithwaite, your . . ."

"Accept my word," he roared, "or do what you please. I will give no other guarantee."

Outside the room she clutched at her head and choked back a deep sob. She could not risk her son's inheritance and he knew that. She had thought him at her mercy, but in reality she was as much in his power as ever. Not until she reached her boudoir did the cruelty of this fact no longer obliterate other memories of their conversation. He had given his word and she would keep him to it by whatever means.

⸙ Seven ⸙

If Joseph Braithwaite's home, with its massive china cabinets, its silken draperies and Turkey carpets, was a temple dedicated to the material rewards of a successful commercial career, his dark and meagerly furnished set of offices was consecrated to the austere nonconformist virtues of thrift and self-denying industry by which these good things had been achieved. Even the pictures on the walls—prints of the Braithwaite mills taken from *Knight's Cyclopaedia of the Industry of All Nations*—were intended not to divert or delight the eye but to stimulate the beholder to still greater feats of application.

George Braithwaite had always viewed his father's dedication with a humility befitting one who derived such benefit from its results; and certainly, before his conversation with Magnus Crawford at Bentley's, the notion that he might one day come to the center of his father's industrial empire, to argue with him about the handling of a strike, would have struck him as too fantastic to merit even a passing thought. And yet, ten days before the election, George found himself walking across the factory yard with this very purpose in mind. George had not lightly decided to try to achieve the all but impossible task Magnus Crawford had set him; only because marriage to Catherine mattered more to him than anything else in life had he dared provoke his father's rage. George's captaincy in the yeomanry, the fact that he would soon buy a commission in a fashionable regiment and later sit in the House as member for the borough, all owed more to his father's expectations than his own wishes; but his proposal to Catherine had been his own independent choice. Having no fortune, she had never been part of Joseph's plan for his son, and paternal indifference to the match had increased rather than diminished George's determination to consummate it.

As George climbed the iron stairs to his father's office, he thought of Catherine to give him sufficient strength to face what would undoubtedly be a testing ordeal. As the price for abandoning his opposition to George's pursuit of his sister, Magnus had demanded that George persuade his father to dismiss the Irishmen who had replaced his striking workers. With neither a full understanding of the reasons why Crawford had made this demand nor any clear idea how it might be achieved, George was a far from confident man as he pushed open the outer door of his father's office.

When George was shown in, his father was seated at a table by the window unsealing letters and sorting papers from a dispatch box. Without looking up, he would dictate occasional memoranda to the elderly clerk perched on a high stool at an adjacent desk. On seeing his son, Joseph broke off in midsentence and came toward him with a low bow.

"A rare honor, George," he murmured with feigned obsequiousness. George was always embarrassed by his father's labored jokes about his gentlemanly son who now looked down on all forms of trade. George did not at all despise the origins of his wealth.

"The honor's mine, Father," he replied, looking absently at the piles of ledgers and the Liverpool shipping lists pinned on the walls. Joseph nodded to the clerk, who picked up a sheaf of bills and checks and went out. When George was reclining in the room's solitary armchair and his father leaning against a tall iron safe, an uneasy silence filled the office. George cleared his throat.

"That was a deuced unpleasant business on the station road. I can't seem to get it out of my mind."

"From what you told me at the time, I can't say I'm surprised; we all owe you a debt of gratitude. I'm proud of you, indeed I am."

"My concern is to avoid the same sort of incident in the future."

"We all are. Quite right we should be."

George watched his father's fat white fingers touching the gold chains across his gray waistcoat. From somewhere outside, he could hear the muted but incessant throbbing of the enginehouse.

"The point is how we can do it."

"Do what?" George saw his father's thick gray eyebrows raised in surprise.

"Stop it happening again." George paused and thought a moment.

Best take the fence straight on; no point in approaching at too oblique an angle and risk being misunderstood. "It seems to me the only way is to settle the dispute before the election."

"A grand idea, George," laughed Joseph, his smooth pink face creasing with merriment.

"If you discharge your Irish hands, I believe the strikers would go back to work for whatever you saw fit to offer them. Learned their lesson in my view."

His father nodded affably and flicked a trace of cigar ash from a lapel of his black swallowtail coat.

"The strike started because I reduced their wages. Now you say they'll return for what they turned down before." He chuckled to himself and shook his head. "A fine spectacle I'd make of myself if I discharged the Irish and found my old work people as obstinate as before. If I go chasing after them, they'll think I'm weakening; and I'll tell you this, I'll pay them nowt more than I offered before unless there's an increase in demand. When profits fall, wages must fall too. They've not learned that lesson yet, lad."

His father's folded arms and omniscient smile made George's heart sink.

"To prevent riots you could surely pay at an artificial rate for a few weeks."

"I'll not tamper with the law of supply and demand come war or famine. How do I pay the false rate? Out of profits, that's how; and what does that do? Drives capital out of spinning, and we'll end the day with thousands seeking less work for lower wages. Let them as wants higher wages seek other work, and, when demand returns, them as stayed in the trade will be few and the capitalist must pay them a high rate. Leave well alone and all comes right."

After his speech Joseph looked at his son with the self-satisfaction of a priest who has successfully defended the true faith from a dangerous heresy and sees the heretic penitent at last. George recognized the look and dug his nails into the palms of his hands.

"But men in Rigton Bridge have no other work to seek. The mills have destroyed the hand-loom trade."

For the first time Joseph's sleek smile faded.

"Come, lad, can I control the size of population in this town? That power rests with the people themselves."

"Our mills drew them here," replied George, driven on only by his determination to satisfy Crawford. He had never opposed his father so firmly and feared that he would not easily be forgiven.

"They came freely and have no claims on me," said Joseph in the incisive, high-pitched tone which George knew was a danger signal. "It's a master's right to seek out those who'll work for the lowest wage. I did that, and I'll discharge not one of my new hands to buy off riots. I thought you had a better head on your shoulders, George."

Joseph paced over to the window and looked out at the towering factory buildings opposite. George glared at his father's broad back, and felt sharp spasms of anger. Would Crawford have made a better showing? No man on earth could move his father when he had made up his mind. Joseph had evidently been thinking, for, when he turned around, his lips were compressed and his brow furrowed. A moment later he told George that he would not after all be required to negotiate with the confederacy of new voters for the sale of their votes.

"I'll look to that myself. It's no job for fainthearts or soft heads. I'm told their leaders have been to see what they can get from the liberal's agent. They'll not double-cross me that way. I'll have answers for that game."

"What answers, Father?"

"Good enough to keep them in line. If they're after honey they can expect some wasps."

George was shaken by the savage way his father had spoken.

"What if people discover what you're up to?"

"It's done in most elections, and I'll make mine no exception. D'you think those as sells their votes would like things done a different way? I'll pay for my election and not with short change either. A borough's lucky when a rich man stands. With the *Independent* out of business, there'll be none to raise a noise, so who's to care?"

George thought of Magnus Crawford but said nothing. His father laughed when he saw his son was about to leave.

"Take heart, man; I've a rough tongue when others tell me what's to be done. Stick to soldiering, George. Learn your trade with the yeomanry and then we'll see what's to do. The best regiments won't be too good for the Braithwaites, not if it's the Guards. I'll run to two thousand, I tell you."

"Thank you, Father."

Before George was out of the room, his father had returned to his letters and papers. As he went down the stairs, George cursed himself for ever having tried to achieve what Crawford had asked of him. Now what could he tell the man? That he had failed as he had known he would? That his father had humiliated him yet again? Better not see Crawford at all and let him draw his own conclusions. Seconds later George had an idea that did a lot to ease his depression. If Crawford was going to blacken him in his sister's eyes, might not he, George, repay the compliment and improve his chances at the same time? He would go to Catherine a week or so before her decision was due and tell her what her brother had said about her motives. After swearing to her that he had never believed a word of these lies, he would humbly renew his proposal. Shocked by her brother's duplicity and deeply moved by her suitor's spontaneous demonstration of trust and loyalty, might she not there and then accept him? Even if this procedure did not bring immediate success, George was hopeful that it might ultimately tip the scales in his favor. Leaving the factory gates, George could not imagine how so simple an idea had previously eluded him.

⮫ Eight ⮪

As Tom Strickland walked along Store Street, a light rain was falling and the narrowness of the thoroughfare made it impossible for him to avoid the dirt thrown up by the wheels of carts and drays. In such conditions the crossing sweepers looked as though they were made of mud and filth. Although the street was partially paved, the numerous rag shops, gin palaces and pawnshops marked it out as a resort of the poorer classes.

The stalls of a street market forced Tom against the entrances of courts and open doorways, through which he could see blackened staircases and backyards piled high with rubbish, some of it floating in slimy water from overflowing rain butts. Pushing past ill-clad groups of haggard women bargaining for scraps of stale meat and frost-bitten vegetables, he came to Conduit Row, and, turning down it, reached a small open space with a horse trough and a pump in the center. On one side was a long windowless wall with a central archway leading to a soap and candle factory, and on the other, a terrace of seedy but still dignified eighteenth-century houses with tall railings, torch snuffers and overhanging lamp brackets. These buildings would once have housed doctors and solicitors, but, with the growth of the town and the flight of professional men to new suburban villas, they were now mostly given over to cheap lodging houses.

The last house in the terrace was slightly larger than the others, but it was not for this reason that Tom stopped and looked up at the dirty windows and cracked brickwork. With an air of surprise he pulled a letter from his pocket and checked the address. Still puzzled, but satisfied that he had indeed come to the right place, he walked up the steps to the door. The day before he had received a note from Magnus Crawford asking him to come here, and, although he had had no idea what the man wanted with him, curiosity had proved stronger than his irritation over Crawford's behavior outside Bentley's the week before. He felt irritated with himself for the hold Crawford had over him, but was honest enough with himself not to deny it.

On the door were two ornate painted signs: *E. J. Clegg, Draper, Clothier and Hatter. Workshop Only*, and, just below it, *B. & J. Truscott & Co., Lithographic and Copper-Plate Printers*. So much smaller was the discolored brass plate next to the bellpull that Tom had not at first noticed it. When he did, he laughed out loud; on it were two words: *Rigton Independent*.

On entering the editorial office, Tom saw no sign of Crawford. The room was long, drafty, low-ceilinged and well lit only at the far end, where a large trestle table stood near the window, covered with a litter of proof and manuscript pages, a dusty pile of books for review and numerous empty soda water bottles and cigar boxes. Balanced on a flat-topped coal scuttle, in front of a small bright fire, sat a youth with ink-smeared arms and hands and similarly marked corduroy breeches. As Tom advanced, the boy lazily doffed his paper hat, but made no move to get up. Not so a large red-whiskered man behind the trestle table, who rose at once and introduced himself as the paper's cashier. Tom explained his business, and, having learned that Crawford was expected shortly, sat down to wait.

Never having been in a newspaper office before, Tom was considerably surprised by what he saw; he had always imagined messenger boys running in and out, compositors busily setting up pages and the steady thump of a steam press in the background. Now he felt acutely embarrassed that he had ever suggested that Crawford should put money into such an apparently run-down concern. The unpleasant thought occurred to him that Crawford might have summoned him to point out the fatuity of his suggestion.

Looking around him, he noticed several broken windowpanes stuffed up with rags. Against the wall nearest him were a dozen or so stacks of unused paper ranged from floor to ceiling, partly blocking a doorway, through which could be seen a hand press and beside it another machine for compressing the printed sheets. It seemed most unlikely that the

Independent would be able to earn much more than would be needed to pay the printer and compositor.

To pass the time, Tom looked at back numbers of the paper. Four pages in length, two were taken up by a melodramatic fiction serial and advertisements for remedies usually excluded by the better papers: "Yoland's Specific Solution for speedily curing gonorrhea, gleets, strictures and expelling bladder stones." The correspondence, he suspected, was entirely written by the staff, since exchanges between "A Cotton Master" and "Vindex," or some such pseudonym, invariably went against the first named. The rest was made up of political articles— always hostile to landlords, manufacturers and magistrates—and local trivia, consisting of sporting events, regional antiquities and a feebly satirical section called "Town Talk." Tom was glancing through an article castigating the missionary societies for idolizing the suffering Negro, while ignoring the white factory slaves at home, when Crawford burst in.

Not seeing Tom at first, Magnus tossed his hat and cape to the ink-smeared youth, and then swept some books off the top of a cupboard and unearthed a bottle of Madeira. He was turning to offer the red-whiskered man a glass when he saw Tom.

"Mr. Strickland, forgive me. I'm late. I'm afraid Madeira serves for port and sherry here. Take a glass?" Without waiting for a reply, he turned to the boy. "If you're awake, Moggs, light some lamps." Then, having handed Tom a glass and introduced him briefly to the cashier, Crawford led his guest into the printing room and shut the door behind them.

Tom watched Crawford walk across to the printing press and slap its greasy metal frame, as a lover of horses might the flank of a favorite hunter.

"Just a poor old Stanhope, but still in working order. Comforting, wouldn't you say, that Caxton changed the world with something still more primitive?" He laughed loudly at Tom's consternation.

"Did you pay the fine?" asked the artist uneasily.

"I did, though not, between ourselves, to control a rag of a radical weekly."

"Why then?"

"Patience, Mr. Strickland." Magnus saw that Tom was looking absently at the compositor's table. "Ingenious how the letters are divided up, wouldn't you say? More than fifty divisions in the lower case alone; how the man finds anything is a mystery to me." He picked up a handful of metal letters, examined them for a moment, and then stared at Tom with unexpected directness. "I'm going to make Joseph Braithwaite sweat a little for his election."

Tom smiled to himself.

"Last time we met, the idea seemed to hold little attraction for you. May I ask your reason?"

"Personal ones, Mr. Strickland." He tossed away the letters and rested a hand on the compositor's stool. "I don't like him, I don't like his methods either." He saw that Strickland was looking at him intently. "Have you ever wanted to atone for anything?" he asked abruptly.

"I don't think so."

"Then serve in a colony." He paused and narrowed his eyes. "I'm bored, Mr. Strickland, perhaps that's the truth of it; bored enough to welcome any diversion, even borough politics, if I can . . . Do you know I've heard it said men used to fight duels for nothing . . . nothing except to make something happen. A man may still gamble for that reason. Absurd in these civilized days, don't you think? An artist has his work, of course, to occupy him; idle minds must seek other panaceas."

"The desire for justice?" murmured Tom with a smile.

"You flatter me, but leave me my imperfect motives. The wish comes first, the reasons merely justify." He refilled his glass and grinned at Tom. "No more metaphysics. I paid the fine because the editor also happens to be the liberal candidate's agent. Before I saved his livelihood, he told me nothing; afterward he became quite confiding." He laughed softly. "You see, Mr. Strickland, I've decided to trust you."

"Then tell me what he told you," said Tom, concealing his excitement. He knew that he was being told these things for a reason and he was filled with a desperate impatience to discover what it was. Crawford's pretense of levity did not deceive him; the man had paid out three or four hundred pounds for information and was certain to use it.

"Last week," replied Crawford, "our editor had a visit from half a dozen anonymous individuals who came to visit him in his capacity as liberal agent. They claimed to represent the interests of seventy others—most of them recently enfranchised voters. These six solid citizens were out to sell their tidy parcel of votes for a fine sum; they'd already taken money from Braithwaite and wanted to see whether the liberal purse could measure up—if it failed, the votes went Braithwaite's way. I'm going to treat with them on the liberal's behalf."

"To collect evidence of bribery?"

"No chance of that," replied Magnus wryly. "Braithwaite will probably pay the money to a tradesman who's recently worked for him; it'll look like an ordinary payment in his books. This honest broker will then disperse it among the voters for a commission. Nobody'll be able to prove a thing."

"So what do you do? You can't intend to outbid Braithwaite?"

"I don't, but I'm going to give that impression. In fact I've arranged to meet our six rogues on Nomination Day. I'll have witnesses with me, and, as soon as they've pocketed the bribe, I'll get it back by threatening to denounce them to Braithwaite for trying to cheat him . . . unless of course they return my money and agree to abstain in the voting."

Impressed for a moment, Tom thought quickly, determined that Crawford was going to have no chance to think him naïve. The flaw seemed so glaring, when he thought of it, that Tom hesitated in case he had missed the point. Then he said quietly,

"But they'll go straight to Braithwaite themselves, tell him that the opposition has tried to bribe them but backed down. Then they'll swear that, whatever's said, their votes are his."

Magnus nodded eager assent.

"Quite true, Mr. Strickland." He came up to him and murmured, "But suppose one of my witnesses is a man whose word Braithwaite would be sure to trust . . . a man, for example, dependent on his patronage; don't you think that might impress our six gentlemen? They'd know Braithwaite would believe such a man's word rather than their own."

Tom's heart was beating fast now that he knew what Crawford wanted. He admired the man's skill for almost making it seem that he had suggested his own participation. He smiled at Magnus, who was watching him anxiously.

"When do we meet them?" he asked, feeling his cheeks tingle and a surprising constriction in his throat.

"Nomination Day. I'll write with the time and place."

The understated calmness of this reaction annoyed Tom.

"You're very confident, Mr. Crawford," he said with a trace of bitterness.

"Why not? They'll know better than to touch us; I'll have left an excellent account of our movements with those who'll know how to avenge any insult. Your best protection will be some papers connecting you with Braithwaite."

"Are you very used to people doing what you want?"

Magnus suddenly looked at Tom with such frankness and sympathy that he forgot his resentment.

"By no means. Surely you don't think I've done this before? Isn't that the attraction: a new taste, a new drink? I'm just as worried as you are."

"Now you're making fun of me," laughed Tom.

"Really I'm not, but I had to seem certain, didn't I? Otherwise why should you have agreed? You like to seem persuadable but your questions were sharp enough."

"Now you're just making sure I won't change my mind."

Magnus lowered his eyes in a parody of being shocked.

"Isn't that just a little cynical of you, Mr. Strickland?"

As Tom caught the humorous sparkle in Crawford's eyes, he could not understand how he had ever thought him cold and forbidding. The thought that he was part of a plot to balk Joseph Braithwaite no longer struck Tom as frightening but as ludicrously funny. Wanting to laugh, he controlled himself and said,

"What if word gets back to Braithwaite about my part in this?"

"It won't, but if it does, all you have to do is play the loyal employee who joined the conspirators only to be able to reveal their baseness to his master."

"How easy," replied Tom, with a disdainful toss of the head.

"If you persuaded me to trust you, surely you can do the same with Braithwaite?"

They both laughed, and Magnus moved toward the door. As he was leaving, Tom caught sight of a pile of printed handbills.

LORD GOODCHILD WISHES IT
TO BE KNOWN THAT WHEREVER
HIS NAME IS USED TO BIAS

VOTERS IN MR. BRAITHWAITE'S
FAVOR, IT WILL BE DONE
WITHOUT HIS LORDSHIP'S
AUTHORITY AND CONSENT.

Underneath appeared the name of a solicitor to give the spurious document greater authenticity. Magnus picked up one of the bills and shook his head.

"A little unethical perhaps. I'll have it stuck up all over town a couple of nights before polling. Braithwaite won't have much time to print a denial."

"Who's going to believe it?"

"Fools, Mr. Strickland, but doubtless Rigton Bridge has its share." Magnus opened the door and ushered Tom through the office. They paused on the dark landing and shook hands.

"Till Nomination Day, Mr. Strickland."

"Indeed, Mr. Crawford."

Outside in the smoke-laden twilight Tom listened to the distant strains of an organ-grinder for a moment, and then, with a shrug of the shoulders, began to walk. It was impossible, absurd, fantastic and yet it had happened. He, Thomas Strickland, had made a decision that might decide the election. He thought of the way Goodchild had brushed him aside in the hall at Hanley Park and how George Braithwaite always counted on his docile agreement. If Crawford's plan worked, it would be a pity that those who suffered by it should never know the means of their discomfiture. As he passed the street market in Store Street, he changed his mind. To share that knowledge as a secret with Crawford would be better still, and they would never know. A moment later he realized that he had been walking in the muddiest part of the street without noticing.

~ Nine ~

For several weeks, Lord Goodchild had dreaded the steady approach of the day appointed for the nomination of candidates; but, now that the moment had actually come, he felt much calmer than he had expected, calm enough in fact to walk through the massive crowd assembled in the market square. A fine driving rain, blown by a gusty wind, made the profusion of party flags and banners around him flap and fill like carelessly furled sails in a crowded harbor. In the center stood the sturdy wooden platform of the hustings from which he would soon be obliged to propose Joseph Braithwaite.

Goodchild was well aware of the deep resentment which his support of the millowner's candidature had occasioned among the local gentry. Because the Tories were so closely associated with agricultural and landed interests, very few manufacturers had sought adoption as Tory candidates in the past. But with the repeal of the Corn Laws, it had seemed obvious to Goodchild that the principal obstacle to an alliance between the urban factory owner and the rural landowner had been removed. The manufacturers had wanted cheaper bread to keep down wages, and, this aim achieved, could surely be relied upon to oppose further reforms with die-hard conservative vigor. The futility of agricultural opposition to the nation's manifest destiny as the workshop of the world had been an argument often used by his lordship in persuading his tenant farmers to pledge their votes to Braithwaite. Fortunately, few of them had known about his indebtedness to the manufacturer.

On Nomination Day there was never any polling, only formal speeches by the candidates and their proposers, and then, after a farcical "show of hands"—meaningless because those showing their preference in this way were rarely qualified voters—the day of the actual poll would be announced, in this case for the following week. The only satisfaction Lord Goodchild derived from the proceedings was that they would cost Braithwaite the two hundred or so pounds needed to pay and transport, from neighboring villages, a body of men large enough to give him token support in the square and to prevent an assault on the hustings.

Goodchild had never been unhappy in crowds. The garish bandanna head scarves of the mill girls, the small boys clambering up lampposts, and the cries of the hot potato sellers, brought to mind other large gatherings, like those at the racecourse rails or at the prizefiights of his youth. That there were whores and pickpockets about, he had no doubt, but, taking such things for granted, he was neither surprised nor affronted. Never having doubted his own position, he had always been comparatively unmoved by popular agitation. And yet this crowd was different from any he had seen in recent years. He did not expect to be liked by working people, but he was surprised to be hated, and, although nobody had struck him, he noticed little of the mixture of deference and mild resentment to which he was accustomed. Instead the strike and the suppression of the riots had produced the same smoldering anger he remembered from the worst period of the Chartist troubles. Not often given to feeling guilty, the discomforting thought still occurred to Goodchild that if he had been truer to his obligations, and less attentive to his pleasures, Braithwaite would not have gained his present provocative ascendancy. Goodchild had not raised his rents for a decade, but gangs of boys still weeded his fields for less than Braithwaite paid his child piecers. His lordship's disquieting sense of failure, however, owed less to a humanitarian's bad conscience over his omissions than to the realization that if he, and others of his caste, had done more to defend the interests of the people, the rapid encroachments of the new plutocracy* would have been checked.

A few yards to his right the crowd was denser where a juggler was performing, spinning two basins, one above the other, on the top of a long cane. The man's silver satin coat and sequined trousers were soaked by the rain, and his gilded slippers were splattered with mud. A barefooted boy with a running sore under an eye was collecting coins in a wooden bowl. Goodchild tossed in a gold sovereign and strode off at once so he did not hear the amazed gratitude of the recipient.

When he reached the Swan, Braithwaite's headquarters, he saw Joseph himself talking to the high sheriff and the returning officer in the entrance hall. He also noticed two Light Dragoon troopers doing sentry duty at the door. There would be other soldiers in the hotel kept tactfully out of sight. Goodchild was thankful that as yet his own regiment had not been sent for. The town's chief magistrate, the Reverend Francis St. Clare, came up to him with a gravely bowed bald head.

"An ugly mob, my lord, and painfully agitated."

Goodchild glanced out at the line of special constables keeping the crowd back from the front of the hotel with enthusiastic use of their staves and truncheons. He looked back at St. Clare's soft and pudgy face that reminded him only of a fat schoolboy suddenly overtaken by middle age before his beard had had time to grow. He smiled reassuringly.

"Ugly? Surely not. Excited perhaps, but not ill-disposed."

Seconds later a stone crashed through the window of the adjoining dining room.

"Not ugly, my lord?" asked St. Clare quizzically. Goodchild laughed easily.

"What would Nomination Day be without a few broken heads and windows? An immemorial custom, Mr. St. Clare."

"Perhaps you would have been less sanguine had your lordship been in the under sheriff's chaise when the door was torn off and horse soil thrown in."

"I would have resented stones and bottles more. Dung has the merit of softness." He paused and went on in a more serious manner, "I have walked in the crowd . . ."

"My Lord?" St. Clare's amazement was not feigned.

"And I found them sullen but peaceable. Should the high sheriff or the mayor ask you to read the Riot Act, I would advise refusal unless the hustings are in danger." From the corner of his eye, Goodchild saw Joseph coming toward him. Braithwaite's face was flushed, and although he seemed calm and composed, Goodchild guessed that he owed some of his courage to the hotel's brandy. The millowner took his proposer's arm.

"Harry, I see you've been acting the Christian among the lions or perhaps I should reverse the order, only there seems little sanctity out there." He let out his strange, high-pitched laugh, which pained Goodchild almost more than the man's use of his Christian name. Goodchild felt the pressure of the hand on his arm tighten and saw the millowner's face darken. "There's deception afoot, Harry—a scheme to poach our votes. But I'm wise to it. They'll not make fools of us, my lord, not that way, I tell you."

Goodchild was about to make an appropriate reply when the band, which was to lead Braithwaite's procession to the hustings, launched into "See the Conquering Hero." From the efforts being made by the special constables to clear a path through the crowd, Goodchild judged that their departure for the center of the square must be imminent.

Five minutes later, after some irksome jostling and jeering, both Goodchild and Braithwaite, and the Liberal candidate and his proposer, took their places on the platform, next to the high sheriff and the town clerk. The returning officer stepped forward and appealed for silence.

"I have received her Majesty's writ for the election of a new member for the borough of Rigton Bridge in the Eastern Division of the County and have appointed today for the nomination. I must beg that both sides are heard with considerate attention and true English impartiality and must remind . . ."

Goodchild listened to very little of this preliminary address but waited patiently for it to finish. As soon as it did, he moved forward to the rail to make his speech proposing Braithwaite and extolling his virtues. He was greeted by a deafening roar of opposition. He had expected hissing and groaning but this full-throated howl of derision took him by surprise. Nevertheless he began his speech calmly, aware that he was inaudible even to those nearest him. Within seconds eggs and rotten vegetables were raining down on the hustings. A bag filled with water burst against his chest, and when he was subsequently hit with flour, he began to resemble a snowman in a thaw. He saw a man below him in the crowd piss into a bottle and hurl it up at the platform, but he finished his speech without being hit by anything more substantial than a potato; then, taking Braithwaite by the arm, he led him forward, as a king might present his son and heir to his loyal subjects, but there were no acclamations for the prince of commerce. Joseph had barely opened his mouth before he was hit on the cheek by a piece of glass. The wound was not deep but bled profusely. The Liberal candidate vainly appealed to the crowd to hear his rival, while Braithwaite glared at his attackers with a scornful sneer made more grotesque by the blood that streaked his face and shirt front. Goodchild was impressed that Joseph did not for a moment leave the front of the platform.

By the time the Liberal and his proposer had had their say too, the crowd was more peaceable, and the "show of hands," although over-whelmingly against the Tory, provoked no further violence. The returning officer announced the poll for the following Tuesday and the proceedings were at an end.

Braithwaite was trembling with suppressed rage as they reentered the Swan, but Goodchild and most of the others in his party, while being in no pleasant frame of mind, were nonetheless relieved that no worse trouble had occurred. Their most fervent hope was that polling day itself might pass as uneventfully.

* * *

As Tom Strickland entered the labyrinth of streets and alleys south of Market Street on his way to meet Magnus Crawford, his former mood of lighthearted adventure had long since been dispelled by the violent scenes he had witnessed earlier near the hustings. A man like Crawford, who had suppressed a native rebellion might take angry mobs for granted, but to Tom, in spite of his far from sheltered childhood, the rumbling fury of that vast crowd with its threat of ungovernable power had been a chastening spectacle. The idea that he and Crawford, or for that matter Braithwaite himself, could influence such a swelling tide of disaffection now seemed arrogant and unreal. Not even the great institutions of state could survive if cut off from the mass of the people. And yet the Chartists had been defeated and the vast majority of the people was still unrepresented in Parliament. Tom was in an anxious and thoughtful mood as he picked his way toward the river. Could Crawford be involving himself for no better reason than a craving for new experience, as he had claimed? He had spoken of atonement too, and hatred of Braithwaite's methods, but which was the truth? And through what misguided romanticism, Tom wondered, had *he* committed himself? Because of reckless courage at the hazard table, and the intangible attraction of the man's presence, with his strange shifts from melancholy to gaiety, from indifference to ardent involvement? Perhaps it had been no more than an artist's habitual feelings of inadequacy in the face of men of action. He smiled disdainfully at the idea, but could not utterly dismiss it.

The note Crawford had sent him, two days after their meeting, had been brief and factual. Because Braithwaite's agents were by now likely to be watching the offices of the *Independent*, Magnus had asked Tom to meet him by the old packhorse bridge on the river. From there, they would go by a circuitous route to the small flint-glass factory where the meeting with the new voters' representatives was to take place. Tom was not to come in at once but was to remain in an adjacent timber yard midway between the gasworks and the glass factory. He would be joined there by the Liberal agent, who would have set out separately for the rendezvous, to split up and confuse possible pursuers, and would have with him half a dozen laborers, hired in case of trouble. Magnus would go on alone to the meeting place, followed at a distance by the boy Moggs. If Crawford suspected no foul play, he would send back Moggs to summon Tom and the others from the timber yard.

It being Nomination Day, Tom was jostled as he walked by large numbers of men and women who would otherwise have been at work. Groups were lounging at street corners and outside taprooms from which floated the sound of singing and the music of pianos and seraphines. The next street he passed along was swarming with drunken workmen ejected from a nearby gin shop, and with young mill girls and piecers shouting and playing kiss-in-the-ring. Closer to the river the dark and crowded back streets opened out into wide muddy tracts of undeveloped waste ground, trampled bare of grass and covered with piles of blackened bricks, ashpits and mounds of decaying rubbish. Tom saw some pigs rooting about for rotting vegetables and so saving their owners the expense of feeding them. The desolation, the drizzle and the smoky grayness of the sky, which washed out all colors brighter than brown and dirty ocher, filled Tom with a leaden numbness—sharpening to active pain when he saw, outside a small coarse-thread mill, a young mother squatting on the step suckling a baby. The infant had been brought to the factory by a child minder, herself no more than eight or nine years old. The woman seemed oblivious of the fine steady rain and the heavy drips falling from the porch.

Reaching the medieval packhorse bridge, long since made redundant by the wide iron bridge half a mile upstream, Tom sat down on the parapet and waited for Magnus. Below him, from the two open brick drains, the effluent from a bone works and a tannery spewed out into the dark brown water, joining the discharge from a slaughterhouse on the opposite side. A little farther downstream, where the river skirted the parish burial ground, was a weir, affording the funerary angels and saints a less than heavenly view of the bizarre variety of floating debris, as it plunged down a vertical curtain of water into the foaming maelstrom below: dead cats, discarded skins from the tannery, offal from tripe houses, bones from the glue factory and odd lengths of timber from the sawmills.

Nauseated by the stench, Tom was relieved to see Magnus approaching a few minutes later, walking beside a massive, broad-chested man whose muddy corduroy breeches and heavy, tall, lace-up boots suggested that he was a navvy, evidently brought along as their bodyguard. A few paces behind came Moggs, the ink stains on his smock frock showing no signs of washing out in the rain.

"Just the weather for Nomination Day, Mr. Strickland," said Magnus by way of greeting. His hair was plastered down by the rain and his soaking patelot cape clung to his shoulders like a second skin. "I fear it'll take an Indian monsoon to keep them so quiet on polling day."

"They seemed lively enough to me."

Magnus noticed his disapproval and smiled easily.

"Wait and see how cavalry enlivens them. Though I don't deny they raised a fine chorus when Braithwaite's band struck up. He could have spared himself the hire of so many trombones."

Tom made no reply as Magnus led them onto the towpath. Ahead, the river narrowed into a dark brick gorge where warehouses lined both banks, the wharves silent and deserted because of Nomination Day. Magnus glanced sideways at Tom as they walked.

"Why so pensive, Mr. Strickland? You mustn't be so hard on a man for making light of grave matters. You'd be surprised how many soldiers before a battle seize on any trifling incident if it helps them laugh."

Tom looked down at the mud and cinders on the path.

"I'm no soldier as you know quite well."

They went on in silence past heaps of merchandise, shapeless under sodden tarpaulins. Magnus said quietly,

"If you regret coming, you'd best speak your mind."

"Regret coming?" Tom returned sharply. "Did I need much persuading?"

"No, that's why your moodiness worries me. Unless we can act together—better not act at all."

They had reached a coal depot, where the canal joined the river. Tom kicked savagely at loose coals that had spilled onto the path from the huge mounds bordering it.

"Secret meetings . . . payments of money, threats . . . power over others." He stopped and looked accusingly at Magnus. Moggs and the navvy walked on a few yards and leaned against the walls of a lock-keeper's hut. "Are we so different from Braithwaite? Or is it just to make things happen . . . a new drink? What was it you said?" He paused and said in a lower voice, "I didn't find that crowd this morning amusing. . . ."

"What did you find it?"

"Frightening . . . sad . . . I can't tell you."

"Then tell me this," said Magnus urgently, "if a man has a gun, must I fight him with my bare fists to prove my superior virtue? If you don't like my way, go back."

Tom's dark eyes flashed with anger. Magnus often thought Strickland, with his gentle voice and sensitive, high-cheekboned face, too tranquil and bloodless to oppose him, but, for all his aesthetic pallor, the man had spirit too.

"Me go back? Are we not here because *I* suggested you should pay a fine?"

Magnus looked away toward the lock gates, where a constant cascade of water foamed through the sluices.

"Then why are we arguing?" he murmured. "I need your support."

"If this is personal vengeance against one man, then I *will* go back."

"What do we gain if we succeed?" cried Magnus. "Praise, wealth, gratitude? Nothing, except how we stand in our own eyes. Forget my reasons. If you value honor, obligation, call it what you will, don't look to others for a code; only look to yourself, and *do* as you wish to be."

Tom met his eyes and smiled.

"Thank you. I know all I need to."

A few minutes later they had left the warehouses behind and were following the river through open meadows. Ben Craske, the navvy, told them of occasions when he had come here as a boy to watch bullbaiting and dogfights. After half a mile, Magnus, having satisfied himself that they had not been followed, led them across a deserted tile-yard back in the direction of the town.

The glass factory, where the meeting was to take place, was near the center of a complex of industrial buildings dominated by the intricate and ornate ironwork frames of the town's largest gasholders and the chimneys of the coking furnaces. The cobbled street, leading past the gasworks to the glass factory and neighboring timber yard, was narrow and flanked by smoke-blackened, windowless walls. Tom was trying to imagine how Magnus would conduct the meeting, when, ahead of them, he saw a cart piled high with sacks of coal, blocking the entrance to the gasworks. He noticed too that Magnus hesitated for a moment before walking on at the same pace. After all, there was nothing to be suspicious of, there would be sure to be dozens of coal deliveries to the gasworks every day. They were now only minutes from the glass factory. Because of Crawford's momentary indecision, Craske reached the cart first, strode on a few paces more and saw, less than fifty yards away, a dozen men leaning casually against the wall. By the time he had also caught sight of the daunting array of sticks and clubs in their hands, the rest of the party had passed the cart too. Magnus yelled to everyone to run, but, as they spun around, four men came out from the entrance to the gasworks and blocked the narrow gaps on each side of the cart. Only Moggs moved, darting forward under the cart and running.

Tom realized with a paralyzing sense of shock that the men they had agreed to meet had almost beyond doubt been instructed by Braithwaite to lead into a trap whoever came to treat with them; their openness to bribery had never been more than a pretence. As this came to him, Tom caught a glimpse of Crawford's eyes turned on him with such hatred that he knew at once that Magnus was sure that he had betrayed him. But there was no time to deny anything, since by now the dozen men were advancing, intent on forcing them back onto the cart, so they could be attacked from both sides. Ignoring Tom, Magnus grabbed Craske's arm.

"Split up. Take the cart; I'll try the entrance."

The men were now barely twenty yards away. Tom's heart pounded as he registered details in dreamlike isolation: an unshaven face, a pair of heavy boots, a greasy, seamless surtout. Craske pulled out a life preserver and Magnus a loaded crop before they began to sprint toward the cart. Tom turned to follow them and heard the men behind break into a run.

Craske reached the cart a second or so before Crawford and landed a brutal kick on the horse's flank. As the terrified animal bolted with the cart, Tom only just flung himself clear in time. A wheel caught one of their pursuers and dashed him against the wall as the cart went over with a thunderous crash, scattering coal across the street. Craske struck down one of the men standing in his path and ran on. Hearing the ringing clash of nailed boots on the cobbles behind him, Tom went on running, but without hope. Just in front of him, Crawford swerved sharply into the entrance to the gasworks. Reckoning that his best chance of escape would be to continue straight ahead, where Craske had already demoralized those opposing him, Tom knew instantly that he would follow Crawford instead. In no other way would he ever convince him that he had not been his betrayer.

As Tom entered the long covered way, which ran under the purifying rooms, into the inner courtyard of the gasworks, the sight of the square of light at the far end gave him fresh heart. The staff in the management office would give them refuge. Magnus had almost reached the courtyard when Tom saw him stop dead. Two thickset men had stepped out of the shadows at the side of the tunnel and were starkly silhouetted against the light. Tom halted too, his head swimming, fear churning in his stomach. Successive waves of panic left him breathless and trembling. Behind, they were cut off; ahead, how many men besides these two were waiting? One blow with a club across the face could melt the mouth into a liquid mess of raw flesh and broken teeth, another smash the cartilage of a nose to pulp . . . just two blows.

Magnus made no move toward his opponents, but, tearing off his cape and holding it in one hand, stood waiting in the center of the covered way. Tom heard the boots of the two men echoing loudly as they advanced. Occasionally drops of water fell from the brick arch above his head, hitting the granite sets with a loud plopping noise. Wanting to run to help Crawford, Tom found his legs would not carry him. One of the men was swinging a length of chain, the other holding a thick knobstick. Suddenly, without knowing how, Tom was running forward, as if wading through flowing water. Before he had covered half the distance, the man with the knobstick hurled himself at Magnus, who flung his cape in his face, dodged and then ran at the man with the chain. Tom saw the dull blue gleam of the descending metal and Magnus's upraised arm shielding his face. Before his assailant could swing again, Magnus wrenched at the chain, catching him off balance, and, as he staggered, brought down the weighted end of his crop on the side of his head. The man thudded against the wall and slipped to the ground, his head knocking against the brickwork. Tom yelled a warning as the other thug leaped at Magnus from behind. They went down together, rolling and punching. Tom caught up the chain from the ground, looped it and struck, catching Magnus's attacker at the base of the neck. As the man released his grasp around Crawford's neck, Magnus swung his knee hard into his stomach, leaving the man thrashing on the ground, fighting for breath. Hearing footsteps and shouting from the end of the tunnel, Tom and Magnus fled toward the light.

In front of them in the center of the courtyard were the offices and countinghouses. Magnus wrenched at a door handle but it was locked, and Tom was no luckier with the next. All the managers and clerks would be off for Nomination Day. They turned and ran around the back of these buildings, only to find themselves in a long, narrow, roofless coal store with no way out. The shouts were coming closer. A vast heap of coal was piled against the blank wall at the end of the cul-de-sac. From the top it might just be possible to reach the guttering of the lean-to at the back of the office buildings. Tom tried to swallow but his mouth was too dry; he was sweating but had trouble stopping his teeth chattering.

"Come on," roared Magnus, running at the coal, but slipping back. He dropped his crop, and with the help of his hands, began to climb. Tom clawed his way up after him, choking as he breathed in the thick coal dust. Looking up, he saw Magnus at the top trying to pull himself up onto the roof by the guttering, but his hand had evidently been hurt in the fight and he could not hold on.

"Wait," yelled Tom, clambering to the top and linking his hands to give Magnus a foothold. With this additional height, Magnus got his chest against the guttering and managed to haul himself up onto the roof. Leaning down he gave Tom his uninjured hand and pulled him up. Both were shaking and breathing in painful gasps. Tom saw that the chain had dragged away the cloth from Magnus's left sleeve, lacerating his wrist which was bleeding freely.

"Believe in miracles?" groaned Magnus, glancing skyward. Tom shook his head. "A pity."

Moments later Magnus was loosening tiles with his heel and was soon sending them slicing downward toward the men mounting the coal below them. Tom reached the crown of the roof on his hands and knees, and, steadying himself against a chimney stack, noticed a heavy metal cowl above one of the pots. He tore at it with all his might, nearly falling as the cowl came away. Below him he saw Magnus kick off the first man to try to get onto the roof, sending him sprawling backward, but others were climbing up farther along. Tom pitched the cowl at one of them, catching him on the thigh and hurling him back onto the coal, taking the man behind with him.

Magnus had slithered down the far side of the roof, loosing an avalanche of slates, which were still clattering down into the yard, when Tom caught up with him. Magnus found a drainpipe and, swinging himself out, began to slide down; Tom followed, tearing the palms of his hands and bruising his knees against the joints in the piping. From the roof, Magnus had thought that the way to the entrance was clear, but, as Tom reached the ground, he saw their way cut off by three more men. Braithwaite had all too clearly paid a large sum to have those who had had the temerity to defy him severely chastised. Magnus looked helplessly at Tom's trusting and still hopeful face, and the thought of what probably lay ahead for both of them made his legs weaken. He was responsible for having got Tom into his present situation, and could think of no way out for either of them. Without the man's help, he would already have been beaten insensible. While he hesitated, Magnus felt a sharp punch between the shoulder blades; looking up, he saw that they had been followed over the roof, where several men were about to throw more slates. He pulled Tom back under the eaves and whispered urgently,

"Swear to me if you get out . . . if you can get out on your own feet, that you won't wait for me. Just go. Leave the town. Don't try to see me. Go. Braithwaite mustn't . . ." He stopped as a dull clanging noise came from the pipe. Within seconds the first men would be down. They ran toward a narrow opening and soon emerged in a smaller yard, flanked on one side by two massive gasholders and smaller cisterns filled with tar and ammonia. Opposite was the door to the retort house, lit by the red glow of the furnaces within. As they ran exhausted toward it, both sensing that they would find help there, the men behind were gaining ground.

The tall metal chamber they entered was lit only by the incandescent glow of the open furnaces. At the far end was a group of all but naked men, working under an overlooker, raking out white-hot coke from the retorts, while others were dragging a metal cart filled with fresh coal across to the furnaces. Magnus shouted to attract their attention, but his words were drowned by the thunder of the furnaces as the new coal was run in. The overlooker tipped water onto the used coke to cool it, causing a deafening, hissing noise and filling the chamber with dense steam. Unused to the red flickering light and now half-blinded with steam, they stumbled forward. Without warning, Tom's foot came up hard against the rails on which the iron carts ran, and he fell. He saw Magnus bend down to help him, then, catching a movement just to his left, he shouted a warning and the next second saw an explosion of white light in front of his face. Gas, he remembered thinking, as he fainted. He came to almost at once to see Magnus grappling with two dark shapes. Tom crawled to his knees, realizing with terrible lucidity that they had been overtaken in the darkness; the splintering pain behind his forehead, where he had been hit, made him reel as he stood up. He saw Crawford catch one of his attackers in the face with a well-aimed punch, and then double up as a club hammered into his ribs. As Magnus staggered back, Tom watched him crumple under a savage, glancing stroke, which caught him on the side of the face and thudded into his shoulder. Tom lurched forward and tried to shout, but no sound came. Fear like an ice-cold knife bit into his entrails. Whatever their original instructions, these men now seemed bent on killing them. He blundered against the man who had felled Magnus and was sent crashing backward by a kick in the stomach. Nothing mattered now, only air, air. His eyes seemed bursting from their sockets, his flesh crawling, until, at last, he gulped in air, which he could not breathe out. It seemed hours before the choking, gasping fight was over and the rhythm of his breathing was restored.

At last, as if through the wrong end of a telescope, Tom saw the overlooker leave the furnaces and start running in his direction; only now with the furnace doors clanged shut had he heard anything from the far end of the chamber. Soon men were fighting all around him; the furnacemen as large-limbed and powerful as the hired thugs. Tom raised himself to his knees, and, after an initial spasm of giddiness, realized that he was not going to faint. As he stood, the hammering pain in his head made him want to scream, but when he caught sight of a group of men bending anxiously over Magnus's inert body, his terror overcame even this pain. Moments later he was overjoyed to see Crawford move his head. He knelt beside him and squeezed his hand, but though he spoke his name several times, he could not get him to open his eyes. The light was too bad to see well, but Tom could tell that he was breathing easily. He had been covered with sacking, and one of the furnacemen was trying to make him drink from a chipped cup. Blood was oozing from a gash that extended from his hairline to his chin. Remembering the man's composure and confidence, Tom wanted to weep; instead he turned and walked toward the doorway. He could do nothing to help him. Sickened, stunned, bewildered, he walked out into the cold air of the yard, thankful to be away from the brutal struggle in the retort house.

He sank down on some sacks of coal and cradled his throbbing head in his arms, knowing as he did so that his peace would be short-lived. It would not be long before the furnacemen overcame the four or five hired men . . . and then? Helpers arriving, summoned by Moggs, constables with them? Tom tried to visualize it. Charges . . . they would ask him what charges he wished to bring. A string of endless questions: why had he been there, why had he been attacked and by whom? Who had been with him? Magnus's vehement plea came back to him to go if he should have the chance, regardless of whether he should be alone. But could he really have meant him to go, even after the danger had passed? Dazed with shock, his head still hurting badly, Tom tried to think. Had Magnus merely been concerned for him, in case Braithwaite discovered his treachery? Or had he had quite different reasons of his own for not wanting it known who had been with him when he had been attacked? Confused, and scared that he might make the wrong decision, Tom walked slowly across the yard, toward the iron framework of the gas-holders. If he stayed and identified himself, might not Braithwaite in some way be able to use his presence to establish what Magnus had intended to do, and so implicate the Liberal in bribery? But already, Tom knew that he did not care enough to think anymore. Even if he did stay, he would achieve little. Better to do what Magnus had asked, and go.

Sick at heart to be leaving his companion behind, Tom also felt overwhelming relief as he left the covered way and headed for the river in the failing light. Knowing that he might easily have been scarred and mutilated for life, he felt thankful to have escaped with nothing more serious than a bad winding and a painfully aching head. Worse than the shock and the bruises was his bitter resentment of the cowardly unfairness of the attack and a corrosive disgust, not for the men themselves, but for their paymaster, who dealt out arbitrary violence from a safe distance, through an untraceable chain of intermediaries. That he and Crawford had been the recipients had been incidental, since their personal involvement had probably not been known. But that made nothing better; it was still less excusable to make men suffer without as much as knowing their names.

As Tom sank down shivering in the long wet grass by the river to rest his shaking legs, he felt defiled. He had sought adventure and action, the opiates with which Crawford had lured him; and instead he had found clumsy brutality, terror and the blind rage in which any act of cruelty could be contemplated and committed. Worst of all, Tom knew that, although Magnus had been trying to protect him when he had been clubbed down, his former admiration for him had gone. For all his courage and style he had been outwitted as easily as a child, and I with him, and because of him, thought Tom. And this hurt him most of all: that he had made him a hero, and now could not gracefully accept his fallibility, because he too was demeaned by it.

Tired, cold and very weak, Tom got up and followed the towpath toward the dark warehouses. In the chill clammy air, the nameless desolation of the deserted wharves and the gray twilight hinterland of waste ground seemed for that moment to have entered and engulfed his soul.

⚘ Ten ⚘

George Braithwaite did not learn what had happened to Magnus Crawford until two days after Nomination Day; and the news shocked and
troubled him. He had recently heard that Magnus had saved the *Independent*; if he had also attempted some more direct form of political
interference in the election, George knew that his father might well have
been tempted to discourage him. No gentleman would have chosen to go
to the part of town where Crawford had been attacked unless keeping a
secret appointment. But though George had mentioned the assault to his
father, he had learned nothing from him. After their argument about the
strike, Joseph Braithwaite had kept his own counsel.

George was acutely aware that if Catherine Crawford entertained
even a fraction of his suspicions, his chances of acceptance would be
remote indeed. He had not intended to see her until after the election,
but, realizing that it would be remarked upon if he did not call to inquire
about Magnus's health, he steeled himself for a meeting.

Driving through the winter woods on the way to Leaholme Hall in his
glistening black and yellow Stanhope phaeton, George took none of his
usual pleasure in the gleaming coats of his perfectly matched pair of
blood horses. Dressed, soberly for him, in a dark brown Newmarket
coat, fawn cashmere waistcoat and white drill trousers, he stared fixedly
at the coachman's back, wishing that he had not foolishly refused to
have the hood put up. The rains of the previous week had given way to
another spell of intensely cold weather, which seemed to promise heavier snow than the few flurries earlier in the month. As the coach sped on,
other thoughts perplexed George. Three days before Nomination Day,
Strickland had completed his father's portrait and had left the house the
same day, and this, in spite of the fact that he had been asked to stay on

to paint George's mother. To refuse this work, when he had failed to secure a commission from Lady Goodchild, seemed willfully contrary behavior. Strangest of all, Strickland was evidently still in Rigton Bridge. Only that morning, George had been told by his valet that he had seen the artist going into the Green Dragon the day before. The only explanation that seemed to account for the man's obtuseness was that he had heard something discreditable about his patron.

As the phaeton came to a halt in the sweep in front of the tower entrance to Leaholme Hall, George threw open the carriage door, without waiting for the groom to jump down, and strode across the gravel, adjusting his stock as he went. In fact he might as well have waited, for he was soon informed that Captain Crawford was in town, Miss Crawford riding and Mr. Crawford too ill to receive anybody.

He was shown to a narrow, low-ceilinged sitting room with oak-paneled walls, and the small mullioned windows, which, in George's view, would have been better replaced with large modern ones. Sitting down by the log fire, he heard a clock strike in another room. A paper was offered him, but, feeling too nervous to read, he gazed abstractedly into the flames of the fire, thinking of Catherine. Having been friendly with prizefighters, gamblers and young men of means, dedicated to sensual amusement with transitory partners, George's views about marriage had become by contrast increasingly exalted and pure; and Catherine Crawford, with her grace and reticence, was the only woman he had ever met who matched his picture of the ideal wife who would redeem him from his former dissoluteness: a woman as different as he could imagine from the actresses and whores who to date had been his only close contact with the female sex. On the rare occasions when he had dared think of a possible marriage night with her, the idea had struck him as almost blasphemous. If they married, he supposed she would put up with his demands to beget children, but matters of that sort would hardly please her. Goodchild might pursue doctors' wives to regain lost passions, but George was resolved to master his own baser instincts if his dearest wish were ever to be granted.

When Catherine entered, he rose at once, encouraged to see that she had come straight to him, before changing out of her riding habit. Her plumed hat, and close-fitting jacket with its ermine collar and cuffs, suited her, he thought, to perfection. The shadow cast by the brim of her hat and her position in front of the window meant that he could not see her face.

"I came to ask after your brother," he began hesitantly.

"To do what?" she whispered.

"I heard that he was hurt. I would have come sooner, if . . ." He broke off as she came toward him, for now, for the first time, he was able to see her expression.

"You dare pretend you do not know how he came by his injuries?"

"On my honor, no."

"Then ask your father on *his* honor."

She tore off her hat and he noticed her pallor and the dark shadows beneath her vivid blue eyes. One side of her hair had come unpinned, and the falling tresses of silvery hair brushing her cheek, far from seeming undignified to George, lent her distracted face a tragic grandeur.

"I did ask him. He told me he knew nothing."

He looked at her helplessly as she flicked some hair from her face, her disbelief and derision obvious.

"How very surprising."

"You must hear me, Catherine," he replied in a choking voice. "I tried to persuade my father to end the strike. Perhaps that's very surprising too." His cheeks were burning with humiliation. "Your brother told me your only interest in me was mercenary." He was angry, but so distraught that he feared breaking down. He looked up from the carpet. "Did I say one word to you against him for that lie? Are my father's doings any fault of mine?" Afraid that he had sounded self-pitying and querulous, he waited without hope for her to speak.

"No fault at all if you make them public."

"I say, Miss Crawford, that's asking a bit, you know."

He saw her clasping her hands together, as if close to screaming at him.

"If you'd seen his face as I did, when they brought him home," she said hoarsely, "you might consider the suggestion less fantastic."

"Damn it," he blurted out, "there's no proof against him one way or the other. If there was, I'd make him sorry for it. I would truly."

He expected more anger, but instead, she sat down facing him, a slight smile playing on her lips.

"*You* make your father sorry?" She let a hand fall limply from the carved arm of her chair and shook her head. "I'm sorry if you knew nothing . . . perhaps you didn't. But ignorance isn't enough. Magnus had no difficulty finding out your father's game, and tried to spoil it for him. Conscience, you see, does not make cowards of us all."

"That's not fair, Miss Crawford."

"It's the truth though." She got up and hid her face in her hands for a moment, then turned to him with sudden exasperation. "I know you can't betray your father, but that's what makes it all hopeless. You're not a bad man; it isn't that. I'd never have thought of marrying you if I'd thought that. You're weak but that's no sin. . . . It's just that it's impossible now. We both know that and there's nothing more to be said."

"I'm no coward," he stammered, dazed by the rapid flow of her words. She swept up her hat impatiently and turned to leave.

"Only you know what you are, Mr. Braithwaite. Your conscience is, I hope, your own."

Seeing her walk to the door, he could not help protesting.

"It's not right, Miss Crawford. I don't even like my father, not at all. I didn't choose him, you know."

Catherine glanced back at him for a moment from the doorway and said gently,

"If I'm hard, George, you'll find me easier to forget."

"I won't at all," he objected, but she left the room without answering and he doubted whether she had heard.

On the way home, at a sharp bend, Braithwaite's coachman nearly knocked down a woman carrying a baby on her back, but George was no more aware of this than he was of the farm laborers digging up turnips in the fields, or the last russet leaves clinging to the trees. Instead he thought of what he might have said but hadn't. Can I be blamed if your brother gets himself beaten about and robbed? The man's old enough to look after himself, I daresay. D'you think my father bothers himself with penniless colonial soldiers with a taste for back-street politics? Strangely these imagined remarks comforted rather than depressed him. Even the contemplation of what might have been was better than facing the reality of what had actually occurred.

* * *

The three weeks since his brother's return had been particularly joyless ones for Charles Crawford. Whenever he was ashore, without immediate prospects of a naval command, he felt lifeless and depressed, but this condition had been much aggravated by Helen Goodchild's long silence, unbroken since his visit to Hanley Park on the day of the hunt. Charles's disappointment was the greater for the strength of his earlier conviction that his words had struck home. He had often thought of calling on her again, but because Helen had made it so clear that she would write if she wanted his help, his pride had prevented him. Besides any woman faced with such a decision would need weeks rather than days to make up her mind. At times he wondered whether she might have acted on her own account, and this led him to entertain a faint hope that, if it were so, and she managed to wring concessions from Goodchild as a result of his advice, he might yet be rewarded by her—if not with affection, at least with a closer friendship. But the occasions on which he felt much confidence of this were very few.

The reason why Charles had been out, when George Braithwaite had called on Catherine, had been a visit to Rigton Bridge, where he had spent a frustrating and entirely fruitless afternoon trying to discover the identity of the man responsible for the attack on his brother. But nothing he had been told by the police commissioner or the chief magistrate had been of the remotest use.

That evening, during the course of a hitherto silent dinner, Catherine remarked that George Braithwaite had come to Leaholme Hall during the afternoon.

"Most thoughtful of him," commented Charles, laying down his knife and fork. "He must have plenty to occupy him with the election so close."

Seeing his sister's hands apparently tremble as she raised her glass, Charles wondered whether a draft had deceived him by making the candles flicker. Catherine took a sip of hock and said in a flat unemotional voice,

"I refused him, Charles."

"What?" he gasped, almost choking on a mouthful of mutton.

"His father is to blame for the attack on Magnus."

Dumbfounded, Charles raised a clenched fist to his brow.

"Impossible!" he exploded at last. "The men in custody were offered their freedom if they named their paymaster. They refused." He threw down his napkin and stared at her triumphantly. "Why?"

"Fear?"

"Fear be damned. They didn't know his name, that's why. Even if they had, he'd still have been some sort of go-between."

"Magnus is certain," she whispered.

Charles pushed back his chair furiously.

"Anyone who stoops to gutter politics can be certain of nothing. If he was so sure, why didn't he tell me?"

"If I believe it," she asked wearily, "does anything else matter?"

He looked at her despairingly across the polished table.

"You lose a husband worth ten thousand a year and calmly ask if anything matters. Dear God, Catherine . . . Throw that chance away because of some inane, unfounded suspicion of your brother's."

Though he had eaten little, Charles pushed away his plate and left the room. He had viewed his sister's probable marriage to George as not only providential for her, but also as a considerable asset to him. Since George had intimated that he had no love for politics, it had brightened Charles's gloomy horizon to hope that, when Joseph finally gave up the seat in the Commons which he would shortly win, this plum would drop into his lap as Braithwaite's only son's brother-in-law. Since three-quarters of the officers on the Navy List were at present ashore on half-pay, Charles had not ruled out the possibility that he would have to spend many years to come in the vicinity of Rigton Bridge. With Joseph's friendship, these years were likely to be considerably more profitable than without it. A few county families might still look upon them as parvenus, but they would soon learn to put self-interest before snobbery. The thought that Magnus had very likely put an end to all this made Charles feel faint with anger. Soon he was stumbling up the stairs in the near-darkness, heading for his brother's room. If Magnus was sufficiently recovered to turn Catherine against the Braithwaites, he would be well enough to listen to another point of view.

* * *

The bedroom was lit only by a single candle, but even by this dim light, Charles could see Magnus's blackened and swollen mouth, his stitched-up chin and heavily bandaged forehead and jaw. He crossed to the bed and pulled up a chair, deliberately waking his brother in the process.

"I'm sorry to intrude," he murmured. "I have been doing my best to discover the identity of the instigator of . . ."

"Don't, Charles. I told you I didn't want to trouble you."

"You would have troubled me less had you confided as much in me as you did in your sister. Has she told you what she did this afternoon?"

"She has."

Charles was not happy to be on the verge of screaming at a sick man, though he had seen too many men die of fever off Zanzibar to be maudlin over comparatively trivial ailments.

"I know Catherine takes a different view of the matter," he began, making a conscious effort to control the pitch of his voice, "but if what she tells me is true, you've made an idiot of yourself . . . as though a paltry radical paper and a few meetings in the back parlors of pothouses could do Braithwaite more harm than a child's pebbles rattling his windows. For God's sake man, is this the sort of thing for gentlemen? People aren't forced to take bribes you know; they do because they want to. If you think you're going to change human nature, you'll have a sad awakening."

Magnus closed his eyes and sighed.

"Tip a stone from your shoe; the world's no better, but your foot's more comfortable. My aims were modest."

"To ruin the best chance of marriage Catherine's ever going to get?"

"I didn't want her to marry him, but I didn't hit myself on the head to stop her."

Disconcerted by the tone of this answer, Charles said sharply,

"But you'll still associate yourself with a rag like the *Independent*. Don't you care anything for Father? For years he's taken no sides in this town and his impartiality has gained him the respect of all."

"And the love of none," replied Magnus under his breath.

"That's a damned lie," hissed Charles.

In spite of the pain it caused him, Magnus could not help smiling.

"I was forgotting you, Charles, I apologize." He rolled over onto his side gingerly, so that he could see Charles better. "Do you actually suppose that because Father subscribes to Low Church missions, while he pays for the restoration of a rood screen, that either the dissenter or the Anglican thinks any better of him for his gifts to the other?"

Now that they were on the timeless ground of their age-old animosity about their spotless father, Magnus almost felt another person, the boy he had once been.

"Does his career mean nothing to you?"

"A great deal, Charles. It killed our mother."

"I saw him weep," whispered Charles in a shaking voice.

"You saw me do the same. His career killed her. He should have wept," Magnus returned quietly. "If you think events in this town are likely to influence their lordships at the Admiralty, I suggest you're mistaken."

"Perhaps, but you wouldn't care either way. Don't tell me you give a tinker's curse for triennial parliaments or the secret ballot, whatever you may have said to Catherine. You couldn't gain enough notoriety in the army, so you sold out to play at the radical demagogue for a while. More honorable paths of advancement were too slow, I suppose." He stopped, furious that he had lost his temper and made himself appear callous. The only point in talking to Magnus would have been to persuade him to get Catherine to reconsider, but that had never been even a remote possibility. "I'd like to sympathize with you, Magnus."

"Do so then, Charles. You have my permission."

"How can I when you tell me nothing?"

"Don't worry, I'll be going when Father gets home."

Magnus lay back exhausted; his night shirt was soaked with sweat and his head hurt him.

"Will we ever stop behaving like children?" sighed Charles, as he walked toward the door, remembering with sudden clarity his mother's mocking voice: "If only you could laugh, Charles . . . really laugh like Magnus does. You're always so serious, so taciturn." Leaving the room, Charles saw himself a pale and awkward boy of twelve being helped up onto the box of the post coach at the start of his first journey to Portsmouth. While he had been fighting his way from gun room to wardroom, from volunteer to midshipman and mate, Magnus had been at home with his mother and sister: taking drives, going on picnics, singing, barely troubled by his succession of tutors. Going down the stairs, another memory: a misty March morning and Magnus weeping, weeping as though he would never stop, their father's letter in his hand: *Free-town, Sierra Leone. Mother died this morning just before six o'clock. The quinine never took effect, but she felt no pain* . . . Mother's boy and father's boy. Charles's anger had spent itself. But still feeling unable to face Catherine, he went to the Billiard Room and rang for brandy and water.

Helen, he thought, running a hand absently over the smooth green baize of the table, if only . . . but, like so many other possibilities in his life, that one too now seemed irrevocably lost.

~ Eleven ~

Lord Goodchild felt weary, depressed and a little drunk. For the past hour he had been drinking claret and arguing with Francis St. Clare, in the chief magistrate's offices in the courthouse. St. Clare's pink face was tinged with gray and his eyelids were puffy with tiredness. During the night there had been a desperate riot at the workhouse, where every window and stick of furniture had been smashed, and hundreds of loaves of bread distributed among the mob. The total number of injured was not yet accurately known, but three men had undoubtedly been shot dead: a soldier and two rioters. With the election only two days away, the situation could hardly have been worse.

At two in the morning, having read the Riot Act without effect, St. Clare had sent to Oldham for two squadrons of the 22nd Hussars to relieve the local yeomanry, and, at the same time, had dispatched a courier to the general officer for the district, asking that the 17th Lancers, Goodchild's regiment, and the 14th Queen's Light Dragoons should receive orders to leave Manchester for Rigton Bridge within the next twenty-four hours.

Lord Goodchild, who three days before had persuaded his mistress to disregard her husband's threats to use further meetings as evidence in divorce proceedings, had been lying naked in bed next to Mrs. Carstairs when his adjutant had arrived at dawn with news of St. Clare's request. Nothing short of such a catastrophe could have led Goodchild to turn his back on the prospect of a day of unhurried lovemaking, punctuated with restful intervals for food and wine. But he had soon been dressed and on his way to Rigton Bridge, hoping to find that panic, rather than necessity, had inspired St. Clare's decision. On arriving, the police commissioner's report and the chief magistrate's personal account of the night's events had quickly brought him close to a reluctant acceptance of

St. Clare's position. He had promised his unreserved support, if the commanding officer of the 22nd Hussars also considered it essential for more cavalry to be drafted in, and had assured St. Clare that he would consult the colonel at the garrison barracks before returning to Manchester.

Shortly before he left the courthouse, Goodchild was shown police reports on several other incidents. The first, he was surprised to see, involved assault and battery against Sir James Crawford's younger son. Out of a dozen or so attackers, five had been detained, three with head injuries.

"The prisoners who could testify, stated independently," he read, "that they are coalbackers from Oldham, and were approached by a stranger in the taproom where they are accustomed to drink after their work; and that they were offered there the sum of five guineas each for a day's unspecified employment in Rigton Bridge. The man who paid them also led them in the affray, but made good his escape with six others. All those detained aver that his identity is unknown to them. . . ."

"Why the devil isn't Crawford bringing charges?" asked Goodchild, finishing the report.

"I don't know," replied St. Clare, "and frankly I've no time to find out. Thought you'd be interested though, my lord . . . Sir James being related to Lady Goodchild."

A certain sly archness, in the way the magistrate had spoken, irritated Goodchild.

"He's only her godfather."

"Just as well he's still at sea," murmured St. Clare with a frown. "Or didn't you know that his son bailed out the *Independent?*"

"You think there's a connection?" asked Goodchild coldly.

"It crossed my mind, my lord," replied St. Clare with a sleek smile and a speculative glance, which Goodchild did not like. "I'm charging them with causing an affray and the gas company will proceed for trespass and damage to property, so the scum may still come to the top."

"Let's hope so," returned Goodchild emphatically.

On his way to the barracks, his lordship was grim-faced. St. Clare thought Braithwaite had been behind the attack on Crawford and had supposed that he too would have been mixed up in it. Disgusted and bitterly angry to be associated, even by implication, with such proceedings, Goodchild realized for the first time the full extent of his helplessness. In case there should be a crowd waiting outside the barracks intent on stoning vehicles arriving or leaving, Goodchild told his coachman to stop in the next street, and finished his journey on foot.

Turning the corner, he saw that the street was empty and the men guarding the gates, troubled only by the insults of a few ragged boys. The road was littered with slates, stones and broken bottles. Over against the parade ground wall, an overturned fly and several splintered carts were evidence of a recently dismantled barricade. A few minutes later he was ushered into the orderly room and found the lieutenant colonel of the 22nd slumped in a chair by the fire, the frogged tunic of his black undress uniform unbuttoned, and his eyes red-rimmed and heavy with fatigue. By the window, an equally weary-looking captain was dictating orders to two copying clerks. The colonel rose with an effort and frowned.

"My lord, you are not in Manchester?"

"I came to see for myself. I return tonight. I want an opinion . . . your opinion."

The colonel sank down into his chair again and rubbed his eyes.

"On St. Clare's request for the reserve regiments?" Goodchild nodded. "The Light Dragoons should be sent but not the 17th."

Goodchild stared at him angrily. No colonel of hussars was going to impugn his regiment without giving good reason for it.

"The 17th knows how to do its duty, Colonel Summers."

"Of course, of course," muttered Summers, tilting back his chair and knocking over a burned-out candle stump on the small table beside him. "It's my opinion—purely a personal one, you understand—that a regiment whose commanding officer happens to be the unpopular candidate's proposer won't find much favor with the rabble of nonelectors." He coughed and cleared his throat. "But doubtless Lord Delamere will know better. Generals usually do."

"Those with responsibilities and interests in a town should be there to keep the peace in time of trouble. I shall recommend Lord Delamere to meet the chief magistrate's request in full."

Summers did not argue, but Goodchild still felt angry, not least because he himself had dreaded his regiment being called upon for that very reason. But now, even without the 17th, there would be at least five squadrons of regular cavalry in the town on polling day, and, after the night's rioting, Goodchild did not suppose that any of them would be popular with the mob. Since Summers would probably be the senior officer present, and Goodchild feared he might turn out a fire-eater, he was determined to be there to try to prevent unnecessary provocation. Wanting to go, but feeling he should find out more about the riot, he asked,

"The rioters had guns, I hear. Any idea how many?"

"My officers found it hard to count them in the dark, my lord." Summers smiled wearily and shrugged his shoulders. "Perhaps ten, perhaps twenty."

Goodchild recognized the hint of contempt in the man's voice. Summers had fought through the Sikh War of 1846, and was probably one of those embittered professional soldiers who had not been rich enough to purchase commissions from regiment to regiment to speed up promotion, and therefore looked upon those who had done so as pampered part-timers who would sell out rather than face dangerous foreign service, or exchange into another regiment so they could spend more time hunting and entertaining than with their brother officers. Goodchild resented this because he had only held commissions in one other regiment before buying the colonelcy of the 17th; and, far from having shirked fighting, he keenly regretted never having had any opportunity to lead his men in battle. Nor, as his wife and son could testify, had he spent most of his time at home. Yet the knowledge that his regiment might very well already be preparing to leave Manchester made it easy for him to dismiss the colonel's opinion of him and devote his thoughts to more pressing matters.

Leaving the barracks, Lord Goodchild saw that the snow, which had seemed imminent for several days, had at last started to fall. Deciding against a journey by road, he told his coachman to drive to the station to meet the four o'clock for Manchester. In the first-class waiting room, he asked the stationmaster for pen and paper, and then, while the snow fell silently on the gabled roof, capping each point and pinnacle of the ornamental ironwork, he wrote to Magnus Crawford, expressing shock and indignation over his treatment and regretting that he had been unable to visit him.

When he had finished, he walked over to the window, and, wiping away the steam from the cold panes, looked out across the empty track; already the sleepers were level with the dividing gravel. He was surprised that the near certainty of his regiment's involvement had not depressed him, but instead he felt quite calm. He imagined the screaming crowds in the market square and the Quadrant and shook his head. Nothing could be more remote from the stillness of the little station under the soft and steady fall of snow.

He walked out onto the platform and breathed in deeply; above him the sky itself seemed to be descending piece by piece. He felt the flakes brush his cheeks and melt on his face. When they landed on his lips, he licked them away as he had done as a child. Later he found himself thinking of the warm dark room he had left early that morning and the smooth softness of Dolly's white thighs; recalling the unabashed way she drew his hands to her breasts when she wanted him to make love, he felt a slight stirring—the green pleasures of adolescence relived voluptuously in the riper landscape of early middle age. He smiled to himself, but not without pain. Dolly, Helen, Braithwaite, Humphrey . . . a fine mull I've made of things, he thought. What Helen would do, when told that he could not settle more than fifteen hundred a year on her, if they separated, he hardly dared guess. Remembering her fury, he wondered whether she would still keep him to his word, even if the price were to be the sale of Hanley Park.

A slight wind blew the snowflakes obliquely, making them whirl and spin. In the distance he heard the engine's whistle, and felt somehow consoled by the long melancholy blast in an otherwise muffled world. The train would come, and polling day just as surely, and afterward, Helen would impose what penalty she chose for his neglect; how stupid, he thought, not to have realized before: everything had already been decided and needed only to happen. He could no more avoid it than he could the election, or the snow's slow silent descent around him.

~~ *Twelve* ~~

For two days following his escape from the gasworks, Tom Strickland had wanted to leave Rigton Bridge, but his badly bruised ribs and stomach had been too painful for him to consider traveling south. He had not felt himself in any danger, since he thought it most unlikely that Joseph Braithwaite would have discovered what he had done on Nomination Day, and, with so many other matters to occupy the manufacturer's mind, still more improbable that he would do anything about it, even were he to possess such knowledge.

As Tom's pains had diminished, his depression had also lifted, and, since the election was now only three days distant, he decided to stay on at the Green Dragon until it was over. In spite of his conviction that Joseph would win the seat, Tom had nevertheless come to see polling day as a fitting last act to his time in the town, involving, as it would, so many of the people he had come to know. The worsening situation did nothing to change his mind, and, in retrospect, he felt mortified that he had come so close to acceding to Crawford's request to run away from events, which he might never again have an opportunity to witness. To leave now, would be, he thought, as absurd as it would have been if Daumier and Meissonier had turned their backs on the Paris revolution in forty-eight, fleeing to the country instead, to paint placid village scenes. To bear witness, to record and maybe even penetrate the external surface of things so they might be apprehended more fully: these were tasks from which he should never have allowed Crawford to lure him.

When therefore, on Monday morning, the boots brought up a note to Tom's room, written by Miss Crawford and delivered by her maid, informing him that her brother wished to see him before noon on polling day, he wrote back at once declining, only to learn that the maid had not waited to take back an answer. Later he felt disquieted. Although he had found out from the servants at the Bull Hotel, where Magnus had been first carried from the gasworks, that the doctor who had attended him there had not considered his condition grave enough to forbid his removal to Leaholme Hall, Tom had still felt guilty for wanting to avoid seeing him. But notwithstanding, in this respect his feelings had not changed since their calamitous failure on Nomination Day. He had allowed personal admiration to get the better of his judgment, and still felt ashamed of himself; and his aches and pains, and the knowledge that he might easily have suffered far worse, had done nothing to make him grateful to Crawford. But, being honest with himself, he had to admit that he had willingly accepted the risks involved. Nor, when he thought about it, did it escape him that Magnus would know how he felt, and would therefore have reasons quite as good as his own for wishing to avoid a meeting. Yet this was what he was asking for. If the man wanted to express his contrition for having miscalculated so badly, Tom foresaw an embarrassing and pointless interview; but he might need to tell him something of importance, possibly to do with court proceedings. After further deliberation, Tom reluctantly tore up his note and decided to call as requested. He would make sure he arrived early enough to be able to get back to Rigton Bridge by midday, to be in time to see the majority of the votes cast in the election.

On the day itself, Tom had left the livery stables, where he had hired his hack, by eight o'clock, and an hour later was nearing his destination. The sun shone from a clear steel-blue sky, casting back a dazzling light from the snow-covered hills. Across the fields were the clearly defined tracks of stoats and weasels, with sometimes the deeper imprints made by a fox or badger. From time to time heavy lumps of snow fell into the road from the laden branches with a soft plump, obscuring the deep furrows cut by the wheels of carriages. From the brow of the next low hill, Tom saw, in the center of a sparsely planted park, a range of low rambling buildings squatting darkly against the surrounding whiteness. His horse's hooves thumped pleasantly on the compact snow and the animal's breath came in steaming clouds. A little closer and he could make out the snow-capped battlements of the squat central tower of

Leaholme Hall. In the stillness of the countryside, Tom found it hard to imagine the frenzied scenes that might already be taking place in Rigton Bridge.

*   *   *

Magnus was lying in a four-poster bed while a woman in a gray morning dress read to him. As Tom entered, her back was to the door, so he could not at first see her face, but knew from her voice that she was young. For several seconds he did not dare look at Magnus in case his expression betrayed shock or pity.

"How are the mighty fallen, Mr. Strickland?" murmured Magnus with a rueful smile which changed at once to a grimace of pain. "In my case not in the high places of Gilboa but on the premises of the Rigton Chartered Gaslight and Coke Company." He looked down at his strapped and bandaged arm. "I'm grateful to you for coming."

Tom lowered his eyes, shaken by Magnus's swollen mouth and the cuts and bruises visible on the unbandaged parts of his face. In the darkness of the retort house, he had not thought him nearly so badly hurt.

"I'm truly sorry."

"At any rate you were more fortunate; not that I can claim any credit for it." He turned to the young woman who had been reading. "Kate, you have not met Mr. Strickland. Mr. Strickland, my sister, Miss Crawford." As Magnus lay back, evidently tired by the effort of supporting himself on his uninjured arm, Tom looked at Catherine with her blonde ringlets and clear blue eyes and was struck as much by her air of sadness as by her beauty.

"My brother has told me what you did for him," she said quietly.

Distressed to find Magnus so much worse than he had expected, and guilty that he had thought so little about him, Tom replied curtly,

"I did very little. You may judge by my face."

"My brother does not praise those who do not merit it."

Still embarrassed and determined not to be taken for a selfless and devoted follower, Tom met her eyes.

"I followed your brother, Miss Crawford, because he thought I had betrayed him and for no other reason."

"I deserve your anger," sighed Magnus.

"I chose to go."

"You think what we did was valueless?"

"I suppose," replied Tom, "that it's better to try and fail, than to do nothing at all."

Magnus lay back and gazed up at the canopy above him.

"Thank you for saying that. I too regret the result but not the attempt. You have every right to have a poor opinion of me."

"If I do, I must have the same opinion of myself."

Tom longed to be able to leave. He had dreaded fulsome apologies and admissions of failure.

"I was worried about you afterward. Kate sent servants to ask at hotels and lodging houses. When I heard you were still in Rigton Bridge, I wished I'd never asked you to leave."

"I'm sure you had my safety at heart," replied Tom, touched by this.

"You were right to stay." Magnus closed his eyes for a moment. "I can understand your reluctance to come here . . . but it makes what I want to ask of you harder to say." He was struggling to prop himself up on his pillows, and Catherine came over to help him. Tom saw her take a damp cloth and wipe beads of sweat from his neck and below the bandage across his forehead. As soon as he was settled, Magnus went on, with a flash of his old spirit, "I've lost . . . made a fool of myself, as my devoted brother delights in reminding me; but I didn't ask you to come to hear apologies or excuses." His eyes were bright and feverish with pain. "You see there's still something to be done. I can cast my vote."

"How, Magnus?" asked Catherine with horror.

"In the usual manner." He turned again to Tom. "Beaten I may be, but not broken. Will you help me cross the square to the polling booths?"

"I am not afraid to be seen with you," said Tom in a low voice, his reluctance quite plain. He wished only to forget the whole affair.

"But will you come?" asked Magnus impatiently.

"You must be mad, Magnus," cut in Catherine. "Only a handful of people will see you in the crowds. It's nothing more than a fool's pride."

"I don't deny," he murmured, "that it would be satisfying to be seen by Braithwaite and his lackeys, but I'll be content to have my name entered in the poll books."

"And who will know it?" she cried.

"You, Kate. Mr. Strickland here. Charles, I daresay. And *I* will, which, being selfish, means most to me."

"Refuse to go with him," Tom heard Catherine whisper in an imploring voice. "He doesn't know how much they hurt him."

"I have a fair idea, Kate." He looked at Tom. "It's strange, but my cracked finger hurts far more than my head or shoulder."

"Neither of which, as you can see, Mr. Strickland, were more than scratched."

Ignoring Catherine's desperate irony, Tom crossed to the window. Through the diamond-shaped panes he could see bright drops of water falling from the eaves above. The sun was already melting the snow.

"All right," he said without turning, "I'll go with you."

Magnus made no comment upon his evident lack of enthusiasm, but said to his sister,

"I shall need clothes. You must cut them; perhaps only a shirt; a coat can be fastened at the neck and I can wear a cape over it."

When Catherine had left the room to fetch her sewing box, Magnus leaned over the small table beside his bed and mixed himself a draft, which Tom supposed would contain laudanum. He would need it, if the heavy strapping around his shoulder meant, as Tom was sure it did, that a bone had been broken.

"You know that misguided women in Rigton Bridge give their babies opium to stop them crying?" Magnus raised his glass and drained it. "I hope it may do the same for me." He lay back, as if intent on concentrating all his reserves of strength for the ordeal ahead. Then he sat up and swung his legs around. Tom saw that he was gritting his teeth to stop himself screaming. After several seconds he let out a long sigh and took a deep breath. When he spoke again, Tom was surprised that Crawford's voice was so steady:

"My grandfather was conscious when the ship's surgeon hacked off his leg. Afterward, or so the story goes, he asked to be carried back to his quarterdeck in a canvas cradle." He braced himself and then stood up, nearly falling, but steadying himself on the arm of a chair.

Appalled that anyone should voluntarily subject himself to such suffering, Tom looked away; his sense of the futility of the gesture Crawford was making increased by his mention of his grandfather. For an admiral to allow no pain to prevent him seeing the issue of the day was understandable. But any such comparison, even if ironically intended, merely emphasized the utterly different circumstances in which Magnus was acting. Because Tom had thought him free of most of the attitudes of his class, he was doubly saddened to see Magnus now prove a slave to a code of honor, pathetic and self-glorifying except in war. Wanting to argue with him, Tom realized that, having promised to come, he would do better to remain silent.

As the brougham swayed out of the lodge gates, Magnus listened with closed eyes to the swish of the wheels. The snow cushioned him from the worst of the jolts and bumps he would otherwise have had to endure, but even the gentle rolling motion of the carriage caused him pain, dulled by the laudanum, but still sharp at times, so that he experienced successively detachment and an acute awareness of his body, enabling him, it seemed, to see matters both in distant perspective and in close personal terms. He knew that Strickland had not wanted to come, and this depressed him. When he thought of their carefree elation at the *Independent*, his gloom deepened. He had thought Tom's determination to search out creditable motives proof of an involvement as great as his own. But now, looking at Strickland's downcast face, paler than usual with the reflected whiteness of the snow, and his remote dark brown eyes, Magnus felt a chilling isolation. He looked toward the ending of the day as though into a lighted tunnel and saw at the end only a wall. Had he not deliberately given to the election a significance it had never possessed, simply to avoid having to look beyond it? Without turning his head, he said,

"What do you think will happen? I don't mean today, but after the election."

Tom said nothing for a moment and then gave a slight shrug.

"Should anything be different? When the strikers give up, won't things go on as before? Wages will rise with demand, tempers will cool . . . how quickly, I suppose, depending on what happens today."

Magnus did not answer, but looked out through the window at the shimmering trees, their branches bent down by the snow. Perhaps whatever he had thought and done, nothing would have been changed. Progress was a lie, history an endless repetition, and no individual able to affect even a part of its vast cycle. Barbarism, wars, despotism, democracy, civilization, decline, anarchy and barbarism once again. And justice? He remembered La Rochefoucauld's mocking maxim: "Love of justice in most men is no more than the fear of suffering injustice themselves." Was it even worth weighing passive acceptance against a more positive philosophy, when both ended in the same inevitable failure? Whether in Ceylon or here, the end would be the same. Most men by the age of thirty abandoned individual ambition, sinking it in class, family or nation, living for others or for nothing in particular. Why not him too? The cottager who cut down a tree for firewood survived as well as the poet who meditated under its branches or the botanist who gave it a Latin name. But Strickland had something else: the self-contained conviction that art mattered—a faith possibly no more reasonable than a belief in the existence of evil spirits, but a faith, and one that enabled a man calmly to turn his face from the world of events without feeling any debilitating loss. In spite of the man's show of concern for what they had attempted, it had been no more than a game to him.

"Do you think," he murmured, "that I'm the fool Catherine said I was to be doing this?"

"If it's what you want, why should I?"

"Because I might want to deceive myself into thinking better of myself. That's what you think I'm doing, isn't it?"

"If you succeed, why should deception come into it? I wouldn't do it myself, but I'm not you. There wasn't much room for pride or heroism at the engraver's where I was apprenticed. My grandfather never lost a leg. My father was a fire insurance clerk. My mother gave music lessons."

Stung by the unfamiliar harshness in Strickland's voice, Magnus still managed a slight smile.

"You said that rather too proudly to be laughing at aristocratic pride. You're forgetting how you came after me the other day because you couldn't bear to be thought disloyal. You said so yourself."

"Can't you see the difference?" asked Tom, with a hint of contrition. "I wanted *you* to think well of me. That's not the same as doing something to be able to think well of oneself."

The carriage slithered slightly at a bend, making Magnus wince with pain.

"If others think badly of us," he sighed, "surely we think the same of ourselves?"

"You don't care what most people think of you." He looked at Magnus sadly. "Can't you understand? I'd never met anybody like you. I cared about your opinion because I admired you."

In the distance Magnus saw the dark sprawl of the town, its harsh outline transformed and softened by the snow. He turned to Tom.

"But you don't anymore?"

"No. That isn't your fault though. I never thought what was possible or likely. I envied you . . . your assurance, manner . . . things like that."

"Which of course aren't worth a brass farthing."

The effort of talking had taken Magnus's mind off his shoulder, but hurt his mouth and jaw.

"I didn't mean that," Tom replied softly.

"You weren't paying me a compliment either."

Magnus was surprised by an almost imploring look from Tom.

"Haven't you ever met somebody, and thought he knew everything that you had wanted to . . ."

"And later found out how wrong you were?" Magnus smiled. "Who hasn't? But I sometimes ended by liking the people I'd expected too much from . . . after I'd forgiven them for my own mistaken estimate." He looked intently at Strickland's handsome face. "Are you too proud to do that, Tom? Perhaps you think I took advantage of you because of my class, asked you to take risks because I considered it my right. I asked you because I liked you; yes, from the night of the riot, when you pointed out so clearly that I had no rights over you. Any favors there may have been were conferred by you. I have no plans, no prospects. You help me today, but I can do nothing for you tomorrow. I'm the debtor, Tom."

Strickland looked away.

"I didn't expect friendship as a reward. You needn't fear that burden."

"Burden?" cried Magnus. "If you'd known a quarter of the loneliness I went through in Ceylon, you wouldn't call friendship that."

"I'm sorry."

From the pained look on the artist's face, Magnus did not doubt his sincerity.

"Didn't it occur to you," he asked, "that I wanted you with me today so I could prove something to you? Just as you once wished to prove something to me?" He fell silent and both listened to the creaking of leather and the muted thud of the horses' hooves. "A pity," he said at length, "that I chose the wrong things. Stoicism's probably no more than a refuge for the lost and scared." He banged sharply on the roof and the coach slid to a halt. "Shall we go back?" he asked Tom, who stared back at him in astonishment.

"No, no, of course not. I didn't explain well, but it doesn't matter. I want to go with you."

"I've made it impossible for you to say anything else."

"It's not that at all. Really."

Soon they were passing through the deserted outskirts; the town seemed silent at first, until they heard a low distant rumble, as might be heard approaching a racecourse at a large meeting. It was not loud at first, but grew as the pure white snow gave way to blackened slush and the wide span of the iron bridge came in sight. Magnus caught Tom's eye, and, though he did not smile, knew that he had changed his mind. The pain in his shoulder was worse, but he suddenly felt happy.

~ *Thirteen* ~

From their headquarters in the Town Hall, Lord Goodchild and Colonel Summers looked down anxiously at the surging crowd in front of the polling booth in the center of the market square. At the next window, beside the town clerk, stood a tense-faced St. Clare. As on Nomination Day, Braithwaite had assembled a paid mob to protect his voters from the vast crowd of non-electors favoring the Liberal candidate, but once again, their presence merely served to cause greater antagonism. Nor were the hundred special constables, employed to keep the two factions apart, a dependable force. Freshly issued truncheons and black and white cockades could not be expected magically to transform an untrained levy of shopkeepers and warehousemen into a body sufficiently disciplined to remain calm for long under the barrage of stones, dead rooks, rats and rotten fruit raining down on them from both sides. So far they had managed to protect Tory voters on their perilous path to the polling booth, but the mood of the crowd was worsening.

By noon the Liberal agent's tactics had become apparent. For the first two hours after the opening of the poll, the Tories had been allowed to establish a narrow lead, but now the Liberals were pushing forward forty or so voters in a rush to achieve a tenuous majority. Their hope being, that, as the Tory vote inevitably rose toward parity, the fury and disappointment of the crowd, whose expectations had been falsely raised, would be enough to discourage the more fainthearted of Braithwaite's electors from turning out. Although to date there had been no violent attacks either on individual electors or on property, Goodchild felt far from confident; the unpopular special constables would not remain for long the sole targets of the stones and bottles being thrown;

and, when Tory voters had to contend with greater intimidation than the spitting, jostling and hooting they were currently enduring, action would have to be taken.

Their problem, as Goodchild and Summers knew very well, was that, if rioting broke out, they would be unable to clear the square without serious repercussions. In Millcroft Fields, an open space just outside the town, the Spinners' Union was holding a meeting of five thousand strikers and had promised a march to the marketplace. To meet this threat five troops of cavalry—two of dragoons and three of lancers—had received orders to seal off the entrances to the High Street and Silver Street, the two principal thoroughfares leading into the square. This would stop the union's procession reaching the center of the town and also prevent the crowd already assembled in the square leaving it en masse and joining the strikers. Clearly, if the situation in the market square did become critical, the mob could not be driven out by either of the main exits, since this would bring them up behind the cavalry sealing off the streets, thus exposing the soldiers to attack from both sides. The square could only be cleared by forcing the crowd out through the three small alleys on the south side—an action that would cause panic and bloodshed, since several thousand people could not rapidly be squeezed through such small openings without terrible crushing and trampling.

As Goodchild watched, two Tory voters were being escorted to the booth from the Swan Hotel, flanked by a dense screen of constables. A flurry of movement passed over the crowd around them, like an angry squall over water. A moment later the police were attacked with staves and bottles, but they managed to get the electors safely to the booth. On coming out, their protectors faltered and both men were kicked and punched, one having his coat ripped off. The idea of bolstering the special constables with a company of foot soldiers had been suggested but rejected, since their appearance in the square would probably start the riot they had been put there to prevent. Also unmounted men were easier to overwhelm, and, if the mob succeeded against one group of soldiers, they would feel confident that the same could be achieved against others. This consideration apart, Goodchild was convinced that it would be madness to place his men in a situation where they might have to fight hand to hand with people from their own class and background; up on a horse they would be more likely to do their duty. That morning a number of pamphlets and posters had been tossed over the barracks wall. One of them Goodchild still had folded in his pocket:

SOLDIERS!

Ask yourselves these questions: Must I, at the word of command, fire at and destroy my fellow creatures, more especially when special constables have aggravated them almost to madness, hired ruffians at five shillings a day, and I as a soldier at little above a shilling a day, harassed almost to death in protecting those very policemen who have been the aggressors? Heaven and Justice forbid it!

Goodchild remembered from the riots of 1842 that troopers, to avoid hurting the crowd, often secretly bit out the ball from their cartridges.

A chaise with shuttered windows had drawn up outside the Town Hall; moments later Joseph Braithwaite leaped out. As soon as Goodchild saw the manufacturer's infuriated face, he knew what to expect. Joseph strode up to St. Clare.

"May I ask whether you intend to wait until murder is committed before reading the Riot Act?"

Summers stepped forward in the same shabby undress uniform Goodchild had first seen him in.

"Mr. St. Clare's restraint has been at my request."

"My voters are being set upon, sir. I demand you clear the square."

"If there is a riot it will be quelled," returned Summers in an even voice.

"Colonel, you are permitting a brutal and vicious mob to prevent my voters reaching the polling booth."

Goodchild disliked Summers, and resented the fact that, as commander of the garrison, he was in overall command of the troops in the town, but he admired the colonel's manner as he said,

"In the present circumstances electors must expect some inconvenience to attend the exercise of their privilege."

"Is that your view, my lord?"

Goodchild turned reluctantly and faced his benefactor, twisting his golden sword knot between his fingers.

"It is."

"I had never hoped, my lord, to see you tolerate intimidation."

Goodchild felt a spasm of choking anger and indignation. How did the man dare speak of intimidation when a quarter of the shopkeepers in the town stood to lose their leases or their custom if they voted against him?

"I believe that money and property have methods of persuasion quite as pressing as the mob's."

A loud cheer rose from the square. Goodchild turned and saw a man with a heavily bandaged head leaving the polling booth supported by several others. He swung around the telescope mounted in the window and picked out Magnus and Strickland. He pushed the eyepiece toward Braithwaite and said,

"There's a man able to vote in spite of certain impediments." The slight intake of breath as Joseph looked through the instrument convinced Goodchild that he had known exactly what had happened to Magnus. Nor would he get much pleasure from seeing Strickland in young Crawford's company. Already his shock seemed to be giving way to anger. Joseph pushed aside the telescope and walked to the door.

"Gentlemen, you will regret it if you fail to do your duty to the electors."

"My duty, sir, is to the whole town," replied Summers, as the door closed after their visitor.

Five minutes later, a young subaltern burst in on them. The union marchers had left Millcroft Fields and were heading for the High Street along Mytongate and Granby Street.

As Goodchild, accompanied by a subaltern and the adjutant, stepped out into the stable yard, the order *Prepare to Mount* was given and men hurried to remove heavy gray blankets from the horses' backs; underneath, the animals were already saddled. The thawing snow in the yard was littered with straw and hay and stained with urine. Goodchild's batman came up with his white gauntlets and black-plumed shako. Horses neighed and whinnied and the cobbles resounded to the clash of hooves as the thoroughbred horses pranced and skittered in the sharp cold air. Without their usual lances and fluttering pennants, the 17th was equipped with carbines and sabers, their scabbards so highly polished that they could be, and sometimes were, used as shaving mirrors.

Goodchild mounted his large, mettlesome, black horse and his servant adjusted the stirrup leathers and checked the reins and girth. The command *Forward!* was given, and, with clanking sabers and clattering hooves, the troop defiled in fours, moved out of the yard. The sun caught the gold lace on epaulets and glinted from the brass ornaments on shakos and pouches, and from numerous buttons. The black plumes spread out and caught the wind as the walk was increased to a trot. At the appearance of the horsemen, with their dark blue uniforms and striking blue facings, a roar of anger rose from the crowd in the square, but this changed to an ironic cheer as the cavalry wheeled toward the High Street. Riding just ahead of the two troop leaders, Goodchild felt thankful to be escaping from the square, where Summers would now be wholly responsible for suppressing a riot, if one started. His lordship's task was now to prevent the strikers' march reaching the center of town; and with four troops of cavalry at his disposal, he was confident that he could halt four thousand marchers without violence.

When Lord Goodchild reached the top of the High Street, he was surprised that, although he could hear distant shouting and the music of the union's band, the signal flag had not been broken out above the Free Trade Hall ahead of him. The flag was to have been hoisted the moment the marchers passed the troop of yeomanry, positioned to prevent them from forcing their way into Horsefair, the street leading into the Quadrant—the open space where the only other polling booths were situated. Either the strikers had turned back or they had overwhelmed the yeomanry.

The captain of the troop of lancers deployed across the High Street, rode up to Goodchild and saluted.

"Did you send out advance pickets?" Goodchild asked sharply.

"My orders forbade sending out small bodies of men, my lord."

Goodchild nodded. How even the yeomanry could have failed to hold the narrow archway leading into Horsefair was beyond him.

"I want you to lead a small scouting party—say ten troopers and a sergeant—to see what's happening in Horsefair. If you're not back in five minutes, I'll send a troop after you and enter the Quadrant from the west with another two troops. On no account must the marchers be penned into Horsefair. If they're in there, we'll get them out from the Quadrant end."

"And the High Street, my lord?"

"We'll still have one troop here and I'll send for another from Silver Street."

The captain rode off to collect his men and Goodchild called over his adjutant and two other senior officers to give them orders. He kept glancing at the flagstaff above the Free Trade Hall, but no flag was hoisted. Ahead the streets were eerily empty and now the band was no longer to be heard. Goodchild's heart was pounding, more with anger than fear. The whole exercise had been perfectly planned, but the yeomanry could have been counted on to let them down. Trust the yeomanry.

* * *

George Braithwaite sat waiting on his horse behind the two closely packed lines of yeomanry troopers blocking the narrow medieval archway of Monkgate Bar. In theory he knew that his two dozen men under the Bar, and the further hundred in reserve behind them, should be able to hold the confined opening into Horsefair against many thousands. Certainly, had his men been on foot with orders to fire if attacked, they could have turned back any mob; but George's orders, as he understood them, only empowered him to use mounted men, and were unambiguous in forbidding any shooting, unless in answer to shots. Although George had been told that there was little likelihood of the marchers trying to force their way into Horsefair, he had his doubts. They would send forward spies who would at once see that the High Street was impassable and would therefore know that their only way of reaching the center of town would be through Monkgate Bar. Nor, when they came level with the line of green uniforms under the Bar, would the marchers be able to see the larger reserve force in Horsefair.

When the marchers arrived and at once started to hack out cobbles with pickaxes and iron bars, George, and the troopers in front of him, knew what was coming, but were powerless to do anything. If they charged with so small a line, they would be surrounded and the crowd would surge through the arch behind them. To have fired at once would have been their only salvation, but their orders ruled that course out.

In the narrow space under the Bar, the first cobbles crashing among the terrified horses caused pandemonium; animals reared up, threw their riders and brought each other down. In the ensuing chaos, the mob poured forward through the archway into Horsefair, and saw the reserve troop facing them two hundred yards away with drawn sabers, preventing their further advance on the Quadrant. The marchers' leaders could not stop because of the pressure from behind, as hundreds pressed on oblivious through Monkgate Bar.

Acutely conscious of Goodchild's repeated exhortations to avoid bloodshed, George did not give the order to charge, but prayed that the forward impetus would slacken, as more and more came to understand that the way ahead was blocked. Deciding to give them room, he ordered his men back, but, when the mob kept coming, he saw that his withdrawal had been interpreted as irresolution rather than design. Simultaneously the thought came to him that unless he charged immediately, he would be unable to meet the mob at anything above a gentle trot. He felt the same sickness and confusion he had experienced a month before on the station road. But now there was no Magnus Crawford to give advice. In training the charge ended with a double flank retirement in column of troops and the re-forming of the first line behind the reserve line; but today, would he even be able to use a second line? And how could the first line clear itself after a charge against such a densely packed crowd? One line would have to be enough.

He screamed out the order for the front line to move forward, and at the trumpet note to trot, rode out in front, noticing that, since there would be no room for the normal four phases of the charge, most of the troopers did not know whether to hold their sabers at the carry or at the engage. As the white sea of panic-stricken faces grew closer, George forgot to give any more orders; it was as much as he could do to keep hold of his saber, but the pace of the line increased to a canter regardless. The ideal was that the squadron sergeant major, in the center of the front rank, should hit the opposition fractionally in advance of the markers on each flank, the whole line going in in an extended arrow shape; but, as the yeomanry neared their target, all orders to dress by the center were ignored, and the line thundered pell-mell into the screaming crowd, now surging and falling back over itself to escape.

The noise around George was the loudest and most awful sound he had ever heard: groans, shouts, curses, neighing horses and the clash of metal. Whatever will the mob had had to reach the Quadrant had now clearly gone. He could see his men hacking wildly with their sabers, drunk with success. "Retire!" he screamed to the trumpeter, as he saw people falling, struck down by hooves and saber cuts. A horse sank to the ground, evidently stabbed or shot. A moment later he heard a distinct shot and the whizz of a bullet. The trumpet notes to retire rang out, and the line wheeled and backed out of the breaking crowd, leaving thirty or forty wounded men on the dirty, slush-covered road. George was shocked to see that one of those struck down was a boy of eleven or twelve. He ordered two troopers to bring him back, but, as the men dismounted, one fell, shot through the shoulder.

Without waiting for more, George cantered back down the street toward the reserve line. The shots were coming, it seemed, from a churchyard to the right of the street, where a length of the railings had been torn down by large numbers of the crowd in their frenzy to escape the charge and to reach the cover of the gravestones in case the soldiers opened fire. A moment later he saw a puff of smoke beside the church tower under some yew trees, and then men swarming up a builder's ladder onto the porch and from there onto the roof of the nave; and from that position, George knew that they would be able to hit his men at almost any point in the street, giving them virtual possession of Horsefair. When another of his men fell from his saddle, he gave the order to dismount and draw carbines.

While they huddled together against a warehouse wall, ramming home cartridges and getting rid of cumbersome gauntlets and sabretaches, George picked twenty men, intending to lead them into the churchyard to clear out the armed strikers. He ordered a squad under the troop sergeant to rip out loose railings when they passed through the gap, his plan being to use them to batter down the locked church door so that he could get men up into the tower. From the top they would need to fire only a few isolated shots down at the nave roof to clear the strikers from it. His legs were trembling with fear at the coming danger, but he also felt sullen resentment and anger. Remembering Magnus's prophecy of disaster, these feelings intensified; doubtless Crawford would laugh at the comic irony that had made George Braithwaite the victim of his father's stubbornness. If Catherine read in the papers that he had dislodged some armed strikers, she would probably think nothing of it; such proceedings had none of the glamour of war. As it was, he was likely to be blamed for allowing the marchers to get into Horsefair.

Sick with bitterness and fear George led his men toward the gaping rent in the railings, walking upright, although his followers were crouching. But, when a bullet hit one of the railings with a sound like a clapper hitting a cracked bell, he found himself following their example. When they reached the gap, bullets cracked and whined about them as they sheltered a moment under the cover of the low wall on which the railings were mounted. George had no carbine, but raising his useless saber, he gasped, "Forward after me!" surprised that what he had intended to be a resounding shout had come out little above a high-pitched whisper. His bowels also troubled him and his legs felt as soft as wax as he hurled himself in a stumbling run toward the nearest gravestones. In threes and fours his men sprang through the gap after him.

On the long grass in the churchyard, the snow still lay thick in places, unmarked save by a thin film of smuts and the footprints of the strikers, most of whom were now either behind the church or up on the roof of the nave. An ominous silence had fallen, as though they were saving their shot and powder for the time when the yeomanry should reach the open grass in front of the porch. But the brief respite from danger gave George time to collect his wits. Beneath the cap of snow on the soot-blackened stone, behind which he was crouching, he made out a banal epitaph.

HERE LIES MARY JANE POTTER
WHOSE MANY VIRTUES
DELIGHTED THE LIVES OF OTHERS,
AND ADORNED HER OWN

George was pleased to be calm enough to manage a wry smile at the possibility of being killed in a graveyard. He darted on again, and this time dropped down behind a raised box tomb. Around him, in an extended line, his men were advancing on the church. When the soldiers reached the last gravestones, George watched the group under the troop sergeant, armed with their railings, dash toward the cover of the porch, and reach it without loss under an intense crackle of firing from the roof, while the remainder of the yeomanry, still kneeling behind the gravestones, did their best to give covering fire.

Seconds later, as the churchyard echoed to the sound of heavy metal hammering and smashing against the locked door, George was not alarmed by the absence of shots from the roof; the overhanging porch provided perfect cover for the work. When the doors gave way, George waited impatiently for his men to appear on the roof of the tower.

Suddenly he was stunned to hear the rattle of musketry coming from behind him. He could not believe it, until a bullet sang past his shoulder, nicking a gravestone and showering him with fine splinters of stone. He threw himself face down in the snow as other shots whipped past. Before he heard the warning shouts from the tower, he realized what had happened. At the first sound of the attack on the door, the strikers on the roof of the nave had crawled to the other side of the leads behind the high parapet and had lowered themselves to the ground by the drainpipes and creepers on the wall of the north transept. Before starting to break down the door, he should first have surrounded the church. The comprehension of his elementary error made his head swim. He had let them escape and steal up behind him, where the gravestones gave them excellent cover. Around him men were cursing and crawling flat on their stomachs, vainly seeking to escape the raking fire. A troop corporal crawled up to George on his hands and knees, his face gray with fear. A long scream came from a few yards behind him.

" 'ave to do summat," he gulped, almost angrily.

"Shut your mouth," snapped George, on the point of telling the man to stand when addressing him. "When I make a move, we'll run for the porch. Tell them that."

As the corporal crawled away, muttering meaningless filth under his breath, the unpredictable direction of the bullets, as they cracked and whizzed off the tombstones, badly unnerved George, so much so that, to stop himself screaming, he forced his knuckles against his teeth until they bled. Then, unable to stand the strain any longer, he leaped to his feet, and brandishing his sword, fled toward the porch. Moments after he and his men had reached their objective, a body of lancers clattered into the street. Thinking themselves surprised from behind, between ten and twenty armed strikers broke from their positions and ran in confusion toward the wall on the far side of the churchyard, their heavy fustian coats dark against the snow.

"Fire, dammit, fire," yelled George, hardly aware of what he was doing after the agonizing tension of the past three minutes. His men, however, seeing their enemies doing their best to get away, had no wish to detain them, and fired high or wide, reloading slowly. Only one man was hit on the wall.

*   *   *

Having left the main body of his men in an adjacent street, Lord Goodchild had ridden through the Quadrant with a small detachment of officers and troopers, and had been greatly relieved to find that, although the crowd there was as excited as the people in the market square, no violence had taken place. On entering Horsefair, he was incredulous to find the street empty and could not understand it; only a quarter of an hour before, he had been told that the yeomanry had been overwhelmed, leaving the mob in possession of the street. He was still more perplexed when he saw sixty or seventy yeomanry troopers smoking and lolling against the wall of a large warehouse. Moments later he caught sight of some bodies in the road and heard the rattle of musketry coming apparently from inside the churchyard. Having sent his adjutant across to ask the yeomanry what they meant by leaving unattended wounded on the ground, he rode on in the direction of the firing.

It now seemed tolerably clear to Goodchild that the mob had broken into Horsefair and had then been dispersed by shooting or a charge. He was completely at a loss to work out how they had forced their way in, since two overturned carts, blocking Monkgate Bar and defended from behind by men with sabers, should have made the narrow entrance impassable. He reined in opposite the churchyard and saw men in the yeomanry's green jackets firing down from the top of the church tower. Answering shots from the ground were puffing out clouds of dust from the stonework around the battlements. Next he saw a group of soldiers, led by an officer with a sword, run for their lives toward the church porch. As the rest of Goodchild's detachment clattered up beside him, some dozen or so men, probably strikers, broke from behind the gravestones and raced toward the far boundary wall. After a pause the soldiers in the porch opened an irregular stammer of fire on them. Goodchild reckoned that the break in the railings had been made by the mob in a desperate attempt to create another escape route when charged by the yeomanry; that the soldiers had then followed these fleeing men into the churchyard made Goodchild almost angrier than the fact that they had incompetently allowed the mob into the street in the first place. The lunacy of risking their own and other lives in an effort needlessly to hunt down armed men in a place providing such a variety and abundance of cover left him speechless. Also shooting tended to attract more guns to an area; the yeomanry were lucky not to be already involved in a battle as serious as the one that had taken place outside the workhouse three nights before. At present there could not be more than half a dozen guns firing regularly at the yeomanry, and these snipers seemed intent only on escaping; if the green-jacketed idiots stopped firing for a few minutes, their adversaries would be able to get over the wall and make a peaceful exit.

Turning, Goodchild saw the yeomanry from down the street removing the wounded under his adjutant's instructions; one of those hurt was little more than a child. So far he had managed to suppress his fury, but the sight of the boy's bloody matted hair and gashed face made Goodchild curse aloud. Without the yeomanry's bungling, the day might have ended without a single serious casualty. One of the fugitives in the churchyard had clambered up onto the wall, and was on the point of dropping down on the other side, when a volley rang out from the porch; the man spun around, twisted in midair and then fell. Goodchild gritted his teeth and touched his horse with his whip.

George and his men watched in open-mouthed amazement as one of the lancers set his large black horse at the railings and coaxed him through in a graceful jump. The sight of this officer, in his plumed shako and magnificent uniform, elegantly clearing the tombstones as if on a steeplechase course, while the snipers fired wildly at him, made the yeomanry hold their breath in anguish. George could not return the fire in case he hit the officer. Each moment he expected to see the horse rear up and fall, or the rider to be flung, broken and bleeding from his saddle, but miraculously he reached the church unscathed, dismounted and calmly tethered his horse to the left of the porch out of the line of fire. Then he strode briskly toward the doorway, his tall boots slapping against his thighs. George gasped as he recognized Lord Goodchild, his face scarlet and contorted with rage.

"My lord?"

"What the devil are you doing, sir?"

"Dislodging snipers. They fired on us."

"If you try to kill armed men, they have a habit of trying to do the same to you."

The scorn and anger in Goodchild's voice amazed George.

"My lord, they fired on us first."

"Before you had charged an unarmed crowd? I think not, sir." Goodchild impatiently flicked the black plume away from his face. "The blame is yours for letting the mob into this street."

The crackle of musketry still echoed across the churchyard from the tower. George was trembling with emotion.

"If my orders had made sense, I could have defended the Bar. I was told to use only mounted men."

"Are you mounted now? Circumstances dictate the method, not general orders. Your orders were to defend Monkgate Bar. How you did so was left to your discretion." Goodchild unhitched his saber which had become caught up with the straps of his sabretache. George's men had tactfully withdrawn to the back of the porch, where they were exchanging grim smiles, leaving only a corporal and a trooper to cover the approach. "You realize an inquiry will be held after the inquests on the men you killed? There will be questions in Parliament."

"I had no choice, my lord."

"For your sake, I hope so." Goodchild turned to go. Another burst of firing came from the tower. "Order your men to stop shooting and you will find you have no further trouble."

George watched blankly as Goodchild left the porch and remounted. Again he ran the gauntlet of fire through the churchyard and reached his destination in safety. After the jump down from the wall into the cobbled street, Goodchild checked his horse and turned him. A moment later Lord Goodchild was thrown forward by what seemed to be no more than a punch in the back; he felt no pain, but for some reason found himself lolling forward with his cheek brushing his horse's mane. He tried to raise himself but merely slipped farther forward, until he was dangling helplessly with a foot caught in a stirrup. Men were running and riding toward him, and he was soon released and carried toward the shelter of the warehouse. Soldiers were shouting and gesturing but he could not make out what they were saying. Above him the wall of the warehouse swayed and tilted across the blue sky like a reflection in moving water; he did not dislike what he saw, but, feeling tired, shut his eyes. Then he thought he would get up to see what had happened in the Quadrant, but he realized that he had forgotten why he wanted to go there. Seconds later he thought he had walked there and could not understand why he could see so much sky and so little else. The place was quieter than he had thought it would be, very quiet except for voices a long way off.

That's good, he thought, opening his eyes again and discovering that he was on the ground. He saw a dark red stain spreading across the white cloth plastron covering his chest and edging toward the row of small gold buttons. He was more surprised than frightened, his strange giddiness making the sight seem quite unexceptional; he did try to tell somebody, but when he attempted to speak he started to choke and no words came out—only a few thick bubbles of blood at the corner of his mouth, and then, as though he were being sick, a great rush. The warehouse wall blotted out the sky.

Soon a fly drew up and he was placed in it and conveyed to the Swan Hotel, to which a surgeon had hurriedly been called. During their brief journey the adjutant held his inert hand and wept openly like a child. There seemed little reason to send for his wife; he could not last long.

*   *   *

In a private room at the Bull, Magnus was resting after his exertions in the square. His head and shoulder hurt him considerably more than they had done that morning, and, now that he had time to reflect, he was convinced that his gesture had not been worth the pain it had caused him. Some minutes before he had learned that Braithwaite had achieved an unassailable lead and was therefore sure of his election. The volume of booing and jeering had increased, but, because of the absence of any strikers in the crowd, the violence, which Magnus had been so certain about, had not materialized. He knew that this ought to have pleased him, and yet he could not help feeling cheated and let down. He had predicted a disaster like Peterloo or the Bristol Riots, but instead a tense and ill-natured contest was drawing toward an uneventful close. Again and again he wondered how he had ever allowed himself to have become so obsessed with his hopeful schemes and plans. He was speculating about what Braithwaite's precise majority might be when Strickland flung open the door; he had gone down earlier to find out whether the votes had come in from the Quadrant; Tom was panting, as though he had run all the way and his eyes were wide and staring.

"Lord Goodchild's been brought to the Swan. He's dying—shot."

"How?" whispered Magnus.

"I don't know. It happened near the Quadrant."

"He may not be so badly hurt."

"Everybody at the Swan seems sure of it."

"Have they sent for his family?"

"I don't think so. He's not expected to live long enough."

The man had proposed Braithwaite and Magnus had despised him for it. Yet now he felt shocked and grieved. The day before he had received a sympathetic letter from him, and today he was dying, or so they said. Outside the crowd still groaned and scuffled, and the sun still formed a clear square on the dusty table beside Magnus's sofa. Tom sat down on a rickety table, his shoulders hunched and his head bowed: a picture of dejection. Magnus remembered his friend's calmness in the carriage as the town had come in view; only three hours ago. He sat up suddenly and said urgently,

"They ought to send for her."

"Lady Goodchild?"

Magnus nodded and let himself slip back onto the sofa.

"You must go for her, Tom."

"Me?" Strickland exclaimed, aghast.

"Would Charles be better? Or Braithwaite, or one of his lordship's brash young officers? I'd do it myself if I could stand the ride."

"If he's dead when we get back . . .?"

"Men expected to be dead within an hour sometimes live for several days." He sighed and let a hand fall to his side. "If he is dead, she'll have done her best to have reached him. There will be some consolation in that. No man ought to die among strangers."

"What can I say to her?"

"You must hurry," Magnus replied abruptly. Tom paused for a moment and then walked to the door. Magnus heard his footsteps grow fainter until they merged with the shouting of the crowd.

❧ *Fourteen* ❧

The sky was a translucent ivory overhead and growing steadily darker to the east when Tom rode over Flixton Ridge and saw the snow-covered roofs of Hanley Park on the far side of the woods below. Since he had left the turnpike, the faint crescent moon had become more distinct and started to shimmer in the sharp cold air. His eyes were streaming and his ears hurt, but Tom did not slacken his pace until forced to do so by the glassy patches of ice which had formed where the snow had thawed earlier in the day. His constant struggle to avoid falling left him little time to worry about what he would say.

When he reached the stables, Tom instructed a groom to get ready the fastest carriage and not to waste time with hammercloths or polished leather. Then he ran up the steps under the portico into the lamp-lit hall and hustled a dozing footman out of the hooded leather porter's chair by the door. The man, sensing the urgency in the visitor's voice, led him out of the hall at once, without the usual formality of taking his card to her ladyship.

Helen and Humphrey were being served dinner by the butler and a footman as Tom was shown in. Apart from the lamp on the sideboard, the dining room was lit only by two candelabra on the oval table. Taking in Strickland's mud-stained clothes and distraught face, Helen rose at once.

"Something has happened in the town," he blurted out, unable to speak more plainly, and hoping to break the news a little at a time. She stared at him imploringly and held out her hands, as if asking, *What has it to do with me?*

"Your husband," he whispered, not daring to look at her, but fixing his gaze on the gleaming silver and glass, glinting in the flickering candlelight. Without asking him anything, she told the footman to send her maid to fetch a mantle, and was on the point of ordering a carriage when Tom told her that he had already set that in hand.

"He must be badly hurt," she murmured, more a statement than a question. Tom nodded and a brief silence followed. She came closer to him and looked at him with unwavering eyes. "Will he live?" As his eyes met hers, Tom knew that he could not lie to her.

"He may be alive when you get there."

Tom had expected tears or faintness, but although she was breathing fast and had become deathly pale, her composure did not desert her. When Humphrey began to sob, she embraced him and held him in her arms until her maid came with her mantle.

In the stable yard the steps of the chariot were already down. Ever since his arrival Tom had been struggling with the unreality of his position; could he, not long since a lithographer's assistant, have brought news of so great a calamity to such a house? He had a sudden vision of being in the coach with her and imagined himself comforting her and felt the weight of her head against his shoulder. Then he saw the boy clinging to her arm as she got into the carriage. An unexpected flicker of resentment caught him by surprise. It was wrong, he knew, but he wished that Humphrey was not there. She leaned out.

"Mr. Strickland?"

Coming to himself, he shook his head and stepped away from the door.

"I shall ride back, your ladyship."

She said nothing, but he sensed from her face that she was relieved and grateful to be left to travel alone with her son. He realized that for the wrong reasons he had behaved impeccably. Tom shut the door and shouted to the postilions to start.

"The Swan Hotel!" he cried, as the carriage rumbled off; then he mounted his horse and rode after them into the darkness.

*   *   *

When she entered the Swan, Helen noticed the silence that her presence brought, and the flow of pity, deference and curiosity. Everywhere people dropped their eyes and yet stared after her the moment she had passed. As she was climbing the stairs, Joseph Braithwaite came toward her with outstretched hands, but she walked past him without a word. Her face conveyed nothing, nor, when she did speak, did her quiet, level voice betray her feelings. She imagined people saying to each other that she was calm because she had not yet realized the magnitude of her loss and was numbed by the suddenness of the catastrophe; she told herself that she did not care what they thought. Let them think me as hard and cold as marble if they choose.

By the light of three candles on a table beside his bed, she saw her husband's white and drawn face and the slight smears of blood at the corners of his mouth, which had been hastily wiped clean before her arrival. The sheets were pulled up to his chin so she could not tell where he was wounded. The only sound in the room was his rasping breathing. Outside she had noticed that the street had been covered with straw to deaden the noise of passing carriages. His eyes were closed and his lips slightly parted. Chairs were placed by the bed and she sat down with Humphrey close to her.

The boy was uncomprehending and frightened, and yet, even in these dreadful circumstances, struggled to imitate his mother's dignity. As he looked at his father, Humphrey could not believe that he was going to die. It was not possible that his commanding voice and overbearing presence should cease to be, on a single day. An event so extraordinary should surely take place over months or years. That he should never ride to hounds again, nor shoot, nor drive his four-in-hand team again seemed inconceivable. When Humphrey remembered his father's promise that they should talk together and walk around the estate, he felt himself shaken by powerful choking sobs, which seemed to rise from the pit of his stomach. Helen too found it hard to believe in his coming death. When scholars, priests or cautious tradesmen died, the process could not be so starkly inappropriate; they had practiced self-denial and foregone present enjoyment for future gain either spiritual or material. Death had lived a little in the pattern of their lives, but Harry's every thought and pleasure had been in the present; his women, his drink and his sports were so entirely of the world that death in his case seemed far more final and destructive. Yet not even this thought made her feel grief and she gazed at him dry-eyed. Only when she saw a smudge of black dye from his hair on his damp forehead did she catch her breath and feel tears pricking. What could his careful attempts to appear youthful avail him now? She remembered hearing of women clinging to their dying husbands and having to be pulled away screaming and weeping when they were dead.

For a time, Helen longed to be able to weep to prove to herself that she could feel her impending loss. Later she reproached herself for the thought. Such self-regarding tears would have nothing to do with the dying man, whose labored breathing filled the room. Her grief could not touch him. She had wished to be separated from him and now she struggled to fight off her guilt for having had that wish; she had never desired his death. At any rate she would never be among that band of women who saw little of their husbands when alive and felt no love for them, but, who, after their deaths, paraded their grief as a belated means of demonstrating the devotion they had never felt, their tears all aimed to convince the living that they had really cared for the departed. Nor would she tell others that he had possessed virtues which she had never noticed.

She saw Captain Ferris, her husband's adjutant, hovering near her chair, and noticed with shock his red-rimmed eyes and tear-stained cheeks. Helen felt a hot blush of shame as she understood how deeply affected he was. But then Harry had given so much more to his beloved regiment than he had ever given to her. But her bitterness disappeared when she thought of the months of their courtship, as she saw him as he had been at twenty-six and herself at twenty, her eyes overflowed. She looked down at the sunken eyes and the gray skin drawn tightly across his cheekbones and remembered the handsome hopeful face she had fallen in love with, recalling his laughing eyes and his smile which had transformed her feelings like sunshine on a winter day. How she had basked in his praise and pride after Humphrey's birth, and how sure she had felt of his love. As her tears flowed silently, she was not thinking of his death, but of the loss of all the hope and happiness she had felt during the early years of her marriage. She wept for her own lost youth as much as for his ebbing life. Perhaps if he had suffered a long illness, they might have been brought closer and their love renewed, but the suddenness of the blow had prevented that miracle. The last time he had left Hanley Park, he had not found time to say good-bye to her.

Shortly after eleven o'clock Lord Goodchild started choking and his eyes opened briefly; Helen took his hand but he did not recognize her.

Seconds later he was coughing blood and then began to hemorrhage. The surgeon rushed forward but could do nothing. In the silence that followed the sudden burst of activity, Helen remained sitting dumbly beside the blood-drenched bed. Nobody moved nor mentioned what everybody in the room was aware of: the painful breathing, which they had listened to for so long, had stopped. Having sat for two hours, it seemed strange to Helen that now there was no reason to remain. Only the knowledge that unless she moved the others in the room would feel obliged to stay made her rise. At length she gazed down at his face, as though memorizing it, and then covered him with the sheet.

In her abstracted state she looked around for Humphrey but did not see him. Outside on the landing she learned from Captain Ferris that her son had fainted and had been carried to the next-door room. She went to him, followed by the adjutant, who remained awkwardly beside her. Later he said quietly,

"If your husband had thought more of himself and less of others, he might yet have been spared to us."

Helen was watching anxiously as Humphrey was persuaded to drink by the surgeon. She knew that Ferris expected her to say something but could think of no reply. The man clearly wanted to tell her exactly how Harry had received his fatal wound; it was as if his need for consolation was greater than hers.

"Tell me what happened."

As Helen heard how Harry, oblivious to his own danger, had crossed the churchyard to stop a pointless gun battle, she felt admiration but anger too. If he had thought of his wife and son, he would have hesitated before taking such a risk; he would not have ridden to the church, but would have gone on foot, presenting perhaps a less impressive spectacle, but also a less inviting target. She thought of his reckless riding as he led the field at every hunt, and of his scornful disregard for caution when riding in steeplechases. In the end he had been killed by his own élan and panache. Ferris was saying,

"Your ladyship may rest assured that the arrangements will be seen to by the regiment."

Helen imagined the bands, gun carriages and firing parties and gripped the banisters. The regiment had had enough of him during his life and she would not have it dictate to her after his death. Had the regiment not killed him? And should she now meekly accept whatever role Harry's brother officers might see fit to allow her in his funeral?

"There will be no military funeral, Captain Ferris."

"I am sure that he would have wished . . ."

"If he has left instructions, I shall abide by them." She turned without looking at him. As she reached the top of the stairs she paused: "After the inquest you may convey his body to Flixton Church; after that he will be buried in private by his family in the mausoleum at Hanley Park."

"He died commanding the regiment, my lady."

"Funerals," she murmured, "should console the living before they glorify the dead."

Ferris watched her go in stunned silence, interpreting her self-possession as callous indifference and her decision as an affront to the dead.

Tom Strickland was sitting in the hall when she came down the stairs followed by her son, who was being helped by the surgeon. He rose and stepped forward so that she would see him if she needed him. She took his hand for a moment and then walked past to her carriage. A buzz of conversation broke out after her departure, but Tom did not wait to hear what was said. Instead he walked out into the deserted square, and eagerly breathing in the cold air, gazed up at the brilliant and indifferent stars. He thought of the dead man lying in his curtained room, and touched his own warm cheeks and felt the moisture of his breath on his hands. Life, he whispered, and an exultant surge of feeling rose within him; he felt greedy for the dawn and for new days and years, and whatever might transpire, he would try to welcome them and to waste nothing.

PART TWO

Return of the Admiral

~ *Fifteen* ~

Running into the Channel in a southwesterly gale, under double-reefed topsails and a single foresail, H.M.S. *Albion* surged forward and steadied momentarily before dropping with stomach-turning speed into the troughs of the mountainous Atlantic rollers; then, more slowly she would rise to the next crest, as the following wave caught her up astern and passed her with a thundering rush, throwing up boiling foam as high as the main deck ports and sweeping on into the darkness with a hiss and a roar under the spray-drenched catheads and bowsprit. Like most tall three-deckers, *Albion* did not steer well when running in a heavy sea, and needed all the strength of four men at the wheel to keep her on course. Throughout the ship, the howling of the wind in the rigging, the rattling of blocks and spars and the creaking of the guns accompanied the more constant and lower-pitched groaning of the timbers. The pitching motion was more pleasing than the simultaneous heavy rolling, which had not been much reduced by lashing the main and middle deck guns amidships. But although the gale was uncomfortable, it was, from a sailor's point of view, quite manageable.

Shortly before three, Rear Admiral Sir James Crawford abandoned his efforts to sleep, and, having clambered from his cot, lit a lamp, and, without waking his servant, pulled a uniform coat over his shoulders; leaving his sleeping quarters, he passed through his dining cabin into his day cabin. Through the streaming windows of the stern gallery he could see the black rollers dwarfing *Albion*'s hull, always seeming to be about to break over the stern and swamp the ship, but then lifting her up and passing under her keel. The only light came from the lanterns on the taffrail above and from the phosphorescent flashes of foam on the crests of the waves. The moon and stars were hidden by a thick layer of low clouds. *Albion* could survive worse weather by far, but the accompanying frigate *Blanche* and the sloop *Rifleman* would be getting an unpleasant pounding. Every so often, when his flagship rose to the top of a wave, Crawford could see the smaller vessels' navigation lights about a mile astern on the starboard quarter, small pinpoints against the black waves.

From the moment of waking, one thought had been dominant in Sir James's mind: this was probably the last night he would ever spend afloat in the admiral's quarters of a line-of-battle ship. His three years of command on the North American and West Indies Station were over and he was homeward bound. Often during his command he had attempted to make light of the excessive respect and awe shown to a naval commander-in-chief; but, although his career had been an unusual one, including, as it had, eight years in diplomacy as Her Majesty's minister in Athens, his lifelong passion for the service held him as firmly as it had when he had joined as a boy forty years before.

When Sir James returned to his sleeping quarters, his servant, Partridge, was up and laying out his clothes for the morning: silk shirt, long underpants, undress frock coat, plain trousers with no gold lace stripe, and a thick pea coat with admiral's epaulets. Before dressing, he shaved while Partridge miraculously contrived to stop the bowl of water spilling, while holding up a lantern and a mirror; it was a tricky operation, but, whatever the weather, Sir James never appeared unshaven on the quarterdeck. Even by the light of the swaying lantern, the exceptional blueness of his eyes was apparent; and their clarity and sharpness, coupled with his heavily lidded eyes, gave him an eager but half-melancholy look. As a young man he had thought his rather full face undistinguished and dull, but now, in his early fifties, his thick profusion of iron gray hair and the deep lines at the corners of his mouth and eyes, while making him look more resolute and serious than he believed himself to be, had given his face an interest and distinction it had not previously possessed; age had embellished rather than marred his looks. After Sir James had shaved himself, Partridge dressed him, finally helping him into his pea coat and boots. He declined the cocked hat held out to him and strode out into his dining cabin toward the companion ladder leading up to the quarterdeck just aft of the mizzenmast and the wheel.

As he emerged on deck, the marine sentry came to attention and the men at the wheel stared fixedly into the binnacle. He walked over to the weather side of the quarterdeck, where the bulwarks afforded him some shelter from the wind and spray, which made his freshly shaven face smart. The officer of the watch nodded deferentially and then moved across to leeward accompanied by a midshipman, leaving him in the dignified isolation always accorded to his rank. No officer, not even the captain, spoke to the admiral, unless addressed first, except on duty when an order concerning a movement of the whole fleet or squadron was to be given.

The ship was glistening wet from deck to trucks, and high above, the two topsails on the main and fore formed sharp black squares against the deep, gray-blue sky as *Albion* ran on with streaming spars and canvas, pursued by pelting squalls. As Sir James heard the faint notes of seven bells flung past on the wind, he saw his flag lieutenant come up the main companionway between the two forward quarterdeck guns to hand him a paper with the apparent time of sunrise and the positions of the ships in company. Not wishing to talk, Sir James walked as steadily as he could on the swaying deck toward the shelter of the overhanging poop.

The last time, he thought again, watching the men at the wheel. During his absence Lord Palmerston had been dismissed from the Foreign Office; and with Sir James Graham, his other patron, no longer first lord of the admiralty, Crawford did not expect another appointment. A few years back, he could have bided his time, but now, with even the largest three-deckers being built with steam engines as well as sails, the day could not be far distant when admirals would have to command fleets entirely composed of screw-assisted vessels, and then no flag officer could hope to remain long ashore without losing touch with constructional and tactical developments. During the thirteen years since Sir James had become a widower, only his work had sustained him. When his flag came down at Spithead that afternoon, it would mean more to him than the simple ending of a command. Idleness frightened him more than the thought of any work, however arduous. Since all his working life, with the exception of four years on half-pay, had been spent at sea or abroad, he could not hope on his return to fall into the comforting routines of an established social life. Nor with an unmarried daughter, and an elder son who idolized him, would he be able to allow himself the comforting indulgence of a mistress as he had during his years in Athens.

Shortly after eight bells Sir James went below and did not return to the quarterdeck until dawn, which came—as so often after stormy nights—sullen and gray, with low, fast-moving clouds and blustery showers. The sea, like the sky, was a dirty chill gray, flecked with white horses. Through his glass he could see the topsails of *Blanche* and *Rifleman* falling in and out of sight as they rose from the deep valleys of the rollers and fell away again out of sight. Already he found himself looking around him with a premature nostalgia, noting the most trivial details of the ship's routine, not because he could ever forget what he had seen so often, but to record them one more time: the gunner's mate coming up on the hour to verify the security of the guns for the officer of the watch, the carpenter's mate reporting the depth of water in the well, and the midshipman on quarterdeck duty returning with a marine corporal from his rounds of the lower decks to repeat anything seen by the lookouts at the gangways and catheads.

By midafternoon *Albion* was running alongside the southern shore of the Isle of Wight, past the lighthouse on St. Catherine's Point, and then reaching in the calmer water under the lee of the eastern side of the island. Another hour and she was close-hauled on the port tack ten miles from Spithead; by then Sir James was below, buckling on his full-dress sword belt, with its embroidered oak leaves and acorns, and submitting to Partridge's careful scrutiny. The stiff gold braid, which edged his high collar, cut into his chin unpleasantly and his trousers felt too tight, but having dabbed at him once or twice with a clothes brush, Partridge seemed satisfied. Holding his cocked hat in his hand and being careful not to trip over his cumbersome ceremonial sword on the companion ladder, Sir James proceeded to the quarterdeck, followed by his flag lieutenant and secretary, both also in full dress.

The ship was approaching her anchorage under topsails, fore-topmast-staysail and spanker. As the admiral came on deck, the officer of the watch was shouting to the men aloft through his speaking trumpet. At his orders the men in the fore and mizzen tops furled their topsails, leaving only the main topsail set. The captain stood by the helmsman as *Albion* edged closer into the wind.

"Down helm! Haul down the staysail!"

As the fore-topmast-staysail came down, the spanker was hauled to windward and the ship came up faster into the wind; at the same time the main topsail began to shake and was then caught aback reducing her speed. Precisely as *Albion* lost all way, the order rang out from the bows:

"Let go!"

The carpenter brought down his maul with a sharp blow, knocking out the pin holding the anchor in place at the cathead. A loud splash was followed by the thunderous rattling of the cable. The rigging was now swarming with men furling sails, before swaying up the lower yards and squaring all yards. Others were far higher up checking that the topmasts and topgallants were still properly stayed and upright after the storm.

"Hands out barge!" resounded through the ship and the massive boat was soon slung out on the booms, while a dozen bluejackets jumped in to get her ready; the lowering tackles were made fast, and, as the boatswain's mate piped shrilly, she was lowered into the sea with a deep splash. Meanwhile the band had been summoned to the poop, and the marine guard marshaled on the quarterdeck where they presented arms as Sir James and his flag lieutenant passed by on their way down to the main entry port on the middle deck. There all the officers were assembled, standing stiffly, swords at their sides and hats in hands. The admiral spoke a few words of thanks to the captain and the first lieutenant, and, while the boatswain whistled perseveringly, Sir James made his way down the lane of side boys to the entry port and stepped out onto the accommodation ladder. From forward a puff of smoke and a loud bang marked the start of his twelve-gun salute. He paused for a moment on the ladder and looked up at the mizzen where he could see a small white flag with a red ball in the corner and a red St. George's Cross slowly coming down as the guns thundered, taken up by the other ships of his squadron.

He knew that it was an empty ceremony addressed to his rank and not his person, but for all that he still felt his eyes filling and had to look away to avoid his flag lieutenant's eye. When he was seated in the stern of the admiral's barge, the boatswain piped, "Away there barge's crew," and the oars dipped and rose in perfect unison as the crew pulled away from *Albion*'s towering black and white sides. The band on the poop with numerous drum rolls broke into the opening bars of "Auld Lang Syne." Looking back, Sir James saw the men lining the lower yards and the hammock netting and raised his hat in acknowledgment of their three cheers. A common enough practice on such occasions, but again he found it hard to maintain an impassive expression.

He thought of the numerous ships he had left after a commission had ended and found it impossible to imagine that this was the last time. Could this really be the final occasion on which he would be rowed past the Round Tower, the Semaphore Tower, the Sally Port and the Point —landmarks that he had first seen from the sea as a boy of thirteen? A short time and they would be at King's Stairs and after Portsmouth, London for a few days; a visit to the Admiralty and then the long train journey to Rigton Bridge, and after that, months, maybe years of wait-ing. A pinnace was putting out from the Victoria Pier; after a few strokes the coxswain's command, "Oars!" sounded across the water, and every oar in the pinnace was raised in the air until the admiral's barge had gone past. In the stern sheets of the pinnace, Sir James saw a young lieutenant off hat and look wistfully after him, doubtless envying him and wondering whether one day he too might attain flag rank. Crawford shook his head and managed a smile. Every age imagined its own particular problems to be the worst; in his own career he had only troubled himself with his own immediate problems, and had never wor-ried about those that might beset him after his next promotion. Only recently had he found it increasingly difficult to live in and for the present, but at Leaholme Hall he would have to do just that if he were to avoid a constant sense of bitterness and disappointment. As King's Stairs came in view, Sir James was aware of his flag lieutenant eyeing him surreptitiously. The young man owed his position to the influence of his father who was second sea lord.

"What's on your mind, Mr. Hay?"

"Nothing at all, sir."

"An enviable condition, Mr. Hay."

Hay laughed nervously and fiddled with the hilt of his sword.

Sir James stared ahead of him; already he could hear the waves slapping against the steps and the quay.

❧ Sixteen ❧

Behind closed blinds in the first of the family carriages, Helen Goodchild gazed tenderly through her heavy mourning veil at Humphrey
sitting beside her. The strain of behaving with the stoicism he thought
expected of him showed in the concentrated frown on his unhappy face
and in the way he sometimes bit his lower lip to keep back his tears. For
Helen, her son's black silk top hat—the first he had ever worn—and
grown-up surtout, stressed his vulnerability. Ahead lay the ordeal of the
public funeral in Flixton parish church, and then the private ceremony
at the family mausoleum. She touched his hand, but he looked away, as
though afraid that any overt sign of affection might break down his frail
defenses.

Helen felt her own eyes filling, not on account of her dead husband,
but with anguish over her boy's future. Three days before, the family
solicitor had come from London at her request. The state of Harry's
affairs revealed by him had been beyond her worst imaginings. Not only
would Audley House have to be sold, as Goodchild had always claimed
it must, but the sum raised would not fully cover another mortgage he
had taken out on Hanley Park. Since Joseph Braithwaite's loan had been
secured against the London house, after its sale other security would
have to be given; and, since Harry's Irish estates were entailed and could
not legally be encumbered until Humphrey's majority, the only possible
surety for Joseph would be Hanley Park itself. Until the loan was repaid, their fortunes would depend on Joseph Braithwaite's whims. Only
knowing this had Helen understood her husband's determination not to
displease the manufacturer. Her only chance of repaying him would be
to borrow from another source and pay the necessary interest; but with
current income falling considerably short of expenditure, there could

only be one way of achieving this. Having so ardently desired her freedom, the realization that she must marry again, and quickly too, if Humphrey's inheritance was to be saved, had been a crushing blow which had tested her courage to the utmost.

She raised the blind a little and saw that they were now over halfway from Hanley Park to Flixton. Already Harry's body would have been brought to the village by his regiment.

Standing in the crowd opposite the church, George Braithwaite was perplexed to see little evidence of grief around him. Even in the worst of the Chartist troubles, the shooting of a peer or magistrate would have been deemed an appalling outrage, but here, although some people were clearly shocked, a sizable minority had evidently come only to see the soldiers and the multitude of carriages blocking the main street. The shops and inns being shut as a mark of respect, many people had brought food and drink with them in case, should the proceedings be drawn out, they might miss any part of them. For those less provident, piemen and hot potato sellers were at hand.

George listened to the tolling of a single muffled bell. On the opposite side of the street a troop of the 17th Lancers was drawn up behind a coffin draped in the Union Jack and resting on a gun carriage. Thinking of the magnificent uniformed horseman riding across the churchyard on polling day, George felt a numbing sadness. Goodchild had taken his father's money, while despising him, but George could not find it in him to remember him with bitterness. His weaknesses had redeemed him. He had not been invited to the funeral, but George had still decided to pay his respects, as much as a farewell to his own old life as a tribute to the dead man. His hopes of marrying Catherine gone, and his relations with his father no longer cordial, George had made up his mind to leave the town as soon as he could buy into a suitable infantry regiment—after the terrible scene in Horsefair, he no longer had any desire to be a cavalry officer.

Bareheaded among the villagers, George watched the family carriages stop outside the lych-gate. The crowd had become silent, and apart from the occasional pawing of hooves and the funeral bell, the loudest noise was made by the road-sweeper's shovel as he passed behind the soldiers' horses disposing of the dung. At a command from an officer, whom George recognized as Goodchild's adjutant, Ferris, six troopers heaved the lead-lined oak coffin from its platform and carried it through the lych-gate toward the church, led by a subaltern with his black plumed shako under his arm. As the procession of mourners moved toward the arch, George heard the rector of Flixton's sharp nasal voice rise above the murmurs of the crowd:

"I am the resurrection and the life, saith the Lord. He that believeth in me, though he were dead, yet shall he live . . ."

George turned away and walked pensively toward his phaeton. Titled, handsome, rich, at least to start with, married to an acknowledged beauty, and yet unhappy. George derived no consolation from this reflection. If Goodchild had failed to gain even a part of what he had desired, how much more unlikely that those less favored would do so either.

After the first part of the service, Helen saw the coffin taken from the church and placed in an ornately carved hearse, surmounted by trembling black plumes and drawn by four black horses with feathers at their heads. While a coronet was being fixed in place on the black velvet pall, substituted for the Union Jack, a woman broke away from the crowd and, before anybody could stop her, had kissed the side of the coffin. She turned to go but was grasped firmly by a coachman. A buzz of excitement and laughter rose from the crowd. Out of the corner of her eye, Helen was appalled to see Dr. Carstairs coming toward them.

"Let her go!" she cried with an urgency and authority that impelled obedience. Released, the woman stared at Helen from behind her veil, and her tear-stained cheeks and anguished sleepless eyes cut Helen to the heart with their hatred and reproach, which said more clearly than words, "What did *you* ever care for him?" A moment later, Carstairs, giving no sign that he recognized Helen, led his wife away. The incident was over in a few seconds, but after it Helen felt a tight choking feeling in her chest and her head swam as if she were about to faint; Captain Ferris took her arm and helped her into her carriage. Against the white facings of his uniform his face glowed scarlet. Although neither he nor Helen said anything, both were perfectly aware that the other knew the strange woman's identity and her former relationship to the dead man.

While the hired undertaker's mutes, with their long mourning coats and black staves, lined up on each side of the hearse, Helen sat alone behind the drawn blinds of her carriage and wept. The endless condolences she had received from Harry's relatives and their compliments about her courage had sickened her before, but now the thought of their repetition was unendurable, and her crape flounces and heavy, black bombazine dress seemed even more hypocritical than she had previously thought them. She imagined herself throwing open the carriage door and screaming hysterically that she did not care and had wanted to leave him; that she could not go on acting out a bereavement she did not feel because her husband had loved and been loved, and she had neither been the donor nor the recipient of that love. What right had she to pretend grief, when another woman was consumed with real sorrow? It took ten minutes to assemble the cortege, and during that time she recovered sufficiently to submit to what was expected of her. When Humphrey got in beside her, she was quite calm again.

In spite of what many people considered a forbidding manner, Sir James Crawford was not without a wry sense of humor, and it had always amused him that Goodchild's grandfather's vanity had so far surpassed his dread of dying that he had built his final resting place on a prominent rise, so that its copper dome and tall pillars could be seen across the lake from every window on the south side of the house. The eye was drawn to it inexorably by an ornamental bridge and a commemorative obelisk on the far side of the water. Sir James was soon to see that aesthetic considerations had so outweighed practical ones that a well-made road had never been built; and this omission made access to the mausoleum a difficult matter, especially when several days of heavy rain had followed a thaw, as was the present case. Although the ditchers had worked hard to drain and sand the track, the hearse still became bogged down near the obelisk, and again on the final slope up to the mausoleum.

Before their destination had been reached, Sir James and Charles, like many of the mourners, had been forced to leave their carriages and walk. By then the black silk stockings of the undertaker's men were splattered with mud and their hardened professional gravity replaced by surly and discontented looks.

Sir James had reached Leaholme Hall only two days before the funeral and had been stunned to learn about Goodchild's death, but some of the sting had been removed by Charles's remarks about the late peer's failings as a husband. Sir James had been very fond of Helen as a girl and young woman. Her father had been a close friend of his, until his death at the Battle of Navarino, an action in which Crawford had also fought. It had been ironic, given his disapproval of the young Lord Goodchild, so recently come into his title, that Helen had first met her future husband while staying with her godfather at Leaholme Hall.

Built to defy time, in just under a century the stonework of the mausoleum had been so eroded by wind and rain that it already had a crumbling and leprous air. Tall iron railings stopped cows getting in from the neighboring fields, and a low wall and paved surround kept the grass and nettles at bay. The building was circular and on two levels: a chapel above, the burial vault below. Descending into the damp chilling darkness of the vault, with its man-sized niches—enough to contain generations of Goodchilds—Sir James shivered. The place looked like a giant's uncared-for wine cellar. Only some half-dozen of the holes had been bricked up. There was no piped gas, and what light there was came from flaming torches in wall brackets.

The comicality of the bogged-down carriages and the strangeness of the vault had to some extent saved Sir James from dwelling upon the family's loss, but when he saw Humphrey's grimly pursed lips, trembling with the effort of repressing tears, Crawford was agonized—and not only by this present image of grief. Through his mind passed another procession: the dead he had known and loved, his wife among them. Remembering her, he had to struggle not to shed tears of his own. The fatherless boy also made him think of his own children, alone in England, their mother dead, and he as usual serving abroad. And had duty and ambition finally justified that sacrifice? Rear Admiral of the Blue at fifty-three and no prospect of further advancement—his life a brief footnote in naval history. He glanced at Charles, whose calm face reassured him; yet, recalling Magnus's rebelliousness and Catherine's present unmarried state, he could not escape a shaming feeling of remorse for having thought so much of his career. If Charles married, he would advise him, whenever ashore, to devote as much time as he could to his children; in his case the opportunity had passed, almost it seemed, before he had known it was there.

As the bearers approached the niche appointed to receive Harry's corpse, Helen managed to dispel her fears for the future. The red glow of the torches, the lingering shadows and echoing footsteps in the macabre Gothic atmosphere of the vault—itself so much a creation of the previous century rather than their own—made it seem the perfect setting for Harry's funeral. Like this building, he too had been an anachronism, belonging more to the age of pigtails and Hessian boots, sedan chairs and prizefights, than to the more staid and pious 1850s. She remembered him telling her with pride how he had once got up on the box and driven the Brighton stagecoach to London the entire fifty-two miles. And now, with the railways supreme, the last three or four stagecoaches in the country would soon be gone. It was not sentimentality or nostalgia that moved her, but the thought that, if she had not married Harry, she would have liked him. She would have enjoyed his stories of Crockford's and relished their humor, if she had not been involved with his debts; so too with many of his other activities. She glanced at the niche next to her husband's, and knew that, unless she married again, the day would come when she would lie there, divided from him in death, as in life, by a wall. A moment later she was surprised to find herself silently crying.

Charles Crawford could not see Helen's face through her veil, but he noticed her shoulders moving slightly, and smiled inwardly, impressed at the way she was acting out the part of grief-stricken and disconsolate widow; the idea that her sorrow might be genuine did not cross his mind; but her hypocrisy did not disturb him; being a convinced conformist, he liked to see the proper moods and feelings conscientiously displayed on the right occasion; that Helen could summon up grief to order seemed to him praiseworthy rather than reprehensible.

Since Goodchild's death, Charles had found it impossible to suppress a stirring of new hope. He alone, of all the people in the vault, would know about her true feelings for her late husband. His very presence at this private burial was surely a clear indication that later she would once again confide in him. Because of the press of mourning relatives at Hanley Park, Charles had delayed calling on her as deliberate policy. But now he regretted this. Two days after Goodchild's death an unwelcome communication had arrived from the Admiralty requiring him to appear as a witness at a dockyard inquiry into the loss of *Euryalus*, his last ship, which had sunk, not under his command, but later during sea trials, following her conversion to steam. He could not very well go to

Hanley Park in the week after the funeral, and therefore could not expect to see her before the New Year, since the inquiry would be sure to last until the middle of December, by which time Helen would have left to spend Christmas with relatives.

As the priest said, "We therefore commit his body to the grave," the bearers removed the pall and coronet and slid the coffin forward, the wood grating unpleasantly on the rough stone. Charles saw Helen handed a silver trowel, not, he thought irreverently, unlike a cheese scoop in shape. It was evidently filled with earth or ashes. At the words "Earth to earth, ashes to ashes, dust to dust," she tipped the trowel's contents onto the lid of the coffin with a hollow pattering sound. Charles gazed at her and felt his heart beat faster. When the New Year came he would renew his quest in earnest. His enforced absence might even prove to his advantage, since she would not be able to accuse him of unseemly haste. This time, he thought, nothing will deter me. Nothing, he murmured under his breath as she passed him a few feet away.

Five minutes later the mourners emerged thankfully into the open air, coughing with the smoke of the torches, which had also served to make their eyes water befittingly. Being downhill, the journey back to the house was accomplished without difficulty, at an almost unseemly speed.

❧ Seventeen ❧

On the morning after Lord Goodchild's funeral, Magnus Crawford threw open the shutters of his room at the Bull Hotel and looked down into the stable yard. In the distance he could hear the notes of a key bugle and then the approaching clatter of a post chaise on the uneven paving. The activity of the posting house pleased and consoled him. People coming and going, children throwing stones into the horse trough, the postboys getting ready fresh pairs of horses, ostlers and waiters running out to attend to new arrivals—everyday life continuing as though the election had never taken place. In this atmosphere of bustling normality, Magnus had been able to think of the future without so many regrets for the past.

For three days after the election he had been laid up as a result of his unwise exertions on polling day. Too weak and ill to face the coach journey back to Leaholme Hall, he had stayed on at the Bull, assuring Catherine and Charles that he was being well looked after and would return home by the end of the week. But before that, he heard that his father had returned, and knowing very well the account Charles would probably have given of his recent doings, Magnus had decided to delay confronting his father until his plans for the future were more fully formed.

Since he had gone down from Oxford without taking a degree, the recognized professions were closed to him; nor did he have any wish to return to the army or the colonial service. Short of becoming a drudging business clerk, journalism seemed not just the best, but probably the only possible occupation for him. In Ceylon he had opened his campaign against the governor with a series of anonymous letters to the *Colombo Gazette* from "A Serving Officer," and had written additional eyewitness accounts of courts-martial and executions, one of which had aroused particular revulsion. The officer in charge, to amuse the firing squad, as Magnus had put it, had placed the condemned men on top of wine casks, so they could be knocked down by the bullets like rag dolls in a fairground shooting gallery. Magnus had suggested that, if the foreign secretary was prepared, when it suited him, to send the fleet to the Piraeus to protect the commercial interests of a Spanish Jew living in Athens, simply because the man had been born in Gibraltar and was therefore entitled to a British subject's rights of protection, the British Government should have been more attentive to the rights of native British subjects in Ceylon. Whether well written or not, the effect of these articles and letters had been considerable. Magnus's recent dealings with the *Rigton Independent*, although not journalistic, had nevertheless made him aware that, if during the past weeks he had had access to the columns of a national daily newspaper, he could have done far more to influence the course of the election than could ever have been achieved by direct action. With the predicted abolition of the newspaper tax, cheaper papers would be certain to increase the power of the press. These reflections had made Magnus feel less fatalistic than he had done immediately after his humiliation. Uncertain whether he would succeed, he knew at least how he intended to begin. He would try to interest the monthlies in a series of descriptive pieces, which would make an asset of his status as a gentleman and former officer. No gentleman, as far as he knew, had ever worked as a railway navvy or stayed in slum lodging houses and then written about the experience from a gentleman's point of view: surprise, genteel disapproval and comparisons with his own way of life, all serving to underline the upper class's woeful ignorance of the conditions in which the mass of people lived and worked. If these articles aroused the interest he hoped they would, Magnus believed that he would in time be offered more influential employment from the editors of daily papers.

During his days of recovery and reflection at the Bull, Magnus had also been forced to acknowledge how much he had come to value Tom Strickland's company. When he had been in too much pain to return to Leaholme Hall, he had been surprised and touched that Strickland had been concerned enough about his condition to remain in Rigton Bridge beyond the date he had previously set for his departure. Apart from his kindness, many other qualities attracted him to Tom: astuteness, a total inability and disinclination to conceal his changes of mood, times of irrepressible enthusiasm, often followed by periods of intense thoughtfulness, and above all, a feeling that, like him, Strickland was prepared consciously to take great risks in the pursuit of an illusive goal. Magnus could not fathom precisely what he himself needed to do, but he knew that he could never accept the clearly defined aims of Charles or his father—their lives marked out with a map's precision. With Tom, the lines were blurred and hard to read, like a pattern that could only be understood when completed, a life so open to change and incident that nothing could finally be certain until the years had rolled back the entire design. Not having come from a background that demanded blind conformity to paternal expectation and social appearances, Strickland seemed free in a way which Magnus envied. Life in the army, the navy and the government service evidently meant no more to him than the habits of Eskimos and probably seemed no more important. Apart from liking him, Magnus's sense that Tom possessed the key to another world made him determined not to lose his new friend when they went their ways from Rigton Bridge.

Unlike the Swan and the Green Dragon, the Bull had entirely retained its original character as a small posting inn. The tavern parlor still had a sanded floor, and old men sat there at oak tables smoking clay pipes, on some evenings singing together. While potage à la bisque, turbot au gratin and côtelettes of this and that could be swilled down with St. Emilion at the Swan, the Bull's landlord stolidly kept to his beefsteaks and pints of port.

Tom Strickland bent his head as he entered the parlor with its wide beams and low bulging ceiling, and looked around almost with nostalgia at the heavy settles on either side of the open fire and the strange selection of prints on the walls: racehorses, theatrical scenes, mezzotints of Radical Members. The barman and the potboy were lounging behind the bar, but busied themselves when the landlord, a bald, corpulent man with an impressive bunch of watch seals at his fob, came in. He nodded to a farmer in a broad-brimmed hat and coarse pepper-and-salt trousers stuffed into muddy gaiters, and then, catching sight of Tom, beckoned to him and led him behind the bar to a small snuggery or private parlor.

Magnus rose smiling from a chair in the chimney corner. A small table was laid with a white cloth and lit by wax candles; on a sideboard sherry and Madeira were comfortably airing themselves. Tom had originally been asked to dine, but wanting to leave the town that evening for Manchester to be able to make an early start for London the following morning, he had accepted for lunch instead. Magnus, to Tom's amazement, was wearing an embroidered smoking jacket over a fine lawn shirt with ruby studs. The effect was more striking since Magnus's arm was still in a sling. Without speaking he handed Tom a sherry cobbler and raised his own glass. After a moment's silence he smiled.

"The future, Tom, and damn the past."

They both drank and then sat down by the fire. Magnus handed Tom a box of cigars and pushed a low stool under his feet. For the first time since their meeting at the *Independent*'s offices, Tom was carried along by Magnus's lighthearted mood.

"Well?" asked Magnus.

"Your clothes," laughed Tom.

Magnus lit a cigar from a candle and struck an elegant pose in front of the fire.

"I sent a man for them to Leaholme Hall. Your last day in Rigton Bridge. Special occasions demand the right rig. Didn't you know what a swell I was before I went abroad? Morning gowns with tassels as large as bellpulls."

"I've hardly met anyone less foppish."

"Ceylon wasn't a place for dandies, I admit." He puffed at his cigar. "No, the point's symbolic my dear Strickland . . . the resurrection of Magnus Crawford, late of the Ceylon Rifles. A few days ago I was ready to crawl out of this town like a whipped dog. Now here I am in my best bib and tucker, ready to face the future as squarely as a man can."

"What will you do?"

"Later," said Magnus raising his glass. "Drink up and I'll tell you something amusing. When Lord Goodchild wanted to keep a railway coach to himself, he used to travel with a boy dressed up as a chimney sweep. Isn't that admirable in a way? He also used to offer maiden ladies cigars if he thought them religious." Tom did his best to laugh, but could not forget Helen Goodchild's arrival at the Swan shortly before her husband's death. "Of course," Magnus continued, noticing Tom's slight reserve, "I realize that eccentricity like that depends on an excellent income and a degree of self-confidence unusual except in madmen, so don't be hard on me. I knew a lot of fledgling Goodchilds at Oxford—their greatest accomplishments being to get roaring drunk and then wrench off door knockers or trip up elderly watchmen; a real wit might bark like a dog in college prayers. I like to think I survived my education rather well. It's a great consolation to know how hard it'd be to be sillier than one was."

"Don't English gentlemen always like a challenge?" asked Tom with a smile.

"Enough of your mockery, sir," replied Magnus, pointing his cigar reprovingly at Tom.

Lunch—the most lavish the Bull had provided for many months—consisted of soup, game, neck of mutton and turnips, followed by Stilton and celery. The maid who served had coal-black ringlets, which Magnus said reminded him of gigantic leeches, and Tom suggested would make her an excellent model for Medusa. Afterward, when the cloth had been removed and port and Madeira set in place, Magnus returned to the fire and sat on the fender.

"What'll you do when you're back in London?"

Tom shrugged his shoulders.

"Pay off some debts and then . . . I know what I want to do, but I'll have to paint some hideous anecdotal subject for the Academy first—a homely and edifying scene. The gambling husband ruined and repentant, his wife tearfully forgiving . . . or perhaps something from literature. There's a black crossing sweeper in Charlotte Street who'll do very well as Othello."

"What happens if the Academy refuses it?"

"There's the British Institution or the Portland. Prices are bad, the hanging worse, but pictures get sold." Tom drank some port and pushed back his chair. "Failing that, I'll be back to woodcuts for periodicals, restoring stained glass or doing two-guinea portraits. I've given young ladies lessons in water color before now."

"Don't you mind that?" asked Magnus.

"Of course."

"Well, then, if the Academy Exhibition is the main chance, why not do three or four for it?"

Tom laughed and cast up his eyes.

"They take time, and time calls for money."

Magnus looked at him with excitement and said urgently,

"I've lost you a patron, the least I can do is see you get another. I'll help you. When you sell the pictures, pay me back. With what I won from George and baubles like these," he went on, pointing to his ruby studs, "I've over a thousand to be going on with."

Tom looked at Magnus with astonishment.

"You've never even seen my work."

"I'm no art critic. I'm sure Joseph Braithwaite's standards were exacting."

"But his taste's abominable."

"All the better," replied Magnus easily. "You satisfied him so you must be versatile." He called for another bottle of port and sat down in the chair next to Tom. "How do artists make money?"

"Society portraits or the sale of engraving rights." He paused and looked at Magnus almost angrily. "I can't take your money. I'd have left Braithwaite anyway. Of course I'd have liked a commission from Lady Goodchild, but I'm still better off than I've often been in the past."

"But you can't do what you want," objected Magnus. "You said that."

"How many people can?"

"That isn't at issue."

"But I'll tell you what is," cried Tom. "Everything changes if I take your money. Surely you see that?"

"Tom," murmured Magnus, shaken by his outburst, "I shan't need more than four hundred in the next year. I'll be starting a new career."

"Then you'll need everything you've got."

"Not if I succeed. If you're only worried about accepting anything from me in case I fail . . ."

"That isn't it at all."

"Then prove it by accepting my offer," said Magnus soothingly. "If I make a good living, the loan won't matter; if I don't, I'll have to try something else anyway. Look, if two people trying to do the same sort of thing stick together, the struggle must be easier. If you're ever in a position to lend me money, *I* won't refuse out of misplaced pride."

"Because you won't be me." Tom looked away. "I'll tell you the job I hated most. To pay my mother's doctor's bills I worked for a coach builder painting coats of arms and crests on carriage doors; I wonder if your father used to order from that firm? Of course I'm grateful to you, and I know there's no condescension in the offer, but it makes no difference."

Tom's blushing embarrassment considerably distressed Magnus who had never intended that he should feel in any way beholden to him.

"I can assure you," he said quietly, "that few younger sons take much pride in their position: too poor to marry in their own class, too snobbish to marry out of it, endlessly striving to keep up appearances on inadequate funds . . . Poor things, they have little reason to feel superior to anyone. Being one myself, I ought to know."

Magnus saw Tom's expression soften, but he still seemed perplexed.

"I could never accept unless you got something in return."

"I'll need somewhere to stay until I find rooms."

"Charlotte Street isn't St. James's," said Tom with a smile.

"Nor were the paddy fields of Ceylon."

Magnus caught Tom's eye and he smiled involuntarily.

"The stove smokes, the skylight leaks and the studio hasn't been cleaned out for years."

"I hate being tidy," laughed Magnus.

"Army officers have no servants to tidy for them?" asked Tom with quizzical amusement.

"They run their masters' lives. I like the idea of an independent existence." Magnus smiled. "I'm sure we could run to a maid of all work. See who's doing the begging now, Mr. Strickland."

Before Tom could answer, the landlord came in and announced that a lady had come to see Mr. Crawford. Moments later Tom and Magnus rose as Catherine entered. She recognized Tom's presence in the room by a slight inclination of the head and then turned to her brother.

"Magnus, I must speak with you."

"Of course, Kate," he replied, offering her a chair. She glanced meaningfully in Tom's direction, but Magnus refused the hint.

"Perhaps Mr. Strickland will excuse us," she said reluctantly.

"Unless what you have to say is . . ."

"Very well," she cut in impatiently. "Father's been asking why you haven't been home to see him."

"Dear father, can't he wait a little longer to tell me I'm a fool to have left Ceylon?"

"Couldn't he just want to see you? You were away a long time and he is your father."

"Then I'm sure he won't have forgotten that I went away because he wanted it."

Catherine was wearing a mantle of green and cream shot silk and Tom noticed the way she was twisting the fringed edge, as though nervous or upset.

"You still ought to come back, unless you want Charles to have everything his own way."

"He will anyway."

Magnus's bland replies infuriated Catherine. How easy for him to spend his time as he pleased, drinking with friends, going where he wished. She resented the fact that he had delayed his return to Leaholme Hall, when a moment's reflection would have told him that she would need his support on their father's homecoming.

"Charles has told father that I refused George because of your lies."

"And you set him right?"

"You know what he's like," she said with unconcealed exasperation, turning coldly to Tom. "You see what a united family we are, Mr. Strickland?" The sadness and anger in her voice made Tom wish that he had after all left the room. Magnus took his sister's arm.

"I'll come tomorrow, Kate. Now don't be so stern or Mr. Strickland will think you're always like it. Do you think Father might like to sit for his portrait? Thanks to me, Tom lost the opportunity to paint Mrs. Braithwaite."

"I'm not wholly disappointed," Tom replied softly.

Magnus thought for a moment and then smiled.

"She always reminds me, with those tight waists of hers, of a sausage tied in the middle, the meat moving where it may."

"Even the iron dictates of fashion cannot quite repeal the laws of nature," Tom answered with a smile.

"I heard that you were to paint Lady Goodchild," said Catherine abruptly.

"Her ladyship took another view of the matter." He turned to Magnus. "I should have told you, she wrote thanking me for riding out to Hanley Park that evening. Your brother, Miss Crawford, told me to go for her."

Catherine smiled briefly at Magnus.

"I fancy Charles might have needed less persuasion, or does Mr. Strickland not know about our brother's devotion to her ladyship?" She turned to Tom with mocking politeness. "But perhaps you do not share Charles's opinion of Lady Goodchild's looks? As an artist would you call her beautiful?"

"As an artist, I would like to have painted her."

Catherine laughed brightly.

"Artists like to paint all manner of things . . . cows by a river, ships at sea. You're very diplomatic, Mr. Strickland. Did you ever have dealings with George Braithwaite when you painted his father?"

"He talked to me sometimes."

"Did you think him the fool Magnus does?" she asked sharply.

"For God's sake, Kate," interrupted Magnus angrily. "How can you possibly expect an answer to that?"

"You refused to speak to me alone, so can have no secrets from him. Should he not repay the compliment?"

"I should not have stayed; I apologize, Miss Crawford." Tom bowed slightly and picked up his hat. Magnus jumped up.

"You were my guest and I made no such request and make none now. Accuse *me* of discourtesy, if you must, Kate."

Catherine sighed and lowered her head.

"Perhaps if you were at home with Charles and Father you might make some allowance, Magnus. I'm sorry, Mr. Strickland."

When Magnus returned from seeing his sister to her carriage, he stood in silence by the window for a moment.

"Unhappy people often say things they later regret."

"I'm not offended. Your sister thinks me her inferior and treated me accordingly."

"I'm sure not. She envies Helen Goodchild's freedom, resents me for neglecting her, felt humiliated at speaking about Father in front of you. I was a fool, but she chose her moment badly."

"It's kind of you to make excuses for her, but I really don't mind." Tom laughed suddenly. "Imagine if I were to fall in love with her and she with me. . . . I wonder what sort of a welcome your father would give me. Why pretend the world isn't as it is? While I was in Paris, a good many gentlemen who had read Murger's *La Vie de bohème* came to the ateliers to live like artists . . ."

"But they had plenty of money and the artists had none. Don't make things even worse than they are, Tom. If you think I'm as stupid, we may as well forget what I said earlier."

"Why should I?" asked Tom, smiling at Magnus. "Don't ask me why, but I've decided to accept your offer; nothing would be very different if I refused, except that I'd lose an opportunity. If you do come to Charlotte Street you'll hate it, but that's your affair."

"I see you've decided to take advantage of me because Catherine was rude to you."

"Perhaps, but really I can't remember why I thought of refusing. The wine, I think . . . I'm very grateful too."

Magnus shook his head, confused by Tom and yet pleased that he had changed his mind.

"Although, of course, I may ask you to paint my crest several times a day and expect you at all times to remain my most humble and obedient servant."

"Which is why I'm so grateful," muttered Tom with feigned servility.

"Deference in the blood."

"No escaping it, sir."

When Tom had gone, Magnus dozed in front of the fire. Occasionally noises from the tavern parlor or the stable yard roused him and he tried without much success to recall the precise manner in which Tom had made his decision. Instead he imagined he saw his pale alert face and sensitive eyes and was happy to think that they would soon meet again. In his mind he pictured the engine looming out of the morning mist and the roofs and chimneys of Rigton Bridge slipping away into the past, as the train, flying its long banner of smoke, sped across the soaring arches of the viaduct toward the open country. The recollection that he had promised to see his father only briefly interrupted his contemplation of the future.

⤚ Eighteen ⤙

On entering the library at Leaholme Hall, Magnus saw his father writing at the round table in the window. When Sir James rose and came toward him, Magnus's dominant feeling was embarrassment. As his father took his hands and gazed at him, he still could think of nothing to say. All the while he felt unpleasantly conscious of his sling and the gashes on his cheek and forehead.

"You've changed, Magnus, and I don't just mean your injuries."

"You look just the same," replied Magnus, aware of the banality of their greeting. Could they really do no better after seven years? As he looked at his father, he was not even sure that he had spoken the truth. Still the same thick gray hair, flecked with silver at the temples and side-whiskers; his mouth as firm, and his jaw as decisive—once again reminding Magnus of the sculpted heads of certain Roman emperors, with flawlessly chiseled features and short-cut hair brushed forward; but in his heavily lidded eyes there seemed a softer almost sad expression.

At first, while they spoke in safe generalities about the election riots and the strangeness of returning home after a long period away, Magnus's uneasiness persisted, but gradually it dawned upon him that his father also felt tense. One trait, which he remembered well, was the casualness with which his father wore civilian clothes: his cravat loosely tied, and a cream silk embroidered waistcoat worn with a faded morning coat. Fastidious in many ways, especially about punctuality, Sir James also had the slightly negligent air often possessed by men used to having everything done for them, and never exposed to any personal criticism. After a short silence, Sir James frowned and said in a low gruff voice,

"You still bear me a grudge, I daresay?"

"Because you sent me away?" The admiral nodded. "You paid my debts; I had no cause to complain."

Sir James, who had been resting against the table, stood up and shook out the tails of his coat.

"So you don't think I had too little sympathy for youthful weakness?"

"I don't think youth ever had much charm for you," replied Magnus with a smile. "Your own may have, but mine certainly never did . . . what little you saw of it anyway."

Sir James pursed his lips and gazed past Magnus at the vellum and calfbound books on the shelves on either side of the doors. His eyes looked distant and sad.

"I often thought if your mother had lived . . ." He broke off almost angrily and shook his head. "In life, like chess, one can't take back the moves already played." He sat down and absently drummed his fingers on the arms of his chair. "Charles says you're not going back to Ceylon."

"He's right," murmured Magnus, surprised that his father did not seem disturbed.

"I read your evidence to the commission and can't say I blame you, though it's a pity to lose so many years seniority in the service." He paused and looked at Magnus with sudden concern. "If you agree, I can probably get you something in the Foreign Office, a civil post . . . possibly in England. Not just influence you understand; your record in Ceylon was excellent."

"I was thinking of something rather different," said Magnus, certain, from the way his father raised his eyebrows with ironic surprise, that he had wanted to see him merely to persuade him to accept some quiet position from which he could cause no trouble in the future. "I'm thinking of journalism."

"To what purpose?" Sir James asked abruptly. Magnus met the searching gaze of his father's flinty blue eyes.

"The influence of the press on the course of public affairs is not negligible."

"Very true, and as often as not that influence is far from beneficial."

Magnus managed an unforced laugh.

"I'm sure you don't think I'll pander only to the most maudlin and vicious public taste."

"Charles expects you to write only in the Radical interest."

"I'll have to find employment before I can write in any interest."

Magnus, who had expected his father to press him on this point, was surprised when he said in an unmistakably conciliatory voice,

"You are not perhaps aware that those who have written most for the public press, and often with the nation's interests at heart, often live in obscurity and die in poverty. A briefless barrister may end a judge, a physician be knighted and come to five thousand a year. Not so the journalist, whose profession gives no social distinction and small financial reward. In society the occupation is not even avowed, except in private. A journalist may be feared, but never respected. I don't pretend to understand why this should be so, but know it to be true." He got up and walked across the room, turning by the antique globe next to a small pair of library steps, this habit of pacing about, Magnus supposed, deriving from the quarterdeck. "Few men are happy, Magnus, unless their efforts are properly appreciated and rewarded."

"I don't want social distinction or to avow my occupation in society, but I'm grateful for your opinion."

Sir James glanced at his son to see that he was not mocking him, but, encouraged by his apparent sincerity, said quietly,

"Allow me to make a proposition . . . treat it how you will. If you decide to pursue a career that I consider worthy of your abilities, I will provide you with sufficient capital to add a further five hundred per annum to your income. On my retirement from the active list, whenever that may be, I will add a further five hundred to that sum." He paused to give Magnus time to take this in. "Of course you will need to consider this."

"I reject it," Magnus replied without hesitation.

"You do?" Sir James stared at him with amazement. "May I ask why?"

It occurred to Magnus that during the past fifteen years, as post captain, ambassador and admiral, his father would have had few opportunities for any conversation other than with subordinates, and was therefore entirely unaccustomed to disagreement.

"I don't think my reasons would please you."

Sir James nodded, as though he had predicted this answer.

"Nor did your absence on my arrival and the discovery from Charles that you chose instead to stay in a posting inn."

"I hope he also told you what it feels like to travel on a country road with a broken shoulder."

"I accept that reason, and would still like to know why . . ."

"If Charles gets this estate and most of your capital, I am entitled to some capital of my own without conditions." Until Magnus had said this, he had not realized how angry he had become.

"There's some logic in that," Sir James conceded calmly. "But what's the use of my settling capital on you when you've never stuck at anything? Prove yourself, and then I'll think again."

His father's evident conviction that every word he had spoken was just and reasonable provoked Magnus almost to the point of screaming.

"When I was twenty," he whispered, "you cleared my debts and for that service I spent seven futile years on a distant island as a criminal might serve a sentence." His voice rose and shook as he said, "I will submit to no further conditions."

"You're perfectly entitled to do as you please, and so of course am I."

Magnus was trembling with rage as he walked to the door.

"Since you have chosen to speak of money . . . you may remember that when Mother died her capital became yours. Do you suppose *she* would ever have withheld my rightful share from me as a bribe to make me please her?" He breathed deeply, horrified that he felt exactly as he had done in his father's presence eight years before. "Your legal ownership of that money," he ended quietly, "gives you no moral right to keep it from me."

"My moral obligation to her is to see that you are saved from imbecile connections such as the one Charles tells me you formed with the *Rigton Independent*."

Magnus paused in front of the mahogany doors, knowing that he should leave before his anger led to a permanent estrangement. Finally he turned.

"I am to understand that if I pursue a secure career you will add to my security, but if I choose a precarious profession, you will guarantee me the poverty which you profess to be so eager to spare me? Like those excellent fathers who cut off with nothing those daughters who marry poor men and need help most."

Sir James listened impassively and turned the antique globe with a ringed finger.

"Forgive me if I reject your comparison," he replied with frigid and urbane politeness. "You have only to change your mind and to act in your own best interests for me to alter my attitude. I have not given you up. The harder the road, the more likely is the traveler to return. One day you will thank me." He looked at Magnus with sudden reproachfulness and pain. "I offered to use my influence on your behalf . . . proposed a capital settlement . . . Great heavens, must I now apologize for being at fault?"

"Of course not. You'd thought hard and long about what I should do; it was ungrateful and selfish of me to have views of my own."

Stung by his son's sarcasm, Sir James came toward him and held out his hands.

"Should a father not encourage a son to follow the course most likely to make him happy?"

The real perplexity with which this had been said calmed Magnus.

"People learn nothing from advice, Father, only from experience. I served the crown long enough to know I want other employment. Since you can't live my life for me, I must go my own way."

"Don't you mean to stay a few days?"

"No."

"Because we disagreed? A day or two and both of us may see matters quite differently." Sir James's tone was almost imploring.

"I intended to go anyway."

"Surely we can . . ." Sir James let his hands fall and looked away.

"What did you say about chess, Father?"

"The comparison was a stupid one."

"But moves can't be taken back, however long ago they were made. We both know that." Magnus opened the doors and looked back over his shoulder. "Look after Kate."

"I am not indifferent to her situation."

"I'm glad, Father."

From the landing Magnus heard his father call,

"When you've proved yourself . . ."

He sighed and shouted back,

"There are no admirals in Grub Street."

Magnus met Charles in the hall. To the right of the door was a trunk and several chests.

"Father going again so soon?" asked Magnus.

"I am ... tomorrow. Damned inquiry at Devonport."

"I'm glad I didn't miss you before you went, Charles. I wanted to thank you for all the helpful things you said to Father about me."

Charles met his eyes without embarrassment.

"I said nothing discreditable."

"Then I'm sure you won't find it discreditable if I tell you what I think of you." Magnus watched the blood rush to his brother's cheeks and asked mildly, "Do you loathe me, Charles?"

"Of course not."

"I could have sworn that my feelings for you were warmly reciprocated. You disappoint me."

"You've failed in a third-rate colony and I expect you'll fail again, but I don't loathe you. I pity you. You're eaten up with envy and bitterness."

"Envy of you, Charles?"

"Among others, yes."

Magnus smiled and said quietly,

"Please don't worry about my unhappiness, Charles. I'd rather be dead than change places with you. Come to think of it, complacency like yours is a kind of death. My father's distorted mirror image, at best a pale reflection, an eager ghost."

Charles walked to the door and said over his shoulder,

"Nothing I could say would damage you more than your own words."

"I wonder where you read that, Charles?" Suddenly Magnus laughed and went over to his brother. "I'm sorry. You did your best to blacken me with Father, but I don't suppose it made much difference. You talked about us being children. . . . Best forget. I hope you get a good command and the widow; I hope you get her too."

"Is there nothing *you've* ever wanted?" murmured Charles.

The unexpectedness of the question disturbed Magnus; it was not something he would have thought Charles capable of asking.

"Many things," he replied softly, realizing with a sense of shock that what first came to mind was to be a boy again, to do what he had told his father was impossible and take back past moves. To be hopeful and confident. To live in the protective mist of a child's half-formed imagination. Better by far to have Charles's crude ambitions than this yearning for a bright lost world. Without looking at his brother, Magnus walked past him.

"I must see Catherine."

Magnus found his sister in the blue morning room. She got up and came toward him, her gray silk dress rustling as she moved.

"I'm afraid my talk with Father went as might have been expected."

"Tell me," she murmured.

"He was reasonable according to his lights . . . I according to mine. There was no meeting." He took her hand for a moment and pressed it before letting it fall. "I'm afraid I've done you little good. I can understand why you felt angry with me yesterday."

"Can you, Magnus?"

Pretending not to have noticed the sad hint of reproach in her voice, he smiled.

"If I had to stay here, I think I'd murder one or other of them."

"Necessity is an excellent pacifier."

He remembered the terror of the future she had expressed on the evening he came to Leaholme Hall. The sight of her sad face and bright eyes filled him with grief.

"We'll see each other soon. You'll stay with Aunt Warren in London; we'll do lots of things."

"I should like that." She hesitated a moment and then said awkwardly, "I'm sorry I behaved badly to your friend." She lowered her eyes. "It's so stupid . . . I liked him, you see." She looked despondent but brightened. "Perhaps I'll have a chance to apologize to him in London."

"I expect so." Magnus was surprised by a definite feeling of reluctance and could not escape the conclusion that, though fond of his sister, he did not want her to become friendly with Strickland. She evidently sensed his misgiving but mistook his reason.

"Are you afraid I may make a fool of myself?" she asked with a reproving smile. "I like him. No more than that. So you needn't worry about Father's disapproval."

The teasing, almost coquettish way in which she had spoken irritated him.

"Father's disapproval never influenced me," he replied, looking at the

French clock on the mantelpiece. "I've a fly waiting," he said, raising his hands helplessly.

"Then you must go."

He did not move for a moment, but then, seeing her come toward him, he kissed her cheek and left the room.

In the departing fly, Magnus was still troubled by his reaction to his sister's interest in Tom, nor could he get Charles's question out of his mind. He thought of the perfect days when Charles and his father had been away at sea, and he living at home with his mother and Catherine: an age of innocence soon ended. Oxford. Some friends, bent on his initiation, had taken him to a notorious brothel. The girls, many of them no more than twelve or thirteen, had been lined up in a row, their expressions bored and listless. His friends lifted up skirts with their canes, prodded breasts and thighs, with as much delicacy as they might have shown inspecting horses for sale at a fair. The slang term for copulation then in vogue was to "spend," an appropriate one, Magnus thought. The customers had been separated from each other by thin partitions. Magnus had thought of animals mounting in a farmyard as he listened to the grunting and oaths of his friends and the whores' feigned squeals and moans of enjoyment. The smells, the blind gropings and the absence of all feeling, except a coarse and brutal hunger for flesh, sickened him. His friends laughed at him, but he did not return. Instead he had showed his nerve in other ways: by gambling and never hesitating to use his fists if insulted. The laughter had stopped, but his personal isolation had begun.

In Ceylon the same. Being attractive and thought richer than he was, he had been pursued by numerous daughters of army officers and planters, who clutched hysterically at every new arrival who seemed at all likely to fulfill their dream of marriage. He remembered pink faces shining with sweat and the touch of damp hot hands at regimental balls. In tropical heat the girls had still danced in seven or eight petticoats. Their trivial jealousies and constant obsession with clothes and etiquette had made them seem absurd and pathetic to Magnus when he recalled his mother's intelligence and serenity.

Some of his brother officers had married out of frustration and boredom; others had taken native mistresses. Magnus had found pleasure in renunciation, lonely at first, but in time deriving positive satisfaction from his self-sufficiency. He alone, the sheltered, cosseted boy, proved impervious to the isolation of remote surveying expeditions and to months away on outstations working on the colony's roads. This sense of completeness, of possessing everything within himself, had been his answer to his inability to find either desire or pleasure with women.

And now? he asked himself in the dark interior of the fly. At the first hint of a close friendship with Strickland, he had behaved with a child's possessiveness. But at least he knew the answer to Charles's question. What he wanted most was to end his long isolation—to recapture lost happiness through true friendship.

Nineteen

Two days after Charles's departure for Devonport, Sir James Crawford visited Hanley Park to call on his goddaughter. On entering the hall he was surprised by the absence of any visible signs of mourning. In fact the atmosphere at first reminded him of the air of bustle and preparation preceding a ball. Doors were open and servants hurrying back and forth, carrying china, dragging furniture aside and shouting instructions to each other. Only when he saw their faces did he realize that their task was not a happy one. While waiting for a maid to fetch the butler, he watched two grumbling footmen stagger past, supporting between them a large gilt-framed mirror surmounted by an eagle. Obviously the main reception rooms were being shut up.

The butler came down with the news that her ladyship was with her bailiff and her agent, but that Lord Goodchild would see Sir James at once. Although he had last seen Humphrey as a boy of nine, the shock of hearing him addressed by his new title passed quickly. Crawford followed the butler through a succession of cold, uncarpeted rooms, past shapeless stacks of furniture under brown hollands and dust sheets toward the library. Even the curtains and pictures had been taken down. Clearly this reduction of accommodation would be followed by a similar reduction in staff. That Goodchild had left debts did not surprise Sir James, but that these drastic economies should be needed, so soon after his death, seemed incredible. A feeling of pity for Helen was followed by one of anger with the dead man.

When Harry had proposed to Helen, Crawford, who had then often advised her widowed mother on many matters, had recommended refusal: a suggestion that had outraged both mother and daughter. Refuse a peer and a man of Lord Goodchild's wealth? He must be mistaken about the young man's character; further acquaintance would prove to him that Harry was anything but the coarse young rake his envious rivals might make him out to be. He was high spirited certainly; surely dashing manliness should not be condemned in one of his years? But Sir James, who had discovered that Goodchild had been scratched from the list of members at Almack's for "insulting" several members' wives—rumor had it that he had tried to rape one of them—had not been impressed. He did not deny that it was common enough for rich young peers to boast of never going to bed till nine each morning, but sensuality apart, he had thought he detected in Harry an arrogant cynicism which would preclude the humility required on the lower slopes of any worthwhile career. And Sir James considered nonfulfillment through pride, neglect and pleasure seeking, rather than through innate incapacity, the worst sin that a man of rank and wealth could commit: a sin against himself. For Crawford it still seemed as reprehensible for a peer to decline the political opportunities opened to him by his position, as for a sailor to desert his ship. But, as Sir James walked through the stripped and echoing rooms, he felt sorrow rather than satisfaction in witnessing so striking a vindication of the opinion he had expressed fourteen years before.

Humphrey walked across the library and held out a stiff hand to his visitor. Ever since early childhood he had been in awe of Sir James Crawford, and although he had seen him less than a dozen times in all his thirteen years, the impression made had been a deep one, less by what the great man had said than by what Humphrey had imagined his part to have been in actions worthy to be classed with those of Howe, Nelson and Collingwood. Sir James would have been surprised to hear that for Humphrey the Battle of Navarino, the Syrian War and the West African blockade evoked images as compelling as accounts of the Glorious First of June, and the battles of the Nile and Copenhagen. To be addressed as "my lord" and treated as an equal by such a man made Humphrey blush with pleasure. He still vividly remembered the day when the admiral had shown him his sketchbooks, full of drawings of places as far away as Valparaiso and Rio, Batavia and Penang.

After expressing condolences for his father's death, Sir James was at a loss what to say; to mention the activity he had witnessed below would merely be painful; instead he picked up the book Humphrey had been bent over when he entered: Book Four of Thucydides's *Peloponnesian War*.

"Did you know that Thucydides wrote an account of the Battle of Navarino?" he asked, knowing that the boy was interested in the action in which his grandfather had died.

Humphrey looked puzzled and embarrassed. Surely the admiral knew that the Greek historian had died two thousand years ago? Guessing his thoughts, Sir James told him how Sir Edward Codrington, being an amateur classicist, had pointed out to his captains, on the evening before the battle, that the Athenians had defeated the Spartans in Navarino Bay in the fifth century B.C.

"Not every admiral reads his captains Thucydides before an action, but that's what we were treated to. The Athenians hemmed in the Spartan fleet between the mainland and the island of Sphakteria; so Codrington wanted us to do the same. We even sounded the channel but found it was too shallow. A pity, we might have attacked the Turks on both sides of their line."

"Like Nelson at the Nile," cut in Humphrey, eager to show his knowledge. Sir James smiled.

"Not quite; that was a great victory against a far more formidable enemy. If you like I'll show you what happened."

Needing no further encouragement, Humphrey held out paper and a pen. Sir James quickly drew in the outline of the coast and islands and then started on the ships.

"Your grandfather was here in *Asia*, here I am in *Philomel*, Bathurst in *Genoa*, and *Dartmouth* . . ."

He looked up and saw Helen smiling at him; she had evidently been watching for some moments. He took in her widow's cap and tight-waisted black dress.

"James, the fools didn't tell me it was you till a moment ago. Forgive me." She inclined her face for his formal kiss. "I'm sure Humphrey would hang onto you all day if I let him."

"We'll go on another time," Sir James assured the boy with a conspiratorial wink, implying that women never appreciated the importance of tactics and battles but that they two knew better. Then wishing him good luck with his translation, Crawford followed Helen from the room.

She led him to a small sitting room dominated by a boulle table covered with letters, notes and account books, and motioned to him to sit on a chesterfield by the window.

"My poor Helen, that it should come to this . . . My dear girl, I am so sorry."

She looked down and sat on the ottoman opposite. No answer was possible or expected. She knew that his sympathy embraced not only her husband's death, but the sadness of her marriage and her present difficulties. Since her wedding she had seen little of her godfather, but enough for him to have realized her unhappiness. Nor would she now have to explain about debts and mortgages for hours before he would believe her pessimism justified.

"When will you leave here?" he asked at last.

"When we have somewhere smaller to go to. It's not yet certain whether the house must be sold, or whether a tenant will suffice. The estates, it seems, have been as badly managed as it is possible to imagine." She smiled and murmured, "I am sure it is no surprise to you." He said nothing but shook his head slightly. "I often thought of the advice you gave me—when it was too late." But then in spite of the gloominess of what she was saying, she felt happy. Seeing Sir James again reminded her vividly of the years before she married. Unlike men of fashion he retained the short Roman hairstyle now replaced by close curled and waved hair. Nor did he care that the "Osbaldiston" necktie was rarely worn by the beau monde. He kept what he liked and added any new style to his wardrobe if it pleased him. Helen remembered that this had been his habit in her childhood and recalled her mother's indignation that Sir James ruined the pockets of beautifully cut coats with an assortment of papers, bank notes and coins. "That manservant of his is useless; he needs a wife," she had often said, after he had become a widower; and Helen had known very well that her mother would have liked to have become the second Lady Crawford. Helen had always admired her godfather's casual attitude to clothes and appearances, thinking it the hallmark of a man of the world to be confident enough to consider an outfit or an opinion invulnerable simply because he assumed it. He entered society as a visitor from a rougher more demanding world and saw no need to make concessions. His ease in any company, she believed, sprang from his having had no permanent home for so long; he could make himself comfortable in any temporary place. She had never been deceived by the sleepy, nonchalant look his heavy eyelids gave him;

often she had noticed a keen darting glance of his blue eyes under his thick gray eyebrows and a slight flicker of amusement or disdain if he were being treated to a pompous or dull speech. Many people had spoken of him as cold and indifferent but this, she was sure, was because they never watched him closely.

"Tell me about the great world," she said after a silence.

"Doing excellently well without me."

"For long?" she asked, lifting her hands in a show of astonishment.

"I fear so."

"Truly?" she whispered, all flippancy gone.

"Palmerston will get back, but not to the Foreign Office, and the first lord has little regard for me."

"First lords come and go."

"So do admirals, but being so numerous, they mainly go."

"Can Palmerston really do nothing for you?"

"Not if I ask at the wrong time."

"But at the right time?"

"Perhaps." He smiled carelessly. "But there are probably better things than satisfied ambition."

"For an admiral?" she murmured.

"I think even for them." She was looking at him questioningly. "The gift of understanding my children would be no mean blessing. The other evening I was foolish enough to suppose that Magnus might like to hear my opinion on his future plans. I was mistaken. But then even those who ask advice rarely follow it." He sighed and shook his head. "But why you should submit to my trivial woes I have no idea." He got up and looked down at her. "If you should ever want to talk to me, send and I shall come. And I promise that I have got over the desire to advise, help, suggest or any such folly."

She got up and came toward him.

"I remember once when you were very cross with me over Harry, you said that nobody was worth anything until life had crushed the conceit and optimism out of them."

"I must have been feeling my age at the time. But now I've become quite as young and foolish as the rest." He shut his eyes for a moment, pained by the recollection. "Crushed did I say? Oh, dear. You must have been particularly pert and insufferable that day."

"Life was very different then."

James nodded and picked up his cane, remembering a young girl in a loose flowing dress with the low décolletage so favored at the time, her eyes glowing with excitement and pleasure, and Harry Grandison's glistening phaeton at the door, complete with crested panels and two perfectly matched black horses. Later, the red plush of a box at the opera, or the bare shoulders and flashing diadems at a ball. A country girl narrowly brought up by a naval officer's widow. Could he ever have imagined she would follow his advice? Picnics of plovers' eggs, prawns and aspic jellies washed down with champagne; young men with polished boots and flowered waistcoats kissing primrose gloves to her in the Row. What a fool he must have been to have tried to dissuade her. And now still beautiful, but pale and careworn; what an impossibly different situation ahead of her. Leaving the room he smiled at her and said,

"When I come next, I should prefer it if you did without your cap."

She laughed aloud and took it off at once.

"My badge of widowhood. Gladly." She took a comb from her hair and shook it free so that it fell to her shoulders. Then she touched the jet brooch which fastened the high collar of her black dress. "My dressmaker tells me that jet trimmings are now considered elegant with full mourning." Sir James recognized the bitterness in her voice, but felt unable to say openly that he understood the cause. Instead he murmured,

"Your life will not remain empty for long."

"It will take a veritable Sir Galahad to burden himself with my debts and anxieties, let alone with my poor boy."

Crawford took her by the arm and led her across to the pier glass.

"Look at yourself, Helen."

She stared at her reflection for a moment and smiled.

"Was this the face that launched a thousand ships, and burnt the topless towers of Ilium?" She took his hand and squeezed it. "You're very kind, James, more than I deserve."

"If reason really governed our actions, there would be no love, no courage and no despair. Men in spite of all that's said are less rational than women. You'll see."

On his way out, they paused in the center of the marble-paved hall.

"You've done me good, James." Suddenly she laughed. "What were those expressions that used to amuse me so? The way sailors talk of women's eyes?"

"Her toplights made my heart jump like a brig's boom in a calm."

"A little loose in stays," cried Helen. "I remember that best."

Sir James looked slightly embarrassed.

"Expressive, I suppose; some women, like some ships, don't come around quickly."

"Promise me, James. You'll come soon and make me laugh?"

"I'll try."

She watched him put on his hat and go out to his coach. Looking back, Sir James saw her solitary figure small under the massive portico. From a single chimney, that belonging to the room where they had sat, a thin ribbon of smoke was rising into the chill air. He stared glumly across the misty park at the bare trees and suddenly smiled. Like a brig's boom in a calm.

Twenty

Charles Crawford returned to Leaholme Hall from Devonport two days before Christmas and learned, as he had feared he would, that Helen Goodchild had left Hanley Park to stay with her sister-in-law until the New Year. Nevertheless his disappointment was softened by the news that during his absence his father had seen Helen regularly. As soon as Catherine had told him this, Charles had jumped to the optimistic conclusion that Helen, with her usual astuteness, was making herself pleasant to his father in order to undermine the numerous objections which he might raise should his eldest son and heir appear keen to connect himself with a widow whose financial prospects were so uncertain. During his reluctant stay in the West Country, Charles had thought a great deal about his chances and had become increasingly hopeful. Few eligible men would take at once to a woman of thirty-three with a thirteen-year-old son and enough assignments, mortgages and debts to keep several hardworking solicitors busy for years. In fact, even Charles had entertained doubts about the wisdom of marrying, until George Braithwaite had told him that less than ten thousand had been raised on Hanley Park itself before Goodchild's death.

After dinner on the day of his return, Charles and his father sat drinking port at the horseshoe table in front of the fire in the dining hall. Moments like these Charles cherished above all others: the vast room lit by a dozen candelabra and the glow of the fire, his father at his side, nodding at what he said and listening carefully. After Charles had regaled him with the technical details of the inquiry and the case against the inspector of machinery at the dockyard, he mentioned that Admiral Phipps Hornby, the second sea lord, had chaired the commission.

"Privately he told me he thought it scandalous that no further employment had been offered you."

"Most kind," replied Sir James ironically. "A pity Northumberland, like most first lords, is deaf to any voice but his own."

"His Grace won't last long. Derby's administration can't survive the next budget."

To Charles's surprise, these words, which he had intended to comfort his father, only made him angry, but the mood was short-lived. Sir James turned to his son with a smile.

"If a man's on the shelf and no spring tide will get him off, he must try something else."

"Superintendent at a dockyard?" asked Charles.

"Damn dockyards." He pushed back his chair and assumed a heroic pose. "How do I strike you?"

"I'm sorry . . . ?"

"My looks, man."

"Little changed," replied Charles with evident confusion. Vanity had never been one of his father's traits, but possibly disappointment would lead to unexpected eccentricities.

"Changed from what? How old would you say?"

"Forty-five. Maybe a year or two more."

"But not fifty-three?"

"Definitely not."

Sir James relaxed and became thoughtful. After a long silence he turned to Charles.

"Whatever I look, I *feel* far older. Just recently it's as if I always have a dead weight on me, the sensation that a great misfortune had just happened or is about to happen to me. I used to have a peculiar elasticity of spirits which resisted constant strain and pressure for long periods without losing its spring. But it's not so now—the spring is gone, quite gone."

Charles could have sustained no greater shock had Sir James told him that he had decided to become a missionary or begin a career in trade. The quality he had most admired in his father was his refusal to give in to pessimism or self-pity, whatever his problems. The confession embarrassed him too, more, he guessed, than would have been the case had his father admitted to immorality or drunkenness. Nevertheless, he felt tears in his eyes.

"You mentioned doing something else."

"I shall be direct with you. Age and experience allow me a degree of honesty which youth rarely permits itself—I want a wife." Charles felt an unpleasant falling sensation in his stomach as he tried to smile. His father looked down at the surface of the table. "I did not expect the news to please you. You may be assured that if I marry and children follow, your inheritance will not be materially affected."

"That was not in my mind. Only that, after so long. . . ."

"No fool like an old one," replied his father. "You must speak your mind, Charles. Nobody else will."

"If you are sure that it would contribute to your happiness, you must marry."

"Who can be sure of that? Marriage, like shipbuilding, is at best an experimental science." He looked at Charles intently and said in a low voice, "You would not turn against me?"

"Never."

"I must be sure. Magnus first and then you. It would be a high price to pay."

"I swear it."

Sir James filled his son's glass and they drank, as if sealing their trust and unity.

"After your mother's death, I felt a great emptiness and then thought it had gone; I was wrong. Absorption with my work only patched over the damage and hid it from me." He stared into the flames of the fire. "Of course at my age, youth's *couleur de rose* has faded, but there should be some bright lights left, some vividness remaining in the landscape—not just an unending gray haze. Even gratified ambition is stale and unprofitable if unshared. Only the affections bring brightness to the void. I not only wish to marry—I must."

Charles coughed uneasily, and shuddered when he thought what Magnus might have made of "youth's *couleur de rose*" if it had ever come to his ears.

"Have you talked to Catherine?" he asked.

"Not yet. She can only benefit if I am more in society."

Charles ran his fingers down the side of the decanter and said hesitantly,

"The lady? You have met . . . ?"

Sir James nodded.

"I have not yet asked her, although I think she may accept . . . in time. I fear I already hope too much—unwisely. You see with her I have glimpsed what I thought lost forever." He shook his head and smiled self-deprecatingly. "Laugh at me for a commonplace fool—she makes me feel young."

"And she *is* younger?" murmured Charles, with an agonizing presentiment.

"Little older than you." And then Charles knew. Who else but her? Who else? A spasm of nausea and then a desire to scream. Sir James did not notice the color drain from his son's cheeks, nor see the deliberate movement that upset the decanter. Charles leaped to his feet, muttering apologies. Port dripped down his shirt front, staining his waistcoat and trousers. His father rang for the butler, but Charles said that he would have to change. In his bedroom, he slammed the door and flung himself face downward on the counterpane, but he did not weep nor make any sound. How could he admit his own feelings now, after what his father had told him? Could he tell him that he had indeed hoped too much, that no father had the right to steal a son's happiness in pursuit of his own? He had had a wife and children already, had known a life that was not empty of affection, and now should he expect his son to stand aside for him to be given a second youth at that son's expense? Charles heard his father saying, "You would not turn against me?" Recalled the great weight of depression he had described; and as Charles remembered his own promise of loyalty, he knew that he could not now say what he should have said before. A lifetime of hero worship and emulation could not suddenly be ended and turned to enmity. For no other man or woman on earth could he have made the renunciation he was now planning. He imagined his father breaking down and weeping years later when he discovered the sacrifice that had been made on his behalf. And then suddenly he sat up and stared in front of him in amazement. Just as he had assumed Helen to be prepared to marry him, he had now assumed that she would accept his father. She could refuse—probably would if he asked too soon, before she had been disappointed by neglect and loneliness. Nor would his father be likely to wait long. Of course, for he himself then to approach a woman who had rejected his father would be a hard thing to do, but he would be patient, and careful not to disclose his intention until Sir James had found another woman or gained a new command. Probably Helen had no idea that her godfather regarded her as a potential wife; when she heard she would be horrified. The thought of his father suffering such a humiliation made Charles forget his own troubles for a moment. Given Sir James's state of mind, he ought to be protected from such an event. While dressing, Charles decided what he would do, what he now firmly believed to be his duty. When he returned to the dining hall, he was calm again. He sat down and smiled at his father.

"Forgive my clumsiness. But at least it has given me time to think who it can be."

"And have you guessed?"

"You mean to marry Helen. I applaud your choice."

"Thank you." He studied Charles carefully to try to gauge his real feelings. "Probably you think twenty years is a great disparity?"

Charles shrugged his shoulders.

"As you yourself said, marriage, like shipbuilding, is at best an experimental science."

Sir James laughed, delighted that Charles seemed able to joke about what he had feared might disturb him.

"My analogy was unfortunate. In fact I feel we have certain advantages. We've both suffered in different ways; and then women who've suffered at the hands of a young man often see much to commend the kindlier, less dramatic qualities of an older one. I also have the advantage of having had children of my own." Charles looked puzzled. "A man who does not understand a mother's love might fear a child from a previous marriage as a rival. I believe the boy likes me, and that will count for something."

"And she herself?" asked Charles, as naturally as he knew how. "Has she given any sign . . . ?"

"I have an instinct, no more than that."

Charles nodded attentively, careful not to betray the definite relief this caused him.

"When will you ask her?"

"When the right moment comes," Sir James replied with an enigmatic twinkle of amusement at Charles's curiosity. "Would you like to tell me when my stars will be right? Perhaps I ought to let a phrenologist feel my bumps." He got up and took his son's arm. "Catherine will think we have forgotten her."

Leaving the room, James stopped Charles and said warmly,

"I am a lucky man to have a son with whom I may talk freely of such things."

* * *

On a clear, crisp January morning, Charles rode through Flixton, apparently in the direction of Hanley Park, but a mile beyond the village he turned left onto the Trawden road and dismounted at a small bridge. Sitting on one of the coping stones, he listened to the stream flowing noisily over a bed of flat rocks. The sun was warm for the time of year and had brought out a number of birds, and Charles noticed some primroses in flower across the water. In the surrounding fields the winter wheat was already covering the bare earth with a pale green film. He pulled out his watch and then glanced anxiously up the road.

Some twenty minutes after his arrival, a dogcart swung into view between the high hedges. The driver was a lady in a dark green habit and a black beaver hat with a veil. Charles raised his own hat and jumped down from his seat on the side of the bridge. Helen reined in her bay mare and waited for Charles to come over to her; she looked flushed and irritated.

"Forgive this irregularity, Helen. I did not want it to be known that we had met."

Her color deepened and she twisted the reins.

"Am I permitted to know the reason for this strange reticence?"

"My father called on you several times before Christmas." She nodded impatiently when he hesitated. His mouth felt dry and his chest constricted. When he went on he spoke rapidly as if to get over a matter too awkward to dwell upon. "My father has recently come to entertain feelings for you, which I fear may prove unwelcome if openly expressed."

"Then do not express them," she replied sharply.

"The matter has become sufficiently important to him to make me dread the effects of disappointment."

She said nothing for a moment; Charles studied her face but learned nothing from it.

"What is your suggestion?" she asked quietly.

Charles blushed and looked down at his polished riding boots.

"Suggestion? It is not for me to guess your feelings in this."

Helen frowned and let her whip fall on her lap.

"Forgive me, Charles," she replied with a forced smile, "but you have already done so. Your fear is that he will be disappointed."

"A fear—precisely. No more than that."

A thrush was singing loudly in the hedgerow; the mare had started to crop the grass at the side of the road. Helen caught Charles's eye.

"I admire your concern, but think it is misplaced. Would you have welcomed his intrusion had your positions been reversed?"

"The desire to spare another humiliation and pain is not an ignoble one. I think your ladyship has misunderstood my intentions."

She held out a conciliatory hand and got down from the box to be at the same level.

"Charles, what am I to do? Refuse to see him unless I intend to marry him? It would be a hard life in which a woman had to turn away every man she did not intend to make her husband." She smiled. "And if she did so, how would she ever know who might suit her, or give that eligible visitor a chance to make himself plain?"

He had listened carefully but had not understood her words; instead his only desire was to tell her that he loved her, to go down on his knees on the grass in front of her and admit his hypocrisy. Say that no words would make him happier than to hear her laugh at the thought of marrying Sir James, that the only purpose of their meeting was for him to discover that he could still hope. She took his hand and whispered,

"I am not unkind, Charles. I will never knowingly hurt your father. You have my word."

"Thank you."

He paused momentarily before walking back toward the bridge.

~ *Twenty-One* ~

In the weeks following her meeting with Charles, Helen noticed nothing different in Sir James's behavior. His visits became no more frequent, neither did his manner seem less relaxed. Without appearing to be making efforts to do so, he fitted in with her moods. When she wished to talk, he was an excellent listener, if she seemed tired, he would make his visit a short one, and when she was depressed he usually managed to divert her with lighthearted reminiscences. One story she had particularly enjoyed had concerned an event in the year after Waterloo, when Sir James had been a midshipman in a frigate stationed in the West Indies. The first lieutenant, who hated the captain, had been rebuked by him for the slackness of the entry-port guard, and had been ordered not to call the same guard again. While the captain was ashore, his subordinate got together twenty-five afterguard and placed them on their hands and knees like horses with swabs for tails and manes, and mounted mizzen-topmen on their backs all armed with cutlasses. Last of all he himself clambered onto the quartermaster, both of them in full dress with cocked hats and swords. This guard received the captain at the entry-port with the usual honors on his return aboard. Having saluted with his sword, the first lieutenant deferentially inquired whether the captain found a cavalry guard more to his satisfaction than the old one. His sense of humor had cost him three years seniority. Humphrey also enjoyed such anecdotes, although, as Helen was aware, he was always disappointed that Sir James so rarely talked about fighting.

By the middle of March, Helen was beginning to wonder whether Charles had been mistaken about his father's intention. But by then Charles had been ordered to Shoeburyness to take part in gunnery trials aimed at discovering the relative resistance of wooden and iron ships to explosive shells, so she had not been able to question him. Through February and March, Helen's attitude to Sir James was ambivalent. She was fond of him certainly, but at times doubted whether this went much beyond the affection and admiration a young girl might feel for a favorite uncle. Her previous relationship complicated rather than simplified matters. She had entertained a particular image of him for so long that now she could not dispel it sufficiently to see him afresh. Often she felt certain that his age was of no account—certainly he did not look old—but at other times she felt unsure. Remembering her overwhelming love for Harry in the early days of her marriage to him, there were occasions when she longed to recapture that same self-annihilating passion. But probably, she told herself, she was no longer capable of love so intense. After twelve years of unhappiness, could any woman hope to feel more for anybody than affection and companionship? Only the young could idealize people enough to love them with that strange mixture of selfless and self-absorbed intensity she recalled so well. Without her past innocence and her blind faith in the future, Helen was certain that she could never have loved Harry as she had. And now, was she too scarred by disillusion, ever again to possess the reckless courage needed for that unthinking leap into the unknown which was the prelude to all great love?

Usually she was prepared to think herself truly past such emotion, and this helped her to see Sir James as a possible husband; yet even then her memories of that other love kept her doubts alive. Only when he went to London in early April and stayed there a month did she discover more positive feelings. His absence taught her how much she had come to rely on his presence. She felt lonely and adrift, and Humphrey too seemed morose. Before his departure her godfather had spoken about his unease over the situation in the eastern Mediterranean. He had said nothing about having been summoned by the foreign secretary or the first lord, but with Derby recently gone, and Palmerston in Aberdeen's new cabinet, she had little doubt that this was what had happened. His part in the Syrian War and then his years in Greece would inevitably make him one of the few men in the country with a detailed firsthand knowledge of the origins of the crisis between Turkey and Russia. Realizing this, it took her little time to conclude that Sir James might suddenly be sent to Constantinople as a diplomat or to the Black Sea as a flag officer. She was amazed to find herself frightened by this possibility, especially since there had been days when she had dreaded his making the proposal which Charles had predicted; but now that it seemed he might leave the country, perhaps for several years, she was bitterly disappointed that he had made no mention of marriage. She mocked herself for being suddenly overwhelmed by Sir James's new power and influence, but knew that this was insignificant in comparison with the simple fear of losing him. She even reproached herself for ever having thought that she might have done better. From that day onward, although it was not her usual habit, she read the papers thoroughly the moment the butler brought them in, still warm from being ironed.

*   *   *

On a sunny day in early May, Sir James called at Hanley Park as though he had never been away. He had brought a new sketchbook, and soon after arriving he suggested with an easy smile that if Helen could face a stern artistic test, she might care to come with him to draw the buds of the unfolding beech leaves. Still laughing at so precise a choice of subject, Helen put on a bonnet, and while a footman brought two chairs and her maid hurried off to fetch her parasol and watercolors, she walked out across the fresh green of the lawn. With the servants following, they headed for the woods on the far side of the meadow skirting the eastern shore of the lake. She lifted her black skirt as they reached the rough grass, and he took her arm, pointing out the golden celandine and buttercups near the water. Occasional butterflies floated past, and as they came closer to the trees birdsong grew louder.

When a suitable clearing had been found, the servants placed the chairs where required and withdrew. Sir James picked some purple flowers from the boughs of an ash tree and looked at the blossom; then with a slight sigh he let the twigs fall and sat down to begin his work on the beech buds on the tree facing him. Helen sat too and watched him choose a pencil and begin to draw. She could imagine the impeccable if lifeless representation that would finally emerge. Sir James, like many naval officers, owed his skill to a training that had included compulsory sketching of coastlines for purposes of recognition. She started a perfunctory sketch of the whole clearing but without enthusiasm; for her, drawing had never been more than a socially expected accomplishment. Five minutes later Sir James saw her come toward him.

"James, I really can't sit drawing beech tress until you've told me what you did in London."

"I saw Sir James Graham and Lord Clarendon among others, and a great relief it is to be here again."

"Can things be so bad that you cannot speak of them?"

In the distance they heard the sounds of a gun: a keeper shooting rooks. Helen had learned enough from the newspapers to know the gravity of the Eastern crisis and to understand that the dispute over the guardianship of the Holy Places was merely a pretext for a possible invasion of Turkey by Russia. Even in her father's lifetime, Helen remembered naval officers talking heatedly about the Czar's ambition to dismantle the crumbling Turkish empire and seize Constantinople, the gateway to the Mediterranean. Sir James frowned.

"Nothing's too bad to talk about until the worst's actually happened." He smiled at her and then continued with his drawing.

"If the Russians invade Turkey," she went on doggedly, "will we fight to stop them controlling the Bosphorus?"

"Hand them the eastern Mediterranean on a plate and Constantinople with it? We've not come to that, I trust."

"So there'll be war if the Czar invades?"

Sir James put down his pencil and gazed across the clearing at a vivid patch of forget-me-nots.

"Undoubtedly."

"But will he?" she asked, finally losing patience.

"Not if we send the fleet to the Bosphorus tomorrow and promise to declare war the moment the first Russian soldier crosses the Danube." He closed his eyes for a moment and sighed. "That might be enough to deter them, but the cabinet's divided about whether to threaten or conciliate. At the moment we're doing just enough to annoy the Czar and nothing like enough to scare him." From quite close they heard the clear inconsequential notes of a cuckoo. "The damned bird's right, I fear."

Helen felt suddenly irritated by his weary fatalism.

"If members of the cabinet disagree with the prime minister's policy, they should resign."

"Quite useless until the public is prepared for war; it'll take a little persuading that Turkey is worth defending."

His dismissive tone hurt her. Either he found the subject too painful to talk about, or he thought her incapable of understanding even the broad outlines of the situation.

When he had finished his sketch, they walked deeper into the wood, the damp leafy soil deadening their footsteps. Only when she saw the dark shadows under his eyes and the hunted preoccupied expression of his face did she sense that he was probably involved personally in the government's deliberations. All around them the ground was dappled with sunlight, filtering golden-green through the delicate canopy of pale new leaves. Helen did not bother to hitch up her cumbersome bombazine skirt, caring little if it caught on briers or brambles. But for most of their walk among the silver-gray trunks of the ancient beeches, there was little impeding undergrowth. Sir James pointed to the moss-covered roots of one of these patriarchal trees and said with an apologetic smile that they reminded him of anchors mooring a ship. Here and there cowslips and bluebells were still in bloom, merging with patches of white ransoms and purple wood anemones. He turned to her and glanced around contentedly, as if responsible for the mass of spring flowers and the gentle crooning of the wood pigeons in the branches above. Certainly without him she would never have visited the beech woods in this their most beautiful season, and yet the calling birds and the gentle rustling of the leaves did not dispel her feelings of anxiety and dissatisfaction. She understood his enjoyment of nature after the stresses of his time in the citadels of power, but for her there were too many unanswered questions to derive pleasure from the pale windflowers and the swooping lapwings. They had stopped to watch some swarming bees finding new quarters in a hollow tree when she took his arm and asked diffidently,

"What will you do, James?"

"Bees never cease to amaze me; the survival of that entire swarm bound up in the queen and all the others blindly following and dying just as blindly when their work is done." He turned over a mossy stone with the tip of his cane and said without looking up, "My lords commissioners are sending me to Constantinople. The Admiralty wants me to be a direct link with Stratford, cutting out the Foreign Office."

Lord Stratford de Redcliffe's reputation was well known to Helen, not only as Her Majesty's ambassador to Turkey, but also as a man of outstanding ability and arrogance, notorious alike for his independence and his hatred of Russia. Sir James's position would be a delicate one.

"Will Lord Stratford approve of the arrangement?" she asked.

"Strangely enough he wants me himself—to advise on what the navy can do as the situation develops. If Admiral Dundas says the fleet can't do something, I'm meant to be able to explain away any disagreements that may follow—a sort of go-between; it'll be little short of disastrous if Dundas and Stratford don't understand each other."

"When do you go?"

"I'm expected to sail on the twentieth."

"I'm very pleased for you."

"Strange, isn't it? One day an unemployed flag officer and the next a glorified naval attaché. With my experience in the area, I'd have had to have been half imbecile for them to have found no use for me."

She shook her head and smiled sadly.

"You needn't be so modest. I'm not a complete fool."

"All right; I'm going to preserve the peace single-handed and if necessary win the war if there is one."

Helen pursed her lips and turned away in mock exasperation. As they walked back in the direction of their clearing, she said in a low anxious voice,

"Humphrey's been talking about joining the navy."

Sir James raised an eyebrow slightly and nodded.

"But now there may be a war, you want to put him off?"

"If he was your only son . . .?"

"I should encourage him."

"Even if he might be killed?" she whispered, amazed by his reply.

"The Russians won't risk a general action with a combined French and British fleet."

"How can anybody be sure of that? The Turks fought a fleet from three nations at Navarino. You know very well how many men died there."

"The Russians will stay in Kronshtadt and Sevastopol. The Turks *had* to fight at Navarino."

"Their fleet might be caught at sea."

"Then he would be present at a great victory."

"Or die at one," she cried, refusing to accept his certainty.

"So I must try to dissuade him," he said with a sigh.

Helen looked away. She had not expected him to take up so rigid a position and she was shaken by it. She had supposed that he would see that without Humphrey she would be quite alone. How could any woman who had lost her father in a naval battle welcome the possibility of an only son suffering the same fate? The thought made her sick with fear. She said urgently,

"It's a hard life and he ought to know it. Can a boy of thirteen, who's read some of Marryat's books and a few of Kingston's boy's adventures know what to expect?"

"I'll talk to him."

"He's been completely sheltered. If he had been to a public school or seen something of the world, I might feel differently."

They walked on again in silence until they reached the clearing. Sir James sat down on his chair and rested his chin on a hand. Then he sat up straight and met her eyes.

"Am I honestly to tell the boy not to enter the service, which I am sure offers the finest career a man can follow? Charles was a volunteer of the first class at Humphrey's age and I wept when his ship sailed; but I would not have prevented him for all the world." He stared at the ground and then said quietly,

"If you wish me to, I will try to discourage him." She came up to him and kissed him on the cheek. He felt the moisture of tears, but could not bring himself to say anything to condone what she had made him promise.

"Thank you. Thank you. I know you think me weak, but I know him, he is not like Charles or you. He is . . ."

"Your son, and you cannot live his life for him." He was about to add more when he thought of his own failure with Magnus and fell silent. Instead he said, "Charles will be made post captain in a month or two and would have been entitled to nominate the boy as a cadet. He could have sailed with Charles."

"When you were alone, you had your work. I am not so fortunate. And soon you will be gone." Helen expected this confession of dependence to draw him out, but instead he asked with a hint of self-mocking regret,

"Do you really think you will find it hard to supply that loss?"

"Do l seem so insincere to you?" she asked with real pain.

"You will spend time in London, and then soon enough you will find that women with your looks are rarely allowed to be lonely, even should they wish to be."

"Would you rather I did not miss you?" she murmured.

"Everybody is flattered to be missed."

"You know very well I did not mean what I said as flattery," her voice a mixture of indignation and sadness. He said nothing for over a minute and then moved tentatively toward her, his eyes filled with tenderness.

"If you really mean that . . . marry me, Helen."

She had anticipated the moment for two months, and yet now that it had come, she was shocked to silence.

"What have I to offer you?" she whispered.

"Yourself. What more can any of us give? Can I provide line-of-battle ships and diplomatic missions for your amusement? These things are only hindrances since they will take me from you."

"I am no great hostess with influence and cachet."

"And for that reason I value you the more." He paused and took her hands. "If you wish to refuse me, do so honestly without any pretense that you are unworthy of me."

"I shall write with my answer."

"In ten days I shall be gone." He picked up his sketchbook and sighed. "Had you never thought that I might ask you?" She nodded and blushed. "But now you must have time?" He brushed a fly from his face. "A short delay never softens a rejection, but by anticipation increases the blow when it falls."

Helen's confusion was complete. An hour before, it seemed, she would have accepted him at once. But an hour before she had not known that he would be leaving the country so soon, nor guessed the nature of his response to Humphrey's intention. She bowed her head and said in a low voice,

"I am not keeping you waiting because of any thought that it is more delicate and decorous not to consent at once. I do not know."

They walked from the woods in silence and took a narrow path along the side of the lake. Before turning toward the house, he stopped, and looking out across the sparkling water, said, almost as if speaking to himself,

"In the past when I thought about marriage, I usually laughed at myself as a fine example of that tendency in middle-aged men to make themselves ridiculous." Helen said nothing as she stared down at their reflections in the water, rippling and dissolving in the gentle breeze. "I was governed, I suppose, by the suspicion that others would think me too old for love. I thought this a true estimate, until my visits here." He turned to her and went on earnestly with no trace of his former reflective tone. "You see I am lucky enough not to feel obliged to marry for any reason other than affection; and with you on those grounds I have no doubt."

"And yet," she replied quietly, "you know that I am not so lucky."

"Yes. And I know too that there are many richer and younger men who might bring you far greater benefit." He smiled at her tenderly. "Love is rarely so overwhelming as to obliterate all other considerations; I would feel suspicious of any love that professed to do so—especially any love for a man of my years."

She stood twisting the strings of her bonnet, lost in thought. Whenever she had imagined him speaking about marriage, she had always thought in terms of what *she* would say; but he had said most and had changed the basis of discussion in a way she had not anticipated. She had never thought that her main preoccupation would be with an absolute honesty. Yet though she was tempted, she found herself unable to make easy answers.

"I feel fondness and affection for you . . . but if love alone is to be your reason . . . I fear we are not suited."

"Affection may become more than that."

"And if it does not?"

He shrugged his shoulders and flicked some pebbles into the water with his cane.

"There will still be affection—rather that than an early passion fading to disillusion and indifference."

"And affection is enough?"

"True affection, certainly."

"True?"

"A desire to be with somebody when they're away, to help them when they suffer, to defend their causes and share their aspirations. An understanding that does not fear openness. Loyalty, trust." He raised his hands. "The meaning's clear enough to me."

They crossed the lawn, walking toward the box hedges and the central pond. Slight flecks of spray from the fountain wetted them as they passed. Near the garden door a maid was beating a carpet and laughing with a young undergardener, planting out dahlias in the bed beneath the dining room windows. Perched on a bough of blossoming syringa, a blackbird was singing. Helen deliberately noted these things in an attempt to remain calm and detached, but she could not control her mounting excitement. She would accept; she knew that now. So why not say? She had been honest and told him she did not love him and he had understood her perfectly. He knew that convenience was part of her reason and accepted that too. Had she not been disappointed and miserable when he had said nothing? She tried to think of the doubts that had distressed her before his visit to London, but could not think clearly. Instead the clear notes of the blackbird and the trumpet-shaped flowers of the weigela by the door filled her with happiness. She thought it strange that she had found no pleasure in the flower-carpeted beech woods, until she remembered that then he had not yet made his proposal. How stupid of me. And then inexplicably there were tears in her eyes and a lump in her throat. Inside she took him by the arm and led him to the nearest sitting room. Standing in the center of the room, she held out her hands to him and murmured,

"I accept."

He took her hands and drew her slowly toward him and held her. They parted without kissing, and running a finger down the line of her cheek, as a blind man might to verify a shape, he brushed away a tear. Outside, the maid was still beating the carpet and the blackbird continued his song.

⮜ *Twenty-Two* ⮞

While he had been involved in gunnery trials at Shoeburyness on the Thames Estuary, Charles Crawford had been offered a new command by the Admiralty: to be captain of *Scylla*, an eighty-gun three-decker at present berthed across the river at Sheerness Dockyard, where work to convert her from a sailing ship to a screw-assisted vessel was about to start.

The day on which Charles visited the dockyard to see his ship for the first time ought to have been among the happiest of his life. The captain superintendent and master shipwright showed him over all the five building-slips and explained every detail of the plans for *Scylla*'s conversion: the manner in which her upper deck would be removed and how she would be strengthened astern and amidships to receive her new seven-hundred horsepower engines. Her launch, he was assured, would be in three months, and after that, the machinery would be installed in half that time, while she was in one of the dry docks. Her final fitting out with masts, yards and standing rigging was expected to be finished by October. But none of this information, nor even thoughts of his father's appointment to Constantinople, relieved his depression. Two days earlier Sir James had written emotionally informing him that Helen Goodchild had accepted and in a year would be the new Lady Crawford.

At the head of one of the slips a completed frigate was standing ready for her launch the following day. Under the shadow of her towering hull, Charles imagined the keel blocks being taken out, and finally the dogshores, the two remaining balks of timber holding her in position, being knocked aside by the falling weights, and the ship going off slowly with steady and stately momentum, entering the water quietly with a whisper of swell at her bows, her length gradually lessening and receding. In three months, *Scylla, his* ship, would slide forward to the cheers of the dockyard workers and the strains of a marine band. Yet he felt no lump in the throat, none of the stirrings of emotion, which even the imagination of such scenes usually engendered in him.

It was late afternoon when he parted with the dockyard officers and walked down to the entrance of the Medway and the long wooden jetty of Port Victoria where a cutter was waiting to take him back across the estuary. The light was silvery and mackerel clouds drifted eastward across the sky. Below him four men-of-war were moored in line, their anchor chains hanging motionless and vertical. The slack of the tide, he thought dully. Looking at the ships he could imagine the slight, drowsy lapping of ripples which would be audible on their decks. In a few hours, darkness and their riding lights would cast long reflections on the black unruffled water.

Attuned by habit to every sight and sound of the sea, Charles took in each detail mechanically; his cheek registered the soft, feather-like touch of the faint easterly breeze, his ears, the slight clink of the anchor cables at the hawse pipes, his eyes, as he walked onto the jetty, the distant smudge of the Essex coast across the estuary, its channels all known to him by name: Queen's Channel, Prince's Channel, Four Fathom Channel—a dreary landscape of low shores and shining mud flats, but one in which he knew the positions of each buoy and lightship from the faint undulations of the land. But no associations of sea or river helped Charles to forget that Helen would marry his father—perhaps bear children to delight his old age—new affections coming between him and his first family.

Sir James had written to Charles asking him to visit Helen during his time in Turkey, his letter forcing on his son the bitter memory of his last meeting with Helen, at the bridge near Hanley Park, and of his failure there to speak truthfully. That was the hardest burden to bear: the knowledge that a few words might have saved him. A few words, only that. Charles seemed to hear Magnus's mocking voice merge with the slight movement of water around the piers of the jetty, "I hope you get the widow . . ." His father's words: "Marriage, like shipbuilding, is at best an experimental science."

He looked down at the smooth planks and the occasional gleam of water seen between them. From the river the clear tinkling of six bells from the anchored ships.

One thought vied with Charles's self-reproach and the acid of his disappointment—if his sacrifice turned out to have been for nothing, and she betrayed his father, or made him unhappy, he, Charles, would make her pay dearly for it. The vow gave him a vestige of comfort as he stepped into the cutter and her crew peaked their oars in salute.

✑ Twenty-Three ✑

Tom Strickland finished his supper of cheese and cold mutton and walked across the studio to a table by the model's dais. The light was no longer bright enough to work by so he cleaned his brushes and later ground a fresh supply of vermilion and chrome yellow on a stone slab for use the following day. Then after he had mixed these crude pigments with oil and poured them into bladders, he sat down wearily in a misshapen armchair by the unlit stove and closed his eyes.

Since his return to London from Rigton Bridge, Tom had worked hard but had not achieved as much as he would have liked. In France he had been particularly impressed by the work of two artists: Daumier and Millet—the first for his simple but dramatic contrasts of light and shade, the second for his stark paintings of working people, which combined a forceful, almost crude, application of paint with muted color and great delicacy of line. Yet faced with the now fashionable Pre-Raphaelite use of flat, bright colors and meticulous detail, Tom knew that work influenced by such originals would be received with hostility and indifference. Nevertheless he had completed one large canvas of the strikers being escorted to the train and had started a smaller one of mill girls leaving work, based on a sketch. Even if exhibited, he did not expect either of these to sell. Art, for most buyers, was something apart from life and not a direct outcome of its everyday events. Few were prepared to hang any modern subjects on their walls, unless they were sentimental, humorous, or pointed a positive moral. With these requirements in mind, Tom had recently executed a medieval subject of a knight clutching his jaws, entitled *Toothache in the Middle Ages*—commissioned appropriately by a prosperous dentist—and for the Academy Exhibition had begun work on an epic historical painting: *Caesar*

Going to the Capitol on the Ides of March. The thought of the weeks of niggling labor ahead of him on this one canvas sometimes kept Tom awake at night wondering whether he would ever have the energy to finish it. At such times he longed for a lucrative portrait commission to save him from such drudgery.

The evening was warm and fine but Tom did not want to go out, nor did he feel tired enough to sleep. He was irritated that Magnus had not yet returned from Portsmouth where he had spent the past two days. Tom had not questioned him about the purpose of his visit, but supposed it would be to gather material for an article about any naval preparations afoot as a result of the Turkish crisis. During the past weeks Tom had been surprised and relieved by the ease with which Magnus had adapted to his new life and by his apparent unconcern over rejections. To date out of ten articles, Crawford had only sold three: two to the *Pall Mall Gazette* and one to *Reynolds's Weekly News*.

When Magnus burst into the darkened studio shortly before ten, he found Tom reading by the light of a smoking lamp. He threw down his portmanteau and sat down on a stool with a bulky brown-paper parcel on his knee.

"Tonight it has to be," he exclaimed darkly, tearing open the paper and taking out a snuff-brown coat that might once have been pale gray; a shirt without cuffs followed, then a battered billycock hat, and finally a greasy moleskin waistcoat fastened with twine in lieu of buttons. Holding these garments at arm's length, he sniffed cautiously and then dropped them rapidly. "Had to try five rag shops before I bought these."

Knowing that Magnus had been putting off spending a night in the Lambeth Workhouse ever since he had promised the editor of the *Pall Mall Gazette* an article on the subject ten days earlier, Tom was not astonished by his friend's purchases.

"Don't you feel too tired after the journey?" he asked.

"Certainly not. Doctors are always recommending sea air to restore vital energies." Magnus smiled and then bent down and picked up a second parcel identical to the first. With a dawning perception of what was to come, Tom shook his head emphatically, but Magnus still threw it to him.

"You're the journalist," laughed Tom, tossing it back.

"And you're the artist," replied Magnus.

"I didn't go to the sea."

"I can't help that. This piece has to be illustrated. If the editor's pleased, he'll publish it as a separate pamphlet as well as in the *Gazette*. Unless you come I lose half the fee."

Tom looked at Magnus skeptically.

"Is this true?"

"As holy writ," replied Magnus, his face a parody of injured innocence.

Tom watched Magnus putting his hands into the coal scuttle and gingerly start rubbing coal dust onto his face, doing his best to avoid touching the scar on his forehead.

"You," said Tom, with slow emphasis, "are a low, scheming, two-faced, devious . . ." Magnus coughed apologetically as Tom searched vainly for the right word.

"I knew you'd try to argue me out of it if I told you sooner."

"I'm not coming."

While Tom started to clear the supper table, Magnus put on the hat and pulled down the brim.

"Please, yer worship," he croaked, extending a hand like a beggar.

"No."

Magnus shuffled closer, stooping like a hunchback.

"For mercy's sake, sir, will you not give an old soldier a chance?"

Magnus's wheedling voice and blackened face under the drooping brim of his hat was too much for Tom. Laughing, in spite of his real irritation, he ripped open the parcel and started pulling out the clothes.

"I once spent a night in a casual ward," he remarked grimly.

"Excellent," returned Magnus, pretending not to notice his tone. "You'll know what to say."

By the time they reached the Kennington Road, the workhouse doors had been locked and Tom thought there was an even chance that they would be turned away. The walk had been bad enough in itself. Although Magnus had been amused that well-dressed passersby had invariably stepped out of their way, Tom had found the experience humiliating. He had been too close to real poverty in the past to enjoy this demonstration of the disgust and alarm with which respectable people viewed the destitute.

Magnus glanced speculatively at the large black knocker on the door.
"Well?"

Tom made a face and then looked down at the pavement.

"Keep your mouth shut or they'll know you're a gentleman."

"Would they set on me?"

"They might."

Magnus grinned at him.

"How many supervisors will there be?"

"The relieving officer and two or three porters."

Magnus laughed aloud.

"Three unarmed men to control fifty tramps. They can't be so very
fierce."

Magnus grasped the knocker and banged hard. Several minutes later a
porter let them in, grumbling that they were too late for their bread and
gruel but would have to bath at once and then sleep in the shed. After a
clerk had written down their fictitious names and trades—they had previously agreed to say that they were out-of-work engravers to explain
the softness of their hands—they were asked which workhouse they had
come from and where they intended to go the next day when they were
turned out. Tom gave prepared answers to these questions and they were
led along a corridor lit by naked gas jets and across an open yard to a
small room containing three baths. The water was the color of mutton
broth; the air reeked of feet. They exchanged glances, Magnus apparently unmoved, Tom angry and nauseated.

"Take yer clothes orf," snarled the porter.

"I'll wash my feet," muttered Tom.

"No bath, no bed," announced the porter. He was a stocky red-faced
man with a bulging neck squeezed into a starched collar stained with a
yellow tidemark of sweat. Since entry to the casual ward was denied to
those with even a single coin in their pockets, bribery was out of the
question. Magnus shrugged his shoulders and undressed quickly, then
without even momentary hesitation he climbed into one of the baths and
lay back calmly. Tom followed his example sullenly.

As soon as they were immersed, the porter tied up their clothes and
threw down two numbered metal tickets.

"Hand 'em over when yer call for yer clothes tomorro'. Put 'em under
yer 'eads or they'll get stole." Then he tossed down a couple of blankets

and two striped blue nightshirts on the wet floor. "The shed's over the yard."

When the porter had gone, they realized that they had not been given towels and would have to use their blankets to dry themselves.

"There's something strangely relaxing about being ordered about by fools," murmured Magnus, putting on his nightshirt.

"Damn you," moaned Tom, whose nightshirt was soaking.

The shed was a large room open at one end, the gap being hung with a mildewed canvas curtain. The shock of seeing so many cadaverous half-starved men in so small a place affected Tom far less than the suffocating stench that filled his nostrils: tobacco smoke, rancid sweat and excrement, laced with a faint tinge of decay, sweet and pervasive. The walls were furred with damp and the floor was so dirty that Tom at first thought it was earth, until he saw the line between two flagstones. In the half-darkness he could make out the recumbent figures of between fifty and sixty men and boys lying jammed up against each other on narrow sacking bags scantily stuffed with hay and straw. A drunk was singing in a corner and several men were smoking pipes which they had somehow smuggled past the porter. A furious argument was raging near the center of the room, ignored by everybody except the participants, both apparently in their sixties or seventies. Half the inmates seemed, unbelievably, to be asleep. Looking around him Tom felt no emotion, pity, compassion, even anger, all obliterated by the smell. When the arguing and talking died down, Tom noticed an extraordinary variety of coughs, ranging from short dry barks to prolonged bubbling wheezes. Magnus had dragged two of the straw-filled bags over to the open side of the shed, where Tom sank down beside him. Without moving, Magnus murmured,

"D'you think our piece will make any difference?"

"You saw how people looked at us in the street."

Magnus nodded and then sighed.

"You're right . . . and I laughed about it."

But though the memory disturbed them both, neither was able to maintain a consistent mood for long. Almost as Magnus finished speaking, a massive stevedore, one of the only healthy-looking men in the room, jumped up roaring because somebody had stolen his tobacco tin while he had been asleep. Two boys were tossing it to each other, leaping out of reach as he rushed at them, falling over sleeping men, who woke cursing. Eventually the tin was returned and the shed settled again, until the next outburst. The scene was sad but at times disconcertingly funny. As a church clock struck eleven, Tom realized that they were going to have to spend the next seven hours in the shed. He looked at Magnus despairingly and sank back onto his sacking. After a few moments, Magnus propped himself on an elbow.

"Want to know what I did in Portsmouth?"

"No."

"I went on your behalf." Tom shut his eyes. "I saw my father before he sailed. Filial devotion you may think." Magnus smiled to himself. "He's going to marry Helen Goodchild." Tom sat up abruptly, several bits of straw sticking in his hair. "Good God, you're actually listening." Magnus's eyes were shining. "I persuaded him to commission you to paint her portrait."

"Thank you," breathed Tom in a stifled whisper.

"Aren't you pleased?"

"Yes . . . yes. It's what I wanted . . . you know that."

A drunk had started to sing what he could remember of a music hall song: "I'd like to be a swell a-roaming down Pall Mall." Tom faced Magnus.

"Do you mind?" he asked after a pause.

"Mind him marrying?"

"She's only your age."

"Oh, that." Magnus pursed his lips and stared up at the discolored ceiling. "It's just a transaction, Tom. She gets relief from Goodchild's debts, Father gets her, and I get nothing." He folded his arms across his chest. "You're not surprised, are you? Women sell themselves every day—from duchesses to whores only the price differs."

The drunk's voice quavered on, punctuated by fits of coughing. Tom knew that he had no reason to admire Lady Goodchild, she had treated him badly, and her dignity on the night of her husband's death now appeared to have owed more to indifference than courage; and yet he could not deny an oppressive feeling of disillusion. He remembered her receiving him in the Red Drawing Room, and could hardly, in his present surroundings, believe that their meeting had been real. Her beauty too—no more than a facade concealing emptiness. Her grace, poise and wit merely the servants of self-interest. But why should that concern me? he asked himself savagely. He would be well paid. Even so, the memories he had of her on that election evening still pained him. The thought that she should be marrying again solely for security, when even the contents of a single small room at Hanley Park would have kept her a world removed from the poverty of the men around him, seemed an outrage. From duchesses to whores. He turned and suddenly took in how disheartened Magnus was at his reaction. Tom felt ashamed. The man had gone to Portsmouth for him, probably without any personal desire to see his father; had succeeded in getting him a commission he had dearly wanted. But had he thanked him warmly? Expressed real gratitude? Nothing of the sort. Instead he had wallowed in self-indulgent revulsion that beautiful women could be as selfish and unscrupulous as any other people, and as prone to waste their lives for no good reason. He touched Magnus's shoulder gently.

"I am pleased . . . It's this place, don't you see? Thinking of a house like that here. . . ." Tom felt guilt and affection when he saw the way Magnus immediately brightened at his words. A moment later he turned to Tom, his old self again.

"I hope," he drawled in a matter-of-fact voice, "your illustrations will be worthy of their text."

Tom aimed an ineffectual punch at him and then lay back smiling, amazed that he had forgiven Magnus for putting him in a position where he had had to wash in water that had made the river in Rigton Bridge seem clean by comparison; amazed too that he had even come in the first place.

PART THREE

The Portrait

❧ Twenty-Four ❧

Before his departure for Turkey, Sir James had summoned Catherine and broken the news of his intention to marry Helen Goodchild. Catherine, who had always found Helen scathing and imperious, had done her best to conceal the shock and dismay she felt at the prospect of subordination to a stepmother less than ten years her senior. Because of the recentness of Helen's bereavement, Catherine had rightly supposed that the marriage itself would not take place for a year; but her assumption that her life would remain unchanged in the meantime had proved overoptimistic. Since Magnus had gone and Charles seemed likely to remain in the south while his ship was being converted and fitted out, Sir James had asked his daughter whether she thought it reasonable for him to be burdened with the expense of keeping up a large country house for her alone, especially while an excellent alternative was open to her. While he was away, Helen would need companionship, and who better to provide it than her future husband's daughter? Since Catherine had known that her father was set on this course, she had not argued.

*　*　*

Almost from the day of Catherine's arrival at Hanley Park a veiled animosity had grown up between the two women. If Catherine thought Helen imperious, Helen thought Catherine secretive and self-righteous. From the beginning Helen had disliked having the girl at Hanley Park, but since Sir James, as well as providing Helen with fifteen hundred a year, had also promised her the benefit of any money saved by the virtual closure of Leaholme Hall, she had hardly felt able to refuse to accommodate Catherine. But financial advantages notwithstanding, Catherine's presence continually irked her. She talked so little and her habitual expression, it seemed to Helen, was a martyred smile. Whether she was dispensing tea, or arranging flowers, or playing the piano—there it was, that faint insipid smile full of tolerance and sweet resignation, but not, Helen felt, without a definite hint of reproach. Her position, it was true, was a difficult one; from being virtual mistress of one house, she was now little more than an unwanted guest in another, and realizing this, Helen did her best to be friendly. But she always felt uneasy with Catherine and knew that the feeling was reciprocated. Both seemed to fear any intimacy in case it should lead to indiscretions which might reach Sir James. Helen was certain that Catherine believed she was marrying her father purely for convenience; and at times when she saw Catherine's deep blue eyes—so strikingly like her father's—following her across a room, Helen thought of the girl as a spy and her presence at Hanley Park Sir James's means of ensuring that his wife-to-be remained well behaved. As a rule she quickly laughed at herself for such ideas, but laughter or no laughter, Helen's relations with Catherine, although they grew no worse, did not improve.

Catherine imagined herself living for years in a house which she hated, an unwanted stranger condemned to wander through tall classical rooms with Aubusson carpets and silk upholstered Empire chairs and sofas, forever banished from the homelier, low-ceilinged rooms of Leaholme Hall with their irregular mullioned windows, paneled walls and solid Jacobean furniture: an inconvenient and unimposing house when set beside the formal grace of Hanley Park, but one where she had felt that she belonged. Her father had never been there long enough to feel the same, and now, according to Helen, he was no longer thinking of a temporary closure, but of finding a tenant. The day she had discovered this, Catherine had known that there would be no limit to her time as Helen's *guest*. Therefore when she heard shortly afterward that Magnus had persuaded her father to commission Tom Strickland to paint Helen's portrait, Catherine looked forward to his coming as an oasis in a desert.

Although both her previous meetings with Strickland had been in unfavorable circumstances, he had still impressed her, not just for his striking looks, but for a directness of manner which had combined gentleness of speech and a refusal to be angered with an unmistakable inner pride. Almost all the men she had met during her London seasons had talked down to her when airing their views or expressing opinions. Strickland, by contrast, had appeared modest even when speaking with conviction. Apart from her admiration for artistic talent, the fact that Magnus, usually so critical of everyone, had formed a close friendship with Tom also weighed heavily with Catherine.

She knew that he would not feel able to make himself pleasant to her, unless she first showed that she enjoyed his company, and with this in mind Catherine decided from the beginning to encourage him. Where this might lead, she had deliberately left vague in her own mind, certain at least that she deserved a brief interlude of happiness in her imprisonment. What in any case could words like "shameless" or "flirtatious" matter to a "lady" with less freedom than the youngest chambermaid in the house? Servants could at least chatter and laugh with grooms and footmen, and walk in the lanes with whom they chose on their afternoons off.

So on the hot and dusty July day on which Tom was expected, Catherine dressed with special care, insisting that her maid spend far longer than usual with her hair. While the girl brushed and combed and curled, her mistress stared at her reflection, noting the effect of certain expressions and swearing to herself that she would not allow coyness or reserve to check her excitement and high spirits. By treating Strickland as a friend and equal rather than an inferior guest, she would be sure to annoy Helen, but this thought pleased rather than disturbed her. Because of his friendship with Magnus, Tom would take her part if Helen decided to be scathing at her expense. For the first time since her arrival at Hanley Park, Catherine joyfully anticipated an end to her loneliness.

* * *

Tom Strickland had not been many hours at Hanley Park before he sensed the tension between Lady Goodchild and Miss Crawford, but though he realized that his hostess was perplexed by Catherine's gaiety —an aspect of her character which he himself had never seen before— he still felt grateful for the relaxed way in which she talked to him, especially since during dinner her ladyship hardly spoke at all.

While answering Catherine's animated questions about Magnus and their life in London, Tom occasionally glanced at Helen, more to acquaint himself with the difficulties he would encounter painting her than because impelled to do so. Her face seemed paler than he remembered. Her cheeks were slightly sunken, not marring her looks but emphasizing the perfection of her bone structure and the intensity of her dark, almond-shaped eyes.

After dinner he gave Catherine a bowdlerized account of his night with Magnus in the Lambeth Workhouse and was surprised that she did not seem at all shocked by anything he said. Later Catherine told him that she had not always confined her visiting to poor villagers, but had occasionally taken food and money to families in Rigton Bridge where she had heard plenty about the local workhouse. All the time Tom was acutely aware of certain differences between the two women: Catherine's fresh complexion and rounded cheeks, Helen's pallor and smoldering eyes, her beauty made more poignant by faint traces of haggardness—the face of a woman who had lived and suffered and found no repose. Looking at her troubled eyes, Tom was stung by the memory of the easy way in which he had condemned her on first hearing that she had consented to marry Sir James.

Catherine's behavior since Strickland's arrival was a revelation to Helen, and the girl's open smiles and unforced laughter seemed to reproach her for having been the sole cause of her former lassitude. The idea that Catherine might wish to captivate Strickland for any reason other than to discomfort her did not at first occur to Helen; although later, her awareness that the artist with his dark curls and slender figure was by no means unattractive did make her change her view of Catherine's motives. Nor did Lady Goodchild understand or approve of Catherine's evident interest in Strickland's excursions into low life. While not averse to indirect charity, Helen suspected that many urban Lady Bountifuls gained a twisted pleasure from visiting squalid rookeries and courts to dispense soup and blankets. Then like Strickland they would return to warm clean sitting rooms to tell their travelers' tales, as if they had been to Africa rather than to Seven Dials. Helen was no more callous than others of her class and would have preferred a world without poverty—provided, of course, there were still servants—but since the poor were always likely to be there, and were openly in evidence to all who used their eyes, she saw no point in discussing them. In truth they bored her. Idealism of all kinds had always irritated her, smacking too much of worthy Low Churchmen and chapels with absurd names like Shiloh and Ebenezer; and perhaps because she had so little herself, she thought those professing to be actuated by ideal motives self-deluded men and women trying desperately to hide their selfishness, not least from themselves. In her view the strong had always taken advantage of the weak, and short of a dramatic change in human nature, to expect them to do otherwise was naïve wishful thinking. The idea that Catherine might be guilty of this offense did not endear her to Helen, who was already starting to think her deceitful for having concealed so much of herself.

Only later, when in answer to a request from Tom, Catherine had sat down at the piano and played and sang, did Helen recognize her true feelings. There was Catherine in her cream-colored silk dress, her silvery hair dressed in ringlets and her face gleaming in the candlelight with the smooth, peachlike bloom only given to women in their twenties, playing and singing so delightfully with her clear small voice, while she, Helen, sat watching her and remembering a time when she too had looked like a figure from an untouched world of innocence and hope. For a while Helen could not believe that she might be jealous and yet the young man's attentiveness to Catherine disquieted her. She had pretended to herself to be above joining in while Tom and Catherine had talked about "the condition of the people," but in reality she suspected that they had not cared whether she participated or not. And now while Catherine sang, she felt excluded once more. Strickland had asked for her opinion from time to time and had addressed remarks to her, but from politeness, she had felt, rather than inclination.

The fondness both of them evidently felt for Magnus formed a bond between them which she could not share. Yet exclusion for that reason did not hurt her. Jealousy of their youth? Not even that precisely. The idea that here were two people who possessed a freedom that she had felt obliged to throw away was what hurt her most. Catherine might still marry a man her own age and truly love him, not just feel lukewarm affection. And Strickland, for all the financial hazards of his work, could leave the house when he had finished and be free to go where he chose, behave as he wished and need care nothing for what others thought of the company he kept or the things he did. And yet Catherine envied her the petty mastery of running the house, and Strickland deferred because of her patronage and position. As soon as Catherine ended her song, Helen rose and told them she was tired. Then she rang for the groom of the chambers to show Strickland to his room.

On reaching the bedroom, Helen sent away the maid who was waiting patiently to undress her, and sat down by the open window. The lamp was smoking a little, but instead of ringing to get it fixed, she took off the chimney and globe herself and turned down the wick. She could hear a faint rustling of branches and the whir of insects. A large moth, its eyes glowing red in the lamplight, bumped against the window and fluttered past her into the room. In the distance the lake shone like a long silver mirror, and the moon cast a soft unbroken light over the fields beyond.

She shut her eyes and tried to recapture the certainty she had felt two months before. A week after James's departure she would not have been troubled by so small a matter as exclusion by an insignificant artist and an inexperienced girl. She thought of James and the responsibilities he had shouldered and wondered what he was doing at that moment. Ten days before, the Russians, as he had said they would, had crossed the River Prut. Now he was in Vienna with Lord Stratford attending a conference of the ambassadors of the great powers. Should any woman engaged to be married to such a man feel distressed by trivial incidents? She stared out angrily into the night and then put her head in her hands. In truth it was not eminence, and the vicarious pleasure of hearing of great events from those participating in them, that she wanted. Sir James had spoken of wanting openness and understanding between them; and yet when she thought of their conversations, all she most vividly recalled was his remoteness and his assumption that politics and international affairs would be beyond her, that smile of weary, slightly contemptuous wisdom when she had questioned about what he had said. With her he would prefer to sketch and chat about matters of no importance, or be read to, or reminisce about the distant past, separating her from his real life and present cares, and so cutting her off from the most essential part of him. He had written from Constantinople before leaving for Vienna, and although a Russian army was already marching toward Turkey's northern frontier, most of his letter had been taken up with a humorous description of an audience with the sultan, and that great man's distress to discover that Sir James Crawford did not smoke—not even finest latakia tobacco in a gold and amber pipe provided by His Sublime Majesty, and lit with glowing charcoal by a kneeling slave.

And when he came home, he would want to forget the stresses and disappointments of his work, so not even then would she be able to share his thoughts. She remembered Harry speaking of a friend who had surprised him by marrying late in life. "Nobody knows why he's bothered; he's been married already for years—to his habits." And would matters be so different for her? She had thought often enough what she might gain from marrying him, but had rarely considered what he really wanted from her. No more than a soothing and ornamental presence to grace his occasional leisure hours? If he were with her, ten minutes of conversation might allay her fears, but there was no means of knowing when he might return. Nor could she go to him so soon after Harry's death without exposing him to embarrassment and gossip. She thought of writing to him about her doubts, but to express them, however phrased, would imply a wounding lack of faith.

She sat a few minutes more by the window, gazing up at the multitude of stars, their radiance softened by the brightness of the moon, in the air the savor of moist earth and falling dew. She was tempted to walk in the garden, but a sudden shiver dissuaded her. Instead she rang for her maid to undress her and get her ready for bed.

～ Twenty-Five ～

After Lady Goodchild's brooding silences of the evening before, Tom Strickland viewed her first sitting with apprehension. Ever since her capricious *volte-face* over commissioning him on his first visit to Hanley Park, he had been confused by her many contradictions. In view of her bereavement he had never expected any appreciation of his ride to tell her about Goodchild's fate, and yet, even before the funeral, she had sent a servant to search him out and to deliver a letter of warm thanks. It seemed incomprehensible to him that a woman capable of thinking of such a thing when so deeply involved in other far more pressing matters should now be ready to marry a man who, by Magnus's account, was obsessed with the austere demands of duty to the exclusion of all human needs.

Helen was to sit for him in the anteroom leading from the hall into the Tapestry Room and Red Drawing Room—the two principal reception rooms on the west side of the house. Tom had chosen this less grandiose room because it was ideally lit, having windows facing both north and west. He had decided to paint two or three oil sketches before starting on the final portrait. For these preliminary works he would not bother with a canvas on an easel, but intended to paint sitting on an artist's "donkey," using a sized but unprimed millboard with a prepared palette fastened onto the corner with a clip. Before coming down to the room he had ground and mixed his colors and set them out on the palette from white, through reds, browns, blues and greens to black. While waiting for Helen he looked around the room identifying pictures and furniture. The Grecian mantelpiece of dark green and white marble he was confident was by Westmacott. Tom had once had to tint and color a manufacturer's catalog of mantelpiece designs. The medallions in the decorative plaster ceiling, he supposed, were Angelica Kauffmann or her husband, Antonio Zucchi. Two portraits by Raeburn and one by Romney posed no difficulty, but the Phillippe Mercier group of the fourth baron's children, he would not have known without the information on the frame. He was glad not to be working in the Red Drawing Room where the *Magdalene* by Titian and Rembrandt's *Head of a Jew* would have inhibited him. He had been amazed that Helen had not pointed out these masterpieces and had made no comment upon them until he had examined them. The Rembrandt he had been horrified to see "skied" over a door. He was looking at one of a pair of ivory chairs when Helen came in.

"They were made for Clive or Warren Hastings. But then you can be sure the owners of any kind of Indian work will tell you that story. One might suppose they were furniture dealers."

Tom did not reply, but gazed at her with a beating heart. The lights shining in her hair, smoothed flat from a central parting and gleaming almost like perfectly matching bands of burnished copper—could he do justice to that? Or the glowing whiteness of her shoulders? Or the complicated richness of the different shades of blue in her shot silk evening dress? At least he would not have to attempt the incredible detail in the lace trimmings of her skirt. Sir James had asked for a kit-cat, or head and shoulders, and not a full length. Here was a subject that Gainsborough or Lawrence might have attempted with confidence, but for him, Thomas James Strickland, the task would be of a different order. He was astonished that he had not envisaged, till the moment she had appeared, the full implications of the work ahead. He had thought, until he saw her now in these clothes, that he would be content to follow the pattern of Winterhalter or Sant and paint her with an expression of conventional aristocratic pride and invulnerability; but the contrast between the grandeur of her appearance and the dissatisfied, uncertain look in her eyes made him determined to try to do more than this, to paint a portrait that would be a revelation rather than a facade. That he might lack the interpretative insight for such a portrayal scared him even more than his technique being found inadequate to achieve a convincing representation of the subtleties of her hair and the changing sheen of her silk dress. If he had learned little about composition, except Reynolds's rigidly precise dicta on the balance of light and dark, he had at least left the Academy Schools with an excellent technical capacity for painting detail, hard and tedious though he might find its execution.

Helen had sat down in the needlework chair placed in position by Tom and had shaken out the looped flounces of her skirt.

"It is very hard of you to insist on evening dress at this hour, Mr. Strickland. Surely you could have managed it in the way of artists who paint military men—painting the man on one day, and placing the horse under him on another, sparing the rider's time and the horse's back."

"I could have draped the clothes on a lay figure, your ladyship, but since you wished to be painted in a décolleté dress, I had to see your neck and shoulders."

"Are women's shoulders so very different?" she asked innocently.

"As different as their eyes and noses," he murmured, blushing slightly under her amused gaze.

"Shall I look at you, Mr. Strickland, or somewhere else?"

Having decided against a full face, Tom asked her to look slightly to his right out of the lower part of the window behind him. He wanted an inward-looking, almost self-absorbed expression, and thought this would be best achieved by giving her nothing precise to focus upon. Then having satisfied himself that her hands and arms were right, he began drawing a rapid outline with charcoal, and occasionally dusting his board with a few light flicks of a cloth. Later he would start to work with his prepared palette, rubbing in the darks with umbers and browns, and then painting on the general lights in masses, accentuating certain features with pure white before softening the effect with blanched reds and lakes. His usual practice in these preliminary sketches was to let the ground of the unprimed board show through to serve as half-tints. He had been working for ten minutes when she turned to him.

"I suppose I may not talk?"

"If you wish, of course . . ."

"I understand; it would spoil the pose. Perhaps you could talk to me? Staring for hours through this window will make me look like a mournful tragedienne, unless there is some diversion."

"Your thoughts?" he countered.

"I think I should prefer yours unless it will hinder you. You have never told me how you became an artist."

At first Tom was irritated to have to divide his attention, but as time passed he realized that her reactions to what he said told him far more about her face than he would have learned had it been constantly in repose. During the next half hour before she rested, he explained to her at intervals how his father, in spite of his humble position in a fire insurance office, had paid to send him to a gruesome private school in Wandsworth, an academy not unlike the one to which Dickens had sent the hapless Paul Dombey. Tom knew what scorn Helen would have for such an institution, where the sons of gentlemen were many times outnumbered by those of prosperous tradesmen. But strangely, although at first he felt embarrassed in that elegantly resplendent room to mention such an ungentlemanly education and pedigree, he came to feel a certain exultation in doing so openly and without apology. He described the meat pie served every Friday and christened, after a tooth had been found in it, Resurrection or Dead Man's pie; he told her about the floggings meted out for failure to conjugate Greek verbs, and about the sadism of the dancing master, whose trousers had been so starched and stiff that, as he walked, his legs looked like a pair of shears. He went on to tell her how he had run away, intending to walk to Portsmouth and go to sea. Besides his jacket, waistcoat, trousers and shoes, he had possessed as working capital a half crown, a watch and a pocket knife. These good things had provided him with food and shelter for two days, and after that hunger had driven him to beg at lodge gates and cottage doors. When his shoes had worn through he had stuffed them with grass, but three nights spent sleeping under hedges in cold wet weather had finally made him turn back. Returning to school a week later, barely able to walk, he had expected a flogging, but to his surprise had been given a slice of seedcake and a glass of wine, while his father was summoned. His flight being considered unforgivable, he had been expelled more in sorrow than in anger, and since his drawings were thought to show some talent, he had been placed by his father in a lithographic office, and a year later was apprenticed to an engraver. His employer there was sufficiently impressed by his architectural drawings to run a series of them, and one day these had been seen by an elderly Academician, who had come to check on the progress of an engraving of one of his own pictures. In this way Tom had been recommended to apply to the Royal Academy Schools, where eventually he had been taken on as a probationer and then as a full student.

While he had been speaking, Tom had seen precisely the expression he wished to catch: her lips just parted in a smile almost on the point of dissolution, her deep brown eyes already resuming an introspective sadness, an expression quite unlike the unguarded lapse of a feigned society smile. When Helen had listened to the details of his story, she had smiled in sympathy with his experience, rather than in superior amusement at his background. A look compassionate rather than remote.

During her first rest Helen came up to Tom, a slight frown wrinkling her forehead. He expected her to ask to see what he had done, but instead she said,

"You have made a great impression on Miss Crawford."

Tom looked up abruptly and put down the brush he had been cleaning. He could feel his cheeks coloring.

"How so, your ladyship?" he asked quietly.

"You are not an unattractive man, Mr. Strickland, and, as you may be aware, Miss Crawford has recently led a retiring life."

The easy and relaxed feeling of unity, which Tom had started to experience with Helen while he had been painting, vanished. Perhaps even when he had seen the smile he had thought so beautiful, she had been thinking of making this implied criticism. He felt a sudden spurt of anger.

"If you consider that my behavior toward Miss Crawford was anything other . . ."

"On the contrary; I meant no criticism—only a woman's intuition that Miss Crawford may make of your natural friendliness more than you intend to convey."

"I am not aware that anything I said last evening could be open to any such misinterpretation. I have not so much forgotten the engraver's shop to suppose a baronet's daughter would welcome anything other than formal conversation from me."

Helen walked to the open window and looked out. Without turning she said,

"Nothing I said deserved this bitterness."

"Your ladyship must nevertheless understand it. Magnus is not ashamed to live in the same house with me, and yet because his sister speaks warmly to me, I must be reminded that my inferior breeding makes such friendliness dangerous. In this house, madam, where even the meanest plate and bowl reminds me of my position, I need no further telling."

"I am not responsible for the world's injustices, Mr. Strickland," Helen replied sharply. "I merely wished to save you from the sort of humiliation which you evidently feel I have already subjected you to. You must have realized the girl finds you attractive. While she is in my house I am responsible for her."

"You may be assured that I will treat her with as much coolness as I can make consistent with courtesy." He picked up another brush and went on with his cleaning. She came and sat down close to him in one of the ivory chairs.

"Tell me, why are you so angry?" she asked gently.

"I hope your ladyship will forget any rudeness I may have been guilty of."

"An honest answer will absolve you."

He looked at her and their eyes met; Tom felt a slight tightening in his chest, but his face remained impassive.

"It might as easily end my employment."

"I swear it will not. But since you evidently disbelieve me, I will save your feelings by hazarding a guess." She looked at him for a moment with a faint ironic smile. "You resent my lecturing you about Miss Crawford because you think me a hypocrite."

"Why should I do so, your ladyship?"

"Surely that needs no explanation?" she murmured reprovingly. "Like many confident young men, you immodestly suppose that any woman marrying an older man must do so solely for gain. Hardly the proper sort of person to disparage a girl's romantic idealism."

Galled by the ease with which she had guessed the cause for part of his resentment, he refused any acknowledgment of this, but replied quietly,

"I was angry because you thought I had insufficient wit to realize that were I to encourage Miss Crawford, I might cause you embarrassment with her father."

"I never thought that. You are quite wrong."

"About what your ladyship thought, but not about why I was offended." Mortified by the sharpness of her tone, he added, "Perhaps I would have done better to have lied."

"If honesty makes you so sour, you would indeed do better to lie."

Feeling like a careless crossing sweeper who had been rebuked for splashing mud on a lady's dress, he held up his millboard and said in a low, controlled voice,

"I fear that your morning is wasted. I have made a poor likeness." Helen looked at the work in front of her in silence. The neck and shoulders were suggested by rough charcoal lines, but the face itself, although in a monochrome of browns with touches of white and black, was painted clearly enough for her to discern the expression: observant but sad liquid dark eyes, lips forming a vulnerable and fleeting smile, a sensitive and poignant face devoid of pride and coldness, a look that was both resigned and uncertain, as if recalling a past conflict, decided, but not resolved.

"No morning was wasted," she murmured, lowering her eyes. "And yet I think another likeness might be more suitable." She looked again at the unfinished sketch and sighed, "You are a clever artist, Mr. Strickland, but not a tactful one."

"I will try to do better, my lady."

She smiled ironically and tossed her head back.

"Of course, you have abandoned honesty after what I said. You mean you will try to do worse." She caught his eye, and, although still angry, he returned a faint smile. "Perhaps we have done enough for one morning."

"As your ladyship wishes."

Helen inclined her head and looked quizzically at Tom.

"You know, Mr. Strickland, I wish you'd be a bit less generous with your 'yes, my ladys' and 'if your ladyships.' Excessive deference is usually a subtle form of insult."

"I shall try to avoid it in future."

"Perhaps I can help you."

Tom was surprised to see Helen go across to a corner cabinet containing Chelsea porcelain and lift out a dessert plate. She held it up to the light and he saw a deep green border edged with gold, encircling an intricately painted pastoral scene after Watteau or Teniers.

"You spoke of plates and bowls, did you not?" she asked with arched brows. Then without waiting for his reply, with a sudden movement of the arm she tossed the plate into the fireplace where it shattered into a myriad of tiny fragments. After a slight shrug of her shoulders, she smiled briefly and turned on her heel. From the doorway she said, "Tomorrow I trust we will both do better."

Speechless with confusion, Tom watched her go out into the hall, his heart still pounding from shock. A moment later, as his words came back to him, he cried aloud at his stupidity. *A house where even the meanest plate and bowl reminds me of my position.* His anger forgotten, he stared at the jagged pieces of china scattered among the fire irons and felt a warm tingling sensation down his spine. Who else but Helen Goodchild, he asked himself, could have conceived an action that was both apology and command, accusation and truce—all in a single movement of her hand?

⤺ Twenty-Six ⤻

During the afternoon following Helen's first sitting, Catherine had tried to recapture the relaxed and friendly atmosphere of the evening before, but had found Tom diffident, remote and eager to find an excuse to leave her as soon as he could do so without rudeness. Thinking that his behavior was probably a result of the strains of beginning work on the portrait of a far from easy sitter, she was not unduly alarmed; because she herself often suffered from moods, she was rarely surprised to encounter them in others.

But when the same thing occurred next day, after Lady Goodchild's second sitting, Catherine felt less confident that all was well. Immediately after lunch, Tom had slipped away, into the cornfields, as Catherine later discovered, to watch the men getting in the harvest and to sketch them. On his return she asked to see his work and was hurt that he seemed reluctant to show her. She found nothing offensive in seeing the men depicted stripped to the waist and the women with their gowns pinned up behind, showing their stays and coarse linsey petticoats. She saw that he had noted how the men wore footless stockings pulled up over their arms to protect them from the stubble. She praised several sketches, especially one of a group of laborers lying sprawled under the shade of a heavy farm wagon eating their lunch, but Tom looked down at his dusty boots and had said little in return. He had thrust a poppy and some cornflowers in his buttonhole and his face was glowing with the wind and sun. His uneasiness had struck Catherine as so uncharacteristic that from the time of this brief conversation, Catherine concluded that Helen had been speaking to him.

Infuriated by this suspicion Catherine sought out Helen at once, but as so often happened, was unable to talk to her because Humphrey was with her. The boy's habit of turning up when least wanted, and his open admiration for Charles and her father, distressed and irritated Catherine. His pathetic desire to please her and his well-meaning attempts to cheer her up if she looked depressed became a great burden to her; and, since he was only occupied with his tutor during the mornings—the time when Tom was painting Helen—Humphrey was always wandering about and wrecking her opportunities for speaking to Tom. In fact Humphrey had taken to inviting the artist to come for walks with him to see "his" estate. The thought that her father might very well be paying off Goodchild's debts, so that the little lord might ultimately enjoy an unencumbered patrimony, added to Catherine's feeling of injustice, especially since she had barely enough money to buy Berlin wools and muslin in Flixton.

On the fourth day of Tom's stay Catherine's anger reached a new pitch. Without consultation or warning, Helen had invited George Braithwaite to lunch that very day. To have to suffer the vicar of Flixton and his wife was a penance, but to be forced to endure George at the same time was altogether worse; indeed Catherine suspected deliberate malice on Helen's part. When faced with this, Helen professed entire ignorance of any rejected proposal or any other past embarrassment and had merely countered by saying that Sir James had been eager to avoid a permanent rift with the Braithwaites. Besides, George had recently bought a commission in the Coldstream Guards and would soon be leaving the county. Catherine had been about to broach her principal grievance when the housekeeper had come in.

The conversation at lunch was monopolized by the vicar and Helen. When Catherine was not angrily staring at the reflections of the tureens and dishes in the polished surface of the table, she watched her future stepmother closely. The vicar, a fervent advocate of self-help and the unique opportunities for mental and moral improvement offered to working men by the Mechanics' Institute, had been airing his pet subject. Catherine saw Helen's lips flicker at the corners as she said with apparent sincerity,

"If a man can redeem his own soul by his exertions, what other improvements cannot be attained?"

Catherine already knew the impact of Helen's sarcasm at firsthand,

and, unlike the unsuspecting cleric, was well aware that he was being made fun of. Helen seemed able to make herself liked even by those she ridiculed. At one point she mentioned having heard that the Society for the Conversion of the Jews, with annual subscriptions totaling over thirty thousand pounds, had only secured twenty converts in the past year.

"But I'm sure, Vicar," she had added with a smile, "that none of your parishioners would become Jews for a mere thousand or so."

Later she had joked about the temperance movement killing more men than it saved, town water being demonstrably less healthy than beer. The vicar had laughed heartily at this. The temperance movement was too much connected with dissent for him to approve. Eventually the vicar told a favorite joke—always a sign that he had enjoyed himself—one concerning an occasion when his cook had asked whether a piece of cheese had "gone too far to be saved." The cleric's witty reply being that, though in an unpleasing sense "alive," the cheese possessed no soul and was therefore past salvation. George and Humphrey both chuckled loudly and the meal ended with goodwill all around. Catherine acknowledged that Helen had a remarkable talent for being offensive without actually causing offense, especially when speaking to men.

Afterward, determined to avoid George, Catherine had taken herself off to the Sculpture Gallery, which Humphrey's great-grandfather had built to house his collection of classical statuary. She was sitting despondently on the broad rim of a large marble sarcophagus when she heard footsteps and looked up to see Tom enter. Her funereal seat was situated in an apse and so he did not notice her at first but started to examine the statues with interest. He was standing absorbed in front of the entwined figures of Bacchus and a satyr as Catherine spoke his name. He started and turned in her direction.

"Miss Crawford, I didn't see you."

"If you had done so, I am sure you would by now have found a reason to leave." She said this softly, concealing some of her bitterness.

"Leave? Before looking at works like these? I had no idea they were here." He gazed from side to side and made a vague gesture embracing the entire room. "Some pieces are superb. That figure of a slave," he pointed. "And there, just to the left, the boy playing a pipe."

"Statues are conveniently silent," she said, determined not to let him so easily evade her implied question.

"On the contrary," he replied as lightly as before. "That figure of Minerva positively screams out that she is no more complete than Lord Anglesey after Waterloo. Look at that crudely replaced leg."

Catherine gave him a tight smile and moved a pace closer.

"What is your reason for avoiding me?" she asked, feeling the blood rush to her cheeks.

He looked down at the large shell pattern inlaid in the marble floor and shut his eyes for a moment.

"I could not risk coming to feel too much."

Tom heard her sharp intake of breath and saw her fingers clutching the fringed border of her silk shawl. At first he thought that she was deeply moved but then noticed her forehead crease with anger.

"Am I so great a fool, sir? You mean you could not or would not risk *me* feeling too much for you."

"I am not guilty of that presumption . . ."

"Is it presumptuous to afford me the courtesy of a few minutes conversation each day?" Seeing that he would not reply, she calmed herself a little and asked more as an entreaty than a command: "Did Lady Goodchild tell you to change your behavior to me?"

"She did not," he replied at once; and although she caught his eye, he did not look away, nor did his gaze waver. Catherine felt her lips begin to tremble and tears spring to her eyes; a moment later a low, powerful sob surprised her. He stepped toward her with outstretched arms, but she turned from him furiously. He saw her lean against the plinth supporting a bust of an emperor, but, though her shoulders trembled, she made no further sound. At last she murmured without turning,

"What must you think of me?"

"I respect and . . ."

"Respect!" she cried. "What use is respect?" Then with a great effort of control she came toward him and said quietly, "I am all right, Mr. Strickland. You may leave me. Please."

He started for the door, but, before reaching it, came face to face with George Braithwaite.

"Seen Miss Crawford, Strickland?" he asked brusquely. "Hell of a house for finding people in." His eyes bulged slightly as he took in some of the female nude figures and Bacchus's priapic pose. Catherine had had time to reach the apse from which she had watched Tom five minutes earlier. Tom's hope was to talk to George and prevent him going into the gallery. "The Romans knew a thing or two I never learned at school," went on George moving forward as he spoke.

"You read Catullus?" asked Tom in a last vain attempt to stop Braithwaite, whose eye had lighted upon the female slave. He took several steps forward and saw Catherine. As Tom heard George embark upon an apparently endless list of places where he had searched for Catherine, he slipped away.

Catherine left the apse and came toward George without betraying her previous emotion.

"Won't keep you long, Miss Crawford. Only came to say good-bye." He looked in embarrassment at the statues, evidently hoping that his remark about the Romans knowing a thing or two had not been overheard. He also sensed that he had come at a bad moment.

"I hear you've bought into the Guards?"

"Hope I get on better in the infantry," he replied with a modesty that surprised her.

"I'm sure you will."

"Truth is, I couldn't stay here after what happened."

"You mean between us?" she asked, distressed to think that he was leaving because of her.

"And the election . . . everything." He moved uneasily and cleared his throat. "Rejection makes a man think . . . I know you won't believe I've changed." He laughed edgily. "Course I can't claim much credit when things did the changing for me." He tapped the top of his hat with his cane. "If we go to war, I'll not turn out a dud, Miss Crawford. Not when I think of you I won't. I'm not the duffer you took me for."

"I never took you for anything of the sort." She moved closer to him. "I'm truly sorry about everything, George."

"Can't be helped," he replied gruffly, gazing past her at a plaster urn in a medallion on the wall. He seemed about to add something, but turned abruptly. Halfway across the room he stopped.

"Damned if I'll feel the same about anybody else, Miss Crawford. Damned if I will."

Then without expecting a reply or waiting for one, he walked out, his riding boots echoing loudly on the marble floor.

* * *

Later the same afternoon Catherine found Helen reading in the arbor at the end of the Pergola Walk. Shafts of sunlight filtered through the overhanging canopy of wisteria and honeysuckle, speckling Helen's straw hat and pale yellow dress with glowing points of light. Helen put down her book and motioned to Catherine to sit down on the rustic bench beside her wicker chair.

They talked for a while about the beauty of the day, and about *Henry Esmond*, the novel Helen was reading, and the vicar's wife, whose chilly manner and pink complexion had always made Helen mentally christen her "the strawberry ice." And in a natural manner their conversation had drifted to Tom Strickland, Helen mentioning that he had started work on the final portrait. Catherine then asked whether Helen was pleased with the sketches.

"He is competent certainly," was her dismissive reply.

"Only that?"

"Competence is not unimportant in an artist."

"To me it means correct but uninspired," objected Catherine.

"Inspiration is rare," sighed Helen, lying back languidly with half-closed eyes. "I'm always sorry for artists. Nowadays they've so little imagination that they spend most of their time dredging their way through history and literature for subjects. Such a labor, and most of them are fearfully uneducated. Imagine knowing no Homer and practicing heroic Greek art." She cast her eyes upward at the absurdity of the idea. "Small wonder they all end up with the same trite scenes from *Don Quixote* and the *Vicar of Wakefield*." She sat up again and smiled at Catherine. "Poor Mr. Strickland went to a deplorable commercial academy in Wandsworth where he learned nothing."

"The same, I believe, has been achieved at Eton," returned Catherine coldly. "Mr. Strickland also went to the Royal Academy Schools."

"A pity that they taught him no conversation there. His boorish silences make sitting very drear."

"My brother would never stay with a taciturn boor."

Catherine saw Helen's raised brows and her questioning look.

"My dear, forgive me. I never thought that my idle criticism of Mr. Strickland would distress you."

Catherine longed to leap at her and slap the superior, slightly contemptuous smile from her face. Her voice shook as she said,

"I think you knew it would. I think that is why you said it. You don't think him ignorant or uncouth but said so to test my reaction."

Helen's smile changed to a look of surprise and misunderstood rectitude.

"But, Catherine, how can my opinion of him, whether true or false, affect you?"

"You belittled Mr. Strickland to make me defend him."

Helen seemed puzzled for a moment and then looked sharply at Catherine.

"Let me assure you, Miss Crawford, if I thought you foolish enough to consider hurling yourself at the feet of an impecunious artist, I would speak plainly enough."

Catherine got up and looked down at Helen.

"As plainly as you have already spoken to Mr. Strickland?"

Helen also rose, being careful as she picked up her book to put a marker in her place.

"You did not answer me, Lady Goodchild."

Helen tried to take her arm, but she pulled it away.

"I had no reason to answer. Having no suspicion of this . . . stupidity, what reason would I have had to *speak* to him, as you put it?"

"I think your memory is at fault, your ladyship," replied Catherine, just managing to keep down her voice.

"It would be better if you thought carefully before continuing this conversation."

Catherine watched some ants crossing the stones and disappearing into a narrow crack. When she spoke again she was more composed.

"I am not your ward and will not be dictated to. I have some jewelry I could sell. I could become a governess and would." She paused and breathed deeply. "I would endure even that rather than stay here against my will."

Helen had listened without evident emotion, nor did she show any as she said,

"Your father must know the reason if you decide to go."

Catherine let out a false laugh.

"I am sure I may depend upon your ladyship to tell him."

"Only if you leave, or continue these threats."

After saying this Helen walked away toward the house. When she had reached the shelter of the rose garden, she covered her face with her hands which were trembling badly, and swayed slightly as if she might fall. Ahead of her a climbing rose had come away from the wall and trailed across the path. With a sudden angry gesture she clasped her hand around the thickest stem and closed her fingers on the thorns.

⤚ Twenty-Seven ⤙

After breakfast, on the day that Tom intended for Helen's last sitting, he had some time on his hands, and not wishing to talk to anybody, went up to his bedroom where he found an underhousemaid at work. The girl started to retire, but being curious to see exactly what she did, he told her to continue. Before starting on the bed she took two velvet chairs out onto the landing—dust, she explained, being hard to get out of velvet. Next she stripped off the blankets and sheets and hung them on a clotheshorse in front of the window to air.

The bed was a large half tester with valance, back curtain and hanging silk side curtains. To Tom's amazement the girl lifted off the two mattresses and feather bed, exposing the rough cloth of the straw paillasse at the bottom. The mattresses were turned and the feather bed shaken and beaten to separate the feathers before being replaced. While the sheets aired, she dusted, brushed, emptied the water jugs and ewers into a slop pail, wiped and rinsed them, looked under the bed to see if the chamber pot needed emptying and then once more turned her attention to the bed. If he had asked for a bath that morning, she or another servant would have had to bring it up, carry cans of hot and cold water from the kitchen and when he had finished, empty it by hand, taking down the dirty water in pails. In winter she would have started by making up the fire. Tom thought of the same or similar processes going on in every occupied room in the house throughout the year; he thought too of the constant work in the dairy and creamery, in the kitchens, washing rooms and pantries, in the plate room, estate offices, stables and gardens, and he felt dazed by the sheer quantity of labor which women like Helen considered to be their right. Knowing that domestic servants were better cared for than factory workers, he did not feel angry, nor did he feel envious, only surprised that during his brief stay, he too had started to take for granted his perfectly laundered shirts, his polished shoes and immaculate room.

Noon, and Helen was looking at her portrait in attentive silence. The background was incomplete, so too her dress, but her face, shoulders and hands were finished. The ambivalent sadness of the preliminary sketches had been replaced by a more assured expression. The uncertain smile had gone, and now, instead of tremulously parted lips, her mouth was firm and slightly compressed with little brackets at the corners suggesting quizzical amusement. Her eyes were no longer looking down, but gazed out confidently at the beholder with a look of challenging inquiry. Here was Helen as Tom had seen her in company: social Helen, the mistress of every situation, never shocked, never at a loss: a proud, self-confident but not insensitive expression, the public face rather than the unguarded private one of the sketches.

Tom had walked away from his work and was staring fixedly out of the window. The portrait in his eyes was a travesty; he also reproached himself for having followed Helen's advice over Catherine. By making himself remote, he had merely increased the girl's infatuation, inaccessibility and mystery often being better stimulants of passion than complete knowledge. Now, wise after the event, he was sure that had he been as openhearted as she, he could hardly have caused her greater distress than that inflicted by his immediate rejection. Nor looking back was he happy to have renounced an intimate relationship that could have brought them both happiness—albeit of short duration. Catherine was undoubtedly an attractive and unusual woman. It would also have been most gratifying to have imagined the fury Charles Crawford would have felt had he ever learned the object of his sister's affection.

But neither Catherine's misery, nor his own sense of a missed opportunity, accounted entirely for Tom's feeling of dissatisfaction. His greatest self-reproach stemmed from the fact that in this, as in the matter of the portrait, he had deferred to Helen Goodchild's wishes. Believing more in an aristocracy of merit than one of heredity, Tom did not consider that he had been overawed by Helen's rank, nor could he explain away his obedience as a means of gaining her ladyship's good opinion in order to secure new commissions from among her wide acquaintance. The simple truth seemed to be that in spite of, or possibly because of, the unpredictability that made her charming one moment and mordantly scathing the next, she exercised a personal influence over him not far removed from fascination. Memories disturbed him· the vicious way in which she had once attacked portraiture as a dead art, her rudeness to him during her first sitting, followed at once by her bizarre gesture of reconciliation, had all left him confused and feeling at a disadvantage.

If he spoke only in harmless commonplaces, she treated him like a fool, but when he spoke his mind, he always ran the risk of being reproved for discourtesy. His solution had been a proud but respectful silence, but this too had failed. Whenever she had been serious with him, he had felt obliged to reply in the same spirit. On more than one occasion she had made fun of him for tentative replies which she had described as "arrogant humility."

When she had finished looking at the portrait, she gestured to him to come closer.

"It will do nicely, Mr. Strickland."

"I am glad to have pleased your ladyship."

"You're nothing of the sort."

"Since I did not please myself, it is some compensation to have satisfied my sitter."

She smiled, evidently amused.

"That perhaps is nearer the truth." She put down the Oriental fan which she had held while sitting and looked at him reproachfully. "I know I've said so before, but it would be such a relief if you could be less careful of your dignity."

"I have little else to take care of."

"Your talent?" she asked with a trace of gentle mockery. He stiffened inwardly.

"Your picture shows how I value that commodity."

"When you return to London I am sure you will be able to paint scenes more to your taste: *Night in the Workhouse* or *Workmen in the Gin Shop*."

"There is little enthusiasm for such work," he replied coldly.

Helen stared at him with a concern which he was well aware was false, and then pretended to be deep in thought. A moment later she looked up brightly.

"Change the names then. Try the *Seven Sleepers of Ephesus* and the *Roman Holiday*. Roman mobs are always much more acceptable; their togas are so clean." Uncertain whether this was an attack on him personally, or on current popular taste, Tom remained silent. "Or a more humorous subject? I have an excellent one for you." She looked at him expectantly, but he did not meet her eye. "Shall I tell it you?"

"Please do."

"A monk gazing at fattened sows in a pen, and called *Thoughts of Christmas*."

"I am sure it would sell excellently."

"I know I can think of others."

"Your ladyship should have been an artist."

Helen laughed delightedly at his heavy sarcasm.

"I really am sorry," she said, still laughing. "But your grand scorn for low storytelling art is more disdainful than anything a duchess could manage."

"Being an artist I cannot share your detachment over the condition of my profession."

"Forgive my deviousness, but I think I've proved us equals in pride if not in possessions." She smiled enigmatically and motioned to him to sit beside her on a chaise longue by the window. A light breeze from the garden was rustling the curtains. "Perhaps you have read *Le Rouge et le Noir?*" she asked in a matter-of-fact voice. Tom shook his head. "The Marquis de la Mole has his secretary, Julien, wear a black coat during the day and a blue one in the evening. In the black coat Julien is a servant, in the blue, a friend." She looked at him thoughtfully. "Could you put on a blue coat, Mr. Strickland? Your black one gives you too many advantages. You talk to me in a tone which says, 'I humor the woman because I'm paid to, not because I wish to.' Contempt is never more apparent than when dutifully concealed."

"All right, my blue coat is on," replied Tom in a resigned voice. He suspected that he was about to be made the butt of some subtle joke. She looked at him admiringly.

"How well it suits you. A perfect fit."

"I'm not so sure."

It had occurred to Tom that the implication behind Helen's literary allusion was, "How charming I could be if you were not who you are. But I am considerate enough to be prepared to imagine you're something different. Naturally since *my* personality is perfect, you must be the one to make changes. Don't expect *me* to."

"What's wrong with it."

"I prefer my old one, and would like your ladyship to wear a coat of the same color."

"But, Tom, I thought you far too democratic to worry about niceties of protocol." This quite unexpected use of his Christian name made Tom catch his breath; the shock was almost as acute as if she had touched him. She smiled at him and held up her hands. "Very well, my coat is black." She turned to him and he was aware of the proximity of her bare arms and shoulders. "Now tell me, Tom, did Catherine ask you whether I had spoken about her?"

"She did, and I denied it."

"She was very angry with me."

"I did *not* tell her."

"Then perhaps you can explain her anger."

"A voluntary rejection is always harder to bear than one that is forced."

"She was angry because she believed you acted solely by inclination?"

"I think so."

Helen appeared to think about this for a few seconds, then she got up and walked over to the mantelpiece. Tom sensed that she was not satisfied with what he had said, but could think of no way to convince her. Also he suspected that the investigation was aimed less at Catherine's thoughts than his own. She appeared to be trying to force some kind of admission. The steady, uninhibited way she was appraising him made him embarrassed. He shifted his gaze from her to the Vulliamy clock behind her on the mantelpiece. He heard her say,

"There is an alternative, isn't there, Tom?"

She was waiting patiently for his reply; he could tell from her tone that his answer would be important and was frightened to say the wrong thing, but his heart was beating too fast and he could not think clearly. All the time he was aware of her remorseless eyes. At last he shrugged his shoulders and let his hands drop to his knees.

"It's stupid, I know." He paused and took a breath. "I suppose she could have thought you wanted me for yourself . . . that you were jealous of her love . . ." He let his sentence end unfinished and felt his cheeks glowing. She crossed the room and sat opposite him in Warren Hastings' ivory chair; the silence while she did so seemed unbearably long to Tom, who could tell nothing from her expression about how she had taken what he had said.

"And that idea seems stupid to you?" The same bland, matter-of-fact voice.

"She knows you're to marry her father," he objected with attempted incredulity.

"And she believes my motive is pure convenience?"

Tom contrived a laugh as he said,

"All the more reason why you would never jeopardize your whole future by such folly."

"A woman in love does not calculate risks." She gave him a half-sad smile. "Supposing me to be in that condition, why should she expect me to be cautious?"

Again Tom was at a loss how to reply; he tried to remember exactly what had preceded her last question but failed. The stupid game over blue and black coats and her use of his Christian name had blurred the clearly defined roles which he greatly preferred to her elaborate pretense of a temporary equality. At last the constant air of tension, present during all her sittings, had brought him close to breaking with all inhibition. All his past experience with women suggested that she wanted him to believe that she was strongly attracted to him—her object probably no more than to make a fool of him to relieve her boredom, just as flirtatious girls will encourage a man to be able to slap his face. Perhaps she really had been jealous of Catherine and was simply striving to assert her superiority over a younger woman.

He had been staring fixedly at the border of the carpet, but, when he looked up, he saw an expression so vulnerably open and so tender that his defensive suspicions instantly melted away. All that his mind seemed capable of grasping was the reality of that look. His heart was fluttering and his breath came quickly.

"What did you ask me? . . . Something about Miss Crawford?"

He guessed at once from her swift glance of reproach and the sudden lowering of her eyes that she had mistaken his genuine inability to reply for a deliberate refusal to allow her the saving grace of an indirect approach. Unable to endure her silence he stammered out,

"Either I'm mad or you intend me to understand . . . that your feelings toward me are . . ."

"Improper?" she murmured. "Shameless? What are the words most often used?" Her cheeks were burning, but she held his eyes with a defiance that astonished him after her anguished reticence. "Now you know the meaning of hypocrisy, Mr. Strickland. But then a lady's most useful accomplishment is her ability to say quite naturally the opposite to what she thinks. Miss Crawford being well schooled understood at once what I have had such labor to acquaint you with." She bowed her head and then looked at him beseechingly, all traces of cynicism gone. "You must not ask for explanations . . . I cannot give them. Think what you wish. Only the guilty feel the need to justify."

A wild elation made his head swim. Goodchild's ethereal wife, proud, inaccessible, capricious Helen, prepared to make herself his mistress? A powerful wave of pride and dominance overjoyed him, only to be succeeded by a piercing shaft of doubt. How many times before during her marriage had this scene been acted out? With houseguests, even her son's tutors as victims? Could he honestly claim that he knew her any better now than he had done after their first meeting? Her instability frightened and fascinated him. Her eyes were glittering and her cheeks still flushed. An overpowering longing to sit by her and touch her caught him unawares. Not happiness now, not exultation, but a yearning more like pain. A terror of future hurt and loss overwhelmed him. He tore his eyes from her face, furious with himself for feeling so much and so soon. An eager schoolboy rushing to thrust his hands in the fire. Fools gave themselves away easily. No longer confused, thoughts came to him with stark clarity. She would tell him nothing, would not explain or justify, disdaining to give assurances to a plebeian artist who would be grateful for whatever crumbs she might let fall. Even when revealing herself she had maintained the privileges of her position, and he, fool that he was, had been on the brink of babbling endearments. Forcing himself to be calm, he started to collect his brushes. At last he moved toward her and said softly,

"A man who loves, where he can have no claims, will suffer; where he may not even ask for a single proof of sincerity, his helplessness is too abject even for pity."

"Proof?" she whispered as though astonished. Her wounded tone pained him but he maintained his show of detachment.

"I have so little to offer you, and you so much to lose that I fear you are toying with me."

She rose and faced him with such sadness that he felt ashamed even before she spoke.

"If what I have to lose is insufficient proof of my sincerity, what other may I give? You could ruin me at will; yes, and my son. Yet you speak of having no claims. You fear you may be unhappy . . ." She broke off, her eyes bright with unshed tears. "My God, do you think me immune from that disease? Am I so jaded that I must risk ruin simply to beguile a few tedious hours?"

The passion with which she had spoken shook him badly, undermining all his previous sense of resolution. Close to surrender, he still resisted.

"To escape intolerable unhappiness and to forget the future, thousands do daily what they very soon regret. . . . Tomorrow I could leave to finish your portrait in my studio."

"Or you may finish it here. The choice is yours."

Why be afraid and not thankful? Why should he run from his strongest inclinations out of fear? Suddenly he was gripped by an intense and vehement pleasure in being where he was, in seeing what was before him, in being close to her and knowing that he would kiss her . . . she in evening dress, he in his paint-spotted clothes. He saw from her apprehensive expression that his face had not betrayed his new mood. Fear? With the returning tide of confidence, he was dumbfounded by his former hesitance.

"You still need proof?" she asked, coming toward him. Before he could answer, she had cut the ground from under him, as she had so often done before. With ceremonious slowness she went down on her knees in front of him.

Never in his life had Tom seen a more defiant act of self-abasement. He was appalled by the thought that somebody might enter. The habit of deferring to her left him hideously embarrassed to see her at his feet; he felt powerless rather than commanding.

"Please don't," he begged.

"Are you convinced?"

"Anybody may come . . . your son . . . Catherine . . ."

She smiled at him as he realized his true position. He had proved him-self more frightened of discovery than she, though she had everything to lose. Her proof was irrefutable. In acknowledgment he too went down on his knees and embraced her, awkwardly at first, too conscious of her naked shoulders. She turned his cheek and kissed him firmly on the mouth, leaving him gasping for breath. Her teeth hurt his lips, but he did not break away.

"Convinced?" she whispered again, her eyes tender and yet mocking.

"Yes, yes," he sighed.

They held each other perhaps ten seconds, but to Tom it seemed far longer, so much did he feel during that time on his knees, beside an ornate ivory chair, under Angelica Kauffmann's painted ceiling, in a room which he had once chosen for the quality of the light.

~ Twenty-Eight ~

Among her letters brought in by the butler, Helen saw the Admiralty seal on one of the envelopes. She did not leave the breakfast table at once but continued talking to Humphrey with apparent unconcern. Afterward she went up to the small sitting room where she kept all her papers and shut the door. Her hand shook a little as she picked up an ivory paper knife and slit open the flap of the envelope above the embossed anchor.

> My dearest Helen,
> How I wish I could be with you in England instead of stifling here, becoming daily more convinced of my inability to influence anybody in this slow drift into war . . .

She put down the sheets of paper and covered her face with her hands, but moments later she got up abruptly from her seat at the bureau and walked over to the open window where she stood looking out at the unchanging pattern of clipped hedges and symmetrical lawns. Nothing there had changed, the room was no different, the sky as blue, the sun shining as brightly, and should she feel sudden shame and guilt because of a letter? He had sent others, and would send more, and they too, she promised herself, would alter nothing. She would be true to her word; she had agreed to marry Sir James, and marry him she would, but until she did, she would please herself. She had been discontented too long to be prepared to surrender any possibility of happiness that came her way in these last months of freedom.

Yet in spite of her determination, the guilt remained: guilt mixed with anger. James had been perfectly aware that her financial problems had increased his chances, and, although she had told him honestly that she did not love him, he had forced an answer from her before he went away instead of giving her time to know her mind more fully. His trump card had been her fear that if she delayed acceptance, the offer might not be repeated on his return, and though others might well have offered, she had needed immediate and certain support to save her son's inheritance. That too he had appreciated. Now was she to reproach herself for failing in his absence to dedicate herself to self-denial and to bow down at the altars of prudence and propriety, those twin goddesses whose one injunction was to pursue material advantage with a cautious single-mindedness that left nothing to chance? Never. Before paying her final forfeit to financial necessity, she would prove to herself that she could still be free, if only for a few brief months; and since all moderate and safely acceptable behavior would merely confirm her slavery, this proof demanded that she risk everything and have the courage to follow a course, which if revealed, would bring disgrace and ruin.

She could imagine the universal incredulity should it ever be known that she had encouraged a man without money, influence and noble blood, and had indeed chosen him for these very deficiencies. He was what he was through no accidental or external advantages. Tom's pride was innate and no mere badge of caste and wealth. She had been more contrary and provoking with him than she had been with any other man, but he had never behaved badly in return, nor had he ever lost his dignity and shown bitterness in the face of her mockery. In the end, in spite of all her wiles, she felt that *she* had become the humble supplicant and he, the penniless artist, her generous judge of bequests. Far from turning his head, her change toward him had revealed a strength of character she had never suspected. When she had offered herself, he had questioned her avowal and had given her the chance to retract; perhaps he had even been trying to protect her. Until that time, she had been as much absorbed by the thought of a daring and unforgivable liaison as with Tom himself, but his attitude had tipped the balance. Briefly, it was true, she had wondered whether his withdrawal had been a calculated attempt to draw her on still further, but the helpless embarrassment he had shown when she had gone down on her knees had disposed of this fear; in fact his bewilderment had touched her deeply. With no possible previous experience of the behavior of true ladies, his attempted calmness and self-possession had been quite remarkable.

Immediately after their kissing she had felt remorse. To make him love her, without being sure of her own feelings, was selfish and wrong. The attraction of his youth, freedom and novelty could not justify causing him suffering. His suggestion that she might have acted as she had to escape the future had worried her; but when they had met again at dinner, the painful tension she had felt in talking to him as though nothing had happened had made her long to see him alone, and sitting close to him she had had to struggle with a powerful impulse to stretch out her hand. The difficulty she felt in fragmenting herself and changing from one role to another finally convinced her that she felt something very close to love; for the first time she felt frightened that she might lack the courage to sustain the part she had begun to play. What would he feel for her when her mystery had gone? Loving her might mean no more to him than an unusual adventure, a pleasing gratification of social ambition. Perhaps in the end he would reject her as revenge for having been forced to seek the patronage of a class he secretly hated. Yet she could not believe it of him. How could such naturalness and candor be false? There was no bitterness in that open face framed by tousled hair. The acid of disappointment and resentment had etched no lines around his mouth, nor dimmed the optimism of his brown eyes. His looks were not exactly innocent, he was too intelligent and had experienced too much for that, but his face still had the purity of expression only given to those unenslaved by fear and thwarted hopes. He was probably no more than five or six years younger than she, but Helen felt an age apart, and this added to her other feelings a poignant nostalgia for what she had lost. For her his true possessions were emphasized by his poverty, a condition which she was sure would have crushed her. Even his faults pleased her: his social uncertainty which at times made him ludicrously formal, and his light, restless gestures and nervous silences made her feel tenderly protective.

When Helen returned to her letter she felt more composed, but James's small precise hand still caused her acute apprehension. If peace could be guaranteed, he would soon be returning; if war became inevitable, that would be equally agonizing, her precarious happiness unlikely to survive the insistent clamor of the outside world. Her marriage would take place earlier, and James, if his post were made permanent, would expect her to join him in Turkey; her distance from England and the thunder of the guns would soon blot out all softer notes.

... We arrived in Constantinople yesterday having traveled from Vienna via Trieste. A hot and disagreeable journey—railways are really good for nothing except to go blindfold from place to place with superior velocity . . .

When she came to details of the diplomatic negotiations, Helen found herself not so much unable to take them in as fearful and reluctant to understand the vast impersonal forces shaping her destiny. Sentences and phrases danced before her. "Stratford will recommend the Turks to reject the Vienna Note . . . evacuation of Moldavia . . . rights of the sultan's Christian subjects . . ." At times she could almost hear Sir James's urbane and wearily ironic voice, and then she read carefully:

... I fear that in two months' time we will still be engaged in the same curious game, tossing a ball—often called a note, declaration or convention—from Vienna to Paris to London to Constantinople and finally, the longest toss of all, to the goal at St. Petersburg. But either it never starts, or falls to bits in the air, or bounces into the seraglio precincts and the sultan kicks it under the table where it vanishes. The worst of it is that each new ball spoils the one already in use, and since we cannot control the number thrown in, this is always happening. Hence the Vienna Note wrecked Lord S.'s plan, which ruined Clarendon's convention, which killed the first French draft; and so we will go on. I could write an Oriental romance entitled the *Thousand and One Notes*, but fear it would be anything but diverting. . . . With every added month of negotiation the Czar will become more sure that we don't intend to fight if he starts a war. . . . In a month or two Turkey will fight willy-nilly. Of course if the cabinet presents the Czar with a clear ultimatum, we may yet escape, but I doubt it. All the time the Russians are building up forces and our own army is footling at Chobham. By the time the fleet is sent for it will be winter, and a cruise in the Black Sea then won't be all pleasure, with gales, snow and ice. A sorry figure we will cut the following spring when the naval war starts. . . . So here I am to advise on naval matters and for all the notice that is taken of me, I might as well be at Timbuktu. If you were here I might even find something good to say of this utterly alien place. On the Bosphorus you constantly hear the muezzin's call from the minarets and the crash of guns announcing that the sultan has gone to the mosque, or that it is Ramadan or Bairam or some other Mohammedan feast, or the day when the Prophet went to heaven on a white camel, or was it brown? . . . In a week I hope to go botanizing on the Asian side of the Bosphorus with Skene and Franklin, two young attachés from the embassy. The others will think us mad to be scrambling about in the heat in eager pursuit of eastern "flora," but there are literally thousands of beautiful wild plants and shrubs—many unknown in England. Also butterflies that make our peacock look a drab clerk by comparison. When I grow tired I shall imagine you by my side with a white parasol in your hand and that lovely smile and I'll soon be pushing on the youngsters and not vice versa.

If God help me I am still here in November, could you think seriously about coming out? You would be carried through the streets in a sedan chair like your grandmother, which would at least be a novelty, and I will be the best guide I can. I am sure Lady Stratford would invite you as her guest, so there would be no impropriety. The wearisome conduct of the crisis would seem a small burden to bear with you to share it—if you could bear to be the recipient of so much irritation and disappointment. . . .

Helen started as she heard the door opening. Looking up, she saw Humphrey entering hesitantly.

"I saw the envelope; couldn't help seeing it." He paused anxiously. "You're not cross? I had to know what's happening. Who else gets letters from embassies in Vienna and Constantinople?"

"Lord Clarendon and Sir James Graham," she replied with a smile, watching his look of awe and pleasure. He came closer.

"Can you read bits to me? Will there be a war?"

"James thinks so." Humphrey's undisguised excitement, which had touched her before, now only irritated Helen. "People will die," she said sharply. At once he looked crestfallen and ashamed, probably, she thought, recalling his father's death. Remorse swiftly followed her burst of indignation. What right had she to judge him? The thought of Humphrey finding her out made Helen's heart race.

"Won't it all be over in a month or two?" he asked apologetically. "Nobody's beaten our navy for ever so long."

A new thought had Helen trembling violently—a sudden impulse more than a rational decision. The answer to her guilt: reparation to her future husband, a free choice for her son.

"Do you still want to join the navy?"

His eyes were shining with pleasure and anticipation.

"Who on earth wouldn't at a time like this? Think of it, Charles a captain, Sir James an admiral and me a cadet. Do you think he'll get the Baltic or Black Sea command?"

"He doesn't expect either."

"But Dundas and Napier are far too old. I read that in the papers."

"I shouldn't depend on the papers." She took his hand and went on in a low urgent voice, "You could be hurt, Humphrey—even killed."

"Does that stop the others?"

"Most of them are much older."

"Not the cadets and middies."

Taking a cushion from the ottoman, he tossed it up and caught it.

"I can't stay here all my life; well, can I?"

"Many country gentlemen find occupation enough on their estates."

"Or lounging away their lives in their clubs living on their means. You don't want me to be like that."

A long silence while he waited expectantly.

"I shall write to Charles," she said at last. "He can nominate you when he gets a ship."

Humphrey threw the cushion wildly with both hands, hitting the chandelier and setting the glass pendants tinkling and spinning; then he kissed and hugged his mother. How strange, she thought, that he should be so happy when he knows he will be leaving me, but when she cried a little, he was more affectionate than she could remember him being for several years.

*　　*　　*

After breakfast Tom had prepared himself for Helen's morning sitting, but an hour later she had still not made her appearance. He tried to persuade himself that he was angry, but at the same time found himself making excuses for her: an unexpected letter from her solicitor demanding immediate attention, some crisis with Humphrey or Catherine, an urgent visit from her bailiff. Yet even in these circumstances she could have sent down a servant to tell him that she had been delayed—nothing could have been easier. How could she be unaware that, by leaving him waiting for an hour without explanation, she would make him fear that he had unwittingly displeased her, or that she had altered her opinion of him for some other reason? But still he could not feel angry with her; instead her absence frightened and depressed him.

Tom paced up and down the room, now and then glancing at the clock, and always listening for footsteps, longing for the door to open, and knowing that if at that moment she were to come in smiling with some transparently improbable excuse, he would at once feel happy again. He despised himself for his weakness, but could not help himself. Nor was he comforted by the thought that her lack of consideration increased his feeling of attachment. He accused himself of being a groveling parvenu, of having allowed Helen's superficial social graces to blind him to her underlying selfishness, of being seduced by the beauty and grandeur of the house, of having had his head turned by a little attention. What if her encouragement, which had led him to hope so fondly, had been a device to destroy his already slender powers of resistance? Everything part of a deliberate plan to humiliate him for ever having supposed himself deserving of being her lover? When he had been sure that her love was genuine, he had felt a god, capable of anything, brilliant, witty, self-assured and entirely worthy of her. Just an hour of doubt and he could not tell how she could ever have seen him as anything other than plodding, gauche and ordinary. He tried to think of something amusing and cutting to say when she might eventually appear, but could only contrive remarks that would sound bitter or spiteful. Lightness of touch was what he believed she valued most, but, obsessed as he was with the seriousness of his emotions, everything he thought of seemed portentous and overearnest. Either that, or he would chatter incoherently because of his nervousness. Lovers always said banal and stupid things to each other and found in the most common-place ideas truth and profundity; but, if one were doting and the other detached, matters were very different.

Tom suspected that his only salvation lay in saying and doing little, in the hope that she would find such inaction enigmatic and perplexing. If he confessed his fears, he was certain he would be lost. Never must he admit that he found it all but impossible to think of anything other than her, that her most trivial actions seemed significant to him, that he could hardly concentrate enough to read a book, that he was in constant dread lest a chance remark of his might destroy the impression of him which had initially aroused her interest.

Just before eleven, Helen's lady's maid came in and told him that her ladyship could not sit and sent her apologies. When the girl had gone, Tom was left with a strong impression that she had looked at him strangely. Was it possible that his feelings were evident even to the servants? *Even* to the servants. The pattern of his thought shocked him. Had he come to think of himself as so different from these people, whose condition was much closer to his own than Helen's or Catherine's? Small wonder if it should be one of them to find him out. The idea of eyes following him and ears listening to him at table or from doorways made him panic. He sank down in a chair and stared blindly at the swirling patterns in the carpet, imagining himself facing the admiral. The thought was so humiliating and terrible that he could not envisage any line of defense or justification. And Magnus—what would Magnus think? Magnus who had become his closest friend, whose friendship until a few days ago had been the single most important tie in the world, whose help had procured him his present employment. Magnus hated his father, but however intense that hatred, he could not be expected to welcome the news that his friend had become a lover of the woman his father intended to marry. As it was, his treatment of Catherine might lead her to try to turn Magnus against him, and given any additional opportunity her success could be guaranteed. Tom foresaw Magnus asking him to promise never to see or write to Helen. In his present state of mind he doubted whether he could give any such undertaking. But lose Magnus's friendship—Tom buried his face in the angle of the back of his chair. He thought of his friend on the night he had watched him gamble at Bentley's, recalled his manner of speaking, his courage on the day of the election, his indefatigable capacity for making plans and carrying them out. For a few minutes Tom was nearly convinced that he would, after all, have the strength of mind to pack his things and leave. A moment later Helen came in wearing her black riding habit; she came up to him, and touching his cheek lightly with the tips of the fingers of a gloved hand, said politely,

"A ride in the gig, Mr. Strickland?"

The easy almost mocking confidence of her gesture coupled with the formality of her address made his heart swell. No doubts of him in her mind. She was looking at him expectantly through her veil, her head slightly inclined, her lips parted. He noticed her breath just moving the thin gauze. The servants, Catherine, Magnus, each and every one of his objections died before he had time to think them. Instead he nodded assent and followed her from the room, trying to disguise the elated spring in his step and the wild happiness which made his face ache from the effort of concealment.

The horse stepping high, the tall wheels whirling so that the spokes blurred and merged, and the light open carriage cracking along at a fine pace with harness ringing and leather creaking, the wind cool in their faces as a long white cloud of dust billowed out behind. The effrontery: to drive him herself in a two-seat gig from the front portico, down the drive through the lodge gates, raising her whip to the gatekeeper as he ran out to open the heavy wrought-iron gates and smiling at his daughter helping him. All the time Tom sat impassively beside her, staring at the stone griffins on the flanking piers and longing to ask her where they were going, but remaining true to his determination to say little. She had taken the initiative; let her keep it.

When Helen had asked Tom to come with her, she had done so on impulse, really having intended to get away on her own to think. Since giving in to Humphrey, she had felt in a strange mood—sad because afraid for him, but carefree because she had appeased her conscience: as if by freeing him, her selflessness had granted her a brief dispensation to think only of herself. One moment she felt like saying outrageous things and laughing wildly, the next like listening to or telling a moving story and weeping without restraint. Although she disliked the tarnished and dull midsummer leaves and the parched, burned grass, everything around her seemed highly charged and significant, as though she had previously seen obscurely through a mist which had suddenly cleared. With no precise plan of where to go, she drove to where she had met Charles early that spring.

A very different scene now, the lane luxuriant with rank grass, cow parsley and flowering dog roses, the stream a mere trickle choked with ivy-leaved crowfoot and fringed with purple loosestrife. But even in this damp place the surrounding rough grass was dry and brittle. Hay cutting had started in late May and the corn had been golden by early June; never could she remember a drier, hotter summer. They crossed the field, Tom carrying a rug, and sat down under the silvery leaves of a willow.

After what seemed to Tom a long silence, she took his hand and raised it to her lips, inclining her head toward him in the same movement; again her initiative sanctioning him, he moved closer and kissed her through her veil, drawing back and then kissing her more lightly several times, once more waiting. Without taking her eyes from his face, she pulled the fine gauze aside with a slow, deliberate gesture, but now both moved together, their lips meeting eagerly. He drew off her gloves and kissed her hands, noticing a few light freckles against the pale skin and the faint blueness of veins.

She held him back for a moment, so that he felt that he had exceeded what was expected and looked away to hide his confusion; but when she placed her palms lightly on his cheeks and turned his face toward her, he understood that she had simply wanted to see him better. She reached forward tentatively, almost in shyness, and touched his hair, letting her fingers trail across his cheek down to his neck, looking at him all the while with a tenderness and longing that set his heart pounding wildly and brought a dull inner roar to his ears. Her lips moved a little but she did not speak. Incapable of remaining still, he pulled her to him, oblivious of the small pointed buttons on her bodice jacket and the brushing feathers of her hat. They slipped sideways, their bodies clinging and colliding, but without pain, as if falling in air like gliding birds—their element the rapt absorption of their misting eyes and their quickening breath: breathing and seeing together, as one. Her eyes were half-closed and her parted lips searching for his mouth, kissing his ears and neck as he turned away, her fingers stroking the hair at the nape of his neck, loosening his neckcloth. He jumped up like a man wrestling to shake off unseen wires that yield a little but still hold him. She rose too and took his arm, understanding and feeling grateful for his restraint. Still breathing deeply, he bent down and picked up the rug. His shirt was soaked with sweat.

They walked beside the stream toward the bridge, Helen patting her hair as they went to see what damage her chignon had suffered. She touched her veil and felt that it was torn; as she tossed it aside, Tom plucked it from the grass, blushing at such an obvious piece of chivalry, but she smiled at him and murmured,

"Those who play at hide-and-seek in love are not worth seeking." She sighed and rested her back against the stone arch of the bridge. "Even if I pretended to care for the diplomacy of passion and all its tactics and intrigues, we would not have time for them." He sensed her changing mood and felt an ache of fear. She squeezed his hand to reassure him. "Coming here together was unwise."

"Are we never to be alone?"

"Except for my sittings, no; at least not at Hanley Park." She paused and went on rapidly, "I have various arrangements to make before the sale of our London house. I had not intended to leave a visit longer than three weeks. We will meet then."

"Perhaps I should go sooner than you suggested?"

"It would be better for us."

His look of resigned sadness pierced her to the heart.

"What will you work at when you get back?" she asked gently.

"God knows. Perhaps I'll stare at the wall or drink . . ." He shrugged his shoulders and stared down at the sluggish stream, already amazed that he could have thought that absence from her would be easier than staying and pretending indifference. "I may paint what you suggested— the monk and his pig."

"I should like that; I should like you to think of me."

She kissed his cheek, but they did not embrace; like sailors, he thought, after a rough passage, getting used to firm ground and stepping carefully. It seemed terrible to Helen deliberately to be stifling emotions which their every wish and longing had been to prolong and which she had feared she would never know again. Ahead of them, only the uncertainty of moments snatched, of plans unexpectedly overturned, of tensions and tears. Foreseeing such a future, why should he wish to go on loving her? The thought weakened her resolve to send him away so soon.

Beyond the bridge, cattle were drinking from the stream, and in the still air numerous bees sought out the white clover in the meadow, their humming interrupted by the sharper chirp of grasshoppers. Clouds were forming above the hazy outline of the distant hills.

Helen imagined arriving in London to discover that he would not see her. Other women would console him; he might confess his unhappiness to Magnus who would mix sympathy with advice to forget her. His work would divert him; being younger than she, he would be more resilient. Although Helen often smiled at the mention of truth and duty, her own honesty did not even now allow her to contemplate marrying a man with the definitely formed intention of deceiving him afterward. Tom's chances for love would come again; this, she believed, might be her last. They had been silent for some minutes when she took his hand and murmured without looking at him,

"Come to me tonight." She felt his fingers tighten around hers.

"I don't know your room," he replied, blushing deeply, keenly aware of the bathos of his reply; his skin was tingling and there was a warm throbbing in the muscles of his calves.

"Then I'll come to you." A moment later she laughed and began pulling on her gloves. "I can't imagine why we should be whispering."

He said nothing but started to pick seeds and dry grass from her long black skirt, finally rising and securing a stray lock of hair at her temple. His care for her appearance and his caution made her eyes fill. He had nothing to gain by preserving her reputation—quite the reverse. Only when they were driving home did she wonder whether he had done such things before to avoid discovery. His regular mistress might be a married woman. I know nothing about him, nothing. Yet tonight we will make love. Helen felt faint with shock. She imagined him showing this other woman her veil, telling her how easily her ladyship had been seduced, how he could now expect more portrait work from her aristocratic friends. She reined in the horse and looked at him beseechingly.

"Never talk about me to anybody. I beg you not to."

"I won't; I swear it."

She shut her eyes for a moment and then nodded.

"I believe you," she replied in a low fervent voice, as she lifted the reins. A few minutes later they were approaching the gates.

*　*　*

That afternoon Catherine stood in the doorway of the library watching Tom reading; in fact he had managed barely three pages during the hour he had been sitting there. Since their conversation in the Sculpture Gallery, they had addressed no more than a dozen sentences to each other. Tom heard the rustle of a dress and stood up.

"How is the portrait, Mr. Strickland?"

"As complete as I intend to make it here."

"Surely you are not leaving already?" Catherine asked, with an innocence which he was certain was ironic.

"I go tomorrow."

"It has taken longer than you thought?"

"A few days."

Her cold scrutiny disconcerted him, but he did not show it.

"By asking you to stay on, her ladyship has paid you a rare compliment."

"I must try to merit it," he replied with a laugh. "I fear she has found sitting very dull. She kept me waiting an hour this morning and then did not deign to sit."

Catherine ran her fingers along the spine of a book and then smiled brightly at him.

"Did you enjoy your morning drive?"

"Should I not have done so?" he asked, meeting her gaze.

"Of course not."

She rested her hands on a marquetry table between them, drumming lightly with the tips of her fingers.

"You must forgive my mistake, Mr. Strickland."

"I cannot recall any mistake, Miss Crawford."

"I believed Lady Goodchild had spoken to you concerning me."

"And now you think otherwise?"

"Of course," she replied pertly. "Her ladyship would hardly have considered a man whose company pleases her so much an unsuitable companion for me."

Tom was still thinking of a reply as she left the room.

* * *

Shortly after dinner, Humphrey suggested billiards, and for once Tom was glad to oblige him, since the alternative was to sit with Catherine and Helen, ignoring the unnerving tensions and undercurrents passing between them and trying to make innocuous conversation. A game of billiards also gave Tom a brief respite from his apprehensive thoughts. In the past his progress with Helen had appeared entirely spontaneous, and this had saved them both from self-consciousness and nerves. There would be nothing unplanned or unexpected about tonight; this time both of them would have had hours in which to reflect.

Between shots, Humphrey lounged on the arm of a leather armchair, sipping claret and talking about the navy; he also lit a cigar and persevered with it in spite of several bad fits of coughing. His valiant efforts to be a man of the world amused Tom and he enjoyed calling the boy "my lord" and in return being called "Strickland"—a token of familiarity, he thought, rather than superiority. They were in the middle of their second game when Helen and Catherine came into the Billiard Room. While Humphrey raised his eyebrows disapprovingly at what he evidently considered an unwarrantable violation of this male sanctum, Tom hurriedly finished his shot before turning to greet the ladies.

They sat down on the long, buttoned-leather sofa in front of the window and watched the play in silence, a proceeding which did not please Tom, since Humphrey began playing with an expertise and determination which he had not shown when they were alone. This was not the first time that Tom had noticed Humphrey's eagerness to impress Catherine, nor did he intend to spoil the boy's attempt by making an exceptional effort to avoid defeat. In the end Humphrey won comfortably.

"I hope you win all your naval battles so easily," said Catherine, as Humphrey put away his cue. "I am sure that I should be frightened of becoming a sailor with everyone speaking of war."

Tom had an uncomfortable feeling that Catherine had really aimed this remark at Helen; he was still uneasy about what she had said in the library, and was determined that if they argued, he would remain neutral.

"Even officers who have been in action ever so many times are a bit nervous," replied Humphrey.

"Of course war is by no means certain," added Helen. "Nobody wants it, not even the Czar."

Catherine got up and on reaching the table, began bouncing the red ball back and forth off the opposite cushion; in the light of the bright moderator lamp above the table, her eyes shone mischievously.

"Why on earth is everybody pretending to be against a war? Lots of promotion for soldiers and sailors, contracts for caterers and shipbuilders, and the whole thing fought out thousands of miles away over somebody else's country by people paid to do it."

"You can't want people to be killed," said Humphrey, genuinely shocked by her apparent cynicism.

"Isn't it rather like cholera—dying in battle? Nobody thinks it'll happen to them, so they don't worry. And anyway, we're going to win, aren't we?"

"I find your attitude a little surprising," said Helen icily, "especially at a time when your father is doing everything he can to preserve peace."

Catherine smiled sympathetically and leaned against the side of the table.

"I wonder if he's told you why he thinks my lord Aberdeen such an old woman?" Helen did not reply. "Apparently his lordship toured the battlefield at Leipzig and was so stricken by the bodies of the slain that there and then he became a Quaker—in sentiment if not in name. Perhaps he had expected to see flowers instead of corpses—my father's words."

"If you are suggesting that your father would encourage Humphrey to become a naval officer, knowing that he stood a high risk of being killed, I think you ought to say so clearly."

"Your ladyship knows his thoughts better than I, but you may have heard that half his crew were dead before he moved out of the line at Navarino. The officers on the gun decks had to threaten to shoot men to keep them at their guns."

Tom noticed that Humphrey appeared animated rather than cowed by this information. To his relief Helen still seemed perfectly calm.

"The circumstances were hardly similar. Your father is convinced the Russians will not leave harbor."

"Perhaps we will send in the fleet to sink them at anchor?"

"Kronshtadt and Sevastopol are too well fortified," said Humphrey, more with disappointment than relief.

"I hope so for everybody's sake," replied Catherine, sweeping one of the white balls into a pocket with a loud thump.

"Your father has repeatedly said so, and I have perfect confidence in his judgment."

Catherine glanced at Helen and said quietly,

"He is fortunate to enjoy such loyalty and trust." She turned to Tom and Humphrey. "I have stopped your play; forgive me, gentlemen."

As Catherine left, Tom was convinced by Helen's expression that she was also aware of the barbed irony in Catherine's parting words to her. Although Catherine's bitterness distressed him, Tom was sure that it owed more to wounded pride and a personal dislike of Helen than to any evidence more damning than their ride together, unaccompanied by coachman or groom. Jealousy could be founded on even less—on a word or a glance. Given time to reflect, Tom was confident that Catherine would see that she had allowed her emotions to distort her judgment. Tom's fear was that Helen might be unable to take such a philosophical view of her future stepdaughter's behavior.

Having played a final game with Humphrey, this time of pyramid, and having lost it badly through inattention, Tom rang for a servant to light him to his room.

He lay fully clothed on his bed, doing his best to prepare himself for what he expected to be a long and anxious wait, made worse by a growing suspicion that she would not come. Their morning by the stream seemed to have happened weeks rather than hours ago; and since then, worries about her son and Catherine would have reminded Helen forcefully of the realities of her situation. The darkness of the room and the deep shadows cast by the candles on each side of the bed made the sunlit fields seem still more remote. He fumbled in the pocket of his frock coat and pulled out her veil, staring at it for several moments before replacing it. Then he undressed rapidly and climbed into bed. For a time he wondered whether he ought to wear his nightshirt but in the end decided not to, its patched condition overcoming his shyness at being naked when she came. A moment later he laughed aloud at the absurdity of worrying about such things. The beautiful kingwood chest, with its intricate brass inlay and gilt bronzes, was filled with his worn shirts, and threadbare underwaistcoats and trouser drawers. Beside the carved sphinxes, supporting the porphyry and marble top of the dressing table were his only pair of new shoes, bought specially for his stay at Hanley Park. After thoroughly impressing on himself the *bizarrerie* of his position, Tom felt less nervous, and fell to thinking about the various conversations he had had with Helen since his arrival. Later, thinking of the future, he imagined himself welcoming Helen in his studio and laughing with her about the cracked skylight and stained floorboards; he saw Magnus come in and was relieved that he did not seem angry or disturbed to see Helen, but embraced her warmly and offered her some wine.

When the clock in the cupola above the stables struck one, Tom was asleep.

Helen entered silently, closing the door with great care and placing her candlestick on the edge of the washstand. At first she thought that

Tom was feigning sleep to impress her with his *sang-froid*, but, on coming closer, she realized, from his light regular breathing and the peaceful expression of his pale, upturned face, that he was indeed sleeping. The candles had burned right down and several were sputtering and on the point of going out. For a moment she felt angry with him, as if for a betrayal. He had not had to endure the nerve-racking minutes she had lived through on the stairs and in the long passageway, listening every few feet, testing each board; discovery could not bring *him* ruin. *Had I waited for him, I should never have been able to sleep.* Yet looking at his closed eyelids and tousled hair, she felt her anger ebbing, respecting him for his calmness. She sat down gently on the edge of the bed, being careful not to wake him until she had laid her cheek against his; for a moment he did not move, but then she felt his eyelashes flutter like the wings of a moth and heard him sigh; he opened his eyes and lifted his head a fraction, staring at her, at first with surprise, and then with horror and mortification. Not wanting to hear his apologies, she kissed him lightly on the lips and slipped into bed beside him.

"Did you think I might not come?"

"I thought perhaps Catherine . . ."

"Stupid boy," she murmured, touching his shoulder with her lips and turning him to her. Perhaps five seconds since he had opened his eyes, and yet Tom felt as wide awake as if he had been plunged into ice-cold water; his chest was aching and his limbs painfully tense. By contrast her body seemed relaxed and yielding under her silk peignoir. Until this moment he had seen her only in tight-fitting bodices, with her hair swept back and to the side from a central parting; now it hung loosely to her shoulders, glowing vividly in the candlelight, softening her features, making her seem like a girl. His tenseness eased a little as he traced the outline of her nose with a single finger, passing on over her lips and chin. Sitting up she undid the ribbon securing her peignoir, letting it slip slowly from her shoulders. They remained still for a few seconds and then lay down facing each other, side by side.

After she had stopped loving Harry, Helen had known perhaps half a dozen lovers, but none had caressed her with Tom's delicate almost teasing gentleness; he would kiss her and then withdraw his mouth to brush her breasts with his lips. Often he came near to entering her, but then slid away, coaxing, pressing, eluding—increasing her suspense to the point of pain, seeking out hollows and angles, molding his slender body to her shape, until she felt that they were merging—his warmth flowing around her, into her, their separateness dissolving; yet there was an element missing; by the stream she had found him as helpless as herself, but now, although aroused by the lightness of his touch, over again she felt the detachment of his wooing, and was filled with an agonizing and humiliating sense of her vulnerability—as if she alone were truly naked and unveiled. He made her burn with the expectation of ecstasy, with the licking of small flickering flames, but not with an enveloping fire, not with a desire which was also close to fear, not with the promise of completeness she had glimpsed beside the stream: the fulfillment of utter surrender.

She turned away from him, raising clenched fists to her eyes, but when she lay back, she saw him gazing at her with eyes full of such concern and sadness that she was sure he had shared her fear of any consummation that fell short of their imaginings; all his efforts aimed to recapture that lost moment.

"My darling, I didn't see your eyes—your eyes were hidden."

A moment later her lips were parting his, her fingers probing and searching, twisting his hair and forcing his hands to her breasts with a desperation that snapped his control, making him echo her sobbing, halting cries of pleasure, annihilating memories of her aloofness, filling him with a fierce and passionate tenderness, as he raised his narrow hips and thrust into her, feeling himself carried with her, almost before knowing that they had begun, almost before the slight resistance to his entrance had ended—so that when it was over, time lay sleeping with them a little while, undisturbed, stirring only with a dull murmuring in their blood, with the quieter rhythm of their breathing.

The candles had all burned out and between the curtains a thin bar of blue light was brightening imperceptibly with a hint of redness. Outside birds were singing. Helen woke with a sudden start, her heart beating violently and then slowing with the understanding that dawn was only just breaking. Beside her Tom was sleeping soundly, his face cradled in the crook of an arm, his fingers trailing in his hair. She hesitated a moment before waking him.

"I must go "

He nodded dumbly, incredulous that he had wasted such precious hours in sleep. They embraced a last time, but he knew that she was eager to be gone. She shivered a little as she pulled her loose gown around her shoulders.

"I'll send for you when I get to London."

He pressed her hand to his lips, loving her as she went, tiptoeing to the door like a thief, a thief in her own house; and as he saw the door close, and heard the faint click of the latch, he felt a leaden and helpless anger that such a night should end so furtively, as if they had cause to be ashamed. He flung himself down across her pillow which still held her warmth and lay as though dead.

* * *

The brougham was waiting, the liveried coachman on the box and footmen carrying out Tom's easels, canvases and boxes.

"I hope your journey is not a tiring one, Mr. Strickland."

"I hope not too, your ladyship."

"Perhaps if you are ever in the neighborhood of Flixton or Rigton Bridge, you will call."

"I would be honored to, my lady. . . . Good-bye, Miss Crawford. Good-bye, my lord. Thank you all for your kindness."

He left them standing at the top of the steps and walked down to the coach without looking back.

In Tom's room, the housemaid, whose labors he had studied two mornings before, had stripped off the bed linen and was emptying the ewer and basin on the washstand when she noticed a fluted silver candlestick. She picked it up and shook her head, evidently puzzled at first, and then thunderstruck. As she replaced it a slow smile spread across her face—a smile of complicity rather than malice.

She was returning the candlestick to Lady Goodchild's room, where she had often dusted and polished it, when she came face to face with Miss Crawford at the top of the main stairs. With a hasty movement she shielded it with her arm and moved past with a slight bob.

"Mathews, are you hiding something?"

"Where, miss?"

"In your hand."

"Only a candlestick, miss."

"Then why hide it?"

"I weren't, miss."

"I saw you hide it. Where are you taking it?"

"To her ladyship's room."

"Where was it?"

"In the corridor, miss."

Catherine's face was ashen and her hands trembling.

"You're lying, Mathews. Must I tell the housekeeper that you are a thief?"

"No, please, miss." The girl's face was scarlet and she was close to tears. Catherine came closer and said gently,

"Did you find it in Mr. Strickland's room?"

The maid nodded and began to cry. Catherine leaned against the wall, her face contorted with anger and grief.

"Go!" she shouted. "Go!" Turning the moment the maid was out of sight, she ran to her room, choking with humiliated pride and hatred.

≈ Twenty-Nine ≈

From his seat in a swaying hansom, Charles Crawford surveyed the midafternoon scene in St. James's Street, his view through the open front of the cab framed by the bony haunches of the horse and the driver's reins sloping down from his perch behind. Opulent barouches, driven by liveried coachmen in powdered wigs, rolled by at a stately pace, little faster than the crowded omnibuses and lumbering brewers' drays, holding up dashing mail phaetons and broughams, but not detaining impudent costermongers' carts and determined cabmen. Behind tall windows Charles saw the glint of chandeliers and yawning clubmen relaxing after heavy lunches, some gazing idly at a group of Creole singers shaking their tambourines on the pavement opposite, the noise of their voices and instruments inaudible above the grating roar of so many iron-rimmed wheels grinding over the granite sets.

The traffic slowed to a crawl near the Piccadilly end of the street and finally came to a halt as a blind beggar lurched out in front of a timber cart. Charles rapped on the roof of the cab with his cane to attract the driver's attention and clambered out. Having paid, he walked along as briskly as he could on the crowded pavement, dodging past a knot of cabmen drinking beer on their stand and chatting with several shirt-sleeved waiters freed from their midday labors. Ballad sellers, orange girls and the occasional early prostitute mingled with shoppers and sightseeing provincials.

Even the distant prospect of a visit to his aunt's Bruton Street house was usually enough to depress and irritate Charles, but on this occasion Catherine's letter asking him to meet her there had barely affected his spirits. Today every newspaper carried the story that the Czar had rejected Turkish modifications to the Vienna peace plan, thus bringing the two nations to the brink of war. In peacetime Charles knew that it might be twenty years before he achieved flag rank; with the help of a full-scale European war, this time could well be halved. His only worry was that *Scylla* might not be ready for commissioning when the war at sea began.

His eager anticipation of hostilities had done much to alleviate his misery over Helen's acceptance of his father. Nevertheless when she had written asking him to nominate Humphrey, his first reaction had been to refuse, but quite unable to think of any way of explaining such churlishness to his father, he had finally been obliged to offer the boy a cadet's vacancy in *Scylla*. Yet though worried in case every sight of Humphrey should remind him of Helen, Charles had found some consolation in the thought that his responsibility for the young peer's welfare would give him power over his mother—not that he intended to treat Humphrey with anything other than perfect impartiality nor use his power in any way. The possession of it would be enough. Charles was also pleased to have been able to appear magnanimous to a woman who had hurt him: the ideal gentleman forever turning the other cheek.

Having half an hour in hand, Charles walked along Piccadilly to the Green Park, hoping to fill in time amusing himself with a scrutiny of the sartorial excesses of any men and women of fashion who might be taking the air. He was therefore disappointed to encounter for the most part clerks and apprentices enjoying an afternoon off with their milliner or shopgirl sweethearts. He smiled at his stupidity; the time he had spent in Sheerness and Chatham had made him forgetful of London habits. Anybody wishing to be thought smart would hide rather than advertise their presence in town in August, with society all but dead, Parliament in recess and everyone of *ton* or consequence in the country. On reflection it seemed strange to him that Catherine had chosen this month to come to London. Originally she had written suggesting that he come to Lancashire, since she had urgent matters to discuss, but he had not wanted to see Helen, and had also been unwilling to leave Sheerness for long during the most critical phase of *Scylla*'s conversion. What his sister might wish to tell him in person, that could not be expressed in a letter, he was at a loss to know; although he suspected something along the lines of a touching personal appeal to him to use his influence with their father to allow her to return to Leaholme Hall. There was another less pleasing possibility. On calling at his club, Charles had found a letter from George Braithwaite, containing hints that during a visit to Hanley Park, George had gained an impression that Catherine was fond of Magnus's young artist friend. Braithwaite had only implied this, and Charles was inclined to think that George's rejection had made him morbid and vindictive.

Toward the end of his walk in the park, Charles saw a park keeper with a stick prodding one of a group of destitute girls lying close to each other on the grass. They were dressed in what had once been finery: dirty torn muslin, grimy shawls and greasy, napless velvet. Their faces were filthy and weather-beaten, all of them in their early twenties and already past gaining a living from prostitution. Charles fumbled in his pocket, and to the keeper's disgust, tossed them some silver; then in a more somber mood he walked out into Piccadilly. He had known too many whores to look down on them.

That very morning he had visited Madame Negretti's impeccably respectable dressmaking establishment and made arrangements for the coming evening. Dressmaking certainly took place on the lower floors of her premises, but the remaining ones housed one of London's discreetest brothels, where clients provided references and made private appointments for particular girls. There was no violent stampede to pick girls from a *tableau vivant*, as in many brothels and burlesque houses, and the careful timing of appointments, and the layout of rooms, meant that patrons rarely, if ever, saw each other. The charges were as high as twenty pounds for a night, paid in advance, or added to an existing dressmaking account. Orgies and flagellation could be arranged, but always took place elsewhere. Madame Negretti also provided girls for other establishments, mainly hotels. She had catered for Charles's occasional needs for nearly ten years in a manner that had left him few grounds for complaint. In truth he would have preferred to keep a woman for his sole use, but his means had not allowed it. His previous first lieutenant had partially solved the same problem by paying his butler to marry a girl from an oyster bar, on the understanding that she would be at his master's disposal during his time ashore, and would be kept happy and provided for by the butler during his employer's long absences at sea. But disliking the idea of complicity with servants, Charles intended to remain faithful to La Negretti and to do so with a clear conscience. The adulterous habits of certain sections of the aristocracy shocked and disgusted him; Charles's stern sense of honor never allowed him to contemplate sleeping with a gentlewoman whom he did not intend to marry.

His aunt's maid led Charles to a small back sitting room on the ground floor, where he found Catherine diligently working at a shell box. The room looked onto a bleak graveled yard backed by a blackened brick wall supporting the gnarled and sooty trunk of an ancient wisteria. Charles embraced his sister perfunctorily and sat down on a frail Oriental chair in front of a cluttered china cabinet. Whenever he came to Bruton Street, he felt cramped by the quantity of furniture in rooms never intended to hold half as much. He moved away a pole fire screen to see Catherine better. The room was hot and airless.

"A fine month to be in London," he said gruffly.

"I needed to see you."

"The work on the ship is only half done, and when it is it'll be another two months before she's fitted out and manned."

"Don't be angry, Charles, I knew that, but could not wait to see you." He watched her lean forward, clasping her hands nervously. "You know that Lady Goodchild is in town?"

"We do not correspond," he replied dryly, moving his weight uneasily on the flimsy bamboo chair. "If she is, why the deuce aren't you staying with her?" He looked around guiltily in case the door was open.

"Don't worry, Aunt Warren is out till six." Catherine moved her chair closer to him. "I couldn't stay with her ladyship because she's only two servants with her and almost every room is given over to the auction. She's selling everything there."

"She has every right."

Resigned though Charles had become to losing Helen, he did not relish a long conversation about her finances or any other aspect of her behavior. If Catherine wanted to leave Hanley Park, she should approach her father. He saw her get up and walk over to the door, where she listened a moment.

"Why such secrecy?" he asked, interest now overcoming irritation.

Catherine tightened the blue sash of her white dress and narrowed her eyes a little.

"What would you do, Charles, if you thought Helen was deceiving Father?"

"How the devil can she be? It's as certain as can be that he's letting her have money. Not to marry him after that would be the most flagrant breach of promise I've ever heard of."

"I didn't mean that she won't marry him," she replied softly.

"Then what *do* you mean?"

"She's been seeing Mr. Strickland since she came here."

"Wasn't he painting her portrait? He's probably putting the finishing touches." The dismissive tone Charles had adopted was a token of doubt rather than confidence. He remembered seeing Helen and Strickland laughing together as he had peered through the window on the day of the last meet before Goodchild's death; yet for his own peace of mind he was determined to avoid jumping to any hasty conclusion. To be ousted by his father had been painful, but to believe that Helen had taken a nondescript painter as a lover would be infinitely more wounding. Surely she would never risk so much, given her debts? Charles was also comforted by George's suspicions. If Catherine had been fond of Strickland, and he had subsequently rejected her, she might well wish to harm him; nor had she any reason to love Helen. He saw that Catherine seemed shaken by his impervious attitude, and said more kindly,

"You must explain more. How can I credit such a thing without hearing your reasons?"

Charles listened attentively as she told him about her intuitive suspicions, which had been borne out by their unaccompanied drive together and by the more critical discovery of the candlestick.

"The maid probably left the thing in the wrong room," he said with crushing indifference.

"With the candle burned right down? The same maid always cleans both rooms and knows exactly what belongs in each."

Never, it seemed to Charles, had he so much wished to prove anybody wrong. He smiled at Catherine and shook his head.

"Suppose she intended to clean it and took it with her to the other room? She sees something else needs doing, does it and then forgets the candlestick and leaves it there."

"But she hid it from me as she passed," cried Catherine, unable to hide her incredulity that he should doubt her.

"You're sure she hid it?"

"As sure as I am of my own name."

"Perhaps she thought you might draw a false conclusion from her forgetfulness—the very conclusion you have drawn."

"She would only have thought that if she had her own reasons for suspecting them."

"Another maid could have put it there without her knowledge," replied Charles, as outwardly unruffled as ever.

"She was very reluctant to tell me where she found it; if any other maid had moved it, she would have found out and sent her to me. I know she would have asked the other servants."

Charles stretched out his legs and undid his waistcoat buttons. He was sweating unpleasantly.

"I can't see," he said, "why the girl should want to go to such trouble to shield her mistress. It seems far more likely that, seeing your distress, she would not wish to involve herself further by questioning other servants."

Catherine got up abruptly and stared down at him angrily.

"You are deliberately refusing to acknowledge the obvious explanation. Why not go through every unlikely possibility? God moves mountains, why not a candlestick? Or perhaps I put it there."

Charles held out his hands in a gesture of submission. He felt numb and sick at heart.

"Father's in love with her and frankly he won't believe any wrong of her on the basis of what you've told me." He caught his sister's eye and went on earnestly, "Suppose I tell him my fears and he asks Helen to explain them. Will she confess and beg to be forgiven?" He smiled grimly and shook his head. "Over the years I have written her a number of letters—some, to put it mildly, were less than discreet. She would not find it hard to cast doubt on my motives."

"But if the evidence were conclusive?"

Charles looked at her searchingly.

"You suggest a private inquiry agent?"

Catherine blushed and looked down at her lap.

"Is there no more delicate way?"

"Somebody must watch them if you want to discover more."

"It would be too heartless to send Father the man's statement. We should tell him first, and if he doubts us, produce the statement as a last resort." Her ill-concealed excitement nauseated Charles and convinced him that George had been right. Did she have any idea of the suffering this would bring her father?

"Matters are not quite so simple," he said condescendingly. "Her ladyship might claim the evidence was bought and perjured."

"How could she support such an accusation?"

"My letters—your resentment of being driven out of your home. She might even tell Father that you had cast eyes on Strickland."

"Father would never be deceived by such a lie." Her flaming cheeks and trembling voice fanned Charles's anger.

"Have no fear, Catherine, it will never come to that."

"We cannot do nothing, Charles."

Charles got up and collected his hat and cane.

"When I know more, I shall acquaint Lady Goodchild with this knowledge. I think she will prove faithful afterward; I daresay she will also treat you with consideration."

"You will let them marry?" she asked in astonishment.

Charles looked at her coldly and began doing up his waistcoat buttons.

"I neither intend to break my father's heart, nor to make him hate me as the instrument of his misery."

"He might thank you for saving him from an old man's folly."

"I think he might consider that we had destroyed his chance to marry a young woman in order to protect our prospects; any children they have will need providing for. I am sure Lady Goodchild would use this argument to explain our behavior. Added to the others, she could mount a creditable attack."

He walked to the door but she laid a hand on his arm.

"But will you end their liaison? Love is not killed by threats."

"You may depend upon me to find a way, unless," he added, with a tight-lipped smile, "you would prefer to do so yourself."

"You will not hurt him?"

"I will do what I must."

Catherine still stood blocking his way to the door, her face frightened, all vindictiveness gone.

"Can you not tell me what you intend to do?"

"How can I before knowing everything?"

"Could Magnus talk to him?"

Charles edged past her and opened the door.

"My dear sister, Magnus hates our father more than the devil himself. He may even have put Strickland up to it."

She called after him in the hall but he did not turn, hurrying out into the sunlight and hailing the first hansom that he saw. He had not meant to attack Magnus, but her changing attitude to Strickland had snapped his patience. At the same time he had felt pangs of his old longing for Helen and disgust with himself for feeling them at such a time; before, he had not imagined her in Strickland's arms; but when he had seen the tenderness in his sister's eyes, as she had asked him not to hurt the artist, he had pictured Helen with the same look in her eyes, and had felt not hatred but desire. Charles banged on the roof and shouted up to the driver to take him to his club; he would not go to Madame Negretti's after all; twenty pounds paid in advance; but now he would not go there for two hundred, no, not for two thousand pounds.

~ *Thirty* ~

On a fine August morning Magnus finished his breakfast in the coffee shop opposite Tom's studio and walked to the barber's where he was shaved each day. But in spite of the sunshine, and the fact that a regular engagement with the *Morning Chronicle* had recently ended his financial problems, Magnus felt far from carefree as the barber began his preparations.

Having been so entirely at ease with Tom during their first months together in Charlotte Street, Magnus had been profoundly shocked to notice a distinct change in his friend after his return from Hanley Park. Where there had once been understanding and openness between them, Magnus now experienced few moments unaffected by an inexplicable tension. In the past week Tom had never asked questions about Magnus's work, as he had always used to do, nor had he said anything about his own painting. In fact he had spent most of his time away from the studio, and during what few hours he did pass there, he was moody and withdrawn.

Recalling Tom's former lightheartedness and the frequent visits of his friends, Magnus assumed that he had unwittingly offended him. But when he had asked whether this was so, Tom had angrily denied that anything had changed. Magnus would certainly have left if treated in this way by anybody else, but Tom was entirely different. His laughter made Magnus feel less downcast when he was depressed, his praise of an article made him think better of it, and his wide-ranging enthusiasms and interest in many kinds of people, whom Magnus would previously have dismissed out of hand, had literally changed the way he viewed the world. For the first time in his life, Magnus had felt entirely free of his father's influence and power—until the Eastern crisis.

The final rejection of the Vienna plan by the Russians, and his father's probable part in this disaster, horrified Magnus. Yet when he had tried to talk to Tom about the dangers of his father's and Lord Stratford's consistent advocacy of a threatening naval policy, he had changed the subject with a finality that had made it impossible for Magnus to reintroduce it. The little fighting that Magnus had witnessed in Ceylon had been quite enough to convince him of the unimaginable catastrophe a European war would be. It seemed inconceivable to Magnus that his country could go to war to protect the interests of the sultan of Turkey, the corruption of whose government would make the most hardened boroughmongerer in Britain blush to contemplate; and yet respectable tradesmen and evangelical spinsters were already reading with evident approval pronouncements of Britain's sacred duty to safeguard the integrity of the Ottoman Empire, and seemed to see no inconsistency in supporting a Mohammedan nation against a Christian one in a struggle where British interests would be at best marginally concerned. The argument was even current that, because Britain would lose rather than gain by a war with Russia, the defense of Turkey would be a heroically disinterested act.

Yet Tom remained apparently indifferent while Magnus waged his losing battle to keep the *Morning Chronicle* in the antiwar camp, and, remembering his friend's incredulity that justice had been defeated at Rigton Bridge, Magnus was cut to the heart not to have his support in this new and infinitely more important struggle.

On returning to the house after his shave, Magnus was not surprised to find that Tom had already gone out. He had come down to the studio and was about to sit down when he saw Lydia, Tom's most regular mistress, step out from behind the screen by the model's dais.

"Where is he?" she asked, coming up to him without the civility of any other greeting. Whenever Lydia was angry, Magnus was chilled by the ugly transformation of her usual pert, Dresden china prettiness.

"Out somewhere," he replied briskly, ignoring the way she sucked in her cheeks and looked at him with angry disbelief. From his earliest days in Charlotte Street, Magnus had sensed Lydia's resentment of his influence over Tom, and knew that had she seen any way of getting rid of him she would not have hesitated to use it. At least it was some comfort to know that she too was just as bemused by Tom's recent behavior as he was.

"He was to meet me at Brandon's yesterday. I waited an hour. I daresay you know nothing about where he was then?"

"Why not ask him?" he replied gently.

"If I'm fortunate enough to see him I will."

Lydia was wearing a tight, frogged, hussar-style jacket edged with fur which matched the trimmings of the insolent little bandeau around her tilted chignon. Normally the impudence of such an outfit perfectly suited her elfish expressions and sly smiles; but with pouting lips and a petulant frown, her military jacket reduced her anger to a caricature of martial belligerence. She brought down the tip of her parasol with a bang on the floor.

"Be so good as to tell him that I will not be treated in this way." She turned and walked to the door, but before reaching it, turned abruptly with a suddenly tragic face. "He makes me so unhappy. Surely he speaks about me sometimes. I'm sure he tells *you* what he really feels for me."

"He's talked about nothing recently." Her wheedling tone irritated Magnus less than her assumption that Tom still confided in him. Months before, he had grown accustomed to Lydia's mannerisms and vanity. Possibly had *he* been the principal singer at the Olympic, applauded to the echo each evening by a pit and gallery glistening with gold chains, eyeglasses and silk hats, he too might have formed the deluded view that his antics away from the theater and the strange world of opéra bouffe would command the same rapturous attention. Less than a year ago, Lydia had been performing in the chorus of Sam Collins's music hall in Islington for a far less affluent audience, and just before that in Caldwell's Dancing Rooms in a Soho back street. To earn more she had worked as a model at evening sessions in the studios of the Society of Artists, and it had been there that she had met Tom. Since then she had so captivated a fashionable barrister that he had set her up in a St. John's Wood villa with a carriage and a weekly allowance, visiting her on two afternoons a week and an occasional night when his wife was out of town. Lydia would never have jeopardized her career by becoming the paid mistress of a man who was not "happily married." Although not quite twenty-two she was saving with exemplary thrift and hoped in a year or two to buy the villa from her barrister. As Magnus had reluctantly come to accept, there was more to Lydia than met the eye.

After a long silence she walked away from him through the clearly defined shafts of sunshine and sat down on the edge of the dais.

"I don't understand why you're so much against me," she said with a wistful little smile.

"I'm not. How can I tell you what I don't know?"

"You're a cold fish, Magnus," she said with a sigh. "Is it just me, or all women?"

Magnus folded his paper and got up.

"I don't like women who conceal calculation with coyness, and think that no man will think them innocent unless they pretend to be trivial."

"Is that how you see me?"

"Sometimes."

She stared at him angrily.

"Unless he tells me what's wrong, I'll find out for myself. Then you'll see how coy I am. Tell him that."

"Certainly."

She flounced to the door and turned.

"Nobody's going to walk out on me without a word. You wouldn't take it either if you'd ever been mashed on a girl, but the Thames'll run dry I daresay before you get spoony over anyone."

When she had gone, Magnus picked up his newspaper, but then threw it down again. Lydia had an uncanny knack of exposing his weaknesses. Her petulant irritation with Tom for his remoteness from her had touched Magnus on a raw nerve. Was his own nagging disappointment and sense of betrayal any less selfishly possessive? His memory of Lydia's disgruntled and self-pitying questions made him squirm. Could Tom view *his* questions in the same light? If he did, the time had come to leave. But go where, when there was nobody else for whom he cared a jot? To no other person had he ever been able to be truthful about the loneliness and fears of involvement that had dogged him since his mother's death, with nobody, besides Tom, feel a simple ease and contentment in doing the most mundane things—sitting reading or working in different parts of the same room, walking together, talking trivia. Never had he shared his thoughts more fully.

Remembering Lydia's suspicious and unhappy face, Magnus saw in a moment of absolute clarity that, if Tom had fallen seriously in love with somebody, there would be no room left for anybody else. The sudden force of his feeling of loss and jealousy shocked and disgusted him; not because he had ever thought the world's prurient divisions between love and friendship in any way applicable to him, but because the full measure of his dependence had at last struck home: a terror that he could no longer face the future on his own. Was this the thing that he had come to? Clutching at other explanations, he blamed his feelings on the uncertainty caused by Tom's secrecy, telling himself that he was not jealous at all, only angry at being excluded and deceived. Recalling vividly that the first impulse of his brother officers in Ceylon on falling in love had been to describe the experience in tasteless detail and at tedious length, Magnus found it still harder to understand why Tom could not tell him something, however veiled. The only possible reason he could think of for his friend's silence was that he had fallen in love with Catherine while at Hanley Park. It was certainly strange that she should be in London at the very time when Tom was so often absent from the studio.

Magnus thought of asking his sister, but decided on the more straightforward course of a direct question to Tom; regardless of what he might answer, Magnus allowed himself to hope that his truthfulness would help banish the humiliating resentment and pain caused by his ostracism. If it did not do so, he had no idea what he could do.

* * *

Having gone out to avoid Magnus, Tom was disappointed to find him still in on his return. It had been all very well for Helen to make him swear not to tell him anything—*she* did not have to live with him; and after their earlier honesty, Tom found lying no easy matter. On many occasions he had felt desperate enough to break his promise of secrecy. From his point of view it might be no bad thing if Magnus *did* warn his father. Helen had made it quite clear that their affair would end with her marriage; so why not let Sir James find out? Because she might reject him at once for betraying her? Because Magnus would most likely be furiously angry and yet do nothing? Tom hated himself for the unhappiness he was causing Magnus, but could not help his behavior.

He had expected Helen's visit to London to be a time of constant happiness, but had been cruelly disillusioned. Since she would not allow him to come to her house in Belgravia, because of the servants, and he could not take her to his studio because of Magnus, they had been forced to meet at a small hotel in Marylebone. Tom hated the furtiveness of going there; he hated the room they used, with its red curtains, heavy gasolier and large cheval glass, its stained carpet and flowered wallpaper; and he hated Helen's insistence on paying for it. She treated the plans and subterfuges as an exciting game, but he had never stopped resenting them.

She would have her coachman take her to a shop, an exhibition hall or gallery, and leave her there; then later she would engage a hansom to take her on to the hotel. She had discouraged Tom from writing to her, and decided at each meeting when the next should be. All her caution brought home to Tom her determination never to sacrifice either wealth or position for love; by cooperating with her he felt himself the engineer of his own ultimate destruction. But he had rarely argued or shown his resentment, even when Helen had written a note changing the time of an assignation too late for him to cancel a previously arranged appointment with Lydia. He knew that Lydia suspected him, and was afraid of what she might do if slighted. His position with Lydia was further weakened by his having borrowed money from her; most of this debt was still outstanding.

Again and again Tom had tried to persuade Helen to spend an entire day and night with him, but she had refused because of difficulties with servants. At any house where she might be expected to accept an invitation, she would naturally have to take her lady's maid. Could she not trust the girl with a secret? Tom had asked. No, even the most trustworthy girl had a best friend whom she would tell, and this best friend would have another best friend and so it would go on. While he for most of their meetings was haunted by the rapidly approaching moment of parting, she seemed able to live entirely in the present. Once he had lost his temper and called her heartless and more concerned with her reputation than with him; he had threatened to break their next appointment, but next day had suffered such an agony of fear that she herself would fail to come that he had broken her commandment against letters and had sent a note of apology with the local butcher's boy. During all this time Tom was unable to work at anything except a grotesque parody of Shakespearean narrative painting: Bottom in the role of Pyramus, kissing a blatantly masculine Flute attempting the role of Thisbe. Tom knew he would never sell it, but continued merely to avoid having to talk to Magnus.

Hearing footsteps on the stairs, Magnus left the studio and caught sight of Tom going up to his bedroom. Tom paused for a moment after Magnus spoke his name and then came down slowly toward him. They went into the studio.

"Lydia came."

"And?"

"She said you left her waiting somewhere."

Tom said nothing, but walked across to a large canvas covered by drapes; he lifted a corner, half-exposing his rendering of Nick Bottom's "most lamentable comedy."

"She talked about finding out what's wrong with you."

"And how does she propose doing that?" asked Tom, letting the drapes fall back into place.

"Why not ask her? She thinks you're in love with somebody."

"She said that?"

"By implication." Magnus moved closer to Tom and smiled encouragingly. Tom's face remained cold and expressionless. "Is she right?" Tom looked down at the stained floorboards. "If she is, you should have told me."

"Why?"

"Because you're unhappy and I might be able to help you. You once helped me."

Tom threw up his hands and laughed harshly.

"Me help *you*. Dear God, I'd have to be the Czar, the sultan and the prime minister to do that these days."

"Is it so ridiculous to be concerned about the probability of a disastrous war?"

"As absurd as stepping into the path of a train in the hope of stopping it."

"You don't believe that, Tom?"

"Because you once disgraced the governor of an unimportant colony, you think you can control the fate of nations?"

"After what happened at Rigton Bridge?" asked Magnus, confused and wounded by Tom's aggression. "Of course I tried to influence my father. In my position would you have done nothing?"

Tom sighed and bowed his head.

"I had no cause to say what I did."

The cries of a costermonger shouting his wares rose from the street. Magnus looked at Tom's hunched shoulders and handsome unhappy face and felt a rush of sympathy.

"Are you in love with Catherine?" he whispered.

Tom slowly met Magnus's eyes, exasperation, pain and contrition in his voice:

"Would to God I was."

"Helen?"

"Yes, Helen." He kicked at the leg of a trestle table and caught Magnus's expression of pity, rather than anger. "Helen, your future stepmother. A fine friend, am I not?"

Magnus shook his head and turned away.

"How can you love any woman prepared so blatantly to marry for money?" He had spoken softly and intensely as if searching for his own explanation.

"The fault is common enough," replied Tom sharply.

"With a man of my father's age and character?"

"She agreed to it for her son's sake."

"So he could enjoy the money Catherine and I should have had?"

"I am sure she intended you no harm." Tom glanced anxiously at Magnus. "What will you do?"

"Do?" shouted Magnus, trembling with anger. "Did you tell me so that I would warn my father? Did you hope to marry that calculating woman yourself? I shan't save them from each other. You told me in confidence and I shall respect that confidence."

"I knew you would."

"She'll use your emotions just as she'll use my father's money. Does she care that you're unhappy? Does she even notice it? All right, serve her lascivious needs, go to her like an obedient footman when she calls and let her use you. You say Lydia's incapable of understanding anything except the manipulation of men—what else does Helen Goodchild understand? Lydia's worked for her achievements. Has her ladyship as much as fastened her own shoes? I know such women, Tom, and she's not fit for you. She has assurance, but think of the narcissistic hours she spent working on it. With years of idleness a milk girl would have learned as much poise and wit and memorized as many polished sentences."

"We are not speaking of the same woman."

"Then no more need be said."

"Are you angry on your father's account?"

Magnus raised his hands to his face and groaned aloud.

"Hang my father. I care about *you*. I thought you more discerning. I thought you proof against the effete charms of aristocratic shams. I thought merit weighed more with you than wealth or blood."

"Must the coincidence of birth preclude all merit? Wealth does not guarantee corruption or poverty, virtue. Your family misfortunes give you no right to brand an entire class with the same mark."

"Her intention to marry my father proves her worth."

"Love has no scales to measure worth. I did not choose to feel as I do."

Magnus no longer felt angry as he looked at Tom's pale drawn face.

"She will reject you."

"I know that."

Magnus nodded and walked to the door.

"She's made a sad man of you."

"I would not change my lot."

Magnus touched his hand and smiled at him.

"Poor Tom."

He gazed at Tom for a moment and then turned the china door handle. Tom followed him to the street door.

"Where are you going?"

"To find somewhere to live."

"Stay here."

"You must have cursed me when you wanted to bring her here."

Tom saw Magnus opening the door.

"I never intended this, Magnus. Don't hate me."

"I don't."

"Will we see each other?"

"If you want to, Tom."

Tom nodded dumbly as Magnus slipped out into the street.

⤳ *Thirty-One* ⤳

The New Burlington Street premises of the private inquiry agency, which Charles Crawford had engaged to report on the movements of Tom and Helen, combined something of the atmosphere of an undertaker's parlor with that of a solicitor's office; in musty files, the records of dead marriages and thwarted loves, once matter for great passions, were now reduced to neatly numbered sheaves of yellowing paper. The staff all spoke in muted sympathetic tones, as if their clients suffered from loss or bereavement rather than jealousy and hatred; but this veneer of consideration concealed a lawyer's love of detailed information and facts. Mr. Featherstone, the principal, also reminded Charles of a skillful physician, never afraid of admitting that his medicine, however delicately administered, might be painful, but always confident that if bravely taken would lead to a final cure. His specialty was the collection of evidence for divorce cases.

Mr. Featherstone's establishment, like Madame Negretti's, was dedicated to discretion. There were three waiting rooms so that clients should never know the embarrassment of being observed during their time of trouble. Charles sat in one of these three rooms staring at the door. In front of him on a small table copies of *Fraser's* and, thoughtfully, the *Army and Navy Gazette*; soldiers and sailors, he reflected, being particularly prone to marital warfare and domestic shipwreck. The room was on the ground floor facing onto the street, but protected from prying eyes by thick muslin curtains. Not liking the idea of having such confidential papers posted to him, Charles had come in person to read the report on the first ten days' surveillance.

On being ushered into Mr. Featherstone's office, Charles experienced the same disconcerting resentment he had felt during his first appointment the week before. Like God, Mr. Featherstone was a deity "unto whom all hearts be open, all desires known, and from whom no secrets are hid." Charles was sure that no crime or moral outrage could be repulsive enough to ruffle his host's benign composure. Featherstone was wearing a black swallowtail coat of a slightly antiquated cut, doubtless intended to suggest old-fashioned service and reliability. He had an unnerving habit of cracking his knuckle joints during silences and stroking his side-whiskers when thinking, but these, in Charles's eyes, were minor irritants compared with his exaggerated solicitude for his clients' feelings—a deference not far removed from parody.

A clerk handed his employer some papers and withdrew. Charles felt an apprehensive fluttering in his stomach, making him want to snatch the papers and start reading them at once.

"There was matter of substance to report?" he asked, attempting to hide his anxiety, while Featherstone glanced through the first and second pages. He looked up and smiled disarmingly.

"No inquiry, Captain Crawford, is ever entirely fruitless. A gentleman comes to us suspecting his wife. We establish her innocence beyond a doubt." He paused and cracked his knuckles. "In doing so we discover his son is a blackmailer, his butler a thief and his daughter planning to elope." He chuckled quietly and tapped the report with two fingers. "The case you have entrusted to us intrigues me."

"I would have thought it perfectly routine," Charles replied coldly, uncertain whether Featherstone was attempting to flatter or confuse him.

"You claim no personal interest in the lady, Captain, and I believe you—although many men are deliberately reticent, suggesting they are acting for friends or using other equally transparent devices to divert attention from themselves." He glanced at Charles searchingly. "I ask this question, Captain, because I wish to serve you well, not, you must understand, to appease any personal curiosity. Is there not some connection you have kept from me? Something of a family nature?"

"I told you all that was needed," returned Charles brusquely. He had not told Featherstone anything of his father's intended marriage.

Featherstone nodded agreeably and stroked his side-whiskers.

"Naturally when we started our inquiries I sent a man to spend several days at Flixton. Of course he visited Hanley Park."

"I must deplore such an uncalled-for intrusion."

"Mr. Kirkup went, I should add, in the guise of a literary man compiling an architectural guide to the homes of the nobility and gentry in that county. The housekeeper welcomed him with perfect trust and civility. I had not been aware that your sister has been her ladyship's guest for several months."

"I did not think it relevant."

"Nor that your brother shares lodgings with the other party?"

"I should like the report, Mr. Featherstone."

"You will find it most satisfactory, Captain."

Charles was stung by the man's tone and the way he was looking at him. A smile of respect, admiration and sly complicity.

"Satisfactory?" he snapped. "Be so good as to explain."

"I would not cause further offense for the world, Captain. Pray accept my apologies for presuming to predict your satisfaction." He handed the papers to Charles and added softly, "There was one discovery my man made in the north. The housekeeper supposed that Lady Goodchild will marry your father. Since this is mere hearsay, it is omitted in the report." He coughed discreetly and moved to the door. "I am sure you would prefer not to be disturbed. Ring when you have finished, Captain."

As soon as Featherstone had gone, Charles brought down a fist on the arm of his chair with all his strength. So that was what the unctuous hypocrite thought, was it? A concerted plot by two brothers and their sister to prevent their father marrying a woman of childbearing age—Strickland their paid instrument of destruction, hired to protect their inheritance by ruining a woman's reputation. A year in Featherstone's line of business and even the most trusting of men would imagine treachery and cunning behind every innocent action. Charles felt contaminated and soiled by his association with him. Whatever the rational justification for paying to have a woman spied upon, such proceedings would still appear mean and dishonorable to any impartial person. For all the public expression of outraged virtue at the behavior of lovers—in private, only hardened hypocrites would not admit to feeling sympathy for them. Better to have gone straight to Helen and stated his suspicions at once, even though risking a scathing denial, than to have resorted to sneaking subterfuge. But Charles's self-doubts soon changed to anger when he began to read. That she should have preferred a socially ambitious parvenu to him and his father made him ache with loathing.

Then, while giving herself to this man, she had written to dear, loyal, unsuspecting Charles, asking him to nominate her son; and now he could not avoid taking the boy without telling his father why. The last traces of Charles's guilt ebbed away, leaving only bitterness and a desire for revenge.

The report was a painstaking document with an appended list of expenses detailing every hansom fare, every drink, meal, tip and bribe incurred by the investigator and his assistant. The first page dealt mainly with the largely abortive trip to Flixton and Hanley Park, and then went on to chronicle some early surreptitious attempts to extract information from the three servants in Helen's London house. Contact had been made in public houses, dancing rooms, and "other places of recreation," but "since these approaches were not attended with immediate results, it was thought best to abandon them as likely to excite suspicion if persisted with." From the bottom paragraph of the second page Charles started reading attentively.

Tuesday August 28th. The lady was observed leaving home shortly before 2 o'clock in a brougham driven by her own coachman, and was put down at the Diorama, 9, Park Square East, Regent's Park—the moving panoramas presented being of the earthquake in Lisbon in 1755 and Etna in Sicily under three effects, evening, sunrise and eruption. After ten minutes the party came out and left in a hansom hailed by the doorman. Due to an accident to an ice wagon and the subsequent press of vehicles, the party eluded pursuit beyond the junction of Baker Street with the Marylebone Road. The party returned home alone in time to dine and did not go out again. No callers were admitted either by the front or mews entrances during the night.

Wednesday August 29th. Many morning callers but none corresponding with description of other party. Most visits apparently connected with forthcoming auction. Late morning some furniture removed by Pickfords. Party remained at home all day and night.

Thursday August 30th. Quarter-past ten A.M. party left in own brougham and was put down at Garrett's Silversmiths in Conduit Street. Coachman left immediately. Engaged sharp boy working with accordionist to stand by the shop door and note the number of the hansom in case party followed Tuesday's proceedings. Party hailed cab herself, but boy managed to slip around the other side of the vehicle and jump onto the step, pretending to beg, and so caught sight of the number and reported back to me. Paid him two shillings. Made no attempt to follow hansom but proceeded to the inland revenue office (hackney carriage department)

Somerset House to ascertain the name and address of the driver and his place of stabling. Same evening repaired to the stable yard of that individual situate in a street leading from Gower Street to Gordon Square. After abuse and acrimony a sovereign and three half-quarters of gin refreshed his memory. He had driven the party to Blandford's Hotel by Beaumont Mews in Marylebone High Street, setting her down about noon.

Friday August 31st. Sent my assistant Mr. Kirkup to observe other party but without results. Repaired myself to Blandford's Hotel and gave the boots a half crown and promised another if he could describe anybody arriving at the hotel about midday on the previous day. He described both parties well, his recollection of the lady's dress and bonnet being faultless, and corresponding precisely with my own observations. On ascertaining that the gentleman had taken a room by the week in name of Sir Peter Rubens, I engaged the next door room and by promise of a sovereign obtained key to gentleman's room from boots. Observed positioning of pictures and measured distances from floor and corner. Returning to my room, I opened a small aperture in the lath and plaster wall opening into next door room behind the picture selected previously. Moved picture in own room about six inches to conceal hole. Remained at hotel but neither party came.

Saturday September 1st. All day at hotel. No developments. Mr. Kirkup followed Mr. Strickland to 17, Rawdon Road, St. John's Wood, where he (Strickland) stayed from 11 A.M. until past 3. Suspecting the house to be another place of assignation used by the parties, Mr. Kirkup knocked at the door, telling the maid he was a country curate trying to trace the daughter of a parishioner, the girl having run away to be a servant in London, last having written from St. John's Wood. He showed the maid a daguerreotype of his niece, which naturally the maid did not recognize. To gain entrance, Mr. Kirkup asked for a glass of water, which he was given in the front parlor where he met the lady of the house, a Miss Emily Pike—a young woman little above twenty. From general conversation Mr. Kirkup concluded female party was unknown to Miss Pike. Neighbor's maid said that man of Strickland's appearance often visits Miss Pike, who is better known as Lydia de Glorion, professional singer at the Olympic. Talking to boy at Vaughan & Tyler Wine Merchants, Mr. Kirkup learned that Miss Pike takes delivery of wine debited to account of Mr. Lionel Curtis Q.C., the owner of 17, Rawdon Road. At this stage the nature of Miss Pike's relations with Mr. Strickland is uncertain. (Further investigation unjustified unless required by client. E. J. Featherstone.)

Sunday September 2nd. Blandford's Hotel. Both parties arrived separately between 2 and half-past. At once left the dining room and went to my own room. Ten minutes later was told by the boots that Sir Peter Rubens had changed his room, not on account of any suspicion, but because of some trivial dissatisfaction with the furnishings—the color of the curtains and the shape of the gasolier, according to the boots. Boots told me new room was at end of corridor and that adjoining room was already occupied. Asked if any balcony or other means of observing parties, but was told no. Parties stayed four hours and left as usual separately. For formal confirmation of Mr. Strickland's identity followed him home to Charlotte Street on foot via the Euston Road and Fitzroy Square. He seemed agitated and collided with several passersby. Bought an apple from coster's cart but threw it away half-eaten. General appearance of being distraught, variable speed of walking, etc. Reached home just after seven. (Client to confirm whether absolute proof of intimacy is required. E. J. Featherstone.)

Charles put down the report without bothering with the sheets detailing expenses. His head was throbbing and his jaws ached with the pressure of his clenched teeth. He thought for some minutes and then rang for Featherstone.

"Your men have been most diligent, Mr. Featherstone."

"May I assume, Captain, that this inquiry is concluded?"

"Not yet."

"Absolute proof cannot be obtained without considerable expenditure both in time and as you will appreciate . . ."

"I do not require it."

Featherstone was looking at him with unconcealed surprise.

"Instruct your men to do nothing for a week, and then to resume their watch the following Monday. I shall call here again in a fortnight."

"What will you wish to establish, Captain?"

"Whether they are still meeting."

"No more than that?"

"No more than that."

Charles smiled icily at Featherstone and picked up his hat. It should be a salutary lesson for him to realize that, clever though he might be, there were still some cases that did not fall within his experience or understanding. Featherstone was smiling again, a knowing, appreciative smile.

"An uncomfortable week for Mr. Strickland, I shouldn't be surprised."

"I am no horsewhipper, Mr. Featherstone."

As he went out, Charles felt that he had partially repaid the man for his impudent deductions about Sir James. Outside, a slight feeling of nausea surprised Charles. He had momentarily thought his dealings with Featherstone had placed him in a region beyond the pale of ordinary sensations. Certainly he was unaware of any desire for vengeance as he hailed a hansom and told the driver to take him to Rawdon Road, St. John's Wood. He felt neither elation, nor even a sense of power; his only satisfaction was the feeling that he was about to perform a duty which was necessary and in his father's interest.

⮐ *Thirty-Two* ⮑

The shower had stopped, but by the time Catherine reached Magnus's new address in Jermyn Street, her pink pardessus and matching skirt were covered with dark spots and splashes of mud. She climbed a cheerless, uncarpeted staircase and knocked on the oaken outer door of her brother's set of rooms. Having told the valet who she was, she was led into the sitting room where Magnus was reading in a chair with a hinged lectern on one arm and a candleholder on the other. As in so many bachelors' rooms there was a hob grate and very little china or ornaments, just two blue Bristol vases with cut-glass pendants on the mantelpiece and a silver fruit basket on a heavy Gothic sideboard. The only pictures were sporting prints. In the center of the room was a large round table covered with a red velvet cloth and littered with a mass of newspapers, proof pages, notebooks and magazines. Magnus got up and took his sister's arm.

"You're wet, Catherine. Shall I have Paul light the fire?"

"Please don't. I walked here and there was a light shower."

"Aunt Warren does not allow you her carriage?"

Catherine undid the damp bow of her bonnet and took it off. Magnus noticed that her fingers were trembling.

"I did not want her to know that I had seen you."

"See your own brother?" he asked, astonished.

"She might tell Lady Goodchild that we have met."

"Must we have that lady's permission?"

She gazed at him with a look of entreaty, a plea for patience.

"I have done something foolish and wrong."

Magnus smiled tenderly at her and shook his head.

"You do something wrong, Catherine? I don't believe it."

"In your last letter you mentioned leaving Mr. Strickland's house but gave no reason. Did you quarrel about something?"

His smile faded and he said briskly,

"The arrangement suited neither of us. There was too little space, and most of that was taken up by his studio." He frowned and came closer to her. "If you've been worried, why have you waited so long before coming here? I wrote saying where I was over a week ago."

She picked up her bonnet and began nervously to straighten the damp fringe of cream lace at the brim. Without looking up she said,

"Charles came to see me . . . two weeks ago; no, a little less than that. I hadn't expected him, hadn't even been aware that he knew I was in town." She paused and then went on more rapidly, "He was friendly and sympathetic, unusually so. I told him how unhappy I was at Hanley Park and he offered to ask Papa to let me return home. I must have been mad to tell him what I did. He was so kind, you see, and I needed somebody to talk to. I'd been demented with worry." Magnus was looking at her with protective concern and anxiety. "Helen has been seeing Mr. Strickland in London; they're in love, I know they are, Magnus. I was terrified what it might do to Father, what it could do to them if Father discovered . . ."

"So you told Charles?" said Magnus in a hoarse, choked whisper. She nodded and started to weep, covering her face with her hands and dropping her bonnet on the floor. "You could have come to me; you knew that, but you went to him. Why? Why?" His voice had risen to a shout.

She fumbled in an inside pocket of her pardessus and found a handkerchief.

"I was afraid," she stammered, dabbing at her eyes. "You were so friendly with him; I didn't want him to think that I had spoken to you behind his back; I knew you hated Father. I was confused and frightened, Magnus."

Magnus sat down and shut his eyes. His head was bowed as he asked,

"Did Charles say what he intended doing?"

"No."

"Will he tell Father?"

"He said he wouldn't."

"Why not?"

"He thought it would kill Papa. He thinks if he tells Helen that he knows, she'll never betray Father again. I think he will have Helen watched."

Magnus managed a relieved smile.

"Sounds as though he's showing remarkably good sense. I'm pleasantly surprised. You frightened the life out of me, dragging it out like that." He looked at her with sudden puzzlement. "What are you so alarmed about?"

"Aren't *you* afraid for Mr. Strickland?" she asked with a hint of reproach.

"Whatever his faults, Charles isn't a murderer."

"He may have him beaten . . . his rooms wrecked."

Magnus considered this without apparent emotion and at last nodded.

"He won't send him flowers, will he? After all he loved the woman himself. I'm sure Tom realized there were risks."

Catherine took his hands.

"Will you warn him, Magnus? I beg you to."

"No," he returned at once, with a harshness that confounded her.

"But is he not your friend?"

"He told me about Helen of his own free will. If I warn him that Charles knows, he will think I told him. Tom knows my opinion of Helen and that I think him a fool." He caught Catherine's eye and forced her to hold his gaze. "If you wish it done, Catherine, you must warn him yourself."

"It is not for a woman to . . ."

"When you told Charles, the subject was not too delicate for your womanly nature."

"I'm not brave enough to tell him to his face. Can't you understand what he would think of me?"

She shrank from the cold hostility of his eyes and the ironic curl of his lips.

"Would his thoughts be so different if anybody else told him what you had done?"

"Have you never been ashamed?" she cried.

"Of course," he replied. "And afterward I don't remember feeling better for having failed to do what my conscience told me I ought to."

"I never thought you so hard," she whispered.

"I gave Tom my word that I would do nothing in this matter, and I do not intend to break that promise."

"Whatever the consequences?" she asked incredulously.

"Bruises heal quickly and leave no marks. Betrayals scar for life."

"Is warning somebody a betrayal?"

"Anything is a betrayal to a man who thinks himself betrayed. I will not have Tom suppose that I gave Charles his secret. The warning would not be worth the hurt it would cause."

"Tell him *I* went to Charles."

Magnus tossed back his head impatiently and leaned forward.

"And who might he suppose had told you? In his place would you not suspect the one person you had confided in?" He got up from his chair, bent down and handed her her bonnet. "Go to him in person; explain why you suspected him and why you acted as you did; otherwise put it out of your mind." He watched her put on her bonnet. "Would you like Paul to fetch you a hansom?"

She shook her head and looked at him miserably, as if appealing for some word of forgiveness, but he merely went to the door and held it open for her.

"It was not easy for me to come," she murmured.

"Do you expect me to applaud you?" Her sad, reproachful face framed by the oval of her bonnet with its little frill of lace moved him to anger rather than pity. "You were not even honest with me."

"Because you humiliated me," she replied, her eyes flashing with anger. "You know I told Charles because I loved Tom. Does it please you to have forced it from me, to degrade me?"

"I degrade you? You call jealousy and spite love, and say *I* have degraded you."

"Why should you judge me?" she shouted. "You feel nothing and never have; even Charles is more human."

When she had gone, Magnus sat down in his reading chair and picked up his book, but the words blurred and merged as his tears blinded him. An hour later the valet brought in his supper on a tray and was surprised to find his master sitting in the dark with a book on his knees.

⟋ Thirty-Three ⟍

Charles paid the cabman and gazed approvingly at the little white Regency villa with its black wrought-iron railings and balconies. He was reminded slightly of a perfectly appointed doll's house. In front was a trim lawn and to the right a miniature conservatory with numerous panes of colored glass, dominated by the dark spiky shapes of a monkey-puzzle tree. As he walked up the graveled path, between narrow beds of dahlias and chrysanthemums, to the small latticework porch, Charles felt distinct twinges of envy for Mr. Lionel Curtis Q.C., whose financial circumstances enabled him to keep his mistress in such congenial surroundings. He was a little surprised that Mr. Kirkup had not commented on the appearance of the house in his report; possibly Featherstone discouraged all mention of architectural or other descriptive details. At any rate, Miss Pike would be sure to wish to retain Mr. Curtis's favor. Charles took off his hat, and after mentally rehearsing his opening lines, rapped on the door with the silver knob of his Malacca cane. A maid wearing regulation black with a white apron and muslin mobcap informed him that Miss Pike had not been expecting anybody and was shortly going out. Charles handed the girl his card.

"Tell Miss Pike that Captain Crawford is Mr. Magnus Crawford's brother and wishes to speak with her on a matter of urgency."

The maid returned several minutes later and led him upstairs to a sunlit front sitting room furnished with gilt chairs and sofas and with a tall Venetian mirror over the mantelpiece. In front of one of the windows was a brightly colored parrot in an intricately made bell-shaped cage.

Mr. Kirkup's report had done nothing to prepare Charles for Lydia's looks. Her pink and white complexion, golden hair and delicate lips took him completely by surprise. She was wearing an open purple jacket bodice revealing a richly figured white shirt with mother-of-pearl buttons and a cambric collar and deep green necktie.

"You must be brief, Captain Crawford. I have to be at the theater in an hour."

Her carefully modulated, slightly husky voice, which Magnus had considered affected, Charles thought delightful. Nor did her fluttering eyelids or feigned demureness irritate him. He studied his shoes.

"You know Mr. Strickland I believe, madam?"

She looked at him with a sudden piercing directness and Charles sensed an iron will beneath her pretty exterior. The revelation came as a shock.

"Come, Captain Crawford. Mr. Strickland is my lover. Your brother will have told you as much."

Charles pretended to be calmly scrutinizing the parrot's green and red plumage and beady eye.

"My brother and I do not sit chattering over other people's affairs." He felt with annoyance that he was blushing.

"Why are you here, sir?"

"You demand brevity and I shall oblige you." He flicked some imaginary dust from the brim of his top hat and caught her eye. "Mr. Strickland is at present secretly meeting a lady of my acquaintance—a lady who is apparently as captivated by him, as he by her. I wish to end this association."

Two glowing red patches had appeared on Lydia's smooth cheeks; at first Charles thought her embarrassed, but quickly saw that she was violently angry.

"Why you should wish to make trouble for Mr. Strickland is your own concern, but you needn't expect me to believe your talebearing. Your brother never liked me, so don't go trusting his lies either." Her velvety musical voice was shot through with a harsh strident edge.

"My brother told me nothing. I engaged a firm to watch Mr. Strickland and the lady. Their observations brought me here. You may recall a curate who begged some water . . ."

"The sneaking bastard!" Lydia hissed through clenched teeth. "A proper goose he made of me with his Methodistical chaff." She turned on Charles and shouted in a strong Cockney accent, "If you don't hook it smart, I'll call up those'll make you." Excited by her raised voice, the parrot let out several raucous, staccato shrieks.

"Can't you see how we can help each other?" replied Charles, horrified by the way matters had gone.

"I can do well enough without help from the likes of you, *Captain*," she returned vehemently with a stress on the final word that made his rank sound like a vile term of abuse rather than a compliment. His face was brick-red as he came toward her menacingly. No jumped-up chorus girl was going to treat him like this with impunity.

"That may be so, but *I* need *your* assistance and by God I'll have it, if I have to tell Mr. Curtis about your dirty little artist."

"Not too dirty for your fine lady. Does she like a man who's more than a pompous bag of wind?"

Charles turned on his heel and made for the door. Before he reached it she said,

"You have not said what you want with me."

With the utmost difficulty Charles contained his rage and faced her. She was smiling with the same innocent but slightly arch expression with which she had greeted him.

"You should not think that your threat changed my mind. There are many besides Mr. Curtis who would like to look after me. I am curious though."

"Then damn your curiosity."

He strode out onto the landing but she followed him at once.

"Perhaps we *can* help each other. I may have been too hasty."

Charles felt exultant. That was how to treat women of her class, blow for blow. A woman such as she neither understood nor deserved courtesy.

"If you were to write to the lady saying that Mr. Strickland has undertaken to marry you, I am sure she would relinquish him."

"Why not send her your clergyman's prying rigmarole?"

"I don't want her to feel *forced* to give him up. If you write, I believe that she will do so voluntarily. I want their liaison ended and not driven into greater secrecy. Threats and restraints increase passion as often as they remedy it. Your revelations would destroy her respect for him."

Lydia shook her head scornfully and compressed her lips.

"Do you think he'd come within a mile of me if he thought I'd written to her? She'd show it him."

Charles gripped his cane more tightly. She was right and he had not anticipated her objection. He thought desperately and then clapped his hands triumphantly.

"Visit her instead. Say you're carrying Strickland's child and beg her to say nothing in case he deserts you." He looked at her expectantly, convinced that there could be no opposition. He was amazed when he saw her dismissive and contemptuous expression.

"I'll win him back fairly or not at all."

"You happily deceive your benefactor, Curtis, but cannot lie to the woman who has stolen your lover? I confess I find your logic hard to grasp."

"If I see her I'll say what I please."

Charles coughed uneasily.

"I need hardly say that you must not mention my part in this."

"Or Mr. Curtis might be hearing from you?" she said with a pert little smile; then with an actress's parody of genteel speech: "I shall be as discreet and ladylike as the Queen herself; so please do not trouble yourself on that account, my dear Captain."

The maid entered with the news that the carriage was waiting.

"I shall be down shortly, Madge."

The girl went out and Lydia came up to Charles.

"The lady's name, if you please."

He went over to a davenport between the windows and wrote out the information; she took it from him before he had time to blot it. He saw her eyebrows rise a fraction.

"Does Lord Goodchild know anything?"

"His lordship is dead."

She thought a moment and he saw the paper tremble in her hand.

"Is Tom after marrying her?" she asked with real pain in her voice.

Charles laughed dryly.

"Make no mistake, Miss Pike, if he entertains any such hopes he is making himself ridiculous. She is already promised to a man of distinction and public note."

She thrust Helen's address angrily into her watch pocket.

"I'm glad I'm no lady," she murmured quietly, with a look of controlled hatred in her eyes. "Your visit has not been a wasted one, Captain."

"You will say what I suggested?"

"Perhaps I will; perhaps I will."

Outside, Charles courteously took Lydia's arm as she stepped into her carriage, then with deliberate irony he raised her gloved hand to his lips. Although he was caught in a heavy shower while in search of a hansom, he felt no irritation, so great was his relief at having saved what had seemed a lost cause. By himself he could have frightened Helen badly enough to have made her stop seeing Tom, but only with Miss de Glorion's help could he destroy Helen's love. Only that could make his father secure; revenge had nothing to do with it, nothing at all; and yet as the rain fell harder and dripped from the brim of his hat onto his shoulders, Charles could not help smiling.

⇜ *Thirty-Four* ⇝

Tom walked out through the stable yard of the Angel where a solitary groom was cranking the pump, the water gushing in spurts and splashing noisily into the metal pail. The sun was just up, but the air still raw with a trace of lingering mist. In the street a string of bleating sheep were being driven toward the market cross, where already the first covered carts and tented stalls were being set in place. He could hear the distant sound of wooden stakes being beaten into the hard ground and men calling out to each other, but apart from a few farmers in their best clothes and the busy stall keepers and tradesmen themselves, there were few people about. The market day crowds would not arrive for another couple of hours.

Tom passed some closed shops, looking into the windows of the cobbler's, admiring briefly the shining leather in the saddler's, and then, beside the smithy, turned down a narrow cut where the bulging walls of the timbered cottages were barely a dozen feet apart. A few minutes later he was in a country lane walking between autumnal hedges bright with red holly and hawthorn berries and the orange hips of wild roses. Occasionally he picked and ate a ripe blackberry, feeling a touch of acid in his empty stomach after swallowing. Spider's webs glistened in the morning light. The lane led down to a ford and a narrow footbridge where some children were playing, swinging on the rails and laughing as they hung out over the water. On the far bank the bracken was already a deep russet, and the trees beyond, yellow and brown, glowing here and there with the deeper fiery red of the turning maple leaves. Few leaves had started to fall, but the winged sycamore seeds were spinning down from a tree beside the bridge. Tom loved the transience of September with a lover's passion for seizing the fleeting moment, enjoying the warmth before the long winter cold, happiness tending to nostalgia, sharpened by an ever-present presentiment of loss.

A peddler, perched on a donkey cart laden with baskets full of seed packets, nuts, cakes and sweets, drove through the ford. Tom stopped him and bought some humbugs, which he tossed up to the children on the bridge, wondering as they thanked him in shrill voices, which were boys and which girls, since all were wearing passed-on clothing, the younger boys in skirts and pinafores once worn by elder sisters. He sat down on a low wall and watched the water flashing over the stones, casting shimmering diamond reflections on the dark underside of the bridge. The sun was growing warmer.

He had been in Barford with Helen for three days, and still it seemed like a dream: walks and picnics together, drives in a dilapidated hired gig, and, above all, her loving tenderness toward him, quite different from the brief embraces of their carefully planned meetings at Bland-ford's Hotel. He imagined her as he had left her, before coming out for his early walk, a white arm hanging over the edge of the bed, her auburn hair spread like a glowing fan on the pillow, her clothes in a heap where she had dropped them over the oak chest at the foot of the bed—and no maid, no footman, no groom nor coachman—just Helen alone. Even if they were married he would not see her dress and wash, these things being attended to by her maid while he skulked in his dressing room. During the few moments of each day when she was not in his thoughts, he was still aware of a warm and delightful feeling of good fortune, the same sensation he had each morning on waking: the sense of guarding within himself a treasure of great value and fragility. Then seeing her, he knew the immense happiness of loving and being loved and could not imagine his life without this joy, could not think what had filled his thoughts before meeting her; everything, including his art, seeming trivial in comparison with his love. He had made one sketch since coming to the Angel, the view from their bedroom, which he had given her as a memento of their time together. When he returned to the room, he would help her to dress, fastening the hooks and eyes at the back of her bodice, perhaps pinning her chignon. And later they would walk arm in arm through the market day crowds, and he might buy some trifling present: a child's penny trumpet or a cottage figurine, and then they would return to their room *together*, without separating or coming in at different times. They called the room "ours," a thought that made his throat choke up; what else save these temporary refuges would they ever be able to share? He got up from the wall and started to retrace his steps. He saw the shape of her life and his own brief part in it: an episode. He thought of the great houses she would stay in, the famous people she would meet, all the world at her service—ideas, paintings, books no more than recreations to divert her, and people the same. A sudden panic made him run toward the street, a feeling that when he returned she would be gone. Then he slowed down, ashamed of himself. How could she leave so early before the post coach and with no word?

He had asked so often in the past fortnight, and she had refused with such regularity to come to a small country town that he had given up hope, until one day to his amazement, for no new reason that he could guess at, she had herself suggested a town, and how they would go there and when. For fear that she might change her mind, he had not faced her with her past objections, but had been thankful for her change of heart, and had deemed it another example of her mysterious and unpredictable nature that she should now do so easily what she had till then resisted with such firm and precise arguments. Yet he had allowed himself the indulgence of hoping that her new lack of caution and her greater affection might mean that she would seek to delay her marriage.

Helen had waked and lay in bed awaiting Tom's return. For her their days at Barford had been agonizing as well as happy. At times during the day before, she had forgotten her anguish: as when Tom had carried her across the thick mud around a field gate and had pretended not to be out of breath when he had put her down; when she discovered that he, and not the hotel staff, had placed flowers in their room; when he had produced cards and books on a day when rain had stopped them going out; on all these occasions she had been entirely absorbed by her love for him. But now, with the curtains still drawn, and his side of the bed empty, she could think only of the week before in London and Lydia's angry, tear-stained face. How perfectly she recalled her repeated questioning: How can you care for him when you know what misery you'll bring him? How can you claim to know the meaning of the word love if you are ready to marry another man merely to protect your wealth and position? How delightful and exciting for a month or two to take a man of a lower class as a lover, how illicit and daring. But never a thought of facing poverty with him or caring for him if he were ill; never the smallest intention of risking social ostracism for his sake or abandoning the selfish habits of a lifetime. Are you any better than those rich old women who pay young men to make up for boredom and their husbands' indifference?

Helen had neither tried to justify herself nor to point out the falseness of the comparison. She had not mentioned her son, or the fact that her acceptance of Sir James had been before the beginning of her liaison with Tom. Lydia had told her how Charles had suggested she pretend to be with child, and she had then faithfully recounted everything else he had said, not, Helen thought, for reasons of honesty or fellow feeling but because she had considered the truth more threatening than the lie. Helen had neither given her word to say nothing to Tom, nor had she made any promises about giving him up, although at the time she had felt shocked and frightened enough to consider going to him at once to end their relationship. But when the girl had gone, and Helen had called her carriage, she had not been able to bring herself to do what she was certain was inevitable. Instead, playing for time, she had written to Charles, in case he acted precipitately, naming a day late the following week for him to come to speak with her "on a matter which I believe has caused you concern." Then she had sent an apparently spontaneous note to Tom, by her own footman, suggesting they go away together. He would at least have some happiness to remember before their separation.

Helen's intention had been to give Tom no hint of anything amiss, until their last day at Barford, when she would tell him that Charles had had them followed and that they could no longer meet with safety. Yet the closer came the day for revelation, the more Helen doubted her capacity for telling him. Apart from her fear of weakening in the face of his sorrow, or of parting in anger or bitterness, she was no longer sure that she could voluntarily commit herself to losing him. She imagined him returning to Lydia and the thought increased her wretchedness. Instead of steeling herself to tell Tom, more often she found herself trying to think of some way in which she might defy Charles, even daring to imagine in detail the consequences of breaking her word to Sir James: her failure to pay the interest on the loans that had saved Hanley

Park, followed by its sale and the inevitable destruction of the rest of Humphrey's inheritance, and culminating with her own financial ruin and social disgrace; possibly Tom would tire of her when she grew a little older and was as poor as he; or she might come to hate him because of everything she had given up and lost forever for his sake. Caught between her inability to surrender her lover and her terror of losing Sir James, Helen abandoned the idea that she could continue to control her destiny. Fate, she told herself, would do that.

Two days before, she and Tom had learned that Russia and Turkey were at war. When he had asked her anxiously whether her marriage would take place sooner if the expected British declaration came, she had reassured him that it would not. Yet even then she had known quite well from Sir James's most recent letter that the Admiralty had promised him a squadron in the Black Sea as soon as Britain's participation became certain; then an early marriage would be inevitable. Unable to bear the thought of Tom's unhappiness, she had kept this from him. In a week or two disclosure would be forced upon her; in the meantime she would not destroy or curtail even by a day the happiness still left to her. If lived fully, a week might be remembered as a year.

When Tom came in breathless and with ruffled hair, wearing the new coat he had bought especially for their trip, she held out her arms and kissed him fiercely, knowing she could no more speak about Charles, or movements of the fleet, than write a confession to Sir James. Suddenly she was laughing. There were no more decisions to be made by her; whatever happened now, would be because others willed it. Whether the stroke was dealt by Charles or James, or by the British Cabinet or the Czar of all the Russias himself, it no longer mattered, still less, when she considered that they too would all believe that their choices had been dictated by forces they had neither understood nor influenced.

⤔ *Thirty-Five* ⤖

By the time Charles had reached Belgravia and was climbing the steps of Helen's palatial stuccoed house, it was already growing dark and the lamplighters were at work. The ground-floor and basement windows were all shuttered, and when he stepped back from the tall twin pillars of the porch and looked up, he could see no lights burning on any of the upper floors. He tugged viciously at the heavy brass bellpull and waited. As he was on the point of leaving, an elderly footman wearing a stained nankeen waistcoat opened the door and held up an oil lamp to get a better view of the caller. Charles pushed past him into the hall and said peremptorily,

"Tell Lady Goodchild that Captain Crawford is here."

"Her ladyship sees nobody, sir. The house is just sold."

"Tell her," snapped Charles.

The footman muttered something under his breath, and then, having lit a candle in a pewter candlestick on an upturned packing case, stumped off up the stairs. By the feeble light of the single candle, Charles could see that the hall was stripped and empty; he picked up the candlestick and pushed open the mahogany double doors of the principal reception rooms on each side of the main staircase. They too were bare and uncarpeted; only the watered, rose-colored silk on the walls recalled the former glory of the house in Lord Goodchild's day. Then no footman in dirty clothes would have opened the door. Charles remembered the tall, yellow-coated flunkeys in their powdered wigs and the brightly lit rooms filled with fashionably dressed people. But he was in no mood for nostalgia or sympathy.

In the early afternoon he had visited Mr. Featherstone's establishment and had been stupefied to discover that not only had Helen continued to see Strickland, but that she had actually spent a week alone with him in a posting house in a Sussex market town. Without even waiting to give further instructions to Featherstone, Charles had at once taken a hansom to St. John's Wood, where he had arrived to find Lydia not at home. He had been obliged to wait two hours for her return. At first he would not believe that she had visited Helen, but when she had described the house and Helen's appearance, he had been forced to concede that she had told the truth. From St. John's Wood he had lost no time in coming to Belgravia, becoming increasingly angry on the way. So that was how she had received Lydia's revelations—and real revelations they had been. The girl had not hidden from Charles the fact that she had told Helen that he had had her followed and watched.

The week before, when he had received Helen's letter, Charles had been in complete ignorance of Helen's knowledge of his proceedings and had thought that the matter she had referred to in her note as having caused him "concern" would be to do with Catherine's unhappiness at Hanley Park or the final arrangements for Humphrey's entry into the navy. Now it seemed that while perfectly aware that he knew everything, she had dared to try to fob him off for a fortnight with her letter, and in the meantime had had the effrontery to spend a week in the country with her lover, and had done so in spite of the knowledge that her every move with Strickland at Barford would be reported back by Featherstone's men.

The footman returned and led Charles up the echoing unlit stairs to a small chamber which had once been Lord Goodchild's dressing room. Helen, who had been writing at a small gate-legged table, rose with a slight frown.

"Have you not mistaken the week, Charles? I was not expecting you today."

"I am aware of that."

The room, like all the others in the house, was uncarpeted. A narrow, metal, framed bed was against the far wall; a dressing table and mirror and an armchair made up the rest of the furniture. When Charles had sat down, Helen resumed her seat at the table and finished the sentence she had been writing, then she put down her pen and said in a low voice,

"Before you start, Charles, I ought to tell you that I received a letter from your father the day before yesterday. He has asked me to join him in Turkey. I intend to go. He wishes us to marry next month in Malta. I have written agreeing to this plan." Seeing he was about to speak, she motioned him to silence. "I give you my word that from the day I leave England, I will never see Mr. Strickland again."

Charles looked at her calm pale face in the candlelight and gripped the arms of his chair. Her hair was hanging loose to her shoulders and she was wearing a simple dark blue high-necked dress, fastened at the throat with a cabochon brooch. Her beauty stirred him against his will.

"I might have known, madam, that you would be well prepared. However your plans are not agreeable to me."

"You intend to warn your father?"

"I have not decided."

"What might help you to a decision?"

"Your compliance with my wishes, or your opposition to them. In the first place you will present yourself at the chambers of my solicitor the day after tomorrow to sign a prepared confession stating that, while engaged to marry my father, you consorted with Mr. Strickland."

Helen had listened with apparent meekness, but when he had finished speaking she leaped to her feet and faced him furiously.

"You have no legal right to force this confession. I am not guilty of breach of contract."

Charles was momentarily taken aback by the violence of her objection. He had only thought of the confession in the hansom on the way from St. John's Wood and had therefore had no opportunity to consult his solicitor.

"I am claiming a moral rather than a legal right. I am aware that since you intend to go through with the marriage there is no call for a *confessio delicti*. The document I want you to sign will be a purely voluntary confession of misconduct."

"May I ask your purpose?" she asked in a choking voice.

"The protection of my father's name and reputation. Should I ever have the slightest reason to suspect you after your marriage, I would not hesitate to show it him. One might call it an incentive to good behavior."

"If I refuse to sign?"

"I shall inform my father of your liaison at once. Your refusal would suggest an intention to deceive him again when you are his wife."

"The evidence of your spies is quite enough to prevent that."

"I do not intend to argue," he replied sharply. "Will you oblige me?"

Helen thought for a moment and then nodded.

"On condition that the confession is destroyed in the event of your father's death."

Charles laughed grimly. How typical of the woman that at such a moment she should think of the inconvenience of such a document should she ever wish to marry again if widowed.

"Very well. You will also write a letter to Mr. Strickland this evening telling him that you will not see him again. I will post it myself. You will be watched until you leave the country, so I would suggest that you do not try to meet him."

She sank back into her chair and stared at him in agonized disbelief. Her eyes were brimming with tears.

"Why are you doing this to me, Charles?"

"Good God, Helen, I have the power to ruin you, yet I choose not to. Instead I ask two concessions on your part. I say nothing of your scandalous conduct and yet you reproach me for cruelty. Must I apologize for doing what I can to protect my father?"

She looked at him imploringly.

"How can it benefit your father for me to be denied a last meeting with Mr. Strickland?"

"You would be tempted to plan further meetings."

"Which your spies will tell you about."

"They are not infallible."

She got up and came closer to him, stretching out her hands in helpless supplication.

"Let me see him and I will swear never to try to do so again. I will sign papers saying it, give any guarantee you wish; only let me see him once more; only that, Charles. One last time."

He hesitated a moment, undecided.

"What if he were to plead with you?"

"I would not weaken. I know I would not."

"You've risked everything for him already. Nothing you say convinces me that you would not do the same again."

She flicked a strand of hair from her eyes and turned abruptly.

"You realize that I will go on writing to him if you prevent us meeting?"

"I consider that a lesser danger. If you see nothing of him before your departure and then remain several months in Constantinople, your infatuation will pass."

A long silence during which Charles saw her stare at him intently and shudder, as though through some secret revelation she had learned a new and terrible truth about him.

"Why have you decided not to tell him about me?" He lowered his eyes. "Because by my marriage I will be separated from Tom? You could not endure my love for him."

"The truth would have destroyed my father. There is no other reason." He got up with trembling legs and shouted, "None, do you hear me? None."

She walked back to her chair and sat down again.

"If you tell him, you lose your power over me. Well, don't you?" He said nothing and she gazed down reflectively, before murmuring, "You loved me once."

He walked to the door, his cheeks still burning.

"Any power I have is dependent on your behavior. I shall return tomorrow for your letter to Strickland and will tell you the time to come to my solicitor's."

As he was going out into the dark corridor, she ran up behind him and caught his arm.

"I will do anything to see him again. Anything; anything you wish."

In the half-darkness of the passage he felt her clutching for his hand, but pulled it away violently, horrified in case she touched his mutilated fingers. With atrocious swiftness he felt her arms about his neck and her lips on his cheek. He shrank from her and groaned, then with a sudden movement seized her around the waist, and pushing her back against the wall, kissed her roughly, angrily, hating himself and yet unable to break away. She had not resisted or flinched from him—a martyr for her love of another man. The thought scorched through Charles's brain as he ran blindly toward the stairs, stumbling in the darkness and cursing himself as he went.

*   *   *

Half an hour after his departure from Helen's house, Charles was in Charlotte Street, knocking wildly at Tom Strickland's door. Tom had barely time to recognize his visitor before seeing a flash of silver and feeling an explosion of pain on the side of his head. The blow from the knob of Charles's cane caught him just above the temple and sent him reeling back into the hall. Charles stepped forward and slammed the door behind them both. Tom leaned dazedly against the wall, pretending to have been hurt more than he actually had been, not in the hope of avoiding further blows but in order to appear too far gone to be able to think or speak if questioned. He did not resist as Charles grasped him by the lapels and shook him.

"D'you hear me, Strickland?" Tom let his head sag forward and staggered as Charles released him. "If you see her again, I'll kill you. Kill you, d'you hear?"

The only light in the hall was that cast by a streetlamp through the fanlight over the door. Charles's face was thrust so close to his that Tom could feel his breath on his cheek. Still trembling with shock, Tom felt flickering sparks of anger fanned to bright rage as he caught Crawford's expression of disgust and moral rectitude. The man saw nothing cowardly in bursting in and striking without warning, a son needing no recourse to fairness when defending his father's honor, especially when the object of his punishment was a lowborn artist—that would be the real cause for his revulsion: the fact that her ladyship had defiled herself by loving a man so far beneath her. In Crawford's face Tom read the physical loathing of one class for another.

"When you come to kill me, perhaps you'll allow me a better chance to defend myself."

Charles stepped back and favored Tom with a derisive bow. Then he tossed him his cane.

"Defend yourself now."

The width of the man's shoulders and his height momentarily sobered Tom but the fierce smarting of his head goaded him on. Charles was watching him with nonchalantly folded arms and a sneer on his lips. The sound of heavy footfalls came from the street, several men passing slowly just outside the door.

"You could shout for help," Charles suggested scornfully.

For answer Tom smashed the heavy silver knob of the cane against the wall and threw down the splintered shaft.

"You're a fool, Strickland."

Tom's throat was as dry as chalk and he could hear the loud beating of his heart. Vague memories from his schooldays: punch straight, don't swing wildly, watch your opponent's hands. As Charles came toward him, Tom jabbed sharply at his white contorted face, catching him on the lower lip where beads of blood welled up at once. The next second Tom was sprawling from a heavy blow in the ribs; he almost twisted clear as Charles bore down on him with all his weight, but found himself pinioned by the ankles. As he writhed to get free, Charles caught his arm and twisted savagely until the joint cracked. Tom locked his teeth so not to scream, certain that he would be forced to beg for mercy, and dreading that humiliation. The pain was agonizing, and his will already weakening, when Charles unexpectedly released his hold and flung him forward, dashing his forehead against the rough wooden floor, stunning him for a moment. Tom lay still for several seconds, seeing from the corner of his eye Crawford's polished boots planted close to his neck.

"All you can take, eh, Strickland?"

The scorn of his voice lashed Tom like a whip. Furtively he braced his elbows on the floor, and then lunged sideways, grabbing Crawford's feet and bringing him down. Tom leaped up, but a scything kick on the shin hurled him back against the door. Charles slowly raised himself on one knee; he had evidently hurt himself in falling and was breathing hard. Seeing his chance, Tom sprang at him, expecting to topple him with ease, but instead meeting a rocklike shoulder. Tom staggered and then backed toward the stairs, knowing he would be no match for Crawford's weight if he allowed him to pull him down.

As Charles advanced on him, head thrust forward and eyes narrowed to slits, Tom gulped in deep breaths and clenched his fists. Crawford came on with slow remorseless steps; his coat had been ripped and was hanging loosely on his massive shoulders; spots of blood dotted his scarf. Tom landed only two ineffective punches before going down under a furious flurry of heavy blows, arms raised blindly to protect himself. As he sank to his knees, head lolling, another punch rocked him and he crashed back onto the stairs, and lay with limbs spread-eagled.

He was dimly aware of the taste of blood in his mouth and the distant sound of his labored breathing. Charles's face floated above him like a pale planet and then vanished.

When Tom regained consciousness, he was propped up at the foot of the stairs and Charles had gone. He listened to the faint hissing of the gas jet on the landing above and closed his eyes. His head was throbbing but not with the splitting pain he knew he would suffer later. Too dazed and weak to move he stayed where he was. Some half-remembered thought or idea troubled him . . . something to be done . . . something important, he knew that now . . . must go, must warn her . . . warn Helen. Helen. He clutched the banisters and raised himself only to fall back again, overcome by dizziness and nausea. He failed once more, and then, sobbing with frustration at his weakness, crawled toward the studio, where he lay prostrate and despairing on the dusty floor.

⮞ Thirty-Six ⮜

Tom paid the flyman before reaching the gates of Hanley Park, having decided to finish his journey on foot. Once again he was looking up at the imposing wrought-iron gates, dominated by the massive central coat of arms and the heraldic griffins on the flanking piers. Only four months since that shimmering morning when he and Helen had driven out between them into the summer countryside. Now the leaves were falling and the air was damp and cold. Through a thick ground mist the elms in the park seemed to be floating rootless in a filmy silver sea. Tom fumbled with the heavy ring handle and pushed the dew-moist metal bars, but even when he had withdrawn the lower bolts, the gates would not move. He was reluctant to bring out the gatekeeper to unlock them, in case the servant asked him his business, and on learning it, told him that he need proceed no further since her ladyship was away. Instead Tom clambered over the stone wall and dropped down onto the grass. A rabbit stared at him, hunched and frozen for a moment, before bounding away into a tangle of bushes. At its zenith, above the mist, the sky was a pearly blue; later the sun would shine. Tom started in the direction of the house, and soon saw the indistinct white outline of the facade.

Tom had not been strong enough to leave his bed for two days after Charles's visit, and on that second day he had received a short cold letter from Helen. In it she had stated that Charles had found out about them, but would take no action against her if no further meetings took place. She had reluctantly promised to abide by this condition and had left London. Tom had been sure that the curtness of the note was no true reflection of Helen's feelings. He had thought it probable that Charles had dictated it; but whether written under duress or not, Helen clearly intended to go through with her marriage. It was the end of their affair, and bitter and upset though he had been, Tom had accepted it. From the beginning he had known the inevitable outcome, yet the manner of its coming had filled him with rebellious anger. He was haunted by the thought that she had known even while they had been at Barford and had not had the courage and honesty to tell him. Now his only happy days with her seemed transformed into a fool's paradise. She had owed him nothing except a single duty: to tell him in person when the moment of parting had come. But she had found it easier to accept Charles's terms, preferring to embalm the memory of her happiness than to risk clouding it with the tears and possible anger of a last meeting. If she had thought of him rather than herself, she would have warned him at once about Charles, and thus have prepared him for that gentleman's sudden appearance. Perhaps, as Magnus had suggested, she had merely used him; perhaps Magnus's picture of her had been the true one. But when Tom thought of her, his resentment melted and he could not accept this. He still loved her, and feared he always might. Regardless of Charles's threats, he would see Helen once more, and whatever the hurt, they would part knowing each other's feelings and openly acknowledging their loss. She had started their intimacy and she should end it—in person.

Tom had thought initially that, in spite of her claim to have left London, she was still there. He had bribed the only remaining servant in the Belgravia house to show him every room, and only then had he been convinced that she had gone. Next he had written to her at Hanley Park in the hope that, if she were not there, his letter would be sent on to her. He had said that if he did not hear from her within two weeks he would come to Hanley Park to make inquiries about her. He had received no answer.

Tom paused a moment as the butler led him through the anteroom where Helen had sat for him. The two ivory chairs, the green and white marble mantelpiece and the painted ceiling reminded him vividly of the tense hours they had spent together in this room and made his heart ache for her. Already the butler had told him that she was away.

With the first shock of hearing that Tom had come, Catherine had immediately feared that Magnus had told him by whom he had been betrayed, but remembering her brother's absolute denial of any intention to warn his friend, she had breathed more freely. She received him in the Red Drawing Room and was at once troubled by his haggard face and shocked to see dark bruises beneath one eye and across a cheek. Tom noticed the direction of her gaze.

"Your brother called on me, Miss Crawford."

"For what reason?"

"You know well enough, madam. You made your suspicions clear even when I was staying here." He fixed her with burning eyes and came closer. "Where is she? Tell me, Catherine. I must know."

"She came a week ago to take Humphrey to Chatham. She will have sailed for Malta by now."

She followed him as he moved blindly toward the door.

"You must not go after her."

"In case your brother kills me?" he shouted.

She shook her head and murmured,

"They would be married before you reached Valletta."

"How do I believe you? Your brother told you to say this if I came here."

Catherine left the room and returned some minutes later with a newspaper. She handed it to him folded back at the middle page; a paragraph was marked under *Service Appointments*.

> Rear Admiral Sir James Crawford Bart., K.C.B., formerly Commander in Chief, North American Station and Rear Admiral of the Blue, to be Second-in-Command Mediterranean Fleet and Rear Admiral of the White, with effect from 1 November. Captain the Hon. H. Broughton C.B., H.M.S. *Retribution*, is appointed Flag Captain . . .

Tom dropped the paper on a chair and remained staring at the floor, thinking that Helen would have known this at Barford, that in this too she had deceived him, as she had done over Charles's knowledge. Even when they had read about the sultan's declaration of war on Russia, she had lied to him, saying that she did not think it likely that the British and French fleets would enter the Bosphorus and the Black Sea for several months. Yet the haste of her departure and Sir James's desire to marry at once was clear proof of the destination of the fleet; and she would have known, and yet had said nothing, nothing. His anger passed and he was paralyzed by a merciful numbness, a feeling of such emptiness and desolation that he felt no more pain, only a strange light-headedness as though he were drunk. He heard Catherine saying:

"If there is anything I can do . . ."

He found himself staring at the portrait over the opposite door—Rembrandt's *Head of a Jew*.

"Do?" he asked, confused.

"Anything you might like me to say to her?"

He shrugged his shoulders and was silent a moment.

"Tell her . . ." He broke off and gazed again at the portrait and felt tears pricking under his lids. Rembrandt, the miller's son, fashionable for a time, then bankrupt, and painting, in lieu of payment, the Jews who lent him money. Two hundred years ago, and he was remembered; and who was rear admiral of the red, vice admiral of the white or lord high admiral then? ". . . tell her," he said pointing, "to hang that painting where it can be seen."

Walking again through the misty park, Tom felt a dull incomprehension. He was sure that Helen's sudden flight and marriage had been hurried on by the approaching war. While *he* had thought only of her, had she been so mesmerized by reading of the comings and goings of diplomats and ministers with their treaties, telegraphic messages and protocols that she had come to believe that such things demanded reverence rather than hatred and derision? If no exchanges had ever taken place between Constantinople, Petersburg and London, would the ordinary people of England and Russia have made up their minds spontaneously to attack one another? The answer was glaringly obvious, and yet nobody derided the ministers and officers, who claimed to be so concerned to prevent events that could never take place if they were to stop preparing for them. But prepare they would, and in due course the fighting would begin.

Sooner or later good-natured men would be leaving homes, some of them only miles from the gates of the silent park, consenting to part with parents, wives and children, and to embark for a distant country where they would try to kill people with whom they could have no possible quarrel. But they would go; they would march, denying common sense and conscience, as all men must who promise unquestioning obedience in the service of a cause they do not understand.

Did life mean so little to so many that they would connive in making shadows of themselves, consigning present passions to forgotten memories; abandoning future hopes as though what they had once wished from life had already gone? No, he thought—for them the bands and flags, the hoarse shouts of command and the hope of glory. How easy for the disappointed lover to see the actions of others only in terms of his own despair. There would be as many reasons for fighting as for loving.

All through the summer, the Eastern crisis had seemed remote and trivial in comparison with his love for Helen. But now he saw its true proportion. Whether brought about by folly or blindness, the results would be real enough. Already his own life and Helen's had been touched and diminished by its lengthening shadow; others would soon feel the same chill sense of their own insignificance.

Tom's memories caused him such pain that he wondered whether even war could be worse than this disease of love, which drained all courage from his heart; the mind might be as empty as a burned church or a wasted town. His happiness seemed already to be part of some long-lost world from which he had somehow strayed into a region belonging to others, where for him there would be no present and no future.

PART FOUR

The War

❧ *Thirty-Seven* ❧

Ordered perfection—a long dining table with polished silver on a spotless cloth; gold braid glinting against dark blue full-dress uniforms by the light of candelabras; scarlet-coated marines with immaculately pipe-clayed belts and cross straps serving wine. A pleasant room with white paneled walls; only the sloping stern windows at one end and the heavy cross beams overhead suggesting that it was the wardroom of a line-of-battle ship. No swearing here on any night, no talking shop or mentioning the names of ladies, except wives or sisters, and tonight an added sense of constraint since Admiral Crawford was dining in the wardroom of his flagship as the guest of his officers.

Two miles from the fleet's anchorage, a world away from white decks and polished wood and metal, lay the Crimean coast and the stinking and polluted inlet of Balaclava, choked with scores of British supply ships and transports, their masts and spars forming a dense floating forest, hemmed in by tall black cliffs. Six miles inland, forty thousand French and British troops were encamped on the heights south of the town of Sevastopol—Russia's great dockyard arsenal and home port of her Black Sea Fleet. Behind the town's massive defenses an unknown number of defenders were waiting, while, somewhere to the north, lurked a Russian field army already defeated by the French and British armies at the Battle of the Alma, but not destroyed. In the minds of many officers on the allied side was the bitter rankling certainty that their commanders, Lord Raglan and Marshal St. Arnaud, should have marched on Sevastopol immediately after their victory at the Alma, instead of waiting to land siege artillery and to establish supply ports. By doing so, they had given the enemy time to complete a system of defensive earthworks and entrenchments more formidable than anything previously encountered by British artillery officers and engineers. These men were not alone in suspecting that the allied forces would now have to mount a siege lasting through the intense cold of a Russian winter with no better shelter than their flimsy tents.

This possibility was rarely far from Sir James Crawford's thoughts, but during dinner he had been preoccupied with other matters. Since hoisting his flag in *Retribution*, he had from time to time been subjected to tactfully oblique questions about whether the new Lady Crawford might be induced to leave the British embassy in Constantinople to visit the Crimea when Lord Stratford next came out. Helen's youth he was sure would already have caused some ribald amusement; but when Commander Berners, the officer next to him at the after end of the table, tentatively broached the subject of Lady Crawford's plans, Sir James's evasion had been good-humored, although tonight this topic was particularly unwelcome.

In an hour's time, Charles's ship *Scylla*, in company with two other vessels, would be steaming in under cover of darkness to attack the Russian shore batteries. On board, under Charles's orders, would be four recently promoted midshipmen, among them Humphrey Grandison, Lord Goodchild. Sir James, who had himself devised the series of night attacks, of which tonight's engagement was but a part, was very well aware of the high risks involved, in spite of his numerous precautions. The commanders of the attacking ships always knew their firing positions from bearings taken on a number of floating lights, unobtrusively laid down by a small paddle sloop earlier in the day. None of the attacks ever took place on consecutive nights or at the same time. So that the flashes of continuous firing did not assist the enemy to calculate their range, ships were only permitted to fire broadsides. To prevent the illumination of one vessel's broadside betraying the positions of the others, each ship was to attack singly, going in at spaced and irregular intervals. But effective engagement of stone forts had to be at dangerously close ranges, making it in part a matter of luck whether an individual ship were to be sunk, set on fire or escape untouched. Surprise being crucial, the first vessel's chances were better than those of the two ships following. Tonight the last ship, and therefore the one most likely to have her range found by the enemy, was H.M.S. *Scylla*. If the boy was hurt, Sir James did not suppose he would be much helped by explaining to Helen that an admiral could hardly be thought to be sending his own relatives into an attack in the least dangerous position. Whether conceding this or not, he knew that she would still reproach him for the rest of his life for having done so little to discourage Humphrey's entry into the navy.

By the time dessert was served, Sir James had spoken very little to the officers seated next to him. Feeling a little guilty about this, he turned to Berners who was delicately peeling a banana with a silver fruit knife, and told him how he had first tasted this particular fruit on the West African coast.

"Of course in the thirties bananas were very rare. Couldn't be bought for love or money in England. Hard to believe today. Fifteen years and now everybody's eating them." Berners smiled politely while Sir James went on to describe the condition of ship's biscuit on the same station. "Had to break it up on deck and mix in raw fish to tempt the weevils out. When we got fresh turtle from Ascension, we were damned glad of it, I can tell you."

Sir James could see that Berners was finding it hard not to grin. He did not blame him. To dine sitting next to the second-in-command of the fleet and to learn nothing about the conduct of the war or anything at all except the food eaten on the West African Station twenty years before would be distinctly unnerving. He was sure he saw relief on Berners' face when the cloth was removed and glasses charged for the Loyal Toast. The president of the mess rose at the head of the table and brought down his silver mallet.

"Mr. Vice, the Queen," that officer said, addressing the vice-president at the opposite end of the table.

"Gentleman, the Queen," came the reply and then everybody, still seated, raised glasses to a general murmur of "The Queen, God bless her."

Ten minutes later, Sir James was on the poop staring through his glass at the dark silhouettes of three two-deckers and a steam tug a mile farther inshore. At four bells he was joined by his flag captain, Captain Broughton, his signals officer and the officer of the watch. By now numerous glasses and telescopes on the three blacked out vessels would be directed toward *Retribution*'s main-top for the appearance of the signal by lanterns: *Weigh and proceed*. Sir James moved away to the port rail to be on his own. Two weeks before, the combined British and French squadrons had attacked Sevastopol's sea defenses by day and had inflicted little damage at a cost of over a hundred dead and three line-of-battle ships towed out of action on fire. Sir James had been certain that failure had been because his own commander-in-chief, Dun- das, and the French Admirals Bruat and Hamelin had been too cautious to engage at decisive ranges. Since the outnumbered Russian fleet was most unlikely to leave harbor, the navy's only remaining role was to destroy the sea forts. Sir James's fervent hope was that these small-scale night attacks would prove to the other admirals what damage could be done to stone fortifications at ranges of less than half a mile. If they failed, he knew that there would be no more general bombardments by day and the Russians would be left free to move guns from their sea defenses to strengthen their land batteries facing the allied armies.

As anxious minutes passed and the time for the signal approached, Sir James grew increasingly apprehensive and often had to remind himself that actions like the one about to begin might be critical in shortening the war. If Charles and Humphrey were to die, they would not do so for an insignificant reason.

Gazing out across the smooth water toward the dark rugged cliffs of the Crimean coast, Sir James thought of a very different shore: the quiet water's edge at a small resort on the Bosphorus—Therapia with its fountains and secluded gardens, its olive groves and vineyards, crowned by the dome and twin minarets of a tiny hillside mosque among cypresses and white flowering strawberry trees. There, before joining the fleet, he had spent several weeks with Helen: a time uninterrupted by anxiety and confusion. Warm hazy days: Helen, in a blue silk dress and broad-brimmed straw hat, sitting on cushions in the stern of a gilded caïque, trailing a hand in the water; Helen, bareheaded in the sun, sketching under the ivy-covered walls of the ruined Genoese castle near Büyükdere; at the embassy at Pera, charming Lady Stratford and even making Lord Stratford laugh, a feat Sir James himself had never achieved.

Sir James shivered and pulled his coat around him. If any harm came to Humphrey, what would she say? What would she do? Fear hit him with a sudden wave of nausea, a feeling of helplessness worse than anything he had ever felt on his own account—far worse even than the chill anxiety he had suffered over the boy's safety when there had been a bad outbreak of cholera in the fleet a month before. At times on the Bos- phorous he had been troubled by Helen's occasional depressions and her air of remoteness at such times. Dear God, if anything happened to Humphrey . . . would she ever recover from it? Still five minutes till the signal, and *Scylla* would not reach her firing position for a further twenty after that. He moved away from the rail and called over the officer of the watch.

"Any activity ashore, Mr. Gaussen? Nothing reported by the lookouts?"

"No, sir."

"Very good, Mr. Gaussen."

Any sign of movement in the enemy batteries and Sir James knew he would be justified in calling off the action. He felt horribly disappointed. He imagined Charles waiting on his quarterdeck surrounded by his ship's officers and envied him. How much easier to go into action than to stand and watch others do so, in the full knowledge that, if they met with disaster, he, as their admiral, would feel himself personally responsible.

* * *

Half an hour before the signal from the flagship was expected, the drum had summoned *Scylla*'s crew to quarters with the additional roll to clear for action. The major preparations had been made several hours before: internal bulkheads taken down, splinter netting set up, royal yards and topgallant masts struck and the lower yards slung securely in chains, to prevent them crashing down should chain shot severely damage the standing rigging. Now only the finishing touches were needed, but these would be enough to occupy the men for at least a part of the remaining period of suspense.

While the hands were running up or down the deck ladders to their respective stations, Humphrey and Colwell, a junior mate, followed the third lieutenant, Mr. Bowen, on his inspection of the airless orlop deck and "cable tiers," below the waterline, checking that all was thoroughly cleared and adequately lit with battle lanterns; that the amputation tables were in place in the cockpit, and platforms and cots placed to receive the wounded. The surgeon and his assistant were getting out their instruments, watched by the loblolly boys—young seamen deputed to heave the maimed and screaming men onto the tables and hold them there until the chloroform took effect. Humphrey swallowed hard as his stomach churned. *Scylla* had not taken part in the general bombardment and the coming engagement would be his first experience of being under fire. Earlier in the day the mates and other midshipmen had placed jocular bets in the gun room about who would be killed and he had been laughed at for not participating. His connection with the captain had not made him popular, since, though Charles was respected, he was not much liked by the junior officers, having outlawed traditional gun-room punishments like *cobbing*—beating cadets and midshipmen with the flat of a scabbard—and reducing to seven shillings a week the amount members of the gun-room mess might spend on wines and spirits. There was, however, as all admitted, a certain humor in Captain Crawford's punishments; any midshipman seen with his hands in his pockets would instantly be sent to the tailor to have them sewn up, a man caught spitting would have to do his work for that week with a spittoon tied around his neck. Humphrey's pockets had already suffered, and it was generally conceded that Crawford showed his stepbrother no favors of any sort, rarely inviting him to dine with him and never excusing him any duty. Humphrey had understood this public impartiality but was wounded that Charles had never spoken to him privately since they had sailed, and this, in spite of the fact that Sir James had often asked him to breakfast with him alone in his quarters. Humphrey's unhappiness about Charles's coldness was made worse by his admiration for him and his certainty that he was one of the most capable captains in the fleet.

Passing on from the cockpit, the low deck beams and supporting pillars throbbed and vibrated more intensely with the slow pulse of the ship's iron heart: her massive steam engines. Level with the boiler room the heat from the fires made the all-pervading smell of oil and bilge water seem thicker and more nauseating than ever. The fires had been alight for several hours, damped down so that steam could be raised at command. Bowen led the way up the fore companion to the main gun deck where final preparations were going ahead with a minimum of noise and without the usual trill of the boatswain's mate's whistle.

Large tubs of water were being filled from the pumps in case of fire, and Humphrey noticed that the deck had already been wetted and sanded to prevent men slipping in pools of blood. Dripping fire screens had been hung around the magazine hatchways and the armorer was going around making a final inspection of gun-locks. Powdermen were hard at work bringing up boxes of friction tubes and cartridges. The racks at the hatchways contained enough shot for ten rounds more than the expected four broadsides. All along the two-hundred-foot deck the gun crews were loading the gleaming ebony 32-pounders to the orders of their No. 1's, the elevation for six hundred yards being fixed with "marked coin" or graduated wedges, inserted under the breech. Cartridges were placed in muzzles and forced home with two smart blows of the rammer, then shot and wads were rammed down firmly on top, and the cartridge pricked to check that it was properly bedded at the bottom of the bore. Between the guns were small stacks of shell boxes with their looped rope handles. The first two broadsides would be with shot, the second two with shell. As Humphrey watched the loading going on, every movement of these muscular, slightly stooping men seemed firm and deliberate, in a way that impressed him more than the stories he had heard about individual acts of heroism. Here was a corporate calmness and obstinate resolution based on an absolute confidence that no man present would let down his fellow. When all the guns were loaded and primed, the lieutenants of the divisions gave the command, "Run out," the crews bent to the side tackles, and the wooden truck wheels rumbled thunderously across the enclosed decks. "Ready," came the repeated cry as the movement was completed from end to end of the deck. The locks were cocked and the lanyards ready in each No. 1's hands. After the rush of activity came a profound silence as the men knelt or stood by their guns; only an occasional cough rose above the continual groaning of the timbers and the distant throbbing of the engine. The gentle rolling of the frigate was not enough to rattle the shot in the racks. For several seconds there was a tension and expectancy in the air, so powerful that Humphrey held his breath, as if the final word, "Fire!" was imminent. Then, when the officers gave the order, "Stand to your guns," a low murmur broke out and the crews squatted and sat, preparing themselves with good-humored resignation for a nerve-racking wait. The sight produced an emotional choking sensation in Humphrey's throat, tearful and yet exalted, a simultaneous feeling of fear, awe and pride, making him expand his chest and hold his head higher although his eyes were full and his heart was pounding.

He followed Colwell and Bowen through the waist where the wreck clearing party was stationed with their saws, axes and tomahawks to be used to clear the decks if masts or spars were brought down during the action. When they reached the quarterdeck, the first lieutenant was standing by the rails of the main companion. While Bowen saluted and reported the orlop deck in order, Humphrey walked across to the portside carronades to join the other midshipmen waiting to carry the officers' orders to all parts of the ship during the engagement. Soon the lieutenants were coming up from the gun decks to declare their divisions ready for action. The only light on deck came from the binnacle compass, but by the stars Humphrey could see the officers' swords and epaulets and the strip of gold lace on the side of Charles's cocked hat. Under their feet the deck was as fresh and white as a tree just stripped of its bark, the black lines between the planks as thin and delicate as threads.

While Humphrey had been below, the flagship had signaled to *Vengeance*, the first ship, to weigh, and already she was moving in on the masked lights. *Vengeance,* an unconverted, sailing two-decker, went in with a steam tug lashed amidships to her port side, in which position the steamer would be protected from the Russian guns by her massive consort's hull. Since only the ship's starboard broadside would be fired, the frigate's fighting efficiency would not be impaired. As *Vengeance* began her slow turn to port, gradually presenting her guns to the batteries, Charles and Mark Wilmot, his first lieutenant, went up onto the poop and scanned the long low silhouette of Fort Constantine with their telescopes, looking for movement or lights. They were relieved to see no signs of any preparation. If the Russians were heating red-hot shot, the smoke from the furnaces should be visible. Fort Constantine alone mounted almost a hundred guns, three times the number *Scylla* could bring to bear in a single broadside. Built on a spit, the fort jutted out from the north side of the harbor, commanding the sea approaches and the mouth. The guns were ranged in three tiers, the bottom two consisting of heavy 42- and 68-pounders in casemates, and above them, in a single row, 32-pounders, *en barbette*, raised on platforms to fire over the parapet. From the south side of the harbor, the ships would face the sixty or so guns of Fort Alexander and the same number in the adjacent Quarantine Battery. Everything, as Charles and Wilmot were painfully aware, would depend upon whether the Russians were taken by surprise. Charles turned to Wilmot and smiled; they had known each other since serving as mids for several months in a brig on the China Station fifteen years before. Wilmot had a wife and two small children; Charles was godfather to the youngest. He wondered whether Wilmot was thinking about them. Charles himself felt impatient rather than afraid; there was nothing for him to do now and he could not bear inactivity.

Humphrey was staring out at the forts through the darkness at the moment when a brilliant flash lit up the white stonework clearly showing the rows of embrasures; during the second it took for the roar of *Vengeance*'s first broadside to reach *Scylla*, the sky was once more plunged into darkness; it was as if, he thought, the sun had been snuffed out without warning on a bright day. Never could Humphrey remember minutes longer than the two or three that now passed. The question in his and every other mind was whether Fort Constantine would open with isolated guns, at full strength or not at all. The flash of the next broadside came and still no answer. Then seconds later, Humphrey saw a sight far more disturbing than the fiery smoke of guns in the casemates would have been; the sky was ablaze with light balls and rockets fired from the parapets of the forts. Figures were distinctly visible moving on *Vengeance*'s decks, now and then obscured by the white smoke of her last broadside. The light balls were bursting at great height, hanging, as though suspended for a moment, and then, still incandescent, falling into the sea.

Charles leaped down the poop steps onto the quarterdeck, and, seizing the master's speaking trumpet, yelled to the signals quartermaster in the main-top.

"Make to flagship: 'May I commence?' "

Before the lanterns had been displayed, *Vengeance* fired again, and a split second later the Russian batteries opened with a beautifully compact flight of shell from the 32-pounders, the fuses describing glowing-red fiery arcs in the black sky. Without waiting for the answer to his signal, Charles was yelling,

"Hands up anchor! Man the capstan!"

The reasons for silence now being gone, the boatswain's pipe repeated the command, and the men on the forecastle leaped to their bars, spinning the capstan around like an enormous top, their feet pounding on the deck. The cable had already been hove in, and the chain was at once grinding and clashing in at the hawsepipe. Light balls were still going up in high, lazy parabolas, climbing rapidly, hanging and then falling slowly. Tall plumes of water, tossed up by the Russian shells, could be seen spouting in line twenty yards short of *Vengeance*. As Charles gave the order to raise steam, the flagship signaled: Leander *and* Scylla *proceed in line abreast*.

Vengeance was moving across the face of the batteries at an agonizingly slow speed of four or five knots, the best the tug could manage when towing alongside. The spaced broadsides had been abandoned and her gunners were firing independently at their best speeds. Every second or so a well-placed shell burst against the walls of Fort Constantine with a violet and orange flash, illuminating the whole structure. The Russians were replying with shell in coordinated salvos, punctuated by random discharges of hot shot from Fort Alexander and the Quarantine Battery on the other side of the harbor. On account of the very close range, the gunners on both sides were using short $1\frac{1}{4}$-inch fuses, which often detonated the explosive in midair, throwing out shrieking fragments of metal and showers of glowing red sparks. Sometimes after a momentary lull, a sharp explosion shook the air, then came more muted sounds, merging into each other, like a rapid roll on a gigantic drum, rising in pitch and crescendoing into simultaneous crashes like thunder directly overhead.

As *Vengeance* began her turn out to sea, she was hit amidships by two large mortar shells, which instantly started a fire. Humphrey gasped as he saw the flames catching the ratlines and shooting up them as though following fast-burning fuses. Every man on *Scylla*'s quarterdeck was gazing in silent horror, expecting a magazine to go up, but after the initial blaze, the flames began to die down as the ship was shrouded in a dense pall of black smoke. No efforts were being made to launch boats, and so Humphrey assumed that the conflagration had looked worse from a distance than it actually had been.

The boatswain's pipe proclaimed that the anchor was at the bows, and a moment later an assistant engineer came running with the news that the steam was up. Within seconds the screw had engaged, and as the vibrations intensified, the master's calm voice was heard: "Turn ahead easy," then, "Half ahead." Humphrey had always liked the master, a bald, potbellied man with red cheeks and small twinkling eyes; unlike the other officers he was wearing a plain faded surtout without a sword belt. His phlegmatic expression and folded arms comforted Humphrey. Charles sent the midshipman nearest to him forward with orders for the 68-pounder pivot on the forecastle to open up at fifteen hundred yards. Astern of *Scylla* two deep folds of water fanned out, their crests creaming and foaming with phosphorescence. On a parallel course, half a mile to starboard, *Leander* was steaming in on Fort Alexander, a long ribbon of dark smoke arching from her tall ungainly stack.

Scylla's forecastle Lancaster had fired two rounds when the Russians found the ship's range with 42-pound round shot. As Humphrey heard the low vibrant whoosh of these balls passing through the rigging, and then the sharper whistle of the first shells fired at them, he felt an icy tingling down his back, as if after sweating he had suddenly been subjected to a chilling breeze. His mouth felt numb and stiff and he was afraid if he was asked something he would not be able to answer. The softness of his hand against the hilt of his useless little sword, made him shudder. He raised a hand to his neck and felt the soft downy skin which he had never needed to shave. If I were hit here, or in the stomach. Nobody lives after a stomach wound. Was it possible that other human beings less than a thousand yards away wanted to kill *him?* He thought of his mother and the servants at Hanley Park, and could hardly remember a word of anger being spoken to him by any of them. He saw his father dying, the blood bubbling at the corners of his mouth. Remembered the men dying ten a day during the worst of the cholera, and how on boat duty he had been sent out with a bayonet or sharpened boarding pike to puncture the bloated, sewn-up hammocks which had raised the 32-pound shot used to sink bodies buried at sea. He recalled the precise slow hiss of escaping gas and the sickening smell as he or another man stabbed at one of these inflated shrouds, sending it down at once, emitting a decreasing stream of bubbles. But few of the officers had died of cholera, and those who did had had time to know their fate, a privilege not accorded by these lumps of metal tearing the air. A soldier might fire his rifle and move his position, urging men on, working out what enemy movements meant, but for naval officers there was nothing but this endless waiting and nowhere to hide. Without moving his head or hands to betray himself, he said a silent prayer. Before he had finished, a round shot smashed down onto the poop, plowing up the planks as though they were paper thin, striking the mizzenmast, leaving the bitts a useless mess of matchwood and going overboard, carrying with it twenty feet of the taffrail. A second shot landed in the waist, killing two men instantly and pitching over a gun, splintering the truck and crushing a gunner's legs. The man's screaming rose above the firing, a shrill, scarcely human sound. Humphrey stared at Charles, as though he could do something to stop this terrible sound, but Crawford gazed ahead of him, apparently deaf to pain and suffering. Next to him, Wilmot said a few words and they both smiled grimly. Humphrey dug his nails into the palms of his hands.

In truth Charles was angry. The first casualties should be moved at once, especially if badly wounded, less for their own sake than for general morale. He found himself wondering why there was a delay. Mangled and shattered limbs caught under a fallen gun or spar? A deck ladder carried away? Something fluttered down to the deck just to his left; he bent down and with a tremor of irrational rage picked up the ensign. The shot that had crashed through the taffrail had severed the stern halyards.

"Secure this to the mizzen truck," he shouted to a member of the nearest carronade's gun crew. Without halyards, no power on earth could restore it to the mizzen peak. Round and chain shot were now slicing through the rigging almost continuously. Charles turned his telescope on *Vengeance* and saw with a shock that her foremast had been brought down. Shells were raining down around her, and although she was still moving, her withdrawal was not fast enough to prevent the gunners registering hit after hit on her upper decks. He had no doubt that the only reason why *Scylla* and *Leander* had not been recalled was the absolute necessity for dividing the Russian's fire as much as possible to save *Vengeance*. Charles knew the terrible dilemma his father would be in, how by trying to spare *Vengeance,* he might well lose one of the other two ships, and if he did, Dundas and the French admirals would not be slow to point out the absurdity of attempting any further attacks on the forts. Charles was determined that come what might *Vengeance* should not be lost—his father would not be let down by him, so long as *Scylla* answered her helm. As another shell burst on the crippled frigate's forecastle, Charles strode to the wheel.

"Starboard two points; full ahead," he said quietly.

"Starboard two points," replied the quartermaster as the course was adjusted, and then as the engine-room bell rang: *Engines full ahead.*

Charles felt the eyes of his officers on him and heard several uneasy coughs. Wilmot came up to him. He looked embarrassed and anxious.

"I understood our orders were to . . ."

"I know our orders, Mr. Wilmot," said Charles curtly.

"Aye, aye, sir."

Charles knew what Wilmot was thinking but could not explain to him without others overhearing and realizing what a gamble he was taking. The orders had been to turn to port at a thousand yards and to engage Fort Constantine from the front. Charles was now steering straight for the harbor mouth, a course that would inevitably expose his ship to close simultaneous fire from the forts on both sides of the entrance. He calculated that only by coming close to the guns on the inner southern face of Fort Constantine could he draw the fire of the western seaward face away from *Vengeance*. That he would also have to risk the fire of Fort Alexander from the other side of the harbor mouth could not be helped, but *Leander* would soon be engaging that battery and should occupy the gunners there. *Scylla* had now reached her top speed of thirteen knots, making her a harder target than the slow-moving *Vengeance*. The high trajectories of the short-range mortar shells told Charles that he was now within five hundred yards of the mouth; several seconds later he was thankful to hear *Leander* going into action. On her new course, *Scylla*'s broadsides would be useless for a few minutes yet, but her bow Lancaster was still firing at three rounds a minute.

From the corner of his eye Charles saw that the seaman he had sent up with the ensign had performed his task and had now climbed down to the comparative safety of the mizzen-top. He was easing himself out by the futtock shrouds onto the top of the ratlines when some chain shot hit him, hurling him from the rigging like a rag doll, his arms thrown out and his back bent double. Charles thought he had gone overboard, but a moment later saw the body impaled on the davits below the poop, stomach ripped open and head lolling forward. Charles heard Wilmot order a mizzen-topman, "Get that thing down!" and he himself was about to send a midshipman down to the gun decks with new orders when a shell hit the quarterdeck. The air was splitting apart in a tornado of whistling and screaming splinters and jagged metal; the deck seemed to lurch and lean upward as he fell. He held his head as every bone in his body danced with the reverberations and shock; he was blinded with smoke, and his nostrils and throat were choked with the suffocating acrid smell of burning powder. As the smoke cleared slightly, and the white popping flashes behind his eyes diminished, he saw that half the

officers and men, who moments before had been standing on that immaculate white deck, were dead or dying. The master's massive body
was lying slumped against the binnacle housing, his head cleanly severed from his body by a bomb splinter, as neatly done as might have
been achieved with a knife. Blood was bubbling and gushing from his
neck. Wilmot was lying on his back, his right side an unrecognizable
pulp of bleeding flesh and torn clothing, his face raw and bloody as
though it had been flayed. The quartermaster's right leg had been
smashed below the knee, and he was sitting looking at the wound with a
surprised and confused expression, the shock still insulating him from
the pain. Charles steadied himself on the only surviving post of the rail
around the main-companion hatch; his stomach was heaving and he
could feel bile in his mouth. Men were running up from the waist with
stretchers and slipping in the spreading pools of blood. Charles himself
picked up a sand bucket and scattered its contents. Another shell exploded on the bulwarks just above the main entry port, hurling large
planks and timbers into the air, but *Scylla* held her course without any
reduction in speed. A red-hot shot had buried itself deep in the forecastle deck planks between the foremast and the gangboard gratings
over the bowsprit. A cry of "Fire!" went up but, from the size of the
flames, Charles did not think it would spread. Shot was now falling on
every side, columns of water shooting up and cascading down in fountains onto the decks. Charles remembered that he had been about to
send orders to the gun decks, recalled too with a paralyzing spasm of
panic that he would have entrusted them to Humphrey to take below to
get him out of the way before the ship was under the full impact of the
forts' fire. He looked around and saw him standing just aft of the port
shot garlands, staring down at the deck as if dazed or in a dream. As
Charles touched his shoulder, the boy started and swung around to face
him. The air was loud with the whistling of shells and the groans of the
wounded. A canister bouquet exploded sharply just astern.

"Don't be afraid, my boy," he murmured. Humphrey made no movement; his eyes looked glazed and there were drops of sweat standing out
on his forehead and upper lip. "Go tell Mr. Machin to let the men fire as
they will after a single broadside. He may fire the moment his guns bear
on either side."

Humphrey raised his hand to his cap mechanically.

"Aye, aye, sir."

As he moved away uncertainly, Charles called out,

"And stay below unless I send for you."

Seconds after Humphrey's departure, shots tore through the starboard gangboard above the waist and another smashed a large hole in the forecastle bulwarks, carrying away deadeyes, cleats, shrouds and foremast ratlines—so much gossamer on the wind. A few more shots like that and the masts would be down. For the first time Charles wondered whether his ship was going to survive. Suppose he had not risked his ship by going in; might *Vengeance* still not have crept to safety? If either *Scylla* or *Vengeance* were to be lost, there was no doubt which the Admiralty would have chosen to sacrifice: *Vengeance*, the unconverted sailing frigate. If he ever survived the loss of his ship, he might well face a court-martial for failing to adhere to his orders. Another fifty yards and there would be no turning back; yet Charles never even considered this option, although he had already vastly increased *Vengeance's* chances of escape. Another shell exploded as it struck the plank-sheer rail, showering the quarter-deck with splinters and cutting Charles's forehead above his left eye. He wiped away the blood and cursed the Russians. The hammock netting had absorbed most of the blast and saved him from certain death. He thought of the deluge of shell and shot which he felt sure would rain down on *Scylla* as soon as she was level with the inner face of Fort Constantine. He imagined the yards and blocks coming crashing down, and felt fury rather than fear: fury that the Russians had blocked their harbor mouth and refused to come out and fight on equal terms, fury with the British public's belief that the Royal Navy was not as it had been of old. The ignorant blockheads thought that the men who won the Battle of the Saints, the First of June and Trafalgar would have had no trouble in leveling a few harbor forts. None of them remembered that Nelson's failures had all been against shore positions: the fiascoes at Turk's Bay and Tenerife and his repulse from Boulogne. Did they ever think that the navy's present impasse in the Black Sea was due entirely to the Russians' fear of a general action? Not they. Well let them read in their comfortable chairs about how a British two-decker acquitted herself against overwhelming odds.

He saw Bowen and Cunningham, the only two officers of wardroom rank to have survived the shell, both looking at him strangely and he did not find it hard to guess their thoughts. Bowen caught his eye and Charles smiled blandly before turning and ordering the men at the quarterdeck carronades to stand to their guns. A few seconds later he gave the order to fire, and the quarterdeck guns were followed by the entire broadside, port first and starboard just after, the ship heeling in the opposite direction after each discharge, engulfed in smoke from stem to stern. By running up onto the poop and leaning out over the shattered taffrail, Charles was able to see shells and shot pitting the stonework, here and there demolishing the dividing walls between the casemates. The crash of *Scylla*'s guns and the continual rumbling of the truck wheels made him shiver with excitement and elation. It was almost a minute before he realized that the enemy had not replied. At first he assumed that they could not depress their guns low enough to hit him as close in as three hundred yards. Even at five hundred most of the shot had gone through the rigging. But at this range it ought to be easy for them to hit *Scylla* firing mortars at their normal 45-degree elevation, loaded with short-fuse shells and low charges of powder. Without such weapons the forts would not be able to achieve a continuous line of fire across the channel. His confusion changed to astonishment when he saw that, although close enough to Fort Constantine to cause problems over the depression of fixed guns, the same reason could not explain the silence of Fort Alexander, seven hundred yards away. Then through gaps in the smoke Charles saw men hauling up light howitzers and field guns to the parapets. Only then did he understand with a chilling shock that he had engaged the face of an empty battery. There were no guns in the casemates commanding the channel at the harbor mouth.

How did I not know it? he asked himself. They sank their ships across the mouth and so would obviously suppose that no ships would try to enter the approach channel. All the guns previously commanding the harbor had evidently been removed to the casemates facing the sea. Charles felt ridiculous and utterly deflated. Moments before he had thought of heroism and probable death; now he was tortured by the sarcastic comments he might expect from fellow captains. *Scylla*'s guns were still blazing on both sides, but he was still too stunned to order them to stop.

The smoke was so thick that he could not see whether *Vengeance* was clear of the seaward batteries, but he supposed that she must be. Then suddenly it came to him that his action, far from being ridiculous, had been inspired. He would say that he had *calculated* on there being no guns commanding the mouth, that he had taken the risk of steaming in so close, only because certain that the guns had been removed. That he had known that the only way to draw the fire from *Vengeance* was to present for a short time, but only for a short time, a more tempting target. He would say that he hoped that his attack on the undefended faces would persuade the Russians to replace guns in these casemates to prevent further attacks on them, which, if carried out regularly, would seriously weaken the whole structure of these forts. His action might therefore ultimately reduce the number of guns in the casemates facing the sea, and this would assist any future general naval bombardment. Charles felt almost lighthearted as he went down to the quarterdeck to give the order to cease firing and to stand out to sea.

By steaming out from the center of the channel, *Scylla* was not exposed to the same intensity of fire which she had faced when heading straight for Fort Constantine. Before Charles was able to order the retreat from quarters, the spanker gaff had been carried away, a round shot had plowed into the captain's day cabin, demolishing the stern gallery, and another had lodged in the lower counter, narrowly missing the rudder head; but no more lives had been lost.

As *Scylla* came in to her anchorage, Charles heard *Vengeance*'s crew cheering and ordered his own men to repay the compliment. Passing down the main companion on his way to visit the wounded, Charles was cheered down the entire length of the main gun deck. Apparently the gun crews had credited him with the foresight he intended to claim for himself. Among those lining the ladder down to the orlop deck, Charles was relieved to see Humphrey, his monkey jacket white with powder and his trousers torn, but otherwise apparently unharmed. Charles patted him gently on the back and continued his descent to the surgeon's bloodstained domain. He wished he had been able to drink some rum or brandy before seeing what he knew he would, but now he would have to face it without. He took a deep breath and entered the cockpit.

⤳ *Thirty-Eight* ⤳

Since dawn, *Brandon* and half a dozen other transports and merchant steamships had been pitching ponderously at anchor within the gentle curve of Balaclava Bay awaiting their respective turns to enter the narrow inlet, in response to signal flags hoisted above the crumbling cliff-top fort at the mouth. During *Brandon*'s passage from Constantinople, Magnus Crawford had shared a cabin with three young British officers who had recently purchased commissions and were on their way out to their first war. Their aggressive self-confidence had saddened rather than annoyed Magnus, when he had reflected on the length of time that would elapse before they would order ices again at Gunter's or walk arm in arm under the striped awnings in Berkeley Square. Nor had he been surprised to be ostracized when they had found out that he was a´journalist, and not, as they had at first supposed, a "Traveling Gentleman" or "T.G.," as the rich young idlers, now visiting the "Seat of War" for amusement, were called. His fellow passengers' contempt for journalists was largely due to Mr. Russell's scathing dispatches to *The Times* and his attacks on Lord Raglan and the commissary general.

Their remarks about Russell distressed Magnus, not because he had ever met the man, but because they once more underlined *The Times*'s supremacy, both in circulation and general repute, over the other dailies, including the *Morning Chronicle*, for which he had come out. There were at least a dozen other correspondents in the Crimea, but to date Russell's dispatches had claimed almost all the public's attention. Yet for all that, Magnus felt fortunate to have been chosen by any paper, knowing as he did that his past military experience had counted for less than the general reluctance of better known correspondents to take on an assignment that seemed likely to last through the winter. Indeed, because of his inexperience, he had felt obliged to accept his editor's decision to pay him no salary, but only his expenses and a fee for each dispatch published. But such poor terms had done nothing to discourage him.

When Magnus clambered up onto one of *Brandon*'s paddle boxes to get his first view of the port, he knew precisely why he had come. Believing that the Crimean invasion would prove a disaster, he placed the principal blame on the senior naval and military officers who had failed to speak out openly about the dangers involved, while there had still been time to hold back. Magnus's certainty that his father had been as guilty as any of these officers had crystallized the issue for him and had added to his determination to record the consequences of their lack of judgment and foresight. At times it had shocked him that the thought of a national catastrophe did not entirely displease him, but brought with it a grim satisfaction; such an event would, he supposed, finally discredit the ruling elite in politics and in the services—nor would his father escape that fate. Without Tom, Magnus's horizons had shrunk to a single objective: to chronicle the self-destruction of his father's caste.

As *Brandon* steamed slowly between the tall cliffs at the entrance to the harbor, the two companies of Turkish infantry, the majority of the ship's passengers, started to emerge on deck, stacking their cooking pots, swords, firearms, prayer mats and blankets in confused heaps between the high bulwarks of the forecastle. None, as far as Magnus could judge, seemed unduly surprised by the extraordinary spectacle of upward of a hundred and fifty vessels moored in two tiers, stem to stern, on both sides of an enclosed inlet, half a mile long and at no point wider than three hundred yards. Ships entering or leaving the harbor did so along a central channel between the shipping barely wide enough for a steamer to turn in. The water was evidently deep since most of the ships were moored hard against the banks, their sloping sterns often projecting over the edge of the quays and jetties.

The town itself was built on a strip of gently sloping land sandwiched between the ships' masts and the cliffs: a wretched cluster of wrecked houses, some of stone, and others of cracked planks, not unlike dilapidated farm outhouses or ruined market stalls. In the center of a network of muddy, unpaved alleys, so narrow that the tiles frequently touched across them, was a burned-out church, the skeletal blackened timbers of its onion-shaped dome still standing. Along the waterfront Magnus could make out separate wharves: one for munitions entirely covered with round shot, piled in vast pyramids many of them ten feet high, another for cattle, a third for forage, a fourth for the disembarkation of troops, and near the head of the harbor, yet another with block and tackle hoists and sheers for unloading heavy guns. From reading Russell's descriptions of the place, Magnus had expected there to be far less order than there was, and, although the water was stagnant and stinking with the bloated carcasses of dead mules and horses, and the offal from the slaughterhouses, he was impressed by what had already been done. To land, at a tiny fishing port on a foreign coast, three thousand miles from home, all the provisions and munitions of war for the largest army ever to have left England at a single time: with its shot, shells, powder, guns, mortars, gun carriages, platforms, fascines, gabions, trenching tools, sandbags, food, cooking utensils, tents, horses and forage, was not an insignificant achievement. On the bare stony hills above the head of the harbor, he saw rows of white tents, and, imagining what living in them would be like when the snows came, he thought angrily of his father in the secure comfort of his flagship.

On landing, Magnus made his way to the commissariat office to try to get a mule or donkey to carry up his tent and boxes to the plateau before Sevastopol. At that office he learned that the commissary general could not authorize transport for civilians without a requisition order from the deputy adjutant general, quartermaster general's department. An hour later he had further discovered that such an order could only be signed by the quartermaster general in person, and for this he would have to walk the seven miles up the Balaclava col to staff headquarters.

Discouraged and angry he called at the post office to see if any of the letters of introduction to influential staff officers, promised by the editor of the *Morning Chronicle*, were waiting for him. They were not. In a corner he saw a large sack of letters marked "Dead." A postal clerk was busy writing in a ledger with ink, which, he told Magnus, was made with vinegar and soot—all the ink originally sent out from England having been used up. With the existing system of requisitions, memos, orders and overlapping departments, it did not surprise Magnus that there was no ink. When he told the clerk about his difficulties, he was informed dryly that had he succeeded in getting a mule, he would have found no nails with which to have the animal shod. There had been a ton of such nails in a transport which had been in the port for two weeks, but since this ship's invoices of cargo had been mislaid by the harbor master's office, and the vessel had outstayed the period allotted by the captain superintendent, the transport had sailed for England with the nails still in her hold.

By now resigned to spending another night in *Brandon*, Magnus walked back along the waterfront in the fading light and sat for a while on an overturned cart outside the main forage yard, watching officers and men passing on their way to and from the various wharves. He was amazed by the contrast between the new drafts in their bright clean uniforms and the condition of the troops who had evidently been in the Crimea since the start of the campaign. But for their swords, officers would have been indistinguishable from their men. Torn and patched full-dress coats now ranged through various shades of port-wine to dirty tints of brown and dull copper. Gold lace and epaulets, where they survived, were black and tarnished, and many officers appeared to be wearing no shirts under their coats. A tiny minority were wearing cumbersome padded jackets lined with rabbits' fur, and hardly a man, whatever his rank, seemed to have continued shaving; their beards, Magnus supposed, providing badly needed extra warmth about the neck and throat. At midday the weather had been warm enough, but now, just before sunset, the cartwheel tracks and hoof marks in the previously yielding mud were freezing into hard ruts and ridges underfoot.

By the cattle wharf, Magnus passed two mounted officers, one riding a donkey, his long legs almost touching the ground on each side. Behind him wound a procession of carts and arabas loaded with shell boxes and cartridges, some dragged by a dozen men, others by mules and oxen, with one even pulled by a dromedary. Magnus was walking on when he felt a touch on his shoulder. He turned and saw that the officer who had been riding the donkey had dismounted and was facing him. The man's hair was unkempt and greasy and the lower part of his face concealed by a fair wispy beard. His pale blue, slightly protruberant eyes looked out anxiously from under a strapless forage cap pulled down over his ears. A thick nose between gray sunken cheeks accentuated his sickly emaciation. On his sleeves were four gilt cuff buttons sewn on in pairs—denoting either the Grenadier or Coldstream Guards, Magnus was not sure which. The officer was staring at him with uncertain, screwed-up eyes. With a gasp of recognition, Magnus remembered the night he had arrived in Rigton Bridge, and in the darkness a very different face under a yeomanry shako.

"George," he murmured, horrified by the change in his once sleek and slightly puffy features.

It took George Braithwaite ten minutes to accomplish what Magnus had failed to achieve in half a day—the acquisition of a pack pony, borrowed in this case from a team brought out by the recently arrived railway surveyor and his party. Magnus was surprised by George's apparently genuine desire to help him, not only because of their past quarrels, but also because of the attitude to journalists displayed by the officers on *Brandon*. Yet George, and Bartlett, the other officer with him, showed Magnus no ill will at all when he told them why he had come out.

"Somebody's got to tell the public what they don't want to hear," was the opinion George expressed, as they rode off together with the carts and wagons following. He laughed mirthlessly as he held up a hand in a worn leather glove. "Forty shillings for a pair of gloves like this, and damned lucky I was to get them. Had to pay a guinea for a small tin of cocoa yesterday . . . It's the same with everything. If you don't believe me, try getting a fur-lined coat under a hundred."

"Nobody'll sell at that price," muttered Bartlett dismissively. Magnus looked more carefully at George's companion. Probably no more than twenty, but already he had sunken eyes and deep lines on each side of his mouth. Three months of war and two major battles and he looked nearer thirty.

"Surely *some* winter clothing's been issued?" put in Magnus quietly.

"Hardly any," replied George. "Haven't changed this coat for six weeks and it can be devilish cold at night too. We've hardly enough fuel to boil a can of water, let alone make a decent fire with."

"There must be plenty of trees to use for fuel," said Magnus firmly, disturbed by George's and Bartlett's resigned, matter-of-fact tone.

"Trees?" Bartlett sounded almost scornful. "The engineers cut them down weeks ago to use in the batteries—gun platforms and props for the magazines mostly."

They rode on in silence for a short distance, until George turned to Magnus with a reassuring smile.

"Nobody can understand it when they come out. . . . Hundreds of ships packed full of stores and every sort of shortage in the camps."

All the way up the long hill from the port to the heights, the un-metalled track was lined with shattered gun carriages, wrecked limbers and the unburied carcasses of scores of mules and horses, which had died hauling up the guns.

"That's one reason," said Bartlett, pointing to a dead mule with a grotesquely inflated stomach. "Too few pack animals. You're lucky to have got the one you're sitting on; wouldn't have had a chance if it'd been here a month. As soon as fresh ones get here, they're worked to death dragging up ammunition. There's hardly any forage up at the camps, stores weren't built up and now something else is always more important—cartridges and shells for a start."

Magnus had read plenty about the army's lack of provisions, but this was beyond anything he had expected.

"What about cavalry horses?" he asked.

"Starving," returned Bartlett flatly. "Tether them near each other and they gnaw each other's tails. The Russians did us a favor cutting up the Light Brigade . . . saved us the trouble of shooting our own horses."

The young man's weary pessimism shocked Magnus, but the small groups of haggard and ill-dressed men they passed and their broken-down animals bore out everything he had been told. The hills around them were bare and rocky with hardly a bush in sight and no trees at all. The only small village he saw had been burned and reduced to rubble; not a door or window frame was in place, all, he supposed, having been used for firewood. Bartlett was humming tunelessly to himself.

"Things could be worse," murmured George. "Men aren't starving and enough ammunition reaches the batteries."

"In a month?" asked Bartlett with the same ironic tone Magnus had noticed before.

"We'll attack before then . . . bound to," replied George with a forced laugh.

"We'd better."

Having parted with Bartlett at the top of the col, George and Magnus went on a further mile to the Second Division's encampment. Outside George's tent they found his orderly frying salt pork over a small fire, having spent an hour, he said, digging up enough roots to provide fuel for the cooking. George had brought up some onions from Balaclava, which were peeled and sliced, ready to be put in with the pork. Still watching the meat, the orderly began grinding up some green-looking coffee beans in the hollow of an 8-inch shell, pounding them with a round shot. The tent was circular and had a sunken floor to exclude drafts, and an external drainage trench to prevent flooding.

Magnus followed George in and saw two officers playing cards by the light of a dim lamp hanging from a bracket screwed onto the central pole. The air was thick with cigar smoke and the fumes from a charcoal brazier. Balanced on the top of this smoking stove was a basin of mulled wine. Horse blankets served as a carpet, and, apart from a broken-down sofa taken from a house in Balaclava, piled-up shell boxes and barrels did duty for chairs and tables. George described how that morning he had waked to find the canvas above him frozen into a stiff glassy sheet and how beads of ice had studded his beard and blanket. George and the officer he shared with—the younger of the two cardplayers—slept on bread sacks placed over straw pallets resting on boards. Magnus was assured that he would be welcome to sleep on the sofa till he had his own tent.

George ladled out four glasses of mulled wine and introduced Magnus to the two officers. When Magnus tasted his wine, he discovered that it contained almost as much rum as claret. Harrington, the older of the two officers, put away the cards and handed over some notes to Towers, a willowy young man with a superior manner and a habit of stroking his drooping dark mustaches when he talked. Harrington was a stout, thick-necked major with pale thinning hair adhering greasily to his pink scalp. He had pleasant hazel eyes, and small plump hands with very dirty nails. Getting up, he strode over to George.

"Well, what do you think of them?"

"Of what, Major?" asked George.

"The boots of course," replied Harrington, clicking his heels together.

"They look very well on you."

Towers smiled to himself and sipped his warm wine appreciatively.

"Care for a pair like 'em?" asked Harrington.

"Wouldn't refuse them at any rate," said George.

Harrington lit a cigar and sat down on the sofa.

"Young Towers here paid one of those sailor boys in the Naval Brigade batteries to dig us up a few Russians—the ones killed in Friday's sortie. Could have had a pair of silk socks too if the Turks hadn't got there first."

"They've been digging up British graves too," said Towers, "for blankets. There's supposed to be a new order forbidding any more men being buried in their blankets."

"Nothing to do with the Turks," replied Harrington. "There aren't enough blankets. That's the reason."

George suddenly reached inside his coat and started scratching fiercely.

"Take no notice, Crawford," muttered Harrington. "We're all crawling here. Ain't that so, Towers."

"Some of us haven't got lice *and* fleas," Towers replied coolly.

"I have," said George, adding with a wan smile, "and there are rats in the latrines. You ought to be on your father's flagship, Crawford."

Once Towers and Harrington had realized that Magnus was indeed Admiral Crawford's son, he was deluged with requests to get them potted meat, dried figs, fresh fruit and numerous other delicacies the fleet was supposed to be enjoying. At this inappropriate moment the orderly came in with two helpings of fried pork and onions for George and Magnus.

As the wine started to take effect, Magnus no longer felt as irritated with George as he had done immediately after his father's identity had been given away; in a predominantly aristocratic regiment, a manufacturer's son would have to take what opportunities came his way for raising his stock. When George had been in the yeomanry, Magnus had detested him for his incompetence, but now when any incompetence might kill him, he felt sympathy for him. His father had forced him into the Guards for social reasons, forgetting that in time of war the Brigade, in its role of shock troops, always suffered the worst casualties. The thought of George leading a bayonet charge was a strange one, but if he had not already done so, Magnus had no doubt that he would soon have to.

While they were drinking some of the most peculiar tasting coffee

Magnus had ever drunk, Towers told a story about his company's cook, who had been carrying down a large jug of coffee to the batteries, when he had been hit by a shell fragment in the back of the neck. The wound had been little more than a nick, but the unfortunate man had fallen and been almost blinded by the scalding contents of his jug. George then chipped in with a conversation he had had with the colonel of the 46th Regiment, who had been suffering from delirium tremens, a complaint he put down entirely to the Russian climate, suggesting that if the army stayed in the Crimea much longer, the "infection" would prove as widespread as typhus fever and cholera.

During the next hour, while Magnus was questioned about public attitudes to the war at home, George became increasingly fidgety and anxious. Shortly before nine the orderly came in and told him that his company had fallen in and was ready to march down to the trenches. Strapping on his revolver, George told Magnus he would see him at breakfast and not to bother to get up if there was an alarm in the night, then, picking up the greatcoat he shared with Towers, he went out into the night.

Magnus followed him at once. Twenty yards away George's men were standing at ease in two ranks, stamping their feet and swinging their arms to keep warm. Only two or three had greatcoats; the rest carried blankets instead. Above the undulating plateau, tiny stars twinkled in the clear frosty sky, and as far as the eye could see, the ground was specked with the widely dispersed, glowing pinpoints of watch fires, which cast a red-gray light on the tents nearest them.

"Poor devils," said George, jerking his head in the direction of his men, "in the trenches two nights out of three, and half of them fall asleep on their feet. In the last Russian sortie, half a company of the Rifle Brigade was bayoneted before they woke. We're supposed to shoot anybody who sleeps on duty. There wouldn't be many left if we did." He buttoned his coat and looked at Magnus awkwardly. "I've learned a thing or two out here, Crawford. By God, I have."

"Good luck," shouted Magnus as George joined his men. He had no difficulty in imagining the awful strain of nights spent in the forward trenches. If any officer did let a sortie get through to the batteries behind the trenches, dozens of guns could be spiked during the ensuing confusion. The thought of spending nine hours in a shallow hole in the ground, straining one's eyes into the darkness and listening for footsteps would be enough to drive a nervous man mad. Then at uncertain intervals during the night each side would be sure to fire grape and canister at each others' advanced posts and rifle pits in the hope of catching working parties digging new trenches or repairing damaged parapets.

Magnus had heard that the Brigade of Guards had come out three thousand strong and was now down to twelve hundred on duty. A betting man, he reflected, would not put much money on George getting home alive. Another battle like the Alma, or even a lesser action such as the defense of Balaclava, and Bartlett, Towers, Harrington and George could very well all be dead. And if they survived that ordeal, dysentery, cholera and exposure were still more formidable enemies to be reckoned with. As he heard a sharp rattle of musketry coming from the trenches, Magnus tensed and only relaxed when certain that it came from the far left where the French held the line. A year ago, he thought, I would not have cared if George had been shot down in front of me. He wondered for a moment whether George's friendliness merely meant that he had not yet given up all hope of marrying Catherine. Remembering his vehement opposition, Magnus felt a sharp twinge of remorse; the animosity he had felt toward George at Bentley's seemed to have taken place in another age. He shook his head and paused a little before lifting the flap of the tent.

⌇ Thirty-Nine ⌇

The morning had as usual been misty and bitterly cold, but by noon the sun had broken through, bringing an almost springlike warmth to the air: a mixed blessing to the three hundred sailors dragging six heavy ships' guns up the Balaclava col. Not long before, their hands had been too numb and cold to grip properly; now their clothes were soaked with sweat and their mouths parched. All those pulling at the drag ropes had discarded their coats, and many had stripped off their shirts as well. The pace achieved earlier in the morning—half a mile in three hours —seemed unlikely to be repeated before the following day.

Charles Crawford walked up and down the line of guns, exhorting his men and trying to get the various ships' crews to race each other: a tactic that had hitherto been successful, but was becoming steadily less effective. Charles hoped to be able to get four 32-pounders and two 68-pounders into No. 2 Battery in the Naval Brigade's section of the British "Right Attack" by the end of the week. If he succeeded, his men would be the first to have dragged such heavy guns up the seven-mile col in under five days—a feat still more remarkable when much of the track was muddy and the 32-pounders on ships' carriages with small, wooden, truck wheels. Knowing that, whether turning the capstan or scrubbing and holystoning the decks, the men always worked better to a song, Charles had placed a fifer or fiddler cross-legged on the breech of each gun, with a boat's ensign flying beside him, and had ordered the playing of accompaniments to well-known marches and shanties. As back muscles tensed and the men strained and heaved at the ropes, the sound of their voices, echoing and dying in the desolate and stony hills, moved Charles to pride and sadness: pride in their confidence and in his responsibility for them; sadness at the undernourished look of many of them, and in the vulnerability of their white bodies, exposed to the glaring, midday sun—seeming whiter still in contrast with their ruddy hands and necks. The softness of their skin, and his, the cold hardness of the gun metal, and the thought of the terrible months they would all be spending in the batteries under fire made Charles shudder as he heard their defiant voices, small in the vast landscape, and the cheerful jokes and shouts of applause greeting the end of each song. He felt paternal toward them but not patronizing. If they were cannon fodder, so was he. Every five minutes or so, if a steeper slope was in prospect, he would call for a brief rest and in that time add a few men to those already at the drag ropes, or rest a few of the weaker ones if the track was leveling off.

The carriages were being pulled up breech forward by means of three separate drags to each gun, with fifteen men to every rope. Three sailors steered from behind with a long handspike inserted in the muzzle, and four more to each crew were employed clearing stones out of the way, laying down planks or sacking when the mud became bad, and placing chocks behind the wheels when there was danger of a gun rolling back. The shot, shells and cartridges had been taken on ahead in carts the day before; Charles had also had to organize tents and stores for his contingent, and all the gun platforms, holdfasts and tackles: arrangements that had occupied him in Balaclava for most of the three weeks since handing over command of *Scylla*.

His decision to offer himself for one of the three captains' posts in the shore-based Naval Brigade had been made after he had learned from his father that no further active naval involvement in the war was likely before the spring. The brigade's fourteen hundred men, on the other hand, could count upon continual action in their shore batteries throughout the winter, fighting alongside the Royal Artillery. Charles's appointment, when it came, had undoubtedly owed something to his father's influence with Admiral Dundas, but more to the marked prejudice among most senior captains against serving ashore.

Detestation of idleness apart, Charles's principal reason for joining the brigade had been his suspicion that his father expected him to go where the fighting was. As a lieutenant on the East African coast, he had gained a reputation for bravery: pursuing well-armed slave dhows into the mangrove swamps in launches and cutters with a handful of men; landing in dangerous breakers and attacking barracoons and burning

Arab boats pulled up on the beaches. His support of *Vengeance* under the guns of Fort Constantine had added to this reputation. The good opinion of others, his father in particular, was vital to him, helping him to forget the doubts and fears of personal weakness which he felt whenever ashore on half-pay. Others might thrive on reflection and periods of tranquillity, but Charles only felt truly himself when committed to a firm course of action, to working within the confinement of a specific task. Danger weakened some men's resolution; in Charles's case it was a stimulant to decisiveness, an opportunity for proving to himself and others that his will was unshakable. Forced on by his need to be admired, and by the expectations of others, he felt no loss of freedom. On the contrary, it was only when acting out the role he supposed was expected of him that he felt free; only when choices were behind him, and a single duty lay ahead, could he face the future with equanimity.

In the afternoon, leaving the guns in charge of a lieutenant, Charles rode up to the Naval Brigade encampment on the plateau, where he drank a glass of hock with Captain Lushington, the senior naval officer ashore, and was then taken down through the communication trenches to No. 2 Battery, which he would in future be commanding. Apart from the occasional crackle of small-arms fire from the advanced saps of the opposing trenches, there was no firing going on and the sailors were leaning back against the traverses, smoking pipes and watching a party of engineers extending the parapets and strengthening them with the usual earth-filled wicker gabions.

From the raised firing step Charles scanned the enemy defenses with a telescope. Never before had he been so close to the principal Russian bastions of the Redan and Malakoff. But the number of guns in these massive batteries, and their formidable chain of connecting earthworks, was not what made him catch his breath; the sight that sent a momentary shiver of fear to his heart was the nature of the ground that would have to be crossed before these batteries could be taken—and they would have to be taken if Sevastopol was to fall. First there was the abatis, a thick tangled barrier of sharpened branches and tree trunks, then a network of trenches and rifle pits, then a long smooth slope with no fold or wrinkle in the earth to give advancing troops cover from the guns in the Redan. His hand shook a little as he lowered the telescope, for that had only been the beginning. A broad deep ditch and a palisade still lay ahead before the ramparts of the batteries could be stormed.

As he jumped down from the firing step, he caught sight of a dark stain on the ground beside one of the guns; the blood was caked and dry, its surface cracked into tiny diamond shapes, lifting a little at the edges. There had been no rain for several days. Charles closed his telescope and walked across to join Lushington who was leaning against the sand-bagged entrance to the magazine.

"Will the brigade take part in any general assault?" he asked as casually as he could.

"Undoubtedly."

Charles managed a dry laugh.

"Let's hope we'll have some reliable reserves behind us."

"Of course they may attack us first."

"Would you in their position?" laughed Charles, certain that Lushington had been joking.

"You and I don't expect them to. But mightn't that be rather a good reason?"

Charles shrugged his shoulders and smiled.

"I don't think I'd put money on it."

Before they left the battery, Charles looked back at the white stone buildings of Sevastopol shimmering in the distance, and saw the sun glinting on the golden dome of a church; the water in the roadstead was a dazzling blue. Near the center of the town, the streets he had been told were pleasantly broad and lined with acacias. And will I be there next spring, he wondered, walking under those white flowering trees?

As he was entering the communication trench leading out of the battery, he heard his name called out from behind, and turned to see Humphrey smiling at him.

"What in God's name are you doing here?"

Lushington laughed, evidently supposing that Charles had spoken roughly as a heavy-handed joke.

"His duty, I hope. Lord Goodchild is one of our new mids."

Charles stared blankly at his senior officer as though he had not heard him aright.

"I left orders with Commander Mason that none of *Scylla's* mids were to volunteer for service ashore."

"Mason was invalided last week. Didn't you hear?" asked Lushington, clearly surprised by Charles's sudden displeasure. "Lord Goodchild asked to join in person on *Britannia*. I cleared it with Buchan, Mason's replacement."

"I see," murmured Charles, thinking of how horrified his father would be when he learned what Humphrey had done. *Scylla* had been on the point of sailing for Malta for repairs and refitting after her mauling, and the boy should have gone with her; he would have been out of harm's way for six weeks at least. By moving to the Naval Brigade, Charles had hoped to escape the constant memories of Helen which every sight of her son had evoked in him. Now, with numerous other worries to contend with, he would always be afraid for the boy's safety; and, short of pneumonia or a wound, nothing could get him out in under four months. His release from *Scylla* would already have gone through Admiral Dundas' office. The realization that Humphrey, by volunteering for service in the batteries, had merely behaved as he himself had done, did not make Charles feel any more sympathetic toward him.

Back at the naval camp, in Lushington's tent, Charles read through the general orders to the brigade and learned more about the precise duties which would be expected of him. When he rose to leave, Lushington took him by the arm. He looked serious and concerned.

"About young Goodchild, Crawford," he said in his gruff, gravelly voice. "You're surely not against middies getting a taste of action? Did neither of us any harm, did it? Boys are insensitive little brutes. I've often thought they feel less than grown men."

Charles listened impassively to these views that he had often heard used to justify the "blooding" of cadets and midshipmen.

"Perhaps, sir, you were unaware that I have a personal concern for Lord Goodchild."

Lushington clapped him on the shoulder.

"Of course I knew that. That's why he's in your battery. As a matter of fact he asked to be under you. He's a great admiration for you, Crawford. Told me about that scrimmage you were in the other week." He broke off and looked down at the sailcloth on the floor of the tent. "Whatever your present-day cynics may say, hero worship's a fine thing in a boy."

"If it doesn't kill him," murmured Charles.

"I don't like to make this observation, Captain Crawford, but he holds Her Majesty's commission and this is a war."

Before Charles could reply, the sentry came in and saluted.

"Four o'clock, sir."

"Then make it so," replied Lushington, who had noticed that Charles, as a captain himself, had been about to give the customary order. Moments later they heard the bell outside the tent struck eight times to mark the end of the watch. The fact that the camp's routine was the same as a ship's would normally have pleased Charles, but now it meant nothing to him at all.

"Perhaps I should tell you," Lushington went on quietly, "that the young man didn't seek me out on purpose; he came aboard *Britannia* to collect mail for his ship and met me at the entry-port. I'd been seeing Admiral Dundas."

"I wouldn't have blamed him even if he'd come here to see you. It's just been a shock, you understand. In his place I'd have wanted to go ashore."

"Pluck deserves commendation, eh?"

"Certainly."

Lushington's genuine relief impressed Charles. It was not every acting commodore who bothered about the feelings of midshipmen. In retrospect he also felt touched and somewhat guilty that Humphrey had been praising him when he had given the boy so little cause to like him.

Charles still felt depressed as he rode away toward the col, but his anger had passed. Humphrey would have to take his chance with the rest. No man on earth could protect any other from the flight of a shell or the course of a bullet.

⮜ Forty ⮞

The heavy rain had stopped, and now a fine dank drizzle was falling. From the direction of Sevastopol, muffled a little by the mist, came the clanging of church bells calling the garrison to early morning service, a dismally familiar sound to the men on night picket duty in front of the British lines. Four o'clock on the morning of 5 November. The fog and drifting mist became whiter as dawn approached, but showed no sign of lifting.

Bored, tired and numb with cold, Magnus was tempted to abandon his original purpose of remaining with the men of the picket until they were relieved. His reason for sharing their discomforts was his editor's insistence that, besides routine dispatches on the progress of the campaign, he produce more vivid first-person descriptions of various aspects of the army's life in the Crimea. To this end he had already spent time in a mortar battery, at the French supply port of Kamiesch Bay, and had described the dawn stand to arms in the Guards' camp and a night in the trenches. For the past six hours he had been with members of a Rifle Brigade picket, posted half a mile in front of the exposed right flank of the British Army's encampments.

Unlike most of the other British journalists, Magnus was not surprised that Lord Raglan had not ordered the construction of batteries and entrenchments to defend his weakest flank from attack by the Russian field army. The ground there was uneven, and so extensive, that to be effective, three or four miles of fortifications would have been needed. This would have reduced the number of guns available for the batteries firing on Sevastopol, and have diverted more men than could be spared from the siege works. The rumor currently rife in British regiments was that a general allied assault on the town had been planned to take place in two days' time. If this attack succeeded, the army would be spared the disaster of a winter in the Crimea. With this in mind, Magnus felt sure that in Raglan's position he too would have thrown all the resources of his small army into an early attempt to take the town, and have gambled on not being attacked first.

The previous day Magnus had taken note of the position the picket was to occupy. A hundred yards in front of them, and now shrouded in mist, a steep slope ran down to a river valley overshadowed on the far side by sheer walls of rock, rising up to the ancient ruins of Inkerman. Behind the picket lay a fissured plateau, half a mile in depth, dominated by a small knoll on which the British had built a battery screened by a tall, ten-foot sandbag wall. There were two embrasures but no guns had been placed in them. Several hundred yards to the rear of the Sandbag Battery, the ground rose steeply to form a long low ridge, the last natural defensive position between an attacking force and the 2nd Division's camp on the British right flank. If Russian troops did manage to reach the camps on the main plateau facing Sevastopol, the allies could well be driven down to Balaclava and destroyed there.

But such fanciful thoughts were far from Magnus's mind as he felt the damp seep through his boots and the clammy air penetrate his thick scarf and sheepskin coat under his waterproof cape. Better by far to endure a hard frost than this moist chilling fog. The ground ahead was covered with dense brushwood and thorn brakes, which seemed to recede and float as new swaths of mist were driven up from the valley by a light wind.

Of the fifty or so men in the picket, only a quarter were on watch, while the rest lay or sat huddled together in their blankets. Magnus could imagine how tired a man would have to be before he could sleep with an empty stomach, under a single sodden blanket on cold wet ground; yet from the sound of quiet regular snoring, it was clear that many were asleep. In spite of the drizzle, their arms had been piled in the usual pyramids, butts on the ground, barrels pointing upward. But nobody, Magnus least of all, expected an attack, so it would hardly matter if many of the rifles were too wet to fire. From in front, where the sentries were spread out in a wide semicircle, came occasional sounds of movement as a man stumbled into a bush or changed his position. The lieutenant in command returned from visiting the sentries and squatted down on his haunches a few yards from Magnus with his back to him. Magnus knew that his presence was unwelcome. Earlier the young officer had asked him what possible interest the dull routine of a night picket could have for newspaper readers. Wouldn't he be better employed collecting tales of heroism from survivors of the Light Brigade or anecdotes about the Alma? Magnus had assured him that for those who had never spent a night out of their beds, picket duties would not seem unremarkable; but now he felt bored enough to agree with the lieutenant. Down in the trenches between the opposing batteries, the rival defenders had been close enough in places to hear each other talking and the atmosphere had been tense and oppressive. Here on the isolated right flank, it was quite otherwise. Probably he would be unable to write anything.

By half-past five the reliefs had still not come and Magnus made up his mind to leave in ten minutes whether they had arrived or not. He was picking up his folding campstool and moving toward the lieutenant when one of the sentries came crashing through the brushwood.

"Rooshians, sir . . . hundreds of 'em," he gasped.

"Which way?" asked the lieutenant, knowing that Magnus was watching him, and making a definite effort to appear calm. The sentry pointed to the front, but the fog was as impenetrable as ever.

An hour before, another sentry had reported hearing wagon wheels in the valley, but when the rest of the picket had listened, nothing had been heard. Magnus knew from his own experience in Ceylon how easy it was for an exhausted man to imagine hearing sounds or seeing movements through moving mist. The officer was skeptical but ordered the entire company to stand to their arms. The noise the waking men made, rolling up their precious blankets, and tripping over each other as they searched for their firearms, ruled out any chance of listening, and the order to load led to the additional sounds of tearing cartridges and clattering ramrods. Men swore as they fumbled with numb fingers for percussion caps and cartridge pouches in the half-light.

Then a sudden stutter of small arms firing came from the right, a noise no louder than rain beating against a window, but probably deadened by the fog and closer than it sounded; absolute silence followed these shots. It was just possible that a relief party had become lost in the fog and had surprised a picket from the valley side.

During the few seconds in which everybody listened tensely for the answering volley which would prove that the enemy was attacking, Magnus was a prey to powerfully conflicting emotions. For the sake of the army he hoped there would be no further firing, knowing that a general action before the predicted allied assault, would make a winter campaign inevitable, but he also knew that if no more shots came he would be acutely disappointed. Probably chance would never again place him in a forward position at the start of what might be a critical battle. During the tedious hours of the night, he had amused himself by trying to imagine what he would do in command of the 2nd Division in the event of an attack. Send reinforcements out to the pickets to help them contest every foot of ground? Or order them back at once, and rely on artillery to shatter the advancing columns, before counterattacking from the higher ground of the ridge? Now he found himself desperately eager to know which course General Pennefather would choose, and what the Russians' tactics would be. There was no doubt at all from their drawn white faces that the men around him had no similar desire to find out such things.

Two crisp volleys followed by a spasmodic crackle of independent fire confirmed that a large sortie or full-scale assault had started. The firing died away and a loud roar of hundreds of voices made every member of the picket shudder; the absence of shots after the shout meant that a bayonet charge had given way to hand-to-hand fighting. Fifty or a hundred men would now be fighting against more than twice their number.

Magnus was standing a few paces from the lieutenant and saw that his face was glistening with sweat. He opened his mouth but no sound came. Magnus could not believe that he would not withdraw his men to the ridge or the Sandbag Battery; he was irritated with himself for not having asked him what his orders were in the event of an attack. A sergeant came over and saluted.

"Shall I send a man back to division, sir?"

The officer licked his dry lips and nodded.

"And, Hill, we'll need to warn the pickets to our left. Better ask their officers to join forces with us."

Magnus watched the young man with his boyish freckled face and curly red hair take several deep breaths to steady himself. Then he set about forming his men into a crescent, two ranks deep, and ordered them to get down behind bushes or rocks. He took out his revolver and as he did so, caught sight of Magnus, whom he had forgotten.

"Better go back now, Mr. Crawford," he said with a trace of soldierly contempt for civilians.

"In a minute or two," replied Magnus with a smile.

"I am not responsible for you. If I'm hit I'm a hero, if you are, you're a fool."

"I agree."

The lieutenant checked the mechanism of his revolver and then loaded it. Magnus's calmness seemed to have reassured him, and he no longer spoke with his previous gruffness as he reached in his pockets and pulled out a gold watch and two letters. He handed them to Magnus, who took them without comment. The top one was addressed to "The Venerable the Archdeacon of Lichfield."

"My father," he murmured, seeing the direction of Magnus's gaze.

"I shall return them to you later," said Magnus, fixing his eyes on the lieutenant's dark green uniform with its black frogging, not daring to meet his eyes in case his face betrayed his doubts.

Before the runners had returned from the neighboring pickets, a sharp crash of firing came from the left, and as Magnus turned he saw a flickering line of tiny flashes, dimmed by the mist, as the second volley rattled out. From the length of the line he reckoned that the nearest picket was being attacked by about three companies. It seemed unlikely that the Russians would attack with whole regiments and brigades until they had thrown out groups of skirmishers to discover the precise strengths and weaknesses of the units on the plateau. Then through a gap in the mist, Magnus saw that he had been mistaken: barely two hundred yards away a dense mass of Russians, at least a battalion, were marching straight at them. Before the mist closed in again, he saw their gray greatcoats and small spiked helmets quite clearly. Many of the men had not seen the enemy, but those who had leaped to obey their officer as he waved them away to the right, preferring, as Magnus thought, discretion to suicidal valor.

Relieved by this decision, and knowing that he would see nothing of the overall pattern of the coming battle unless he got back onto higher ground above the worst of the mist, Magnus started to run toward the Sandbag Battery. He tripped in the brushwood several times but scrambled to his feet and hurried on. When he was almost halfway to his objective, he heard a stammering burst of firing in the direction from which he had come. This was followed by confused shouts and yells, then another ragged volley, followed immediately by a thin cheer. Magnus could see nothing through the mist, yet the skin on his scalp seemed to tighten and a tremor ran down his spine.

The lieutenant and his fifty men had not let the Russians pass unmolested, but had fired into their flank and then charged them with fixed bayonets. For a moment Magnus saw the forms of the sleeping men and the young officer's glistening face and frightened eyes. The shouting went on, punctuated by random shots and screams. Magnus stood gazing into the wall of mist, expecting to see the remains of the picket running terror-stricken toward the ridge, but the confused sounds of hand-to-hand fighting went on for two or three minutes more until an awful quietness came, broken by the shrieking of wounded men and distant firing from other outposts.

Magnus felt tears rise and a low groan broke from his lips. Then suddenly, from the same direction, more firing started; and alone in the mist Magnus cheered. One of the pickets sent for by the lieutenant had arrived too late to save him and were now firing into what would already be a badly mauled Russian left flank. Even if only half the Minié rifles and Enfields had been effective, they would have caused heavy casualties to columns marching in close order. Judging by the sounds coming from all around the perimeter of the plateau, it was evident that similar desperate assaults and blindly courageous rallies were taking place wherever Russian troops met with British pickets. A few hundred men were buying time for the rest of the army at the cost of their lives, delaying an enemy probably ten times their number.

Moved and shaken though he felt, Magnus's earlier determination to see as much of the battle as he could still held, and on finding that his view from the Sandbag Battery was no better, he pressed on toward the ridge below the 2nd Division's camp, intent on discovering whether any efforts would be made to support the pickets on the lower ground.

*   *   *

A few minutes before six o'clock George Braithwaite was awakened by bugles and shouting outside his tent. The previous night he had stayed up late playing cards and losing heavily; the night before that he had been in the trenches. The canvas of the tent was sodden with rain and a drip had soaked the lower end of his blanket. His head was throbbing and he felt sick with tiredness; he wanted to run out and scream his anger to the whole camp. Instead he sat up and flung off his wringing blanket. With no duties to attend to during the morning, he had expected to be able to sleep till midday, but because of some idiotic sortie somewhere, everybody was running about like imbeciles, waking up hundreds of men when only a couple of companies would be needed to repel the attack. He looked angrily at Towers who was still sleeping, and went across and shook him.

"There's a general stand to arms," he shouted, as Towers squinted up at him from between red-rimmed lids. Just then their orderly ran into the tent and told them in a panting whisper that the Russian field army was less than a mile from the camp.

"They might have waited till after breakfast," muttered Towers, stumbling to his feet and tripping over one of his boots. George did not smile at Towers' remark nor at his shouts of anger as he stepped into a large puddle near the tent pole. The nervous shock of being wakened abruptly after only three hours' sleep, followed by the horrifying information about the scale of the attack, had set his heart hammering like a fist in his chest. He also felt a tight choking feeling in his throat. Many times since his arrival in the Crimea he had learned that to "have one's heart in one's mouth" was not an entirely fanciful expression.

As the first sharp wave of panic receded, George felt his exhaustion return. He sank down on his bed and listened to Towers swearing mindlessly as he struggled with his boots. George's feet had swollen so much that for the past four days he had not dared to take his boots off in case he should be unable to get them on again. The thought of a grueling and dangerous day without food and rest brought him close to tears. He wondered whether his absence would be noticed if he slipped away on the pretense of going to headquarters, but the thought of facing accusations of cowardice instantly banished this idea. The orderly brought him his combat sword and his bearskin, which he had not worn since the Alma. The sight of the black fur and red hackle calmed him a little. Was he not an officer in a regiment that had won battle honors in every major British war since the reign of Charles II? A company commander in the 2nd Regiment of Foot: the Coldstream Guards, whose motto *Nulli Secundus* had been chosen as a protest against the Grenadiers gaining the distinction of being the 1st Regiment in the Brigade? For a moment, as he felt the weight of the bearskin on his head and the chain chinstrap cold against his jaw, pride in past glory outweighed present fear.

He was adjusting his sword belt and revolver strap when the first shell fell on the camp. George had not heard the preceding whistle through the wet canvas, so the sudden explosion shocked him far more than it would have done had he been forewarned. He had prepared himself for fighting to come but not for immediate danger. Towers was calmly scooping potted meat from a jar and eating it off the end of a knife; as he saw George leaving, he dropped the knife and shouted to him to wait, but George left without looking back, eager to be out in the open where there was a certain security in being able to hear the approaching projectiles—a round shot fired straight at a man could even be seen in the air and evaded; but today thick banks of mist lay across the lines of tents, and the shot and shells hurtled out of them without warning.

George saw that everybody was running toward the ridge above the lower plateau. The fact that the Russians were able to shell the camp with such ease and accuracy made it certain that they had driven back the pickets and had established a battery of heavy guns on one of the low hills half a mile beyond the Sandbag Battery. As George ran, he saw the body of an officer covered by a cape; he looked away quickly and hurried on. Tents were being ripped to shreds by shell fragments or being bowled over like ninepins by round shot. He saw three horses that had been tethered together, all killed by the same ball. Two had been disemboweled.

A few resourceful officers had managed to get together whole companies and were marching them down to the ridge in an orderly fashion; but most of the men were walking or running in small groups: regiments jumbled together, shouting to each other to find out where they were supposed to go. George joined a major leading two complete companies of Scots Fusiliers and twenty or thirty men from the Coldstream. Since their camp was some distance south of the main 2nd Division encampment, the Guards reached the ridge later than many light infantry regiments, some of which had already been ordered into action to support the survivors from the pickets.

The mist was still lying in dense pockets on the lower plateau, but steadily dispersing with a light breeze blowing from right to left. From what he could see, George guessed that the Russians now had about six thousand men on the plateau and outnumbered the five or six British battalions, resisting them there by at least three to one. As the mist and the smoke from the musketry rolled across, alternately concealing and revealing, George gradually came to the conclusion that the Russians had an army of thirty or forty thousand men on the slopes beyond the lower plateau. The British, he reckoned, were opposing them with perhaps four thousand men and would probably be able to muster twice that number when the 3rd, 2nd and Light divisions had joined them. The 1st Division would have to remain above Balaclava in case of a breakthrough, and the rest of the army would be tied down defending the batteries facing the town. From the dull rumble of heavy firing from the left, it seemed that the enemy was launching diversionary attacks on the French positions to stop them moving troops across to bolster the threatened British right flank. The best odds that could be hoped for in the next couple of hours would be five to one against the British.

But as George looked down at the chaotic fighting taking place below him, he did not abandon all hope. The thick brushwood and small ravines and hollows, which split the plateau, made it hard for the Russians to use their numerical superiority effectively, since the broken nature of the ground split their formations, and the shifting mist served to conceal the defenders' positions and helped them to outflank the enemy columns. Nor, when British lines were broken, could the Russians pursue them easily through the brushwood. Already the battle was being fought not in disciplined formations but in small, widely scattered groups of broken troops, and this also had the advantage of preventing the Russians using the full capability of their field guns without risk to their own soldiers. But the longer George watched, the clearer the final outcome became. For every one British battalion being sent down into the fighting, the Russians were committing two or three, and whether troops fought in rigid formation or in fragmented groups, sheer weight of numbers would finally tell. The point had almost been reached when it would be impossible to reduce the forces on the ridge any further; it would be on this key position that the Russians would mount their principal assault, and if they were to break through in numbers, the British and French camps and batteries would be taken, and the allies forced down to their supply ports and destroyed there.

For the five minutes since his arrival on the ridge, George had been watching the battle with such intense absorption that he had to some extent forgotten his own danger. Then the Russians began firing their heavy guns at the formations on the ridge. For reasons that George could not understand, it seemed that General Pennefather, in command of the 2nd Division, only had 9-pounders at his disposal: guns quite useless against the Russian 24-pounders firing from the hills beyond the lower plateau. The first round-shot fell behind the Guards' position, bouncing and skidding away across the turf like gigantic cricket balls, tearing up large divots. It was a sight that made George's stomach turn over. Then the enemy started firing shells as well as shot.

As a company commander, George was standing slightly apart from his men and a few paces in front. Although he was no more exposed than they, his solitary position made him feel that he was. Ahead of his battalion some field officers were conferring in a group; to his relief, one of them came across and told him to get his company to spread out and lie down. George was annoyed that many officers remained standing to give their men confidence that nothing very terrible was about to happen; he therefore felt obliged to go on standing too, finding it hard not to flinch or lower his head as he heard the shells hissing and whistling overhead. One burst twenty yards behind him and he felt the earth tremble. There were screams and the repeated call for stretchers. Another exploded in the rear rank of the company in front of him, killing three men and showering George with earth and stones, one of which hit his shoulder and bruised him. After this he lay down. Four bandsmen were running with a badly wounded man on a stretcher; a round shot felled the back two, cutting one in half, and pitching the bleeding man from the stretcher onto the ground where he lay twitching and screaming in agony. Over and over again George heard the awful soft thud as a round shot hit a man, a noise like a hammer smashing into damp, rotten wood.

When he had come under heavy artillery fire in the trenches, George had felt comparatively safe; even the shallowest depression or hole quadrupled a man's chances of survival. But the top of the ridge was flat and bare, with none of the thick scrub covering the lower ground. Even a few screening bushes would have helped to stop the round shot bounding on and killing men at the second or third bounce. George found himself staring fixedly at the ground, noting the texture of the soil and the whitish celery color of the coarse grass near its roots. He wanted to cover his head with his hands to cut out the noise of the shells and the frightened yelling of the wounded, but he did not dare in case new orders were given and he could not hear them. At the Alma, the desperate dash down to the river and the breathless tension of the charge up the hill on the other side had saved him from his fear. A charge rarely lasted longer than a few minutes, and one side usually gave ground before bitter hand-to-hand fighting developed; but this bombardment could go on for hours, and all that time there would be nothing that any man under it could do to affect the issue.

Sweat was dripping down George's forehead from under his bearskin and running into his eyes. Every pore in his body seemed to have opened, making his mouth and throat feel parched and swollen. He thought of the churchyard at Rigton Bridge and his overpowering panic after the first few shots, and how he had been almost too weak to get to his feet and order the men to run for the porch. And am I still the same? Still a coward? He imagined hearing the order to advance and saw himself unable to rise, and this brought him closer to hysteria. He recalled Lord Goodchild riding across the churchyard with a calmness bordering on contempt, and felt a furious resentment that he had been constituted so differently. At this moment, he thought, I would do anything, accept any conditions, to escape from this ridge if my departure were to be unknown, even, if need be, live the rest of my life in poverty provided I were safe. No comforts were essential; life was all that mattered. Oh, God, let me live. If I live I will make amends for past pleasure-seeking; I will build model dwellings, open soup kitchens, set aside capital for a charity to assist army widows. I will do anything, God, if I live. But the shells still came down, and at each approaching whistle he felt an iron collar tighten round his throat and his heart leaped in his chest. After every miss he experienced relief so intense that the greatest pleasures he had ever known seemed trivial by comparison; but this emotion lasted no longer than a second, and vanished with every new danger.

Then after twenty minutes of bombardment there was a lull. With the ebbing of his fear George felt disgusted with himself for his collapse; and once, he thought, I believed that proximity to death could change and elevate a man. In hours or minutes I may be dead, yet nothing in me has changed. I am no wiser, no less shallow and indecisive than I was before. My thoughts were not about what may lie beyond death or the meaning of life. I always avoided such subjects and I still avoid them now. Looking back on my life what memories have I, except blurred images of prostitutes, horses and cards? No woman will shed tears at my death. Catherine will receive the news of my passing with mild regret but without pain. Helen would probably smile ironically. Poor George killed by his father's wealth and snobbery. Nothing but the Guards for George; no matter that many of the officers wouldn't talk to him. What did his father care about that, provided he could boast about his son in the Brigade? He vividly recalled his stumbling utterances among the statues at Hanley Park. So that had really been his last chance with her. A fine way to have used it. A fine way. And now he would never see Catherine again.

When the shells started to fall once more, George's anger did not desert him. He was still scared, but the near conviction that he was about to die unloved, without, as it seemed to him, ever having performed a single useful or memorable action no longer filled him with self-pity but with rage. His experience of war had brought him no religious or philosophical revelations but it had at least forced him to recognize the emptiness of his past. And now, when he believed himself capable of leading a better life, he was not to have the chance.

Shortly after half-past seven George saw the duke of Cambridge, his divisional general, and General Bentinck, his brigade commander, ride across the face of the regiment and spend several minutes talking to a group of officers, which included the colonels of the Scots Fusiliers, the Grenadiers and Colonels Wilson and Townshend of the two Coldstream battalions. Knowing that this meeting probably meant that the Guards were soon to go into action, George got up and walked to the front of the ridge.

During the shelling the Russians appeared to have occupied most of the lower plateau and to have driven the British back to the Sandbag Battery, which was now the focus of most of the fighting. The emplacement itself, containing no guns, and with walls too high for riflemen to fire over, was of little or no value; but the elevated spur of land immediately behind it was clearly of crucial importance, since it commanded the lower ground which the Russians would have to cross before launching their final attack on the ridge. George was now certain that the Guards would be ordered to retake the position as soon as the outnumbered defending troops retired. The vicious nature of the hand-to-hand fighting and the hundreds of bodies already lying on the slopes horrified him. Yet suddenly George knew that he *did* have a final opportunity. He could die well, as stoically as aristocrats like Townshend, or any other officer or man in the Brigade. When a shell burst a few yards behind him, its concussion knocking him over as if he had been felled by a violent punch, his panic did not return. The surface of his body felt numb and strangely alien, giving him a light-headed feeling of inviolability. Only a minute or so later did he see that a splinter had cut his left hand. A private in his company ran forward to help him to his feet, but George ordered the man back and then shouted to the men to dress ranks, taking a perverse pleasure in seeing that the lines were as straight as on a parade ground. He heard the advance sounded, and as the battalion began to march, felt a warm glow of contentment, like a man in the first pleasurable stage of intoxication. At the head of the columns the colors were flapping slightly against their corded staves. Around him he could hear words of command after each shell fell into the moving columns: "Close up, close up by the center."

*   *   *

From the high ground immediately in front of the 2nd Division's camp, Magnus had watched the horrifying shelling to which the men on the ridge had been subjected, and had been amazed at the length of time it had taken the Royal Artillery to bring up some heavy guns to silence the Russian 24-pounders on the opposite hills. Later he learned that two ADCs, sent by Lord Raglan with the necessary orders to the commander of the siege train, had been killed on their way there. Generally by the time orders could be conveyed to battalions in the fighting, the situation had changed so drastically that they were useless; and even when they did arrive in time to be acted upon, few commanders in the field were able to communicate them to their widely scattered men. In the past, the voice or trumpets had proved more or less adequate, but in the chaos of fog, broken country and shattered formations, neither was having any effect.

Shortly after the Russians stopped shelling the ridge, Magnus positioned himself close to the commander-in-chief and his staff. Although he could not understand why the regiments defending the Sandbag Battery were not being supported, he could not help feeling a grudging admiration for Lord Raglan's impassive almost weary manner, and his quiet unchanging voice. Staff officers galloped up in alarm and left apparently reassured by this pacific-looking old man in a plain blue frock coat and black cravat—more the clothes of a country gentleman than a British commander-in-chief. Around him clustered his mounted staff with their yards of gold lace and white plumed cocked hats, which attracted a steady fire from the enemy guns; but Raglan remained staring attentively ahead of him at the smoke-filled ravines and dells below the ridge. Magnus, who now had no doubt that a Russian victory was inevitable, did not envy his lordship. The fate of being held responsible, and unjustly so, for the first major British defeat since the American War would be enough to make many men break down and weep; but Lord Raglan showed no visible emotion when a gray wave of Russians poured into the Sandbag Battery and rolled the British off the spur. This Magnus could see was the prelude to a series of attacks on the ridge. He wondered what plans, if any, Raglan had to save the camps and batteries, if the ridge fell before large French reinforcements entered the battle. Seconds later a shell burst among the staff. From the amount of blood on their uniforms, Magnus thought most had been mortally wounded. Going closer with a sinking heart, he saw that a shell had entered a horse and exploded in the abdomen, showering blood and entrails over all those nearby. General Strangways of the Royal Artillery was the only casualty; the lower part of his shin was hanging by a few strands of flesh. Magnus distinctly heard the old man ask, "Will any one be kind enough to lift me off my horse?" He had heard many anecdotes about the stoicism of wounded men, but he was still amazed to witness such calmness. He had heard it said that, when Lord Raglan's left arm had been amputated after Waterloo, he had politely asked for the limb to be returned so that he could remove a ring from a finger. Only now did Magnus believe this story to have been true.

As Strangways was being carried away, Lord Raglan sent an ADC galloping down toward the Brigade of Guards. Even when Magnus saw the direction in which the staff officer was going, he could not believe that the Guards were going to be ordered to retake the Sandbag Battery.

Twelve or thirteen hundred men against two divisions would have no chance at all, if logic played any part in military proceedings. It seemed incomprehensible that Raglan should be committing his elite troops before the ridge came under direct infantry attack. But minutes later, Magnus was convinced that this was what the commander-in-chief intended to do.

With a lump in his throat he watched the Guards move (in perfect columns of battalions, the three regiments of the Brigade marching in echelon. Earlier some of the men had been wearing greatcoats but now these had all been taken off and the red jackets stood out sharply against the sodden dark brown earth. As the Brigade moved down steadily toward the spur, the regiments were advancing in three parallel squares, forming a broken diagonal across the lower slopes of the ridge. Then under heavy shellfire they began a disciplined slow wheel to the left, the Scots Fusiliers, in the leading position on the extreme right, marking time, while the Coldstream, in the center, marched in slow time, and the Grenadiers, behind on the left, continued at their previous pace, until all three regiments were level, and the diagonal of squares had become a straight line. In this formation Her Majesty's Brigade of Guards marched onto the spur toward the Russian divisions drawn up in a wide arc in front of the Sandbag Battery.

And once, thought Magnus, I would have laughed at the months of drill needed to attain such precision, and would have thought the time far better spent in improving marksmanship. But the slow solemnity of the movement he had just witnessed, performed on rough ground under fire, had impressed him beyond words, and he had no doubt about the demoralizing impact the sight of such discipline would have on the waiting enemy.

Three hundred yards from the Russians, the Guards halted to fix bayonets, and moments later, Magnus saw small puffs of white smoke spread along the front ranks, as they fired a succession of volleys, which were immediately answered by the enemy's field guns. Closing ranks, and leaving the wounded where they fell, the Brigade advanced by the center, until fifty yards from their objective, they cheered, lowered their bayonets and charged.

*   *   *

In the couple of seconds after George's company had formed two ranks and fixed bayonets, the Russian field guns fell silent, and George could clearly see the gunners loading again, this time with grape and canister. The momentary stillness after the roar of the guns gave him a strange and eerie feeling of timelessness. Moment by moment he expected his colonel to give the order to fire, moment by moment he predicted the next salvo from the field guns; and the intensity of his anticipation extended his awareness of the present; small sounds, the clink of a sword against a scabbard or a cough seemed unnaturally loud, as though his ears and all his senses had suddenly been sharpened as never before. Under his feet long grass, flattened by the night's rain, above him a low gray sky, around him the last sights he might ever see. One flight of grape, one volley of musketry, and the end of all sensation. Nothing. He wanted to pray but remembered the self-disgust he had felt after his prayer on the ridge. No more hypocrisy. He gazed ahead at the dense mass of men immediately in front of him. How far across that narrow strip of grass will I get? To that bush? That rock? Or to those gray-coated ranks? Till that moment he had been certain that he would be killed before reaching the enemy. But I may not be, he thought, feeling an agonizing constriction in his chest. To be shot was one thing, but to be stabbed or bludgeoned to death was very different. He clutched at memories of sword exercises which he had never fully mastered: "right guard," "parry," "cut," "left guard." Thrust and twist upward to make the wound worse. Go for the stomach. A sharp sword properly wielded can take a man's head or arm off at a blow. He felt the swooning numbness a man feels being beaten unconscious, when he can resist no more. Then he heard Colonel Wilson's clear resonant voice:

"When I give the order to fire, don't hurry your shots. Be steady. Keep silent and fire low. Ready. Present. *Fire.*"

The crash of the first volley was still in George's ears as the Russian field guns flashed out, tearing the air with hissing and shrieking metal; the musket balls did not whistle as with single shots but hummed and whirred like a swarm of bees. Men were falling on every side. From the moment the firing started, time leaped forward again and seemed to race with mad inconsequence. From the corner of his eye George saw General Bentinck's white horse rear up and sink down, while the adjutant general was flung bodily from his saddle by the same round of canister.

George saw Colonel Wilson a few yards away, sword in hand, his mustache looking very white against his brick-red face. He was gazing along the ranks of his battalion, as if trying to fix the sight in his mind. Then he took hold of his bearskin and, placing it on the point of his sword, held it aloft and yelled at the top of his voice,

"Three cheers for the Queen!"

The cheering rapidly spread from those in earshot to the entire battalion. The Scots Fusiliers and Grenadiers were also cheering. George never heard the command to charge, but seeing the men in the company to his left running forward, he waved his sword and ran too, hearing his men following, their cheers rising to a blood-chilling scream and ending in a low fierce moan.

Just before the charge began, George had noticed a tangle of brambles halfway across the intervening space, and after what seemed a few strides, saw that he was already level with them. By now some of his company had overtaken him and were firing random shots as they ran. A bullet snicked against a button on his sleeve and another passed inches wide of his face, but in spite of the bursting pressure in his lungs and a paralyzing ache in his thighs, George did not slow down; the fatigue of his body helped to dull the awareness of his brain. He had a peculiar sense that *he* was standing still and the ground under him was moving; the men who fell appeared to be tumbling away backward. A moment later George came down hard and thought that he had been hit until he realized that he had tripped over a body. Colonel Wilson's sightless eyes were a few feet from his own. One bullet had entered the colonel's chest and another had passed through his cheeks, ripping out his tongue and his upper teeth. Little spurts of blood still pulsed from the mess of flesh and bone that had been his mouth. *Be steady. Keep silent and fire low.* Blinded with tears and retching painfully on an empty stomach, George leaped to his feet. A faint sound came from his lips and then a sobbing roar of rage; he pulled out his revolver with his wounded hand, and gripping his sword more tightly in his right, ran on, drunk with hatred and the desire to maim and kill.

The Russians' faces were now clearly visible, pale and high-cheekboned, under strange, flat, muffin-shaped hats, utterly unlike the spiked helmets George remembered from the Alma. George singled out a tall officer with a sharp nose and a wiry black mustache. Before he could reach him, one of the leading men in his company, swinging his rifle by the barrel like a club, had caught the officer a crunching blow on the side of the head with the full weight of the stock. Another few yards and George was almost blinded by dense smoke and the flashes of rifles. All around him men were jabbing and thrusting at gray-coated figures with their bayonets as if mad. A wounded Russian caught one of George's legs and held him firmly. George lashed out with his free leg, but the man tightened his grasp, glaring up with clenched teeth and burning eyes. George brought down his sword on the soldier's skull with all his strength, splitting it from crown to jaw and splattering brains and blood all over his uniform. He tried to strike at another man but for a moment could not move his arm, so densely packed were the men around him. He managed to fire his revolver into the stomach of the Russian immediately facing him, noticing every detail of his face: the curling reddish hairs on his chin and a sore on the side of his nose. The man quivered and slipped to his knees, his face expressing surprise and fear rather than pain. A massive color sergeant was smashing his way forward with short sharp blows of the butt end of his rifle, and George followed him until his burly leader fell, bayoneted in the side. A man lunged at George with his bayonet and the blade ripped through his sleeve, gashing his arm; he fired and missed, but his assailant slumped down, shot with a Minié bullet. A few more strides and George saw that he had passed through the enemy's lines. All sensation was leaving his left arm, so he sheathed his sword and transferred his revolver to his right hand. In front, a group of Russian gunners were trying to drag away a field gun and doing their best to fight with sponge staves and rammers against fully armed infantry. One by one they were hacked down.

Ahead of George was a hundred yards of open ground and then three Russian battalions drawn up immediately in front of the Sandbag Battery. The hopelessness of charging these columns seemed obvious to George, but nothing that he or any other officer shouted could stop the men charging on, cheering like madmen after their initial success. Then George saw that the men were right. Hundreds of Russians were hurling themselves back toward the Sandbag Battery to the security of their own lines. When these panic-stricken soldiers collided with their own advancing troops, three hundred Grenadiers and Coldstream Guards flung themselves into the disordered Russian ranks. George watched the line waver and then start to break; he saw enemy officers vainly trying to rally their men, threatening and even pleading with them, but to no purpose. Within minutes Russians were crashing away through the brushwood on the slopes of the spur and into the valley below. Two companies retreated to the Sandbag Battery and held their ground bravely. The men who had broken through the lines of the Russians' second division had expended all their ammunition by the time they reached the battery, but they outnumbered the defenders and killed them with rifle butts and stones. From a hundred and fifty yards away, George even saw men fighting with their fists.

When he reached the emplacement, the ground was thick with dead and wounded of both sides. From every part of the battery came cries for water and continual moans of pain interspersed with screams. Guardsmen were embracing each other, shouting excitedly about what had happened to them. The air was reeking with smoke, and the soldiers' sweat-streaked faces were blackened with it. A Russian near George had been shot in the throat and was gurgling and spitting blood, as he fought for breath. A private from his own company was lying pressing his hands against a gaping stomach wound, trying to hold in his escaping intestines.

To George's amazement several of the most aloof and reserved officers in his battalion were sobbing like children, less in grief at the carnage around them than with relief at the ending of the unendurable tensions of the past ten minutes. George too felt the reaction; his legs trembled uncontrollably and he was aware of the pain in his arm and hand, dully at first, but then with a sharper edge. During the next quarter of an hour some of the men who had been in the trenches the night before lay down and slept. George could feel the stickiness of blood drying on both his hands, some of it his own, some belonging to others. A dark stain outlined the rent in his sleeve; he felt very thirsty; after drinking some water from his canteen, he gave the rest to several other wounded men from his company. Then he sat down next to a mortally wounded major in the Grenadiers, who tried to convey some wish to him, but failed owing to a natural lisp much aggravated by a perforated lung. George had been sitting some minutes when he saw Towers on the other side of the battery. He was lying next to an embrasure, one leg twisted sharply out of alignment, his thigh smashed by a bullet: the sort of complicated fracture that inevitably meant an amputation. George had a vision of Towers cursing because he had got his feet wet in a puddle; recalled his ironic tone of voice, "They might have waited till after breakfast." With the help of another man, George managed to pull Towers up into a sitting position with his back against the rampart, an action that caused the wounded man such anguish that he clawed up handfuls of stony earth to stop himself screaming. His eyes were glittering and his face white, and beaded with sweat.

"I want to see it."

George shook his head, but Towers was so insistent that he gave in, cutting away the upper part of the trousers with a bayonet. There was not much blood since the ball was still in the thigh, and had evidently hit no artery. Two dark purple ridges showed where the bone had snapped and was pressing against the skin. Towers twisted his neck to see it, and touched the swellings with his fingers, then he rested his head against the sandbags and shut his eyes. There was no sign of any stretcher parties.

"Braithwaite," he murmured. George bent close to him, expecting some personal request in case Towers died of shock during the amputation. The corners of his handsome mouth lifted slightly. "Braithwaite," he whispered, "you owe me eighty-seven pounds from last night." George nodded and looked away as tears sprang to his eyes. "No surgeon's going to get you off."

"Course not."

A long silence followed.

"Why d'you go rushin' out this morning without waiting? Couldn't wait to get at 'em, eh?"

"Thought I'd be killed in the tent."

Towers smiled, apparently thinking George was being modest.

"You're not so bad, Braithwaite. Good fellow, in point of fact."

Not trusting himself to speak, George squeezed his friend's hand, and then, seeing that he had no revolver, left him his, with his ammunition pouch. Russian "corpses" had a habit of coming to life and shooting French and British wounded.

Shortly after ten o'clock the Russians attacked in overwhelming numbers and drove the Guards out of the Sandbag Battery, forcing them to leave their wounded where they lay. The Guards made a stand farther back on the spur and repelled the first counterattack. Several officers advanced, calling on their men to follow them, but very few did. George himself tried to lead his company forward, but seeing the annihilation of several other small groups, he ordered them back. Not long afterward the Brigade, or what was left of it, retired to the ridge.

Toward noon, the Guards with two regiments from the 4th Division managed to retake both the spur and the Sandbag Battery, but George Braithwaite was not with them. At the beginning of this second advance he fainted through loss of blood from his wounded arm. He did not therefore see the heroic charge of the 77th on the principal Russian battery, nor witness the critical intervention of fresh French troops and the decisive attack by the Chasseurs d'Afrique and the Zouaves, which finally swung the battle in the allies' favor.

George had heard much of this by nightfall, but not until the following day did news of what the Grenadiers had found when they stormed the Sandbag Battery for the last time reach George's hospital marquee. All the wounded officers and men left behind had been hacked to death. Lieutenant Towers had escaped this fate; he had shot himself with an Adams service revolver.

Of the fifty-two men in George's company who had gone into action, only nineteen returned to the camp on their own feet. The Brigade of Guards lost six hundred men: half their strength. The whole army suffered less, but was still reduced by a third. The victory was named the Battle of the Inkerman after the ruins on the cliffs overlooking the eastern side of the plateau. The Russians left almost five thousand dead on the battlefield, a total nearly twice the combined British figure for killed *and* wounded. Russian wounded were thought to be over ten thousand. Yet in relation to the total numbers each side could dispose in the Crimea, the British had lost a higher proportion of their fighting strength. Since the defenses of Sevastopol had not been significantly weakened by the defeat of the Russian field army, Inkerman would prove a Pyrrhic victory.

The choice facing Lord Raglan was no longer when to attack the town but whether to raise the siege, or to subject the remains of his army to a winter campaign. Against the advice of three divisional commanders, he decided to stay.

⮜ *Forty-One* ⮞

Tom Strickland clambered up from the caïque onto the crowded landing stage at Galata and paused to gaze back across the waters of the Golden Horn at the twin minarets of the Yeni-Cami and the distant dome of the Suleymaniye on the Stamboul skyline. As he pushed his way past the fruit sellers and money changers at the end of the quay and skirted the fish market, large drops of rain started to fall from a leaden sky. Dodging between a heavily laden donkey and a porter bent double under a gigantic swordfish, Tom hurried on toward his hotel, stuffing his sketchbooks under his coat as he went.

* * *

Two months before, Magnus had told Tom of his own plan to go to the Crimea, and had offered to recommend him as a potential war artist to various newspaper editors, but Tom had refused to consider this at the time. He had not yet forgiven Magnus for his criticisms of Helen, and had thought pity responsible for his friend's kindness. Only a week later he read in the papers that Sir James Crawford's squadron had sailed from the Bosphorus for Balaclava; from this Tom had concluded that Helen would already be on her way home. Miserable though he had been in the months after Helen's marriage, her residence in Turkey had saved him from the temptation of trying to see her. But as soon as he had thought her back in England again, his old longing to force from her the final meeting, which he had previously been denied, had returned with obsessive force. And when this happened, his work, which until then had kept him sane, no longer served to divert him. Soon he had started to give in to compulsions he had hitherto resisted.

He had revisited Blandford's Hotel, walked past the Belgravia house, and even spent a day at Barford. But his most frequent waking dream had been to return to Hanley Park. Only the fear that Catherine would see him there had prevented him going at once, and then he had forced himself to imagine the horrifying consequences of discovery for Helen. Unable to decide what to do, incapable of work and finding his only pleasure in thinking of the past, Tom had finally decided that his duty to himself and to Helen was to leave the country. Though Magnus had by then left for the war, his suggestions had still been fresh in Tom's mind; and while he had not supposed that even the novelty and horror of war would destroy his every memory of Helen, he had been unable to think of anything more likely to help him see his loss in a more rational perspective.

With contacts of his own from the days when he had worked for an engraver, Tom had not been defeated by Magnus's absence. After several failures, he had managed to persuade Colnaghi to commission him to produce a series of portraits of senior officers serving in the Crimea, with supplementary drawings of other aspects of life in the camps and trenches, the end result to be a book of chromolithographs.

Tom had arrived in Constantinople a few days after Inkerman, his intention being to spend a week in the Turkish capital before embarking for Balaclava.

* * *

The rain was sheeting down by the time Tom reached Myserri's Hotel. The hall was as crowded as usual, and resounding to the clink of spurs and the clatter of scabbards. A number of officers were evidently sailing for the Crimea later that evening, since porters were dragging out trunks and portmanteaus. Ever since the first shiploads of wounded from Inkerman had started arriving at Scutari on the other side of the Bosphorus, the mood of the guests had been one of unrelieved gloom, and the presence in the hotel of the members of the Sanitary Commission, sent out from England to inquire into the state of the army hospitals, did little to improve morale. Three days before, the commissioners had found that the barrack hospital's entire supply of drinking water had been flowing through a conduit partially blocked by the decaying carcass of a horse; the day after that, the scandal had been latrines sited next to water tanks in the courtyard. But while stories of rats gnawing at the hands and feet of dying men had not improved Tom's appetite, they had at least increased his respect for the determination of Dr. Sutherland and his fellow commissioners and inspectors to change matters. In fact he had quickly come to enjoy their company more than that of most of the officers in the hotel.

On entering the smoking room, Tom saw Dr. Sutherland and his colleague Mr. Milroy sitting at a table on the far side of the room, drinking brandy and water with other members of their party. After Sutherland had invited him to join them, Tom pulled up a chair. A heated dispute was in progress about whether the Inkerman victory banquet, held the night before at the embassy, should ever have taken place. While some claimed it had been a necessary gesture to bolster Turkish confidence, others argued that it had been inexcusable for the ambassador to lay on a feast for five hundred guests when, scarcely a mile away across the Bosphorus, thousands of wounded were dining on salt pork and watery broth.

Apart from Tom, the only other person at the table taking no part in the discussion was Dr. Padmore, a slim, pale-faced man in his late thirties, who Tom liked for his slightly wistful sense of humor and retiring manner. Padmore, the commission's chief medical officer, was also a keen archaeologist, and had accompanied Tom on several of his sketching expeditions which had involved visits to Roman monuments in Stamboul such as the Cisterna Basilica. Because of Padmore's mildness, it had come as a surprise to Tom to hear that his cross-questioning, when the commission sat taking formal evidence, was merciless.

A servant in a red fez and matching cummerbund had just brought more brandy when Milroy began to bemoan the five to one discrepancy between men and women at the ball that had followed the embassy banquet.

"My God, man, didn't you dance with Lady Stratford?" asked Sutherland.

"Her ladyship dance with a sanitary commissioner? My dear Sutherland, the cabinet may have given us certain powers and priority, but there are limits, you know."

"What about her daughters then? Nice looking girls too."

Tom was usually amused by Milroy's stolid refusal to see anything amusing in Sutherland's good-humored mockery, but tonight the ex-

changes between the former borough engineer and the government inspector of hospitals had a quite different effect on him—all talk of the
embassy banquet serving to remind him of Helen's time as the ambassador's guest. So certain had Tom been that she would return home after
her husband's departure for the Crimea that he had never entertained
any serious suspicion that she might have stayed on, until his second day
at Myserri's when he had seen her name listed in a recent number of the
United Service Magazine, as one of those present at an embassy reception attended by the sultan. This function had taken place just over a
month earlier, but by then Crawford's squadron had undoubtedly sailed
for the Black Sea. Though disconcerted, Tom had not abandoned his
previous conviction; after all there was nothing very surprising about her
staying for another week or so after the fleet's departure. Yet though he
fought against it, a needling doubt had entered Tom's mind, not sufficiently disturbing to make him seriously reconsider his plan to remain a
full week in Constantinople, but a source of underlying tension nonetheless.

As he listened to Milroy and Sutherland, Tom became painfully
aware that a word from either of them could set his mind at rest.
Presumably they would have heard somebody mention the fact that Sir
James Crawford's wife was there, if such had been the case. He stared
fixedly through the cigar smoke at the crudely painted pattern of birds
and pomegranates on the opposite wall. Not having eaten since midday
the brandy had made him light-headed, but not enough to save him from
a mounting feeling of agitation. Several times he was on the point of
asking a direct question, but on each occasion he had sat back before
speaking. It was absurd, he told himself, to be sitting with a thumping
heart unable to make an inquiry that he could have made at any time
since his arrival. But before this moment he had never been presented
with such a direct temptation to find out. Now it seemed quite plain to
him that unless he appeased his craving to know one way or the other,
his remaining days in the city would be ruined by the continuing uncertainty. If she was still in Constantinople, it would not be so very terrible,
although the thought of being obliged to leave earlier than he had intended was an irritating one. But every moment that he delayed told him
more clearly that he would gladly give up far more than three days'
sketching to have his doubt resolved.

Tom turned to Padmore who had just finished saying something to John Rhodes, one of the junior inspectors.

"Did you go . . . to the banquet, I mean?"

"Do you think I shouldn't have done?" asked Padmore with a convincing show of guilt.

"Of course not. I didn't mean that at all. I wanted to ask whether somebody was there, a lady." Tom saw Rhodes raise his eyebrows and felt the blood rise to his cheeks. "I painted her portrait, you see . . ." He hesitated awkwardly, having lost the thread of whatever justification he had intended to give. Angry with himself for showing his embarrassment, he added with unnecessary abruptness, "Her name is Lady Crawford, Admiral Crawford's wife."

Padmore smiled apologetically.

"I'm afraid the nearest I came to anyone so exalted was a colonel's lady. Not even the right service. Sorry."

Rhodes, who Tom had noticed liked to appear to know the answer to every question, put down his glass and pursed his lips thoughtfully.

"Tell you what," he said, "see that fellow over there with Major Pearson?" He glanced in the general direction of the door. "Skene's his name. Captain Skene. He's some sort of attaché at the embassy. He'll know. Ask him."

Tom felt suddenly dizzy and weak.

"Mightn't he find it rather strange . . . somebody he'd never met, asking him just like that?"

Rhodes considered this for a moment, puffing at his cigar.

"See your point, Strickland. Awkward one this." He drummed on the table with his fingers for several seconds and then raised a hand authoritatively. "I've got the answer. Leave it to me."

He got up and Tom watched him walk over to a young man in a black evening coat sitting with a group of army officers to the right of the door. Tom strained to catch what was said but there was too much noise in the room. The triumphant smirk on Rhodes's face as he returned showed that at least he had not been rebuffed.

"Said we were having bets on how many generals' and admirals' wives were at the banquet. Obliging fellow told me straight off, no questions asked. Four generals and two admirals . . . their wives, you understand."

"He wanted to know which wives," interjected Padmore.

"All in good time." Rhodes favored Tom with a self-congratulatory grin. "Lady Stewart and Lady Crawford."

Tom gripped the edge of the table to steady himself.

"Thank you," he muttered, pushing back his chair.

"Nothing to it, if you know who to ask."

When the others rose to go to the dining room, Tom slipped out into the darkness of the courtyard with its trellised arcading and orange trees. Standing alone under the shelter of the eaves, he watched the rain pattering down on the gravel around the central fountain. The following day he had previously set aside for finishing several oil sketches of the Sultan Ahmet mosque and the Church of the Pantokrator, but now the thought of any kind of work seemed ridiculous. The definite answer he had received, far from bringing him the peace of mind he had predicted, had left him a prey to a new and frightening indecision. Though pained by his reviving memories, he was also animated by a pulsing nervous excitement, akin to fear but not without undercurrents of pleasure.

In this strange mood he could clearly recall his thoughts before Rhodes's revelation, but not the feelings and motives behind them. His firm intention had been to leave the city if Helen turned out still to be there, a simple matter of arranging the earliest possible passage to Balaclava. The correctness and inevitability of this course had seemed too obvious to question then, but now . . . ? In England he had persuaded himself that only fear for her reputation had prevented him going to Hanley Park. Yet here he was, planning to sail at once from a foreign city where the risks of any meeting with her being discovered were a fraction of those which would have been encountered in England, with Catherine still at Hanley Park. The plain implication of this astonished him. He had left England, just as he was now planning to leave Turkey, not out of consideration for her, but because of his *own* fears. If she were to receive him with anger and hostility, his world of memories and makebelieve would be shattered. Far easier to leave for the East, dressing up cowardice as gentlemanly concern for a lady's good name, than to risk an angry and painful confrontation which might destroy past illusions. Yet such a confrontation would be far more likely to cure him than this endless running away.

He stared at the drops of rain falling from the dark leaves of the orange trees and breathed deeply to control a sudden surge of panic. See her, he told himself. See her. Wasn't that the only way he would ever lay the ghost she had left with him? Perhaps he would discover after this lapse of time that the ideal figure he had made her in his mind had owed more to a lover's selective imagination than to the woman herself. Anger also came to buttress his resolution. Helen had loved him, and yet he had never once argued against her decision to marry, but, like some scared lackey eager to keep his place by acquiescence, had politely handed her the knife to use whenever it might please her to sever their connection. Should he now continue to sacrifice himself for the minimal risks to her reputation which a meeting might involve?

Later, sitting in his room, Tom had no difficulty in thinking of the most suitable place in which to see her. Only the previous Sunday, Dr. Sutherland had mentioned that the *Morning Post*'s correspondent in the city had placed his house in Orta-köy at the commission's disposal for its members' use while he was with the Turkish troops at Silistra. The village was seven miles from Constantinople, a journey that not even the deplorable roads could extend much beyond an hour in a decently sprung carriage. Since Sutherland had already suggested that Tom make use of this offer to get a sight of the neighboring countryside before he left, there seemed little possibility of any difficulties being raised.

He would write a letter tomorrow. No—best write it at once before his mood changed. Possibly in wartime letters not arriving with the diplomatic bag or service mails would be opened and read by the embassy staff. He would have to write the sort of note that a friend of the family might be expected to send, but one still making it clear that he did not intend to be fobbed off with a refusal to see him. Since Helen would be most unwilling to risk his coming to the embassy, in case Charles or Sir James should hear about her receiving a young man having nothing to do with the navy or the diplomatic corps, he would need to imply that, if she rejected his choice of day and venue, she could expect him to seek her out at his own time and pleasure. By asking her to lunch with him at Orta-köy, he might be able to prevent her leaving after a few words.

Still apprehensive, but by now elated too, Tom paced across to his window and gazed out over the glistening roofs, seeing the distant lights of Stamboul reflected in the black waters of the Golden Horn; his thoughts though were not of what he saw, but of a building scarcely a mile away, overlooking the Bosphorus. Somewhere in that gigantic, square, neoclassical palace faced with gleaming stucco, Helen Crawford was living her life in total ignorance of his proximity. Outside her windows would be spacious gardens, guarded by soldiers in white and red sentry boxes; each morning bands would play in the central courtyard at the base of the tall flagstaff. A new life, utterly removed from her old one. A nervous flutter of doubt assailed Tom, but his mind was made up. She had owed him a final meeting and he would have it.

He had not moved from the window when his opening lines came to him.

> Dear Lady Crawford,
> I was sorry not to be able to bid you a personal farewell before you sailed for Malta. But Charles Crawford came to my house and kindly acquainted me with your immediate plans, so saving me a wasted visit . . .

Quite prepared to run to many drafts before reaching a final version, Tom sat down, picked up a pencil and started to write.

~ Forty-Two ~

Magnus had seen sights on the battlefield which, at the time, he had thought impossible to surpass for the depths of suffering and degradation revealed: a Zouave roughly pulling the boots off a screaming Russian soldier, whose legs had been shattered by a round shot; a sergeant of the Connaught Rangers, who had died in such pain from bayonet wounds to the stomach that he had bitten into the earth—when Magnus had seen him, his limbs had stiffened and one arm was held aloft, the fingers still clutching tufts of earth torn up in his last agony. Only the faces of men killed instantly by bullets in the head or heart looked peaceful in death. A French chasseur had crawled to quench his burning thirst in a ditch, but had fallen forward exhausted and had drowned in the few inches of muddy water he had so painfully fought to reach. Worst all to watch had been the gangs of Turks clearing the Russian dead from the field, dragging the corpses by the heels toward the shallow communal pits, bumping their heads on the ground, not caring that skulls were split open on stones, and partially severed limbs wrenched clean off. Outside a hospital marquee he had seen a pile of amputated legs with boots and stockings still on them; as he had passed, an orderly tossed out a dozen fingers and toes as coolly as if they had been fowl's feet.

Yet within a week of Inkerman, Magnus had described scenes of greater horror for his newspaper; no scenes of death were as heartrending as the processions of wounded on their way down to Balaclava for embarkation to Scutari. At first it had been intended to let the dying remain in the camps rather than subject them to the additional suffering of a futile journey, but, when a week after the battle, a night of heavy snow had been followed by three days of torrential rain and finally a prolonged and intense frost, the hundreds of cases of frostbite, pneumonia and rheumatism could only be accommodated in the hospital tents by evacuating all the battle wounded, whether recovering or sinking, to the port.

* * *

When George Braithwaite had seen the surgeons working through the night after Inkerman, and for most of the following day, he had been ashamed to ask these men, red with blood to the elbows, to turn their attention from gravely wounded soldiers to deal with his torn hand and lacerated arm. For a while he had sat in line, and many times had seen the fearful cut made, the white flesh spring back and the saw laid against the bone. The surgeons had been so hard-pressed that they had often pinched the arteries together with their fingers, only tying them with ligatures when the limb was off and tossed aside. Men with similar wounds had been able to see every movement and had writhed and groaned not so much with pain as with terrified anticipation. The chloroform had soon been exhausted, and then the roars and screams of men under the knife had been more than George could bear and he had fled to his tent, having his servant bind up his wounds with an old shirt. Next day his arm was swollen and caused him such pain that he had been forced to return to his regiment's hospital marquee. Later the surgeons had been pleased by the steady ooze of "laudable pus" from his arm, but when this suppuration had shown no signs of diminishing, and the inflammation had grown worse, he too had been ordered down to Balaclava with the rest.

The shortage of stretchers and the absolute impossibility of dragging the heavy British ambulance wagons, with their gun-carriage wheels, through the quagmire of mud on the sloping track meant that many of the wounded had to be carried on the backs of men often themselves suffering from exposure. Others were strapped to mules and horses, but the lack of forage had so decimated the army's baggage train that even with teams from the artillery and cavalry, there were far too few, and most so weak that they constantly stumbled, causing terrible agony to men with freshly amputated limbs and open wounds.

George had initially been fortunate enough to be strapped to one of the upright mule seats lent by the French; but on seeing many far more severely wounded men struggling through the mud on foot, he had asked to be taken down so that the seat could be given to one of them. He did not feel heroic to have made the sacrifice, since, just as in the hospital tent, he had felt shamed by the greater distress of others; now he was unable to allow himself to be carried when his legs were whole and men in crude splints were limping by, using their rifles as crutches. In spite of his sling, his arm hurt him with each step, and the half-frozen mud was so thick and adhesive that every few yards he was obliged to rest for several minutes before once more lifting his soil-clogged boots and squelching on. He thought of the impeccable uniforms of the regiments that had embarked with the Coldstream at Portsmouth and looked around him in incredulity. Some of the officers had tied hay in sacking around their rags of trousers to keep out the cold; others had made leggings of sheepskins and horsehides. He saw a colonel on a stretcher with a mess-tin cover pulled down over his ears. To save their faces from frostbite, a number of private soldiers had bound strips of old blankets around their heads, layer upon layer, leaving only the mouth and eyes exposed, making their skulls appear swollen and deformed.

Many of those on the mules were almost past pain and caring, with eyes sunk deep in their sockets, dull and dead, mouths open and faces gaunt and gray, tinged with blue. A Turk was carrying a handsome, dark-haired man roped to his back; the blanket covering him had slipped, exposing the bandaged stump of his left arm, cut away a few inches from the shoulder. The only way of knowing which of the worst cases were alive was the film of their breath, visible in the raw cold air. One who passed by, strapped upright in a mule seat, was obviously dead, his head lolling drunkenly with every lurch of the animal, and teeth clamped hard on his already blackened tongue. Often a death remained unnoticed for several miles, when the fixed stare of an eye or the rigid set of an arm would announce that all was over. If the eyes were closed, the lids would be prized open and the pupils peered into for any signs of life. If dead, the man's body was lifted down and left by the side of the track, while another took his place in the seat. Many seats and stretchers had had several occupants before Balaclava was reached.

George's arm burned and throbbed sharply, but the sight of so much suffering on every side gave him strength, convincing him of his own insignificance in comparison with so many deaths and so much pain. He was also humbled by the uncomplaining stoicism of the ordinary soldiers, men whom in England he would never have glanced at a second time, but whose courage in two battles, and now, on what would for many be their last journey, made him wince at his past arrogance and blindness. Only once had he entered the workhouse at Rigton Bridge, and had almost vomited at what he had then considered a subhuman stench only possible among derelict working men; and now he stank more vilely than any pauper in that workhouse, and could not write on a sheet of paper without it being covered with lice. He remembered the hatred he had felt for the mob on the day of the election and could no longer understand or remember his reasons. His only anger left was for those responsible for sending an army to fight in these conditions with woefully inadequate supplies and so small a chance of survival.

* * *

Early in the morning Magnus had learned with misgiving that just over a thousand wounded were to be transferred from the 2nd and 4th Divisions' camps to the port. On previous occasions, he had heard it said that, when as few as two hundred had been embarked, they had been left unattended by the landing stage for hours on end while two or three boats ferried them out to a hospital ship in an endless relay of trips.

When Magnus arrived at the quay, he passed within twenty yards of the spot where George Braithwaite was lying, but did not see him. All around on the muddy ground were prostrate men, some groaning feebly, others too weak to make a sound. A light rain was turning to sleet, slanting across the harbor with freezing gusts of wind. No awning had been erected, and Magnus saw only three covered stretchers; the vast majority of the men were lying on the bare earth, without as much as a blanket under them. Two assistant surgeons and half a dozen medical orderlies were wandering among their charges doling out water.

Magnus went up to an orderly and asked why the men were getting no food, since many would not have eaten since the previous evening; he was told that they would have all they required on board. Estimating that less than half of those waiting would have left the quay by midafternoon, Magnus asked why they could not have some arrowroot and beef essence at once. The orderly explained wearily that ground rice and sago was all that was left in store, and that since the principal medical officer had not given any instructions, none would be issued.

A man near them was moaning softly, a low, rhythmic, plaintive sound, not unlike an exhausted child sobbing itself to sleep. The orderly bent down to adjust the loose bandages around the soldier's hand and wrist; as he unwound the cloth, the man's frostbitten thumb and two fingers dropped off. Calmly retying the bandage, the orderly told Magnus that the hand of a rifleman he had just looked at had come away at the wrist in the same way.

At the landing-stage itself, Magnus saw badly wounded men roughly bundled off their stretchers, lifted up under their armpits and carried down to the boats where they were laid on the bottom boards between the thwarts in several inches of slopping water. The slightest movement caused them acute pain, but when they were hauled along the quay and slung down bodily by Turkish porters, accustomed to tossing around barrels and boxes, to the seamen in the boats, they suffered unendurable agony and roared out like men under the lash. Although Magnus realized that they were taken off the stretchers because these would be needed again to carry down more men, he was outraged that they were being packed so tightly in the boats. If even a small proportion of ships' boats from the fleet had been used, there would have been no need for such barbaric cruelty.

The unmoved and dignified indifference of the assistant surgeon supervising, with pipe in mouth and hands in pockets, made Magnus shudder; this spectacle, which he was witnessing for the first time, had obviously been taking place several times a week on a reduced scale. The surgeon was probably no more callous than others of his calling, but, hardened by familiarity, had come to look upon such torture as a regrettable but inevitable part of the medical department's routine. As Magnus was walking away, a young officer with fair curly hair matted with blood begged him to cover his face so he would be spared seeing what was going on.

At the commissariat wharf Magnus found a Maltese boatman prepared to take him out to *Medway* in midharbor.

Even on the open upper deck of the hospital ship, the putrid fecal smell emanating from the hatches made him feel sick. On the enclosed decks below, the air was so foul that he was afraid of fainting. *Medway* was a troop transport and had never been converted for her present use. There were perhaps twenty cots and fifty mattresses for six hundred men and no additional lavatories beyond the heads in the bows, which had been barely adequate for the needs of healthy soldiers but were ludicrously unsuitable for sick and wounded, most of them barely able to crawl and many suffering from dysentery. The few bedpans in use on the middle deck had been emptied into a portable bath near the main companion, and Magnus did not have to use his eyes to know that it had not been emptied since the day before.

The men were lying at random all over the decks, the majority on the planks. One man who had had both his legs amputated was crying out and dashing his head against the bulwark behind him. Disgusted and furiously angry, Magnus sought out the surgeon in charge and told him that unless the man were placed on a mattress and attended to, he would do everything in his power to make the *Medway*'s name a national byword for criminal neglect. The surgeon listened in silence; his eyelids were inflamed and swollen, and his unshaven face yellow and pinched with fatigue. When Magnus had finished, he asked quietly,

"Do you suppose it makes any difference to a delirious man whether he's on a mattress or not? The one you saw has gangrene in both stumps and won't last the day."

"What will happen if there's a storm on the crossing?"

The surgeon looked at Magnus with sudden anger.

"Men will be thrown across the decks. If I waited for this ship to be put in order, she wouldn't sail for a month. The navy chartered her from a shipping company, the army is meant to equip her and the Medical Department to provide staff; who found the crew, I've no idea. How can you expect anybody to accept responsibility with such a system? I'll tell you something else. There are three hundred stoves in one warehouse ashore—just three or four of them would save lives on the voyage, but the harbor master can't spare dock labor to move the stores on top of them; he needs every man he's got to unload food and ammunition for the men in the camps. Why not blame him? Blame who you like, but it'll make no difference."

Two hours later Magnus was aboard H.M.S. *Retribution* intent on seeing his father.

The beautiful whiteness of the decks, achieved by the use of lime juice and constant scrubbing and holystoning, the ebony gloss of the guns, the glistening pikes and tomahawks strapped to the beams, and the polished brasswork, seemed to Magnus to belong to another world from that of the mud and ordure of Balaclava and the military camps. The sailors' low-crowned, varnished hats were immaculate, their deep, turned-back collars, edged with white tape, were spotless, and their clean-shaven faces glowed with health, making them seem men of a different species from the bearded and emaciated wretches serving ashore.

The sentry at the entry-port marched Magnus to a petty officer, who brought him to a mate, who in turn led him up to the quarterdeck to see the commander; and every man in this meticulously ordered hierarchy seemed politely surprised that a civilian, in a tarred canvas coat and patched trousers, should have the temerity to ask to see the admiral. It was after evening quarters and the marine band was playing on the middle deck, the music wafting up to the exalted heights of the quarter-deck and poop. Having explained to the commander who he was, and having noticed the distinct alteration in that officer's frigid manner, Magnus was led down the after companion and entrusted to his father's flag lieutenant, who finally ushered him to the admiral's quarters, past the marine sentries and through a pair of maplewood veneered doors with china handles, into his father's day cabin.

Ahead of him, through a doorway in the paneled bulkhead, Magnus could see the graceful, square-paned stern windows. On a small round table were several decanters in coasters and some glasses on a silver tray. The day cabin itself was comfortably furnished with three arm-chairs, a long Regency sofa and an oval mahogany table in the center. The ports were covered by wooden blinds, and, had it not been for the curve of the beams supporting the deck above, and the white planks showing at the edge of the carpet, Magnus might have supposed himself in an ordinary, low-ceilinged room ashore. The flag lieutenant went through into the stern gallery and after some murmured words returned with Sir James, and then withdrew.

Father and son shook hands formally, and Sir James said, with an overt jocularity that did not conceal a real grievance,

"I suppose a son, who refuses two invitations to dine without giving his father a single reason, can't be expected to send a note asking whether a casual visit will be convenient."

"Remembering your views on my profession, I thought it better not to embarrass you at your table. . . . I need your help, Father. I want you to go aboard a hospital ship in the harbor. Lord Raglan can't know the conditions the wounded are living in."

"If an admiral complains, everything will be put right?"

Magnus ignored the gentle mockery in his father's voice.

"If you see for yourself, you'll move heaven and earth to bring a change."

"While there's a shortage of medical supplies in the camps, there's bound to be the same in the hospital ships."

"I'm not talking about a shortage. There are three bedpans for every hundred men, no mattresses for men who've lost arms and legs. Scores of them are starving because they can't eat hard biscuit, and there's no soft bread."

"The whole army's starving, Magnus."

"Because of official lassitude and incompetence."

"The truth is far simpler. Nobody planned for a winter siege; everything stems from that disastrous underestimate of the enemy's strength. All other failings are subordinate."

His father's sad philosophical tone maddened Magnus.

"Have you been to the port recently?" he asked, seeing his father stiffen defensively.

"I was there yesterday and everything I saw bears out what I said. Quays choked with timber for huts and no chance of getting it to the camps until the railway is finished. If it could be got there, there'd still be no carpenters to put the huts together. Every plan was made two months late and now everything has to be done at once with chaos the inevitable result. Three months will set matters right." Sir James frowned and swept a lock of silver-gray hair from his forehead.

"In three months there'll be no army left," cried Magnus.

Sir James cleared his throat and looked down at the floor.

"Large reinforcements will arrive in the New Year."

Magnus looked at him in disbelief and horror.

"But the men in the trenches now are going to die . . . every man of them dead by the spring? Are you resigned to that?"

Sir James turned away without speaking. A moment later Magnus was shaken by the emotion and anger in his voice.

"I'm resigned to nothing. Charles and Humphrey are in those

trenches. If you knew how I hate this cabin and my own security . . . yet you speak as if I have no personal stake in events ashore. Do you think we don't hear when the batteries are in action? There are days when I've blocked my ears or gone down to the orlop deck to escape the noise."

Moved by this outburst and mortified that he had spoken harshly, Magnus said gently,

"If either of them is wounded, mightn't you wish you'd gone aboard one of the hospital ships? Even if great changes are impossible, small things can be done."

Sir James sighed heavily and walked away toward the doorway into the stern gallery.

"Suppose I see your ship and go to Lord Raglan, there'll be a board of inquiry and the wretched surgeon in charge will be censured. The principal medical officer at Balaclava may be dismissed for clearing the vessel. To what purpose? Will anybody better take his place? Will the ships suddenly be transformed?" He gazed at Magnus with sympathy and sorrow. "The system of supply is woeful; the confusion between departments even worse, but the whole edifice can't be knocked down and built up again during a war."

Magnus sat with bowed head, knowing that his father was right. He looked up and caught Sir James's eye.

"If you do one thing, I'll never forget it. Send half a dozen launches from the line-of-battle ships to ferry out the wounded."

"Gladly. If the captain superintendent had mentioned . . ." He broke off and looked at Magnus with sudden pain. "Why in God's name didn't you stay in the army? Why, Magnus? Isn't that what's wrong . . . too many officers who think transport and supply too far beneath them to concern themselves with the most basic needs of their men? Too few men like you holding commissions. Instead like the rest of the press you're searching for scapegoats and lowering the nation's morale. It's a waste, a useless waste."

"But we'll make sure it never happens again, Father. No waste in that."

Sir James shook his head sadly.

"Every government neglects the army in peacetime and always will."

"Not after this war."

"In twenty years even the best memories fail; you'll see, even if I don't."

As Magnus rose to leave, his father took his arm and walked out to the companion ladder with him.

"You won't believe me perhaps," he murmured in a low voice, "but every hour I spend on this magnificent ship fills me with humiliation and shame at the navy's impotence to cut short the war. I have attempted repeatedly to persuade Dundas and the first lord to sanction another naval bombardment at close range and for my pains I have earned the reputation of an unstable hothead. When Dundas goes home, Sir Edmund Lyons will succeed him and I shall remain second-in-command."

"I'm sorry."

His father shrugged his shoulders and smiled at Magnus before calling his flag lieutenant to take him to the entry-port. As they were leaving, Sir James called after them,

"I've not forgot the launches, Magnus."

As the gap of water widened, and Magnus gazed back at the towering masts and rows of gun ports, he felt an aching sadness. The war held them all captive, his father as much as any. Magnus thought of him in his splendid but solitary quarters and no longer felt resentment. Charles or Humphrey might die; the chances were that one of them would; and what consolation would his marriage be if that happened? Ignorant of his wife's infidelity and probably doting on her, the man was to be pitied rather than envied. After witnessing such terrible suffering earlier that day, Magnus was surprised that thoughts of his father's marriage had any power to move him; and yet as he sat back against the transom, listening to the regular squeak of the oars in the rowlocks, he felt a stirring of compassion close to forgiveness. Ahead the sea and sky were dark and gray except for a faint streak of red beyond the besieged city.

⤳ Forty-Three ⤳

An old, white-bearded man got up from the turbaned group of coffee drinkers sitting under the plane trees, and, taking his long-stemmed chibouque from his mouth, stared at the small black carriage clattering into the village square, and at the unfamiliar uniforms of the two mounted soldiers following. The women filling their earthenware jars at the marble fountain would not have abandoned their work to gaze at a richly ornamented araba or a pasha's teleki preceded by a retinue of kavasses, but many had never seen an English brougham before, and, although ignorant of the meaning of the crown on the door panels, did not doubt that the traveler was an important one. The brougham came to a halt and the Turkish coachman jumped down from the box and went across to the coffee and sherbet stall under the trees to ask directions.

As the brougham moved off again, Helen looked out at quiet streets and verandaed wooden houses with closed lattices. Not a fashionable summer resort like Therapia, Orta-köy had a sad neglected air made worse by the grayness of the day and the blustery winds. The gaps between the houses were dotted with fig trees and choked with weeds. By the side of the uneven muddy road, a blind woman sat on the doorstep of a small unkempt cemetery surrounded by a rusty iron railing. Inside, under the cypresses, some goats were browsing among the headless Janissary stones. Helen's head was aching with the continual rattling of the windows and the groaning of the springs. At times the roads had been so poor that she had been obliged to cling tightly to the corded strap handles to prevent herself being thrown from the seat. She felt irritable and intensely apprehensive.

* * *

There had been many reasons for Helen's protracted stay in Turkey: a desire to be close at hand in case any harm befell Humphrey; a horror of returning to live with Catherine at Hanley Park; and, just as pressing, a strong feeling that, the longer she stayed away, the less likely it would be that Tom might try to see her again. At the time of her marriage, Helen had been terrified in case his initial grief and anger, at the cruel suddenness of her departure, might drive him to follow her, but as the months had passed, this once disturbing possibility had come to worry her less, becoming in the end little more than a memory—until she had opened his letter.

On first reading it, Helen had been afraid. Never for a moment believing that he had been surprised to learn that she was still in Pera, she had at once concluded that Tom had come out for the sole purpose of seeing her: impelled either by love or a desire for revenge. The letter gave her no positive indication which, although the chillingly sarcastic reference to Charles with its implied criticism of her for having failed to warn Tom, made her for a time consider vengeance the likelier of the two. Yet when she recalled being with him, her memories of his tolerance and touching uncertainty gave the lie to this. She had done much to provoke him, but he had never repaid her with anger or reproach. She thought of him by the river, as he stooped to pick up her veil—brushing grass from her skirt—sitting miserably on their ugly bed in Blandford's Hotel, head in hands, under the hissing gasolier—radiant beside her in the autumnal woods near Barford—memories that brought back not love or pain, but a nostalgic tenderness mingled with regret.

A year ago, a war ago, a world ago—before her daily fear for Humphrey's safety, before the bombardments and assaults, the diplomatic banquets and receptions, before poor James had first made love to her in Valletta, apologetically, as though his body had belonged to someone else. A century it seemed since she had traded her old self for a new name, and, so different had her new life been, that recalling the past, even with Tom's letter in her hand, she had found it hard to understand that events from a distant world might still have power over her, that figures from an English summer might touch her in a Levantine winter.

But, rereading the letter, fear had once more returned, replacing tenderness and nostalgia, and soon turning to anger. The facetious formality of tone, the absence of any thought for the difficulties she would face in contriving a meeting outside the city and finally his veiled threat to call unannounced at the embassy, unless she complied with his wishes, had filled Helen with furious indignation.

To explain why she should need a carriage for a whole day, she had been forced to work out an elaborate excuse about visiting a distant relative, who had fallen sick on his way to the war, while staying with friends in Orta-köy. Had she made no mention of illness, it would have been thought extraordinary that any gentleman should ask her to travel in winter when the roads were at their worst, instead of calling on her at the embassy. Lord Stratford had then raised difficulties; his dear Lady Crawford could not travel alone with a groom and footman, she must have a small military escort; then, by offering her sick relative the services of the embassy's physician, his lordship had placed her in a situation from which she had only extricated herself with the greatest difficulty. But angry though she was, Helen knew that if she handled the meeting badly, she might face far greater inconvenience and danger than that arising from the few lies she had so far been obliged to tell.

*　*　*

Tom started nervously as Fuad, the cook, opened the door and shuffled across the coarse matting, carrying a bowl filled with a messy-looking pilaf of red mullet, rice and herbs; glancing absently at the food, Tom gave a brief nod of approval and turned with a troubled and preoccupied expression to gaze out at the dark yews and myrtles in the garden. When nothing had turned out as he had imagined, what did it matter that the fish had been inexpertly boned and would have to be washed down with a sour and watery local wine? Having assumed that the house in Orta-köy would be well built and comfortable, it had shocked him to find it no more than a wooden summer kiosk, evidently only used by its owner when the flies and smells of the city compelled a brief exodus during the hottest months of the year.

The warped window frames and lattices were no defense against winter winds, and a few pans of glowing charcoal produced nauseating fumes and little heat. Apart from a long divan in the window of the principal room, the furniture was rudimentary: two campstools, a deal trestle table covered with a dirty embroidered cloth and several hard, upright chairs. Fuad's gaunt face and ill-fitting English tailcoat, worn with a green hadji's turban and baggy traditional trousers, were at one with the makeshift air of the house. Only the tubs of tree geraniums and jasmines in the hall saved the place from utter drabness.

But no surroundings, however congenial, could have eased the taut expectancy of Tom's nerves, nor have helped him recapture the determined and aggressive mood in which he had written his letter. He could no longer understand how he could ever have believed that simply by seeing Helen he would be able to break her hold over him. Even before his arrival in the village, he had dreaded that her coming would merely remind him of the magnitude of his loss. She might prove understanding and tender, not callous and indifferent to him, as he had imagined. What if she were to confess to unhappiness comparable with his own? He had seen himself shaming her, forcing her to admit that she had wronged him, led him on, lied to him and ended their affair with a brutal unconcern bordering on contempt.

But now, with her arrival imminent, every vestige of his former certainty had vanished, leaving him agitated and overwrought. The thought of her physical presence both scared and stirred him, bringing panic and elation, confusing and alarming him in case he should prove unable to think or even speak coherently when she arrived. And soon it came to him with a sudden clarity that shook him: this is what hope feels like— the dread of disappointment a man feels when he has rashly allowed himself to hope against the odds. And Tom knew with sinking certainty that if Helen showed him any trace of love, he would surrender unresisting, gladly, and that his past intentions had meant nothing, that time since his parting from her had been no more than an interval, a pause before this inevitable admission of frailty.

It rained heavily shortly before midday, and afterward the sun shone fitfully for a while. Tom had put on the best clothes he had brought with him, but feeling the absurdity of appearing in such surroundings wearing a "half-dress" morning coat and quadrilled velvet waistcoat, he changed into leather trousers, untanned Napoleon boots and an old brown frock coat. Then, to make it appear that he had just come in from a walk or ride, he went out into the garden and stamped about until his boots were convincingly muddy, tousling his hair to add further conviction. Opening the lattice commanding the veranda and the road, he sat down to wait, and partly to calm himself, partly to soften the possible disappointment, pretended to believe that she would not come, that he had been mad in his presumption ever to have supposed she would. From the imam's school beside the mosque he could hear the faint sound of children chanting; closer at hand, sparrows were splashing in the newly formed puddles on the road. A veiled Armenian woman, munching a cucumber, rode past on a milk-white mule carrying long wooden troughs of bread to the bakery; two street dogs began a desultory fight. As time passed, his feigned pessimism turned to a genuine despondency, so that when at last he heard the clatter of hooves and saw the approaching carriage, he felt a breathless shock of real surprise. He was also stunned to see in addition to the liveried coachman and groom, two British hussars in full dress trotting beside the coach: living symbols of the now even greater gulf between their respective stations; and he felt a humiliating sense of guilt for having dared to summon her. Then his pride lived again. This cavalcade had come at his bidding to the very place he had chosen, at his appointed time; and the meanness of the house, and those around it, merely enhanced this victory. Tom clapped his hands to summon Fuad and sent him out to welcome his guest; then, turning abruptly, he thrust his hands deep into his pockets and walked stiffly across to the divan, where he stood staring out blindly at the yews behind the house.

On hearing the soft rustling of a dress, he remained motionless for several seconds, as if lost in thought. From the corner of his eye he saw Fuad bowing low, his hand raised to his face in a profound salaam. As the servant withdrew, Tom turned with lowered eyes, not daring to look at her face, taking in at a glance a cream-colored merino dress and astrakhan-trimmed pelisse. He moved forward several steps, trying to slow his movements to convey confidence and ease, praying, in the lengthening silence, that she would speak first. With burning cheeks and lips too stiff and tight to form a smile, he heard himself murmuring banalities about being glad that she could come, assuring her that had he known about Turkish roads and summer kiosks he would never have subjected her to the journey. And then he had stopped, shocked by the grating artificiality of his voice and the fact that he had apologized. He looked up and her expression robbed him of further words; expecting, if not sympathy for his predicament, at least understanding, he saw only

an icy indifference which pierced him to the heart. A year ago, only a
year, and she would have run to him with open arms, parting as at
Barford with tearful kisses. He shot her a look of tortured resentment,
but the set of her features remained the same, the pale gold of her skin
and the warm rich lights in her hair mocking by contrast the freezing
hostility in her eyes.

"Why have you forced me to come here?"

The slightest tremor of suppressed anger ruffling the precise, polished
surface of her voice, her tone an absolute denial of any claim he might
suppose he had on her. Humiliated and outraged, he burst out awkwardly,

"I did not think our former association so bereft of meaning, so far
beneath consideration . . ." The thread of his sentence had gone. "Because," he went on, his voice rising, "I deserved better than to learn
with the cut of cane in the face what should have come from your lips
when we were together. Or did Captain Crawford come as your personal
messenger?"

She raised her brows and inclined her head as if surprised by such an
immoderate and ungentlemanly outburst. She said with only a hint of
questioning,

"You wish revenge for what was no fault of mine?"

"No fault that you kept silent, knowing what that man knew?" He
stared at her with incredulous fury. "No fault that you left me in a fool's
paradise . . . did that knowing the appointments for the Black Sea,
knowing what they meant?"

For the first time he saw her hesitate, noted a slight movement of her
hands as if impulse had almost broken her studied reserve, but she
replied with the same distanced blandness:

"Nothing could have been changed, whether you knew or not. A
sudden death is less painful than a lingering one."

"Dead I may have been to you after our parting, but a living death . . .
I did not cease to feel when you had gone. Did it not cross your mind
that I might wonder how it was that you never found time to see me
before you left? Was I supposed to shrug my shoulders and go on as if
ours had been no more than a casual encounter in a crowded summer?"
His legs were shaking and he could feel tears starting to his eyes.

"How you choose to remember me is your concern, but one thing I will remind you. Nothing that I ever said could have given you reason to hope that I might break my word to the man I had pledged myself to." She raised a hand to the brim of her feathered hat, a gesture half-nervous, half-mannered elegance. The ghost of a smile played on her lips. "No sweet farewell could have brought any alteration."

"That did not excuse . . . I had a right to see you knowing it was for the last time."

She met his gaze easily, as if unaware of the burning reproach in his eyes. A trace of mockery in her voice as she said,

"And you have claimed that right today. I trust you are satisfied."

"If there is satisfaction in learning how easily you forgot . . ."

"Forgot?" she said sharply. "How could I forget? You mean, did I suffer continually? You wanted to hear that I am still sad and discontented. You brought me here to gratify your vanity, to hear me say that losing you I lost hope and happiness, shutting the door on life, the angel chained to a satyr pining for youth and beauty." She stared at him defiantly, challenging him to deny the truth of her accusation, glorying in his silence. "The opposite is true. You are quite ignorant of the natural dignity of men used to the obedience of others, but I, who have lived among such men and am proud to be married to one, count myself privileged. I enjoy my husband's strength and his position and will not stoop to the hypocrisy of denying it."

He saw a frightening light of triumph in her eyes and felt his powers of resistance ebbing like blood, felt that another onslaught would annihilate him utterly, yet something stubborn in him could not give way.

"And would that natural dignity," he asked, "survive the knowledge that your ladyship had given herself to a man as mean and insignificant as myself?"

"By threatening me, Mr. Strickland, you stigmatize yourself as I never did. Should not a proud little upstart's adoration please a worthless, sensual woman's vanity and pass an idle hour? Sentimental shopgirls *give* themselves. Perhaps you gave yourself, but I did not. So do not threaten to punish me for your innocent self-deception."

"You risked everything!" he cried, moving toward her.

"I enjoyed the excitement, as men like to risk their fortunes at hazard." He stood motionless, staring with wide eyes as if hoping by the concentration of his gaze to burn out the image before him. "You see how much better it would have been never to have seen each other again?" He heard the sudden change of tone, the softness of her voice, a softness that was almost tender, and stifled a swelling inward groan. He had survived her hostility, but this final hint of kindness, recalling everything her harshness had blotted out, everything he had wished for and dared to imagine possible again, broke him, and he turned away, clutching hands to his face, feeling hot tears wetting his palms. He did not see the light die from her face and her lips tremble as she moved toward the door.

Among the jasmines and geraniums in the hall she paused, breathing deeply, horrified at what she had done, yet still sure that her only safety had lain in killing his love, in making herself despicable to him. A few steps from the door and the hussars would see her and after that no going back; but still she hesitated, consumed with grief and shame; she had feared the encounter, but how terribly easy it had been; and worst of all, even while tortured by doing such forced injustice to her motives, she had felt a wild exultation in her capacity for so absolute a denial of her true feelings, even believing that she was hurting him not for her future security but only for his peace of mind, only to help him forget her as unworthy of his regard; and his resistance had sharpened her resolution and pride in her control until she had gone far further than she had ever intended, oblivious to his pain until his final surrender. On a peg by the door hung some coats, a wide-awake hat and a leather pistol holster. A cold fear struck her; that he might kill himself had not occurred to her before; yet he had come from England to engineer this meeting, had probably spent more money than he possessed in doing so, had dreamed of what they would say—and she had treated him thus. It was horrible. Yet to go back, to risk undoing what had been so painful to achieve . . . From the dark hall she could see the coachman and the groom smoking on the grass under the trees across the road. An araba pulled by two oxen lumbered past; a woman carrying a child; the sun was shining. She longed to be gone, and yet—and yet had not the power to go. A moment later she sensed him behind her and heard his dry, faltering whisper,

"Did you ever love me?"

She nodded dumbly, her eyes misting, filling slowly, but never leaving his pale, tear-stained face. Burning with shame, she saw the transformation of his eyes and the flame of joy set there by that slight, pitiful inclination of her head.

"Yes, yes, I did, truly, I did," she repeated fervently, and yielding to the swooning melting of her heart, held out her hands, but he did not move to take them. For a moment of pain she was close to explaining that she had kept silent at Barford only for his sake, that she had begged Charles on her knees to allow a last hour with her lover, but then she saw his slow gentle smile and knew that she had no need.

This confirmation had been all he sought. He looked at her in perfect stillness for perhaps a minute before walking back into the room. Choked by scalding tears she moved after him, disgusted that she had dared speak of dignity, but then she stopped and bowed her head. Everything had been said; she was already forgiven. His going had also been a request to her. Longing to remain, she wiped her eyes, and, with an outward composure, maintained she knew not how, walked out into the sunlit road. The coachman got up from the grass and stretched, then ambled across to the brougham.

"Get on!" she shouted to the man's amazement, and again, as the groom scrambled to secure the steps, "Get on!"

❧ Forty-Four ❧

A perfect winter morning with scarcely a breath of wind, and across the Bosphorus, on the farther shore, the hospitals at Scutari, transformed by the sun to shining oblongs of blanched ivory; high in the crystal sky a frieze of wispy clouds like decorations on a Chinese screen. Sitting with Milroy and Padmore in the stern of the commissioners' launch, Tom was keenly aware of the visual beauty around him, but it evoked nothing in him—unreal because outside and independent of his misery.

In two days he would be sailing for the Crimea, and, in what time remained, had decided to visit Scutari—something he had been previously unwilling to do: afraid of what he would see, and ashamed to be thought a callous experience seeker, prepared to stare at those for whom he could do nothing. Now in his confused and untypically introspective state, he hoped to find in the greater suffering of others a personal cure, an end to his sense of helpless captivity within a timeless moment. He repeated to himself that the fixed point of despair, which fate had led him to, had been no ending, but an accident of time, a single milestone on a longer road. If, in the constant backflow of change, even great disasters could not claim the name of tragedy as a lasting appellation— then how much less could an individual instance of disappointed love? Whatever the intensity with which desire sought to embalm experience, time would soon enough deny those wishful efforts. Yet in his heart, Tom recognized the deception in such thoughts of universal transience.

He had lost what he most wanted, that fact remained—*now*, today, tomorrow and, as he feared, always; and if peace of mind could come only with the certainty that there was nothing else ahead except time's slow erosion, then he would rather suffer than accept that nothingness.

Tom had heard so much from Sutherland and Milroy about conditions at Scutari that the reality did not distress him as acutely as he had supposed it would. Pus-filled bowls, saturated and verminous floor-boards too rotten in places to be scrubbed, and condensation-streaming walls shocked and sickened him, as did the thick, sweet smell of putre-faction, but far greater was the shock of seeing the scores of men with dysentery, apathetic and indifferent, dying, apparently without a strug-gle, and, according to Padmore, without pain: doomed by the absence of proper food. But in wards filled entirely with wounded there was more active suffering, but also much more hope, even in cases where recovery seemed impossible. When Padmore, who had acted as Tom's guide, prepared to leave him in a ward, Tom made as if to follow, but was prevented.

"Stay and talk to them. They like to see a sympathetic face."

"But what could I say?" he asked, feeling not only deep sympathy and respect for the sufferers, but also a dread of offending them by saying too much or too little.

"Ask them how they got their wounds, where they're from . . . Ask things and listen. It won't bother them who you are or why you're here."

Unconvinced by this, Tom watched Padmore go with mounting dread. On the mattress nearest him a man was breathing raspingly through cracked parched lips, one arm thrown back in a way that showed ter-rible pain, his leaden eyes staring upward into space. The room was some fifty yards long, and near the far end a man was sitting up, propped against the wall, reading a description of the Alma from an old weekly. His voice was strong and clear and those around him were listening attentively. When he had finished, the paper was handed around and a conversation started, which made Tom wince with em-barrassment.

"Them as writes the words ha'e bin ter war right enough. More than cans't say for the painters."

The speaker, a powerful red-faced man with massive shoulders, and the remains of his right thigh resting on a stained stump pillow, tossed the paper to his neighbor, who looked at it for a moment, his sallow face wrinkling with mirth.

"They think our horses bin fit for nowt but brewers' drays . . ."

"Drays?" cut in a third. "Ours weren't fit ter pull a barrow."

"See here," went on the soldier with the paper, stabbing at it with his thumb, "there's not a smite o' smoke; a battle wi'out smoke . . . Lot o' tomfoolery, isn't it?"

"What can y' expect?" asked the man with the amputated leg. "Damned painters niver come nigher the Rooshans than Brighton beach."

Surreptitiously Tom got out his small sketch pad and with a soft pencil hastily drew a caricature artist, such as *Punch* delighted in: a foppish young man with a comic-opera pointed beard, floppy, broad-brimmed hat and palette in hand standing languidly on a beach beside his easel, peering out to sea through a telescope—on his canvas a half-finished cart-horse pulling a gun. It was a rapid but fluent piece of drawing: the work of three or four minutes. Tom looked at it thoughtfully and added a passing steam tug belching smoke and a small boy gazing critically at the artist's work. Underneath Tom wrote:

Insolent Boy: "Where's the smoke, mister?"

Offended Artist: "Smoke? There's none I can see."

In case some of the men could not read, Tom walked over to the soldier who had been reading the paper aloud and handed him the cartoon, waiting in acute suspense while he examined the drawing. Then the man laughed loudly and, reading out the words for the others, handed it around. A young soldier with a cropped and bandaged head beckoned Tom over to him after he had examined the sketch with dark shrewd eyes.

"Can ye make my picture?" he asked.

"Your portrait?"

The man nodded.

During the next two hours Tom made some twenty quick sketches of men, and time and again was brought close to tears by the gratitude shown for such rough-and-ready work. He asked the sort of questions that Padmore had suggested, and with most who were well enough to talk found that he had no need to say much himself. Once, three corpses sewn up in blankets were carried past from the dead house on their way to burial, but this evidently commonplace occurrence hardly caused a break in the conversation. When supper was ladled out from a vast copper, Tom saw that the meat was doled out solely by weight, so that some men got helpings almost entirely of bone and gristle. Those who did better sometimes gave bits to others less fortunate. Men with scorbutic gums, unable to chew or swallow, sucked their meat to extract the juice, and what they spat out was eaten eagerly by those with healthy mouths. If he were fighting for survival, Tom did not suppose he would be any more fastidious. The thought that most of these maimed men, so resolutely clinging to life, would return home to a life of appalling poverty with little or no hope of improvement made him burn with anger. Before leaving, he made some sketches of the general scene in the ward, and resolved to do more work of this sort for publication, and also more portraits for men to send home to their families.

When Tom returned to Myserri's that evening, his personal unhappiness, which constant work and involvement had kept at bay during the day, returned with undiminished force. The sights he had seen, far from consoling him, or reducing by comparison the significance of his own distress, had merely deepened his depression, making him wonder how he could ever have been naïve enough to suppose that evidence of suffering on such a wide scale could reduce the impact of individual pain. It was true, Padmore had said on their way back, that orderlies could cope best when dealing cursorily with hundreds; but, when charged with responsibility for a few desperately sick men for days at a time, the personal involvement in these individual cases moved them far more deeply and broke their spirits more quickly than work that had daily seen them walking past miles of accumulated pain and misery. In that way, Tom had passed an afternoon with a mere handful, in twenty yards of a single ward, and had been affected, like the orderlies, by the fate of men with names and faces.

*　*　*

Although life in the officers' wards at Scutari was far removed from the stinking hell in which the men were obliged to live, George Braithwaite had found much to complain of, especially when the pain in his arm had ceased to absorb the greater part of his attention. He had formed a mess with ten other officers, but much of the food, which they had paid their orderlies lavish sums to bring over from Stamboul, was pilfered en route, and what they finally ate was often half-cooked or burned. So far all his efforts to obtain a mosquito net to keep the flies off his face had proved unavailing, as had his attempts to get new sheets and bedding; but compared with his loneliness these were minor irritants. True, his father wrote frequently and had dispatched numerous comforts: potted meats, books, a dozen cases of claret, cigars and some stone hot-water bottles—none of which had yet arrived; but the expectation of these good things did not compensate George for a more fundamental privation.

The favorite activity of most of his brother officers was writing to and receiving letters from wives or fiancées—a pleasure denied to George, and one, the lack of which, continually brought to mind his painful failure with Catherine. Immediately after his arrival at Scutari, when too weak to write himself, George had dictated letters to be sent to Magnus and Charles, telling them what had happened to him, in the hope that they would mention his present situation when next writing to their sister, and that this in turn might lead Catherine herself to send a note of commiseration, thus making it possible for him to reply. A correspondence started, he might even succeed in convincing her of the change circumstances had wrought in him.

When thinking about Catherine, George was haunted by a recurrent fear. Remembering the scene he had interrupted in the Statue Gallery at Hanley Park, he did not care to reflect on the fact that Catherine, alone in that vast house, would have ample opportunity to arrange further meetings with Strickland. In fact, on one of the few occasions when he had seen Charles Crawford before Inkerman, George had expressed astonishment that Catherine was not staying with her stepmother at the embassy in Constantinople, suggesting that, since so many eligible young officers dined with Lord Stratford on their way out to the war or returning home, Catherine was being denied an excellent matrimonial opportunity. Charles had not argued but had observed dryly that, given a certain personal antipathy between the two women, such an arrangement would be inappropriate. George had then asked Charles whether he was happy that Catherine had so much freedom. To his amazement, when he had gone on lightly to allude to his former suspicions of Strickland, Crawford had become furiously angry, dismissing the idea with abusive contempt. So distressed had George been that, until receiving a letter of condolence from Charles, he had feared his friendly relations with Crawford to be at an end.

As soon as George had been strong enough to walk unassisted, he had taken to visiting men from his regiment in different parts of the barrack hospital, offering to try to secure extra comforts and in several cases writing to his father, asking him to employ wounded men on his estate.

On a bitter morning in the first week in December, George was returning to his own ward after such a visit, considerably upset that a corporal from his company, for whom he had brought a game pie and a port-wine jelly, had died during the previous night. Walking through the neighboring ward, George had passed a group of men examining something; on moving closer, George saw that they were admiring a drawing, an admirably executed sketch of one of them. Surprised to find such talent among common soldiers, he asked the artist's name, and was disappointed to hear that he had been a civilian. No longer feeling the same interest in the sketch, George nevertheless felt obliged to show some enthusiasm when it was held up for his scrutiny. Glancing at it, a mild curiosity led him to look at the signature, and, with a sudden shock, he made out the name: *Thomas Strickland.*

That evening, feeling guilty that he had misjudged Strickland, and greatly relieved that his suspicions had evidently been mistaken, George wrote to Charles Crawford, describing the extent of his recovery and relaying general news about the state of affairs in the hospital. In a postscript he apologized for having linked Catherine's name with Strickland's. If she had been seeing the man, she could not be doing so anymore, since the artist was at present staying in Constantinople.

⤸ Forty-Five ⤹

Squinting along the line of sight, Humphrey could feel the heat of the 32-pounder's massive iron barrel scorching his cheek, but he did not move from his task until he saw, through the pall of white smoke hanging over the opposing batteries, a small bright jet of flame. Provided with this mark to train on, he raised his head and called out to the gun's No. 1,

"With two handspikes muzzle right three inches."

Then, hurrying on to the second of his three guns, he gave similar orders; reckoning his third to be pointing true, he left its line unchanged. Immediately after his No. 1's reported back, "Ready," Humphrey shouted, "Fire!" covering his ears before the lanyards jerked down the detonating hammers. A split second and the platforms danced and shuddered underfoot, the shock waves from the reports thumping his chest with the force of physical blows.

"Stop the vent and sponge!" he cried, still reeling, eyes smarting and ears ringing. Through the powder smoke he saw his men sponging, and ramming home the fresh charge, then, staggering slightly, he bent once more to the trigger line and neck ring, watching tensely for the answering flash. When none came from the same point, he chose a new mark to train on.

For two days the naval batteries had been exchanging fire with the Quarries, a recently established Russian battery which owed its name to its cleverly concealed position among the mounds of waste from a disused gravel pit. This new emplacement was not only closer to the allied lines than any other enemy battery—so enabling Russian sharpshooters to pick off men passing by the embrasures in the British batteries—but also lay directly in the path of any future assault on the principal enemy bastions behind it. Since a prolonged shelling had not yet persuaded the

Russian gunners to withdraw, it was widely assumed that the position would have to be stormed with inevitable heavy loss of life.

On this, the second day of constant firing, Humphrey had been surprised and relieved to discover that terror, like other powerful emotions, did not last long at the same level of intensity, and, although likely to return in sharp, bowel-loosening spasms with the approach of well-flighted shells or the infliction of a ghastly wound, it would recede again under constant pressure of laying guns, pointing them and checking that his exhausted crews always entered the shells correctly, fuses outward with the correct charges. Although Humphrey was responsible for three guns only, in a battery mounting twenty-seven, he was rarely without an immediate task to attend to.

As the morning brightened, a light wind began to clear the smoke, making it possible to see the effects of the firing. Now, instead of watching for flashes, Humphrey was able to direct his guns from the raised banquette, observing through a telescope where the shots fell, shouting out, "Twenty short . . . fifteen left!" or whatever most precisely described the point of impact. A man standing on the banquette was partially exposed, but Humphrey felt far safer when he could see the Russian positions. Often after a perfect shot, fired right into an embrasure, he found himself wondering what his father would have thought, had he ever lived to see his milksop son, who had rarely been able to hit a partridge on the wing, engaged in sending 8-inch shells and 32-pound shot with deadly aim into an enemy battery. Such thoughts left him feeling both proud and sad. But although sure that his bearing under fire would have met with his father's wholehearted approval, Humphrey had noticed few alterations in Charles's formal coldness.

Three or four days after Charles had assumed command in the batteries, a mortar shell had crashed down on the sandbagged roof of the magazine, setting the sacking alight. There had been six feet of earth, timber and sandbags between the flames and the powder, but the sight had momentarily paralyzed everybody, until Humphrey had jumped up and started stamping out the fire; a moment later he had heard somebody behind him, and had looked around to see Charles helping, his eyes dark with anger, not directed at him, but at the men who had watched a boy do what they should themselves have done. Later, after only the briefest words of commendation, Charles had taken Humphrey aside and told him that, in future, if tempted to risk his life on a sudden impulse, he should remember that there would be many occasions, unlike the one just past, when the least dramatic course of action would be the best to pursue. An officer who lived longest always served his country best. "Bravery without discretion, my lord, is as much use as modesty without clothes." Still greatly admiring Charles, Humphrey had been deeply wounded by what he took for a rebuke. Especially since, the week before, Charles had picked up a shell, its fuse still burning, and had rolled it over the parapet into the ditch where it had instantly burst—an action undoubtedly saving lives, but one which had involved a risk many times greater than any to be encountered stamping out flames on the magazine roof. Humphrey was also hurt and perplexed that Charles, after being more friendly, had recently become as cold as ever.

Having loudly cheered a shot, which had lifted an enemy gun clean off its carriage, Humphrey heard the lookout yell, "Mortar right!" and, flinging himself to the ground from the banquette, heard the sharp whistling of the revolving shell rise to a piercing, tearing shriek. With a deep, earth-splitting roar a section of the parapet vanished in a red-black inferno of spouting soil and stones. In the choking dust, Humphrey saw a powderman's arm hanging by his side, shattered from wrist to elbow; an assistant sponger had been killed outright, almost torn in two pieces. Seeing the fierce bright flow of the dead man's blood, Humphrey vomited and sank to his knees; but, as usual, within minutes of such an escape, relief soon outweighed shock and horror. An officer gave him some watered rum, and by the time the stretchers had left the battery, everybody's spirits had started to rise again, as they latched onto inconsequential things to laugh about—anything unrelated to the incident. This soothing collective forgetfulness recurred after every casualty. Whenever obliged to leave his guns, Humphrey took deliberate care to avoid catching sight of the already darkening stains—just as, when a child, he had denied the power of a frightening picture in a book by averting his eyes, or slamming it tight shut. To a greater or lesser extent, every man present survived by doing the same.

*   *   *

Charles rode past the artillery depot, and, dismounting near the Light Division's camp, tethered his pony and squelched through the mud toward a huddle of tents and huts erected near the wall of the engineers' siege park. Here on the heights, the rumble of gunfire from the batteries echoed and reverberated like distant thunder, at times sounding deceptively close.

The shelter Charles made for was neither hut nor tent, but resembled the skillfully improvised structures put up by the Turks, having low stone walls, banked up with earth, and a crude but effective roof of planks, brushwood and clay, covered over with skins and tarpaulins. Thrusting aside the canvas door flap, Charles fumbled with a box of lucifer matches in the windowless gloom, and lit a candle stuck to the top of an empty ammunition box. Then he sat down on the bed, a straw-filled mattress resting on an old door, raised off the mud floor on wooden chocks. The bedclothes consisted of a filthy quilt and a matted sheepskin. Next to the bed, a large, black tin chest, balanced on two casks, evidently served as a writing table; on its lid stood a brass candlestick, an inkpot and a mess of papers. On another empty meat cask was a cracked mirror, a razor and a broken horn comb full of greasy-looking hair. Two threadbare Turkish carpets had been nailed to the walls to keep out the drafts. Charles shifted his position to take out his watch, dislodging as he did so a pyramid of empty bottles at the foot of the bed. After passing five minutes inside, he went out again and paced up and down impatiently.

Charles had visited Magnus's hut for the first time on the day before the start of the bombardment, but, having failed to find his brother, had left him a note asking him to be there at ten o'clock two days later. It was now nearly twenty-past ten, and Charles did not have unlimited time to spare, since his turn of duty in the batteries began at noon. On the previous day he had spent sixteen hours under fire and afterward the tautness of his nerves and a painfully throbbing head had kept him awake most of the night. Feeling as he did next morning, Charles would normally have gone to any lengths to avoid seeing his brother, but the arrival of George Braithwaite's letter had left him in a state of such perplexity that he looked upon the coming interview as an absolute necessity.

When a disheveled and bearded figure appeared, plodding up toward him from the direction of Balaclava, Charles did not at first recognize his brother until he was some twenty yards away. Their only meeting since Magnus's arrival in the Crimea had been a chance encounter on the col—a brief and ill-tempered affair, since Charles had thought it all but certain that his brother's sole motive in coming out was to embarrass his father.

Before going into the hut, they shook hands with awkward formality; and as their eyes met, Charles was once more shaken by his inability to hazard even an imprecise guess as to what Magnus might be thinking, a failure which at once made Charles feel uneasy and defensive. Inside, Magnus lit more candles and poured some Madeira into a couple of chipped cups; having taken his, Charles handed his brother George's letter without comment, except for a thumb marking the relevant paragraph. Magnus read it without apparent interest or surprise. Charles watched him intently, wishing that there was a window in the hut so that he could note his expressions better.

"Did you know Strickland was in Turkey?"

"No."

"Does it not surprise you?" snapped Charles. Magnus drained his cup, and moving, Charles thought, with exaggerated slowness, poured himself more Madeira and held out the bottle to him.

"I asked a question," returned Charles, covering his cup with his hand.

"You did. The answer is, no. I am not surprised."

"How so?"

"Because I suggested he come out with me as a war artist."

"But he didn't."

Magnus got up and offered Charles a cigar, which he declined.

"That's right. He obviously changed his mind later." Magnus smiled. "Not everybody's as decisive as you, Charles."

"George seems to think he's been in Stamboul for some time."

Magnus bit the end off a cigar and removed a few strands of tobacco from his lips.

"I doubt that. Otherwise he'd have sailed with me."

Charles leaned forward and said with emphasis,

"He seems to have preferred to be alone there."

"That's certainly possible."

"What reason did he give for rejecting your suggestion?"

"Professional pride."

"What?"

Magnus laughed at Charles's confusion.

"Artists can be very fastidious. He thought it would be hack work."

"Strange that he changed his mind. War doesn't alter much."

Magnus lit his cigar with a candle, puffing and sucking slowly to make it burn evenly. His expression softened.

"I can't help you, Charles. Perhaps he went to Turkey to see Helen, perhaps he didn't. If he did, I can't understand why he should have waited so many months."

"He waited until Father had sailed for Sevastopol."

"You could be right."

"And that's all you have to say?"

"With men dying like flies, I have to admit that the thought of a few embassy attachés sniggering at Father's expense doesn't pose an immediate threat to my sanity. Obviously I'd rather it didn't reach his ears, but I should imagine Helen will do her best to see that it doesn't."

Charles got up and lifted the flap. Magnus followed him out into the open. The guns were still firing. Charles straightened his sword belt and sighed.

"Couldn't stand it in there. I'm sorry." He turned to Magnus with sad, careworn eyes. "I know we all have other things to think of. It isn't all fun in the batteries at the moment. . . . I know you don't understand Father's feelings for her, but you ought to try. If there's any sort of scandal the humiliation would finish him, and I don't mean his career." A ragged company of men were marching from the Light Division's camp in the direction of the trenches, their boots making no sound on the damp earth. Over the brown treeless plateau the sky was darkening with a definite hint of sleet or snow. Charles looked at Magnus imploringly.

"Couldn't you go to Stamboul for a few days . . . write something about the hospitals so your time's not wasted. Do that and talk to Strickland. I'm in no position to go."

"Suppose I go," murmured Magnus, "and suppose he tells me he's seeing her, do you really expect me to tell you? You'd never betray a friend's trust, so you can't expect me to."

"Then I'll have to go to Father. I can't leave him to find out through casual rumors."

"You may be wrong."

"How can I be? One week he refuses to come with you and the next promptly changes his mind when he knows the fleet's sailed. Did Catherine tell you he once went looking for Helen at Hanley Park?"

"Why not wait till he gets here? He's sure to arrive in a week or so. Talk to him then. He'll tell the truth."

"And betray her?"

"Why not? If you wanted more than a casual flirtation with a married woman, wouldn't it serve your interest if her husband cast her off? He's nothing to lose, no position to protect."

While Charles considered this, Magnus blew on his fingers to warm them.

"It won't do, Magnus. All you've proved is that neither of us would know whether he was telling the truth. The plain fact is that I ought to have told Father months ago and was a coward not to."

"Wait, Charles."

"There'd be no point. You can't even be sure Strickland's coming out here."

"And you can't know whether Father will ever hear anything."

As Charles walked toward his tethered pony, Magnus went on gently, "Before you do what you spoke of, you ought to ask yourself whether it's because you hate Helen, or care for Father."

"I don't have to ask myself that," replied Charles, as he mounted.

Magnus watched his brother for a few seconds and then walked slowly back to his hut.

*   *   *

When Charles stepped into the brigade's No. 2 Battery, shortly before midday, he hoped that the constant activity there, and the tense, almost claustrophobic atmosphere of suspense and fear, would divert his thoughts; but, almost immediately he was aware of Humphrey's piping unbroken voice rising above the crash of the guns and the roar of the trucks on the platforms, and noticed the smiles of the gunners: not smiles of condescension but of admiration for the dash and high spirits of their youngest officer. Charles could easily understand their feelings. The sight of a slender boy, with flushed powder-stained cheeks and long fair hair curling about his temples, striving all the time to make his voice sound gruffer and lower than it was, made men twice his age feel that war could not after all be so terrible if a young aristocrat, straight from his mother's care, could endure it so readily. As Charles thought of what he had finally decided upon, during his conversation with Magnus, his heart was torn with pity for the boy.

Humphrey was calling out the positions of shots, steadying his right hand, holding a telescope, on the muzzle of an 8-inch gun not in action, and his left on the shoulder of John Crawley, first class boy. Charles had been surprised from the outset by Crawley's immediate devotion to a youth two years younger than himself, with prospects so entirely different from his own, and one moreover who had replaced him as youngest sailor and darling of the battery. Humphrey's other most devoted follower was Daniel Pascoe, a massive, barrel-chested man, a tin miner before joining the service and now undoubtedly the best No. 1 in the battery.

As Charles watched, Pascoe was priming the gun whose shots Humphrey was observing. A man was handing around grog to the gun crews out of action. When Crawley was offered the pannikin, he asked Humphrey to move his elbow, so that the telescope was not jogged while he drank. As Crawley stood up to drink, Pascoe fired his gun, and the shock made the boy spill most of his precious grog down his monkey jacket. Humphrey was laughing at Crawley's grimace of displeasure when he heard the whoosh of a round shot, and, too late to yell a warning, saw the flashing iron decapitate his friend, hurling his headless body to the ground at his feet.

Since Humphrey was plastered with blood and brains, Charles thought that he too had been hit, but, seeing him move, enjoyed only momentary relief; with an electrifying shock he took in the fact that at the very moment Crawley had died, Pascoe had been stopping the cannon's vent. Like Humphrey, Pascoe was red from head to waist with the contents of the boy's skull; if he moved his finger from the vent, even for a moment, Charles knew that the current of air admitted would fan to life any sparks remaining in the barrel after the previous firing, thus igniting the fresh cartridge and killing the loader and sponger then "ramming home." Charles leaped forward, but Pascoe did not flinch. Keeping one hand firmly on the vent, he calmly wiped the brains from his eyes with the other and shouted to the loader,

"Are you home, Bill?"

"Yes."

"Run out then."

The crews strained at the side tackles, and when No. 2 cried, "Ready!" Pascoe jerked the firing lanyard sharply.

The silence following the report was broken by Humphrey's hysterical sobbing. A number of men were standing gazing at Crawley's bleeding trunk as if mesmerized.

"What the hell are you looking at?" shouted Charles. "If he's dead take him away." Then he led Humphrey back to the shelter of the traverse screening the entrance to the magazine. He stood for a while with an arm around the boy's shaking shoulders, while deep choking sobs wracked his thin body. Another round shot thudded into the parapet showering the battery with flying earth and dust. When Humphrey seemed a little calmer, Charles said gently,

"Go up to the camp and tell Commander Chapman to bring down his crews at six bells and not at eight."

"A seaman should do that."

"I want *you* to."

"I'll stay."

"I'm ordering you, Humphrey. Then go to the right siege train magazine and find out how many rounds we're likely to get tomorrow."

"I'm all right," murmured the boy, immediately starting to sob again.

Several minutes later, Charles dipped a handkerchief into a tub of water and handed it to him. Still shocked and dazed, Humphrey took the cloth without seeming to know what to do with it.

"Your face," whispered Charles, looking at the thick dark clots drying on his cheeks.

Half an hour after Humphrey's departure, Charles was still upset by Crawley's grisly death and Humphrey's grief. He longed to be able to get away from the dust and smoke, and the crash of the guns so that he could wrestle with his now violently conflicting emotions.

Ten minutes earlier he had sent up to the main magazine in the rear for more powder, and, seeing the first cart arrive, he went over at once to supervise the unloading. As he began giving orders, he saw a round shot smash the wheels and rear axle of the following cart, pitching its lethal load onto the ground in full view of the Russian gunners in the

Redan. A glance was enough to tell him that there were at least two dozen of the zinc-lined hundredweight boxes out there, enough powder, if hit, to send up half the battery. A second later a shell crashed down onto an araba heaped with 68-pound shot, tossing the heavy iron balls high into the air, as if no more substantial than a child's marbles. Another mortar bomb struck a mule full in the chest, and, exploding, ignited the powder kegs roped to the animal's flanks, hurling the disintegrating carcass thirty yards to the right, showering the surrounding ground with shredded flesh. In an instant Charles made up his mind not to give a direct order to a junior officer to bring in the hundredweight boxes with his gun crews, but called for volunteers. When none stepped forward, Charles roared,

"Come on, Daniel Pascoe, the devil looks after his own!" and, without looking back, ran out into the hail of shell and shot falling around the ammunition boxes. As soon as Charles and Pascoe had sprinted from the shelter of the parapet, a dozen others streamed after them, and the powder was quickly brought to safety at the cost of one man being wounded.

Afterward, still panting, Charles sat with his back to a traverse, feeling his entire body suffused with a delicious throbbing weakness—a sensation as pleasurable as any he had ever known—his quiescent limbs tingling after the brief burst of violent physical exertion. Waves of relief lapped through him after the ending of the nerve-splitting tension. He breathed deeply, enjoying the memory of that gasping dash through the bouquets of flame, relishing the feeling of the sweat growing cold on his face; he felt exhausted but complete, fulfilled, almost wishing to live through the same danger again.

But the afterglow faded quickly. Why had he asked for volunteers instead of issuing a peremptory order? Had it really been because he had feared resistance, which would have damaged discipline and morale? Or because he had known all along that none would come forward and that he would therefore be able to shame his officers and men by going himself?

Some officers gained a loyalty based on affection, but he had never been able to do that. Instead he had learned to rule by exacting a forced respect bordering on fear and resentment. It had taken him years to acquire the necessary self-discipline. As a midshipman at the storming of Sidon, fifteen years before, he had led twenty marines across a bridge enfiladed by a battery of six guns; his men had hesitated, but, although terrified himself, he had gone on, and, when a shot had thrown up a cloud of dust just in front of him, he had stopped, and, coolly pulling a handkerchief from his pocket, had dusted his boots before waving on his marines.

Charles clambered slowly to his feet and stepped up onto the banquette. As he gazed through the smoke toward the broken, shell-pitted ground in front of the Quarries, the last vestiges of his elation ebbed away. The thunderous detonation of the guns jarred his ears and dulled his mind. A shell burst thirty yards short of the ditch but he did not move. In a few days the Quarries would be stormed; he was sure of that. Perhaps the Naval Brigade would take part, perhaps not. He felt an icy detachment; others would make that decision and he would merely carry out orders.

In one way he was glad. The coming attack made it far easier for him to tell his father about Helen's betrayal, since its imminence compelled him to act without delay—a few days and death might stop his mouth forever. The thought buttressed his resolve. Through courage his father would survive the truth—if not, to live in despair would be better than to remain a lascivious woman's fool. With time, Humphrey would forget his mother's disgrace. Time and courage would save them. Nothing would save the first men to stumble up the slope beneath the Quarries.

～ *Forty-Six* ～

Because of its elevated situation on the cliffs midway between the French and British supply ports at Kamiesch Bay and Balaclava, the Russian Orthodox monastery of St. George had been occupied by the allies within days of their arrival south of Sevastopol as an ideal headquarters from which to concert operations involving the combined fleets and armies of both nations. But with the fleets doing little more than blockading, councils of war had become purely military and had therefore taken place more often at Lord Raglan's or General Canrobert's inland headquarters. On 18 December, however, St. George's was once more the setting for an important conference attended by senior officers from both services.

At noon the same day, Charles Crawford received a note from his father asking him to come to the monastery. In conclusion, the admiral wrote,

> I am sending by the bearer of this message a request to Commodore Lushington enjoining him to see (other duties notwithstanding) that you are free to come. I make no apology for the lack of prior warning since the matters I wish to acquaint you with were not finally resolved until this morning.

At no time during the three days since his conversation with his brother had Charles been able to get away from the batteries for long enough to go to Balaclava and from there to *Retribution*'s anchorage. Yet although his father's note now spared him that inconvenience, Charles was far from certain that he was pleased. During his brief periods away from the pandemonium of the batteries, his former *sang-froid* about revealing Helen's behavior had given way to acute anxiety. While such a disclosure might be accepted philosophically enough by a man with shells bursting around him, it would be most unlikely to strike an admiral living in enforced idleness on an anchored warship in the same mercifully distanced light.

By midafternoon Charles's pony was picking his way between the jagged rocks and loose stones littering the precipitous track leading from the camps to the monastery. Below him on the far side of a marshy valley, Charles could see the blue and gilt dome of the monastery chapel, framed by the dark leafless branches of the surrounding trees and the lead-gray sea beyond. With mounting nausea at the thought of the brutal disillusionment awaiting his father, he rode on across flatter ground dotted with broken vine stumps.

Challenged by the Zouaves on sentry duty outside the main archway, Charles showed his pass and was admitted to a large courtyard. To the right was a low block containing the monks' cells, and next to it a two-storied house flanked by rhododendrons and myrtles. In front of the vine-covered colonnade the Tricolor and Union Jack were flying from neighboring flagstaffs. Only the archimandrite and a dozen other monks out of the hundred-strong community had remained after the allied landings, and now the tall stovepipe hats and black robes of these bizarre prisoners of war contrasted strangely with the more numerous military uniforms.

Since the council of war was still in progress, Charles was taken by an ADC to a room where he was expected to wait. The walls were white-washed and a bright coal fire was burning in the grate. Beside the single recessed window hung a small icon. Charles sat down on a carved oak chair.

*　*　*

By four in the afternoon, the arguments for and against a full-scale assault on the Quarries had been resolved in favor of immediate attack —Lord Raglan as usual giving in to the French generals for the sake of the alliance. Sir James Crawford appreciated his dilemma very well. After the British Army's catastrophic losses at Inkerman, there had always been a real risk that the French, with their greater numbers, would act independently, and so cause furious indignation in London.

Sir James and Admiral Lyons—the new naval commander-in-chief— had learned from Raglan before the conference started that they would be asked to authorize the Naval Brigade's participation if the French were to press for an assault. Knowing too, from an earlier conversation with Lushington, that Charles would be picked to command any naval contingent committed to an attack, Sir James had summoned his son to tell him in person. His own view was that the Quarries would be taken, but not held long enough for the storming party to throw up new parapets—vital not only for successful resistance of counterattacks, but also as cover from the heavy guns in the Redan. Whatever the outcome, the casualties would not be light.

When Sir James, along with others, had voiced this fear, General Pélissier—the French second-in-command—had murmured to Lord Raglan, "On ne peut pas faire des omelettes sans casser des oeufs." Since Charles was likely to be one of the eggs, Sir James had not relished the analogy. It was as well that he had other preoccupations besides his son's probable fate. During the morning session of the conference he had at last gained support for a venture of his own, one in his opinion likely to have a greater impact on the course of the war than the capture of the Quarries.

In the earlier more optimistic days of the campaign, Sir James's plan for a naval raid on the narrow isthmuses connecting the Crimean peninsula with the Russian mainland had been rejected by Admiral Dundas. With Sevastopol expected to fall within weeks, an exceptionally hazardous attack on the town's military supply routes had held scant appeal —especially since only one of the two essential roads could be reached by water, and even then by no vessels larger than paddle sloops, corvettes and gunboats. To cut this road, at the point where a long wooden bridge linked two spits of land, these small ships would have to enter the inland Sea of Azov and then navigate a shallow channel under the guns of powerful shore batteries. If the squadron succeeded, all the grain at present reaching Sevastopol from the east would be delayed for two to three weeks, causing the defenders of the town as much hardship as a bombardment of similar duration. After approving the operation, the allied admirals had lost little time in choosing a flag officer to command the squadron.

As commander-in-chief, Lyons could not appropriately transfer his flag to a ship in a small detached squadron; nor, given the French fleet's deficiency in shallow-draft steamships, could either of the French ad-

mirals advance a claim. Rear Admiral Sir James Crawford, the author
of the plan, had been their inevitable choice.

*   *   *

With nothing more to divert him than the chimes of the monastery
bells and the harsh echoing tramp of the sentry's boots passing and
repassing outside the window, Charles's nerves were badly strained by
the time his father made his appearance. Sir James's troubled and sympathetic eyes made Charles's heart sink within him when he thought of
what he had to say. The admiral stared into the fire and said softly,

"There's to be an attack on the Quarries. You must know why I
asked to see you?"

"How many men will I be leading?" asked Charles after a brief
pause.

"Two hundred. The brigade will be providing the ladder parties. Five
thousand men will be attacking the Quarries and two thousand more
used in diversionary sorties. I'm afraid it'll be a hard business."

Charles could imagine clearly how it would be—the shouting, men
falling, the crash of gunfire. In recent days he had thought of the assault
so often that at times he could hardly believe that something so vivid in
his mind had not already happened. He shrugged his shoulders.

"It won't be worse than Inkerman."

After this matter-of-fact reply, his father said in a thick emotional
voice,

"You mustn't think the choice had anything to do with me. That was
Lushington's doing." He put down his cocked hat on the chair Charles
had vacated and sighed. "At least there'll be no question of Humphrey
being in on this. I've never known such anxiety as during this bombardment. Never."

"Three weeks and he'll be back with the fleet."

"And you too, Charles."

"Me too," he murmured, painfully conscious of the doubts underlying
his father's confident tone. He braced himself to tell him in the heavy
silence that followed, but drew back, unable to speak until Sir James
was less bowed down. When he is more composed, not thinking about
the war or death . . . tell him then.

At first when his father began talking about an expedition to destroy the Tchongar Bridge on the eastern military road, Charles listened only fitfully, supposing it to be some distant project: a device to set them both thinking about the time after the attack on the Quarries; and because Charles wanted to draw his father's thoughts away from that area, he was glad to encourage this new topic. After this is finished, he told himself, I will say what I must; but wanting to delay a little longer, he began to ask questions. Yes, a squadron might pass undetected into the Sea of Azov, but how could it possibly enter the approaches to the bridge in the same way? The channel at Genichesk was barely a hundred yards across. Even the most ineffectual batteries could inflict terrible damage on ships trying to force the straits. Wasn't there a risk too that the shallow water in the area of the bridge would already be frozen over? In any case the operation would involve landings from ships' boats and an overland march to the target.

Charles himself had often thought of methods for interrupting Russian supplies and so knew the difficulties well; but as he listened to his father's detailed answers to his questions and noted suppressed excitement breaking through the calm surface of his speech, Charles felt his heart begin to pound.

"When do you sail?" he asked in a numb small voice.

"Four days."

"Four days?" he cried. "Assemble your marines, equip the boats, give orders to the commanders of the escort ships . . . in four days?"

"I think the officers of a navy that landed thirty thousand men at Kalamita Bay can manage it."

Charles knew that he should show excitement, should say that the plan was excellent, inspired—that it presented a chance for distinction that few flag officers ever dared hope for—that the prize far outweighed the danger—that . . . But Charles found himself unable to say a word. How could he speak of Helen now and thus mar what could well be his last meeting with his father? He might die at the Quarries, his father under the batteries at Genichesk. And, if his father were to die, what futility it would then prove to have told him needlessly. Yet matters might fall out quite differently; Charles himself might be killed and his father survive, to learn from others that his favorite son had known of his wife's betrayal but had deliberately concealed it from him. His mind a tumult of doubts, Charles forced himself to think. The attack on the

Quarries was set for dawn on New Year's Day. His father could have returned by then, assuming that Genichesk could be reached in three days under steam; but there were many imponderables, perhaps too many.

Seeing the expression of dismay and sadness on his son's face, Sir James felt keen pangs of sympathy. He himself dreaded the possibility of returning from the Sea of Azov to find Charles dead, and knew that Charles would be feeling similar fears for his safety; and he thought, how typical of Charles to shrug off his own peril so lightly, and then to be plunged into a black depression because I face an equivalent risk. Wanting badly to tell Charles how he admired him for this, Sir James could not find the words. For years they had been bedeviled by this same incapacity, their mutual affection only hinted at by looks and gestures, by what was left unsaid rather than by what was openly admitted. And after every failure, Sir James had told himself that next time he would finally break the barrier of reserve and reticence which they had allowed their own natures and the traditions of their service to impose upon them. But in the past there had always been the promise of future occasions on which to achieve this closeness. And now? Sir James asked himself. And now? A brief silence.

"Do you remember, ever so many years ago," Sir James began hesitantly, "how we walked around looking at the ships building in the Gosport yards before your exam?"

"I hardly saw a thing," murmured Charles, with the ghost of a smile.

"Then it was my turn to get into a state—though God knows I'd told you a thousand times there'd just be some simple dictation and a few rule-of-three sums; but you wouldn't have it."

"I thought they'd slip in some Euclid or something quite beyond me."

"There I was pacing about waiting for you to come out ages after all the other boys had finished."

"I checked everything twice."

"I should have known . . . Oh, dear, such years ago." Sir James reached out and took Charles's arm. "You remember the journey? All the way I was thinking of how I first came down by coach on that same road when I'd been on my way to sit the exam, and now it was you. I remembered my own feelings so vividly, my father beside me, just as I was next to you and I couldn't believe the time had gone . . ."

Sir James paused hopelessly, knowing that he had utterly failed to convey what he had tried to put into words: the long dusty journey and the sense of personal loss at the memory of his own departed boyhood, all this added to his protective longing to delay his twelve-year-old son's entrance into that harsh austere world of ships and men. The evening before Charles had gone aboard his first ship, they had dined with the port admiral, Charles immoderately proud of his new uniform, and Sir James remembered so clearly the precise expression of fury and dismay on his face, when, after the cloth had been removed, Lady Erskine had taken him out with the ladies. Sir James still felt a blush of embarrassment that he had not asked that he should be allowed to stay. Then next day, after a night at the George, they had taken the boy's chest, bedding and carpetbag to the Sally Port and gone out to *Electra* in Talbot's gig. Poor boy, he held up so well all the way out in the boat, but the handshake on the main deck had been the last straw; to spare him, Sir James had gone straight down into the gig before saying anything he had meant to, but as they shoved off and pulled away from *Electra*, he had seen Charles running aft on the upper deck to cry on his own. Sir James found himself blushing fiercely as he said,

"Lord, how I wept on the way back to the Hard when I'd left you. I never landed with such a heavy heart and touch wood haven't done since."

He saw Charles looking at him with bewilderment.

"You never told me that before."

"No, no, I didn't. So many things we never say." Sir James was horrified by the pain these last few words seemed to cause Charles.

A few minutes later they walked out under the colonnade and crossed a terrace bordered on one side by acacia trees. The light was fading fast but they could see below them the steep fall of the cliffs, and, at their base, jutting from the dark water, tall, fantastically shaped rocks. A little to their right the monks had cut terraces into the cliff face and made gardens there, planted with vines and shrubs; from the lowest terrace a zigzag path led down to a small pebbly beach. The air was windless but very cold. From the chapel came the sound of singing; the monks were at vespers. Turning, Sir James saw a glimmer of candlelight and reflected gold from the icons under the darkened porch. A single strong bass voice seemed to hang and linger in the air after the rest had stopped. He found himself both moved and troubled by the feeling the sound had evoked. Beneath them the tall black rocks, symbols both of permanence and of a lost faith, within their core, fossils innumerable proving . . . he knew not what precisely, except that the Bible, that onetime cornerstone of his belief, was now cracked and chipped by the geologist's remorseless hammers, and scratched by the pens of scholars challenging the truth of the New Testament itself. Remembering his own father's certainty, Sir James felt a passionate longing to share it still, to say with him that any man who does his duty and trusts in God need fear no danger; do what you can as well as you can, and let the rest remain with Him. But now he could not; and those simple words, once so reassuring, held no comfort. People say that this war is different because of the journalists, the Minié rifle, a steam navy and the overland telegraph, but these are small changes. This war is different, truly different, he thought, because of the weakening of belief; because men's attitudes to war itself are governed by their faith, or lack of faith, in immortality. The war's true terror lay, not in the Lancaster's rifled barrel and the moorsom shell, but in the sense that death, under an empty heaven, in an indifferent universe, was final.

Yet looking out across the darkening sea, he found some comfort; if that were so, it had been always so, whatever men had believed. Seeing Charles's despondent face, he longed to console him. If death comes to all, soon or late, he thought, the manner of it may not be so unimportant, since it is the only embellishment a man can give to its inevitable coming; and as this thought formed, some lines of Browning came back to him, and turning, he said them out loud,

> "I would hate that death bandaged my eyes, and forebore,
> And bade me creep past."

Even before coming out onto the terrace, Charles had known that he could not tell him; and, as they rode together part of the way toward the Balaclava col, he felt more lighthearted. His father also seemed less burdened, and during their remaining time together he repeated an artillery officer's explanation of why so few men were killed by shells, bursting even within six feet of them. Because their bodies exposed no more than eight square feet in all, their chances of being struck were as eight to one-tenth of the surface of a sphere in square feet of six feet radius: or in layman's language, chances of seven to one in favor of escape. They laughed because Sir James was sure that he had got it wrong, but had tried to remember the gist of it as some consolation during the bombardment. Charles said,

"I wonder what happened to the artillery officer?"

But Sir James merely shrugged his shoulders and smiled. At the top of the col they shook hands and parted without tears, both remembering that other parting on *Electra*'s deck so long ago. As Sir James reached a sharp descent where the track turned, he called back,

"God bless you, God bless you, Charles."

❧ Forty-Seven ❧

He had arrived at Balaclava under an inky sky, pierced here and there by narrow shafts of white light, where the booming northeaster had torn ragged holes in the heavy clouds. Above the harbor, the cliffs and hills were black, brown and gray, as if rinsed of all warmer colors by the storm; but Tom was not displeased by his first sight of this somber landscape, since it so well accorded with his mood. Whether the grief he had known in Turkey had been worse than the emptiness he now felt, Tom could not judge, since the occasional stabs of active pain he still suffered came with an almost retrospective feel, like the sharp twinges a man "imagines" in a limb already hacked away. But at these moments, his mood was angry as well as leaden. The knowledge that she had truly loved him, and probably still did, had not, as he had expected, brought peace of mind but a deeper hopelessness.

Few men, passing for the first time under the overhanging sterns of the ships moored along the wharves, found consolation in the sights and smells around them, but Tom was relieved to be where he was. Here at least, at the war, among these thin, gray-faced men in their patched and filthy uniforms, there would be no room for "High Art's" heroic themes. Among the men of a devastated army, Tom thought his inner desolation would serve him well in his task.

Confronted with scenes such as those he had already witnessed at Scutari, and feeling as he did, he would not be tempted to impose lofty sentiment or add elevating moral tags to his subjects. Let other artists back in England paint men with clean hands and faces, writing letters by a campfire's light, entitled *Thoughts of Home*, or companion pictures of *A Soldier's Death* and *A Widow's Sorrow*—this last selling in thousands as a print: the young woman gazing with tearful but beatific eyes at her husband's last letter, sword, epaulets and lock of hair, sent home from

UNTIL THE COLORS FADE   **449**

the fatal battlefield; no anger at a life thrown away, no haggard, grief-contorted face, but an expression of sorrowful and yet proud acceptance of a death so noble.

For him, Tom reflected, a brief flirtation with improving themes was over. If assuring him of no other benefit, his personal emptiness would save him from false sentiment. He would not portray heroes fighting for Queen and Country, but merely men killing other men, some shooting, others being shot. That would be all. No more for him "High Art's" agonizing imperative: to make a picture say and be more than a literal presentation of certain facts. For scenes of war, there should be no artist's interpretation, however morally impeccable, between the beholder and these facts. He should be given nothing more. Why should he be, when there was nothing else to give?

On his first night in the Crimea, Tom slept under the table in a cramped cabin used as an office by the assistant agent for transports. Next day he intended to make other arrangements. One more brush with the past was inevitable: he would have to visit Magnus, rather than be sought out by him; but with Magnus, as with all Crawfords, Goodchilds and Braithwaites, the future demanded, if not an absolute severance, at least a new distance and detachment. Never again could he allow himself to depend upon Magnus's help. A new life, even if it were to be an empty one, required that caution.

* * *

After several days of high wind and sleet, Magnus woke to see a clear sky and the plateau bathed in soft sunlight. The air was sharp and cold, and the puddles around his hut still frozen. After lighting a small fire to boil some water, he pulled his sheepskin blanket around him and lay down with a flat stone for a pillow, enjoying the smell of woodsmoke and the sound of the larks overhead. Far away, two guns were firing at each other at lengthy intervals, like talkers involved in a dull conversation, demanding no heated or urgent replies, their occasional thudding making the intervening stillness seem more pleasantly tranquil than on mornings of unbroken silence. From the Light Division's camp, away to his right, blue wisps of smoke from breakfast fires curled upward in slow spirals. By the time the water on his own fire was boiling, Magnus had started to doze.

On hearing his name, he opened his eyes and saw Tom looking down at him; the pan of water had slipped down, extinguishing part of the fire. He jumped up, and still slightly dazed, clasped his friend's hands, and began asking him about his journey: when he had arrived, where he had spent the night, what his work would involve, how long it would take and many other questions. Had he eaten that morning? Perhaps he would like some ham or dried fruit? He had a pound of excellent raisins —good ones were very rare, even at extortionate Balaclava prices.

While Magnus was speaking, Tom was saddened almost to tears by the sight of such obvious pleasure. Couldn't he see that everything had changed? That the past lay between them like a wall? Magnus's inability to understand his love for Helen, and his own failure to speak openly of it, had irrevocably destroyed the trust they had once shared, Helen's marriage merely setting the final seal on what had been already over.

But when Magnus offered to show him the layout of the batteries and trenches from Cathcart's Hill, Tom did not feel able to disappoint him so soon after their reunion. Afterward, by the time they reached the hut again, the sun had melted the ice in the ruts and puddles on the track and the ground was soft underfoot. The distant strains of a band came from the direction of the French camps; no guns were firing in the batteries.

Sitting on empty ammunition boxes on either side of the embers of the fire Magnus had lit an hour earlier, they faced each other in silence. Just outside the siege park an 18-pounder was being limbered up, its team of skeletal horses waiting to drag it down to the batteries. At first, Magnus had tried to persuade himself that Tom's uncommunicative mood had been due to the strangeness of his new situation, but when all his attempts at cheerfulness met with the same lack of response, he could bear it no longer.

"Why did you come to see me?"

"I didn't want you to find out I was here and hadn't told you."

"That was all?"

Tom stared at the patchy grass at his feet.

"We can't go back, Magnus. . . . I can't separate you from your family. I wish I could."

"Can't separate me from *them?*"

"Unless I forget her I'm done for. You didn't understand then; how can you now? It isn't your fault. . . . Charles, Helen . . . your father. You're part of the pattern. Nothing can alter that."

"Part of the pattern," echoed Magnus quietly, then with bitter anger, "Was I part of any pattern when I came to Charlotte Street; when we went to the workhouse? On election day? Strange I never knew it. I thought I was myself."

"Nothing was your fault. I said that. If Goodchild had lived . . . if I'd never painted her portrait . . . Just chances."

Magnus gazed across the plateau toward the Light Division's white sprinkling of tents.

"I suppose you saw her in Turkey?"

"Yes, once."

"Will you again?"

"No."

"Charles knows you were in Constantinople. He says he'll tell Father about last summer. Do you want to stop him?"

"Do you think your brother would believe a word I said?"

"The truth can be quite persuasive. I told him you'd see him. I don't think he believed you'd have the guts."

"I don't care what he believes."

"Nor do I." Magnus paused. "But then I don't much care what happens to Helen."

Tom bowed his head.

"All right. I'll see him."

Magnus got up and kicked over the box he had been sitting on.

"I'd like to know what happens . . . to complete the *pattern,* you understand. I'm sailing with the Azov squadron and'll be away for a week. Perhaps you could meet me here on New Year's Day? Easy to remember. Say nine?"

"All right." Tom moved away and then stopped. "I'm sorry, Magnus."

Magnus walked a little way with Tom toward the col. They paused at the brow of the next hill and saw the forest of masts in the distant inlet, and, beyond the black rocks at the mouth, the brilliantly sparkling sea. Far out, a warship under all plain sail was gliding across the bay, a cluster of signal flags below her ensign at the mizzen peak. When Tom moved, Magnus remained where he was.

"I'm glad we were friends once."

Tom turned as though about to reply but then walked on.

⇜ *Forty-Eight* ⇝

From H.M.S. *Curlew*'s poop, Magnus watched the sharp rise and fall of the foreshortened bowsprit as the small corvette's blunt bows thumped into the short choppy waves combed up by the freshening wind. The jarring thud that accompanied each sudden drop into the narrow troughs made every timber shudder and hurled up clouds of spray which flicked in foaming streaks across the forecastle. The bow wave rolled outward on each side, its breaking crests whipped off into the air by fierce squalls racing like dark clouds across the gray broken water. Seas, which would scarcely have wetted the middle-deck ports of a three-decker, were seething in the low-lying *Curlew*'s scuppers and hissing ominously by, a few feet below the main-deck rail. The light was slowly seeping out of the sky, changing the identifiable shapes of the accompanying vessels into dark smudges, their presence only revealed by the plumes of smoke arching astern and the faint gleam of their navigation lights. Darkness came quickly and with it flurries of snow, lashing faces already wet and caked with brine. Behind the spokes of the wheel, the face of the steersman stood out grotesquely, lit by the glow of the binnacle lamp. His eyes stinging and watering, Magnus clambered down the deck ladder and paused a moment under the break of the poop before going into the commander's cramped, battened-down cabin.

By the light of a smoky lamp hanging from a beam, Commander Hislop, his master and first lieutenant were staring at a damp-looking chart spread out on the central table; Hislop looked up irritably as Magnus came in and then forced a smile. Magnus sympathized with him; to be taking a journalist as passenger was bad enough, but to be responsible for a journalist who was also the admiral's son was an even worse burden for a man to carry when he had many other thoughts on his mind. But since the little *Curlew* had no wardroom, and the gun room was occupied by sleeping marines, the commander's cabin was the only place where Magnus could reasonably be expected to go. Hislop called him over to the table and explained where the squadron's first rendezvous was to take place, just before dawn the following day. Latitude 44°54′, longitude 36°28′: a position a few miles south of the Straits of Kertch. Now, a few minutes before 1:30 A.M., they were steaming past Sevastopol in the opposite direction NW by W½W, within sight of land, all usual lights displayed, to give the enemy the impression that they were bound for Odessa and not the Sea of Azov. In an hour's time, just below the horizon, with lights extinguished, they would alter course.

Until reading his father's detailed instructions to his commanding officers, Magnus had neither understood the risks of the operation, nor had he known that his father intended to go in with the gunboat flotilla deputed to silence the batteries commanding the straits. Half an hour of explosive violence would produce success or virtual annihilation. If the batteries survived the gunboats' attack, the marines, following in their open boats, would be blown out of the water before getting within five miles of the bridge.

Sitting on a slatted locker lid, while the master checked the chronometers for the last time before giving orders for the alteration in course, Magnus felt a rush of emotion. His father's note had said nothing about the chance that they might never meet again. His request to him to accompany the squadron had combined reconciliation with a challenge: an insistence that he finally recognize the worth of the service he had often derided in the past. Magnus suspected that if in the end he had to write an account of an important action, which was also Sir James Crawford's obituary, this possibility would have been foreseen by his father.

As *Curlew*'s movement changed to a steep roll on the new course, Magnus reproached himself for past misunderstandings. With relationships, no reversal, however seemingly conclusive, should be taken as final. If true of his dealings with his father, why not of his friendship with Tom? While the wind harped in the ship's rigging, Magnus resolved that whatever else he might achieve before leaving the Crimea, he would heal the breach with Tom; and this determination, above all others, absorbed him as *Curlew* steamed on remorselessly through the night toward the rendezvous.

❦ Forty-Nine ❧

Although Tom had visited the Naval Brigade's camp on the day after his conversation with Magnus, he had not found Charles, and, not wishing to prepare him for their meeting, had left no message. On the day Sir James Crawford's squadron sailed, Tom had returned once more to learn that Charles was down at Balaclava and unlikely to return until evening; but Captain Crawford, he had been assured, would be on duty in the "Right Attack" the following morning. On this second visit to the camp, Tom had called on Captain Lushington—one of the officers on his list—and had arranged two sittings. He had already managed to get provisional dates out of Generals Pennefather and Estcourt, and felt pleased with this progress. If he satisfied Estcourt and Airey, he would be better placed to approach Lord Raglan's ADC. While not enabling him to forget his coming encounter with Charles, making these plans had done something to reduce Tom's anxiety.

On the morning when Tom first visited the batteries, the icily penetrating wind, which had been howling for two days, had dropped considerably, and the clouds seemed higher, but the ground was still frozen hard and occasional sharp gusts from the north brought sudden showers of hail. There was no firing anywhere along the line and the men in the Naval Brigade's batteries sat crouched listlessly behind traverses or huddled together for warmth in the larger of the two bombproofs.

A bluejacket led Tom into a shallow trench behind the battery and asked him to wait there, while he ducked down between two posts into a low oblong hole cut into the side of the hill and banked up on each side with sandbags. Less than a minute later his guide reappeared and told Tom that Captain Crawford would see him. As Tom entered, an officer was leaving, and Charles did not acknowledge the presence of his new visitor until the old had departed. The shelter was dark and smelled of damp earth, stale sweat and cigar smoke. By the light of two candles Tom made out thick timbers supporting the earth above, and a crude turf ledge along one wall, covered with sacking. Charles did not get up from his campstool on the far side of a small table.

"A pity, Mr. Strickland," he said, pointing to a chair, "a pity you should see us so idle—a little activity makes better pictures, I daresay?"

"Magnus told you I would come?"

"He did." Tom saw the hatred in Charles's brisk smile. "Briefed you well, has he, Strickland?"

"I'm here under no obligation," replied Tom, glancing toward the door to emphasize his point, noting as he did so the effort of control Charles needed to stop himself arguing.

"I'll not interrupt your piece."

When Tom had finished his account of what had happened at Orta-köy, he read the same hatred in Charles's face—hatred mixed with contempt for the upstart who had sullied the purity he had once prized in Helen.

"But why stop there?" snapped Charles. "Having willingly seen you once—why not again?"

"She did not see me willingly."

"You carried her from the embassy by force?"

"I threatened to call there in person unless she agreed to meet me. She came to avoid scandal, not to cause it."

"And why pray did that convenient blackmail not compel her again?"

"I wanted to see her once more—something you denied me in England."

"Forgive my lack of consideration." Charles rested his elbows on the table and cupped his chin in his hands. "It's a strange story, Strickland. You come three thousand miles to spare yourself the temptation of seeing a woman—yet when you discover your honorable attempt has proved a sad error, what do you do? Take the first ship home? Sail at once for the war?" He cast up his eyes at the roof timbers. "Quite the reverse. Suddenly all the inconvenience and expense you put yourself to count for nothing and you actually seek out the very person you had taken such extravagant precautions to avoid."

"Chance can change the strongest resolution."

"Chance be damned, sir. You knew quite well she was in Turkey and came specially to see her."

"There's little point, but I'll tell you what happened. There'd been a ball at the embassy. A number of people at my hotel were invited. That's how I found out she was still there. Do you want to know the date and the name of the man who told me?"

Charles sighed deeply and stared for some seconds at the ammunition returns on the table. He looked suddenly tired and apathetic. At last he murmured,

"I accept your word. After all you came, and I never thought you would. . . . To tell the truth, I don't think I care. You don't matter anymore. Everything changes. I've other things to concern me." He got up and put on his greatcoat. "A sad and sordid liaison." He looked past Tom at the shafts of light admitted by the sacking curtain at the door. "You should have come last week, Mr. Strickland. You could have painted men dying. Did you see the 'artists' impressions' of Inkerman? Colonel So-and-So planting the colors on the parapet—that sort of thing . . . as though they were trees. Too bad most of the line regiments hadn't time to get theirs out of their cases. Watch us from Cathcart's Hill when we attack the Quarries. You should be quite safe there. You won't see much; not at dawn with the mist and the smoke. But you'll use your imagination, I daresay."

"I suppose you could arrange a better view for me?"

"My dear Strickland, a thousand men are going to die. You wouldn't want to be one of them. You stay on the hill."

"You'd like me killed, wouldn't you, Crawford?"

"With so many dying, one more death wouldn't break my heart. Magnus ever tell you he was with the pickets at Inkerman? Russell and Kinglake went forward at the Alma. You please yourself, Strickland."

"I don't care what you think of me."

Charles looked up from the beaten earth floor and smiled.

"I'm sure you don't. I knew from the start you'd never think of putting yourself in danger. That's why I taunted you; no risk of having you on my conscience. If you see some blue coats with the red, we'll be the ladder parties—to bridge the ditch. Don't draw too many ladders though. Perhaps three or four will get us far as the works." He lifted the sacking. "Good-bye, Strickland."

"Didn't you hear me? I said I didn't care what you think. I wouldn't risk a button on my coat to gain your good opinion." Tom walked toward Charles; his heart was beating fast, but his head felt quite clear. "That's why I'll come. You'll go because you have to . . . your duty, your honor, this code and that . . . I'll go for nothing. So who's the hero, Crawford?"

Charles stepped away from the door.

"Don't be a fool."

"You thought you'd humiliate me . . . have me crawl away feeling a coward. Either that or you want me killed. If I knew which I'd do the opposite, but I don't know, and you won't tell me. So I'm pleasing myself instead."

"You're trembling, Strickland."

"I'm scared. Aren't you?"

"I've learned to live with it. Habit takes the edge off everything. You've had your gesture. Now go."

"If you don't send me word where to go, I'll find out somewhere else. I want to see Colonel So-and-So planting his colors and the blue coats among the red."

Minutes later Tom was breathing the sharp fresh air in the trench. *Like an angry child,* he thought, as he started back toward the camps— *like a child.* But he did not care; it made no difference at all. *Afterward,* he said, *I shall have nothing to regret. Afterward I will be free of them all, free of their valor, their two-faced honor and their miserable pride. Yes, afterward.*

∽ *Fifty* ∽

At five in the morning the twenty-seven ships of Sir James Crawford's squadron lay at anchor in the Sea of Azov three miles off the town of Genichesk. The admiral's final conference was over now and all the commanders ready to leave the flagship for their own vessels. Having shaken each one by the hand, Sir James returned to the quarterdeck utterly drained by the hour he had just spent inspiring confidence and concealing his personal doubts from his officers. Above him, between the tall swaying masts, bright stars seemed to hang suspended like jewels in the spidery web of topping lifts and halyards. Already, almost two hours before dawn, a slight glow of light was discernible to the east. Soon the stars would begin to pale. The squadron was to attack at sunrise.

With his glass Sir James could make out an insignificant-looking break in the long line of coastal sandhills. This narrow opening separated the northern shores of the Crimean peninsula from the Russian mainland. Through these straits lay a hundred miles of shallow water and marshes, crossed ten miles inland by the Tchongar Bridge. The size and number of the batteries commanding the straits bore witness to the bridge's strategic importance. Just north of the sandhills was the town of Genichesk, defended by a garrison estimated at two battalions.

Immediately after anchoring, Sir James had sent two cutters inshore to sound the approaches to the narrow channel. The news their crews had brought back had been bad. Although there was no boom obstructing the entrance, the water was not deep enough for the steam frigates to stand in closer than two thousand yards. The squadron's six shallow-draft gunboats would therefore have to destroy the batteries without significant assistance from the larger ships. If they failed, the marines following in their open boats would never get through to the bridge; before leaving the straits, every single launch and pinnace would be smashed to matchwood. He had thought of using the gunboats themselves as transports, but the vulnerability of their magazines had ruled this out. With a total marine force of six hundred men, he could not afford to lose many before the landings. In forcing the straits, he expected at least two of the gunboats to be sunk or crippled. Because the whole operation depended on their success against the batteries, Sir James intended before the action started to transfer his flag to H.M.S. *Hesperus,* the gunboat that would lead in the flotilla.

Apart from the silencing of the batteries, one other objective would have to be achieved to avoid disaster: the town's garrison must be prevented from marching to the defense of the bridge until after the marines were well on their way to it. Loath though Sir James had been to contemplate splitting his small landing force, a diversionary attack on the northern side of the town seemed the only way to pin down the garrison. This attack would therefore begin the action, Sir James's hope being that it would not only occupy the garrison, but also give the main attack on the straits an element of surprise.

At the end of the middle watch the admiral went below and sat down at the small table in his cabin. *Sampson,* his temporary flagship, was a very different vessel from *Retribution,* having but a single gun deck and no admiral's quarters. Sir James was occupying the captain's cabin which was half-filled by a 32-pounder—an indispensable part of the steam frigate's broadside.

In front of Sir James lay the pages he had written to Helen earlier that afternoon.

> My dearest,
> If you receive this letter I will be dead, and the overland telegraph will already have brought you that news. This is a sad and solemn thought, but that is not my mood as I write. I see myself as an overcautious man who takes an umbrella with him on a sunny day. You see I do not believe I will die tomorrow and this belief robs the possibility of all fear. Death only terrifies those due to die at a fixed time. I have no such inexorable appointment. . . .

He folded the paper slowly and sealed the envelope. During the voyage across the Sea of Azov he had also written to each of his children.

Only in his letter to Charles had he admitted his strong premonition that he would die.

In an hour's time a single blue light at *Sampson*'s fore would set in train the embarkation of the first party of marines. Though exhausted Sir James felt the strange lucidity often produced in him for a few hours after tiredness had passed a certain pitch. In the stillness the thump of the lookout's footsteps on the poop overhead seemed very loud. He imagined the boats' crews pulling silently for the shore, thrum mats around the looms of the oars to deaden the sound they made against the tholepins.

And after the long quietness of the night, such unimaginable noise— the air screaming and hurtling in the straits.

* * *

Shortly after dawn the ships had steamed in and anchored less than a mile offshore. Half an hour after the boats had landed the marine diversionary force, Magnus, and the officers crowded together on *Curlew*'s quarterdeck, heard the first sputter of musketry from the land, at first isolated shots and then a regular muted rattle. Just above the horizon a ridge of cloud was beginning to glow, its edges scalloped with gold. The sun was rising, but the western sky above Genichesk was still dark, and the low hills behind the town, black with touches of silver and gray. Soon came some deeper crashes—the field guns were going into action. Moments later the wind brought the thin notes of bugles, and more distinctly the clanging of church bells. The enemy was mustering his forces.

"Deck there!" Magnus heard a midshipman call from the main-top. "Flagship signaling."

A string of black dots, like beads on a thread, raced up *Sampson*'s signal halyards. As the flags were broken out, telescopes were raised to read the signal before it was hauled down. Hoist followed hoist, twenty-two in all. Already ships were acknowledging, and within minutes launches were being slung out and lowered from the squadron's largest ships. The second party of marines was embarking.

The sky was growing lighter by the minute and through his glass Magnus could clearly see the white cross straps and scarlet coats of the marines mustering on the frigates' upper decks. Next he noticed a gig being lowered from the davits over the flagship's mizzen channel, and above the noise of the waves he could just catch the squealing of blocks as she went down fast and met the water with a flat splash. Men were now swarming down the rope netting on the steam frigates' leeward sides and clambering into the tossing launches and pinnaces. Looking again to see what had happened to the gig, he saw that she was now making for the six gunboats riding at anchor ten cables south of the main squadron.

Magnus was about to ask Commander Hislop whether any changes had been made to the written instructions, when the signals lieutenant shouted,

"Flagship again, sir. Tugs and steamers to weigh at once." He paused, waiting for the next hoist. "Our number, sir. Follow in steamers and pick up survivors if launches hit. That's it, sir. Instruction seventeen."

As the hands on *Curlew*'s forecastle leaped to the capstan bars to heave in the cable, Magnus saw the gig reach one of the gunboats. He asked her name.

"*Hesperus*," replied the quartermaster who had been talking earnestly to the master. Magnus recalled from the General Orders that *Hesperus* was the name of the ship detailed to lead through the straits.

Ten minutes later the gunboats were steaming in line astern of *Hesperus* bearing down on the entrance to the straits. The firing from the shore had become louder and almost continuous. Two rockets rose steeply into the sky from the direction of the fighting, and hung for a moment before falling earthward. The marines were unable to hold their position and were being forced to retire. The diversion seemed to have failed. Magnus studied *Hesperus* again through his glass and saw a single black dot rise to her mizzen truck and break out there. The flag looked like a small St. George's Cross. Within minutes the gunboats would be in range of the shore batteries.

"What's that signal?" he asked Hislop, who was conning the helmsman as *Curlew* steamed to her new station.

"I don't see one," replied Hislop, studying *Hesperus* with his glass.

"At the mizzen."

Hislop lowered his telescope.

"That, sir, is your father's flag."

* * *

Sir James had gone forward to get a better view of the entrance, and already with the naked eye could make out the white line of surf where the waves were breaking against the southern spit. On the northern side he saw the first two batteries: one a substantial stone fort with a single row of casemates, the other an earthwork raised up on a tumulus-like mound—mounting between them he supposed a dozen guns. Above the tumulus a red flag was flying from a tall staff. Farther inland was a windmill, its sails turning rapidly. The sun was shining now, casting long shadows from the rigging across the deck, but bringing no discernible warmth. The breeze still cut through the seams of his coat like a knife.

On both sides of the straits, strips of lighter colored water, brown or yellowish gray, betrayed the positions of shoals. For ten minutes the leadsman had been swinging his line in the chains, Sir James listening tensely to his shouts.

"By the mark two," came the next call.

Barely six cables back the depth had been five fathoms; if it shelved any more they would have to reduce speed; the thought of having to kedge off a shoal within enemy gunshot was spine-chilling.

"By the deep one and half one."

Sir James turned to *Hesperus*'s captain, Commander Seymour.

"Be ready to hoist *Reduce to five knots*," Mr. Seymour."

Seymour repeated the command to the quartermaster's mate who ran aft with it. Another five minutes and they would be in action. With a bow pivot, two 68-pounders on metal slides amidships, and two truck 24-pounders astern, Gleaner Class gunboats mounted heavier ordnance than any other shallow-draft vessels in commission. Sir James doubted whether many of the batteries would contain pieces larger than 24-pounders. In the narrows, where the channel was no more than a hundred yards across, they would be engaging at point-blank range. If the gunboats were still afloat, no battery, earth or stone, would survive double-shotted 68-pounders at such proximity. But with magazines only partially protected by water tanks, and no more than a token forecastle above the shell room, Sir James was very doubtful that all six gunboats would reach the narrows. If a ship went down in the main channel, it would be the end for those astern.

"By the mark two," shouted the leadsman.

"That's better, sir," murmured Seymour, with obvious relief.

Sir James nodded. Seymour's habit of raising his right hand to his cocked hat—an apparently nervous gesture—irritated the admiral terribly because of his own ragged nerves.

"For God's sake, man, take that thing off or leave it alone."

Seymour tossed it away toward the rail and explained that he had been afraid it would blow off. Normally he wore one of the new flat peaked caps, but with his admiral aboard had borrowed his first lieutenant's full-dress hat; unfortunately the lieutenant's head was smaller than his own. Sir James smiled and was glad of an excuse to do so.

Sir James was gazing aft at the five gunboats keeping perfect station a cable's length apart in line astern, when the fort opened fire. He swung around his glass to count the puffs of smoke.

"Five guns, sir," said Seymour.

The shots fell six cables wide, throwing up tall waterspouts.

"Keep watching in case a gun fires late."

"Aye, aye, sir." Seymour tried to remain silent, but failed. "Pretty jumpy I'd say to fire so early, sir."

Seeing Seymour's fresh and eager face, and remembering his own unlimited confidence before his gruesome blooding at Navarino, Sir James felt a wave of sadness.

"Let's hope so."

"Will you give the order to fire, sir?"

"Your ship, Mr. Seymour."

Seymour saluted with a smile and loped down the companion to the gun deck, where he moved quickly from gun to gun having a word with each No. 1. A mile out to sea Sir James could see the tugs steaming in with the launches and pinnaces in tow; in each of these dozen boats would be thirty-five marines—only a handful would live if the gunboats did not completely destroy the majority of the batteries. The guns in the fort roared out again—their shots this time sending up plumes of green water fifty yards ahead of *Hesperus*.

In spite of his earlier determination to let Seymour have absolute control over the ship, Sir James was on the point of shouting to him not to fire until directly opposite the casemates when the deck leaped under his feet and the air was filled with shrieking fragments of wood and metal. A shot had carried away *Hesperus*'s bowsprit like a match, snapping the bobstay and chain guys as if they were threads, knocking out the port knighthead, and ripping up the forward deck planking like the staves of an old barrel. As the forestay parted with a whipping twang and the jib halyards and downhaul flew free, the foremast swayed but did not fall. The pivot gun had been tilted from its circular mountings and was now pointing drunkenly into the water. The next salvo ripped through the rigging, splintering the mizzen gaff and bringing the spanker boom crashing to the deck a few feet from Sir James. In a daze he watched Seymour coolly wait another thirty seconds until every one of the starboard guns bore on the fort. Then at seventy-five yards he gave the order. As *Hesperus*'s 68-pounders hurtled back along their slides, the whole ship seemed flung over onto her beam as if capsizing. Being used to line-of-battle ships, the force of the recoil astounded Sir James. His eyes streaming with the fumes of burning saltpeter and sulfur, he could see nothing through the thick white smoke.

"Stop your vents!" he heard Seymour roaring, and, as the smoke billowed away to port, saw the gun crews laboring with their sponges and the powdermen handing fresh charges to the loaders. Two shots crashed back from the fort, one smashing into the hull just aft of the boiler room, the other tearing through the foremast backstays. Forward, three men were hacking at the wrecked bowsprit, now trailing alongside. The smoke cleared very slowly from the fort, but when it did, Sir James saw that three casemates had become a single cavernous hole. *Hesperus* had surely knocked out three of the five guns. No sooner had Sir James congratulated the gun crews than he felt the deck tilting under his feet. All available hands were ordered to the pumps and the carpenter and his mate ran below to try to plug the hole. The list was only improved by moving one of the 24-pounders to port and heaving the damaged pivot gun overboard.

Her starboard broadside now reduced to three guns, *Hesperus* steamed on. Looking astern, Sir James watched *Recruit*, the next gunboat in the line, open fire on the fort and clearly saw large lumps of masonry flying as the shots slammed home. Highly satisfied with events, he was turning his attention to the next battery, three hundred yards ahead, when he heard a muted blast, and then, after several staccato detonations, a deep prolonged roar. Where seconds before *Recruit* had been steaming purposefully forward was an orange-white inferno of flames crowned by a black mushroom of smoke filled with fragments of timber; forward of the mainmast she had simply ceased to exist. Her stern, with the mizzen still somehow standing, remained upright for a moment, and then tilting sharply, sank with a boiling hiss. The disaster had been so sudden, and the silence so complete after the explosion of the ship's magazine and shell room, that Sir James could not take it in for several seconds. By then *Hesperus*'s gig was being slung out to pick up any survivors from the stern.

"Mr. Seymour," he shouted, "reduce to four knots until *Sphinx* is in station astern."

"Aye, aye, sir."

Altering course to avoid the floating wreckage, *Sphinx* came on steadily, and opened fire on the fort, bringing down a dust-laden avalanche of stones and dirt. No answering shots were fired.

The next batteries were a half-moon-shaped earthwork on a low cliff, easily visible since the grass had not grown over the recently thrown-up parapet, and a far more formidable stone fort on a slight promontory. From its size, Sir James thought it would mount at least a dozen guns.

Approaching the half-moon work, *Hesperus* was hulled again, this time more seriously and just below the waterline. Immediately after firing her broadside, she began to list so dangerously that it was obvious she was sinking.

"Hard aport!" yelled Seymour, running up onto the poop, and then, through his speaking trumpet to the men still cranking the pumps, "Belay that nonsense and hoist out the cutter." He looked around him at the remains of the spanker boom. "And get this rubbish overboard. Quartermaster, make to *Sphinx, Admiral coming aboard.*"

Hesperus grounded hard twenty yards from the shore, and, as she hit the shelving bottom, steaming at five knots, every man on her not holding fast to something was flung to the deck. Seymour and Sir James fell side by side, and the younger man helped his admiral to his feet.

"This won't be your last ship, Mr. Seymour."

"I hope not, sir."

Sir James glanced up at the wrecked mizzen gaff and the empty halyards streaming out above it.

"No need to strike my flag."

As the cutter pulled away from the stricken gunboat, *Sphinx* came level with the half-moon battery and discharged her broadside. Fountains of earth sprang up all along the parapet as the shells exploded. When the smoke cleared, nothing but the bleeding bodies of the gunners and the debris of shattered carriages and overturned cannons remained of what moments ago had been an ordered battery. Never having seen 68-pounders in action against an earthwork at such short range, Sir James was stunned by what he saw.

Only the last and largest stone fort remained.

Two minutes after the admiral had gone aboard *Sphinx*, a shell burst on her gun deck, instantly killing twelve of her forty-strong crew, and knocking one of her 68-pounders clean off its slide mountings. Only two guns were left in action. Sir James had only just exchanged courtesies with *Sphinx*'s commander, and now, along with the boatswain, the master's mate and the quartermaster, the man was dead. If he had not gone aft seconds before, Crawford realized that he would have shared the same fate. After the sheeting flash of the explosion, yellow and black spots were dancing in front of his eyes. As if waking from a dream, he saw a hideously maimed man dragging himself to one of the guns. The deck was running with blood. Grabbing the first lieutenant by the arm, he shouted,

"Cease firing! Engines full ahead."

Astern, *Amphion* silenced two guns with her first broadside, before she was holed and started to list sickeningly to starboard. Just clearing the channel she went aground immediately under the battery. Sir James screwed up his eyes in anguish as her decks were raked from stem to stern with canister and grape, dashing men to the deck like paper figures in a wind. *Simoon*, the next in line, engaged the fort seconds too late to prevent a second murderous volley mowing down the few men left alive on *Amphion*'s gun deck.

Sir James was not looking at the precise moment when *Simoon*'s second broadside roared out, bringing down a long section of the fort's wall, and sending up the magazine—not a large one to judge by the explosion, but large enough. The terrible slaughter caused by shells bursting in the confined space behind the casemates was better not imagined. No shots troubled *Leopard,* the last gunboat, as she lowered boats to take the wounded off the sinking *Amphion.*

Under ten minutes after *Hesperus* had fired her first broadside, the straits lay open for the marines. The cost had been three gunboats and just over a hundred lives. As the rockets soared upward requesting the steamers to come in, Sir James looked around him in astonishment, the coastline just the same, the sails of the windmill still turning, no smoke, no gunfire, a clear sky, some men killed. Everything he had expected and yet as always quite different. He felt numbed rather than elated. The losses had been trivial in comparison with those of any large land battle, but the small size of the ships had reduced them to a comprehensible scale. Certain sights in the past had left scars in his mind, which had closed but never quite healed. The simultaneous death of *Recruit's* entire crew at the center of that glowing ball of fire would leave just such a mark.

Leaving *Leopard* in the straits to pick up men from *Amphion* and *Hesperus*, and to stop the enemy righting guns in the ruined batteries, *Sphinx* and *Simoon* steamed on toward the bridge, their crews still standing to the undamaged guns and the leadsman calling out the depth.

Beyond the next point the straits widened rapidly, forming a long tongue of sparkling water a mile across, stretching almost out of sight. With his telescope Sir James could see a distant mass of shimmering whiteness—the ice over the shallower water—and even farther away, where two low headlands almost met, the thin black horizontal line of the bridge and beneath it, no thicker than matchsticks, the supporting uprights. To the left were flat salt marshes, to the right of the ships, two miles of low-lying agricultural land rising gently to a chain of gray-green hills. A thousand yards from the water's edge a dike, running parallel with the shore as far as the eye could see, aroused Sir James's interest; looking back in the direction of the town, he saw on its surface what at first looked like long dark patches of vegetation. Keeping the telescope on them he waited and within thirty seconds was sure that they were two dense columns of marching infantry. The sunshine and the crisp clearness of the air had brought no warmth but a far greater blessing: a perfect field of vision. Besides protecting the farms from flooding during easterly gales, the dike was also the principal road linking Genichesk with the Tchongar Bridge. A moment later some shouts from the lookout in the mainmast shrouds confirmed Sir James's discovery. The enemy was marching to protect the bridge. Let them march, he thought, imagining how harmless and small the gunboats would look to these men on the road. Few soldiers had any conception of the range of ships' guns, their own heaviest fieldpieces being mere popguns in comparison with 68-pounders. Even if they were coming on at the double, they still would not be a good target for another twenty minutes, but then the survivors would be left a good deal wiser about the effects of a well-directed broadside fired at a range of just over half a mile. Sir James hoped to kill a number of them, but his principal concern was to get them off the road. Marching across fields they would be enormously delayed and would have no hope of bringing any field guns up in time to oppose the landings. Having shelled the advancing troops, the road itself could be reduced to rubble at its nearest point to the shore. Ideally it would be best to wait till the infantrymen reached that point, but Sir James did not like that idea. Time was still important. The tugs and steamers with their string of boats would get through, but he also had to guarantee that they would get out once the bridge had been destroyed.

Soon Sir James could see the columns quite clearly, and the frequent glint and flash of bayonets catching the sun. The men's usual long gray greatcoats hid their legs and made their movement seem unnaturally smooth, as though they were sliding rather than marching along the road. Two hundred yards ahead of the infantry was a troop of cavalry and behind it two or three batteries of horse artillery, the slight swing of the gun barrels behind the limbers just perceptible through a steadily held glass.

The two gunboats anchored in a carefully angled line fifty yards from the shore, with additional stern anchors to prevent them swinging. Their guns were loaded with shell and elevated for nine hundred yards. As the marching men entered the line of fire, *Sphinx* and *Leopard* discharged their broadsides together with a hideous crash. Through breaks in the smoke, glimpses could be caught of jets of earth and stones springing up around the road quite silently, for it was several seconds before the explosions were heard by the gun crews and by then they were reloading. Two wide gaps had appeared in the first column of infantry, but for a moment the men on the road seemed frozen. Shouts of triumph went up from officers who had been watching through glasses. Sir James was glad to be distanced from the carnage; when the men started to hurl themselves from the road down the banks on either side, he saw them as dots no larger than matchheads. With a more dispersed target, shots going too long or falling short would kill at random. He reckoned that three or perhaps four of the shells had exploded on the road. As the guns thundered again, he could imagine the terror of the men hearing the approaching, tearing shriek of the shells; many of them would only just have realized that the two small, smoke-shrouded ships on the shimmering sheet of water were responsible for what was happening to them. Sir James could not rid himself of a vision of Charles advancing on the Quarries under a similar rain of shells from the Redan and Malakoff. After each ship had fired four broadsides, he turned to the first lieutenant:

"Signal: *Discontinue*."

Already the tugs and steamers were rounding the point, with the ships' boats strung out astern. He had thought the first diversionary attack a failure, but he had been mistaken. Without it, the men now dead and dying on the road would have marched from the town half an hour earlier, and would already have reached a position from which they would have been able to cut off any force attempting to get to the bridge overland. Now the survivors would arrive too late, and the worst the marines could expect to encounter would be an isolated company stationed in a guardhouse at the bridge; perhaps not even that. Nothing could go wrong now, and Sir James knew it.

For the first time he could feel a little warmth from the sun on his cheeks. The sky was dappled with small white clouds, which cast racing shadows on the sage-green hills. Small waves ruffling the water sparkled like thousands of tiny mirrors. Across the salt marshes the black smoke from the tall stacks of the tugs was dispersing in thin floating streaks. Yet at the back of his mind a vague discontent.

I'm a vainglorious fool, he thought, as it occurred to him with a shock that he had half hoped that the landing would be opposed. For what would almost certainly be his last close action with an enemy, he had imagined a spectacular ending: landing with his men under fire to encourage them, the water around them plowed up by grape and round shot . . . He shook his head, suddenly ashamed of the contradictions in his thoughts. Disgust with war one moment and then infantile dreams of romantic heroism. At any moment passing through the straits he could have been killed or mutilated, and instead of being thankful, he had wanted more. Dear God, at my age. He thought of the letters he had written to his family. Now only the most extraordinary misfortune would make their dispatch necessary. For a moment he thought of sending a boat for Magnus once the marines had landed, but a little later the first waves of tiredness hit him and he remembered the many other things that would have to be done after the bridge was destroyed. In imagination he was already back in *Sampson*'s captain's cabin bent over the mahogany table.

Sir,
I have the honor to inform you that this morning I hoisted my flag in H.M.S. *Hesperus*, and having under my direct orders the ships named in the margin, passed through the straits of Genichesk. . . .

❧ *Fifty-One* ❧

Earlier there had been flurries of snow and sleet, but by four o'clock in the morning, when Tom arrived at the Naval Brigade Camp, the sky had cleared and he could see the glittering points of stars and a full moon silvering the lines of tents. Groups of men were squatting around the watch fires, eating salt pork from mess tins, the flames lending to their pale gaunt faces a mocking counterfeit of ruddy good health. By one fire sailors were queuing for tots of rum from a large brassbound barrel. Already officers were calling out names and telling men off into parties in readiness for marching them down to the trenches. All around him Tom could sense the taut air of anticipation and fear, which mirrored his own feelings. He had little confidence that the pounding given the Russian works by the British and French siege guns during the past two days would turn out to have been any more effective than previous long-range bombardments. Only surprise could materially assist the attackers, and Tom doubted whether Russian vigilance would have been reduced by their two days under fire. The general opinion was that the Quarries would only be taken after fierce and prolonged fighting, and Tom saw no reason to doubt its correctness.

Charles's note had told Tom to find Mr. Parnwell, assistant paymaster, who would tell him where he should go and who would take him there. From previous visits to the camp, Tom knew that the paymaster's office was in the group of huts where the brigade's stores were housed—the paymaster himself, besides dealing with wages, performing for the sailors ashore the job done in the army by the commissariat and regimental quartermasters. Tom eventually found Parnwell overseeing the paymaster's clerks in the crowded armorer's hut, where they were entering in ledgers the number of pistols, revolvers and rounds of ammunition being issued to the members of the ladder parties. The armory was dimly lit by two hanging lanterns and had the sharp, bitter, greasy smell that Tom had always associated with guns. To the left the yeoman was taking down weapons from the racks and checking them before shouting out the type of firearm and the name of the recipient. Ordinary seamen were getting pistols, warrant officers revolvers.

Parnwell, a young man with a large nose and a sandy-colored mustache, glanced cursorily at Charles's note to Tom, and came out from behind the table.

"I'm sorry, sir, but you're not to go down."

"What?"

"I saw Captain Crawford an hour ago and he was quite explicit."

"I must see him then."

"I'm afraid he's already gone down to the first parallel."

Relieved at first and very much tempted to accept this rebuttal as final, Tom felt suddenly angry. He vividly recalled Charles's certainty that he would not have it in him to watch the attack from the advanced trenches. Parnwell's prohibition was just another attempt to dissuade him so that Charles could later stigmatize him as a coward.

"What if I refuse to take Captain Crawford's advice?"

"I think it was an order, sir."

Once again Tom was very close to giving in.

"Civilians aren't under orders. I have a pass for the trenches."

Parnwell looked at Tom with unfeigned bewilderment and then shrugged his shoulders.

"He said if you insisted you could go down with the surgeon's party. They'll be leaving for the second parallel in half an hour."

"Where can I find them?"

"The hospital marquee."

As Tom walked out into the darkness he smiled grimly to himself. So Parnwell had merely been an unwitting actor in another of Crawford's tests. If Charles had genuinely meant to prevent him going on, he would never have given Parnwell instructions to say anything else after advising him not to go. The possibility that Charles had had a real change of heart occurred to Tom, but he dismissed the idea at once. Even if Crawford's conscience *had* troubled him, Tom did not care. The venture had come to mean more to him than a simple victory over Charles. For his own sake he wanted to prove that he could overcome his lifelong terror of physical danger. He had come out to the war affecting to despise the outlook and mentality of the officers there, considering their notions of honor and duty, maintained in the midst of a starving army, as absurd as their habitual pride of caste. And yet, though owing their positions to influence and money rather than to aptitude and merit, he had not been able to deny their courage, and he still felt awed by it. When free of this final vestige of admiration for men who made no secret of scorning his calling and who felt superior by right to every self-made man, however great his gifts, Tom was also sure that he would lose the last traces of humiliation caused by Helen's rejection. With fear conquered, let whosoever wished look down on him. Let them, for he would not care. Never again would any new Captain Crawford have power over him.

Tom was almost at the hospital tent when he saw Humphrey, or at least thought he saw him; he was running past about ten yards away, probably carrying some message, and in the moonlight it was hard to be sure; but when the boy hesitated as if recognizing him, Tom turned abruptly and walked behind the row of tents immediately to his left, unable to face talking to Helen's son; afraid too that Humphrey would ask what he was doing and would argue with him to prevent him going down. Tom waited several minutes, and then, approaching the marquee from the other side, went in. He was not followed.

Shortly before five, an engineer officer led the naval surgeon's party from the batteries through a confusing series of zigzagging trenches, angled to avoid enfilading fire, into the wider first parallel, already crowded with troops—reliefs, the engineer explained, for the first two storming parties. The men were all silent, leaning against the walls of the trench, and some, to Tom's amazement, lying sleeping on the frozen mud, huddled together in their greatcoats, a strange jumble of arms and legs, looking to Tom like bodies awaiting burial. Some of the medical orderlies were already crouching low, as if afraid of a sudden storm of bullets, and this amused the engineer, who pointed out that they were in no immediate danger, being still fifty yards behind the second parallel and a hundred from the third; while beyond that, even closer to the enemy, were the advanced saps leading to the British rifle pits. Tom imagined Charles and the ladder parties somewhere in those more hazardous trenches and felt grudgingly certain that he would not be cowed by thoughts of the coming ordeal. As Tom followed the stretcher bearers and orderlies into the next network of approach trenches, he felt a terrible wave of loneliness. Around him in these man-made fissures were hundreds of other men, and yet this thought brought him no comfort; they at least had good reason to be there—for them refusal would have meant the firing squad. Yet he was moving forward all the time, every second bringing him closer to the most advanced works, closer to the enemy. Men of action, he told himself, did not think, and lacking imagination could not envisage future horror until actually involved in it. But I am quite different; never having felt an innate superiority to other men, I am under no obligation, as officers are, to justify their self-esteem with acts of valor. For the first time since parting from him, Tom longed to be with Magnus, to see his heavy-lidded, gray-blue eyes, and above all to hear his reassuring voice. Magnus had been a soldier and yet combined pride with sensitivity, the power to act with the capacity to imagine. Perhaps there were others like him, but Tom only knew that he had never met them. In the dark confines of the trench, Tom remembered the wide skies and open hills above Balaclava, and his friend walking by his side. If their positions were now exchanged, Tom was sure that Magnus would not be at a loss, would feel no self-pity, and no sense that his lot was different from that of the men around him, but would face whatever was to come with the same calmness he had once shown facing George across the oval hazard table, and walking toward Joseph Braithwaite's hired thugs between the tall, soot-blackened walls of a narrow cobbled lane.

They paused in the second parallel and the surgeon repeated that they would not under any circumstances cross the open ground between the advanced saps and the Russian rifle pits until it was clear that the storming parties had not only taken the Quarries but were able to hold them. But Tom was not much reassured by this. The only reason he could think of why surgeons should be sent to the Quarries was that a heavy fire from the Redan and the Malakoff would prevent the wounded being carried back to the trenches for many hours after the position had been taken.

They entered the third parallel on the heels of the three hundred men of the 7th Royal Fusiliers, who were to form the right wing of the second body of attack. Some dark ragged clouds had obscured the moon for several minutes, but when they blew over, Tom saw the blue-silver gleam of bayonets and the badges on shakos. A field officer pushed by, his polished steel scabbard bumping against his thigh. From the trenches behind them came a faint smell of latrines wafted on a slight but piercingly cold breeze. The proximity of so many men and the absolute stillness broken only by an occasional muffled cough and the clatter of a ramrod was one of the strangest experiences Tom had ever known. Sensing so much fear around him, his own started to diminish, and feeling calmer, he tried to memorize the scene around him: the pale glow of moonlight on faces and shoulder straps, making them seem to float, detached from solid bodies, in a dark void; the myriad gradations of light and shade ranging from evanescent silver through varying depths of chiaroscuro to velvet blackness. How could it ever be possible to paint the transition from the highlights to such darkness while giving a sense of the underlying masses? Because there *were* masses; the points of light did not, as he had at first thought, exist in isolation; many of the shadows he had seen as of a single tone, now seemed softer and less uniform; and the mood, that too must be conveyed . . . by a face, a face close-up, the whole being seen in perspective along the trench, two or three figures dominating in the foreground.

When a further two hundred men of the 33rd Regiment started to move along the parallel from the left, the naval surgeon's party, which had now joined forces with two army surgeons from the Highland Division, was escorted forward by their guide into an advanced sap to the right of the area from which the assault would be launched, and led to the saphead where they were to wait until the Quarries had been taken.

At half-past five the moonlight was as bright as ever, and, clambering up the side of the sap, Tom looked out over the top of the gabions at the gentle slope leading up to the Russian rifle pits in front of the Quarries. The silvery radiance of the light and the unbroken stillness made the coming violence seem impossible. When he dropped down into the sap again, he found himself next to a young assistant surgeon to whom he had talked briefly in the hospital marquee. The man, whose name was Watts, had complained about the way medical officers were treated in the navy. Watts offered Tom some brandy, which he was grateful to take, being stiff with cold.

As the sky grew paler, the moon lost its luster, and men and earth and grass seemed steeped in a chill gray wash. Near his feet Tom noticed a dead leaf, stiff with frost, its skeletal veins starred with minute crystals. He thought of the new leaves of an English spring, pale and translucent; of a green tunnel enclosing a slow dark stream, its surface skimmed by water boatmen; recalled the slow change of the landscape through a dusty north country summer, until the sycamore wings had come spinning down in Barford's autumnal woods.

Above the dark rim of the horizon the sky was whitening, dimming the moon to a flat thin disk.

Shortly after six o'clock several sharp cracking reports came from the direction of the Russian rifle pits as the British covering party sprinted across the open ground and took up positions in shell craters and folds in the ground to keep the Russian marksmen's heads down while the sailors leaped out from the trenches and dashed forward to place their ladders against the tangled branches of the abatis. Immediately behind the bluejackets came a long scarlet wave of infantry—the first storming party. Only a few shots came from the Quarries and none at all from the rifle pits. The infantry surged over the abatis, like horses taking a jump, and ran on, soldiers and sailors pressing forward side by side, up the slope of the glacis toward the irregular ramparts of the Quarries. Behind them several companies of sappers were hacking at the abatis to clear the way for the second body of attack.

Immediately after the first shots Tom had been choked with anxiety, but seeing the attackers sweeping toward their objective so easily, relief and elation replaced all former misgivings. There seemed no way they could be stopped; no way at all. For the first time since the start of the attack, Tom thought of Charles, his sword drawn, striving to outpace those around him. Only a hundred yards.

Then from end to end of that dark ridge of broken earth spurted orange tongues of flame, as grape, canister and mitraille were sent screaming into the attackers' faces, filling the loud air with death, cutting wide lanes through the advancing columns. As the second body of attack left the shelter of the sapheads to support the first storming party, the Redan opened up, flipping mortar shells over the heads of the defenders in the Quarries, sending up plumes of earth as the new formations ran toward the abatis.

Paralyzed and frozen at first, the whole living mass on the glacis began to reel and sway, fragmenting while some still went forward and others started to fall back. Above the crash of gunfire a bugle sounded and the second wave of infantry began to shake out into extended order, company by company, section by section, to avoid the shells still whistling down from the Redan. Had the supports been withheld even minutes longer, the wavering storming party on the glacis would have broken and fled, but, seeing their compatriots already swarming over the abatis, the survivors pressed on. From five hundred yards away Tom saw the leaders scrabbling at the ramparts with their bare hands, struggling to tear down the rubble-stone work revetting the parapet in order to form a ramp for the final ascent. The Russian riflemen had now mounted the firestep and were discharging volleys at the men beneath them, now too close for the field guns to be effective. The guns in the British "Right Attack" were at last answering the fire from the Redan and Malakoff. Two more minutes and the second body of attack had reached the parapet, many, in their broken formation, having survived the gusts of grape that had worked such havoc with the storming party. The Quarries was now completely hidden behind dense white clouds of smoke, frequently lit from within by flashes. There was continual shouting and the accelerating rattle of musketry often drowned by the deeper crash of the British siege guns shelling the Russian bastions. The small-arms fire slackened and then there was a loud cheer, which was soon taken up by the men in the forward British trenches. Since no men were running back, it was clear that the Quarries had been taken.

His eyes glistening with excitement, Tom turned to Watts, who had been watching impassively beside him.

"They've done it."

"They'll try to get it back, don't you worry."

Regardless of their own wounded in the battery, the gunners in the Redan now started firing on the Quarries. A large working party with spades and picks streamed toward the captured position past the heaps of dead and dying near the ditch; ahead of these sappers lay the formidable task of reversing the work's defenses under fire. After two companies from the reserve had followed the working party across the open ground to the Quarries, the senior engineer officer spoke to the surgeons, and five minutes later they were picking their way across the shell-pitted ground toward the glacis. Since the Russians now seemed to be concentrating all their fire on the captured battery, and none on the approaches to it, there was now talk of getting the wounded back to the trenches, and indeed the stretcher parties busied themselves with this task the moment they reached the abatis.

Never having seen the immediate aftermath of even a single violent death, the scores of mutilated bodies and still trickling blood, the moans and hysterical cries for help, made Tom's legs quake under him and his head swim. Yet in spite of himself he could not look away from shattered and torn limbs with bones sticking out through sleeves and trousers, and from chests torn open like carcasses in a slaughterer's yard. He wanted to but could not; and, although feeling that he had come and seen and was now free to return, he did not at once do so.

In the saphead, he had told himself that he would go as far as the ditch and then return at once to the trenches, but within moments that option seemed a more dangerous one than remaining where he was. Having seen the stretcher parties taking back the wounded, the Russians now started to drop shells around the abatis to discourage this proceeding and to prevent the men in the trenches thinking that they could reinforce their comrades at will. The ditch beneath the parapet, although choked with corpses, was now the safest place for the living to be, and the surgeons and their orderlies were soon at work there, binding up wounds as best they could to stop men bleeding to death. On the other side of the parapet, shells were continually falling into the battery, and before long a steady stream of casualties was being brought back to the ditch for attention. Tom caught sight of Watts, the front of his tunic splattered with blood and his hands as red as if his wrists had just been cut.

Still a little dizzy and finding it hard to check occasional sobs of shock, Tom felt firmer on his feet. Soon he was filled with a powerful urge to look inside the battery itself—not merely to see it, or even to be able to say that he had set foot there, but because he was intuitively certain that he would come across Charles's body. He did not wish him dead, but was convinced that he would be, and was sure that he would find him. Even if the living man would never know that the artist he had taunted and despised had reached the Quarries, there would still be, it seemed to Tom, a fitness in the confrontation, even with one party dead. Crawford might even be dying, and he could give him water. Tom wondered what Helen would make of that if she were ever to hear of it. The day before, he had learned about Admiral Crawford's successful coup on the Tchongar Bridge and imagined the pleasure this would bring Helen. Then he pictured her opening the papers to see sketches of the scene in the Quarries minutes after their capture and before the first counterattack. Magnus would see that such sketches were published and properly credited. Colnaghi's could not complain about what would later boost the sales of the lithographs. Tom suddenly felt happy; I must be mad, he thought, to be feeling like this. Death and suffering around me and I'm happy. But his light-headedness remained; the shock and his fear and the strangeness of the trenches, the unreality of the moonlight —everything until now had hidden from him the remarkable fact that he was at a spot, that within days would be the focus of the nation's interest, not just one nation's, but the world's. What he had just seen and was still seeing with his own eyes would be described at second-hand, or reconstructed out of what various soldiers said, and written down for millions of people to read about. It was at once obvious and extraordinary, and all the more so because until this moment he had thought of everything only as it concerned himself and Charles, and Magnus and the men fighting and dying yards away. You're an idiot, he thought; but if anything his surprise increased, because now he was thinking of the extraordinary sequence of events that had brought him to this spot. Helen, of course; Charles too; but, before either of them, George Braithwaite and a visit with him to Bentley's. So many chances; yet was any life different? He remembered reading some words in a book of maxims, but could not remember the author: "In the writing upon the wall, we may behold the hand, but see not the spring that moves it." His sense of his own littleness, even within the pattern of events that had directly shaped his life, increased his light-headedness. The parapet . . . the battery . . . Charles's body. Of course. The decision was already made for him. Without fear he clambered up onto the rampart and dropped down into the Quarries.

Behind a temporary screen of gabions the members of the working party were digging like men possessed, desperately attempting to throw up a breastwork, thick enough and tall enough to stop the shells and round shot fired at flat trajectories from the Redan. Other men were hastily dragging the Russian field-guns from one side of the battery to the other and placing them at the embrasures in the new breastwork. Gunners were feverishly working at the breeches of pieces that had been spiked too hurriedly by the departing Russians to be irreparably damaged. It seemed extraordinary to Tom that men who had just fought so fiercely to take the position should now be working harder than he had ever seen men work before. Every so often those with spades sank to their knees and others at once snatched up the tool and went on digging, tossing up so many spadefuls a minute that Tom lost count. After a shell had killed three sappers, he dived behind a traverse, affording him some shelter from the splinters of shells falling short. Everybody in the work seemed so taken up with what they were doing that none appeared aware of the constant danger and the devastation around them: overturned guns, shattered balks of timber and the scarred and pitted earth they moved upon. Nobody spoke to Tom or seemed aware of his existence. He pulled out a small pad and started hastily drawing the men digging, sensing, as he drew, the urgency of their task but still not understanding the need for them to work at such a frenzied pitch. The idea that the Russians might counterattack within half an hour of being driven out had not occurred to him.

Whenever a shell did any damage to a section of the breastwork, the hole was at once plugged with gabions and no time wasted filling in with earth. During Tom's first five minutes in the battery, no shell burst closer to him than thirty yards, and the impact of that one had been entirely absorbed by a traverse. Feeling much bolder, he began to move about, still sensing that he would find Charles. On one occasion he was cursed for getting in the way of a man carrying ammunition boxes across to the guns, and on another was pushed aside by a group pulling on a rope trying to right an overturned, truck-mounted gun. But everywhere he looked there was no sign of Charles's corpse. He had given up his search when he heard an officer scream,

"They're coming!"

Other orders came with bewildering speed: "Load with case, stand to the parapet . . ." Riflemen were rushing over to the new breastwork and kneeling or crouching behind it. Seconds later he heard the hiss and crack of bullets and was no longer in any doubt of what was happening. The blood rushed to his head as he leaped back toward the parapet he had climbed over ten minutes before. From somewhere he heard a frightened cry,

"To the right . . . They're behind us to the right."

From the corner of his eye he caught a glimpse of gray uniforms and a gunner swinging his sponge stave in a wide arc. Tom was on the parapet, jumping and then falling, the ground rising sharply to meet him—a burning numbness in his side. He twisted slightly as he tumbled down into the ditch, and banged his leg on something hard; for a moment he was more frightened by the thought that he had broken it than by the creeping numbness in his chest. He had fallen across a corpse and was trying to move away when he fell back and saw bright blood on his hand and on his coat. Faint and thirsty he looked for his water bottle but his eyes were not focusing. Feeling little pain, he was not afraid. The surgeons could not be far away. The firing from behind the parapet had become indistinct, a pleasant sound like heavy drops on canvas or the beat of distant hooves. Men were running past and clambering into the battery. Fresh troops, he thought joyfully; then, frightened they would tread on him, he tried to shout and was surprised to hear a choking groan. Seconds of fear were followed by a delicious floating sensation and a vision of flickering golden rods in front of his eyes.

Later he saw the crystals of frost and the moonlight again and realized that he was crying. If I could paint those rods, but how? So much work, when I get home. Just remember what they looked like. That was the thing. He imagined himself on a stretcher being carried back. Everything was taking so long though; already it seemed hours since the men had passed him. Time hung brooding in the air, its seconds marked only by the small fountains of warm pain now spurting in his chest . . . filling him with pain. Lapping wavelets and then pouring like an incoming tide: an engulfing ocean. A dark ocean, himself a tiny light.

He writhed with a sudden convulsion; a heavy heated iron was pressing down deep into his flesh. So much heat and yet he was shivering; his limbs felt like ice. His mind lapsed, and, when he came to again, he felt better: no longer immersed in pain, but floating in clouds, dispersed and separate from him.

I never understood any of them, he thought. *Never. Not really.* But it did not trouble him. Thirst again; parched earth. Rain would be nice, a light fine rain. But above him the sky was clear and very bright.

He was being moved. Somebody was bending over him, a blurred face—like a gargoyle eroded by wind and rain. So many gargoyles and carvings and none of the artists known; no names at all. The face loomed closer and then withdrew.

The secret was to seek even the smallest improvements at whatever cost of time; that way he could capture the moonlight. *The secret was . . . to treat a trifling matter with gravity—a child's seriousness in play. Treat what? Art? Life?* He could not remember. Those rods again— fragmenting now. *Try to remember. No. Best enjoy them in case they disappeared.*

Watts returned with a stretcher party ten minutes after first looking at Tom's wound—a bad one, but men had survived worse: Major Bailey with eight bayonet stabs in the chest at Inkerman and not found for fifteen hours. Others died of shock after no more than a graze. It was hard to tell, but Watts prided himself on his powers of prediction.

He let Tom's hand fall in irritation. Dead all right, and he'd had a definite feeling that he'd come through. Some surgeons said the more they saw, the less they knew, but Watts didn't feel like that, and he was angry to be proved wrong. A man was groaning farther along the ditch.

"Let's get on then!" Watts shouted.

Thirty hours already without sleep, and God only knew how many more to come if they went on attacking, and they would. He could count on that.

⮂ *Fifty-Two* ⮀

By quarter-past eight Magnus was beside himself with irritation and anxiety. He had left Cathcart's Hill to keep his appointment with Tom still uncertain of the outcome of the attack on the Quarries. The British had then still been in possession but were being increasingly hard pressed by determined Russian sorties. As Magnus waited impatiently for Tom, the ceaseless sound of gunfire, echoing across the plateau, increased his agitation.

Magnus had called at the Naval Brigade's camp on his way to his hut and had learned that Charles had not returned. Out of the one hundred and twenty members of the ladder party only thirty had come back unscathed and less than a dozen wounded sailors had so far been brought in. The day before, when his father's squadron had anchored off Balaclava, Magnus had not even known that an attack was imminent, let alone that Charles would be involved. But when in possession of these facts, he had at once done his utmost to find Tom to postpone their ill-timed meeting. Not only had he failed to find him, but had even been unsuccessful in his attempts to discover where he was billeted.

At half-past eight Magnus decided that Tom had forgotten, and returned to Cathcart's Hill in time to see the British repulse the largest counterattack to date, but only by committing half their reserve. Two more determined enemy sorties and the Quarries seemed destined to be back in enemy hands by the early afternoon.

Shortly before ten o'clock, Magnus took advantage of a temporary stalemate in the fighting to return once more to the naval camp to make further inquiries about his brother. He learned from a group of officers congregated outside the commodore's tent that three more wounded sailors had had been brought back but as yet no officers. The Russians were still shelling the ground between the advanced British trenches and the Quarries to prevent reinforcements reaching the work, and the sever-ity of this fire had all but stopped further efforts to bring in wounded. There was an air of deepening despondency throughout the camp.

Magnus was walking away when he saw Humphrey sitting on the ground at the side of Lushington's tent. His eyes were red-rimmed with crying and he looked wretchedly unhappy. Magnus came over and sat down beside him.

"He's sure to be dead, isn't he?"

The boy's bitter personal grief made Magnus feel momentarily ashamed of his own less vehement feelings.

"If he was hit crossing the glacis, he's probably still alive."

"But if he reached the parapet?"

Magnus sighed.

"His chances won't be so good."

Humphrey nodded and swallowed hard. After a brief silence he said, "Your father's in with the commodore."

"I don't think I'll see him till we know what's happened."

"I haven't been in either."

Not wishing to build up false hope, Magnus could think of nothing to say; his own belief was that Charles had been killed shortly after the attack began. He was imagining what it would have been like to have been among the first to reach the ditch, when he heard Humphrey saying something about having seen Tom in the camp several hours before dawn.

"Doing what?" he asked in astonishment.

"I don't know. I saw him near the armory and then lost sight of him."

"Have you seen him since?"

"No. I don't suppose I'd have remembered unless I'd seen you."

Magnus felt a knot of fear tightening in his stomach. Of course there was nothing ominous about an artist or journalist coming to see the men marching down to the trenches, but then why had Tom not been on Cathcart's Hill when the attack started? Possibly he *had* been there; with over a hundred officers clustered around the lookout post and the light so bad, it would have been easy enough to have missed him; and yet Magnus had made a point of looking for him to put off their meeting. He turned to Humphrey.

"Do you know the name of the officer on duty in the armory last night?"

"No, but they'd tell you in the paymaster's office."

Once Magnus had found the assistant paymaster, it took him few questions to discover that Tom had gone down to the trenches with the surgeon's party, none of whom, with the exception of a few stretcher bearers, had been seen since. Sick with fear for his friend, he rounded furiously on Parnwell.

"Why in Christ's name did you let a civilian go down?"

"I don't have to answer your questions."

"My brother is Captain Crawford. Now, why did you let him go down?"

"I tried to put him off. I had no powers of arrest, sir. I told him what the captain had said. What else could I do?"

Parnwell's face was ashen with tiredness and his hands were shaking.

"The captain?" repeated Magnus.

"Captain Crawford, sir."

A trace of exasperation had broken through Parnwell's deferential facade. Magnus moved toward him threateningly.

"You mean my brother asked Mr. Strickland to come here in the first place?"

"He had a letter from him," stammered Parnwell, evidently frightened by Magnus's fury. "I suppose he did. Then he told me to stop him going down. He must have changed his mind."

"But instead you arranged for him to go with the surgeon?"

"He wouldn't listen to me. The captain said if he couldn't be dissuaded, I was to send him down with the surgeon's people."

Outside the hut, Magnus covered his face with his hands. His mind was reeling. The tents, the huts, the gray sky, seemed to spin around him. It was a dream; he was running . . . but where? *Where?* Magnus stopped and stood in an agony of indecision. Must find him. *Find him.* As the first wave of panic receded, he was again aware of the guns. Charles sent him to his death, and I sent him to Charles. I sent him to Charles. Grief and anger clashed in his head, reverberated with the distant din of battle. He could be alive . . . wounded. If only I could think. Find one of the stretcher bearers or one of the ladder party.

Without a guide there would be no hope of finding the saphead from which the naval surgeon's party had gone forward.

Within half an hour Magnus had persuaded a member of the ladder party to lead him through the trenches. Many of those asked had refused, and Ordinary Seaman Hayles had only been won over by the promise of twenty guineas. Before setting out, Magnus went with Hayles to the hospital marquee to find out as much as possible from the surviving stretcher bearers of the first party.

A hundred yards from the long low tent, Magnus saw men gathered around the entrance flaps and his heart leaped with new hope. He began to run, taking in bloodstained stretchers on the ground, their bearers lying exhausted beside them. Two men were dragging a large tub of water into the marquee. A little closer and he heard ringing screams and moans coming from inside. Let him be safe, pray God, let Tom be safe. For the first time Magnus really felt what his friend's death would mean to him.

Nobody tried to stop Magnus as he pushed his way toward the cots and amputation tables. Stupefied by the constant cries and the shouts of the surgeons and orderlies, he moved along the tent in a daze, glancing cursorily at sights of appalling suffering, searching only for one face— dismissing all else. Orderlies were administering chloroform as fast as they could, but the sudden flood of wounded had taken them by surprise. For most of those brought in, the initial shock and numbness no longer saved them from the pain of stiffening wounds and the revival of lacerated nerves. He saw a large man lifted down from a table and water hastily sluiced over its red surface before another victim was placed on it and stripped; fragments of metal had forced bits of the cloth of this sailor's jacket into his flesh and the blood had clotted and caked around the wound, making him roar out as the material was ripped and cut away. Somebody shouted, "Wet it, you fools." Nearly at the far end of the tent Magnus gave up hope; if Tom was still alive, he would be out there somewhere. Magnus was making for the entrance when he saw his father's tearstained face; he was talking to a surgeon, a small bald man with a bunch of silk ligatures threaded through a buttonhole of his spattered coat. Charles was writhing in a cot, his neck arched back and his teeth sunk into his pillow to stop him crying out. His right arm had gone and the bandages covering most of the upper part of his chest were already darkening with new blood. Magnus stood gazing down at him aghast, feeling no more anger, only a surge of desperate pity. The muscles under his brother's white skin tensed convulsively with each new spasm of pain, and there was a feverish glitter in his wild, unseeing eyes. An assistant surgeon covered him with blankets and held a cloth firmly to his mouth until the chloroform left him drowsy and limp. The effect would not last though, and Magnus shuddered at the eternity of pain ahead of him. Magnus heard his father's voice:

"They think he may live if he survives the shock."

Magnus nodded dumbly, feeling a suffocating sickness. Somewhere a man was screaming, his voice sticking on a single piercing note. He felt his father's hand and returned the pressure as their eyes met. Knowing that he should stay a little longer, Magnus knew that he could not endure it, could not help shoulder even a small portion of his father's grief with the task that lay ahead of him.

"He'll live," he said quietly and then turned without another word.

Outside Hayles was talking to one of the bearers. Magnus sank to his knees and pulled out his hip flask, washing down the bile with large gulps of brandy. Then he got up slowly and called Hayles over to him.

"Better be going."

The man did not move. Magnus thought he looked suspicious and uneasy. Then he remembered the money. *He thinks he won't get his money if I'm killed.* Magnus started to laugh hysterically as he fumbled through his pockets, spilling out coins and notes. A slight smile lit Hayles's leathery face and he dropped to his knees and started counting.

When Magnus and Hayles reached the approach trenches between the second and third parallels, they found themselves caught between the chaotic stream of wounded now being carried to the rear, and the reserves and working parties pushing forward laden with ammunition boxes, trenching tools and gabions—both movements being due to the sudden slackening of the fire from the Redan. This left Magnus in a state of painful uncertainty; by the time he reached the glacis, Tom might already be being carried back down one of the advanced saps.

In the third parallel itself the confusion was at its worst. Here shells had burst, bringing down large sections of the trench walls, choking it with earth and debris; at some points bearers were having to lay their stretchers across the trench, resting the ends on the parapets so that reserves could get by underneath. Magnus asked some of the bearers whether they had seen a young civilian with the naval surgeon but none could remember; probably none would have recognized one surgeon from another. Progress was horribly slow and all the time the thought that Tom might be lying wounded barely a quarter of a mile away tortured Magnus.

All around him he heard the confused and angry shouts of men going forward who had been separated from their companies and officers. The sound of so many country dialects made him want to weep; most of these cold, hungry and sleepless men had been farm laborers a few years past in quiet English villages. At a cost of millions they had been shipped three thousand miles to fight against Russian peasants, who had once led lives almost identical to their own, and had most of them also come thousands of miles from home, in their case having endured the horror of forced marches along snow-covered roads, across frozen rivers and through high mountain passes. What could the Czar's claims in Moldavia mean to these men half crazed with passive suffering? No more than "the integrity of the Ottoman Empire" meant to the British soldiers. At least the enemy was sustained by the thought that he was defending his own soil; the French and British had no such incentive, only a blind instinct, a tenacity that was almost a faith, that it was better to die than yield. And although every rational impulse in him cried out that such sacrifices were senseless folly, on a level of pure emotion Magnus was stirred by the nobility of men fighting without hope or belief in their cause. The fighting madness of these men, whose lives had brought them such hardship, was not so much directed toward human adversaries as against fate itself—fate that had cheated and savaged them, but from which they would not run.

Magnus was still trapped in the third parallel when the Russian shelling started again, not with its former intensity but regularly enough to be terrifying to men moving slowly along a trench, unable to see the trajectories of shells until they were passing overhead or exploding among them. One burst a hundred and fifty yards ahead at the junction of the parallel and one of the main advanced saps, causing indescribable chaos and carnage, and bringing everybody in the trench to an immediate standstill. A number of officers climbed up onto the parapet and called on their men to follow. When Magnus suggested the same course, Hayles vehemently rejected it; so he scrambled up the muddy side of the trench and went on alone.

Even before reaching the abatis, Magnus knew the futility of his mission; the dead lay in heaps in front of the barrier or hung impaled on the sharpened branches, like seaweed thrown up against a breakwater in a storm and left there by the receding tide. Ahead on the glacis there were three long lines of bodies, recording the positions the storming party had reached when the Russians fired each of their perfectly co-ordinated volleys of grape. Although stretcher parties were busy, there were far too few of them to make any noticeable impact on the square mile over which the wounded were spread. In the distance Magnus saw that one man had managed to fix part of his shirt to his bayonet and had raised this flag to try to attract help. Magnus gave brandy to several wounded men and then threw the empty flask away. One of those to whom he had given a drink had been a very young man in great pain holding open a locket containing a miniature of a gray-haired woman, evidently his mother. Everywhere Magnus tasted the acid reek of salt-peter and blood in his throat and nostrils, carried on the icy wind, which ruffled patches of pale dead grass, small islands in the surrounding ocean of frozen mud. The sky was a whitish-gray but darkening to the north.

On the glacis there were places where the corpses were three deep. Dead or alive, Tom would never be found until an armistice allowed hundreds of men to come forward in safety. All the time Magnus was keeping one eye on the sky and listening for the whistle of approaching shells. Whenever he sighted one, he did not move or lie down until sure where it would fall. He had seen men run at once, often toward the point of impact. The occasional whine of rifle bullets did not distress him, since he knew that these had already missed. The victim never heard the sound of the bullet that killed him. When the shelling suddenly intensi-fied, Magnus did not feel able to face the scenes of panic and fury in the trenches, but instead dropped down into what had hours before been a Russian rifle pit and waited.

He thought of Charles and wondered how long it would be before gangrene set in; if the amputation did not kill him, his chest wounds surely would. The thought hardly moved him at all. Seeing his brother's shattered body he had taken in his death at once. His father's grief would be enough. A feeling of terrible sickness and impotence overwhelmed Magnus as he thought of Tom's capacity for excitement; he saw him setting out in the darkness toward the trenches in the same mood—an adventure, a test, an experience. Of course he would have known that men would be killed, but it was one thing to expect something but something quite different to live through it. Perhaps he went down looking for subjects, effects of light: like a country child on his first visit to a great city, looking around him memorizing, impressed and frightened at the same time. Other memories hurt Magnus more. Tom's wide-eyed disbelief when they had been ambushed at the gasworks and his immediate faith that Magnus had predicted the disaster and would know what to do. Tom's faith in him had been the greatest gift he had bestowed; now it was a torment. Who did he have to turn to four hours ago? Was he alone? Did he suffer? *And I sent him to Charles; sent him to see him when I had gone and could give him no advice.* Earlier occasions: the day Tom had told him he loved Helen. If he had been in my position, and I in his, would he have curtly told me that my love was a charade, its object worthless? Yet I did that; yes, and thought my *honesty* quite natural. And when Catherine came I sent her away . . . denied all responsibility . . . though I had caused him to go to Hanley Park. The evening at the Bull—our last in Rigton Bridge—I promised to help him, pledged myself to it . . . and afterward I turned against him.

So fragile a thing friendship, so few the times that any man or woman senses in another human being an understanding of his or her inmost, half-realized thoughts—something less tangible than thoughts, something beyond definition, a yearning that has been there since birth—its object sometimes glimpsed but never captured. At times music, the smell of burning leaves, a landscape, a memory—almost . . . a second of completeness, of harmony and then—nothing. Whatever I searched for and aspired to I sensed the same quest in you, Tom.

A week ago you came and we were strangers. Perhaps you *wanted* to die. Did I fail to read even that despair? Magnus started to his feet. The shock of seeing Charles and the scenes on the glacis had so confused him that he had failed to do the one thing he had known was possible— the shock and the shells. He had *accepted* Tom's death without proof, without trying to find where the surgeons were working. He felt several light flakes of snow on his cheeks and imagined the horror of bringing back the wounded if thick snow fell. To the north the sky was dark enough.

A few seconds after leaving the rifle pit he knew that something was wrong, knew it the moment he realized the Russian shells were no longer whistling overhead, knew it before hearing the shouts and shots a hundred yards away and seeing the men running for their lives from the Quarries. The Russians had retaken the battery and were now dashing on in mad pursuit. Furious with himself for not having understood what the renewed bombardment had meant, and then for having failed to notice its sudden ending, Magnus began to run toward the British lines. Looking back he saw Russians bayoneting wounded men. Trembling with hatred, he ran on, and seeing an officer's corpse, bent down, ripped the dead man's revolver from its holster and broke open the breech—it was loaded, with one chamber empty: five shots. He dropped down on one knee and, steadying the gun on his left forearm, fired twice, hitting a man in the leg. If he'd had time to load he would have used a Minié. Men were running past him already—the Russians no more than thirty yards behind. He fired again, missed and then went on running.

Where were the men's officers? Probably most of them dead. Nobody was trying to form them up. No more than a hundred Russians had charged on beyond the battery and they were now driving before them twice that number of British soldiers. All from light infantry regiments; madness to have used them after what they had gone through at Inkerman. Glancing over his shoulder, Magnus saw that a sergeant had got together half a dozen men and formed them in line. They fired, bringing down three Russians and then reloaded, one man so scared that he fired with his ramrod still in the muzzle. After the second volley, four of the six started to run. Magnus saw the sergeant point his rifle at the head of the man nearest him, threatening to shoot if either of the remaining two moved before his order. The farthest man turned and the sergeant jerked around his rifle and shot him; a moment later he too fell, killed by a Russian bullet.

Fifty yards from the trenches Magnus slowed down, convinced that the Russians would not come much closer and risk hand-to-hand fighting with far greater numbers. Determined to fire his last two shots, he flung himself down and, steadying his hand on a rock, aimed and squeezed the trigger. Nothing. The empty chamber. He tried again but the gun had jammed. Hurling it away in disgust he sprinted on. A man just in front of him was hit in the thigh, ran a few paces more and then fell. The ground was rough and slightly uphill, making Magnus's breath come in sobbing gasps, but he could see the ridge of the third parallel and the mounds of earth and gabions at the sapheads. Bullets were still whining and humming past. Looking back he was shaken to see that the Russians had not slackened their pace. They couldn't think that they could succeed . . . but they were going to try to take the third parallel . . . they were. A few panicking men in the trench started to fire, regardless of their own troops fleeing toward them, terrified by the thought of the Russian bayonets. Magnus saw the puffs of smoke along the parapet but heard no sound. By the time the echo reached him, a Minié bullet had torn through his brain.

~ *Fifty-Three* ~

At the end of January 1855, Mr. John Roebuck Q.C., the Radical member for Sheffield, moved a motion of censure in the House of Commons. One question put by him particularly disturbed the House. If fifty-four thousand men had left Britain for the war since the outbreak of hostilities, and there were now only fourteen thousand in arms before Sevastopol, what had become of the missing forty thousand? Heavily defeated in the vote, Lord Aberdeen resigned and the Queen invited Lord Palmerston to form a government. The war went on. Not until the completion of the Balaclava railway and the coming of spring did the army's numbers stabilize at around twenty-five thousand.

In late February—a time when the British had been able to muster no more than five thousand men fit for duty—the French had renewed the attack abandoned on New Year's Day. They took the Quarries and the neighboring low hill: the Mamelon, but were driven out after forty-eight hours. These works remained in Russian hands until captured and held by the allies on 9 June.

What was hoped would be the final attack on the Redan and Malakoff was planned to take place nine days later, the anniversary of Waterloo. The French attacked too soon and the British in insufficient numbers. Six thousand men were sacrificed to no effect. Ten days afterward Lord Raglan died—some mentioned a broken heart, his doctors cholera.

But in spite of allied reverses, the Russians' position deteriorated during the summer. From May onward the Royal Navy's squadron in the Sea of Azov cut off all seaborne supplies from the east, and at the same time allied reinforcements built up rapidly. In mid-August the Russian generals gambled and took the field. They were decisively defeated by the French Army. On 9 September the allies once more attacked the principal Russian bastions. Instead of waiting until the French had taken the Malakoff, whose guns commanded the approach to the Redan, the British attacked simultaneously and were driven back, leaving two thousand dead and wounded on the ground. The French captured and held the Malakoff. During the night the enemy evacuated Sevastopol and blew up their magazines. The fighting was at an end.

In the first week of October Sir James Crawford returned home at his own request and Rear Admiral Houston Stewart was appointed in his place.

⤠ Fifty-Four ⤟

Early one April morning, seven months after the fall of Sevastopol, Helen Crawford walked down through the dewy meadows golden with celandine toward the lake, and watched the high, wispy cirrus clouds reflected in the smooth water. Among the reeds, coots and moorhens were nesting, a yellow butterfly fluttered past. Spring, she thought, yes, spring; and how strange to be still in the midst of such purposive and abundant life when I feel that I am already over, my words habit, my thoughts, everything now mere habit. How strange to feel tired and at the same time scared of a life of absolute certainty unruffled by the hot chase of experience. And yet when I accepted James was that not what I wanted? Peace, and an easy passage through the years without pain or passion. Was that really what I felt in the beech woods before Tom came, before the war?

She had left the house to escape the frenzy of the wedding preparations; the frequent arrival of the carter's wagon with boxes and packages, the comings and goings of the dressmakers fussing over the bridesmaids' dresses. Had their white satin boots arrived? Would there be enough old point lace for this dress? Were the ostrich feathers for the bride's going-away hat not a little yellow? The size and magnificence of Catherine's trousseau almost suggested that some new law had been enacted forbidding ladies to buy any clothes after they married. Helen had seen enough cambric and Valenciennes peignoirs to last several women a lifetime. Passing Catherine's door earlier that morning she had glimpsed a floor strewn with bonnet boxes, trunks and packing cases. On the table had been mother-of-pearl glove boxes, inlaid caskets, embroidered pincushions and a boudoir inkstand in lapis lazuli. On the sofa: a heap of silk, moiré, muslin and cashmere receiving the attention of the French

milliner summoned from London. Catherine had wanted to be married
from Leaholme Hall, but, shortly before the outbreak of the war, Sir
James had let it on a four-year lease.

In the midst of this finery, Helen had been choked to see Catherine in
a simple morning gown which she had often worn during her first summer at Hanley Park. Later in the day the men from Gunter and from
Fortnum would be arriving, bringing with them the usual monuments of
crystallized sugar decked with silver foliage and orange blossom. Helen's
own kitchen staff had already been driven half mad by the army of
invaders; but in two days it would all be over, and Catherine, Miss
Crawford no longer, would be departing for Dover and a continental
honeymoon, her trunks all neatly labeled *Mrs. George Braithwaite.*
Looking across the water at the green copper dome of the mausoleum,
Helen thought of her own marriage to Harry Grandison when she had
been a girl of not quite twenty.

Leaving the lake she made for the woods. Birch and sycamore were in
leaf, some elms and chestnut too, but the beeches which Sir James had
been so eager to sketch three springs ago had not yet unfurled their pale
green-yellow leaves. In the distance she heard the dull thump of an ax
and imagined the white sappy chips of a young ash flying to the ground.
A thrush was singing very close to her but it was still too early for the
cuckoo's mocking notes she had heard so clearly on the day Sir James
had proposed. Walking among the delicate white windflowers, she recalled James's predictions of a distant war. The sameness of the woods
and so great a human change. Tom and Magnus dead, her son a boy no
longer, serving in the Caribbean. Catherine marrying.

Time and again during the first weeks after her husband's return,
Helen had heard him reproach himself for having failed to find the time
to talk to Magnus on the voyage back from Genichesk. For days on end
he had seemed to think of nothing else, often reliving the harrowing
circumstances of their last brief meeting. Trying to comfort him, she had
never reached him in his private world of grief. And then he had been
gone once more. First to attend the exploratory sessions at Vienna and
after that the Paris Peace Conference—his head filled with the Bes-
sarabian frontier, the neutralization of the Danube's mouth and the
limitation of Russia's Black Sea Fleet.

Even now he was away in London at the Admiralty, preoccupied with his new obsession, perusing plans for ironclads and turret ships; his only passion: to see a new navy building before his retirement, so formidable that no nation on earth would dare during his lifetime menace any part of the Empire by sea. Then blind folly and forgetfulness alone would have the power to persuade the country's rulers to involve her in another land war with a European nation.

And yet Helen knew that even if he had remained quietly by her side, she would still have felt no closeness. In time perhaps, as the memory of Tom's death faded, and she forgot the misery she had suffered during Charles's long convalescence at Hanley Park, she would feel differently. Now, his sea days over, Charles had gone to Pembroke Dockyard as captain superintendent; and with Catherine's departure for her new home, more links with the past would be severed.

In a very few months, Helen herself expected to be making the journey south to take up residence at Admiralty House, Portsmouth, where Sir James would be appointed port admiral at the next vacancy. By the time he retired, Hanley Park would be Humphrey's, and Leaholme Hall, Sir James had hinted, would be made over to Charles. After Portsmouth Helen tried to imagine a house in Clarence Parade, Southsea or in the Hampshire countryside within easy reach of her husband's beloved Solent, on whose gray waters he would watch through his declining years the death of old navies and the birth of strange new ships beginning their voyages into the future—without us, she thought; for we, like the sailing ships of yesterday, are now becalmed and will never beat past the point we sought to reach or make the landfall we desired. Already the tide was ebbing fast. The youthfulness of the wood's springtime haunted her. She could not bear it.

On the way back to the house she was surprised to think of Tom without pain—his youth embalmed by death, her vision of him unchanged and unchanging; time cheated at last. Age would find other faces on which to exercise his mocking artistry, her own among them; but Tom would always be as he had been that summer before her marriage.